Extraordinary acclaim for Dan Simmons's

THE CROOK FACTORY

"If Ian Fleming, Graham Greene, and Hemingway himself sat down to collaborate on a novel, the result might have been *The Crook Factory*... a work so strong, so original, that it may have other writers in the genre saying, 'Wish I'd written that.'... A fast-paced tale of espionage that pays homage to Papa, doles out a quick history lesson, and offers up plenty of action and intrigue, it is a book to be recommended to anyone who loves a superb thriller."
—*Dallas Morning News*

"A literary thriller that is sure to win Simmons another batch of readers and place him on the short list for more awards.... A remarkable blend of fact and fiction... filled with just the right amount of action, humor, suspense, and compassion.... In the end, what resonates deepest are the characters.... Readers will come away from this book feeling as if they actually lived alongside the great writer.... A tale that will echo in the mind long after the last page has been turned... *The Crook Factory* exemplifies the kind of fiction that Hemingway held in high esteem, writing that is 'truer than true.'"
—*Denver Post*

"The essence of good historical fiction is not being able to tell where history ends and fiction begins, and in this *The Crook Factory* succeeds extraordinarily well. Simmons adds to this a brilliantly realized portrayal of Hemingway—a daunting and difficult task—and embeds it all in a straightforwardly gripping narrative: the result is a wonderful read."
—Iain Pears

"A gripping read from start to finish.... Dan Simmons is, in many ways, the reincarnation of Robert Louis Stevenson.... *The Crook Factory*, a fast-paced spy thriller rooted in recent history, is yet another milestone in the career of one of America's finest writers."
—*Des Moines Sunday Register*

"A carefully wrought and immensely entertaining espionage yarn that manages to involve Hemingway and his motley crew in the machinations of the FBI, the OSS, the Abwehr, the Gestapo, British and Russian military intelligence, and corrupt agents of both Cuba and Brazil." —*Charleston Post & Courier*

"A first-rate espionage thriller that can do nothing but enhance Simmons' already considerable reputation as a storyteller."

—*Denver Rocky Mountain News*

"Dan Simmons makes you truly feel that you are with Hemingway in one of his real-life adventures as the great writer hunted Nazi agents and chased German U-boats off the coast of Cuba in 1942. Every Hemingway fan will love this book, as will every fan of espionage novels that tell it the way it is."

—David Morrell, *New York Times* bestselling author of *First Blood* and *Creepers*

"Exciting…entertaining…amazing….Novelist Dan Simmons has uncovered perhaps the most eccentric chapter in Mr. Hemingway's life." —*Detroit Free Press*

"A gutsy speculation on Ernest Hemingway's exploits in wartime espionage….As vividly depicted by Simmons, pre-Communist Cuba is an exotic locale whose volatile wartime intrigues are comparable to those of the cinematic Casablanca. It's the perfect milieu for Hemingway, whose larger-than-life evocation must be accounted one of Simmons's sterling literary achievements."

—*Publishers Weekly*

"Extraordinary entertainment…laced with amazing historical vignettes….I was mesmerized by Dan Simmons's brilliant and unique period thriller." —*Philadelphia City Paper*

"An excellent thriller….Simmons skillfully builds his story into the ambiguities in actual history through solid writing and research….The result is fiction true to the spirit of Hemingway and his times." —*Portland Oregonian*

"A real page-turning espionage story complete with corrupt police officials, double agents, secret codes, and multiple murders. Simmons offers one of the best fictional portraits of Hemingway without falling into hero worship.... A fun read for both Hemingway aficionados and spy novel enthusiasts."

—*Library Journal*

"A sophisticated historical espionage thriller... ambitious and thoroughly researched.... A born storyteller... Simmons has over the last decade repeatedly shown himself to be one of the most versatile, intelligent, and unpredictable novelists around."

—*Locus*

"This fabulously compelling and humorous rendering of the little-known war operations and secret agent skullduggery in the Caribbean in the summer of 1942 will surely charm readers who love history, suspense, and intrigue."

—*Booklist* (starred review)

"Hemingway would like this thriller."

—*Milwaukee Journal Sentinel*

Also by Dan Simmons

Flashback
Black Hills
Drood
The Terror
Olympos
Hard as Nails
Ilium
Worlds Enough & Time
Hard Freeze
Hardcase
A Winter Haunting
Darwin's Blade
The Rise of Endymion
Endymion
The Fires of Eden
Lovedeath
Summer Sketches
Children of the Night
The Hollow Man
Summer of Night
Prayers to Broken Stones
The Fall of Hyperion
Hyperion
Carrion Comfort
Phases of Gravity
Song of Kali

Mulholland Books / Little, Brown and Company
Hachette Book Group
237 Park Avenue, New York, NY 10017
mulhollandbooks.com

Originally published by Avon Books, March 1999
First Mulholland Books edition, February 2013

Mulholland Books is an imprint of Little, Brown and Company, a division of Hachette Book Group, Inc. The Mulholland Books name and logo are trademarks of Hachette Book Group, Inc.

The Hachette Speakers Bureau provides a wide range of authors for speaking events. To find out more, go to hachettespeakersbureau.com or call (866) 376-6591.

Library of Congress Cataloging-in-Publication Data
Simmons, Dan.
The crook factory / Dan Simmons.
p. cm.
ISBN 978-0-316-21345-5
1. Hemingway, Ernest, 1899–1961—Fiction. I. Title.
PS3569.I47292C76 2013
813'.54—dc23 2012033885

d in the United States of America

THE CROOK FACTORY

DAN SIMMONS

MULHOLLAND BOOKS

LITTLE, BROWN AND COM

NEW YORK BOSTON LON

"Ernest immediately assembled a crew of eight from among his most trusted confederates. The code designation for the scheme was *Friendless,* the name of one of his favorite cats at the Finca. As his executive officer he chose Winston Guest, a large millionaire athlete who had recently been staying at the Finca. Colonel Thomason recruited a Marine master sergeant from the American Embassy to serve as gunner. His name was Don Saxon and he could field-strip and reassemble a machine gun in the dark in a matter of seconds. The others were all non-Americans: Juan Dunabeitia, a tall, thin, merry-eyed Basque who knew the sea so well that he was called Sinbad the Sailor, later shortened to Sinsky; Paxtchi, one of the jai-alai-playing Ibarlucia brothers, who had frequented the Finca for years and often vanquished Hemingway at tennis; the Canary Islander Gregorio Fuentes, Ernest's veteran mate and cook aboard the *Pilar;* Fernando Mesa, an exiled Catalan who had once been a waiter in Barcelona; a heavyset, pale-faced Spanish Cuban named Roberto Herrera, whose elder brother Luis had been a surgeon for the Loyalists; and a silent man, known only as Lucas, whose origins remain obscure."

—Carlos Baker, *Ernest Hemingway: A Life Story*

GUIDE TO INTELLIGENCE SERVICE TERMS AND ACRONYMS

German

Abwehr: German Military Intelligence—oldest of the various intelligence services—headed in 1942 by Admiral Wilhelm Canaris. While charged by Hitler to work in cooperation with Heinrich Himmler's SD/RSHA Nazi political intelligence wing, the two agencies were deadly enemies.

RSHA: Reich Nazi internal security agency—*Reichssicherheithauptamt*—headed by Heinrich Himmler. Himmler, who was also in charge of the SS and eventually the SD, had as his primary goal the destruction of Canaris and his Abwehr network: actual espionage and counterespionage came second.

SD: Sicherhetsdienst. The intelligence and counterintelligence wing of Himmler's RSHA, headed (until his assassination in May 1942) by Himmler's ruthless protégé, Reinhard Heydrich. Upon Heydrich's death, Himmler took direct charge of the SD as well as the SS and overall RHSA.

AMT VI: "Department 6"—the division of the RHSA's SD devoted to conducting espionage in foreign countries.

Department D4 of Amt VI: Commanded by Grüppenleiter Theodor Päffgen, the section responsible for SD/RHSA political espionage in Latin America.

SS: Schützstaffel. Unit of Nazis originally created to serve as a personal bodyguard to Adolf Hitler and whose responsibilities, under Himmler, were widely expanded to include intelligence, internal security, policing action, and the extermination of undesirables. Some antique typewriters in Germany still have the "twin-lightning-bolt" key denoting the SS.

Gestapo: Dreaded secret police of the Third Reich. Actually RSHA Amt IV controlled by Himmler.

Marine Nachrichtendiest: German Naval Intelligence. As with the Abwehr, an independent military intelligence service not directly controlled by the Nazi political wing.

Vertrauensmann: German Abwehr secret agent or "V-mann."

micropunkt: microfilm used by Abwehr agents, developed at the Institute of Technology in Dresden.

British

MI6: British Foreign Intelligence.

MI5: British Internal intelligence/counterintelligence.

XX Program: Literally "Double Cross"—British intelligence's highly successful attempt to "turn" enemy agents. By the end of the war, all German agents in England were working for the British.

NID: Naval Intelligence Division. Headed by Admiral John Godfrey, who personally hired the young ne'er-do-well, Ian Fleming, who excelled in espionage and rose to the rank of commander in the NID.

Assault Unit 30: One of Ian Fleming's many outrageous and successful ideas—a group of felons and misfits trained for wildly improbable missions behind German lines. Later the basis for the film *The Dirty Dozen.*

BSC: British Security Coordination. A branch of MI6 run out of New York City to provide counterintelligence operations in North and South America. Its secret goal prior to Dec. 7, 1941, was to help draw the United States into the war. The BSC was headed by William Stephenson, code-named "Intrepid," arguably the most successful secret agent of WWII.

Camp X: BSC special training and operations center near Oshawa in Canada. Many FBI/SIS counterintelligence operatives were also trained there by British experts. The plot to assassinate Reinhard Heydrich, head of the German SD, was worked out at Camp X.

American

FBI: Federal Bureau of Investigation, J. Edgar Hoover, Director.

SIS: Special Intelligence Service: counterintelligence division of FBI created during the war, especially involved with Latin American operations ("Joe Lucas's" special area of expertise).

COI: "Coordinator of Intelligence"—foreign intelligence and counterintelligence service of the U.S. created and headed by William "Wild Bill" Donovan. The COI (later the OSS and eventually the CIA) was known for its bold operations and for hiring "unlikely" secret operatives—such as Marlene Dietrich, Julia Child, famous American writers, etc.

OSS: Office of Strategic Services: name change for Donovan's COI in June of 1942. According to an arrangement made that year, the OSS was to be in charge of "foreign intelligence"—i.e., overseas spying—while the FBI/SIS was to retain jurisdiction over all counterintelligence operations in the Western Hemisphere. In reality, the two agencies clashed constantly. J. Edgar Hoover's goal was nothing less than total control of all U.S. intelligence operations, foreign and domestic.

CIA: Central Intelligence Agency: descended directly from the OSS, one of many agencies now charged with gathering intelligence for the U.S. government. Bill Casey, the head of the CIA during the Reagan era, was a protégé of Bill Donovan's.

ONI: Office of Naval Intelligence. Early in 1942, the ONI was very concerned by an illicit affair between one of its young intelligence officers in Washington—John F. Kennedy—and an older woman under suspicion of being a Nazi secret agent. Kennedy was transferred overseas.

The Latin American division of ONI was run in 1941–42 by a hunchbacked dwarf named Wallace Beta Phillips, a consummate spymaster who left Naval Intelligence after his work there in cooperation with the BSC was constantly compromised by the FBI. He later joined the OSS.

G2: U.S. Army Military Intelligence. In 1942, G2 was spending much of its time and energy following, wiretapping, and investigating such probable enemy agents as the Vice President of the United States, a former Secretary of State, Eleanor Roosevelt, and young Lt. John F. Kennedy.

SDI: Intelligence service of the U.S. State Department.

Russian

NKVD: *Narodnii Kommissariat Vnutrennikh Del*—the People's Commissariat of Internal Affairs—Stalin's intelligence service and de facto secret police, run by the psychopath Lavrenty Beria.

GPU: Soviet internal secret police until 1935, later the MVD.

Other

DOPS: (*Delgacio Especial de Ordem Politica e Social*) Brazilian political police specializing in counterintelligence, often in liaison with the FBI/SIS.

THE CROOK FACTORY

1

HE FINALLY DID IT on a Sunday, July 2, 1961, up in Idaho, in a new house which, I suspect, meant little to him, but which had a view up a valley to the high peaks, down the valley to the river, and across the valley to a cemetery where friends were buried.

I was in Cuba when I heard the news. There was some irony in this, because I had not been back to Cuba in the nineteen years since my time with Hemingway. There was more irony in the fact that July 2, 1961, was my forty-ninth birthday. I spent it following a greasy little man through greasy little bars, and then driving all night—still following him—as he drove three hundred and fifty kilometers out into the boondocks, out beyond where the armored train in Santa Clara marks the road to Remedios. I was out there in the cane fields and palm forests for another day and night before my business with the greasy little man was done, and I did not hear a radio until I stopped at the Hotel Perla in Santa Clara for a drink. The radio there was playing sad music—almost funereal—but I thought nothing of it and spoke to no one. I did not hear about Hemingway's death until I was back in Havana that evening, checking out of the hotel near where the U.S. embassy had been until Castro had kicked the Americans out just a few months before, in January.

"Did you hear, *señor*?" said the seventy-year-old bellman as he carried my bags out to the curb.

"What?" I said. The old man knew me only as a businessman from Colombia. If he had personal news for me, it could be very bad.

"The writer is dead," said the old man. His thin cheeks under the gray stubble were trembling.

"What writer?" I said, glancing at my watch. I had to make a plane at eight P.M.

"*Señor Papa,*" said the old bellman.

I froze with my wrist still raised. For a brief moment, I found it hard to focus on the dial of my watch. "Hemingway?" I said.

"Yes," said the old man. His head kept bobbing up and down long after the single syllable was uttered.

"How?" I said.

"Gunshot," said the bellman. "In the head. By his own hand."

Of course, I thought. I said, "When?"

"Two days ago," said the old man. He sighed heavily. I could smell the rum. "In the United States," he added as if that explained everything.

"*Sic transit hijo de puta,*" I said under my breath. A polite translation might be "There goes the son of a bitch."

The old bellman's head snapped back on his scrawny neck as if he had been slapped. His servile, usually rheumy eyes flashed a sudden anger bordering on hatred. He set my bags down on the floor of the lobby as if freeing his hands to fight. I realized that the old man might well have known Hemingway.

I raised my right hand, palm out. "It's all right," I said. "It's something the writer said. Something Hemingway said when they threw Batista out during the Glorious Revolution."

The bellman nodded, but his eyes were still angry. I gave him two pesos and walked out, leaving my bags near the door.

My first impulse was to find the car I had been using—and had left abandoned on a street just outside the Old Section—and drive out to the *finca.* It was only twelve miles away. But I realized that this was a bad idea. I had to get to the airport and get out of this country as soon as I could, not go wandering around like some goddamned tourist. Besides, the farm had been confiscated by the revolutionary government. There were soldiers standing guard out there right now.

Standing guard over what? I thought. Over his thousands of books that he hadn't been able to get out of the country? His dozens of cats? His rifles and shotguns and hunting trophies? His boat? Where was the *Pilar*? I wondered. Still berthed in Cojímar or pressed into service of the state?

At any rate, I knew for a fact that the Finca Vigía had been closed up for this past year with a battalion of former orphans and beggars receiving military instruction on the grounds. Word in Havana was that the ragtag militia was not allowed in the house—they slept in tents near the tennis courts—but that their *commandante* slept in the guest house, almost certainly in the same bed that had been mine when we ran the Crook Factory out of that same building. And I had film in the false lining of my suitcase that showed quite clearly that Fidel had stationed an antiaircraft unit on the patio of the Steinharts' home on the hilltop next to Hemingway's farm—sixteen 100-millimeter Soviet AA guns to defend Havana from the heights. There were eighty-seven Cuban gunners at the site and six Russian advisers.

No, not the Finca Vigía. Not this hot summer evening.

I walked the eleven blocks down Obispo Street to the Floridita. Already, just a year and a half after the revolution, the streets seemed empty compared with the traffic I remembered here during the early '40s. Four Russian army officers came out of a bar across the way, obviously drunk and singing very loudly. The Cubans on Obispo—the young men in white shirts, the pretty girls in short skirts—all looked away as if the Russians were urinating in public. None of the whores approached them.

The Floridita had also become property of the state, I knew, but it was open this Tuesday evening. I had heard that the bar had been air-conditioned in the '50s, but either my informant had been misinformed or the cost of cooling the place had become prohibitive after the revolution, for this evening the shutters were all up and the bar was open to the sidewalks, just as it had been when Hemingway and I drank there.

I did not go in, of course. I pulled my fedora lower and looked away for the most part, glancing in just once when I was sure my face was in shadow.

Hemingway's favorite bar stool—the one on the far left, next to the wall—was empty. This was not a surprise. The bar's current owner—the state—had ordered that no one could sit there. A goddamned shrine. On the wall above the empty stool was a bust of the writer looking dark, amorphous, and ridiculous. Hemingway's kiss-up friends had given that to him, I had heard, after the writer had won the Nobel Prize for that stupid fish story. A bartender—not Constante Ribailagua, the *cantinero* I had known, but a younger, middle-aged man in dark-rimmed glasses—was mopping the bar in front of Hemingway's stool as if expecting the writer to return from the *baño* any moment.

I turned back toward the hotel on narrow O'Reilly Street. "Jesus Christ," I whispered, mopping the sweat from under my hatband. They would probably turn Hemingway into some sort of pro-communist saint down here. I had seen it before in Catholic countries after a successful Marxist revolution. The faithful were kicked out of their churches, but they still needed their fucking *santos*. The socialist state always scrambled to provide them—busts of Marx, giant murals of Fidel, posters of Che Guevara. Hemingway as the patron saint of Havana. I smiled as I hurried across a connecting street so as not to be run down by a convoy of military trucks with Russian drivers.

"La tenía cogida la baja," I whispered, trying to pluck the phrase from half-forgotten bits of Havana slang. This city, above all others, should "know his weak points"—see the code under the surface.

I flew out of Havana that night, thinking more about the implications of my visit to the camouflaged camp south of Remedios than of the details of Hemingway's death, but in the weeks and months and years to come, it was those details, that solitary death, which grew to an obsession with me.

The first reports from the AP said that Hemingway had been cleaning one of his guns when it had accidentally discharged. I knew immediately that this was bullshit. Hemingway had cleaned his rifles and shotguns since he was a young boy and would never make such a mistake. He had—as the news reports soon confirmed—blown his own brains out. But how? What were the details? I remembered that the only fistfight Hemingway and I had ever had came as a result of his demonstration at the *finca* of how to kill oneself. He had placed the butt of his Mannlicher .256 on the rough rug of his living room, pulled the muzzle near his mouth, said "In the mouth, Joe; the palate is the softest part of the head," and then pressed the trigger down with his big toe. The hammer had dry-clicked and Hemingway had raised his head and smiled as if awaiting approval.

"That's fucking stupid," I had said.

Hemingway had propped the Mannlicher against the ugly floral chair, balanced on the balls of his bare feet, twitched his fingers, and said, "What did you say, Joe?"

"That was fucking stupid," I had repeated. "And even if it wasn't, putting the barrel of a firearm in your mouth is something only a *maricón* would do."

"Fag" or "queer" is too-polite a translation for *maricón*. We had gone outside by the pool and fought then—not boxed, but gone at each other with bare fists and teeth.

Hemingway would not have needed the barrel in his mouth in Idaho that July day in 1961. Within days of his last wife's report of death by accident, it became clear that he had used a shotgun to kill himself; a double-barreled twelve-gauge Richardson. His first biographer reported that it was the double-barreled Boss twelve-gauge with the slow choke, Hemingway's favorite gun for pigeon shooting. I think it was the Boss. The Richardson with its gleaming barrels was a beautiful show gun, but too flashy for such work as blowing the top of one's head off. I remember once on the *Pilar*, Hemingway reading a piece in a two-week-old *New York Times* about the twin pearl-handled pistols which General George Patton carried. Hemingway had laughed: "Patton will be pissed off. He's always correcting these shit-stupid journalists. They're *ivory-handled* pistols. He says that only a pimp would carry pearl-handled revolvers, and I agree." The silver-barreled Richardson would come too close to that for serious work, I think.

But as the weeks and months and years passed, I realized that it had not mattered so much which gun he had used that morning as did the other details.

In the months before his death, Hemingway had become convinced that the FBI was bugging his phones, following him, and preparing a tax case against him in collusion with the IRS which would ruin him financially. It was this delusion of FBI persecution, above all others, which had prompted his fourth wife to decide that he'd become paranoid and delusional. It was then that his wife and friends had taken him to the Mayo Clinic for a series of electroshock treatments.

The treatments destroyed his memory, his sex drive, and his writing ability, but they did not free him from his paranoia. On the night before he killed himself, Hemingway's wife and friends took him out to dinner at the Christiana Restaurant in Ketchum. Hemingway insisted on sitting with his back to the wall and became suspicious of two men at a nearby table. When his wife and a friend, George Brown, called over the waitress, named Suzie, and asked her to confirm who the strangers were, Suzie said, "They're probably salesmen from Twin Falls."

"No," said Hemingway. "They're FBI."

Hemingway's sometime friend A. E. Hotchner wrote about an almost identical incident in the same restaurant, but eight months earlier, in November 1960. Hemingway had previously explained to Hotchner that he was being following by the FBI and that his phone was tapped and his house and car were bugged. Hotchner and Hemingway's wife, Mary, had taken the writer out to dinner at the same Christiana Restaurant. Hemingway was in the middle of an amusing story about the days when Ketchum was a wide-open gold rush town when he suddenly stopped in midsentence and said that they all had to leave. Their meals were unfinished. When Hemingway's wife asked what was wrong, he said, "Those two FBI men at the bar."

Hotchner had gone over to a nearby table where an acquaintance—Chuck Atkinson—and his wife were having dinner and asked if Atkinson knew the two men. "Sure," said the Ketchum native. "They're salesmen. Been coming here once a month for the last five years. Don't tell me Ernest is worried about *them*."

I know now that the two men had been coming to Ketchum for the five years previous to that day, where they went door to door in the area, offering encyclopedias for sale. They *were* FBI men, special agents out of the Billings office. As were the two other men on that Saturday evening in Christiana's on July 1, 1961. They were following Hemingway. They had tapped his phone. His house was bugged, but not his car. Earlier that winter and again in the spring, other FBI agents had followed Hemingway as he was flown in a private plane to Rochester, Minnesota, where the writer was to receive his electroshock treatments. On that first trip, in November 1960, just two weeks after Hemingway's "paranoid delusions" in the restaurant, the FBI men landed in a private plane just minutes after the Piper Commanche carrying Hemingway and his doctor had set down. But four agents from the Rochester office had already followed the Hemingway party into town, using two unmarked Chevrolets—one ahead of and one behind the car transporting the writer and Dr. Saviers.

On that first trip in November 1960, according to the "unfiled" FBI report—one of the thousands of J. Edgar Hoover's Personal OC Files ("OC" for "Official/Confidential") "lost" in the month after the death of the FBI director in May 1972—the FBI men tailing Hemingway had followed the writer into St. Mary's Hospital, where he was admitted under the alias of George Saviers, but they had stopped at the door of the Mayo Clinic when Hemingway was transferred there. They did not stay outside for long. Later files show that the FBI had interviewed Dr. Howard P. Rome, the senior consultant in the Section of Psychiatry who was in charge of Hemingway's "psycho-therapeutic program." Those same files show that Dr. Rome and the FBI men had discussed the advisability of Hemingway's electroshock treatment even before the writer or his wife was presented with the option.

As I mentioned earlier, J. Edgar Hoover's Personal File sections of the OC files—all twenty-three file cabinets' worth of them—were "lost" in the days and weeks after the director's death, at age seventy-seven, on May 2, 1972. That morning, less than an hour after the discovery of the director's death, Attorney General of the United States Richard Kleindienst, after conferring with President Nixon, summoned Assistant to the Director of the FBI John Mohr to the attorney general's office, where Kleindienst ordered the assistant director to seal Hoover's office and to keep all files there intact. A little after noon on the same day, Mohr sent the attorney general the following memo:

"In accordance with your instructions, Mr. Hoover's private, personal office was secured at 11:40 A.M. today. It was necessary to change the lock on one door in order to accomplish this.

"To my knowledge, the contents of the office are exactly as they would have been had Mr. Hoover reported to the office this morning. I have in my possession the only key to the office."

Within the hour, Kleindienst reported to President Nixon that "the files were safe"—meaning the "secret files" that everyone in official Washington presumed must exist in Hoover's office.

What John Mohr had not told Attorney General Kleindienst, however, was that Hoover kept no files in his office. All of the FBI's most secret files were kept in the office of Hoover's secretary of fifty-four years, Miss Helen Gandy. And even by the time Hoover's office was being sealed that morning, Miss Gandy had begun reviewing the director's Personal OC Files, separating them, culling them, shredding many, and placing the others in cardboard boxes to be hidden in the basement of Hoover's home at Thirtieth Place NW.

With six weeks, those secret files would be moved again, never to be seen again by anyone within the FBI or in official Washington.

But I am ahead of myself. What matters at this point are the events on the morning of July 2, 1961, my forty-ninth birthday and Ernest Hemingway's last moments on the planet. Those events made me vow to do two things before I died. The first of those—to track down and liberate the FBI's secret files on Hemingway and his counterespionage ring in Cuba—would take me more than a decade of effort and would entail danger to my life and liberty. But the second promise I made in July 1961 would be, I knew even then, infinitely harder to keep. That was to write this narrative. In spite of the thousands of case reports I had written over the decades, nothing prepared me to tell this story, in this manner. Hemingway the writer could have helped me—indeed, he would have been wryly amused that I was finally forced to try to tell a story using all of the sneaky tricks in a fiction writer's repertoire. "Fiction is a way of trying to tell things in a way that is truer than truth," he said to me that night along the coast as we waited for the German U-boat to appear.

"No," I had said then. "Truth is truth. Fiction is a pack of lies masquerading as truth."

We shall see.

The events of the morning of July 2, 1961, in Ketchum, Idaho...Only Ernest Hemingway knew the truth of those few moments, but the results seemed obvious enough.

According to the testimony of his fourth wife and many friends, Hemingway had made several clumsy efforts at suicide in the months before and after his second series of electroshock treatments in May and June. Once, as he was returning to the Mayo Clinic, he had tried to walk into the spinning propeller of a small plane warming up on the tarmac. Another time, a friend had to wrestle a loaded shotgun away from Hemingway at his home.

Despite all this, Mary Hemingway had locked the writer's guns in the basement storage room but had left the keys to the room in plain view on the kitchen windowsill because "no one had a right to deny a man access to his possessions." I thought about this for years. They—Miss Mary and friends—had felt that they had the right to authorize a series of electroshock treatments which all but destroyed Ernest Hemingway's brain and personality, but she decided that she could not keep his guns locked away from him when he was depressed to the point of suicide.

That Sunday morning of July 2, 1961, Hemingway awoke early, as he always did. This morning was beautiful, sunny and cloudless. Miss Mary was the only other occupant of the Ketchum house, sleeping in a separate bedroom. She did not awaken as Hemingway tiptoed down the carpeted stairs, took the keys from the windowsill, went down to the storage room, and chose—I believe—his faithful Boss twelve-gauge. *Then he went back upstairs, crossed the living room to the tiled foyer at the foot of the stairs, loaded both barrels, set the butt of the shotgun on the tiled floor, set the muzzles of both barrels against his forehead, I think—not in his mouth—and tripped both triggers.*

I emphasize the details because I think it is important that he did not simply load the gun in the storage room and do the deed there, in the basement, where even the sound might have been swallowed by the intervening doors and carpeted floors and cinder-block walls. He carried the gun to the foyer, to the base of the stairs, to the one place in the house where it was guaranteed that Miss Mary could not get to the phone or the front door without stepping over his body and the pool of blood, splintered skull, and blasted brain tissue that had been the source for all those novels, all those stories, all the lies he once tried to convince me were truer than truth.

Some months earlier, Hemingway had been asked to write a simple sentence or two for a book commemorating JFK's inauguration. After hours of futile effort, Hemingway had broken down and sobbed in front of his doctor: the great writer could not complete a simple sentence.

But he could still communicate, and I think that the place and manner of his death were a last message. It was addressed to Miss Mary, of course, but also to J. Edgar Hoover, to the FBI, to the OSS... or the CIA, as it was now called... to the memories of those who were there that year between late April and mid-September 1942 when the writer played spy and became entangled with Nazi agents, FBI snoops, British spooks, Cuban politicians and policemen. Spanish priests and noblemen, ten-year-old secret agents and German U-boats. I do not flatter myself that Hemingway was thinking of me that last morning, but if his message was what I think it was—a last, violent move to declare stalemate to a decades-old game rather than suffer checkmate at the hands of a patient but relentless enemy—then perhaps I was woven into the tapestry of his thoughts that morning, a minor figure in a baroque pattern.

I hope that on the morning of my forty-ninth birthday, in Hemingway's last moments, he might have been thinking, if his sorrow and depression allowed him such a luxury as coherent thought, not only of his final, decisive, twelve-gauge gesture of ultimate defiance but also of any victories he had won in his long-running war against invisible enemies.

I wonder if he was thinking of the Crook Factory.

2

MR. HOOVER SUMMONED ME to Washington in late April 1942. The cable caught up to me in Mexico City and ordered me to report to the director "by the fastest possible means." This gave me pause for a moment, since everyone in the Bureau knew how penny-pinching Mr. Hoover could be. Normally, a summons back to Washington, even from Mexico City or Bogotá, would entail travel by burro, car, boat, and train, while requiring a careful eye on the expense account.

On the morning of my appointment with Mr. Hoover, after hops through Texas, Missouri, and Ohio, I landed at Washington's National Airport. I looked out the window of my silver DC-3 with some interest. Not only was it a beautiful spring morning with the dome of the Capitol Building and the Washington Monument gleaming cleanly in the rich April light, but the airport itself was new. In previous flights into Washington I had landed at the city's old airport, Hoover Field, across the Potomac River in Virginia, near Arlington National Cemetery. I had been out of the country since the previous summer, but I had heard about how—even before Pearl Harbor and without presidential authorization—the army had started work on a huge, new, five-sided headquarters where the old airport had been.

As we circled once before landing, I could see that the new National Airport was much more conveniently located near the downtown. It was obvious that the modern airport was not yet finished: the brand-new terminal still had construction equipment and workers swarming around it like ants. I also caught a glimpse of the new army headquarters going up. The press had already started calling it "the Pentagon," and the name seemed appropriate from my vantage point three thousand feet up, for although only about half of the monstrosity had been completed, the foundation and rising walls clearly showed the five-sided shape. The parking lots alone covered all of what had been Hoover Field and its next-door amusement park, and I could see lines of army trucks rolling in toward the completed part of the building, presumably delivering all the desks and typewriters and other bureaucratic detritus of the new, expanded army.

I sat back as the drone of the two engines changed pitch for landing. I had liked old Hoover Field, although it had been nothing more than a grass strip between an amusement park on one side and a dump on the other. A county highway, Military Road, had run across the landing strip—not parallel to it, but *across* it—and I had read a few years earlier that the airport manager had been arrested and convicted for trying to put up a stoplight there to halt traffic while commercial aircraft landed. The county highway department had torn the illegal stoplight out. It had not seemed to matter; the times I had flown in, the pilots seemed adept enough at gauging their landings between the crossing cars and trucks. I recalled that there had been no control tower as such and that the windsock had flown from the highest point on the roller coaster next to the field.

We landed, taxied, and I was the third person out, rearranging the .38 on my belt as I moved quickly down the stairway to the warm tarmac. I carried a bag with a change of underwear, a clean shirt, and my other dark suit, but I did not know if I would have time to find a hotel, check in, shower, shave, and change before my meeting with Mr. Hoover. The thought worried me. Mr. Hoover had no patience with special agents who showed up in less than their Sunday best, even if those agents had spent a day and a night catching planes across Mexico and the United States.

Passing through the new terminal that still smelled of paint and fresh plaster, I paused to look at the papers on the newsstand. One headline of *The Washington Daily News* read ENOUGH VD CASES IN D.C. TO OVERFLOW THE STADIUM. I tried to remember how many people could fit into old Griffith Stadium. Thirty thousand, at least. Glancing around at the mobs of crisp new uniforms—Army, Navy, MP's, SP's, Marines, Coast Guard, most of them kissing at least one girl goodbye—I was surprised that the VD problem since the beginning of the war was that small.

Passing through the new terminal, I headed for the telephone booths near the exit doors. My one chance to get a shower and a change of clothes would be to get in touch with Tom Dillon, a friend who had gone through Quantico with me and shared a bit of Camp X training before he had been transferred to Washington and me to the SIS. Tom was still a bachelor—or had been when I had talked to him ten months earlier—and his apartment was not far from the Justice Department. I plugged in my nickel, asked the operator to connect me with his home number, hoping that this was his day off, knowing that as a field agent Tom was probably not in the office if this was a workday for him. I listened to the phone ring. Dispirited, I was fumbling for another nickel when a hairy hand came over my shoulder, took the receiver out of my hand, and hung it up.

I spun around, ready to deck the soldier or sailor who had made the mistake of fooling with me, only to be confronted by Tom Dillon's smiling face a few inches from my own.

"I heard you ask for my number, Joe," said Dillon. "I'm not home."

"You never were," I said with a grin. We shook hands. "What are you doing here, Tom?" I did not believe in coincidence.

"Mr. Ladd sent me. He said that you had an appointment at the Department at eleven-thirty and that I should give you a ride. Give you time to clean up at my place if you want."

"Great," I said. Mr. Ladd was D. M. Ladd—"Mickey" to his friends in the Bureau—one of the director's assistants and now head of the Domestic Intelligence Division, in which Tom worked. Dillon had not said that I had an appointment with the director and probably did not know that bit of information. It was not my place to tell him.

"Your plane was early," said Tom as if in apology for not meeting me at the gate.

"Didn't have to wait for traffic to cross the landing strip," I said. "Let's get out of here."

Tom grabbed my bag and led the way out through the crowds to where his Ford coupe was parked at the curb just beyond the main doors. The Ford's top was down, and Tom tossed my bag into the back seat and jogged around to the driver's side with the same boyish energy I remembered from Quantico. I settled back into the thick cushions as we left the airport and drove toward downtown. The air here was warm and humid, but much less warm and humid than I had been used to for the past few years in Colombia and Mexico. It was too late in the season to see Washington's famous Japanese cherry trees in full bloom, but the scent of their remaining blossoms still filled the broad avenues, mixing with the rich perfume from the magnolia trees that gave the city its familiar Southern feel.

I say familiar, but in actuality this might have been a completely different city from the Washington I had lived in for part of '38 and '39 and visited briefly the previous summer. That Washington had been a sleepy Southern town, its broad avenues never crowded with traffic, its demeanor more relaxed than many South American villages I had spent time in since then. Now everything was changed.

The "tempos" I had heard about were everywhere: ugly, drab buildings of gray asbestos board, each about half a block long with five wings extending from one side, each thrown up in a week to house the invading hordes of war workers and bureaucrats for the duration of the war. Tempos ran along both sides of the Reflecting Pool in front of the Lincoln Memorial, blocking the view of the pool itself, the ugly structures connected by rickety-looking covered bridges crossing and recrossing the water. More tempos filled the area along Constitution Avenue, obliterating a pleasant park where I had often grabbed a hasty lunch, and a pack of aggressive tempos circled the Washington Monument like so many gray, scabrous scavengers closing in for the kill.

The avenues were as wide as I remembered, but now they were packed with cars and trucks, including more convoys of olive-green Army trucks, in the backs of which I could see the desks and chairs and typewriters and filing cabinets which I had only imagined from my airplane window. America was going to war. In triplicate. The sidewalks were crowded, and while there were still many uniforms visible, the majority of people were dressed in the civil uniform of the day—gray and black suits, the women's skirts shorter than I remembered, shoulders emphasized on male and female alike. Everyone appeared young and healthy and seemed to be hurrying to important meetings. Briefcases were ubiquitous; even some of the women carried them.

Trolley cars were still evident despite the heavy automobile traffic, but I noticed that the trolleys seemed *older* somehow. It took me a minute to realize that they *were* older—that the city must have brought old cars out of retirement to meet the demand of all this added population. I watched as a quaint, double-ended, wooden relic from the 1800s screeched by, glass windows along the roofline, its running boards crowded with men hanging on to brass bars and leather straps. Most of the men were Negroes.

"Yeah," said Tom Dillon, looking over to catch my gaze. "Even more niggers in town now than before the war."

I nodded. Someone looking at us from one of those trolley cars might think that we were brothers, perhaps even fraternal twins. Tom was thirty-one and I was only twenty-nine, but his skin was smoother and he still had a hint of freckles along the brim of his nose. And his nose had never been broken, unlike mine. We were both wearing the dark suits required by Mr. Hoover, with white shirts—admittedly, Tom's was crisper than mine at the moment—and nearly identical snap-brim hats. We each had our hair cut the regulation two inches above our collars, and if our hats had blown off, a viewer would have noticed how carefully we combed our hair on the top to avoid the "pointy-headed look" that Mr. Hoover disliked. Each of us carried the Bureau-required white handkerchief in our right front trouser pocket so that we could wipe our hands before a handshake if we were nervous or had been exercising strenuously. Mr. Hoover hated encountering "damp palms" and did not want that stigma attached to any of his special agents. Both Tom and I carried matching Police Positive .38-caliber revolvers in black holsters on our belts, shifted to the right side so that they would not bulge too noticeably against our suit jackets. Unless Tom had gotten a raise, we each earned $65 a week: a solid sum in 1942 but not impressive for the college and law school graduates who met the minimum Bureau requirements for employment. Both of us had been born in Texas into Catholic families, had gone to second-rate Southern colleges, and had attended law school.

But there the similarities ended. Tom Dillon still spoke in a slow, West Texas drawl. My family had moved to California when I was three, then to Florida when I was six, and as far as I could tell, I had no discernible accent. Tom had gone to college on his family's money. I had squeaked by on a football scholarship, supplemented by a part-time job. Tom had graduated from law school before being recruited, thus meeting Mr. Hoover's requirements, but I had been an exception, recruited at the beginning of my second year of law school, just as I was about to drop out because of lack of funds and motivation. The reasons for the exception were simple: I spoke Spanish fluently and Mr. Hoover had needed Spanish-speaking special agents for the Special Intelligence Service he had been planning—counterintelligence agents who could blend into the crowd, talk to informants, and say "Thank you" in Spanish-speaking Latin America without pronouncing the word as "Grassyass." I qualified. My father had been Mexican, my mother Irish. Which led to another difference between Tom Dillon and me.

When Dillon had said "even more niggers in town now than before the war" I had stifled the impulse to reach across, grab the back of the other agent's head with both hands, and smash his face against the steering wheel. I didn't give a damn about him insulting Negroes—I hadn't worked with any blacks or known any well enough personally to avoid the bias we all had against these fourth-class American citizens—but when Tom Dillon said "nigger," I heard "beaner" or "spic" or "wetback."

My father had been Mexican. My skin was light enough, and I had inherited enough of my Irish mother's bone structure and features to pass for a typical Anglo-Protestant American, but I had grown up being ashamed of my father's Mexican heritage and fighting anyone and everyone who referred to me as "Mexican." And because my father had died when I was six years old and my mother less than a year later, I felt even more deeply ashamed of my shame—of having never told my father that I forgave him for being non-pure-white American and having never begged forgiveness of my mother for hating her for marrying a Mexican.

It was strange. As I grew older, I wished more and more that I had known my father better. I had been not quite five when he went off to the Great War, and I had turned six before we learned he died over there—of the flu, three months after the war ended. How could I miss someone so much whom I had never really known?

There were other differences between Tom Dillon and Joe Lucas. Tom's work in the Domestic Intelligence Division entailed what the vast majority of FBI agents did—investigation. The Bureau, as Mr. Hoover repeatedly had to point out to eager congressmen and senators, was not in the business of police enforcement. It was an *investigative* agency. Tom spent most of his time doing interviews, making reports, cross-checking leads with other leads, and occasionally following people. He had some experience in carrying out black bag jobs, planting bugs, and other illegal surveillance techniques, but for the most part, that was left to the experts. I was one of those experts.

And Tom had never killed anyone.

"So," said Tom as we drove past the White House. "You still with SIS?"

"Uh-huh," I said. Noticed that they had put up some sort of security post at the Pennsylvania Avenue entrance to the White House. The gates were still open, but it looked as if the policeman at the gate might check your credentials if you tried to walk onto the White House grounds. When I had visited the city the previous summer, anyone could still stroll through the grounds without being challenged, although a Marine guard might ask your business if you walked into the executive mansion itself. When I had first come to the city in the mid-'30s, there had been no gates to the White House and entire sections of the grounds had no fence. I remembered playing baseball on the South Lawn that first summer.

"Still in Mexico?" said Tom.

"Hmm," I said. We stopped for a red light. White House

workers hurried by, some with brown lunch bags in their hands. "Tell me, Tom," I said, "what's been happening here in Domestic Division since Pearl Harbor?" If queried by someone, Tom Dillon would probably say that he and I had shared confidences from the beginning, speaking openly about almost everything. The truth was that *Tom* shared confidences. "Caught any Nazi or Jap spies?" I said.

Tom chuckled and shifted the coupe into gear as the light changed. "Heck, Joe, we've been so busy being sicced onto our own people, we don't have time for Nazis or Japs."

"Which people?" I knew that Tom loved name-dropping. It would probably cost him his job someday. "Who's the Bureau been sicced on since the war began, Tom?"

He peeled a stick of Wrigley's and began chewing loudly. "Oh, the vice president," he said casually.

I laughed. Vice President Henry Agard Wallace was an idealist and an honest man. He was also known as an idiot and a dupe for the Communists.

Tom looked hurt at my laughter. "I mean it, Joe. We've been on him since last spring. Bugs, taps, tails, black bag jobs... the man can't take a piss without Mr. Hoover getting a lab report on it."

"Uh-huh," I said. "Wallace *is* a threat...."

Tom missed my irony. "Damned straight," he said. "We've got proof that the Communists are considering using him as an active agent, Joe."

I shrugged. "The Russians are our allies now, remember?"

Tom glanced over at me. He was shocked enough that he had quit chewing his gum. "Jesus, Joe... don't joke about things like that. Mr. Hoover doesn't—"

"I know, I know," I said. The Japanese had attacked Pearl Harbor and Adolf Hitler was the most dangerous man in the world, but Mr. Hoover was famous for his desire to deal with the Communist menace first. "Who else is taking up your time these days?" I said.

"Sumner Welles," said Tom, squinting in the bright sunlight as we stopped for another red light. A streetcar rumbled and screeched its way in front of us. We were only a few blocks from Tom's apartment, but the traffic was almost solid here.

I pushed the brim of my hat back. "Sumner Welles?" I repeated. Welles was undersecretary of state, as well as a personal friend and close adviser to the president. Welles was an expert on Latin American policy and crucial to the intelligence community there; his name had come across the Colombian embassy desk a dozen times in decision-making situations that had affected me. There had been rumors that Sumner Welles had been recalled from his embassy post in Colombia long before I had arrived, but no one was sure of the reason.

"Is Welles a Communist?" I said.

Tom shook his head. "Uh-uh. A fruit."

"Come again?"

He looked at me and the old Tom Dillon smirk was back. "You heard me, Joe. A fruit. A queer. A fag."

I waited.

"It started almost two years ago, Joe. September 1940. On the president's special train coming back from Alabama after Speaker Bankhead's funeral."

Tom looked at me as if I was supposed to ask eager questions at this point. I waited.

The light changed. We ground forward a few yards and then stopped behind a mass of trucks and cars. Tom's voice rose to be heard over the honking and engine noises. "I guess Welles had too much to drink, rang for the porter... several of them showed up... and then he, well, exposed himself to them and suggested... well, you know, Joe, fag stuff." Tom was blushing. He was a tough G-man, but still a good Catholic boy at heart.

"That's been confirmed?" I said, thinking about how it would affect the SIS if Welles were to be replaced.

"Hell, yes," said Tom. "Mr. Hoover put Ed Tamm on it, and the Bureau's been watching Welles for a year and a half. The old fag gets drunk and trolls the parks for little boys. We've got SA reports, eyewitness reports, depositions, wire recordings of phone conversations..."

I tugged the brim of my hat lower to shade my eyes. According to the embassy people I trusted most, Sumner Welles was the smartest man in the State Department. "Has Mr. Hoover briefed the president?" I said.

"A year ago this January," said Tom. He spit his gum out over the side of the coupe. Traffic began to move. We turned right off Wisconsin. "According to Dick Ferris, who worked with Tamm on this, Mr. Hoover didn't make any recommendations... wasn't asked for any...and the president didn't really say anything. Dick says that Attorney General Biddle tried to take this up with the president later and FDR just said, 'Well, he's not doing it on government time, is he?' "

I nodded. "Making homosexual overtures is a felony," I said.

"Yeah, and Dick says that Ed Tamm says that Mr. Hoover pointed this out to the president and explained how it opens Welles up to blackmail. The president's just sitting on it for now, but that won't last for long...."

"Why not?" I said. I saw the block where I had lived four years ago, sharing an apartment with two other special agents. Tom's apartment was only three blocks west.

"Bullitt's after Welles now," said Tom, turning the wheel with both hands.

William Christian Bullitt. A man whom one of the columnists had once called "an Iago of Iagos." I had never read Shakespeare, but I understood the allusion. Mr. Hoover had a file on Bullitt, as well, and in one of my earlier jobs in Washington I had been forced to review it. William Christian Bullitt was another buddy of FDR's, an ambassador who made enemies in every country he was assigned to, and the kind of opportunist who would fuck a woodpile in the off chance there might be a snake in it. At the very least, according to the file I'd read, Bullitt had seduced FDR's adoring and naive secretary, Missy LeHand, just so he could get a little better access to the president.

If Bullitt was after Sumner Welles, he would bring him down someday...by leaking stories to FDR's political enemies, by whispering to the columnists, by expressing his shock to Cordell Hull, the secretary of state. Bullitt would destroy Welles come hell or high water, and in so doing destroy the Latin American desk at State, sink the Good Neighbor Policy that was working down there, and weaken the nation in time of war. But a man who had homosexual urges when drunk would be out of government service and Mr. William Christian Bullitt would probably gain some leverage in the never-ending power game.

Ah, Washington.

"Who else is the Bureau after?" I said tiredly.

Amazingly, there was a parking spot right in front of Tom's apartment building. He swept the coupe into the little space, left the engine running, but pulled on the parking brake. He rubbed his nose. "You'll never guess, Joe. I've been involved in this one personally. I've gotta work on it tonight. I'll leave you the keys... maybe see you tomorrow."

I probably won't be here tomorrow, I thought. I said, "Great."

"Go ahead, guess." Tom still wanted to play his game.

I sighed. "Eleanor Roosevelt," I said.

Tom blinked. "Damn. You've heard about the investigation?"

"You have to be fucking kidding," I said. Mr. Hoover had Official/Confidential files on most of the important people in Washington—in the United States—and everyone knew that he hated Eleanor Roosevelt, but the director would never go after a member of a sitting president's family. He was too concerned about his own job for that.

Tom saw that I was in the dark. He pushed back the brim of his hat with a confident gesture and laid his arm on the top of the steering wheel as he faced me. "No joke, Joe. Of course, we're not following Mrs. Roosevelt personally, but..."

"You had me going, Tom."

"No, no," he said, leaning closer so that I could smell the spearmint on his breath. "For the last three years the old lady's been nuts about a kid named Joe Lash..."

I knew all about Lash, had seen his file in relation to a case I had worked on in 1939 regarding the American Youth Congress, even interviewed him once myself while pretending to be a student interested in his organization. Lash had been national secretary of the Youth Congress then, a perennial student himself, older than me but decades younger in every way that counts—one of those boys in a man's body, going on thirty but with all the wisdom and sophistication of a ten-year-old. The Youth Congress was a left-wing debating society, just the kind of organization the Communists loved to fund and infiltrate, and it was a pet of Mrs. Roosevelt's.

"They're lovers..." Tom was saying.

"Bullshit," I said. "She's sixty years old—"

"Fifty-eight," said Tom. "Lash is thirty-three. Mrs. Roosevelt has her own apartment in New York, Joe. She *refused Secret Service protection*."

"So?" I said. "That doesn't prove anything except that the old broad has sense. Who wants those Treasury assholes breathing down your neck twenty-four hours a day?"

Tom was shaking his head. "Mr. Hoover knows that it means something."

I had a headache. For the briefest of seconds, I again had the urge to grab Tom's tie and slam his face into the coupe's dash until that pert, freckled nose was a shapeless, bleeding mass. "Tom," I said softly, "are you telling me that we're doing black bag jobs on Mrs. Roosevelt? Chamfering her mail?"

He shook his head again. "Of course not, Joe. But we're photographing *Lash's* mail, bugging *his* phone and apartment. You should read the letters that our dear First Lady Nigger Lover sends that Commie jerk... hot stuff, Joe."

"I bet," I said. The thought of that homely old lady writing passionate letters to this boy made me sad.

"That's where I'm going tonight," said Tom, adjusting his hat again. "Lash got drafted a couple of weeks ago, and we're handing over the investigation to the CIC."

"It figures," I said. The army's Counter-Intelligence Corps, a branch of its Military Intelligence Division run by General John Bissell, might have been generously described as a drunken chimpanzee cluster fuck. Bissell's group might also have been described as a bunch of right-wing assholes, but not by me. Not this day. One thing was for sure, I knew—the CIC would have no hesitation in tailing, bugging, tapping, or black bagging Mrs. Eleanor Roosevelt. And I also knew that FDR, for all his patience with sad fools like Sumner Welles, would have Bissell's ass transferred to the South Pacific in a minute when he discovered that the army was after his wife.

Tom tossed me his keys. "Could beer in the icebox," he said. "Sorry there's no food. We can go out for dinner tomorrow when I get off duty."

"Hope so," I said. I jingled the keys in my fist. "Thanks for this, Tom. If I have to leave before you get back tomorrow..."

"Put 'em over the door, just like the old days," said Tom. He leaned over to shake hands above the hot metal of the car door. "See you later, buddy."

I watched him pull the coupe out into traffic before I hustled up the stairs. Tom Dillon was the perfect FBI man—eager to please but basically lazy, willing to eat shit if Mr. Hoover or Mr. Hoover's men said to eat shit, quick at following orders and slow to think on his own, a defender of democracy who hated niggers, spics, kikes, wops, and greasers. Without doubt Tom fired his .38 religiously at the Bureau firing range in the basement of the Justice Department Building and would be proficient with submachine guns, shotguns, high-velocity rifles, and hand-to-hand combat. On paper, he was a competent killer. Tom would last about three days in SIS field operations.

I climbed the stairs to my shower and put him out of my mind.

3

THE MAIN ENTRANCE to the huge Department of Justice Building was at Ninth Street and Pennsylvania Avenue. The classic porticoes, each with four massive pillars on each side of that corner, started above the second-floor windows and ran all the way to the roofline, four stories above. On the Pennsylvania Avenue side, near the corner, the only balcony was outside the fifth-floor window to the left of those pillars. This was Mr. Hoover's personal balcony. Already, in 1942, he had watched eighteen years' worth of U.S. presidents pass by in inaugural parades, then had stood there to watch some of them returning in funeral processions.

I knew the building, of course, but I had never had a desk in it, having been relegated to various field offices or undercover work during my earlier stays in the District of Columbia. This worked in my favor as I came in ten minutes early for my eleven-thirty appointment, looking showered, shaved, hair pomaded, wearing a clean shirt and suit, shoes polished, hat carried carefully in my not-damp hands. The place was huge, and there were a few faces I would have recognized and who might have recognized me, but I did not encounter them as I got off the elevator on the fifth floor and headed for the director's sanctum sanctorum.

Mr. Hoover's office was not at the center of the building, but actually almost hidden away. To find it one had to traipse down a long hallway, then through a large conference room with ashtrays set along a polished table, then through an outer office where Miss Gandy waited like the proverbial dragon guarding the legendary virgin. In 1942, Miss Gandy was already a legend herself:

Hoover's one indispensable employee, part protector, part nursemaid, and the only human being allowed to see, catalog, index, and read Hoover's Personal Files. She was forty-five years old when I walked into that outer office in 1942, but Hoover already referred to her as "that old biddy" to his male friends and closest assistants. And it was true that there was something of the biddy hen about her.

"Special Agent Lucas?" she said, glancing up at me as I stood there with my hat in my hands. "You are four minutes early."

I nodded.

"Take a seat, please. The Director is running on schedule."

I resisted the impulse to smile at the sound of the capital letter on "Director" and took a seat as ordered. The room was almost dowdy—two over-stuffed chairs and a sprung sofa against the wall. I sat on the sofa. I knew that this was the only glimpse of J. Edgar Hoover's office that most special agents ever saw: the director (I thought of him with no capital letter) usually met his lower-level subordinates in the conference room or in this outer office. I looked around, expecting to see John Dillinger's scalp on one of the few shelves of the display case across from me, but the exhibit Tom and my other SA friends had described in loving detail was absent. Only a few plaques and a dusty trophy sat there. Perhaps the scalp was out at the cleaners.

At precisely eleven-thirty, Miss Gandy said, "The Director will see you now, Special Agent Lucas." I confess that my pulse rate was higher than usual as I went through that inner door.

Mr. Hoover leaped up as I came in, bustled around his desk, shook my hand in the center of the room, and waved me to a chair to the right of his desk while he returned to his own place. I knew from hearing other special agents talk that this was the invariable routine if one were lucky enough to meet with the director in his inner office.

"Well, Special Agent Lucas," said Mr. Hoover as he settled back in his throne. I say throne without sarcasm, because his office was set up that way—his desk and chair were on a raised dais, his own chair was much more substantial than the low guest chair in which I sat, and the tall window was at his back, the blinds open so that if the sun were shining, Mr. Hoover would be little more than a massive silhouette against the light. But the day had become partly cloudy since the glorious morning, the light behind him was muted, and I could make out Hoover's features easily enough.

J. Edgar Hoover was forty-six years old on that April day in 1942—the only time I ever met with him, before or since—and I took my assessment of him at the same time he was assessing me. When meeting other men, it was a habit of mine—although *weakness* might be a better word—to judge them according to how I would deal with them in a fistfight. Physically, Hoover would not have been a problem. He was short for an agent—exactly my height, I'd noticed as we had shaken hands—and while I still would have qualified in the light heavyweight category, he must have outweighed me by at least twenty pounds. He was probably around five foot ten and 183, well above the weight-for-height guidelines he had set for his FBI agents. The first impression was of squatness, and that impression was enhanced by the fact that his broad upper body tapered down to the smallest feet I had ever seen on a man. Hoover was well dressed, his dark, double-breasted suit impeccably tailored, his silk tie showing hints of pink and burgundy which no SA would have dared wear, and I made note of the matching pink silk handkerchief puffed out in his breast pocket. His hair looked black and was slicked back so firmly on his head that his characteristic scowl and squint looked like they were caused by a flat wig pulled too tight.

The popular caricature of Hoover was of a bulldog—the squinting or popped eyes, the squashed-in nose, the massive, clenched jaw—and all those elements were visible in that first moment of encounter with him, but my own thought was more of a Chinese pug than a bulldog. Hoover moved fast—his walk out to the center of the room, his handshake, and his retreat to his chair had taken less than fifteen seconds—but his was a nervously purposeful energy. If I had to fight the man, I would have gone for his belly—obviously his softest part, second only to his gonads—but I would have made damned sure not to turn my back on him when he went down. Those eyes and that set of mouth belonged to a man who would try to bite you to death after you'd cut off his arms and legs.

"Well, Special Agent Lucas," he said again, flipping open a thick personnel file that I was sure was mine. Except for a few other files and a black, leather-bound book a few inches from his left elbow—the Bible that had been a gift from his mother, an artifact all of us had heard about—his desk was bare. "Did you have a good trip to Washington, Lucas?"

"Yes, sir."

"Do you know why I've called you here, Lucas?" Hoover's speech was fast, clipped, staccato.

"No, sir."

The director nodded but did not go on to enlighten me. He thumbed through my life as if it was the first time he had ever seen it, although I was certain that he had studied it carefully before I arrived.

"I see you were born in 1912," said Hoover. "In...ah... Brownsville, Texas."

"Yes, sir." Despite the uselessness of guessing about the reason for my summons, I had done some speculating during the trip from Mexico. I did not flatter myself that I was in line for some sort of promotion or special recognition. What set me apart from most of the other four thousand or so special agents working for J. Edgar Hoover that year was that I had killed two men... three if he chose to count Krivitsky from the previous year. The last man in the FBI to get a reputation as a killer had been Special Agent in Charge Melvin Purvis, the agent credited with shooting both John Dillinger and Pretty Boy Floyd, and while it was common knowledge in the Bureau that Purvis had not actually killed either of those criminals, it was also understood that Hoover had forced Purvis into resigning in 1935. Purvis had become famous... more famous than his director, who had never shot at a crook or actually arrested anyone. The public was to associate only one name with the FBI—J. Edgar Hoover. Purvis had to go. This was one reason I had been damned sure never to claim special credit for anything—not for the cases when we had rounded up the last of the Abwehr agents in Mexico, not for the two shootings in that dark, adobe house when Schiller and his hired assassin tried to kill me, not for Krivitsky.

"You have two brothers and a sister," said Hoover.

"Yes, sir."

He looked up from the file and stared at me. "Seems like a small family for Mexican Catholics," he said.

"My father was born in Mexico," I said. "My mother was Irish." This was the other possibility, that the Bureau had only recently discovered my father's nationality.

"Mexican and Irish," said Hoover. "Then it's a miracle that there were only four children in the family."

A miracle called the influenza epidemic and pneumonia, I thought, my face showing nothing.

Hoover was looking at the file again. "Did they call you José at home, Agent Lucas?"

My father had. He had not become an American citizen until the year before he died. "The name on my birth certificate is Joseph, Mr. Hoover," I said.

If this was the reason I had been called to Washington, I was ready for it. Not that the Bureau discriminated. There were 5,702 Negro FBI special agents in 1942—I had seen the number in a report at the Mexico City field office less than a week earlier. About 5,690 of these SAs had been appointed in the past six months—all of them black drivers, janitors, cooks, and office help whom Hoover had not wanted drafted. Hoover had worked hard to make sure that special agents of the FBI were immune from the draft, at the same time he had let it be known to every special agent in the weeks after Pearl Harbor that they could enlist if they wished but that there would be no place waiting for them in the Bureau if and when they got back.

I knew that there had been at least five Negro G-men before Pearl Harbor—Mr. Hoover's three chauffeurs, of course, as well as John Amos and Sam Noisette. Amos was an old man. He had been Theodore Roosevelt's valet, personal bodyguard, and friend—TR had literally died in Sam Amos's arms—and when Hoover had become director of the Bureau of Investigation in 1924, Amos was already on the payroll. I had seen the old black man once at the firing range, where his job was to clean the weapons.

Sam Noisette was a more recent Negro success story, a special agent assigned to Mr. Hoover's personal office—I was surprised that I had not seen him on the way in—who was often held up as an example of the Bureau's generous policy toward blacks. When someone once showed me an article in *Ebony* magazine trumpeting the close working friendship between Special Agent Noisette and Mr. Hoover, I had to smile at the sentence "The relationship between the two men virtually sets the race relations pattern for the huge agency." It was true, but perhaps not in the way the *Ebony* writer had meant it. Noisette—"Mr. Sam," as Hoover and everyone else called him—was the director's personal assistant and majordomo, given the responsibility of handing the director a dry towel when Hoover emerged from his private bathroom, of helping him into his coat, and—most important—of swatting the flies which J. Edgar Hoover loathed with a passion matched only by his fear and hatred of Communists.

Did they call you José at home? Hoover was telling me that he knew...the Bureau knew...that my father had not been an American citizen at the time of my birth, that technically I was the son of a beaner, a wetback.

I looked the pug dog of a little man in the eye and waited.

"I see you moved around a lot as a boy, Special Agent Lucas. Texas. Then California. Then Florida. Then back to Texas for college."

"Yes, sir."

Hoover still looked at the file. "Your father died in 1919, in France, I see. As a result of war wounds?"

"The influenza," I said.

"But he was there in the army?"

"Yes, sir." *In a labor battalion. Which was the last to be shipped home. Which is why he was still there to catch the influenza at the height of the epidemic.*

"Yes, yes," said Hoover, dismissing my father without looking up from the file. "And your mother died the same year." Now he looked up, one dark eyebrow rising slightly.

"Pneumonia," I said. *A broken heart,* I thought.

Hoover shuffled the papers. "But you and the other children weren't put in an orphanage?"

"No, sir. My sister went to live with my aunt's family." *In Mexico,* I thought, and prayed that this detail was not in my dossier. "My two brothers and I went to live with my father's brother in Florida. He had only one son to help him on his fishing boat. My brothers and I worked with him on it for several years while we were in school—I used to return and work every summer with him while I was putting myself through college."

"So you are familiar with the Caribbean?" said Hoover.

"Not really, sir. We fished on the Gulf side. One summer I worked on a charter boat that sailed around to Miami and then to Bimini, but we never saw the other islands."

"But you know boats," said Hoover, his popped eyes staring blackly at me. I had no idea what he was thinking.

"Yes, sir. Enough to get by on one."

The director looked back at the file. "Tell me about the Veracruz incident, Special Agent Lucas."

I knew that he was looking at my ten-page, single-spaced report in the file. "You're aware, sir, of the details of the operation up to the point that Schiller was tipped off by an informant in the Mexican police?"

Hoover nodded. The sun had come out for a moment, and its glare through the blinds behind the director gave the effect he liked. I could no longer see Hoover's eyes—only the silhouette of his burly shoulders extending to either side of the dark shape that was his chair...that and the gleam of sunlight on his oiled hair.

"I was supposed to meet them at the house on Simón Bolívar Street at eleven P.M. to make the drop," I said. "Just as I had a dozen times before. I always came at least an hour before the meeting to check out the place. Only this time they had come ninety minutes before the rendezvous time. They were waiting in the darkened house when I let myself in the front door. At the last minute, I realized that they were there."

"What tipped you off, Special Agent Lucas?" came Hoover's voice from the dark silhouette.

"The dog, sir. There had been an old yellow hound that had barked every time I'd come before. Usually dogs in Mexico aren't all that territorial, but this was a bitch who belonged to the peasant who watched the house for Schiller. It was chained up in the side yard. The peasant had been picked up in our sweep two days previously, and the dog was starved."

"So you heard it barking?"

"No, sir. I *didn't* hear it. My guess is that it had been barking since Schiller had arrived, and he told the man with him to cut its throat."

Hoover chuckled. "Just like that Sherlock Holmes case. The dog in the night."

"Pardon, sir?"

"Haven't you read Sherlock Holmes, Special Agent Lucas?"

"No, sir. I don't read make-believe books."

"Make-believe books? You mean novels?"

"Yes, sir."

"All right, go on. What happened next?"

I creased the brim of my hat as it sat in my lap. "Not much, sir. Or, rather, quite a bit, but very quickly. I was already at the door before I realized that the dog wasn't barking. I decided to go in. They weren't expecting me that early. They hadn't found good firing positions yet. I went in fast. They shot at me, but it was dark and they missed. I shot back."

Hoover folded his hands as if in prayer. "The ballistics report said that between the two of them they fired more than forty bullets. Nine millimeter. Lugers?"

"Lopez, the hired gun, had a Luger," I said. "Schiller was firing a Schmeisser."

"Machine pistol," said Hoover. "It must have been loud in that little room."

I nodded.

"And you fired only four bullets from your .357 Magnum, Special Agent Lucas?"

"Yes, sir."

"Two head shots and an upper body hit. From a prone position. In the dark. Amidst all that noise and confusion?"

"Their muzzle flashes gave them away, sir. I wasn't trying for head shots, necessarily, just firing above the flashes. One usually shoots a bit high in the dark. And I think that the noise rattled Schiller. Lopez was a professional. Schiller was an amateur and a fool."

"A dead fool now."

"Yes, sir."

"Are you still carrying the .357 Magnum, Agent Lucas?"

"No, sir. I have the regulation .38 with me."

Hoover looked back at the file. "Krivitsky," he said softly, as if to himself.

I said nothing. If I was here because of a problem, this could be it. Hoover turned pages in the thick file.

General Walter Gregorievitch Krivitsky had been chief of the NKVD, the Soviet Secret Service in Western Europe, until late in 1937, when he had come out of the shadows at The Hague, seeking asylum in the West and telling reporters that he had "broken with Stalin." No one breaks with Stalin and lives. Krivitsky was a follower of Leon Trotsky, who had become a prime example of that dictum in Mexico City.

The Abwehr, Germany's military intelligence group, had been interested in what Krivitsky knew. A crack Abwehr agent, Commander Traugott Andreas Richard Protze—formerly a counterespionage expert in the old *Marine Nachrichtendienst*, the German Naval Intelligence Office—had put his people to work on turning Walter Krivitsky, who had decided that a high-profile life in Paris was his ticket to safety. There was no ticket to safety. With GPU assassins on their way from the Soviet Union and Protze's Abwehr agents all around—one got close to Krivitsky by posing as a Jewish refugee being hunted by both the Nazis and the Communists—the ex-NKVD agent's life was becoming cheaper by the moment.

Krivitsky bolted from Paris to the United States, where the FBI and the U.S. Office of Naval Intelligence soon joined the Abwehr and the GPU in following the small, thin, shaggy-browed Krivitsky. Once again, the ex-Soviet decided that being in the eye of the public was his best defense. Krivitsky wrote a book—*I Was Stalin's Agent*—published articles in the *Saturday Evening Post*, and even testified before the Dies Committee on Un-American Activities. In every public appearance, Krivitsky announced to everyone who would listen that he was being tailed by GPU assassins.

He was, of course—the foremost among them being a killer known as "Hans the Red Judas," who had just come from Europe after murdering Ignace Reiss, Krivitsky's old friend and another deserter from the Soviet Secret Service. By the time the war broke out in Europe in 1939, Krivitsky could not go to the corner newsstand for a copy of *Look* without half a dozen agencies, foreign and domestic, reading it over his shoulder.

My job was not to follow Krivitsky—I would have had to have taken a number and gotten in line to do that—but to tail "Hans the Red Judas," the Abwehr agent who was following Krivitsky. This was Dr. Hans Wesemann, a former Marxist, a debonair European man-about-town, and a specialist in kidnapping or killing former émigrés. Wesemann was in the United States on a journalist's passport, but although the FBI had been tipped to his presence almost immediately upon his entering the country, the Bureau had ignored Wesemann until it became obvious that he was closing in on Krivitsky.

So in September 1939, I was brought back to the States as part of the FBI/BSC operation to turn the Krivitsky–Red Judas–Hans Wesemann situation to our advantage. Wesemann must have sensed the crowds gathering around his attempt to grab Krivitsky, because the Abwehr agent asked his superior, Commander Protze, for permission to get out of the country and lie low. We learned this later because the British had broken the German code and would occasionally drop us such crumbs. Protze then conferred with the Abwehr director, Admiral Canaris, and in late September 1939, Wesemann was on his way to Tokyo on a Japanese ship. We could not follow him there, but the British ONI and BSC could—and did—and they let us know immediately when Wesemann arrived in Tokyo only to receive a cable from Protze ordering him back to the United States.

This is the point where I came into play. I had been brought to Washington the previous autumn because we had hoped that Wesemann might go to ground in Mexico, the center for most of the Abwehr's operations in this hemisphere. Instead, the German ended up spending October and November 1940 in Nicaragua, waiting for his re-entry into the United States. The Abwehr organization was skimpy in Nicaragua, and by this time, Wesemann's concern for his own safety was approaching Krivitsky's level. One evening the debonair Wesemann was jumped by three thugs and managed to escape serious injury only by the intervention of a disrated, expatriate American merchant seaman who jumped into the fray and managed to get a broken nose and a knife blade along his ribs before he succeeded in driving the assailants off. The BSC and SIS had paid the three thugs to attack Wesemann, trusting my training in hand-to-hand combat to triumph when I joined the brawl. The three idiots almost killed me.

My cover was simple and deep—I was a not-very-bright but frequently brutal able-bodied seaman and ex-boxer who had been cashiered for striking his bosun, who had managed to lose all of his papers and his American passport while getting the Managua police looking for him, and who was willing to do damned near anything to get out of that hellhole and back to the States. In the next two months, in Wesemann's employ, I *did* have to do damned near anything—including acting as a courier to the desultory group of Abwehr agents in Panama who had been watching the canal for two years and once again acting as bodyguard for the aristocrat, this time fighting off a real attack by a ham-handed Soviet agent—before Wesemann grew to depend on me and speak freely in front of me. Brain-damaged old Joe could barely understand English, but Special Agent Lucas had no trouble with the group's German and Spanish and Portuguese.

When Wesemann received the green light to slip back into the United States, in December 1940, I was the only hired hand he brought in with him. The Abwehr was kind enough to forge a replacement passport for me.

I could see J. Edgar Hoover flipping the last few pages of this Official/Confidential report. It had been Hoover himself who had set up the SIS—the Special Intelligence Service—early in 1940 as a separate subentity of the FBI designed to work closely with the British Security Coordination to manage counterespionage in Latin America. But the SIS worked in ways more similar to British military intelligence than to FBI procedure, and I would have been amazed if it had not made Hoover nervous. Case in point—FBI agents were on call twenty-four hours a day; it was cause for dismissal for Tom Dillon to be out of reach of a call from his office for more than an hour or two. When I was working the Wesemann case in Nicaragua, New York, and Washington, there had been intervals of a week or more when I had not been in contact with any of my superiors or controllers. That was the reality of deep-cover counterespionage.

At any rate, I had spent New Year's Eve of 1940 in New York with Dr. Wesemann and three other Abwehr agents. The good doctor and his friends went to half a dozen of the best nightclubs in New York—hardly the low profile one expects of serious spies—while old Bodyguard Joe stood out in the snow next to the car, hearing the cheers from the direction of Times Square and hoping that his ass would not freeze off by the time the celebrating Krauts called it a night. By this time, poor Walter Krivitsky had become an embarrassment not only to the NKVD and Joseph Stalin, but to the Abwehr and the FBI as well. The terrified agent had blabbed all he knew about the now-five-years-out-of-date Soviet intelligence network in Europe, so he was planning to stay in the safety of the limelight by going into detail about the German network he had once been in charge of ferreting out. The GPU killers were still closing in on him. Now the word came down from Canaris via Protze to Dr. Wesemann that Krivitsky was no longer a target for abduction and interrogation, only for elimination.

Wesemann gave the job to his most trusted, naive, ignorant, and violent hired thug. He gave it to me.

By the end of January, Krivitsky bolted New York and made a run for it. I followed him to Virginia, where I made contact with him, identifying myself as an FBI and SIS agent who could protect him from the Abwehr and the GPU. Together, we traveled back through Washington, D.C., where—on the night of Sunday, February 9, 1941—he checked into the Hotel Bellevue, near Union Station. It was a cold night. I went down to the nearest diner and came back with a greasy white sack of sandwiches and two rancid coffees. We ate the sandwiches together in his fifth-floor room.

The next morning, the maid found Krivitsky dead in his bed, a gun that was not his own next to his hand. The door to his room had been locked and there was no fire escape outside his window. Detectives in the Washington police department ruled it suicide.

Dr. Hans Wesemann was as good as his word; he had said he

would get me out of the country and he did—by train, car, and foot to Mexico, where I was told to report to a certain Franz Schiller for further duties. I did so. In the next ten months, with the help of the BSC and the regular FBI office there, we rounded up fifty-eight of the Abwehr agents in Mexico, effectively destroying their operation in that country.

Hoover looked up from the file. "Krivitsky," he said again, looking at me. The sun had gone behind the clouds again, and I could see the director's dark eyes as they bored into me. My report described how I had talked to Krivitsky for three days and convinced him of the hopelessness of his position. The gun found near his hand had been mine, of course. I could see the question in Hoover's black eyes—*Did you kill him, Lucas? Or did you hand him a loaded gun, not knowing whether he would use it on himself or you, and sit there while he blew his brains out?*

The moment stretched. The director cleared his throat and flipped pages in the file.

"You trained at Camp X."

"Yes," I said, although it had not been a question.

"What did you think of it?"

Camp X was the BSC special operations center in Canada, near Oshawa, on the north shore of Lake Ontario not too far from Toronto. Despite the center's melodramatic name—"Camp X" always sounded like something from a cheap movie serial to me—the place was deadly serious in its work: training British guerrillas and British counterintelligence experts for deployment all over the world, and sharing that training with some FBI personnel who were new to this harsher, meaner world of spycraft. All of us in the SIS received our initial training at Camp X. The basics included chamfering mail—intercepting and photographing it, then returning it to the normal delivery channels—as well as the art and science of carrying off black bag jobs; physical, photographic, and electronic surveillance techniques; training in lethal hand-to-hand combat; advanced cryptography; exotic weapons training; radio procedures; and much more.

"I thought it was very efficient, sir," I said.

"Better than Quantico?" said Hoover.

"Different," I said.

"You know Stephenson personally," said Hoover.

"I've met him several times, sir." Stephenson was William Stephenson, a Canadian millionaire and head of all BSC operations. Winston Churchill had personally sent Stephenson to the United States in 1940 with two objectives: the public one was to set up an extensive MI6 operation in the United States to keep track of Abwehr agents; the private one was to get America into the war come hell or high water.

I did not guess at these objectives. One of my goals while at Camp X was to spy on the British, and I did this—it was the most difficult and dangerous work of my career to that point—and I photographed not only Churchill's private memo to Stephenson but also the special operation center's plans to insert guerrillas into Czechoslovakia in 1942 in order to assassinate the Gestapo chief, Reinhard Heydrich.

"Describe him," snapped Hoover.

"William Stephenson?" I said stupidly. I knew that Director Hoover knew Stephenson, had worked with him when the Canadian had first come to the country. Hoover liked to brag that it had been he who had suggested the name British Security Coordination for the operation.

"Describe him," repeated the director.

"Good-looking," I said. "Short. A bantamweight. Likes to wear three-piece Savile Row suits. Quiet but very confident. Never allows himself to be photographed. He was a multimillionaire by the time he was thirty...invented something to send photographs via radio. No formal background in intelligence, but he is a natural, sir."

"You boxed with him at Camp X," said Hoover, looking at the file again.

"Yes, sir."

"Who won?"

"It was just a few rounds of sparring, sir. Technically, neither one of us won because—"

"But in your mind, Agent Lucas, who won?"

"I had the reach on him, sir. And the weight. But he was the better boxer. He would have won every round on points, if anyone had been scoring. He seemed to be able to take any amount of punishment without going down and liked to work in close. He won."

Hoover grunted. "And you think that he is a good director of counterintelligence?"

Almost surely the best in the world, I thought. I said, "Yes, sir."

"Do you know some of the well-known Americans he has recruited, Lucas?"

"Yes, sir," I said. "Errol Flynn, Greta Garbo, Marlene Dietrich...a mystery writer named Rex Stout...and he uses Walter Winchell and Walter Lippmann to plant items he wants aired. He has a couple of thousand people working for him, including about three hundred American amateurs like those I named."

"Errol Flynn," muttered J. Edgar Hoover, shaking his head. "Do you go to the movies, Lucas?"

"Occasionally, sir."

Hoover twitched that smile of his again. "You don't mind indulging in make-believe as long as it's on the screen, not on the printed page, eh, Lucas?"

I did not know how to answer that, so I said nothing.

Hoover sat back in his chair and closed the thick file. "Special Agent Lucas, I have a job for you in Cuba. I want you to fly down there tomorrow morning."

"Yes, sir," I said, thinking *Cuba?* What was in Cuba? I knew that the FBI had a presence there, as it did everywhere in the hemisphere, but fewer than twenty agents, certainly. I remembered that Raymond Leddy, a legal attaché at the embassy in Havana, was the Bureau's chief liaison from that island. Other than that, I knew nothing about operations in Cuba. Certainly the Abwehr had not been very active there—at least to my knowledge.

"Do you know about a writer named Ernest Hemingway?" said Hoover, leaning on his right elbow in the heavy chair. His jaw was clenched so tightly that I could almost hear his teeth grinding.

"Just newspaper reports," I said. "Big game hunter, wasn't he? Makes a lot of money. Friend of Marlene Dietrich. His books get turned into movies. I think he lives in Key West."

"Used to," said Hoover. "He moved to Cuba a few years ago. Has been spending time there for years. He and his third wife live there now, just outside of Havana."

I waited.

Hoover sighed, reached over and touched the Bible on his desk, and sighed again. "Hemingway is a phony, Special Agent Lucas. A liar and a phony and probably a Communist."

"How is he a liar, sir?" *And why does it matter to the Bureau?*

Hoover smiled again. It was the briefest upturn of his lips and an even briefer glimpse of his small, white teeth. "You'll see the file in a minute," said the director. "But one example... well, this Hemingway was an ambulance driver in Italy in the Great War. A trench mortar round exploded near him and put him in the hospital with shrapnel wounds. In the years since, Hemingway has told reporters that he was also hit by heavy-caliber machine gun bullets—including some that hit his kneecap—after which he carried a wounded Italian soldier a hundred and fifty yards to a command post before he collapsed himself."

I could only nod. If Hemingway had said this, he *was* a liar. A knee wound is one of the most painful injuries imaginable. If this Hemingway had received shrapnel in the knee and walked even a few yards, much less carried a wounded man, he was a tough son of a bitch. But machine gun bullets are massive, high-velocity nightmares, designed to smash bone and muscle and spirit. If this writer said that he was machine-gunned in the knee and leg and had carried someone a hundred and fifty yards, the man was a liar. But so what?

Hoover seemed to read my expression, even though I was sure that I had shown no expression except polite alertness.

"Hemingway wants to set up a counterespionage ring in Cuba," said the director. "He talked to Ellis Briggs and Bob Joyce at the embassy there on Monday and has an interview with Spruille Braden on Friday to formally propose it."

I nodded. This was Wednesday. Hoover had cabled me on Tuesday.

"You know Ambassador Braden, I believe," said the director.

"Yes, sir." I had worked with Braden when he had been stationed in Colombia the previous year; now he was U.S. Ambassador to Cuba.

Hoover said, "You have a question?"

"Yes, sir. Why is a civilian...a writer...being allowed to

take up the ambassador's time formally proposing the asinine idea of running an amateur spy ring?"

Hoover rubbed his chin. "Hemingway has a lot of friends on the island," said the director. "A lot of them are veterans of the Spanish Civil War. Hemingway claims that he set up a network of covert operatives in Madrid in 1937—"

"Is that true, sir?"

Hoover blinked at the interruption, started to speak, then shook his head before saying, "No. Hemingway was in Spain, but only as a correspondent. The intelligence network seems to be a figment of his imagination, although he was in touch with more than a few Communist agents there. The Communists used him quite shamelessly to get their message out...and he allowed himself to be used quite shamelessly. It's all in the file I'll give you to read today."

Hoover leaned over his desk and folded his hands again. "Special Agent Lucas, I want you to go down to Cuba and be a special liaison to Hemingway and his silly operation. You will be in an undercover role, assigned to Hemingway by the embassy but not representing the FBI."

"Who am I supposed to be representing, then, sir?"

"Ambassador Braden will tell Hemingway that your involvement will be a condition of the embassy's approval for his scheme. You'll be introduced as an SIS operative specializing in counterintelligence."

I had to smile. Hoover had said that this was an undercover role, but that was my real identity. "Won't Hemingway recognize that SIS is FBI?"

The director shook his massive head so that his oiled hair caught the overhead light. "We don't think that he understands even the most basic facts about espionage and counterespionage, much less the details of organizational jurisdiction. Besides, Ambassador Braden will assure Hemingway that you will take orders only from him—from Hemingway—and that you will not be reporting to the embassy or any other contacts without Hemingway's permission."

"And who will I be reporting to in reality, sir?"

"You'll be contacted once you're in Havana," said Hoover.

"We'll work outside the embassy and local FBI chain of command. Essentially, there will be just one controller between you and me. The contact details will be in the briefing papers that Miss Gandy will give you."

My expression did not change, but I was shocked. How could this be so important that I would have only one buffer between me and the director? Hoover loved the system he had created and hated people who went around it. What would justify such a violation of chain of command? I kept my mouth shut and waited.

"You have a reservation on tomorrow morning's flight to Havana by way of Miami," said the director. "You'll make contact with your controller briefly tomorrow, and then be present at Friday's meeting when Hemingway presents his plan to the ambassador. The plan will be approved. Hemingway will be allowed to play his silly game."

"Yes, sir," I said. Perhaps this was the demotion I had been expecting—being channeled into a completely irrelevant sidewater, asked to play silly games until I could not take it any longer and resigned or enlisted in the army.

"Do you know what Hemingway told Bob Joyce and Ellis Briggs he wants to call his organization?" said Hoover tightly.

"No, sir."

"The Crime Shop."

I shook my head.

"Here are your orders," said Hoover, leaning farther over the desk toward me. "Get close to Hemingway, Special Agent Lucas. Report to me on who the man is. *What* he is. Use your skills to ferret out the truth about this phony. I want to know what makes him tick and what he really wants."

I nodded and waited.

"And keep me updated on what this silly organization of his is doing in Cuba, Lucas. I want details. Daily reports. Diagrams, if necessary."

The director seemed finished, but I sensed that there was something else.

"This man is meddling in an area where various sensitive operations or national security initiatives may be contemplated," said the director at last, sitting far back in his chair. Thunder rumbled from beyond the blinds behind him. "All Hemingway can do is foul up things," continued Hoover. "Your job is to let us know what he is doing so that we can minimize the damage his amateur meddling is bound to create. And—if necessary—intervene at our command to stop much meddling. But until that command is given, your job will be what it will be sold to Hemingway as—adviser, aide, assistant, sympathetic observer, and foot soldier."

I nodded a final time and lifted my hat from my lap.

"You'll need to read the O/C file on this writer today," said the director. "But you will have to commit it to memory."

That went without saying. None of the O/C files ever left this building.

"Miss Gandy will sign the file out to you for two hours," said Hoover, "and show you to a quiet place to read it. I believe that Associate Director Tolson is out of his office today. It's a large file, but two hours should be adequate if you read quickly." The director stood.

I stood.

We did not shake hands again. Hoover came around the desk with the same quick efficiency he had used to greet me, only this time he crossed the room and opened the door, calling to Miss Gandy for the file while keeping one hand on the doorknob and using the other to fiddle with the handkerchief in his breast pocket.

I stepped through the door, turning as I walked so that my back would not be toward the director.

"Special Agent Lucas," said Hoover as Miss Gandy hovered nearby.

"Yes, sir?"

"This Hemingway character is a phony, but he's reported to have a certain crude charm. Don't get caught up in that charm so you forget who you are working for and what you might have to do."

"Yes, sir... I mean, no, sir."

Hoover nodded and shut the door. I never saw him in person again.

I followed Miss Gandy into Tolson's office.

4

THE FLIGHT FROM Washington to Miami was crowded and loud the next morning, but the connecting flight to Havana was almost empty. In the few minutes before Ian Fleming sat down next to me, I had time to think about J. Edgar Hoover and Ernest Hemingway.

Miss Gandy had stayed in Associate Director Tolson's office with me long enough to make sure that I took a seat in one of the guest chairs, not in Mr. Tolson's seat, and then she almost tiptoed out, closing the door softly. I took a minute to look around Clyde Tolson's room: the usual Washington bureaucrat's office—walls covered with trophy pictures of the man shaking hands with everyone from FDR to a very young Shirley Temple, lots of photos of citations and awards being handed to him by J. Edgar Hoover, and even one photograph of a nervous Tolson standing behind a massive movie camera in Hollywood, obviously there as an adviser for some FBI-sanctioned film or documentary. Hoover's office had been a noticeable exception to this standard photographic, office-wall busyness: I remembered that there had been only one photograph on the wall—an official portrait of Harlan Fiske Stone, the former attorney general who had recommended Hoover for the job of Bureau of Investigation director in 1924.

There were no photographs in the associate director's office of Clyde Tolson and J. Edgar Hoover kissing or holding hands.

As far back as the 1930s, there had been rumors, innuendos, and even a few nasty published articles—one especially in *Colliers* by a writer named Ray Tucker—suggesting that Hoover was a fairy and that something funny was going on between the director and his closest associate, Clyde Tolson. Everyone I knew who had known the director and his assistant for years thought that the stories were unadulterated bullshit. So did I. J. Edgar Hoover was a mama's boy—he had lived with his mother until her death when he was forty-two, and both he and Tolson were said to be shy, socially inept types out of the office—but even in my few minutes with the director I had sensed an undercurrent of Presbyterian Sunday school correctness that would have made such a secret life all but unthinkable for him.

Both my personality and my SIS training had theoretically made me an expert in assessing people—in getting close to a possible deep-cover agent and sensing the submerged personality deep within the carefully constructed persona. But it was absurd to think that a few minutes in Hoover's presence and even fewer minutes in Tolson's office could tell me anything about the two men. Nevertheless, after that day I never again questioned the director's and associate director's relationship.

Finished with admiring Tolson's walls, I had flipped open Hemingway's file and begun reading. Hoover had signed the file out to me for two hours. It was not an especially thick file, but it could have taken the full two hours for someone to read all the single-spaced field reports and the tear pages of printed articles. It took me less than twenty minutes to read it all and remember it all perfectly.

In 1942 I had not yet encountered the phrase "photographic memory," but I knew that I had that talent. It was not a skill...I had never learned it...but remembering pages of print or complex photographs with absolute precision, actually *seeing them again* in my mind when I called them back, was a talent I had possessed since childhood. Perhaps this was one reason I had been repelled by make-believe storybooks: remembering tomes of lies, word for word and image for image, was a tiresome burden.

Mr. Ernest Hemingway's file was not especially titillating reading. There was the standard dossier background bio sheet—which I had learned to assume was filled with factual errors: Ernest Miller Hemingway had been born in Oak Park, Illinois—

then a separate village just outside of Chicago—on July 21, 1899. It was noted that he was the second of six children, although none of the siblings' names were listed. Father's name: Clarence Edmonds Hemingway. His father's occupation was listed as "Physician"; his mother's maiden name had been Grace Hall.

Nothing on Ernest Hemingway's early years except the note that he had graduated from Oak Park High School, worked briefly on the *Kansas City Star*, and had tried to join the army during the Great War. There was a copy of his rejection form—defective eyesight. Handwritten at the bottom of that army rejection form, obviously by someone in the Bureau, was "Joined Red Cross as ambulance driver—Italy—wounded by trench mortar at Fossalta di Piave, July 1918."

The bio sheet concluded the personal information with "Married Hadley Richardson 1920, divorced 1927; married Pauline Pfeiffer 1927, divorced 1940; married Martha Gellhorn 1940..."

Under "Occupation/employment" the form was succinct: "Hemingway claims to make his living as a writer and has published such novels as *The Sun Also Rises, A Farewell by Arms, To Have and Have Not,* and *The Great Gatsby.*"

The writer seemed to have come to the serious attention of the Bureau in 1935, when he had written an article titled "Who Murdered the Vets?" for the leftist journal *New Masses*. In 2,800 words—torn out and included in his FBI O/C file—Hemingway had described the effects of the hurricane that had raged through the Florida Keys on Labor Day 1935. It had been the biggest storm of the century and had killed many, including nearly a thousand CCC workers—most of them veterans—in camps along the Keys. The writer evidently was on one of the first small boats to reach the devastated area, and he almost seemed to take pleasure in describing two women, "naked, tossed up in the trees by the water, swollen and stinking, their breasts as big as balloons, flies between their legs." But most of the article was polemic about the politicians and Washington bureaucrats who had sent the workers to such a dangerous place and then failed to rescue them when the storm came.

"Wealthy people, yachtsmen, fishermen such as President Hoover and President Roosevelt" avoid the Keys during hurricane weather so as not to endanger their yachts and property, Hemingway wrote. "But veterans, especially the bonus-marching variety of veterans, are not property. They are only human beings; unsuccessful human beings, and all they have to lose is their lives." Hemingway was making a case of manslaughter against the bureaucrats.

There were field reports, but these were just copies of reports on other people—mostly Americans or Communist agents, or both, involved in the Spanish Civil War—in which Hemingway was mentioned only in passing. Leftish intellectuals had converged on Madrid like flies circling shit in 1937, and making a big deal of Hemingway's involvement seemed naive to me. Hemingway's primary source for material and background at Gaylord's Hotel there had been Mikhail Koltsov, an intellectual, young correspondent for *Pravda* and *Izvestia*, and the American writer appeared to have taken everything the Communist had fed him as pure gospel.

There were more reports pointing with alarm at Hemingway's involvement with the propaganda film *The Spanish Earth*—the writer had narrated it and spoken at fund-raising parties involved with the leftist project—but this hardly seemed subversive to me. Two thirds of all the Hollywood stars and ninety percent of the New York intellectual crowd had been fighting for Marxist credentials since the height of the Depression; if anything, Hemingway had been slow to get on the bandwagon.

The most recent reports documented Hemingway's contacts with other Communists or leftist-leaning Americans, including an FBI surveillance report from just last month in Mexico City. Hemingway and his wife had been visiting an American millionaire at his vacation home there. The millionaire was described by the Tom Dillon–like special agents as "one of the many rich dupes of the Communist Party." I knew the millionaire they were talking about, having checked him out myself two years earlier in a totally different context. The man was no one's dupe, just a sensitive person who had gotten rich during the

Depression while millions were suffering and who was still trying to find some easy path to redemption.

The last item was a memo.

CONFIDENTIAL MEMO
FROM FBI AGENT R.G. LEDDY, HAVANA, CUBA
TO FBI DIRECTOR J. EDGAR HOOVER, JUSTICE DEPT., WASHINGTON, DC.
APRIL 15, 1942

> It is recalled that when the Bureau was attacked early in 1940 as a result of the arrests in Detroit of certain individuals charged with neutrality violations for fostering enlistments in the Spanish Republican forces, Mr. Hemingway was among the signers of a declaration which severely criticized the Bureau in that case. In attendance at a Jai-Alai match with Hemingway, this writer was introduced by him to a friend as a member of the Gestapo. On that occasion I did not appreciate the introduction, whereupon he promptly corrected himself and said I was one of the United States Consuls....

I laughed out loud. The memo went on to describe Hemingway's most recent proposals to Robert Joyce, first secretary of the embassy, about setting up his counterespionage ring, but Leddy kept circling back to the perceived personal insult at the jai alai match. The FBI was, of course, the American Gestapo, and that introduction was driving Raymond Leddy crazy with rage, all of it hidden behind the clumsy doublespeak of Bureau memoese.

I shook my head, imagining the introduction amidst the roar of the jai alai game and the shouting of the bettors. Mr. Hoover had been right. If I wasn't careful, I might learn to like this writer.

"JOSEPH? JOSEPH, OLD BOY. I thought that I glimpsed the back of that familiar skull. How are you, dear boy?"

I knew the voice immediately—the clipped yet drawn-out Oxbridge accent and the drone of someone who knew very well how to amuse himself.

"Hello, Commander Fleming," I said, looking up at the lanky figure.

"Ian, Joseph, old boy. We left it at Ian off at camp, remember?"

"Ian," I said. He looked the same as when I had last seen him more than a year earlier: tall, thin, curly forelock hanging down over his pale forehead, long nose, and sensuous mouth. Despite the season and the heat, he was wearing a quintessentially British wool tweed suit that looked expensive and well-tailored enough, but as if it had been tailored for someone twenty pounds heavier. He was smoking a cigarette in a cigarette holder, and the way he clenched the thing in his teeth and waved it for emphasis reminded me of someone doing an impression of FDR. My only hope was that he would not sit down in the empty aisle seat next to me.

"May I join you, Joseph?"

"By all means." I turned away from the window, where the green of the coastal shallows was giving way to a deep Gulf blue. I glanced over my shoulder. There was no one sitting within four rows of us; the plane was almost empty. Any conversation we would have would be covered by the drone of the engines and the propellers.

"Fancy meeting you here, dear boy. Where are you headed?"

"The plane's flying to Cuba, Ian. Where are you bound?"

He tapped ash into the aisle and flicked his wrist. "Oh, just heading home by way of Bermuda. Thought I might do a bit of reading."

Cuba was still far out of his way if he was flying back from the BSC headquarters in New York via Bermuda, but I did understand his mention of reading. One of the most successful operations the British Security Coordination had been running the past three years was its huge chamfering center in Bermuda. All mail between South America and Europe, including diplomatic pouches from all of the embassies, was routed through that island. William Stephenson had set up an intercept station in Bermuda where the mail was diverted, copied or photographed, dealt with on the spot by a large team of code breakers, and occasionally altered before being sent on to Berlin or Madrid or Rome or Bucharest.

But why Fleming was talking out of school like this was another matter.

"By the way, Joseph," said the Brit, "I saw William just last week and he said to say hello to you should our paths cross again. I think you were a bit of a favorite of his, old boy. The best and the brightest and all that. Only wish that more of your chaps were so quick on the uptake."

I had met Commander Ian Fleming through William Stephenson at the BSC Camp X in Canada. Fleming was another of these gifted amateurs whom the British—especially Churchill—loved to promote over more plodding professionals. In Fleming's case, it had not been Churchill who discovered him but Admiral John Godfrey, head of England's Naval Intelligence Division and a counterpart to the German Abwehr's Admiral Canaris. As I had heard the story, Fleming had been a thirty-one-year-old London fop marking time in his family's brokerage business when the war broke out in 1939. Fleming was also one of those perpetual British public school boys, always up to pranks and seeking excitement on ski slopes or in fast cars or in beautiful women's beds. Admiral Godfrey had seen the creativity in this dandy, for he had given the young stockbroker a commission in the navy and hired him as his own special assistant. Then he turned him loose to come up with ideas.

Some of those Fleming-inspired ideas had been discussed openly at Camp X. One of them was Assault Unit Number 30—a group of felons and misfits trained for wildly improbable missions behind German lines. A group of Fleming's Assault Unit Number 30 characters had been sent into France when the Germans were overrunning that country and had hijacked entire shiploads of advanced military equipment. Rumor had it that Ian Fleming had recruited Swiss astrologers to consult with the wildly superstitious Nazi Rudolf Hess, telling him that his destiny was to please the Führer by arranging a peace between Germany and England. The outcome had been Hess's insane solo flight from Germany to England; he bailed out over Scotland and had been a prisoner ever since—telling MI5 and MI6 great quantities of detail about the inner workings of the Nazi hierarchy.

And from my three A.M. black bag jobs at Camp X, I knew that it had been Commander Ian Fleming who had been sent to North America to help Stephenson get the United States into the war.

"The problem with the chaps Edgar has been sending to camp since you, old boy," Fleming was droning on, referring to Director Hoover as "Edgar," "is that the fellows are sent out into the field with no brief other than 'to go and have a look.' All of Edgar's chaps are good at looking, Joseph, but very few have learned to *see*."

I nodded noncommittally. I tended to agree with Fleming's and Stephenson's assessments of the FBI's espionage capabilities. Despite Hoover's protests about *investigation* rather than *enforcement*, the Bureau was essentially a police organization. It arrested spies—Mr. Hoover had even wanted to arrest William Stephenson when it became clear that the BSC leader had ordered a Nazi agent killed in New York. The agent had been in charge of reporting convoy routes to U-boats and sinking thousands of tons of Allied shipping, but Mr. Hoover saw that as no reason to break U.S. laws. But with the exception of a few SIS operatives, no one in the Bureau really thought in terms of espionage—of watching and turning and burning spies rather than just arresting them.

"Speaking of seeing, old boy," said Fleming, "I see that an American writer chap down in Havana may be getting into our line of work."

I am sure my face was impassive, but in my mind I was blinking in shock. It had been—what?—less than a week since Hemingway had first proposed his idea to the embassy people in Havana. "Oh?" I said.

Fleming removed his cigarette holder and gave me his lopsided smile. He was a charmer. "Ah, but that's right, Joseph, dear boy. I forgot. We discussed that in Canada once, did we not? You don't read fiction, do you, old cock?"

I shook my head. *Why the hell was he contacting me in the open about this? Why would Stephenson and the BSC be interested in this dead-end assignment of mine?*

"Joseph," said Fleming, his voice softer now, more serious, with less of an insufferable accent, "do you remember the chat we had about the Yellow Admiral's favorite ploy against business competitors?"

"Not really," I said. I remembered the conversation. Fleming had been at the camp when Stephenson and a few others were talking about the German Admiral Canaris's—Canaris was called the "Yellow Admiral"—uncanny ability to drive a wedge between rival intelligence services that opposed him: in this case, between MI5 and MI6, England's internal and foreign intelligence services, respectively.

"No matter," said Fleming, flicking ashes off his cigarette. "It just came to mind recently. Would you like to hear the story, Joseph?"

"Sure," I said. Fleming might have begun the intelligence game as an amateur, but he had never been a fool—at least not in espionage—and after three years of war, he was an expert. This story was the reason he had "accidentally" arranged to fly down to Cuba with me—I was sure of that.

"Last August," said Commander Fleming, "I happened to be in Lisbon. Ever been to Portugal, Joseph?"

I shook my head, confident that he knew I had never been out of this hemisphere.

"Interesting place. Especially now, during the war, if you take my meaning. At any rate, there was this Yugoslav chap there by the name of Popov. I happened to bump into him several times there. Does the name ring a bell, dear boy? Popov?"

I pretended to search my memory and again shook my head. This "story" must be of critical importance if Fleming were using someone's real name in a public place like this. Even with the almost-empty cabin and the loud drone of the propellers, I felt like we were doing something almost indecent.

"Not even a little bell, Joseph?"

"Sorry," I said.

Dusan "Dusko" Popov had been born in Yugoslavia but had been recruited by the Abwehr as a deep-cover agent in England. Almost immediately upon being inserted into the country, Popov had begun working for the British as a double agent. By the time

Fleming was talking about—August of the previous summer, 1941, Popov had been passing along real and false information to the Germans for three years.

"Well, again it doesn't matter," said Fleming. "No reason for you to have heard of the chap. Anyway, to get back to my story—I was never good at telling a story, dear heart, so bear with me, please—this fellow Popov, whom some called by the nickname 'Tricycle,' had been given sixty thousand dollar in Lisbon by his continental employers to pay his own employees. In a burst of benevolence, this Tricycle chap decided to turn the money over to our company."

I was translating as Fleming droned on. Word had it that the British had given Popov the code name "Tricycle" because the double agent was quite the woman's man, rarely went to bed alone, and preferred a woman on either side of him. The "continental employer" was the Abwehr, who still thought that Popov was running a network in England. The $60,000 the Abwehr had given him in Lisbon was to pay Popov's mythical sources in England. "Turning the money over to our company" meant that Popov was going to turn the cash over to MI6.

"Yeah?" I said in a bored tone, popping a stick of gum into my mouth. The cabin was supposedly pressurized, but changes in altitude were playing havoc with my ears.

"Precisely, yeah," said Fleming. "The problem was, our Tricycle friend had time to kill in Portugal before he could deliver the money. Our fellows in Five and Six were at sixes and sevens as to who would have the pleasure of entertaining the poor man there, so it fell to me to spend time with him until he could come home."

Translation: MI5 and MI6 had become embroiled in a jurisdictional battle over who should tail Popov and ensure that the money was delivered. Fleming, who worked for the more-or-less jurisdictionally neutral Naval Intelligence Division, had been ordered to follow Popov for the few days last August until the double agent could return to England to hand over the money.

"All right," I said. "Some guy came into some loot in Portugal and is going to give it to charity in England. Did you have fun showing him around Portugal?"

"He showed me around, dear boy. I had the opportunity to follow him to Estoril. Ever heard of it?"

"No," I said truthfully.

"A lovely little Portuguese resort town along the coast, dear boy," said Fleming. "The beaches are adequate, but the casinos are more than adequate. Our Tricycle knew the casinos quite well."

I resisted the impulse to smile. Popov was famous for having balls. In this case, he had taken Abwehr money promised to his controllers at MI6 and gambled it.

"Did he win?" I said, interested in the story despite my caution.

"Yes, rather," said Fleming, fussing with inserting a fresh cigarette in his long, black holder. "I sat there all night and watched him quite clean out a poor Lithuanian count whom our Tricycle friend had taken a dislike to. At one point, our three-wheeled chap counted fifty thousand dollars in cash onto the table...our poor Lithuanian could not match that. Had to leave in humiliation, actually. I found it all quite edifying."

I was sure he had. Fleming had always admired daring above most other virtues.

"And the moral of this tale?" I said. The engines were changing pitch. We were beginning to descend toward Cuba.

Commander Fleming shrugged with his cigarette holder. "Not sure there is a moral, dear boy. In this case, our agencies' quarrel provided me with a wonderful night out in Estoril. But sometimes the results are not so benign."

"Oh?"

"Do you know that other interesting William?" said Fleming. "Donovan?"

"No," I said. "We've never met." William "Wild Bill" Donovan was, of course, the head of America's other espionage/counterespionage outfit, the COI, Coordinator of Intelligence, and Hoover's greatest rival. Donovan was a favorite of FDR's—had consulted with him the night of Pearl Harbor—and tended to do things more in the vein of William Stephenson and Ian Fleming; that is, extravagantly, daring, slightly crazily, rather than in the plodding, bureaucratic method approved by Mr. Hoover and his

Bureau. I knew that Stephenson and the BSC had been making more and more overtures to Donovan at the COI as Hoover's interest in cooperating with the British continued to cool.

"You should meet him, Joseph," said Fleming, looking me straight in the eye. "I know that you liked William S. You would like William D. for the same reasons."

"And does William D. have something to do with your gambling story, Ian?"

"Yes, actually," said Fleming, glancing past my shoulder at the green island seeming to rise toward us. "You're aware of Edgar's...ah...disapproval of this William's methods, are you not, dear boy?"

I shrugged. Actually, I probably knew more about Mr. Hoover's hatred for Donovan than did Fleming. One of the most successful coups the COI had carried off in the past six moths had been to break into Washington embassies—of allies as well as enemies—to steal their code books without the embassies' becoming aware of the intrusions. In a few weeks, Donovan was planning to break into the Spanish embassy, which should be a treasure trove for U.S. intelligence because Fascist Spain routinely passed along intelligence to Berlin. What I knew from my SIS contacts was that Mr. Hoover planned to show up the night of the COI bag job with the Washington police—sirens wailing and lights flashing—and to arrest the COI men in the act of breaking into the Spanish embassy. Once again, jurisdictional battles took precedence over the national interest in Mr. Hoover's eyes.

"Well, all that aside," said Fleming, "it seems that our friend Tricycle came to the United States shortly after my delightful evening with him last August."

This was accurate, I knew. The files I had seen reported that Dusan "Dusko" Popov had entered the United States on August 12, 1941, arriving on a Boeing 314 Flying Boat, the so-called Pan American Clipper, from Lisbon. Popov had been sent to the States by Canaris and the Abwehr to set up the same sort of successful spy network he had "run" in England. Six days later, on August 18, Popov had met with the FBI's Assistant Director Percy "Bud" Foxworth. According to Foxworth's report,

Popov had shown him $58,000 in small bills given to him by the Abwehr in Lisbon and an additional $12,000 which Popov said he had won in a casino. Popov was ready to play the same game with U.S. intelligence that had worked so well for him in England.

The report had mentioned some "promising information" which Popov had turned over, but had not gone into detail—which was, as I thought about it, unusual for a Bureau report.

I knew from friends in SIS and the Washington end of the Bureau that William Donovan and the wild crew at COI had been clamoring for access to Popov and the information passed along by Popov. Donovan had sent FDR's son, Jimmy, as a liaison to Mr. Hoover to try to shake loose some hard information. Hoover had been polite but had shared nothing. Nor had the information been distributed through the Bureau's own counter-intelligence network.

Ian Fleming was watching me very carefully. He nodded slowly, leaned closer, and whispered above the rising roar of the motors, "Tricycle brought a questionnaire into the country, Joseph. It was a helpful gesture from the Yellow Admiral to their yellow allies..."

I translated: Canaris and the Abwehr had sent questions via Popov to Abwehr operatives in America, the answers to which would help the Japanese. It was a rare occurrence, but not unheard of. Then again, this was four months before Pearl Harbor.

"A microdot, actually," whispered Fleming. "It was finally translated by Edgar's chaps...your boys, Joseph...on September 17. Would you like to see the questionnaire, dear boy?"

I looked Fleming in the eye. "You know I have to report every word of this conversation, Ian."

"Quite right, dear boy," said Fleming, his gaze cold and steady. "You shall have to do what you have to do. But would you like to see the questionnaire?"

I said nothing.

Fleming took two folded sheets of paper out of his suit pocket and handed them to me. I shielded them as the stewardess walked by, announcing that we were almost ready to land at

José Marty Airport and could we please fasten those seat belts? She would help us if we did not know how.

Fleming got rid of her with a joke and I looked at the two sheets.

Photostats of the enlarged microdot. The original was in German. The other was a translation. I read the original questionnaire. Popov's orders to help their Japanese allies in August 1941 were—

1. Exact details and sketch of the situation of the State Wharf and the power installations, workshops, petrol installations, situation of Dry Dock No. 1 and the new dry dock which is being built in Pearl Harbor, Hawaii.
2. Details about the submarine station at Pearl Harbor (plan of situation). What land installations are in existence?
3. Where is the station for mine search formations? How far has the dredge work progressed at the entrance and in the east and southeast lock? Depths of water?
4. Number of anchorages?
5. Is there a floating dock in Pearl Harbor or is the transfer of such a dock to this place intended?

   Special task—Reports about torpedo protection nets newly introduced in the British and U.S. navy. How far are they already in existence in the merchant and naval fleet?

I looked up at Fleming and handed the two papers back to him as if they were coated with acid. A Nazi agent seeking such facts about Pearl Harbor—as a favor for the Japanese—in August 1941. It might not have tipped us to the attack, but I knew for a fact that Bill Donovan had been working a large team of COI analysts trying to figure out Japanese plans through the summer and fall of last year—a puzzle solved most publicly on December 7. Would this have provided the missing part of the puzzle for that team if Mr. Hoover had sent over the microdot information?

I did not know. But I did know that the microdot questionnaire in Fleming's hands—obviously not a forgery; I could see the familiar Bureau stamps and signatures—could have blown J. Edgar Hoover's job right out of the water if it had been released during the post–Pearl Harbor hysteria and blame-calling this past winter.

I stared at Fleming. The aircraft pitched and bucked as it came in low over heated land, feeling for a runway. I could see green hills, palm trees, blue water through the small window across the aisle, but my gaze stayed on Fleming.

"Why tell me all this, Ian?"

The NID man put out his cigarette and slowly, gracefully set the long cigarette holder into the same pocket in which he had put away the photostats. "Just a cautionary tale of what happens when one agency becomes... shall we say... too preoccupied with its own preeminence and forgets to share."

I continued to stare. I did not have a clue what this had to do with me.

Ian Fleming put his long-fingered hand on my sleeve. "Joseph, if by any chance you were heading down to Havana to have anything whatsoever to do with this writer chap and his little escapades, have you given any thought as to why Edgar would have chosen *you* as liaison?"

"I don't know what you're talking about," I said.

"Of course not, dear boy," said Fleming. "Of course not. But you have one unique skill which may apply to this writer's circumstance. One bit of job experience which Edgar might value in this situation, if, for instance, your writer friend stumbles onto something he ought not to. One bit of experience which sets you apart from Edgar's other employees."

I shook my head. For a second I honestly did not understand what Fleming was saying. The plane touched down. Wheels screeched. The propellers roared. Air rushed into the cabin.

Amidst all that noise, without leaning perceptibly closer, in a soft voice which I could barely make out, Ian Fleming said, "You kill people, Joseph. And you do it on command."

5

WE MET AT MID-MORNING on Friday in Ambassador Braden's comfortable office at the American embassy. I had arrived early and discussed the situation with Spruille Braden, who had known me in Colombia as a troubleshooter for the State Department working with the SIS and who understood that he would introduce me to Hemingway as such. After my private conference with Braden, Robert P. Joyce and Ellis O. Briggs showed up. Joyce was one of the first secretaries at the embassy, an urbane, well-dressed man with a firm handshake and a soft voice. Briggs had been ranking officer at the embassy until Braden's arrival, but he showed no resentment at being dropped down a rung, and the atmosphere in the room was cordial. Ten A.M., the time for the ambassador's appointment with Hemingway, came and went. Ten more minutes passed. No Hemingway.

The three of us chatted. Both Briggs and Joyce seemed to accept my cover story of being a State Department counterintelligence expert attached to SIS. They had probably run across my name in memos from Colombia or Mexico, and my exact position was always murky in such communications. Talk turned to the tardy writer, and Briggs spoke about the interest he and Hemingway shared in shooting—skeet-trap and live pigeons, both at a local club and out in the marshes near Cienfuegos. I had to sort through my mental file of maps of Cuba to recall where Cienfuegos was—the image appeared in my mind as Briggs went on to talk about going after *yaguasas* in Pinar del Río Province. Cienfuegos was a bay, port, city, and province on the south coast.

While Briggs went on about Hemingway's shooting ability, I

glanced covertly at my watch. Twelve minutes past the hour. I was surprised that Ambassador Braden put up with such impertinence. Most ambassadors I had known would have canceled the meeting if the person requesting it was so much as a moment late.

The door burst open and Ernest Hemingway swept into the room, moving quickly on the balls of his feet like a fighter floating to the center of the ring, his booming voice sounding very loud after the muted tones of our conversation.

"Spruille, Ambassador... sorry... I'm goddamn sorry. All my fault. The damned Lincoln was out of gas and I had to drive way the hell out past the university to find a station open. Bob... sorry I'm late. Ellis." The big man shook the ambassador's hand, then floated to Joyce to grip his hand in both of his, then moved quickly to Briggs, clapping him on the back while enveloping the First Secretary's hand in his. Then Hemingway turned to me with a smile and a quizzical look.

"Ernest," said Ambassador Braden, "this is Joe Lucas. The State Department thought that Joe might be of help in your Crime Shop plan."

"Joe," said Hemingway. "Nice to meet you." His handshake was solid but not crushing. His eyes were bright, his smile unfeigned, but I saw the briefest glimmer of wariness there as he calculated what my presence might really mean.

Braden gestured us all back to our chairs.

My assessment of Hemingway was quick. He was a big man—six foot or six one, probably about 195 pounds, but most of that weight was concentrated above his waist. The rest of us had dressed in suits, but Hemingway was wearing stained chinos, old moccasins, and a light cotton shirt—what the locals called a *guayabera*—worn untucked. He had massive, squared shoulders that gave much of the impression of size on him, and his arms were long and well muscled. I noticed that his left arm was twisted slightly at the elbow and that there was a jagged scar there. Hemingway had a deep chest and showed a hint of belly, but even though the loose shirt and chinos there was the impression of almost no hips or thighs: he was all upper body.

As he sat down and looked across at me, I noted that his hair was straight and dark—a brown almost sliding into black—and that there was no gray in his heavy but carefully trimmed mustache. His eyes were brown. He had a ruddy complexion—tanned from long days out in the Caribbean sun but still flushed with sunburn and high spirits—and a small web of laugh lines radiated from the corners of his eyes. His teeth were white as he smiled, and he had dimples in both cheeks. His chin and jawline were solid, not at all blurred by fat or middle age. I had the impression that Ernest Hemingway could be charming to the ladies when he so chose.

As always, I could not help myself from assessing another man in terms of a possible matchup between him and me. In his brief movements around the room, Hemingway had moved like a fighter, even standing poised on the balls of his feet when he was at rest. His head bobbed slightly from side to side as he spoke and even as he listened, giving others the impression that his attention was tightly focused on what they were saying. As he and Braden exchanged pleasantries, I noticed that despite years of living abroad and in Canada, Hemingway's accent was still solidly midwestern, Chicago flat. He seemed to have the slightest of speech impediments, pronouncing his *l*'s and *r*'s a bit like *w*'s.

Hemingway was taller, heavier, and more muscled than I was, but the hint of belly under the *guayabera* suggested that he was not in full fighting trim. The damaged left arm—probably an old injury, since he seemed not to favor that arm—would weaken his jab and allow an opponent to move to his left. I remembered that years before, Hemingway had been rejected from service in the first war because of poor eyesight. He was probably a close-in fighter despite those long arms, grappling with his foe and slugging short and hard, going for a knockout before he ran out of wind. It would pay to keep Hemingway moving, moving to his left, bobbing, never being a still target in his vision, keeping out of his reach until he tired and then to move in and work on that belly and those ribs...

I shook the thoughts away. Bob Joyce and Ellis Briggs were laughing at a joke Hemingway had made to Braden about the embassy staff's propensity to lose money at the jai alai games. I smiled. There was no doubt that there was a powerful sense of fun and well-being coming off this man. Hemingway in person had a great physical presence which no dossier or photograph could express—he was one of those rare human beings who could dominate any room he entered.

"All right, Ernest," said the ambassador when the laughter had ebbed. "Let's talk about your Crime Shop idea."

"I changed the name," said Hemingway.

"Pardon me?"

The writer grinned. "I changed the name. I think I'll call it the Crook Factory. Crime Shop sounded too high-falutin'."

Ambassador Braden smiled and looked down at the papers on his desk. "Very well, the Crook Factory." He glanced up at Briggs and Joyce. "Ellis and Bob have filled me in on the details of your initial proposal, but perhaps you would like to elaborate a bit."

"Sure," said Hemingway. He stood up, moving easily and bobbing his head as he began to speak. His blunt hands stabbed, molded, and jabbed softly as he made his points. "Mr. Ambassador, this island is ninety miles from U.S. shores and it's filling up fast with Nazi fifth columnists. Passport control in Cuba is a joke. The FBI's got a presence here, but it's understaffed, it doesn't have a real mission, and its agents stand out like undertakers at a street festival. Bob and I figure that there are more than three thousand Falangist sympathizers right here in Havana and many of them are in positions to help Nazi agents get onto the island and to keep them out of sight once they're here."

Hemingway was pacing softly, walking to within a yard of me before turning back, his hands and head moving, but not so much as to be distracting. He never took his dark eyes off the ambassador.

"Hell, Spruille, most of the Spanish clubs on the island are openly anti-American. Their little newspapers cheer on the Axis every chance they get. Have you read the important Cuban daily yet?"

"The *Diario de la Marina*?" said Braden. "I've glanced at it. The editorial stance does not seem very sympathetic to the United States."

"Its owner-editor would dance in the streets if the Nazis invaded New York," said Hemingway. He held out one blunt, callused palm. "This wouldn't be such a big problem, I know, if the Caribbean weren't swarming with wolf packs even as we speak. But it is. Allied tankers are going down almost every day. Hell, you can't cast out a line for marlin without hitting a U-boat conning tower." Hemingway grinned.

The ambassador rubbed his cheek. "And what could your proposed Crime Shop... Crook Factory... whatever you want to call it... do about U-boats, Ernest?"

Hemingway shrugged. "I'm not trying to oversell this, Spruille. But I have a boat, you know. A beautiful, diesel-powered thirty-eight-footer that I bought in 'thirty-four. Twin screws with an auxiliary engine. If we turn up information about German subs, I can head out to check on it. I have a good crew."

"Ernest," said Bob Joyce, "tell the ambassador about the intelligence network you set up in Spain."

Hemingway shrugged again, as if from modesty. I knew from his dossier that he had a lot to be modest about in that area.

"It wasn't much, Spruille. When I was in Madrid in 'thirty-seven, I helped to organize and run a private intelligence operation. About twenty full-time operatives and twice that many temporary sources. Brought in some useful information. Amateur stuff, I know, but they would have shot us in a minute if we'd screwed up."

I heard Hemingway's voice shift to a rougher, more staccato style as he recounted these exploits. Was that a habit of his when he lied? I wondered.

Braden was nodding. "And who would you work with here, Ernest? Ellis mentioned a priest."

Hemingway grinned again. "Don Andrés Untzaín. Good friend of mine. He may be a bishop someday. He served as a machine-gunner for the Loyalists in Spain. He'd as soon shoot a Nazi as give him absolution for confession. Probably do both if he got a chance."

I tried not to show any expression, even though Hemingway's back was turned toward me at that moment. Naming one of your agents or sources in an open meeting like this, without even being asked to, was the rankest form of amateur idiocy.

Ambassador Braden seemed both amused and satisfied. "Who else?"

Hemingway opened his hands in a wide gesture. "I've got dozens of good contacts in Cuba, Spruille. Hundreds. Waiters, whores, newspapermen, rummies, jai alai players, fishermen who see German subs every week, Spanish noblemen who'd love to get back at the bastards who drove them into exile... they'd all love to get into the game and turn in some of these Nazi rats who are coming ashore like flotsam."

The ambassador steepled his fingers. "How much would this cost us?"

Hemingway grinned. "Nothing, Mr. Ambassador. It'll be the cheapest counterintelligence organization the U.S. government has ever had. I'll bear the brunt of the expenses myself. I mean, I may need some small arms or other minor supplies... radios maybe, some gear for the *Pilar* if we use her... but everything else is volunteer work or funded by me."

Braden pursed his lips and tapped his fingers.

Hemingway leaned on the ambassador's desk. I looked at the scar on the left arm and noticed how strong and hairy those forearms were—not my image of a writer of novels.

"Mr. Ambassador," Hemingway said softly, "I believe in this project. It's a serious idea. I'm not only ready to put up most of the money myself, I've turned down an invitation to go to Hollywood and write a script for their stupid 'March of Time' series about the Flying Tigers in Burma. Two weeks' work. A hundred and fifty thousand dollars. And I said no because I think that the Crook Factory is more important."

Braden looked up at the big man hovering over him. "I understand, Ernest," the ambassador said softly. "And we think it's important as well. I'll have to talk to the Cuban prime minister to receive permission, but that's just a formality. I've already cleared it with State and the FBI."

Hemingway nodded, grinned, and went back to his chair. "Great," he said. "Great."

"There are only two conditions," said Ambassador Braden, looking back at the papers on his desk again as if the conditions were printed there.

"Sure," said Hemingway, and he lounged back comfortably, smiling and waiting.

"Firstly," said Braden, "you'll have to send me reports. They can be short, but at least weekly updates. Bob and Ellis can work out some way you can meet them privately... secretly."

Bob Joyce said, "There's a back way up to my office on the fourth floor, Ernest. You can go in through the store on the corner and come up that way without being seen entering the embassy."

"Great," said Hemingway. "No problem there, Mr. Ambassador."

Braden nodded. "Secondly," he said softly, "you'd have to take Mr. Lucas here into your organization."

"Oh?" said Hemingway, still smiling but staring at me with a flat, cold gaze. "Why is that?"

"Joe is a consultant for State on counterintelligence issues," said the ambassador. "And an accomplished field man. I knew him in Colombia, Ernest. He was very helpful there."

Hemingway held his flat stare on me. "And why would he be helpful here, Spruille?" Without waiting for an answer from the ambassador, Hemingway said, "Do you know Cuba, Mr. Lucas?"

"No," I said.

"Never been here before?"

"Never," I said.

"*Habla usted español?*"

"*Sí*, I said. "*Un poco.*"

"*Un poco,*" repeated Hemingway in a mildly disgusted voice. "Do you carry a gun, Mr. Lucas?"

"No."

"Know how to fire one?"

"Theoretically," I said.

"Theoretically," repeated Hemingway. "But you know all about German spies, I suppose."

I shrugged. This job interview had gone as far as it was going to go. Evidently the ambassador agreed, because he said, "It's the only other condition, Ernest. State insists on it. They want a liaison."

"Liaison," said Hemingway, savoring the word as if it were a French obscenity. "So who will you report to, Joe... may I call you Joe?"

I twitched a smile. "I'll report to no one but you," I said. "At least until the operation is over. Then I'll write up a report to my superiors."

"A report card," said the writer, no longer smiling.

"A report," I said.

Hemingway rubbed his lower lip with a knuckle. "And you won't be reporting to anyone else while we're working together?"

I shook my head.

"That will be your job, Ernest," said the ambassador. "You'll deal with Bob and Ellis... or contact me directly if events warrant it. Joe Lucas can be your second in command... or use him in any capacity you choose."

Hemingway stood abruptly and walked toward me. Towering over me, he said, "Let me see your hands, Joe."

I held out my hands.

Hemingway turned them palms up, then rotated them back. "You've done real work, Joe. Not just typed reports. Are these old line burns?"

I nodded.

"You know your away around a small boat?"

"Well enough," I said.

Hemingway dropped my hands and turned back to the ambassador. "All right," he said. "Conditions and new crewman accepted. When can I get the Crook Factory cranked up, Spruille?"

"How about tomorrow, Ernest?"

Hemingway flashed that broad grin. "How about today?" He moved quickly and lightly to the door. "Bob, Ellis, I want to buy you two a drink over lunch. Joe... where are you staying?"

"The Ambos Mundos," I said.

The writer nodded. "I used to live there. Wrote most of a damned good book there. But you're not staying there any longer, Joe."

"No?"

He shook his head. "If you're going to go to work in the Crook Factory, you have to live at the factory headquarters. Get your stuff together. I'll be by to pick you up about three. You'll stay at the *finca* until we catch some German spies or get tired of each other." He nodded to the ambassador and left.

6

I WALKED FROM THE EMBASSY, taking the long way back to Hotel Ambos Mundos, wandering through the streets of Old Havana, buying a paper at a tobacconist, strolling out to the harbor road, and then walking down Obispo Street. I was being followed.

Nine blocks from the hotel, I saw a black Lincoln pull to the curb and Ernest Hemingway get out with Bob Joyce and Ellis Briggs. They headed into a bar called the Floridita. It was barely eleven o'clock in the morning. I glanced into a storefront window to make sure the man half a block behind me was still following, then I turned right off Obispo and turned back toward the harbor. The man turned, too. He was good—always staying behind others, never looking directly at me—but he also did not care if I knew he was there.

Next to the Plaza of the Cathedral I stopped at a bar called La Bodeguita del Medio and took a stool near an open window that looked out on the sidewalk. The man following me paused directly outside, leaned back against the windowsill, and unfolded a *Diario de la Marina* to read. His head was no more than a foot from me. I studied the coppery hairs on the back of his shaven neck and the line where the heavy tan ended just above the stiff white collar of his shirt.

A waiter hurried up.

"*Un mojito, por favor,*" I said.

The waiter went back to the bar. I opened my own paper and began reading the box scores from the States.

"How did it go?" asked the man outside.

"It's on," I said. "Hemingway is taking me out to his *finca* this afternoon. I'll be living there."

The man nodded and turned the page of his newspaper. His panama hat was pulled low over his face, throwing even the cheek and chin visible to me into dark shadow. He was smoking a Cuban cigarette.

"I'll use the safe house for contact," I said. "Same timetable we agreed on."

Delgado nodded again, tossed away the cigarette, folded his paper, looked away from me, and said, "Watch that writer. *Era un saco de madarrias.*" He walked away.

The waiter brought my *mojito.* It was a drink that Delgado had recommended the night before, a cocktail made with rum, sugar, ice, water, and mint. It tasted like horse piss, and I rarely drank before noon anyway. *Era un saco de madarrias.* A difficult guy. We would see.

I left the drink on the table and walked back to Obispo Street and my hotel.

I HAD MET DELGADO THE NIGHT BEFORE, leaving the Ambos Mundos to walk into a run-down section of Old Havana where tenements gave way to shacks. Chickens and half-naked children ran mindlessly through the weeds, dodging through holes in the unpainted fences. I recognized the safe house from the description in my briefing papers, found the key where it should be under the sagging porch, and let myself in. The interior was very dark and there was no electricity. The place smelled like mold and rat droppings. I felt my way to the table that was supposed to be in the middle of the room, found it, felt the metal of the lantern on it, and used my cigarette lighter to get it going. The glare was soft but shocking after the darkness outside and in.

The man was sitting not four feet from me, the wooden chair turned, his forearms resting easily on the back of it. In his right hand he held a long-barreled Smith and Wesson .38. The muzzle was aimed at my face.

I held up my right hand to show that I was not going to make any sudden moves and reached into my left coat pocket to pull out half of a torn dollar bill. I set it on the table.

The man did not blink. He opened his right fist and set his half of the bill next to mine. With my right hand still raised, palm out, I moved the two pieces together. A perfect fit.

"It's amazing how much this buys here," I said softly.

"Enough to take presents home to the entire family," said the man, and lowered the pistol. He slid it into a shoulder holster under his white suit jacket. "Delgado," he said. He did not seem embarrassed by the bullshit identification ritual. He did not apologize for aiming the weapon at my head.

"Lucas."

We talked about the mission. Delgado wasted no words. His manner was rough and efficient, just short of rudeness. Unlike so many of the FBI or SIS agents I had worked with, he did not want to speak about himself or irrelevant matters. He talked about the alternative safe house, drop sites, why the FBI people and places in Havana had to be avoided like the plague, mentioned the opposition briefly—lots of pro-Facists and German sympathizers but little in the way of a coherent Nazi network in Cuba—and gave me a description of Hemingway's *finca,* where the nearest pay phones would be, which numbers to call in Havana and elsewhere, and why to avoid dealing with the Cuban local or national police.

While he spoke I studied him in the lantern light. I had never heard of an SIS agent named Delgado. He seemed a serious person and a serious professional. He seemed dangerous.

It is strange how different men strike you in such different ways. J. Edgar Hoover had seemed like a mean fat boy dressed in nice clothes—a vindictive sissy who had cultivated the speech and mannerism of a tough guy. When I finally met Hemingway, he immediately struck me as a complex, charismatic man who probably could be simultaneously the most interesting person you'd ever meet and a tiresome son of a bitch.

Delgado was dangerous.

His face was tanned and flat in the light: his nose obviously once broken and now crooked, traces of scar tissue on his high cheeks and left ear, heavy brows—also scarred—with small, smart rodent eyes watching everything from the shadows under those brows, and a strange mouth. Sensuous. Amused. Cruel.

He was just an inch or so taller than me, I saw when he finally stood up—halfway between my height and Hemingway's—and it was obvious from the way the white suit hung on him that he had no body fat whatsoever. But when he had set his half of the dollar on the table and then holstered his weapon, I had seen the muscle on his forearms. His other movements were the opposite of what I had seen in Hemingway. Delgado wasted neither motion nor energy, conserving them the way he did his words. I had the profound impression that he could slip a knife between your ribs, clean the blade, and pocket the knife again in one smooth motion.

"Any questions?" he said when he had finished covering the details of safe house timetables.

I looked at him. "I know most of the SIS people down here," I said. "Are you new?"

Delgado smiled slightly. "Any other questions?"

"I report to you," I said, "but what do I get in return?"

"I'll watch your back when you're in Havana," he said. "Or off the *finca* grounds. I'll lay three-to-one odds that the writer will make you live out there."

"What else?" I said.

Delgado shrugged. "My orders were to funnel any information you wanted."

"Files?" I said. "Complete dossiers?"

"Sure."

"O/C files?" I said.

"Yeah. If you need them."

I think I blinked at this. If Delgado could supply Hoover's O/C files to me, then he was way outside the chain of command of either the FBI here in Cuba or the SIS as I knew it. He would be reporting to and taking orders from Hoover directly.

"Anything else you want me to do for you, Lucas?" he said as he walked to the door. The sarcasm was just audible in his voice. He had a very slight accent, but I could not place it. American... but where? The West somewhere.

"Can you recommend any place good here?" I said.

"Restaurant? Bar?" I was curious if Delgado knew Havana or if he was as new to all this as I was.

"The Floridita is where Hemingway and his cronies hang out," said Delgado. "But I don't recommend it. They make a mean drink called the *mojito* at La Bodeguita del Medio. Used to call it the Drake, after Francis Drake, but now it's a *mojito*."

"Good?" I said, just to keep him talking so that I could trace the slight accent.

"Tastes like horse piss," said Delgado, and went out into the hot, weedy night.

HEMINGWAY HAD SAID THAT he would pick me up at the Ambos Mundos at three P.M.—I had expected a chauffeur rather than the writer himself—and I was ready, checked out, and sitting in the lobby by three, my duffel and garment bag at my feet, but neither writer nor servant were to show up. Instead, the hotel manager bustled over in person, a message flimsy in his hand. From his torrent of Spanish and his frequent bows, I was made to understand that I had become a much more important guest now that it was understood that I had received a personal telephone messenger from *Señor* Hemingway and it was a tragedy that they—the manager and staff of the modest but excellent Ambos Mundos—had not known this earlier so that they could have made my stay even more magnificent.

I thanked the manager, who bowed away as if retreating from royalty, and read the flimsy: "Lucas—Thought you might want to take in some local color. Catch the bus to San Francisco de Paula. Climb the hill. I'll meet you at the *finca*. EH"

The manager and two porters hurried back as I carried my bags to the door. Would *Señor* Lucas allow them to carry his bags to the taxi?

No, *Señor* Lucas was not headed for the taxi. He was headed for the goddamned bus station.

It was about twelve miles from Havana to the village where Hemingway's farm was located, but the bus trip took me more than an hour. It was the usual south-of-the-border travel experience: grinding gears on a bus with such a sprung suspension system that I was sure we would tip over; stops every few hundred yards; shouting people; the cackle of chickens and the snorting of at least one pig amidst the gabble; snores, farts, and laughter of the passengers; the carbon monoxide fumes of the bus and a thousand other vehicles wafting in the barred, open windows; men hanging in the open door; luggage being tossed to the waiting boys on the roof.

It was a pleasant afternoon, and I would have enjoyed the local color well enough if it had not been for the small, white sedan following us. I had moved to the rear of the bus out of habit, checking out the rear window without fully turning my head, and had spotted the car immediately upon pulling away from the downtown bus depot. White '38 Ford, two men in it, heavy man driving, much thinner man with a snap-brim hat in the passenger seat, both watching the bus with a passionate disinterest. It was difficult to trail a bus without looking conspicuous—especially difficult in riotous Havana traffic—and they were doing the best they could to hang back, turning down side streets when the bus stopped, talking to newspaper and vegetable hawkers out the window at intersections—but there was no doubt that they were following the bus. Following me. Distance and the glare on the windshield prevented me from making out their features very well, but I was sure that neither one was Delgado. Who, then?

FBI possibly. As per instructions, I had not checked in with Special Agent in Charge Leddy or anyone else in Havana other than the ambassador and Delgado, but the local FBI almost certainly had heard that an SIS man had been inserted into Hemingway's crackpot scheme. But why follow me? Hoover must have sent some instruction to leave me alone. Germans? I doubted it. Delgado had reinforced my impressions that the Nazis had little or no network in Cuba, and it would have been unlikely that their disorganized fifth columnist sympathizers would have connected with me so early. Wild Bill Donovan's COI outfit? I had no idea what their presence was in Cuba, but they had avoided crossing Hoover's path in Colombia, Mexico, and the other areas of FBI/SIS hegemony with which I was familiar. Perhaps Ian Fleming's BSC? The Havana police? The Cuban National Police? The Cuban military intelligence?

I chuckled to myself. This whole situation had gone from slightly farcical to pure buffoonery. Hemingway had me riding a bus to teach me a lesson, to assert his place in the pecking order. Hell, I would be lucky if I didn't end up being assigned to clean his swimming pool...if he had a swimming pool. And as I rode to professional oblivion on this stinking, brawling, wheezing bus, at least two paid agents of *someone's* government were wasting their own time and effort in the afternoon heat to follow me.

The bus made its two-hundredth stop since we had left downtown Havana, the driver yelled something, and I grabbed my bags and climbed off with two women and their pig. The three of them hustled away across the Central Highway, and I stood there breathing the fumes and dust of the departing bus for a few minutes. There was no sign of the white car. I took my bearings and headed uphill.

I could have been in Colombia or Mexico. The same smells of beer and cooking from the open windows, the same glimpses of wash on the lines and of the old men on street corners, the same bold beginnings of paved streets that quickly turned into dusty alleys within twenty yards of the main road. A little boy had been watching me from his post in a low tree up the road, and now he leapt down and ran madly up the road, his bare feet kicking up its own cloud of dust. One of Hemingway's secret agents? I thought perhaps yes.

San Francisco de Paula was a small town with crooked streets, and within minutes I was out of the tumble of buildings and following the only road up the hill. There were several small houses visible on the hill, but the boy had run between two gateposts that led to a longer drive and a bigger building. I walked in that direction.

Hemingway came down to meet me. He was wearing Basque espadrilles, wrinkled Bermuda shorts, and the same sweaty *guayabera* he had worn to the embassy that morning. He had strapped a thick belt around his waist outside the loose shirt and a .22 pistol was tucked into the belt. He had a drink in his right hand. His left hand was on the boy's dark head. "*Muchas gracias, Santiago,*" said the writer. He patted the child, who looked up worshipfully and ran past me down toward the town.

"Welcome, Lucas," said Hemingway as I came through the gates. He did not offer to take my bags as we turned and continued up the dusty drive toward the house. "What'd you think of the bus ride?"

"Local color," I said.

Hemingway grinned. "Yeah. I like to take the bus now and again... reminds me not to get too uppity around my Cuban friends and neighbors here."

I looked at him and caught his eye.

Hemingway laughed. "All right. Hell. I've *never* taken the fucking bus. But it's still a good idea."

We had come to the front entrance to the Finca Vigía. A huge ceiba tree grew to the right of the entrance and threw shade across the wide steps. Orchids grew from the rough trunk of the tree, and I could see where the thing's thirsty roots were heaving up the tiles of the terrace. The house itself was an older limestone villa, solid and sprawling enough in its own way, but it seemed low and unimposing compared to the ceiba tree.

"Come on," said Hemingway, leading me around the side of the house. "We'll get you installed in the guest palace and then I'll show you around."

We followed a path around the main house, through a gate into an interior compound, down a tiled path past a swimming pool, through the shade of mango and flamboyan trees, and past a row of plantains and royal palms standing like weary sentinels in the afternoon heat, and stopped at a small, white frame house.

"Guest house," said Hemingway, sweeping open the low door and leading the way in. "Headquarters for the Crook Factory in this room. Bedroom's back there."

The "headquarters" consisted of a long wooden table with a large map of Cuba spread out on it—conch shells and stones holding it down—and some file folders stacked nearby. Hemingway gently kicked open the door to the small bedroom and gestured with his drink hand to a low dresser. I set my bags there.

"Did you bring a gun?" he asked.

He had asked me that morning if I had a gun and I had said no. Now I said no again. It was the truth: I had hidden both the .38 and the .357 at the safe house that afternoon.

"Here," said Hemingway, pulling the .22 from his belt and offering it to me butt first.

"No thanks," I said.

"You should keep it in a drawer here in the bedside table," said Hemingway, still holding the weapon by the barrel so that the muzzle was aimed at his belly.

"No thanks," I said again.

Hemingway shrugged and tucked the little pistol back in his belt. "This is for you, then," he said, holding out the drink.

I hesitated only a second before reaching for it, but before I could take it, Hemingway raised it, nodded at me, and took a sip himself. He offered it again.

I realized that it was some sort of ritual. I took the drink and swallowed the rest. Whiskey. Not especially good whiskey. It burned behind my eyes. I handed the glass back. It was not yet four-thirty in the afternoon.

"Ready for the two-cent tour?"

"Yes," I said, and followed him out of the relative coolness of the Crook Factory's central headquarters.

THE TOUR STARTED at a well where a man had drowned himself.

Hemingway led me up past the tennis courts, past the swimming pool, past the main house, away from the gardens, and through a field of weeds to a small but dense copse of bamboo. In the miniature jungle of bamboo there was a low stone circle with a metal screen across it: *An old well,* I thought, judging from the cool air and dank scent rising from it.

"Last year," said Hemingway, "an ex-gardener for the *finca* threw himself down this well and drowned himself. His name was Pedro. An old man. It was four days before anyone found him. One of the servants saw vultures circling the well. Damndest thing, Lucas. Why do you think he did it?"

I looked at the writer. Was he serious? Was this some sort of game?

"Did you know him?" I said.

"Met him when we first moved in. Asked him not to prune the plants. He said that was his job. I said that from then on his job would be *not* to prune the plants. He quit. Couldn't find other work. Came back a few weeks later and asked for his job back. I'd already hired another gardener. A week or so after I told him that, the old man threw himself down this well." Hemingway crossed his hairy arms and waited as if this were a puzzle that I would have to figure out if I wanted to work for him and the Crook Factory.

I felt like telling him to go fuck himself, that I already had the Crook Factory job and used to have a better one—a real job in espionage. Instead, I said, "So what's the question?"

Hemingway scowled. "Why did he throw himself down *this* well, Lucas? Why *my* well?"

I smiled slightly. "That's easy enough," I said in Spanish. "He was a poor man, no?"

"He was a poor man, yes," agreed Hemingway in Spanish. In English, he said, "Didn't have a pot to piss in."

I opened my hands. "He didn't have a well of his own to drown himself in."

Hemingway grinned and led me out of the dim light of the bamboo thicket and back toward the main house.

"Did you drink it?" I said as I followed him back down the path. I could see the slightly ragged ends of Hemingway's hair just above his collar. He did not go to a real barber; perhaps his wife cut it for him.

"The corpse water?" he said with a chuckle. "The water from the well where old Pedro lay rotting for four days? Is that what you want to know?"

"Yes."

"Everybody wanted to know that when it happened," he said brusquely. "It's no big deal to me, Lucas. I've drunk from ditches where corpses were rotting. I'd lap water from the hollow of a dead man's throat if I had to. Doesn't make a goddamn bit of difference to me."

"So you did?" I persisted.

Hemingway paused at the back door of the house. "No," he

said, opening the door and beckoning me to enter with an angry sweep of his slightly twisted left arm. "That well just provided water for the pool. May have pissed in the corpse water, though. Never can tell."

"MARTY, THIS IS LUCAS. Lucas, this is my wife, Martha Gellhorn."

We were in the kitchen—the old Cuban-style kitchen rather than the new electric one. I had been introduced to six or seven of the score of cats that seemed to have the run of the place, and I had already met most of the servants and the Chinese cook, Ramón. Suddenly this woman was there.

"Mr. Lucas," said Hemingway's wife, extending her hand in an almost manly way and giving me a quick handshake. "I understand you will be staying at the *finca* a while to help Ernest play spy. Are your accommodations acceptable?"

"Very nice," I said. *Play spy?* I had seen Hemingway's cheeks and neck redden at that comment.

"We have some company coming tonight," Gellhorn was saying, "but the gentleman is staying in our extra room here in the main house and the lady has to return to Havana late, so we won't be needing the bedroom in the guest house. You're invited to dinner tonight, by the way. Has Ernest invited you?"

"Not yet," said Hemingway.

"Well, you're invited, Mr. Lucas. It won't be a constant thing—dinner here in the main house, I mean. You may have noticed that the guest house has a quite serviceable little kitchen area, but we thought you might be amused by tonight's gathering."

I nodded. She had put me in my place quite nicely—*You're invited to dinner, but don't get used to it.*

She turned away from me as if I had been checked off her list. "Juan's driving me to town in the Lincoln," she said to Hemingway. "I have to pick up the meat for dinner. Do you need anything?"

Hemingway did—typewriter ribbon, foolscap, his suit at the cleaners—and while he spoke, I studied the woman's profile.

Martha Gellhorn Hemingway was, I knew from Hemingway's O/C file, the writer's third wife. They had been married a little less than two years, but had lived in sin for at least three years before that. Gellhorn had supplanted Pauline Pfeiffer Hemingway, who had taken the place of Hadley Richardson Hemingway.

Gellhorn was tall and had blond hair that was just shorter than shoulder-length and permed to a frizz. Her features were strong and honest-looking in a solid, midwestern way, although she spoke with a pronounced Bryn Mawr accent. This day she was wearing a seersucker skirt cut to mid-calf and a soft blue cotton shirt with a white collar. She did not seem especially happy, but I had the impression that this was her regular demeanor.

When Hemingway was done with his list of things for her to pick up for him—he had been in town only hours earlier—Gellhorn sighed and looked at me. "Do *you* need anything in town, Mr. Lucas?"

"No, ma'am," I said.

"Good," she said crisply. "Then we'll see you for dinner around eight. Suit or jacket and tie will be adequate." She went out the door.

Hemingway watched after her for a silent moment. "Marty's a writer, too," he said eventually, as if in explanation.

I said nothing.

"And she's from St. Louis," added Hemingway, as if that was the final word on the subject. "Come on, I'll show you the rest of the house."

THE FINCA VIGÍA WAS one of those large, sloppy, classical one-story, Spanish-style homes that had popped up around Cuba in the last decades of the previous century. The living room was huge—probably fifty feet long—and it sported bookcases and various hunting trophies on the walls and floor. An elk head hung next to an oil painting of a bullfighter at one end, there were the heads of two impalas—or some kind of African ungulates looking startled to be there—hanging on the wall at the other end of the room, and still more stuffed heads above the long row of low bookcases on the window side of the space. The furniture in the living room was old and comfortable-looking and not what one would expect in a rich writer's home. In the center of the room were two overstuffed armchairs, the one on the left obviously the writer's favorite—the cushion was sagging, there was a threadbare embroidered footstool within a leg's reach, and next to it was a small table absolutely filled with liquor bottles and mixers. A table behind these two chairs held two matching lamps and some wine bottles. It would be a comfortable place for reading, I thought. Or for getting stinking drunk.

Hemingway saw me looking at the wall trophies as we left the living room. "Went on safari for the first time in 'thirty-four," he said brusquely. "Want to go back as soon as this goddamned war is over."

The library was just off the long living room, and although most of the walls were taken up by floor-to-ceiling bookcases, all crammed with books, bones, and mementos, there were a few more heads of grazing beasts on the small bit of free wall space. The floor was polished tile, but in front of a long, low couch, a lion-skin rug snarled up at me. A wooden stepladder stood to the right of the entrance, and I saw that this was how Hemingway would reach the upper tiers of books.

"I have more than seven thousand books here at the *finca*," said Hemingway, his arms folded, his weight balanced lightly on the balls of his feet.

"Really?" I said. I had never heard anyone brag about books before.

"Really," said the writer, and walked over to one of the lower bookcases. He pulled out some volumes and tossed one to me. "Open it," he said.

I looked inside. It was titled *The Great Gatsby* and there was an effusive inscription on the title page signed—"Love, Scott." I looked up in mild confusion. According to Mr. Hoover's O/C file, Hemingway had written this book.

"First edition," said Hemingway, holding up the other volumes in his large hand. With his other hand, he raked his fingertips down the spines of the books on three of the long shelves. "All inscribed first editions. Joyce, Gertrude Stein, Dos Passos,

Robert Benchley, Ford Madox Ford, Sherwood Anderson, Ezra Pound. Knew 'em all, of course."

I nodded blankly. A few of the names were familiar to me. There were thick O/C files on Dos Passos, Pound, and several of the others whom Hemingway was now mentioning, but I had never needed to read them.

He took *The Great Gatsby* back, roughly shelved it, and led the way through the house to his bedroom.

"Bedroom," he said. "That's Juan Gris's *Guitar Player* over the bed there. You probably saw the other Gris in the living room, along with the Klee, the Braque, Miró's *Farm*, and the Massons."

It took me a second to realize he was talking about the strange painting over the bed. I assumed the other names were artists or the names of paintings as well. I nodded.

There was a large desk in his bedroom, but it was covered with newspapers, mail, magazines, several unwound clocks, some wooden carvings of African animals, and heaps of other junk. Cups overflowed with pencils. Fountain pens littered a blotter. Stacks of paper littered the floor. The huge head of a water buffalo hung on the wall opposite the bed and seemed to be looking out with a mixture of scorn and anticipation.

"So this is where you write books," I said, looking back at the cluttered desk and trying to sound impressed.

"Nope," said Hemingway. He nodded toward the top of a chest-high bookcase near his bed, and I saw the portable typewriter and a small stack of typing paper there. "Write standing up," he said. "Mornings. Don't talk about writing, though. No reason to."

That was fine with me.

As we left the bedroom, I caught a glimpse of Hemingway's bathroom: as many pill bottles on the shelves there as there had been bottles of whiskey and gin in the living room. A blood pressure cuff hung from a towel rack. On the white walls were scribbled notes that I guessed were daily blood pressure counts, weights, and other medical information. It seemed obsessive to me. I filed it all away for future consideration.

There were eight large rooms in the *finca*, not counting the two kitchens. The dining room was long and narrow with a few more dead animals staring down at the mahogany table.

"We always set an extra place in case someone shows up unexpectedly," said the writer. "This evening I guess it'll be you."

"I guess it will," I said. I had the impression that Hemingway was slightly embarrassed at having given me the tour. "Mrs. Hemingway said 'jacket and tie'?" I asked. It had surprised me, given Hemingway's careless appearance at the embassy that morning and the dirty clothes he was wearing now.

"Yeah," he said, looking around the room as if he had forgotten something. "We try to look civilized for dinner." His brown eyes swept back to me. "Damn, it's getting late. You want a drink, Lucas?"

"No, thanks. I'll go settle in and get a bath."

Hemingway nodded in a distracted way. "I'm going to have one. I generally drink three Scotches before dinner. You drink wine, don't you, Lucas?"

"Yes."

"Good," he said, scratching his cheeks. "We're having some good stuff with dinner tonight. Special occasion, y'know."

I did not know, unless he was talking about the go-ahead for his Crook Factory.

He looked up suddenly and grinned. "We'll have several people over tonight, but the two guests Marty mentioned..."

I waited.

"They're going to surprise the socks off you, Lucas. Surprise the fucking socks off you."

"All right," I said, nodded in appreciation of the tour, and found my way out the back door and down the path to the guest house.

7

YOU'LL NEED TO CUT YOUR HAIR, Daughter," said Hemingway. "And show your ears. I hope you have good ears."

Bergman pulled her hair back tight and tilted her head.

"You have good ears," said the writer. "Perfect ears, in fact. Maria's ears."

"How short, please?" said Bergman. "I read the passage a dozen times before they turned me down for the part, but now I cannot remember how short."

"Short," said Hemingway.

"Not as short as Vera Zorina cut her hair," Cooper said dryly. "She looks like a rabbit caught in a thresher."

"Hush," said Bergman, touching Cooper's arm tentatively but affectionately. "That is a terrible thing to say. Besides, Vera *has* the part. And I do not. And all this discussion of hair length is silly. Isn't it, Papa?"

She was talking to Hemingway. It was the first time I heard anyone call him Papa.

From the head of the table, Hemingway frowned and shook his head. "It's not silly, Daughter. You *are* Maria. You've always been Maria. You're *going to be* Maria."

Bergman sighed. I saw tears in her lashes.

Martha Gellhorn cleared her throat from the opposite end of the table. "Actually, Ernest, Ingrid has not *always* been Maria. You remember you said that you wrote the description of Maria thinking of me."

Hemingway frowned at her. "Of course I did," he almost snapped. "You know I did. But Ingrid has always been the one to *play* Maria." He jumped to his feet. "Wait here. I'll bring the book and read the description of Maria's hair."

Conversation was suspended as we all sat at the long table, waiting for Hemingway to return with his book.

I HAD HEARD THE CARS pull up while I was still in the bathtub down in the guest house. It was only six-thirty. Then laughter lilting across the lawn and pool, the sound of drinks being poured. I could hear Hemingway's clear tenor telling some story and then much louder laughter after the punch line. I sat in my underwear and read a Havana paper until a quarter till eight. Then I dressed in my best linen suit, made sure the knot in my silk tie was perfect, and strolled up the path to the main house.

The houseboy, René, let me in. One of the maids led me into the long living room. There were five guests—four men and a young woman—and from their rosy expressions and easy laughter, it looked as if they all had been drinking freely since they arrived. Everyone was dressed nicely—the writer in a wrinkled suit with a clumsily knotted tie, but looking clean and alert with his hair slicked back and his cheeks freshly shaven, the other four men also in suits, Gellhorn and the young woman in black dresses. Hemingway introduced me.

"I want you all to meet Mr. Joseph Lucas, on loan to us from the American embassy to help me with some oceanographic studies I'll be doing in the coming months. Joseph, this is Dr. José Luis Herrera Sotolongo, my personal physician and fine friend since our days together in the Spanish Civil War."

"Dr. Herrera Sotolongo," I said, bowing slightly before shaking his hand. The doctor was dressed formally in a style from twenty years past. He wore pince-nez glasses. The only sign that he had been drinking was a rosy flush along the line of his high collar.

"*Señor* Lucas," said the doctor, returning my bow.

"This short, disgustingly handsome gentleman is *Señor* Francisco Ibarlucia," said Hemingway. "Everyone calls him Patchi. Patchi, say hello to Joe Lucas. It looks like we'll be spending time on the *Pilar* together."

"*Señor* Lucas," said Ibarlucia, springing forward to shake my hand. "*Encantado.* It is my pleasure to meet a scientist of the ocean." Patchi Ibarlucia was not a big man, but he was physically magnificent. Besides the perfect tan, the oiled black hair, and the pearly teeth, he had the coiled steel body of a consummate athlete.

"Patchi and his brother are the best jai alai players in the world," said Hemingway. "And Patchi is my favorite tennis partner."

Ibarlucia's huge grin grew even larger. "*I* am the best jai alai player in the world, Ernestino. I allow my brother to play with me. Even as I sometimes allow you to beat me in tennis."

"Lucas," said Hemingway, "I'd like you to meet my friend and favorite executive officer on the *Pilar*, Mr. Winston Guest. We all call him Wolfie or Wolfer. He's one of the best yachtsmen, tennis players, skiers and all-around athletes you'll ever meet."

Guest lumbered to his feet and came forward to grip my hand in a friendly vise. He was a big man and he gave the impression of being even larger than he was. He reminded me a bit of Ian Fleming, and his face was full, ruddy, eager, open, and almost rubbery with drink. His jacket, tie, slacks, and shirt were beautifully tailored, or exquisite material, and worn with that elegant sloppiness which only the very rich can carry off. "Pleased to meet you, Mr. Guest," I said. "Why do they call you Wolfie?"

Guest grinned. "Ernest started it. Ever since Gigi said that I looked like that guy in the wolfman movies. You know...whatshisname." I had taken him for an American, but he had a slight English accent.

"Lon Chaney, Jr.," said the attractive young woman. She had a strangely familiar voice and a Swedish accent. Everyone was standing now, ready to move into the dining room.

"Yeah," said Guest. "The Wolfman." He grinned again.

He *did* look like that man from the movie.

"Gigi is Ernest's youngest son," said Martha Gellhorn. "Gregory. He's ten. He and Patrick come down every summer."

Hemingway touched the young woman's arm. "Daughter," he said, "I apologize for abandoning protocol in these introductions, but I am saving the best for last. The jewel in the crown, as it were."

"I guess that means I go next, Mr. Lucas," said the last male guest. He stepped forward and held out his hand. "Gary Cooper."

For a minute it did not register. I said earlier that I have always had a photographic memory, but recognizing the photograph in my mind does not always mean recognizing the proper name. For a moment everything seemed wrong—the tall, handsome man, the Swedish woman—as if they were suspects I had run across in an O/C file and I knew that it was wrong for them to be here, in this house. I just could not place them.

Cooper and I exchanged handshakes and pleasantries. He was a tall thin man, mostly muscle over bone, and looked to be in his early forties—about Hemingway's age—but he seemed more mature in some quiet way. Cooper's eyes were very light, he had the deep tan of a full-time athlete or someone who worked outside, and his voice was soft, almost deferential.

Before I could connect the memory of having seen him somewhere to the proper context, Hemingway was pulling me toward the young woman.

"And the jewel in our crown tonight, Lucas. Ingrid, I would like you to meet Joseph Lucas. Joe, Mrs. Petter Lindstrom."

"Mrs. Lindstrom," I said, shaking her large but delicate hand, "it is a pleasure."

"And a pleasure to make your acquaintance, Mr. Lucas," she said.

She was lovely, with the solid bone structure and clear complexion so common to Scandinavian women. But her hair was a dark brown, her eyebrows were thick, and from the full lips to the straightforward gaze she exuded more warm sensuality than most Swedish women I had met.

Martha Gellhorn said, "You might already know her as Ingrid Bergman, Mr. Lucas. *Rage in Heaven? Dr. Jekyll and Mr. Hyde*? Soon to be in... what was the name of the one you've just signed for, Ingrid? *Tangiers*?"

"*Casablanca*," said Mrs. Lindstrom with a musical laugh.

It took me a second or two to realize that these were the names of movies—none of which I had seen—and then I placed their faces with their contexts. I rarely paid much attention to movies, often using them to help me forget whatever I was obsessed with at the time and then forgetting the film as soon as I left the theater. But I had enjoyed *Sergeant York*. I had never seen the woman in a movie, but I had caught glimpses of her photographs on magazine covers.

"Well, now we all know each other," Hemingway said, holding out his arm and bowing like a maître d'. "Shall we absent ourselves from felicity for a while and go to dinner before Ramón comes after us with his Cuban longknife?"

We filed into the dining room.

"Absent ourselves from felicity," hissed Gellhorn at Hemingway as she took Dr. Herrera Sotolongo's arm and followed Cooper and Bergman into the long room. Hemingway shrugged at me, offered his arm to Ibarlucia, took a punch in the shoulder, and bowed Winston Guest and me in ahead of him.

IT WAS THE MAIN COURSE NOW, roast beef in a decent sauce with fresh vegetables, and we were waiting for Hemingway to return with his book, when Bergman said to me across the table, "Have you read his new book, Mr. Lucas?"

"No," I said. "Which book is that?"

"*For Whom the Bell Tolls,*" said Gellhorn. She had been a gracious hostess throughout the meal—a surprisingly formal meal with servants in white gloves standing near the wall—but she could not conceal the impatience in her voice when she spoke to me. Obviously, everyone there was supposed to be intimate with all of the host's works and deeds. "It was the best-seller in 1940 and last year and would have won the Pulitzer Prize if that old bastard, pardon my French, Nicholas Murray Butler, hadn't vetoed the board's unanimous recommendation. They printed more than two hundred thousand copies as a Book of the Month Club Selection and Scribners has printed more than twice that."

"Is that a lot?" I said.

As if to head off Martha Gellhorn's acerbic response, Bergman said, "Oh, it is a *wonderful* book, Mr. Lucas. I have read it many times. I am in love with the character of Maria in it—so innocent yet so determined. And so madly in love. My dear friend David Selznick thought that I would be perfect for the part—David's brother Myron is Papa's film agent, you know...."

"He sold it to Paramount for a hundred and fifty thousand

dollars," said Cooper, his fork raised halfway with a modest portion of roast beef on it. He ate European style, fork inverted. "Incredible. I'm sorry, Ingrid. Go ahead with what you were saying."

She touched the other actor's arm again. "That is correct. It was amazing. But it is an amazing book."

"You are then to be this Maria?" asked Dr. Herrera Sotolongo in his soft voice.

Bergman lowered her gaze. "Alas, it is not to be, Doctor," she said. "I tested for the part, but Sam Wood—the director who took over from Mr. DeMille—thought that I was too tall, too old, and had too large a behind to be running around in trousers for the whole film."

"Nonsense, *Señora* Bergman," said Patchi Ibarlucia, his wineglass raised as if in toast, "your behind is a work of art...a gift of God to the world's worshippers of all beautiful things."

"Gracias, Señor Ibarlucia," said Bergman with a smile, "but my husband agrees with Sam Wood. At any rate, I did not get the part. They gave it to the Norwegian ballerina Vera Zorina."

"Over my protests," said Hemingway, who had returned to the table with his book and was scowling down at them all. "We're not finished with this yet. I'm not finished with Paramount. Daughter, you will be Maria." Hemingway looked at the jai alai player, the doctor, and me. "That's why Coop and Ingrid came down here for this quick visit. All in secret. If they're confronted with it, they'll deny it. We're conspiring in secret to cast the right people for this damned movie. Coop is right...I knew from the beginning that he had to be Robert Jordan. Now Daughter has to be Maria."

"But they have already begun shooting, Papa," said the actress. "Last April. Up in the Sierra Nevada Mountains."

Cooper raised one long finger as if he were asking to be recognized before speaking. "Only the preliminary shots and battle scenes." The actor chuckled. "I heard that Wood and his people were up there working overtime in the deep snows in December, trying to get the scene in where the planes come to blow up El Sordo—Sam had gotten a loan of some fighter-bombers from the army air force just for that scene—and they were sitting up there all day on a Sunday freezing their keisters off, wondering what had happened to their planes, when word came that there weren't going to be any planes... if they saw any, report them and hide. It was December 7."

"Pearl Harbor," Gellhorn said to me, Winston Guest, and the doctor, as if we were retarded. She smiled at the actress. "Actually, Ingrid, you might remember from our conversation in San Francisco two years ago that it was I who first recommended you for the part of Maria. Long before Ernest mentioned it to *Life*. Before we were married, actually." She looked at her husband. "Do you remember, dear? I was sailing on the *Rex* from Italy and had been reading the book and I saw Ingrid there—you had your baby on your back in a little carrier, Ingrid, like some beautiful peasant woman fleeing the Nazis, and then I saw you in that movie with Leslie Howard..."

"*Intermezzo*," said Bergman.

"Yes, and I told Ernest... that has to be your Maria. This girl *is* Maria."

Hemingway sat down. "Does anyone want to hear the goddamned description?" he said.

The table hushed. "Please," said Bergman, setting down her wineglass.

Hemingway rubbed his chin, opened the book, and read in a rather toneless tenor: "Her teeth were white in her brown face and her skin and eyes were the same golden tawny brown.... Her hair was the golden brown of a grain field that has been burned dark in the sun but it was cut short all over her head so that it was but little longer than the fur on a beaver pelt." He stopped and looked at Bergman. "Short, Daughter. To show your ears."

Bergman smiled and ran her fingers through her thick hair. "I would cut it short, but I would get the best hairdresser for short hair in Hollywood. And then I would tell everyone that I cut it myself... with a kitchen scissors."

Everyone laughed politely.

Ingrid Bergman dipped her head again in a shy, almost self-effacing gesture that seemed both studied and innocent. "But Vera Zorina has it and I wish her luck. And you, of course, Mr. Cooper," she said, touching the tall man's arm again. She brightened. "But I was chosen for another part just a few days ago, and now I am on my way to shoot *Casablanca*."

"Won't that be dangerous?" I said. "With the Germans in control of that entire region, I mean."

Everyone laughed heartily. I waited for the gaiety to die down.

Bergman reached across the table and touched my hand. "The movie will be shot in Hollywood, Mr. Lucas," she said, smiling toward me rather than at my ignorance. "No one has seen the script yet, but the word is that the farthest we will go is to the Burbank airport."

"Who is your leading man, Miss Bergman?" said Winston Guest.

"It was supposed to be Ronald Reagan, but now it is Humphrey Bogart," said the actress.

"Are you looking forward to working with him?" said Gellhorn.

Bergman dropped her eyes again. "In truth, I am terrified. He is said to be very private, very demanding of his co-stars, and very intellectual." She smiled at Cooper. "I had so looked forward to kissing *you* in front of the cameras."

Cooper smiled back at her.

"You're Maria, Daughter," growled Hemingway, as if jealous of the growing intimacy between the two actors. "Here," he said, and he scrawled something in the book he held. He handed it across to her.

She read the inscription and smiled brilliantly at him. Her eyes were moist. "May I read it to the others, Papa?"

"Sure." Hemingway's voice was gruff.

"It says—'To Ingrid Bergman, who is the Maria of the book.' Thank you. Thank you. I will treasure this more than I would have treasured the role itself."

"You'll *get* the part, Daughter," said Hemingway. "Ramón!" he thundered toward the kitchen. "Where the hell is dessert?"

OVER COFFEE AND BRANDY, talk turned to the war and its leaders. Gellhorn, at her end of the table, beyond Patchi Ibarlucia, to my left, was saying that she had spent quite a bit of time in Germany in the mid and late '30s and that she had never seen anything as loathsome as the Nazi thugs—both in the streets and in government. Patchi Ibarlucia waved his brandy snifter and declared that Hitler was a *puta* and a *maricón* and a coward and that the war would be over before Christmas. Dr. Herrera Sotolongo, on my right, suggested softly that many Christmasses might pass before the fighting would be over. Winston Guest took a second helping of Key Lime pie and listened.

Gary Cooper said little, but offered the quiet opinion that the Japanese were the true enemy—it was the Japs, after all, who had bombed Pearl Harbor, not the Germans.

Hemingway literally growled. Turning to Bergman, he said, "You see why Coop and I can't talk politics, Daughter? He's to the right of Attila the Hun. Damned strange choice to play my Robert Jordan—a man who gives up everything to join the Lincoln Brigade to fight the Fascists...." As if to take the sting out of the words, Hemingway grinned at Cooper. "But I love him and wrote the goddamned character with him in mind, so I guess he'll just have to play Jordan and we'll just have to avoid talking politics."

Cooper nodded and raised his coffee cup in salute. To Gellhorn, the actor said, "You're good friends with Eleanor Roosevelt, aren't you, Marty?"

Gellhorn shrugged, but nodded.

"Have you and Ernest been to the White House since the war started?" said Cooper. "How are the Roosevelts holding up under all this?"

It was Hemingway who answered, laughing harshly. "Marty bumps into Eleanor all the time, but the last time we had dinner with His Presidentialness in the Casa Blanca was in the summer of 'thirty-seven when we showed everyone there *The Spanish Earth*."

Everyone waited politely. I could see Ingrid Bergman's eyes gleaming as she leaned forward to set her chin on the back of her interlaced fingers.

"The food at the White House is terrible." Hemingway laughed. "Goddamned inedible. Marty warned us...she was eating sandwiches at the Newark airport snack bar. It was July and the White House was a steam bath. Everyone at the table was sweating like a pig. And the place looked like a ratty old hotel—worn carpets, sprung cushions, dusty drapes. Am I exaggerating, Martha?"

"No," said Gellhorn. "Eleanor doesn't care about her surroundings, and the president never seems to notice them. And their chef should be shot."

"What were your impressions of the evening?" asked Bergman, enunciating each syllable with care. Along with her sweet accent, some effects of the alcohol had begun to creep in.

Hemingway laughed again. "I liked Eleanor and Harry Hopkins," he said. "If Hopkins was the president and Eleanor the secretary of war, we might get this war over with by Christmas."

"And the president?" queried Cooper. For such a tall and imposing man, his voice was almost diffident.

Hemingway shrugged. "You've been around him, Coop. He's sort of sexless, isn't he? Rather like an old woman...an old society dame, what with that stuffy Harvard accent." Hemingway pronounced it "Hah-vahd."

"And all that work to get him into and out of that goddamned wheelchair," continued the writer, frowning now into his brandy glass. "It must take up half the day just to wheel him around."

I admit that I blinked at this. Everyone knew in the backs of their minds that the president was crippled, but no one mentioned it and his wheelchair and braces were never shown in newsreels. Most of us in the country had forgotten about his condition. It seemed a rough thing for Hemingway to say.

The writer looked up at the sudden silence. "But...hell..." he said. "He's our war leader, like it or not, and we back him against that moral cripple, Hitler, right?"

There was a chorus of assent, and Hemingway refilled our brandy glasses whether we wanted more or not. We were not quite finished with politics. Dr. Herrera Sotolongo wondered what Adolf Hitler was really like.

"I did several films in Germany a few years ago," Bergman said hesitantly. "It was in 1938. I was pregnant with Pia. Karl Fröhlich took me to one of those huge Nazi rallies in Berlin. You know...the enormous stadium, floodlights and torches everywhere, bands playing, the steel-helmeted storm troopers. Hitler was there. Right in the center of all that organized madness. He was beaming. And returning that *Sieg Heil* salute..."

She paused. We waited. I could hear insects and night birds through the screens.

"Anyway," continued Bergman brightly, with what I heard as a subtly false note in her voice, "everyone in the huge crowd was *Sieg Heiling*, arms thrusting out like marionettes, and I was just looking around. I was, you understand, *amused*. But Karl Fröhlich almost had a fit. 'Inga,' he whispered, '*Mein Gott*, you're not doing the Heil Hitler salute!' 'Why should I, Karl?' I replied. 'You're all doing it so marvelously well without me....'"

Everyone laughed politely as Bergman looked down at her brandy snifter. Her lashes were long and lovely, and her cheeks colored very nicely with pleasure as the chuckling continued.

"That's the form, Daughter," boomed Hemingway, putting his right arm around her and squeezing her. "That's why you *have* to be my Maria."

I sipped my own coffee. It was interesting—watching and hearing Bergman slip from her shy actress persona into actual acting. She had been lying about the *Sieg Heil* incident—I was certain of that—although for what reason and in what way I had no idea. It occurred to me that there were only four of us at the table—Winston Guest, Dr. Herrera Sotolongo, Patchi Ibarlucia, and myself—who lived in the real world. Hemingway and Gellhorn created fiction; Bergman and Cooper acted it out.

Then I almost laughed out loud. I was there under false pretenses, hiding even my real reason for being there—a spy who lied and cheated and was asked to kill for a living. So there were only three real humans at this table of six: the physician, the athlete, and the millionaire were real. The rest of us were aberrations, distortions—shadows of shades—empty silhouettes, like those Indonesian shadow puppets dancing and posturing behind thin screens for the delight of the crowds.

EVENTUALLY HEMINGWAY UNCORKED another bottle of wine—our fourth for the dinner, counting the brandy—and suggested that we enjoy it on the terrace. Bergman looked at her watch, exclaimed that it was almost midnight, and insisted that she had to get back to the hotel—she said that she had an early flight in the morning, connecting in Miami for a flight to Los Angeles to meet with Michael Curtiz, her director on *Casablanca,* and to do some preliminary wardrobe tests even though actual filming would not begin for almost a month. There was a flurry of hugs and kisses on the front terrace—Bergman telling Cooper and Hemingway that she was so sorry that she would not be in *For Whom the Bell Tolls,* Hemingway stubbornly assuring her that she *would* be—and then Juan, the black chauffeur, closed the rear door on her and the black Lincoln was gliding down the driveway. The rest of us followed Hemingway and Gellhorn to the rear terrace.

Before I could make my excuses and escape to the guest house, Hemingway had refilled my wineglass and we were sitting in comfortable chairs on the terrace, enjoying the night sounds, the cooling air, the stars, and the distant lights of Havana.

"A very, very nice lady," said Patchi Ibarlucia. "Please, Ernesto, who is this Lindstrom she is married to and why does she keep a different name?"

Hemingway sighed. "Her husband's a doctor…Petter with two *t*'s. At least he's a doctor in Sweden. Now he's in Rochester, New York, trying to get certified and accredited or whatever the hell foreign doctors do to get their parchment. She's Mrs. Petter Lindstrom in Rochester, but she kept her maiden name for movies."

"We met them for the first time at dinner in San Francisco two years ago," said Gellhorn, shaking her head impatiently as her husband offered to pour her more wine. "Petter is very nice."

Hemingway only grunted.

"Well," Cooper said slowly, "I'm glad that I came down to meet her. It's too bad that Sam Wood chose Vera Zorina instead of Ingrid. Of course, Mr. Goldwyn didn't want to loan me out to Paramount either…"

"Loan you out?" I repeated.

Cooper nodded. He was an elegant man, I realized, as comfortably at home in his expensive jacket and slacks and perfectly knotted silk tie as Hemingway seemed uncomfortable in his formal clothes. Where the writer seemed rumpled after the evening, the actor looked as cool and sharply pressed as he had before the dinner had begun. Throughout the evening I had noticed Gellhorn glancing at Cooper and then at her husband, frowning slightly as if she were comparing the two. Cooper was sitting next to me, and I caught a hint of soap and a subtle cologne or shaving lotion as he turned his face in my direction. "Yes, Mr. Lucas," he said politely. "The movie business is a bit like slavery before the Civil War or major league baseball today. We're under ironclad contract to our studios and unless we're loaned out—usually as some sort of trade—we can't do projects for other studios. In this case, Sam Goldwyn made a deal for me to go to Paramount to do this movie largely because of Ernest's insistence to the press that I was the right man for it."

"What kind of deal?" asked Winston Guest. "Was something or someone traded?"

Cooper smiled. "Mr. Goldwyn told Sam Wood—he's the director who took over from DeMille for Paramount on this project—that I could do *For Whom the Bell Tolls* if Wood would direct me in a baseball picture."

"When do you make this picture, *Señor* Cooper?" asked Dr. Herrera Sotolongo.

"It's already made, Doctor," said the actor. "Mr. Goldwyn wanted it to be finished before I went to Paramount for this project. It will be released soon. It's called *The Pride of the Yankees.* I play Lou Gehrig."

"Lou Gehrig!" cried Patchi Ibarlucia. "Yes, yes. But you are not left-handed. *Señor* Cooper!"

The actor smiled and shook his head. "They tried to teach me to throw and bat left-handed," he said ruefully, "but I am afraid that I was very clumsy. I was never that good at baseball anyway. I hope they can save it by skillful editing."

I stared at Cooper. He did not look all that much like Lou Gehrig. I had followed Gehrig's career since shortly after he joined the Yankees in 1925. I had been listening to the radio in June 1932 when Gehrig hit four consecutive home runs in a single game. In his seventeen years for the Yankees, the Iron Horse had played in 2,130 consecutive games, and he left baseball with a career batting average of .340, 493 home runs, and 1,990 RBIs. On July 4, 1939, I had taken my only vacation in four years so that I could go to New York's Yankee Stadium—I had paid eight dollars for a ticket, a fortune—to see his farewell to baseball. Gehrig had died just a year ago, in June 1941. He was thirty-seven years old.

I looked at Cooper and wondered at the arrogance of someone imitating Lou Gehrig for a mere movie.

As if reading my thoughts, the actor shrugged and said, "I probably wasn't the right person for the role, but Mrs. Gehrig was very nice about it and I got to spend time with Babe Ruth and the other—"

"Shhh!" hissed Hemingway.

In the sudden silence we could hear the crickets, the night birds, a single car on the highway below the hill, and laughter and music from the farmhouse on the adjacent hilltop.

"Goddamn it!" cried Hemingway. "That bastard Steinhart has a party going. And after I warned him."

"Oh, Ernest," said Gellhorn. "Please don't…"

"Is it war, Ernesto?" shouted Patchi Ibarlucia in Spanish.

"*Sí*, Patchi," said Hemingway, getting to his feet. "It is war." To the house, he cried, "René! Pichilo! The weapons! Bring the weapons and the ammunition!"

"I'm going to bed," said Martha Gellhorn. She stood, bent to kiss Cooper on the cheek, said "I will see you in the morning, Coop" to the actor and a curt "Good evening, gentlemen" to the rest of us, and went into the house.

The houseboy, René, and Hemingway's gardener and the keeper of his fighting cocks, José Herrero—whom Hemingway had introduced me to earlier as "Pichilo"—came out of the house with boxes of fireworks and long, hollow, bamboo stalks.

"It's getting late," I said, setting aside my wineglass and standing up. "I should…"

"Nonsense, Lucas," growled Hemingway, handing me a bamboo stalk about a meter and half long. "We need every man. Choose some ammo."

Cooper, Winston Guest, and Ibarlucia had already doffed

their jackets and rolled up their sleeves. Dr. Herrera Sotolongo looked at me, shrugged, removed his jacket, and carefully folded it over the back of his chair. I did the same.

The "ammo" consisted of two crates of fireworks—skyrockets, cherry bombs, strings of firecrackers, bottle rockets, stink bombs, and St. Catherine pinwheels. Ibarlucia handed me a rocket with a short fuse. "These are very good with your launcher, *Señor* Lucas." He grinned and nodded toward the hollow bamboo stalk.

"You all have lighters?" said Hemingway.

Both Cooper and I did.

"Is this a long-term feud, Ernest?" said Cooper. He was trying to suppress a smile, but it kept creeping around the corners of his mouth.

"Long enough," said Hemingway.

Piano music and laughter came from the other house, to the northeast. Steinhart's house was the only other large building on the hilltop—slightly lower than Hemingway's *finca* but apparently much older and grander, judging from the blaze of electric lights and the glimpses of art noveau wings and gables seen through the screen of trees.

"Patchi, you and Wolfer and the doctor know the drill," said Hemingway, crouching at the edge of his terrace and sketching a map in the moist soil of the garden with his finger. He had already taken off his jacket and tie and looked happier with his collar unbuttoned. His finger sketched lines and loops as if he were drawing a football play in the mud.

"We go down here through the trees, Coop," he whispered. We were all crouching around him. The actor was grinning. "This is the *finca*... here. This is Steinhart's mansion... here. We go down through the trees here... single file... and cross the enemy frontier, here, at the fence. Stay low until we get on the other side of his wall here. No one fires until I give the word. Then blow the shit out of his soirée."

Cooper raised an eyebrow. "I take it that you object to his dinner parties, Ernest?"

"I warned him," growled the writer. "All right. Everyone fill your pockets."

We did: skyrockets, stink bombs, cherry bombs, and the

large firecrackers. Guest and Ibarlucia both strung strings of firecrackers over their shoulders like bandoliers. Then we were following the writer through the garden, out through the weeds, over a low stone wall, and down the hill and through the screen of trees that separated us from the light and noise of Steinhart's party.

I knew this was all childish nonsense, but my adrenal glands evidently had not been informed. My heart beat quickly, and I was filled with that sense of slowed time and heightened sensory awareness that always accompanied me into some sort of action.

As Hemingway held the wire fence open for us to crawl through, he whispered, "Be careful after we fire. Steinhart's been known to unleash the dogs and open up with his twelve-gauge."

"*Madre de Dios,*" whispered Dr. Herrera Sotolongo.

We crouched there until Hemingway took the lead again—I made note of our willingness to let him lead and of his easy assumption of the role—and we followed him up another slight rise, through thinning mango trees, across a fallow field, stopping to crouch behind a belt-high stone wall that must have been at least a century old.

"Another twenty meters," whispered Hemingway. "We'll move around to the left to get a clear shot at the dining room and terrace. Coop, follow me. Wolfer, stay with Coop. Then the doctor, then Patchi, and Lucas you'll bring up the rear. Every man for himself coming back. I'll cover your retreat at the fence."

Gary Cooper was smiling. Winston Guest's cheeks were flushed. I could see Ibarlucia's white grin in the dark. The doctor sighed and shook his head. In Spanish, Herrera Sotolongo whispered, "This is not good for your blood pressure, Ernestino."

"Shhh," hissed Hemingway. He went over the stone wall with the grace of a cat and moved silently up the hill.

We had taken up positions in the weeds less than fifteen meters down the hill from Steinhart's brightly lighted terrace and broad dining room glass doors when Hemingway gave us a hand signal to load. Everyone fumbled for rockets and stink bombs. I shook my head and turned my back to the target. There was no chance that I was going to have to admit that I had fired incendiary devices at one of Havana's more important local citizens.

It was just as I turned that I saw the movement at our left, behind the low stone wall that Hemingway had called the "pig fence" during our tour earlier in the day.

In military training—and at the BSC Camp X in Canada—combat instructors emphasize that the best way to see the enemy in the dark is to look slightly away from where they might be. Peripheral vision is more effective than straight-on viewing in the dark. Wait for movement.

I saw the movement—the briefest of occultations as a human form eclipsed the lights of Havana through the trees. Again. Someone in black flanking us to our left. The form was carrying something too thin to be one of our absurd bamboo stalks. A glint of reflected light on glass told me that it was a rifle with a scope and that it was aimed in our direction... in Hemingway's direction.

"Now!" cried Hemingway, and rose up. He fit a rocket into the bamboo stalk, lit the fuse with his gold lighter, and fired directly at the Steinharts' dining room window. Ibarlucia fired a second later. Guest threw a long string of firecrackers. Cooper hurled a cherry bomb onto the terrace. The doctor shook his head and fired off a rocket that flew high, disappeared onto a third-story terrace, passed through an open window, and exploded deep within the house. Hemingway had reloaded and was firing again. The skyrockets—designed to explode into starbursts hundreds of feet above the ground—exploded and then exploded again in magnesium and sulfur rosettes across the terrace and walls. There were screams and shouts and the sounds of breaking crockery from the house. The piano playing stopped.

I had never quit watching out of the corner of my eye for the shape beyond the pig fence. Now the silhouette rose and the light of exploding cherry bombs reflected on the glass scope.

Cursing myself for not bringing a pistol or serious knife, I lit the short fuse to the rocket, stuffed it into the bamboo stalk, and fired in the direction of the pig fence and the highway. It missed high and exploded among the lower mango branches. I loaded another and began running toward the pig fence, trying to put myself between the silhouette with the rifle and Hemingway.

"Lucas," came the writer's shout from behind me, "what the hell are you..."

I ran on, crashing through corn stalks and leaping tomato plants. There was the impression of movement beyond the pig fence and something buzzed past my left ear. I lobbed a cherry bomb and flicked the short-bladed gravity knife open in my left hand, holding it low, and then I was hurtling over the fence in the dark, dropping the bamboo stalk and crouching with the knife loose and ready.

This side of the fence was empty. High weeds rustled ten meters toward the road. I rose, began to move in that direction, and then threw myself flat as gunshots erupted behind me.

A shotgun. Two blasts. Shouts. The hysterical barking of large dogs—Dobermans from the sound of them. The barking stopped as they slipped their chains. Strings of firecrackers went off, confusing the dogs and driving them into a frenzy of barking.

I hesitated only a second and then jumped back over the fence and ran in a fast crouch toward Steinhart's wall and the low area separating the two properties. The shotgun exploded again just before I hurtled over the stone wall. It came from Steinhart's mansion and had been aimed high... either deliberately over our head or at the Hemingway house.

There were huddled shapes at the wire fence. Men were shouting on the Steinhart terrace, and at least two searchlights stabbed out through the smoke. Another cherry bomb went off.

"Goddamn you, Hemingway," a man was shouting up the hill. "Goddamn you! This isn't funny." The shotgun roared again, and pellets tore leaves off the mango tree above us.

"Go, go, go," Hemingway was saying, patting the other pale forms on the back. Guest was breathing heavily, but he jogged quickly up the hill. I could see Cooper's grin. He had torn the knee of his pants and his shirt was streaked with mud or blood, but he moved off briskly. Ibarlucia helped the doctor run up the slope and through the trees.

Hemingway grabbed my collar. "Where the hell were you going, Lucas? Why were you shooting toward the road?"

I removed his hand from my shirt. Men shouted behind us and underbrush snapped as the Dobermans crashed down the hill toward the fence.

"Go!" said Hemingway, and tapped me on the back. I ran, pausing only long enough to look back and see the writer take a slab of raw steak from his trouser pocket and toss it over the fence toward the sound of the approaching dogs. He calmly lit and threw his last cherry bomb, then started up the hill in a slow trot.

STEINHART AND HIS GUESTS did not follow the pursuit beyond the fence. The dogs were called back in the dark. Shouts echoed across the fields for a while, then the piano music started up again.

Cooper, the doctor, Patchi, Guest, and Hemingway collapsed in their chairs on the terrace, laughing and talking loudly. The actor had torn his hand on the fence, and Hemingway brought out bandages and whiskey—pouring the good whiskey on the wound before bandaging it, then filling Cooper's glass.

I waited just beyond the edge of light from the terrace for some minutes, but there was no sign of movement toward the road. I came back, picked up my jacket, and said my good-nights. Gary Cooper apologized for the bandage and shook my hand. "It was a pleasure meeting you, fellow commando Lucas," he said.

"Likewise."

"Good night, Mr. Lucas," said Winston Guest. "I'll see you aboard the *Pilar*, I guess."

The doctor was panting, still out of breath. He bowed in my direction. Patchi Ibarlucia smiled and squeezed my shoulder.

"No whiskey before you turn in, Lucas?" said Hemingway. His face was serious.

"No," I said. "Thanks for the dinner."

I went back to the guest house, changed into dark slacks and a dark sweater, took a small flashlight out of my duffel, and slipped out again to the pig fence and the road. A car had been parked there, just on the wet grass near the road, only a short time before. There were broken branches in the shrubs. At the foot of the pig fence, trampled in the mud, I caught the gleam of a single brass shell casing—a 30.06 I saw as I held it in the thin beam of the flashlight—and recently fired from the smell of it.

I went back up to the *finca* and stayed outside, just beyond the lights of the terrace where Hemingway and his friends spoke and laughed softly until Cooper finally led the retreat to bed and sleep. Ibarlucia drove the doctor away in a red roadster. Guest left a moment later in a Cadillac. The lights of the *finca* stayed on another twenty minutes or so and then winked out.

I crouched there in the darkness under the mango trees just below the dark shape of the guest house, listening to the tropical night and the sounds of insects and feeding birds. I thought about actors and writers and boys and their games for a while, then I concentrated on not thinking at all as I listened and waited.

A little before dawn I went in to bed.

8

ON MONDAY MORNING, Hemingway drove us both to the harbor town of Cojímar, where his boat, the *Pilar*, was anchored. Winston Guest, Patchi Ibarlucia, and Hemingway's Cuban first mate and cook, Gregorio Fuentes, were waiting to go out with us. From the sideways glances the men gave me and the tone of Hemingway's voice, I knew that this was going to be some sort of test.

Hemingway had told me to dress for the water, so I was wearing canvas deck shoes, shorts, and a blue work shirt with the sleeves rolled up. Hemingway had on his baggy shorts, the Basque espadrilles he had worn to the embassy the previous Friday, and a tattered sweatshirt with the sleeves cut off. The mate—Fuentes—was a lean, squint-eyed man with dark skin and a quick, hard handshake. This day the man was wearing black trousers, a loose, long white shirt worn outside his belt, and no shoes or socks. The millionaire, Guest, had on hemp-colored trousers and a short-sleeved, yellow-and-white-striped shirt that emphasized his ruddy complexion. He shifted from one foot to the other and jingled the change in his pocket as we all came aboard. Ibarlucia was dressed like a bullfighter on his day off in tight, white pants and an expensive cotton sweater. As Hemingway showed me the boat and made ready to shove off, I could not help but think that it was a motley crew.

The tour took only a few minutes—the writer was eager to get on the water while the weather was still good—but I could sense the pride Hemingway took in the boat.

At first glance, the *Pilar* was not overly impressive. Thirty-eight feet long with a black hull and green roof, it looked like any one of a hundred pleasure-fishing boats one would find tied up in Miami or St. Petersburg or Key West. But stepping aboard and following the writer to the bridge, I noted the varnished hardwood in the cockpit beyond the bridge and the bronze plaque on the counter near the throttle and gearshift:

HULL 576
WHEELER SHIPYARD
BOAT MANUFACTURERS
1934
BROOKLYN, NEW YORK

The Wheeler Shipyard made good boats. Hemingway paused by the wheel long enough to point out the controls, watching me all the time to see if they meant anything to me. The instrument panel by the wheel had another plaque—which read NORSEMAN POWERED—and four dials beneath it: a tach, an oil level gauge, an engine temperature dial, and an ammeter. There was a vertical lights panel to the left of the helm with the buttons reading, from top to bottom: ANCHOR LIGHT, RUNNING LIGHTS, BILGE PUMP, WIPER, SEARCHLIGHT. A chronometer and a barometer had been mounted on one of the cabin pillars.

Hemingway held out his hand as if introducing me to the boat. "You saw the flying bridge I added?" he said.

"Yeah."

"You can steer and handle the throttle from up there, but you have to start the engines here." His toe pointed toward two buttons on the deck.

I nodded. "Two engines?" I said.

"Uh-huh. Both diesel, of course. The main motor's a seventy-five horsepower Chrysler. Second one's a forty-horse Lycoming. After we get up to speed, I cut off the smaller one to damp vibration. The Chrysler is rubber mounted." He put his large hand on the throttles. "She stops in her own length, Lucas, and idles in gear with the prop turning."

I nodded again. "But why the second engine?"

"It's always good to have an auxiliary," growled Hemingway.

I did not agree—I doubted if it would be worth the extra weight and maintenance if one took good care of the main engine—but I said nothing.

He stepped back into the sunshine. Guest and Ibarlucia moved aside. Fuentes had gone around to the bow and was kneeling there, ready to untie the bowline.

"Cockpit's twelve feet wide and sixteen feet long," said Hemingway.

I looked at the comfortable seats and benches around the long space.

Hemingway walked back and tapped a rear access hatch. "She can carry three hundred gallons of gas and has a hundred-and-fifty gallon tank for potable water. Can load a couple of hundred more gallons of demijohns and drums here in the cockpit if we had to. Forward cabin has two double berths—and there are two more compartments with bunks. Two of 'em have their own heads. Warning, though, Lucas... if you use toilet paper in either of the heads, put it out the porthole, not down the crapper. Paper clogs the goddamned pumps. Anyway, the galley has an icebox and a three-burner alcohol stove." He gestured aft. "You can see I added a built-in fishbox here and had the stern cut down to within three feet of the water."

I blinked in the sunlight and waited. Guest and Ibarlucia were watching me.

"Any questions?" said Hemingway.

I shook my head.

"The little compartment forward has two shelves we call the Ethylic Department," said Winston Guest.

I looked at the big man. "Why is that?"

"It's where we keep the booze," said the affable millionaire, and grinned.

"She can do about sixteen knots on a flat sea—I like to hold her down to about eight, usually—and she has a cruising range of about five hundred miles with a crew of seven," continued Hemingway, ignoring Guest's comment. "Any questions?" he said again.

"Why did you name it *Pilar*?" I said.

Hemingway scratched his cheek. "In honor of the shrine and *feria* at Zaragoza," he said. "And now I have a character in *For Whom the Bell Tolls* with that name. I like the name."

Patchi Ibarlucia had opened a cooler and taken out a cold beer. He popped twice with an opener, raised it, and grinned over the top of the can. "And I think you told me once, Ernestino, that it was a secret pet name for your second *Señora—Señorita* Pauline—is correct?"

Hemingway glared at the jai alai player. Turning back to me, he said, "Why don't you cast off the stern lines, Lucas. Wolfer, you get in the bridge and start her up. I'll go on to the flying bridge to take her out. Patchi, you just drink your goddamn beer—nine-thirty in the morning, for Godssakes—and lounge around in the shade. We'll wake you up when we get out to where the marlin are running."

Ibarlucia grinned and slurped his beer loudly. Guest ambled into the cockpit bridge, still jingling his change. Fuentes watched impassively from the bow. Hemingway clambered up the ladder with surprising agility for so stocky a man. I went aft to handle the stern line.

Something was up. There would be some test for me before this cruise was over.

Fuentes and I untied and coiled our lines, shouting the fact to the flying bridge. The *Pilar*'s engines both fired, the twin screws turned, and we moved slowly out, turning toward the harbor entrance and open water.

SHORTLY AFTER DAWN ON SATURDAY, I heard Cooper and Hemingway splashing around in the pool, then conversation on the terrace, and finally the sound of Hemingway's Lincoln driving Cooper away. I had no food in the guest house yet and was expected to eat in the old-fashioned kitchen of the main house—where the help ate—but I still gave Hemingway and his wife time to breakfast before I went around to the kitchen.

Hemingway came into the kitchen briefly as I was having my second cup of coffee under the disapproving eye of the houseboy, René, and Ramón, the cook.

"I'm writing this morning," Hemingway growled at me. "I'll try to finish by lunch so you can meet some of the Crook Factory agents." He was carrying a glass of what looked to be Scotch and soda. It was 7:45 A.M.

The writer noticed my glance. "You disapprove, Lucas?"

"It's not my place to approve or disapprove of anything," I said softly. "You want to drink before eight o'clock in the morning, it's your business. Plus, it's your house...which makes it doubly your business."

Hemingway held up the glass. "This isn't a drink," he said roughly. "This is the goddamned hair of the goddamned dog that almost bit us last night." Suddenly he grinned. "That was fun...attacking Steinhart's...wasn't it, Lucas?"

"Sure," I said.

Hemingway came over and took a bit of the bacon and a piece of toast that I had made for myself. He crunched them for a minute. "You think this Crook Factory thing is all a game...a joke...don't you, Special Adviser Joseph Lucas?"

I said nothing, but my gaze did not contradict his statement.

Hemingway finished the bacon and sighed. "I'm not working on a book of my own now, you know," he said. "I'm editing an anthology. A book of war writing called *Men at War*. For the last couple of months, I've been reading bargeloads of bullshit that a guy named Wartels up at Crown—he and his toadies—think is crackerjack war writing. They've already set a lot of it in type. Things like a stupid, totally phony story by Ralph Bates—all about women machine gunners at Brunette. Didn't happen. Pure bullshit. While they leave out a beautiful story by Frank Tinker about the Italian disaster at Brihuega."

Hemingway fell silent for a moment, but I had no opinion on any of this. I said nothing.

He sipped his Scotch and soda for a moment and then looked hard at me. "What do you think of war, Lucas?"

"I've never been in a uniform," I said. "I've never fought in a war. I don't have a right to an opinion."

Hemingway nodded. His gaze never left mine. "I've been in a uniform," he said. "I was badly wounded on a battlefield before I was twenty years old. I've probably seen more wars than you've seen naked women. And you want to know what I think about war?"

I waited.

"I think war is a fucking old man's trick pulled on young men," snarled Hemingway, breaking the lock of our eyes at last. "I think that it's a giant grinder that ball-less old farts cram virile young men into so as to eliminate the competition. I think it's bold, grand, wonderful, and a fucking nightmare." He drank down the last of his Scotch and soda. "And I think that my oldest boy will be old enough to fight in this fucking, useless war," he muttered, as much to himself, it seemed, as to me. "And that Patrick and Gigi may have to go as well, if it drags on the way I'm sure it will."

He went to the door and looked at me again. "I'm going to be working on this introduction until about noon. Then we'll go around and see some of the field agents working for the Crook Factory."

HEMINGWAY'S "FIELD AGENTS" turned out to be pretty much the motley crew of cronies, drinking buddies, and old acquaintances that he had described to Bob Joyce and about which I had read in Hoover's O/C file: Patchi Ibarlucia and his brother were to act as spies between jai alai games; also included were Dr. Herrera Sotolongo's younger brother, Roberto; a sailor named Juan Dunabeitia whom Hemingway introduced as "Sinsky"—short for Sinbad the Sailor; an exiled Catalan named Fernando Mesa, who worked as a waiter and also helped crew Hemingway's boat at times; a Catholic priest named Don Andrés Untzaín, who spat each time he mentioned Fascists; some fishermen down along the Havana docks; two rich Spanish noblemen who lived in large houses on hills closer to the city than Hemingway's farm; a covey of whores in at least three Havana brothels; several wharf rats who smelled of rum; and a blind old man who sat in the Parque Central all day.

Once we were downtown, we spent the rest of Saturday afternoon and evening meeting more "operatives" in the various hotels, bars, and churches that met with Hemingway's approval:

a bellman at the Hotel Plaza, near the park; a bartender named Constante Ribailagua at El Floridita; a waiter at La Zaragozana; a doorman at an opera house called Centro Gallego; a house detective at the Hotel Inglaterra; another priest—this one very young—in the incense-smelling vaults of the Iglesia del Santo Angel Custodio; an ancient Chinaman-waiter at the Pacific Chinese restaurant; a Cuban girl who worked in a beauty parlor on the Prado of Havana; and the old man who ground and roasted coffee beans in the little shop called the Great Generoso, across the street from the Cunard Bar. He introduced me to Angel Martinez, the owner of La Bodeguita del Medio—the bar where I had tried the lousy drink—but evidently this was just a social call, because Martinez was not introduced as "one of my best field agents" as the others had been.

It was about seven P.M. and we had stopped for drinks in half a dozen bars when Hemingway led me into the Café de la Perla de San Francisco—a small restaurant just off the town square with a trickling fountain. The bar was nice enough, made of polished stone, but Hemingway led me past it into the tiny restaurant area.

"Are we eating here?" I said.

"Hell, no. The best thing here is the twenty-five-cent blue-plate special. We'll go back to the Basque Center for supper.... Marty's got friends coming to the *finca* tonight and it'd be better if we don't get back until later. Uh-uh, I brought you here to show you that fellow." He nodded toward a man standing near the kitchen doors. The man looked to be Spanish or Cuban, but sported a waxed mustache in the Austrian style, had short-cropped hair, and was glaring at us as if demanding that we either sit down and eat or get the hell out.

"*Señor* Antonio Rodriguez," said Hemingway. "But everyone calls him Kaiser Guillermo."

I nodded. "Another field agent?"

"Hell, no," said Hemingway. "He's the owner. Doesn't know me from Adam, although I've had lunch here quite a few times. But if we can't find any real Nazi spies, I suggest we come back and arrest the Kaiser."

With that our tour of the Crook Factory personnel was

essentially over, except for one busboy at the Basque Club whom Hemingway introduced as "our finest...and our only...courier" as we were waiting for our table to be cleared.

ON SUNDAY, there was no Crook Factory business. At least none that I was invited to attend.

There was a serious party going on all that Sunday afternoon, with people swimming and lounging around the pool, cocktail chatter through the screen doors, the smell of a pig being roasted, and cars coming and going. I identified the Ibarlucia brothers as well as half a dozen other jai alai players, several expatriate Basques, Winston Guest, other wealthy athletes including one I would learn was named Tom Shevlin, and many others I did not know. From the U.S. embassy there was Ellis Briggs with his wife and two children, Bob and Jane Joyce, Ambassador and Mrs. Braden—she was a Chilean aristocrat, I knew, and looked the part, visibly elegant even from fifty paces away.

Earlier, I had asked Hemingway if there was a way other than a bus that I could get into Havana.

"Why?" he said. Meaning, perhaps, that the bars were closed on Sunday morning.

"To go to church," I said.

Hemingway grunted. "Hell, you can take the Lincoln when Juan or Marty or I don't need it. There's an old Ford coupe, but it's in the shop right now. Or you could use the bicycle we bought for Gigi."

"That would be good," I said.

"Remember, it's ten miles to the suburbs," he said. "Twelve to the Old Section."

"The bike would be fine," I said.

It was. I left in mid-afternoon when the party was in full swing, calling Delgado from a pay phone in San Francisco de Paula. We met at the safe house.

"Quite a tour you two had yesterday," said the other SIS man as we stood in the shadowed heat of the little room. Delgado was wearing a white suit with only an undershirt beneath the linen jacket. I could see the butt of his pistol in his waistband.

"You weren't exactly invisible," I said.

He rubbed his jaw. "Hemingway didn't make me."

"Hemingway wouldn't catch on if he was being followed by a three-legged ox," I said. I handed him my report in a sealed envelope.

Delgado broke the seal and began to read. "Mr. Hoover likes his reports typed," he said.

"That report is for the director," I said.

Delgado looked up and showed his long teeth. "I'm supposed to see everything that goes to him, Lucas. You have a problem with that?"

I sat down on the rough chair across the table from Delgado. It was very hot and I was very thirsty. "Who were the two men who followed me out to the *finca* on Friday and were in the Buick behind us yesterday?"

Delgado shrugged.

"Not local FBI?" I said.

"Uh-uh," said Delgado. "But the tall man following you on foot was Cuban National Police."

I frowned. "What tall man?"

Delgado's sharp smile broadened. "I didn't think you saw him. That's why I'm here to watch your back, Lucas. You're too busy boozing it up with that alcoholic writer." He looked back at my report. The smile faded. "Somebody actually took a shot at you with a thirty-aught-six?"

"Or at Hemingway. Or at one of the other clowns in our party."

Delgado looked at me. "Who do you think it was?"

"Where were you on Friday night, Delgado?"

The smile returned. "In the best whorehouse in Havana. And if I were shooting at you, Lucas... you'd be dead."

I sighed and rubbed the sweat out of my eyes. I could hear the sound of children playing in the weedy lots nearby. An aircraft droned overhead. The air here smelled of gasoline fumes, the sea, and sewage. "Hemingway's giving me a typewriter tomorrow," I said. "To type up the Crook Factory reports. My next report to Mr. Hoover will be typed."

"Good," said Delgado, slipping the report back into its

envelope. "We wouldn't want you fired from the SIS and the Bureau for the want of a typewriter, would we?"

"Do we have any other business?" I said at last.

Delgado shook his head.

I said, "I'll let you leave first."

When I was sure he was gone, around the corner and out of sight, I went into the back room, removed the loose board, and pulled out the wrapped package I had left there. I checked both weapons for any moisture—they were both dry except for the oil from the fabric—and then I set the .357 Magnum back, removing and cleaning the Smith and Wesson .38. I loaded the revolver, leaving one chamber empty, slipped two boxes of cartridges into my jacket pocket, and slid the weapon into my waistband far enough back that it would not interfere with my pedaling on the bike.

Then I went out to hunt for a café that was open. I planned to drink at least three ice-cold lemonades before heading back to the *finca* through traffic.

AS SOON AS the *Pilar* was into the Gulf Stream we picked up a heavy swell. The glass had been falling all morning, and a dark bank of clouds was moving in from the northeast. Hemingway's boat had no radio, but the chalked forecast on the bait shed at the marina had warned of an afternoon front coming in from the northeast and a possibility of heavy squalls.

"Lucas!" Hemingway bellowed from the flying bridge. "Come on up."

I clambered up the ladder. Hemingway was at the wheel, bare legs wide apart and braced, while Winston Guest clung to the railing. Ibarlucia was drinking another beer in the shelter of the cockpit bridge. The first mate, Fuentes, was still sitting on the bow, bracing his bare feet on the forward railings as Hemingway brought the bow into the tall waves.

"Any *mal de mer*, Lucas?" said the writer. He had a long-billed cap pulled low over his eyes.

"No thanks," I said. "I'll wait for lunch."

Hemingway glanced at me out of the corner of his eye. "Why don't you take her for a while?"

I did. Hemingway gave me the compass heading and I swung the bow accordingly, throttling back a bit to minimize the roll of the small craft. Guest went down to the cockpit, and in a few minutes he and the jai alai player, helped by Fuentes, had rigged lines to the two outriggers for fishing. Fuentes also dropped a big horn teaser off the stern and played out line. I watched the teaser skip around in the center of our wake, attracting nothing but the occasional seagull.

Hemingway stood with one hand on the rail, easily keeping his balance even when he gave me headings that required me to steer at the worst possible angle to the heavy swells. Cuba was the faintest hint of smudge on our starboard side, and the line of black clouds grew closer and more substantial to port.

"You *have* handled a small boat before, Lucas."

I had already told him that I had, so there was nothing to say to that. Beneath and behind us, Guest and Ibarlucia were laughing at something. The sea was too rough for fishing.

Hemingway slid down the ladder and returned a moment later with a bundle wrapped in oilcloth. Waiting until the spray had passed us, he removed the rifle from its protection. I glanced at it: a Mannlicher .256.

"We were going to anchor off a buoy I know," he said, sighting on flying fish leaping ahead of the boat. He lowered the weapon. "Do some target practice. But this sea fucks that idea."

Perhaps that was to have been my sea trial—bring the *Pilar* to the proper coordinates and then get in a target-shooting match with these three men who had been drinking all morning. Or perhaps I was just being paranoid.

Hemingway wrapped the rifle and stowed it away beneath the console. He pointed to the coast. "I know a nice little cove there. Let's put in, have a good lunch, and get back to Cojímar before it gets bad out here." He gave me the heading and I swung the bow of the *Pilar* toward land. She was a nice enough little craft, although she rode a bit light and handled a little loosely for my tastes. If he wanted to avoid the storm coming in, it was my opinion that he should have turned back then rather than dawdled around for lunch. But he hadn't asked me my opinion.

It was easier going in a following sea, and by the time we

anchored in the broad cove, the sun was bright again and the storm was less on everyone's minds. We sat in the shade of the wheelhouse and ate thick roast beef sandwiches ladled with horseradish. Guest and Ibarlucia each had another cold beer with lunch, but Fuentes had brewed up some rich, black Cuban coffee, and he, Hemingway, and I drank that out of chipped white mugs.

"Ernesto," said Fuentes, rising from his place on the rail, "look at that. On the boulder there on the beach. He is very large."

We were about a hundred and twenty yards out from the beach, and it took me a second or two to see what Fuentes meant.

"Gregorio," said Hemingway. "Get the glasses, please."

The four of us took turns looking through the binoculars. The iguana was indeed very large. I could see the membranes of its eyes flashing occasionally as it blinked slowly while sunbathing on the black rock.

Hemingway clambered up the ladder and we followed. He unwrapped the Mannlicher and wrapped the sling around his left arm in approved infantry firing range fashion, bracing his legs wide against the slight chop and pulling the stock tight against his shoulder. "Lucas, you spot."

I nodded and studied the iguana through the glasses. The rifle barked.

"Low," I said. "About a yard. He hasn't moved."

The second shot was high. On the third shot, the iguana seemed to levitate and then disappeared behind the rock. Ibarlucia and Guest cheered. Fuentes said, "A purse for Miss Martha, no?"

"A purse for Miss Marty, *sí*, old friend," said Hemingway. He led us down the ladder to the deck.

"It's a shame we left the *Tin Kid* behind," said Guest, referring to the little rowboat Hemingway had left tied behind rather than tow it in rough seas.

Hemingway grinned. "Shit, Wolfer, you can almost touch bottom out here now. You afraid of sharks?" He peeled off his sweatshirt and shorts, standing naked except for a tattered pair of underwear. His body was very brown and more muscled than I had thought. There was no gray in the hair on his chest.

"Ernesto," said Ibarlucia, who had stripped to a very small pair of shorts. His small body was all lean muscle, the planes and ridges of a consummate athlete. "Ernesto, there is no reason for you to get wet. I will swim ashore and finish the reptile while you finish your lunch." The jai alai player lifted the rifle.

Hemingway had slipped over the side and now lifted one arm. *"Dame aca, cono que a los mios los mato yo!"*

I thought about what he had said: *Give it to me, damn it; I kill my own.* It was the first time I had felt any kinship with Ernest Hemingway.

Hemingway took the rifle, held it high, and began stroking with his left arm toward the distant beach. Ibarlucia dove in without making a ripple and soon passed the writer. I pulled off my work shirt, kicked off the deck shoes, and stepped out of my shorts. The air was hot despite the approaching storm and the sun burned at me.

"I'll stay aboard with Gregorio," said Guest.

I swam easily in to shore. The surf was negligible in this broad cove. Patchi and Hemingway were walking up and down on the dry sand behind the tall pile of rocks where the iguana had been sunning itself.

"There is no sign, Ernesto," said Ibarlucia. "The shot must have just frightened the reptile." He squinted toward the northeast. "The storm is coming, Papa. We should think about going."

"No," said Hemingway. He pored over the rock, feeling it as if hunting for blood spoor with his fingertips. For twenty minutes the three of us moved up and down the beach and shoreline studying every rock and imperfection. The black clouds moved closer.

"Here," called the writer at last, crouching on the sand some twenty-five yards up the beach from the rocks.

We stood over him as the writer snapped a dried stick into pieces, marked the tiniest drop of blood on the sand, and began crawling inland, studying the ground so closely that he resembled a bloodhound sniffing for a scent trail.

"Here," he said again, ten yards farther up the beach, marking the faintest of red spots. "Here."

The spoor trail ended at a pile of boulders where the cliffs began. We crowded under a low overhang and looked at the tiny, black opening to the small cave. Blood smeared the rock.

"He's in there," said Hemingway, dropping the last of his sticks and unslinging the rifle from his shoulder.

I stepped aside as he aimed the Mannlicher at the small hole.

"It is likely to ricochet, Ernesto," said Ibarlucia, also stepping aside. "Do not shoot yourself in the stomach. The handbag, it is not worth it."

Hemingway only grunted and fired. There was the noise of violent thrashing in the cave.

"It's dead," said Hemingway. "Get a longer stick."

We found a four-foot length of branch washed up on the rocks, but no amount of poking could locate the iguana.

"Perhaps it crawled further in," said Ibarlucia.

"No," said Hemingway, "I gave it the gift of death." He studied the hole. It was narrower than his shoulders.

"I will go, Papa," said the jai alai star.

Hemingway put a hand on the smaller man's brown shoulder and looked at me. "Lucas, you'll probably fit. Want to give Marty a handbag?"

I dropped to all fours and slid forward, scraping skin off my shoulders as I went into the hole arms first. My body blocked the light. The cave angled downward so that rock cut at my scalp as I bent forward to follow the angle of the hole. I had no intention of going deeper than they could reach to pull me out. About eight feet in, my fingers encountered the scaled ribs and belly of the iguana. I felt sideways toward the throat and my fingers came away sticky with blood. It did not move. Holding it firmly by the ridges on its back, I began inching backward, stopping as my shoulder became stuck at the bend in the tunnel.

"Pull me out slowly," I called. "I've got it."

Strong hands grabbed my ankles, skin tore from my knees, back, and shoulders, and I was slowly pulled into the light.

Hemingway handed the Mannlicher to Ibarlucia and patted

my arms rather than my bloody back as I handed him his trophy. He was grinning very broadly, as happy as a boy.

We swam back to the *Pilar* with Ibarlucia carrying the rifle above the rising waves, Hemingway kicking on his back while holding the large iguana out of the water, and me wincing as the saltwater rolled over my lacerated back and shoulders. Once aboard, there was much commotion about the size of the lizard, a ceremonial beer for everyone as the iguana was stored away in the fish box and the anchors were pulled up, and then we fired up the engines and pounded back into the heavy swells beyond the cove.

Three miles out, the storm hit us. Hemingway had called me down to the forward compartment, where he opened a first aid kit and smeared some unguent on my back. He pulled rain ponchos from a cupboard and we went up on deck just as the first squall hit us.

For the next hour we beat back to the northwest, the boat rolling and pitching constantly. Ibarlucia went below to lie on a cot, Guest sat on the upper step looking pale, while Fuentes and I braced ourselves on either side of the enclosed bridge and watched the towering waves as Hemingway expertly handled the tiller.

I had the feeling then that this was a place where Ernest Hemingway—a man I had seen thus far mostly as a series of poses and personae—was most comfortable being himself. The waves continued to get rougher and the *Pilar* pounded through them with spray that all but obscured the windscreen, but Hemingway's comments were calm and quiet. Rain hammered on the roof above us and made the open deck behind us slick.

"Another hour or so and we'll see the—" began Hemingway, and stopped. We had moved out of the squall and into a brighter patch of sea, but rain showers moved like curtains across the ocean on three sides. Hemingway snatched up the binoculars and looked to the northeast. "Well, I'll be goddamned," he whispered.

"*Que?*" said Fuentes, leaning out of the enclosed bridge to stare into the spray as we rose to the top of the next tall wave. "Ahh... yes, I see."

I saw the lights first, flashing a mile or so apart, almost lost against the ripples of lightning behind them. It was not Morse code. There was a large shape off the starboard bow, about three miles away, almost concealed by the shifting walls of rain. At first glance, I thought it was large enough to be a destroyer, but the lines were wrong. To port, moving away from us and the larger ship, was the faintest hint of gray metal rising from the gray seas in front of the gray clouds.

"Damn, damn, damn," said Hemingway, obviously delighted and excited, handing the binoculars to Fuentes. He opened both throttles to two thirds, pounding into the waves so hard that Guest was almost thrown from his seat on the stairs and Ibarlucia cried out from the forward compartment.

"Do you see that, Lucas?" said Hemingway, advancing the throttles another notch.

Fuentes handed me the binoculars. I tried to bring the larger form into focus, but the high waves and pounding of the hull made it difficult. "Yeah," I said after a minute. "Some sort of huge yacht. I've never seen a private boat that size."

Hemingway shook his head. "Uh-uh," he said. "The other one. To port. The shape just entering the squall line."

I swung the glasses, found it, lost it, and found it again. I stared.

"It's a submarine," said Hemingway, voice full. "A goddamn Nazi U-boat. See the shape of the conning tower? See the number on it? A Nazi U-boat. It was signaling to that monster yacht. And I'm going to catch up to it."

"To the yacht?" said Winston Guest, stepping up into the bridge, his face flushed and almost rigid with excitement.

"No, Wolfer," said Hemingway, advancing the throttles again before taking the binoculars from me and refocusing on the conning tower. "We're going to catch and board that submarine."

9

WHY DO YOU WANT INFORMATION on the *Southern Cross*?" said Delgado.

We had met on a deadend dirt track south of San Francisco de Paula. An old, abandoned farmhouse sagged in the heat. In the weedy field, a single burro watched us with friendly suspicion. My bicycle was propped against a torn fence. Delgado's old motorcycle stood next to a wireless telephone pole.

"According to Mr. Hoover's brief to me," I said, "your job is to funnel information that I need, not to ask why I need it."

Delgado looked at me with his flat, dead gaze. Despite the heat, he was wearing a faded, leather A-1 jacket over his undershirt. The buttons on it were as expressive as his eyes. "When do you need it?" he said.

This was the problem. In Mexico, Colombia, and Argentina, it usually took ten days or more for regular files to be forwarded from Washington. If they were sensitive files that had to be vetted, we might not see an extract from them for a month or more. Usually we had gone on to other things by the time we received the paperwork we needed. In this case, the *Southern Cross* would probably be gone by the time this request was processed. "As soon as possible," I said.

"Tomorrow afternoon," said Delgado. "At the safe house. Seventeen hundred hours."

I said nothing, but I could not believe that the files would be in Cuba by the next afternoon. If they did arrive...how? Courier? Why expedite sensitive information to me in this dead-end job? Who *was* Delgado, anyway?

"Just about the boat?" he said, making a note in a tiny spiral notebook.

"And anything that would be directly related to her," I said. "Any current investigations relating to her crew, owners...anything that might be of help."

Delgado nodded, went to his motorcycle, and straddled it. "What would your writer have done if he'd caught that sub, Lucas?"

I thought of that insane chase through the rising seas, the gray conning tower disappearing first into the rain and then into the waves, Hemingway standing wide-legged at the wheel, his face hard and set, throttles pushed so far forward that I thought the *Pilar* was going to break her back or bow on the waves, spray dousing the ship and everyone in it. Everyone there...Patchi Ibarlucia, Winston Guest, the unflappable Fuentes, even me... had been roaring with adrenaline and urging the thirty-eight-foot pleasure craft on as if it had been a thoroughbred in the home stretch. And then the sub was gone...completely, totally gone...and Hemingway had cursed, slammed the bulkhead with the flat of his hand, and throttled back, swinging the bow north to close the distance between the *Pilar* and the impossibly large yacht, shouting at Fuentes to read the name on the stern through the binoculars.

"If you'd challenged the submarine," continued Delgado, "it would have blown you out of the water."

"Yeah," I said. "Tomorrow afternoon at five? I'll try to be there."

Delgado smiled and gunned the motorcycle alive. Still straddling it, he shouted, "Oh, did you see the Buick and its two men watching you leave port yesterday. From the hill above Cojímar?"

I had seen them. The car and its two occupants had been in the shade, so that even with binoculars I had not been able to make out more than silhouettes in the front seat—that tall man and the short man again. Mutt and Jeff.

"I didn't make the driver," continued Delgado, "but the passenger was a certain hairless, hunchback dwarf. Sound familiar?"

"You're joking," I said. "I thought that he had been transferred to London."

"He has been transferred," said Delgado, twitching the throttle of the motorcycle so that he had to shout even louder. "And I never joke."

The "hairless, hunchbacked dwarf" had to be Wallace Beta Phillips, the brilliant Latin American chief for the U.S. Office of Naval Intelligence. In truth, Phillips *was* hairless and hunchbacked, but not a true dwarf...merely short. I had worked in more than one operation out of Mexico City that had been designed and run by Phillips, and I had much respect for the man. Under his leadership, the ONI, SIS, FBI, and the fledgling COI of Wild Bill Donovan had begun to work as a team against the Nazi agents in Mexico. But Phillips had been urging an expansion of such interagency cooperation all through the winter of 1941–42, even while J. Edgar Hoover was demanding that the COI cease operations in the western hemisphere and the ONI restrain its activities to naval matters. After the January showdown in Washington in which Hoover had won full control of all SIS and other counterintelligence operations in the Western Hemisphere, the hunchback's effective leadership had been undercut by resident FBI agents.

Through the past few months, culminating in two failed missions in the spring, Phillips's ONI operations and operatives in Mexico—and throughout the rest of Latin America—had been under increasing harassment from Hoover. In April, I had been ordered to follow and report on Phillips's men, who were working with Donovan's men, to watch the last Nazi agents in two of Mexico's busier seaports. Soon after, Hoover had gone straight to FDR demanding that Donovan's entire COI organization be dissolved and that Wallace Beta Phillips be reprimanded for cooperating with them.

Donovan, who was recuperating from a serious automobile accident in New York the previous month—and who had a potentially fatal blood clot in his lung at the time—protested to the president that Hoover's charge was a "dirty and contemptible lie," and Roosevelt believed him. The COI was safe for the time being, but all interagency cooperation in Mexico and throughout

Latin America had evaporated like dew in a desert morning. The hairless hunchback, Wallace Beta Phillips, had asked for and received a transfer from ONI to the COI and had—the last I had heard before I had flown to Washington—departed for London.

What the hell was he doing in Cuba watching me go out in a fishing boat with Ernest Hemingway and his motley crew?

I did not ask Delgado. "Tomorrow at five P.M.," I said.

"Don't ride your bicycle into a tree in the dark." Delgado laughed. He revved his motor and roared up the road toward San Francisco de Paula in a cloud of dust that settled on me slowly, like ash from a slow cremation.

"UP AND AT 'EM, JOE LUCAS!" cried Hemingway, shouting through the screen door of the guest house that Tuesday afternoon. "Put on your best spymaster tie. We're going to the embassy to sell a man an idea."

Forty minutes later we were in Ambassador Braden's office with the thick light of Havana afternoon filtering through the blinds while the fan overhead worked to move the sluggish air. There were five of us present. Besides the ambassador, Hemingway, Ellis Briggs, and myself, there was the new Chief of Naval Intelligence for Central America, Colonel John W. Thomason Jr.—a trim, solid man who spoke quickly and precisely in a Texas accent. I had heard of Thomason, but it was obvious from the relaxed conversation before the business part of the meeting that Hemingway had already met the man—indeed, that he had been using Thomason's technical expertise for the anthology of war stories he was editing. In fact, the colonel was a writer himself—Hemingway twice referred to Thomason's biography of Jeb Stuart and suggested that one of the colonel's short stories should be in the war anthology.

Braden finally called the meeting to order. "Ernest, I understand you have another proposal for us."

"I do," said Hemingway, "and it's a good one." He gestured toward me and turned toward the colonel. "John, Spruille's probably told you that Lucas here is a State Department expert on counterintelligence assigned to my Crook Factory operation. I've already discussed this idea with Lucas and worked out the details..."

Hemingway had not discussed the idea with me at all except to explain what he planned to propose as we drove hell-bent-for-leather toward Havana in the black Lincoln. Thomason squinted at me with the suspicion any military or intelligence man feels toward the State Department.

"I think Spruille or Ellis has told you about our encounter with the German submarine yesterday," Hemingway was saying.

Colonel Thomason nodded.

Ellis Briggs said, "You're sure it was German, Ernest?"

"Goddamn, absolutely sure," said Hemingway. He described the conning tower, the deck gun, and the numerals on the side.

"Almost certainly a seven-forty-class German sub," said Colonel Thomason. "And what was the last heading you saw it on before it submerged?"

"Lucas?" said the writer.

"North-northwest," I said, feeling like an actor with a bit part in a bad melodrama.

Thomason nodded. "Early this morning a seven-forty-class sub was sighted off New Orleans. It's thought that they might have dropped three or four German agents at the mouth of the Mississippi River. Probably your same boat, Papa."

I looked at the military man. *Papa?* Thomason was forty-eight or forty-nine years old. Hemingway was forty-one. What was this "Papa" crap? Why did everyone want to play the writer's idiotic nickname games...*all* of his childish games? Now we were playing the submarine game. The tone was manly and serious in the quiet room.

Hemingway was on his feet again, bobbing and weaving, using his hands to jab home his points as he moved lightly on the balls of his feet. Ambassador Braden looked polite and pleased, like a housewife who has bought the Electrolux vacuum from a friendly salesman and who is now ready to fork out more money for some labor-saving attachments.

"So here's the plan," said Hemingway, sweeping his arms as if to bring us into his huddle. "My agents in the Crook Factory have reported that quite a few local boats have been stopped and boarded by Nazi subs in the last month or so. Hell, one old man who fishes out of Nuevitas had to hand over all his catch and fresh fruit to a German boat. Anyway, I think that this seven-forty boat was checking out the big yacht we saw...the *Southern Cross*...to see if they should board it or sink it with gunfire. The *Cross* looked suspicious...almost destroyer size. But the sea was too rough and then we came on the scene..."

What is he talking about? I wondered. We had seen a signal light on the yacht and on the sub's conning tower. It had not been in Morse but in a private code. All the way back yesterday, following the huge yacht past Cojímar to where it had anchored in Havana Harbor, Hemingway had speculated that the ship and the sub were in cahoots. He had theorized that the private ship was a refueling vessel for the U-boats, what the Germans called a "milch cow," and had worked out a plan to gain intelligence about the *Southern Cross*'s crew, cargo, and purported mission. He had worked until midnight siccing his Crook Factory wharf rats, waiters, and bartenders onto the fact-gathering project. And now this. What was he up to?

"Here's the plan," he said again. "We take my craft, the *Pilar*, and disguise it as a local fishing boat...or maybe as some sort of scientific mission. Hydrographic survey mission or somesuch. Drape a Woods Hole sign over the side or something. Let the Germans take a look at us through their periscope, incite their curiosity, lure their boat to the surface, and when they close to board us...*blooey!* We hit them with small arms fire, grenades, machine guns, bazookas...everything."

"A Q-boat," said Ambassador Braden, obviously enjoying the idea.

"Exactly," said Hemingway.

"It would be dangerous, Ernest," said Ellis Briggs.

The writer shrugged. "I'll get a good crew. Seven or eight good men should do it. You can send somebody along if you want, Spruille...maybe a Marine to handle the fifty-caliber and the radio."

"Does the *Pilar* have a radio, Papa?" asked Colonel Thomason. "Or a machine gun?"

"Not yet," said Hemingway, and grinned.

"What else would you need?" asked the ambassador, jotting notes on a pad with a silver fountain pen.

"Just the small arms I mentioned. Some Thompson submachine guns would be good. Grenades to lob down their hatches when we close on them. A bazooka or two maybe. A military radio. Oh…and Radio Detection Finding gear. We could work with the naval bases along the coast and any destroyers in this part of the Caribbean to triangulate on a wolf pack's signals. I'll provide the food. We'd need gas, of course. With the shortages and rationing, I couldn't buy enough to patrol for five days, much less the weeks and months this operation would demand."

"What about the rest of your…ah…Crook Factory's operation?" said Ambassador Braden. "You're just getting it up and running, I presume. Would you set that aside for this Q-boat mission?"

Hemingway shook his head. "We can do both. In fact, if the subs are sniffing around here because…as our early intelligence indicates…they're landing more agents on Cuban as well as American shores, well, we'll need both aspects of the operation to find them and stop them."

Colonel Thomason cleared his throat. He spoke slowly, but there was no laziness in his dialect. "Suppose you pull off your innocent fishing boat routine and the German submarine gets suspicious and stands off and blows you and the *Pilar* out of the water with his deck gun? What then, Papa?"

"If he does that, we've had it," said Hemingway. "But why should a submarine risk attracting attention with gunfire when the skipper can send sailors aboard and scuttle us by opening our seacocks? He'll be curious about fishermen in wartime. He'll want to know what kind of profiteers are trying to tag marlin in the Gulf Stream with the war on."

"What if he recognizes you?" asked the colonel. "The *Pilar* is pretty well known in these waters. And if the German sub is involved with intelligence matters, as you suspect, he may know about the crazy *gringo* writer and his fishing boat."

"So much the better." Hemingway grinned. "Carry enemy sportsman back to Berlin to write dirty limericks for the Führer. Feather in the bonnet for *der Kapitan*. Fame and promotion for the crew. Why not? Those underwater boys are suckers for publicity."

The colonel nodded but obviously was not in full agreement yet. "Look, Papa, even if you get ordered alongside, your Nazi skipper isn't an idiot. He isn't going to pipe you aboard to have a glass of schnapps with him. He'll have men on deck…they've been fighting this war at sea for three years, remember…and they won't be holding slingshots."

"That's right," said Hemingway. "That's why along with the grenades we need a machine gun. I shoot a machine gun good, John. Practiced on my grandmother. Nazis won't know what hit them. Now, what Lucas and I need to know is…how big is a conning tower on a typical German sub? How wide is the hatch? And what we really need to know is…how much damage will the grenades do inside a submarine? Is there any chance we could put a prize crew aboard and sail that sucker back into Havana Harbor or one of the U.S. naval bases?"

I quite paying close attention somewhere around there. This was not just fantasy…it was nonsense. But Ambassador Braden, First Secretary Briggs, and Chief of Naval Intelligence for Central America Colonel John W. Thomason Jr. were treating it seriously. Another thirty minutes, and despite the ambassador's comment that he would have to consult with others before getting back to Hemingway, it was obvious that the writer would get his fuel, grenades, machine guns, and license of marque. Insanity.

"Oh, Ernest," said the ambassador after we had all shaken hands again and I was at the door with the writer, "is this officially part of your Operation Crook Factory?"

"Different code name." Hemingway grunted. "Let's call it Operation Friendless."

"Friendless…yes…very good," said the ambassador, jotting notes on his pad.

Outside in the heavy afternoon sun, I said, "Friendless?"

Hemingway rubbed his chin, looking up and down the street as if he had lost something. "You met Friendless," he said, distracted.

"I did?"

"You did. The big tabby cat in the kitchen. The one with the mean disposition." He brightened as if remembering what he had lost. "The Floridita," he said, checking his watch. "We have four hours until dinner. Daiquiris."

THREE HOURS AND too many daiquiris later, I told Hemingway that I would take an evening bus back to the *finca.*

"Nonsense. The last bus going that way leaves the downtown at seven."

"I'll walk, then."

"That'll take all night, Lucas. You'll miss dinner at the *finca.*"

"I didn't know that I was invited to dinner at the *finca.*"

"'Course you are. At least you will be after I talk to Marty. Probably."

"I'll eat in town and get back somehow," I said.

Hemingway shrugged. "Forgot. You have to report to your masters. Whoever they are. Fine. Good. Fuck it."

I watched the Lincoln drive off and then strolled toward the Plaza de la Catedral. I zigzagged back and forth from Obispo Street to Obrapia, back two blocks to O'Reilly, and then back to Obispo. There was no sign of Delgado or the tall man Delgado had said was from the Cuban National Police, but at the corner of Obispo and San Ignacio, the dark Buick pulled up alongside and the hairless humpback in the back seat said through the open window, "Need a ride, Mr. Lucas?"

"Sure."

I sat next to him in the back seat. I did not recognize the only other occupant, the driver, a thin man about my age. He was wearing glasses and a tweed suit more suitable to a New England autumn than to spring in Havana. Something about the driver's alert, overly tense posture and grip on the wheel told me that he was no field agent.

"This is Mr. Cowley," said Wallace Beta Phillips, nodding toward the driver. "No relation to the late special agent in charge from Chicago. Mr. Cowley, Mr. Joseph Lucas."

"Pleased to meet you," said the driver.

I looked at the back of the nervous man's neck for a moment and then back at Phillips. The phrase "hairless humpbacked dwarf" sounds almost bizarre, but in person Phillips was not all that strange-looking: short, yes, but not shockingly so, and his expensive panama suit was tailored to minimize the sight of his curved spine. The most striking things about Phillips were his hairless skin, intelligent eyes, and the fact that he did not seem to sweat. We had never met, but the little man was behaving as if we were old acquaintances.

"Mr. Cowley is in Mr. Hemingway's line of work," said Phillips. He offered me an American cigarette, and I shook my head. Phillips used a lighter on his and exhaled toward the open window on the opposite side of the Buick. We were driving along San Pedro Avenue past the docks. "We thought it might be useful to get another literary gentleman's point of view on Mr. Hemingway's operation," continued Phillips, lifting his little finger in a delicate motion to remove a fleck of tobacco from his lower lip.

"Why?" I said.

Wallace Beta Phillips smiled. He had perfect teeth. "Mr. Cowley is new to our organization. An analyst, actually, not a field man. But we thought that this might be mutually enlightening for his first outing."

"Who is 'we'?" I said. "Not ONI."

"The OSS," said the former Latin America chief of naval intelligence.

"Never heard of it," I said. "It sounds German. And I thought that you were joining COI and going to London."

"Yes, yes," said Phillips. "Mr. Donovan is renaming the office of the Coordinator of Intelligence the Office of Strategic Services. The name will become official soon... no later than June, I believe. Our guess is that Mr. Hoover will refer to us as 'Oh So Stupid.'"

"Probably," I said. "I hear that Donovan refers to the Bureau as 'Foreign Born Irish.'"

Phillips made a gesture with his palms up. "Only on bad days," he said. "I believe that the stereotype originated with the belief that Mr. Hoover—although quite Protestant—prefers hiring Catholics."

"There's the equally strong stereotype that Mr. Donovan enjoys hiring dilettantes and rank amateurs," I said.

Mr. Cowley glanced sharply at me in the rearview mirror.

"No offense meant toward anyone here," I said. "I was just thinking that 'Oh So Social' might be the Bureau's take on your new acronym."

Phillips chuckled. "It is true, it is true. Mr. Donovan does work at bringing unlikely lambs into the fold. Count Oleg Cassini and Julia Child, for instance."

"Never heard of them," I said. They could not have been actual operatives if Phillips was telling me their names. More of Donovan's "analysts," probably.

"Of course you have never heard of them," said Phillips. "One is a fashion designer and the other a chef. I shall not divulge which is which for reasons of national security. Then there is Mr. John Ford."

"The movie director?" I liked John Ford westerns.

"Precisely," said the hairless man. We were moving quickly along the central highway now, the breeze cooling us. "And many, many literary sorts. Besides Mr. Cowley here—who evinces a strong literary interest in Hemingway the writer, as opposed to Hemingway the spy—we currently enjoy the services of several of Mr. Hemingway's former friends, including Archibald MacLeish and Robert Sherwood."

The names meant nothing to me. This entire conversation made no sense to me.

"Mr. Hemingway betrayed both of these gentlemen," continued Phillips. "As friends, I mean. I do hope he does not betray you, Mr. Lucas."

"Hemingway and I aren't friends," I said. "What do you want, Mr. Phillips?"

"Just this chat, Mr. Lucas. I understand that Commodore Fleming had a chance to speak to you on your flight down here."

Jesus H. Christ, I thought, looking out at the small home and shops flashing by. *Every spy agency in this hemisphere seems interested in Hemingway's clown circus. WHY?* I said, "What do you *want*, Mr. Phillips?"

The man sighed and arranged his small, pink hands on his knees. His trousers carried a perfect crease. "The unfortunate event on Simón Bolívar Street in Veracruz," he said very softly. "You know that I was involved in the initial planning stages of that operation?"

"Yes."

"Well, then, Mr. Lucas, you must also know that the ONI was removed from active involvement about the time of your... ah...incident on Simón Bolívar Street. The deaths of Schiller and Lopez surprised me. Before leaving the country, I took time to visit the house on Simón Bolívar and to review the SIS report on the incident."

I felt my heart rate accelerate. The SIS and the Bureau had checked the bodies, read my report, but had never ordered a shooting board review.

Wallace Beta Phillips was looking intently at my face. "I believe that in your report you stated that the gunmen were waiting for you in the house, Mr. Lucas. That you arrived early, sensed something wrong, and went in quickly. They shot and missed. Forty-two bullets, I believe. You fired four times."

"Lopez had a Luger," I said. "Schiller was firing a Schmeisser on full automatic."

Phillips smiled. "They were firing at the front door and the front of the house, Mr. Lucas. They were shot in the backs of their heads and upper torsos."

I waited.

"You *did* get there early, Mr. Lucas. You went in the back door, past the dog. The dog knew you, but you still had to cut its throat so it would not give you away as you came in through the kitchen and crept down the hallway in the dark. Once in the room, you created a diversion at the front door...I do not know precisely how, although one of the neighbors mentioned seeing a child throw a rock at the door and then run quickly away. Messieurs Schiller and Lopez began firing. You shot each of them in the back of the head. You *executed* them, Mr. Lucas—with premeditation and skill, I might add."

There was nothing I could say to that. I watched the scenery go by. We were taking the long way to San Francisco de Paula. I noticed Mr. Cowley's eyes flicking to the rearview mirror; they were wider than they had been a moment before.

"We do not know about General Walter Krivitsky a year ago February," continued Phillips after a moment. "Perhaps you shot him. Perhaps you gave him your pistol and waited while he shot himself. Either way, you impressed Dr. Hans Wesemann and the rest of the Abwehr apparatus left in this hemisphere, and they still consider you a lethal freelance operative. Had you been in ONI, I would have used you for more double agent operations."

"I'm not in ONI," I said. "Nor in your soon-to-be OSS. What do you want, Mr. Phillips?" I was suddenly and totally tired of all this talk: Hemingway's palaver rather than action, Delgado's threats and ironies, Colonel Thomason's hearty man-to-man absurdities about sinking submarines, and Phillips's accusations. At this moment, somewhere out there in the Pacific, good Americans were being marched to their deaths and beheaded by strutting Japanese assholes carrying samurai swords. In Europe, innocent men and women in a dozen countries woke up every morning with swastikas flying over their occupied civic buildings, with jackbooted Wehrmacht goons driving through their empty, rainy streets. Only a few miles from here, good young men in the merchant marine were being drowned by torpedoes they never even saw.

"Mr. Stephenson and Mr. Donovan think that you understand our way of fighting this war, Mr. Lucas," said Phillips. "They believe that you will not let inter-agency rivalry blind you to the larger issues."

"I don't know what the hell you're talking about," I said. "What does that have to do with Hemingway's little game down here?"

Phillips gave me another long, appraising stare, as if trying to assess whether I was lying. I didn't give a shit what he thought. Perhaps he read that in my poker face. "We have reason to believe," he said at last, "that Mr. J. Edgar Hoover is up to something unorthodox here in Cuba. Probably something illegal."

"Bullshit," I said. "The BSC and ONI *taught* the Bureau

how to chamfer and carry out black bag jobs. And if that's going on here, I sure don't know about it. Hemingway's so-called operatives don't know any tradecraft."

Phillips shook his hairless head. "No, no, I don't mean the run-of-the-mill stock-in-trade of all of our agencies, Mr. Lucas. I mean something that may endanger the national security of the United States of America."

I gave Phillips a disgusted look. This was melodramatic garbage. J. Edgar Hoover was a liar and a consummate infighter, protecting his bureaucratic turf at anyone's expense, but if the man had any religion beyond his own career, it was the safety and security of the U.S.A.

"Give me a specific example with corroborating evidence," I said flatly, "or stop the fucking car and let me out." We were within a mile of Hemingway's *finca*.

Phillips shook his head. "I have none yet, Mr. Lucas. I was hoping that you would provide it."

"Stop the car," I said.

Cowley pulled over. I opened the door and got out.

"There is Mr. Delgado, as you know him," said Phillips through the open window.

"What about him?" A Cuban truck roared by, music and horns blaring.

"We have reason to believe that he is Special Agent D," said the humpback.

This gave me pause.

Every agent in the Bureau and the SIS had heard of Special Agent D. Some believed in him. These are the facts as I knew them:

At 10:30 P.M. on the night of July 21, 1934, the criminal John Dillinger and two women—one of them the infamous "Woman in Red," Ana Cumpanas, aka Anna Sage, who had betrayed the gangster—walked out of the Biograph Theater in Chicago. The squad of Bureau agents waiting in ambush for Dillinger was officially headed up by SAC Sam Cowley, but the real leader of the group was Melvin Purvis, who had already received more public attention than Mr. Hoover could tolerate in a subordinate. Purvis identified Mrs. Sage (since it was he who had made the deal with her to betray Dillinger) and tipped off the rest of the SAs waiting around the theater by the prearranged signal of lighting his cigar. Rather, Purvis *tried* to light his cigar; his hands were shaking so badly that he could hardly hold the match, much less light the stogie and then pull out his pistol.

Dillinger ran. Purvis reportedly shouted, in his thin, squeaky voice, "Stick 'em up, Johnny. We have you surrounded." Instead of surrendering, Hoover's so-called Public Enemy Number One pulled a .380 Colt automatic from his jacket pocket and was gunned down by four special agents.

Melvin Purvis was credited by the press and the public for the kill, and the fact that several other agents also fired was public knowledge. But what everyone in the Bureau had heard were the real details of the shooting: Purvis never pulled his gun, much less fired it. SAC Cowley—who was later gunned down by Baby Face Nelson—also did not fire. The four men who fired were Special Agents Herman Hollis, who missed; Clarence Hurt and Charles Winstead, who might have wounded Dillinger; and a fourth agent, referred to in reports only as "Special Agent D," who was thought to have fired only one shot—the fatal one. In later reports, Special Agent D had disappeared completely, and although Hoover's credit for killing Dillinger went to the late Sam Cowley and unofficial credit went to Charles Winstead, rumors continued to spread about Special Agent D.

According to Bureau lore, Special Agent D was a young psychopath—a former hit man for the Mob—whom Mr. Hoover and Greg Tolson had turned to in desperation, paying him ten times the annual salary of a special agent in charge, to fight Dillinger and the others on their own terms. Also according to this water-cooler myth, Special Agent D had been responsible in that bloody year of 1934 for the shootings of Pretty Boy Floyd and Baby Face Nelson, although once again credit went to the late Cowley and also to SA Herman Hollis, who also had been killed in the gunfight with Baby Face Nelson.

The legend of Special Agent D had grown to the point that he was credited with solving the Lindbergh kidnapping case in 1934—although in his own inimitable way. Special Agent D was said to have followed the actual kidnapper—a fag who had befriended one of the Lindberghs' maids before kidnapping and killing the child—to Europe and, in a white rage, put a .38 in the fag's mouth and pulled the trigger. This would not have been a proper public solution to the case for J. Edgar Hoover, so the Bureau had arrested Bruno Hauptmann, a friend and very minor accomplice of the dead fag, to cover it up.

In the eight years since that bloody year, Bureau agents had quietly embroidered the legend of the psychopathic ex-Mob killer Special Agent D, giving him credit for several of the more spectacular but confused killings of various "public enemies." Special Agent D was the stealthy but rabid dog Mr. Hoover kept in his closet for special assignments, unleashing him only when serious problems required quick, serious solutions.

This was the boogeyman with which Wallace Beta Phillips was threatening me. Special Agent D equaled my SIS contact, Delgado.

I laughed out loud and stepped back from the Buick. "It was nice meeting you, Mr. Phillips," I said.

The hairless humpback in his expensive suit did not smile. "If you need us, Mr. Lucas, call room three-fourteen at the Nacional, any time, day or night. And be careful, Mr. Lucas. Be very careful." He nodded to Mr. Cowley, the driver, and the Buick moved off.

I walked into San Francisco de Paula and trudged up the hill to the *finca*. Lights were on in the main house, the Victrola was playing, and I could hear the clink of glasses and soft conversation.

"Shit," I said softly. I had not eaten in town and there was still no food in the guest house. Ah, well... it would be only ten hours or so until breakfast.

I WAS STILL RAVENOUS when I was awakened shortly after two A.M. as someone fumbled at the guest house lock, opened it, and padded softly into the outer room. I remained lying down but shifted slightly in bed so that the pillow was between me and the bedroom door, the .38 beneath the pillow, muzzle aimed at the open door, hammer back.

The dark shape filled the doorway. I knew from the familiar tread that it was Hemingway, but I did not lower the hammer until he spoke in a loud whisper.

"Lucas, wake up!"

"What?"

"Get dressed. Hurry."

"Why?"

"Someone's been killed," Hemingway whispered, the dark bulk of him leaning in from the doorway, his voice excited but under control. "We have to get there before the police do."

10

I HALF EXPECTED THIS to be another one of Hemingway's games, but the man was dead, all right. Quite dead. His throat had been cut from ear to ear. He was lying on an unmade bed in a tangle of red sheets and pillows dyed crimson from the bleeding that had matted in his chest hair and stained his baggy Boxer shorts an obscene pink. His eyes were open and staring, his mouth was locked wide in a silent scream, his head was slammed back into the red pillows in an arch of final agony, and the ragged lips of the sliced throat gapped open like a shark's bloody grin. The knife—pearl handled, a five-inch blade—lay amidst the tousle of sopping bedclothes.

Hemingway took charge and reviewed the scene with the tight-lipped silence men assume in the presence of violent death. He and I were the only men present. Four or five women—whores all—milled about. The death scene was a seedy, windowless room on the second floor of a downtown whorehouse—one of the several where Hemingway's "field agents" worked on their backs—and the whores stood there in chemises and gauzy robes, some staring in dull apathy, others with their hands fluttering to their mouths in shock. The beautiful whore, Maria, was one of the latter, her pale fingers trembling against her cheeks. Her silken underwear was soaked through with the dead man's blood.

Until now "beautiful whore" had been an oxymoron to my way of thinking; all of the whores I had ever known were unattractive and stupid, with pasty complexions, splotchy blemishes, dull eyes, whose lipsticked mouths were about as attractive to me as this corpse's slashed throat. This whore—Maria Marquez—was different. Her hair was rich black, her face thin and fragile but enriched with full lips and large brown eyes. Her gaze was terrified at the moment, but obviously intelligent, and she had the delicate fingers of a pianist. She looked young—certainly not yet twenty and perhaps as young as sixteen or seventeen—but she was definitely a woman.

The oldest woman present was Leopoldina la Honesta—"Honest Leopoldina"—a prostitute to whom Hemingway had introduced me a few days earlier with all the solemnity and ceremony appropriate to a meeting with royalty. In my book, an honest whore would have been more rare than a beautiful one. In truth, Leopoldina la Honesta had a regal bearing, lovely dark hair, and proud bones. She must have been beautiful in her youth. Even in the confusion of this murder scene, she comported herself with dignity and calm.

"Get these others out of here," said Hemingway.

Leopoldina shooed away all of the girls except Maria and closed the door.

"Tell us," said the writer.

Maria still seemed too shocked and shaken to speak, but Leopoldina la Honesta spoke slowly in elegant Spanish, her voice a rich mixture of whiskey and smoke. "This man came in about one this morning. He asked specifically for a young girl—unspoiled—and naturally I sent him to Maria...."

I looked at the younger whore. She did seem unspoiled, her skin as smooth as a baby doe's. Her hair had been cut at shoulder length but was rich and black, framing the thin face and large eyes.

"Sometime later we heard the shouting, then the screaming," finished Leopoldina.

"Who was shouting?" said Hemingway. "Who was screaming?"

"The man...or men...were shouting," said the older prostitute. "Another man had come to the room. Maria was screaming from the bathroom, where she was when the murder occurred."

Hemingway was wearing a light canvas jacket, which he took off and draped over Maria's shoulders. "Are you all right, my dear?" he said to the girl in smooth Spanish.

Maria nodded, but her hands and shoulders were shaking.

"The child had locked herself in the bathroom," said Leopoldina. "She would not come out for some minutes. She was very upset. The man who was with this man"—Leopoldina gestured toward the body—"had left by the time the other girls and I responded to Maria's cries."

"How did he leave?" said Hemingway. We both glanced at the open window. There was a twelve-foot drop to the alley, and no fire escape.

"He walked out," said Leopoldina. "Several of us saw him."

"Who was he?" said the writer.

The older whore hesitated. "Maria will tell you."

"Tell us what happened, little one," said Hemingway, taking Maria by the elbows and gently turning her away from the body and blood.

The young woman's chest was convulsing with sobs, but after a moment—with Hemingway stroking her back through the jacket as if he were petting one of his cats—she was able to speak.

"This *señor*—this dead man—he was very quiet...he came up to the room with the valise you see there..."

The bag was on the floor, its contents scattered everywhere. Papers and notebooks lay on the carpet and on the bed itself, some soaking in pools of blood. I crouched slightly and saw a hypodermic needle and a 9-millimeter Luger under the bed, both evidently spilled from the bag. I touched nothing.

"Did he open the valise in front of you, Maria?" asked Hemingway.

"No, no, no," said the girl. Her lustrous hair touched her cheeks as she shook her head. "He set the valise on the table. He...he did not want to...to make love immediately. He wanted to talk. To speak to me. He took off his shirt, you see..."

A blue blazer and white shirt were neatly draped over the back of a chair. The dark gray trousers were folded on the chair.

"And then?" prompted the writer. "What did he want to talk about?"

"He spoke of how lonely he was," said the girl, taking deep, slow breaths now. She did not look in the direction of the body. "How far from home he was."

"He spoke in Spanish?"

"Yes, *Señor* Papa. Very poor Spanish. I know a little English, but he insisted on speaking to me in bad Spanish."

"But he also spoke English?"

"Yes, *Señor* Papa. He negotiated with *Señorita* Leopoldina in English."

"Did he tell you his name?"

Maria shook her head.

Hemingway stooped, lifted the billfold from the dead man's trousers, removed a passport and a card, and handed them to me. The passport was American, in the name of Martin Kohler. The card was an able-bodied seaman's union card made out to the same name.

"Did he tell you where his home was?" asked Hemingway.

Maria shook her head again. "No, *Señor*. He was just telling me how lonely it was on the large boat and how long it would be until he would see his family again."

"How long?" said Hemingway.

The girl shrugged. "I was not really listening. He said something about months."

"Which boat?"

The girl pointed to the window. There was a hint of moonlight on the bay glimmering between the brick walls there. "The big one. The large one that came in yesterday."

Hemingway glanced at me. The *Southern Cross*.

Leopoldina la Honesta rubbed her arms. "*Señor* Papa, we have not called the police yet, but we must any minute. I do not allow such things in my house."

Hemingway nodded. "Maria, tell us about the man who came to the room and the murder."

The girl nodded and looked at the far wall as if the scene were being projected there. "This man was talking. He was sitting on the bed in his underwear... as you see him. I was thinking that this would take too long, but that he must have paid very much to have so much time with me. There was a knock. The door was unlocked, but the man went to the door to open it. He gestured me into the bathroom, but I left the door open a crack."

"So you saw what happened next?"

"Only bits of it, *señor.*"

"Continue, Maria."

"The other man came in. They began speaking very sharply to one another...but not so that I could understand it. Not in Spanish or English. In a different language."

"What language, Maria?"

"I think that it was German," said the girl. "Or perhaps Dutch. I have not heard either before this night."

"So they argued?"

"Very violently, *Señor* Papa. But only for a moment. Then I heard the struggle and peeked through the crack in the open door. The larger man had pushed my...my client...back onto the bed. The other man was going through the valise on the table, throwing things as you see them. Then the man on the bed cried out and reached for his pistol—"

"Where was the pistol, Maria?"

"In his jacket."

"He aimed it at the other man?"

"He did not have time, *Señor* Papa. The other man's arm swung quickly. I saw this through the crack in the door. Then my client dropped the pistol and fell back as you see him. The bleeding was very bad."

I looked at the arterial spray across the bedclothes, carpet, and wall. The girl was not exaggerating.

"What happened then, Maria?"

"I screamed. I closed the door and locked it. This is the reason that this room has a bathroom—none of the others do. Special clients are brought here. But if they request something...not appropriate...the girl can hide in the bathroom and call for help. The door is very thick. The locks are very strong."

"Did the killer try to get in?" said Hemingway.

"No, *Señor* Papa. I did not see the door handle turn. He must have just left the room then."

"I saw him pass through the lobby," said Leopoldina la Honesta. "He was very calm. There was no blood on his uniform."

"Uniform?" said Hemingway. "Was he a sailor?"

"No, *Señor* Papa," said Maria. "He was a policeman. *Un guardia jurado.*"

Hemingway's dark eyebrows arched very slightly. He looked at the older madame.

"Caballo Loco," said Leopoldina la Honesta.

I had understood the girl's comment. *Guardia jurado* was Cuban slang for a policeman on private duty, such as a cop who acted as a bouncer for a bar. But *Caballo Loco* meant "Crazy Horse," and I did not understand this. I looked at Hemingway.

"Oh, fuck," said the writer tiredly, glancing at his watch. To Leopoldina he said, "Get the girl out of here and dressed. Pack her things. She'll come with us."

The older whore nodded and took Maria out of the room. Hemingway closed the door behind them. He stood scratching the stubble on his cheek and looking at the corpse.

"'Crazy Horse'?" I said.

"The man who did this, evidently," he said. "*Caballo Loco* is a local nickname for a certain Lieutenant Maldonado of the Cuban National Police. Maria said '*guardia jurado*' because everyone in Havana knows that Maldonado does private work for various rich families and government agencies."

"What kind of private work?" I said.

"He kills people," said Hemingway. "And he takes orders from Major Juan Emmanuele Pache Garcia, 'Juanito, the Jehovah's Witness,' the real power in the National Police. Garcia orders that people be killed. Sometimes he does it as a favor for the local politicians or friendly agencies."

"What friendly agencies?"

Hemingway looked at me. "The local branch of the FBI, for one, Lucas." He looked back at the corpse and sighed. "Maldonado killed a young friend of mine."

I waited. When someone says something like that, he always wants to finish the story.

"Guido Perez," continued the writer. "He was a good boy. He used to take part in our rocket attacks on Frank Steinhart's place. I taught him boxing at the *finca*."

"Why did Maldonado kill him?"

Hemingway shrugged. "Guido was a passionate boy. He hated the type of Havana bully that *Caballo Loco* represented. He said something to someone about his contempt for the lieutenant. Maldonado hunted him down and shot him." He rubbed his chin again. "But why this?" Hemingway gestured at the corpse.

I glanced at my watch. "We only have a few minutes. Word will travel. The cops will be here, and Maldonado might be the one investigating."

Hemingway nodded and crouched by the notebooks and documents lying in the blood on the carpet. "Let's see if any of these things suggest a reason for the murder."

I shook my head. "Maldonado wouldn't have left them if they did." I went over to the valise and looked inside. It was empty. "Do you have a knife?"

Hemingway handed me a pocketknife with a three-inch blade. I shook the valise, cut through the false bottom. There was a single notebook hidden there. It was small—about six inches by four. Hemingway took it.

"What the hell?" he said.

The pages were flimsy and perforated like a Western Union message tablet. Some pages held a grid with ten blank squares across and five rows down. On some of the pages, the grids were wider, rectangular, with twenty-six empty blocks across and four rows down. It was obvious that about a third of the book's perforated pages had been torn out.

The grids were all empty except for the one of the first page. On this one, the second square in the first row, the last two squares in the second row, and the fifth square in the fifth row were blacked out. Written in heavy ballpoint pen in the other squares was the following cipher:

h-r-l-s-l/r-i-a-l-u/ i-v-g-a-m / v-e-e-l-b / e-r-s-e-d / e-a-f-r-d / d-l-r-t-e / m-l-e-o-e / w-d-a-s-e / o-x-x-x-x

"All right, Lucas," said Hemingway, handing me the book. "You're my official consultant. Tell me what the hell this is. And what this says."

I did not even glance again at the book. I knew exactly what it was, of course. My mind was racing, trying to decide what to tell the writer. What was my charge exactly? To spy on Hemingway, of course. To see what his idiotic Crook Factory was up to, to report to the director via Delgado, and to await further orders. I was supposed to *play* at being a consultant, an expert on counterintelligence. But was I supposed to provide Hemingway and his team with real information? No one had briefed me on that. Obviously no one had considered that the Crook Factory might uncover any actual intelligence.

"It's a German cipher book," I said. "Abwehr. Two types of transmission blocks there—both book-based. The first one's based on the first word or phrase on a specific page of a book both the transmitter and receiver are using. The second one uses the first twenty-six letters on the page of the book they're using that day. The message on the first page was probably a recent one that he had either received or was ready to transmit."

"What does it say?" said Hemingway, taking the book back and frowning at the cipher. "It looks like a simple letter-substitution code."

"Simple," I said, "but almost impossible to decipher unless one knows what book it's based on. And it's not just simple letter substitution. Before the actual text of the message, German intelligence operatives send their ciphers in clusters of five. The letters each represent the number of its position in the alphabet."

"What do you mean?" The writer was frowning at me.

"Say *k* was equal to zero," I said. "And there will be a dummy letter. Say *e*."

"Yeah?"

"So this cluster..." I said, pointing to *v-e-e-l-b*, "would stand for eleven thousand one hundred and seventeen."

Hemingway shook his head. "No book has eleven thousand plus pages."

"Right," I said. "So that's not the page code. Several of the clusters will be false. But with each transmission, there will be a new page of the book cited. Usually the key word for the cipher is the first one on that page of the book."

"What book?" said Hemingway.

I shrugged. "It could be anything. They could change it weekly or monthly. Use different books for different types of transmissions."

Hemingway took the book back and rifled through the blank pages. "Where are the missing pages?"

"Destroyed after each transmission," I said. "Probably burned."

Hemingway looked at the corpse again, as if he wanted to ask the dead man some questions. "His seaman card said that he was a radio operator."

"First class," I said.

"The *Southern Cross,*" said Hemingway. He put the cipher book in his shirt pocket. "Do German agents use this sort of code to communicate with subs?"

"Sometimes," I said.

"Do you think the book or books that would be the key for this cipher are on the yacht?"

"Probably," I said. "Kohler would have wanted to keep it nearby for his deciphering. It's almost certainly a common book. Something a seaman would keep in his berth, maybe even something common to Kohler's radio shack, if the entire crew is in on this." I looked at the corpse. The man's eyes were beginning to film over. "Or maybe your Lieutenant Maldonado took his reference book when he killed him."

Hemingway turned toward the door. "Let's get that young whore out of here before Maldonado and his friends come back and kill *her.*"

THE GIRL BABBLED in Spanish all the way out to the *finca* in the dark. The purr of the Lincoln's strong motor threatened to put me to sleep, but I listened to Maria's nervous chatter and the writer's occasional questions with a small part of my mind, while simultaneously trying to sort things out for myself.

This was all very melodramatic. The radio operator for the *Southern Cross,* the same luxury yacht we had seen near the German U-boat, murdered in a Havana cathouse by a National Police lieutenant with an absurd nickname. *Caballo Loco* my serene ass.

But the cipher tablet was real. I had seen them before in spy nests we had cleared out in Mexico City and Colombia. Basic Abwehr issue. Or *Geheimaus ruestungen fuer Vertowenslaute*, as the ever-literal Germans would call it: "Secret equipment for confidential agents." If this poor, dead Martin Kohler—or whatever his name was—had been a real agent, especially a *Grossagenten* or "super agent," then the rest of his standard-issue equipment would include a manual for assembly of a wireless set, a cipher reduced to film size by microphotography, a set of call letters, a prayer book or other standard German book on which his code was based, chemicals for making and developing invisible inks, a powerful magnifying glass for reading microfilm, a Leica minicamera, and an ungodly amount of currency in traveler's checks or gold coins or jewelry or stamps or all of the above.

Melodramatic. But I had seen this corny stuff strewn near the bodies of dead Abwehr agents before.

Or perhaps Martin Kohler was just a radio operator who happened to be freelancing for the Germans. It was possible. But whichever possibility was true, the cipher book looked authentic. It held some message, either from Abwehr headquarters to him or vice versa. Or perhaps to or from the sub. We would never know if we did not find the book he had used as a basis for the cipher.

Maria was explaining that she had come from the tiny village of Palmarito, near the village of La Prueba, on the far part of the island, a few hours' walk from Santiago de Cuba, and that her older brother Jesus had attempted to have carnal knowledge of her, but her father believed her brother's obscene story instead of her truthful one and had disowned her and threatened to cut off her nose and ears if she ever returned—which he would do because he was known as the most violent man in Palmarito—and she had come with the last of her money all the way to Havana, where *Señorita* Leopoldina had been kind to her, asking her to meet with only a few clients a week—those willing to pay for her unspoiled beauty—but now if she went home her father would kill her and if she stayed in Havana *Caballo Loco* would kill her and even if she tried to hide, the National Police or her father or her brother would track her down and cut off her nose and ears before killing her....

It was a relief when the stone gates of the *finca* rolled past the cone of headlights. Hemingway cut off the engine and coasted into the last bit of driveway so as not to wake his wife.

"Take Xenophobia to the guest house, Lucas," said the writer. "Get some sleep. We'll head down to the bay when it gets light and check out the boat."

Xenophobia? I thought. I said, "Is the plan to keep both of us in the guest house?"

"Just for a few hours," said the writer, going around to open the door for the young whore just as if she were another movie star visiting the *finca*. "We'll find a safer place for both of you before the day is out."

I was not pleased to have my future plans mixed up with this terrified whore's, but I nodded and led the girl across the courtyard and under dripping palms to the guest house.

She looked around with wide eyes when I switched on the lights.

"I'll get my stuff out of the bedroom," I said. "You can have it to get some sleep. I'll nap out here on the couch."

"I will never sleep again," said the girl. She glanced shyly in at the bed and then at me. Something knowing and calculating entered her dark eyes. "Does this place have a bath?"

"A bath and a shower bath," I said. I took her in and showed her the bathroom and extra towels. I lifted a pillow, using it to cover the pistol I had left there, made an effort to toss the bedclothes right, slipped the revolver under my jacket when she was looking the other way, and said, "I'll be out here. Feel free to sleep as long as you want. I'll be going with *Señor* Hemingway as soon as it gets light."

Lying on the couch, watching the predawn light come up, I heard the bath running and then the shower pounding and then a muffled exclamation. Perhaps it was her first shower. I was half dozing when the door opened and she stood there, backlighted by the soft light from the bathroom, black hair wet and shiny. She was clad only in a towel. She let the towel drop open and looked down in a study of modesty.

Maria Marquez was beautiful. Her body was slim and firm with youth but had retained none of the baby fat of childhood.

Her skin was as light as any Norte Americana's. Her breasts were larger than I would have thought, even after having seen her in a blood-soaked negligee, and they actually rose to the brown-tipped nipples in the way an adolescent male's imagination would hope. Her pubic hair was as dark and thick as the hair on her head, and beads of water glistened there. Maria's eyes remained downcast, but her lashes fluttered in a perfect and silent invitation.

"*Señor* Lucas..." she said huskily.

"Joe," I said.

She tried the word but found it difficult.

"José," I said.

"José, I am still frightened. The sounds of that man's screams are still with me. Could you... would you consider..."

When I was a very young man, on my uncle's fishing boat, I had heard him tell his own son, who was only a year older than me, "Louis, do you know why we call a prostitute *puta* in our own language?"

"No, Papa," said my cousin Louis. "Why?"

"It comes from an old word in the mother tongue of our mother tongue—the old language from which Spanish and Italian and all of the lovely languages descend—and that word is *pu*."

"*Pu?*" said my cousin Louis, who had bragged to me many times of his visits to whorehouses.

"*Pu,*" said my uncle. "It is the ancient word for 'rot.' For the smell of decay. The Italians call a whore *putta*. The French say *putain*. The Portuguese also say *puta*. But it all means the same—the smell of rot and decay. Putrid. The smell of pus. Good women smell of the sea on a clean morning. A *puta* always stinks of dead fish. It is the dead semen in them... the anti-life wombs of whores."

In the decade and a half since that day, usually through my work, I had known my share of whores. I had even liked a few of them. But I had never fucked one. Now Maria Marquez stood there naked in the dim light, her eyes downcast and demure, but her nipples staring boldly.

"I mean," she was saying, "I am afraid to sleep alone. José. If you could just lie with me and hold me until I fall asleep...."

I walked over to her. She glanced up as I came within arm's length. Her dark eyes were gleaming.

I picked up the towel and handed it to her in a way that covered her breasts and belly.

"Get dried off," I said. "Sleep if you can. I'm going out now."

HEMINGWAY AND I STOOD ON THE HILLSIDE, leaning on the dark Lincoln to hold our binoculars steady, and watched the *Southern Cross* catch the first, low rays of the rising sun. The yacht was absurdly long—a football field in length—but it was also sleek and subtle in execution, its bridge swept back in a sweet, post–art deco curve, its decks of teak gleaming, the rectangular portholes of its many above-deck salons reflecting the tropical sunrise. The ship had not put in to the Havana Yacht Club or any of the commercial moorings, but had dropped anchor far out in the bay near the open sea. It took a special exemption from the harbormaster for ships to park there.

The writer lowered his glasses. "Big son of a bitch, isn't it?"

I kept watching. The cluster of radio antennae behind the bridge suggested serious communications facilities. The radio shack would be there. The yacht was naval in its cleanliness. Two officers in blue blazers had stepped out of the bridge to take in the breeze that came with the sunrise, and there were half a dozen men standing guard, two on either side, one at the bow, another at the stern. As if that were not enough, a fast motorboat purred slowly in circles around the big craft. Besides the man at the wheel, two large men in canvas jackets lounged in the back of the motorboat and kept watch on everything that moved in the harbor. Each man had a pair of powerful naval binoculars slung around his neck, as did all of the lookouts aboard the yacht. Hemingway had parked back under some trees on the hilltop, behind a low stone wall, in a position where our own binoculars would not reflect the sunlight and where we would be two shadows next to the shadowy car.

"Marty was awake when we got home," said Hemingway, looking through his field glasses again.

I glanced at him. Was he going to pass along a reprimand for our waking the mistress of the manor? I realized that I was not fond of Martha Gellhorn.

Hemingway lowered his glasses and grinned at me. "I helped her wake up," he said in his low tenor. "Irrigated her twice so as to get the day off to a good start. Maybe that whorehouse gave me ideas."

I nodded and looked back at the yacht. *Irrigated her?* Christ, I hated this supposed man-to-man locker room talk.

As if on cue, a tall, bald man in a dark blue bathrobe and an equally tall blond woman in a white bathrobe came out of a stateroom door halfway back along the hull and stood on the sunlit side of the superstructure, peering into the orange sun. The tall man said something to one of the guards on that side, who knuckled his cap, fetched the other guard, and lowered a rope-and-wood ladder over the port side. Both men saluted again and disappeared from sight.

The man in the blue bathrobe peered up at the bridge and superstructure as if checking that no one was watching from there. He spoke to the blond woman, who did not look at him but who dropped her white robe to the deck. She had been naked under the robe. Her skin was bronzed by the sun, her breasts and lower belly as tanned as the rest of her, and I could see the pinkness of her nipples from three hundred meters away. She was not a natural blonde.

The woman stepped to the open gate in the railing, but instead of going down the ladder, she paused only a second and then dived gracefully, skillfully, barely leaving a ripple as she disappeared beneath the calm gold of the harbor surface. I expected the man in the bathrobe to follow her, but instead he moved to the railing, removed a silver cigarette case from his pocket, took out a cigarette, tapped it the way I had seen only actors in movies do, set the case away, and lit the cigarette with a silver lighter from the same pocket. He stood and smoked as the woman broke the surface ten meters farther away from the yacht and proceeded to swim back and forth with steady strokes. Neither the lookout on the bow nor the one on the stern turned her way as she dove to reverse course, her long, tanned legs and marginally whiter ass turning skyward at each lap. When she did a backstroke, her breasts and small white belly and shadowy navel and pubic hair were perfectly visible to us.

I had seen more naked women in one day than I had in the past six months. And the sun was barely above the horizon.

Ten minutes, exactly, and then she swam to the manladder, climbed it without modesty, and stood dripping as the bald man wrapped her white bathrobe around her. They went through the nearest hatch. A moment later, the two port lookouts returned to their posts. I saw no snickering or exchanging of leers from the men as they resumed sweeping the harbor with their glasses.

Hemingway set his binoculars on the hood of the Lincoln. "Interesting."

I was studying the deck. There were crates and cartons lashed under tarps ahead and behind of the main superstructure. Some of the cartons had stenciled writing on them, but none were exposed enough or at the correct angle to be read from here. Of more interest, near the bow and at several places along each side on the railings were reinforced metal mounts with complicated brackets. I pointed these out to Hemingway.

"Gun mounts?" he said.

"Machine guns, I think," I said, although I was certain enough. I had worked an operation on a Mexican Coast Guard Q-boat which had used similar mounts. "Fifty caliber," I said.

"Six of them," said Hemingway. "Could that private yacht actually be carrying six fifty-caliber machine guns?"

"Or one gun," I said, "and six places to mount it."

Hemingway lowered his glasses again. His face had that serious, tight-lipped expression it had carried while looking at the corpse. I understood it. Fifty-caliber machine guns were frightening things. Even at this distance, there was nothing we could hide behind—not even the huge Lincoln—that would stop such a heavy, high-velocity slug. I expected Hemingway to start in about his "machine gun wounds" in the Great War, but instead he said softly, "You're the consultant, Lucas. What would it take to find out what book Kohler was using as his cipher base?"

"Someone would have to get aboard the yacht and take a

look," I said. "Before the police roust Kohler's berth or someone on the ship tosses the book."

"No sign that the cops have been there yet," said Hemingway. "And maybe they won't bother."

"Why is that?"

"If *Caballo Loco* did the killing, he and his pals don't have much incentive to investigate it," said the writer.

"But they didn't find the notebook," I said, tapping the pocket where I had put the notebook when Hemingway handed it to me during our drive downtown.

"Do you think that was what Maldonado was looking for?" said Hemingway.

"I have no idea." I studied the yacht again. Crewmen were turning out to scrub down the decks. It was late for that; most naval craft would have seen that chore completed before the sun was fully up. But this was not a naval craft. And perhaps the blond woman's morning skinny-dip was part of the regular routine when the ship was at anchor.

"I think we ought to take a look at Kohler's berth and the radio shack before the cops toss the place. I'll make the arrangements today, Lucas," said Hemingway. "We'll see if the Crook Factory can do its job. Should we steal the book if we find it?"

"No need for that," I said. "Just check the titles there. It would probably be a common book."

Hemingway grinned. "If I create the diversion and arrange to get one operative on board, do you want to be that operative? You're supposed to know about this crap."

I hesitated. It would be silly for me to risk arrest or worse by playing at this game—this was not a cherry bomb attack on a neighbor's farm. Whatever the *Southern Cross* was up to, its crew looked efficient, and there was a military feel to the yacht's operation. I could imagine Mr. Hoover's face if he received a memo from the Havana branch of the Bureau saying that its special SIS agent needed to be bailed out of the Havana jail...or had been fished out of the harbor after the crabs had feasted on his eyes and soft parts.

Still, it was a basic black bag job, and I was almost certainly the only one in Hemingway's ragtag counterespionage ring who had actually been trained to do such a thing.

"Yeah," I said. "I'll do it if there's a sensible plan to get me aboard and off without getting shot."

Hemingway tossed the binoculars into the back of the Lincoln and slipped behind the wheel. I went around and got in the passenger side. The sun had been up less than thirty minutes and already the interior of the big car was baking.

"I'll tell you the plan while we have breakfast at Kaiser Guillermo's Café de Perla de San Francisco," said Hemingway. "When we get back to the *finca*, we'll get people busy on it. And we'll find Xenophobia another place to live where we can keep an eye on her. Tonight, when it's dark, we'll go see what Herr Kohler likes to read."

As we drove into an Old Havana redolent with the previous night's garbage and rich with that morning's light, Hemingway was singing a song which he said had been taught to him by his friend the priest, Don Andres. He said that he was dedicating it to the fucking big yacht and all who sailed on such:

No me gusta tu barrio
Ni me gustas tú
Ni me gusta
Tu puta madre.

The second verse was the same as the first:

I don't like your neighborhood
And I don't like you
And I don't like
Your whoring mother.

11

I WAS SURE I would not have time to make the rendezvous with Delgado at the safe house at five P.M., but as it turned out, my Crook Factory errands took me into Havana that afternoon and I had twenty minutes to spare. It was one hell of an informative twenty minutes.

When we had returned to the *finca* after a huge breakfast at Kaiser Guillermo's that morning, Maria was sitting out by the pool in shorts and a halter top obviously borrowed from Gellhorn, reading a *Life* magazine and chewing gum.

Gellhorn intercepted us at the back door of the main house and said softly, "Is *Señorita Putita la Noche* another permanent guest, Ernesto?"

Hemingway grinned. "I think we'll offer her the other guest house," he said, waving at Maria over Gellhorn's shoulder.

"What other guest house?" said his wife.

"La Vigía—Grade A," said Hemingway. He glanced at me. "Maybe Herr Lucas could spend some of his time there as well."

La Vigía—Grade A turned out to be a dairy across the road from the *finca*. Hemingway took me to it before moving Maria there. He said that it had been a working dairy when he moved in—the milk sold in long bottles marked "La Vigía—Grade A"—but that the owner, Julian Rodriguez, had shut it down and sold the property to Hemingway the year before. The writer said that he had no plans for the property, but that he liked the idea of owning all of the hilltop except for Frank Steinhart's house, which he fully planned to burn down one night on one of his rocket raids.

"Also," said Hemingway in his soft Spanish, "the rich man Gerardo Duenas and I run a *gallera* just across the field there and it is good not to have too many neighbors."

I understood. A *gallera* was a cockpit—a pit for cockfights. I could easily imagine Hemingway caught up in the art and science of breeding fighting cocks, even more easily imagine him grinning in bloodlust as the shouts of the men rose around the pit.

The Grade A guest house was a small shack just off the abandoned dairy barn, only about two hundred meters from Hemingway's farm. The entire complex was empty, but it still smelled of manure. The cottage Hemingway had in mind had been the caretaker's home. It was a tiny, whitewashed shack, two bare rooms, one fireplace, an outhouse behind the little house, a woodstove for cooking, an outside pump for running water, no electricity. The floors and walls were relatively clean, but spiders had woven webs in the corners, and it looked like a pack rat had been living in the fireplace. One of the windowpanes had been shattered, and rain had stained the ceiling and wall along the west end of the main room.

"I'll send René and Juan and a couple of the other boys over this morning to get it cleaned up," said Hemingway, scratching his cheek and creaking the old door back and forth on sagging hinges. "We'll put in a couple of pieces of furniture, a little icebox we have in the old kitchen, a chair or two, and two cots."

"Why two cots?" I said.

Hemingway crossed his hairy arms. "Xenophobia isn't totally full of shit when she says that everyone's out to kill her, Lucas. If Maldonado finds her, he'll cut off more than her nose and ears before he kills her. Do you know why he's called *Caballo Loco*?"

"Could it have something to do with him being crazy?" I said tiredly.

Hemingway scratched his cheek again. "He's a big guy, Lucas. And he's hung like a horse. And he likes to use his equipment, especially on young girls. I don't think we should let him find Maria Marquez."

I stood at the fireplace and looked at the mess in it. I was thinking about the plans for the evening. "Won't the whores at the house tell?" I said. I had never known a whore who could keep a secret.

Hemingway shook his head. "Leopoldina la Honesta is as good at keeping her word as her name implies. She swore to me that she and the other girls would say that Maria had run off and that no one knew where she went. She'll frighten them until they will be more terrified of her than they would be of the National Police; I guarantee none of them will tell the police that we were there last night."

I made a rude noise. "From the way you describe him, Lieutenant Maldonado could make any one of those *putas* talk in thirty seconds."

"Probably," agreed the writer, "but Leopoldina shut down the house and sent the whores who know anything back to their villages and home cities an hour after we left last night. They're not exactly licensed, you know. It will be hard for the cops to track them down, and I don't think they'll try. It's not as if there's any mystery involved in this killing... except for where Maria's fled. And if *Caballo Loco* or his boss, Juanito the Jehovah's Witness, show up to ask if we know anything about her... well, she's certainly not at the *finca*."

"No," I said, "she's a couple of hundred yards away in this stinking old dairy."

"Being guarded day and night by an expert on counterintelligence and hand-to-hand combat," said Hemingway.

"Fuck you," I said.

"And your mother," said Hemingway in an agreeable tone.

ALL THE REST OF THAT MORNING and afternoon the operatives of the Crook Factory came and went. Maria was bundled off to the Grade-A guest house by Juan and several other servants, Hemingway and I cleared the large table in the living room of the real guest house, and there was a solid procession of his motley crew reporting, getting orders, reporting again, arguing, drinking, making suggestions, and then disappearing only to reappear.

Winston Guest, "Wolfer," was there all day when he was not running messages; as was Juan Dunabeitia, "Sinsky the Sailor"; not to mention the first mate, Fuentes; Patchi Ibarlucia; Father Don Andres Untzaín, the composer of Hemingway's morning song, and Felix Ermua, El Canguro, "the Kangaroo," a friend of Ibarlucia's and another jai alai player; as well as a weasellike little man named José Regidor who talked tough and whom I guessed would fold like a cheap accordion in a real fight. Also in attendance were Dr. Herrera Sotolongo and his brother Roberto; Hemingway's gardener, Pichilo, who seemed more intent upon talking to Hemingway about the Spanish jerezano cock he was breeding and training than about the intelligence operation; and a dozen others, including some of the Havana wharf rats and waiters I had met on our first inspection of the Crook Factory and just as many that I had never met.

By four-thirty in the afternoon, cars had been coming and going since ten o-clock that morning, the guest house was knee-deep in beer cans and filled ashtrays, and I was sure that we were no closer to realizing Hemingway's half-assed plan than we had been at eight o'clock that morning.

"We still need plans of the yacht," I said. "Without an exact diagram of where Kohler's radio shack and berth are, all this elaborate scheming is so much jerking off."

"Please, Lucas," said Hemingway, looking around at the eight or ten grizzled rumrunners, longshoremen, sailors, and fallen-away priests standing around the room, drinking and arguing. "Watch your language," he said, "there are children present."

"I won't disagree with that," I said with a sigh. My head hurt.

"Lucas, do you want to do something indispensable?"

I looked back at the writer through the blue haze of cigar smoke. Hemingway did not smoke, but he didn't seem to mind the constant puffing around him.

"What?"

"Martha wants to go into town for a few hours. We need the Lincoln back here by six to send out the final communiqués. Could you drop her off and bring the car back? Juan's still cleaning up Grade-A for Xenophobia."

I glanced at my watch. I had not been able to get Delgado

on the phone to cancel our rendezvous. Perhaps I would be able to make it after all.

"Sure," I said. "I'll drive Mrs. Hemingway."

DELGADO WAS THERE and waiting, wearing the same white linen suit and undershirt as before. He smiled his mocking smile as I came into the dim room.

"You're a busy man, Lucas."

"Yeah," I said. "And I don't have much time to waste. Did you get the file?" I did not expect it to be there. Over the past twenty-four hours, my skepticism about the rapid delivery of such highly classified material to Cuba had grown into almost absolute doubt. Delgado had been showing off his clout. And wasting my time in the process.

Delgado reached into a battered briefcase under the table and brought out a dossier. It had the pink file cover and green stamps of an O/C file. It was about the size of a Chicago phone directory.

"Jesus Christ," I said, and sat down heavily. One look at the subheadings in the dossier directory showed me that this would be more than twenty minutes' reading: *The Southern Cross/Howard Hughes/The Viking Fund/Paul Fejos/Inga Arvad/Avard: contacts with Hermann Goering/Adolf Hitler/Axel Wenner-Gren (aka "the Swedish Sphinx")/Threat analysis: COI-Donovan, Murphy, Dunn/ Arvad: surveillance tapes and transcripts, sexual liaison with Ensign John F. Kennedy (U.S. Navy—Division of Naval Intelligence, Foreign Intelligence Branch).* "Jesus Christ," I said again.

"Be careful what you wish for, Lucas," said Delgado.

"I have to take this file with me," I said. "Read it later."

Delgado chuckled. "You know better. It has to be back in Washington by midnight."

I rubbed my chin and glanced at my watch. I had twenty minutes before I had to get the Lincoln back to Hemingway. *Goddamn it to hell.* I flipped open the dossier and began scanning pages.

The *Southern Cross*: Three-hundred and twenty feet long. The largest private ship in the world. U.S. registry. It had been owned and specially modified by Howard Hughes (a referral here to Hughes's complete dossier).

I had seen Howard Hughes's dossier before. The thing was encyclopedic. Everyone knew of the millionaire aviator and inventor. Howard Hughes was precisely the kind of loose cannon that drove Director Hoover crazy—rich, involved in half a dozen top-secret U.S. military projects, erratic, a risk taker. The government kept giving the man top-secret clearance and increasingly more important war projects while doubling and tripling the surveillance and wiretaps on him. I wouldn't be surprised if the director had nightmares about Howard Hughes at least once a week.

In this case, Hughes's ownership and modification of the *Southern Cross* was suspicious, but not as suspicious as his sale of the boat to Axel Wenner-Gren. This was also a name I knew well.

Axel Wenner-Gren was one of the richest men on the planet. He was also—the FBI, the BSC, the COI, the ONI, and every other intelligence agency in the Western Hemisphere was certain—a Nazi spy. Wenner-Gren had his own nickname in the counterintelligence community—"the Swedish Sphinx." The millionaire had founded Swedish Elektrolux and was a chief shareholder in the Bofors gun-manufacturing corporation. Wenner-Gren's contacts with Hitler's lieutenants and German intelligence filled, I knew, a separate dossier larger than that of Howard Hughes. In the past few years, the Swedish industrialist had come into my sphere of SIS concern in Mexico and the Latin American region.

At the outbreak of the war between Germany and England, Wenner-Gren had established his own bank in the Bahamas and become close friends with the Duke of Windsor, becoming so trusted that the duke appointed him as his personal banker. I knew from my own midnight chamfering that British Security Coordinator Stephenson and his second in command, Ian Fleming, considered the Duke of Windsor a traitor and maintained a constant surveillance on Axel Wenner-Gren as the duke's primary liaison with Nazi Germany.

During the week in which the Japanese had attacked Pearl Harbor, six months before, the U.S. government had blacklisted Wenner-Gren, denying him a visa and an entry permit. The multimillionaire had moved his base of operations to Mexico, where my group of the SIS noted his contacts with Admiral Canaris's Abwehr agents in that country. Specifically, we had become convinced that Wenner-Gren was financing an attempt to overthrow Mexico's current president.

After buying the *Southern Cross* from Howard Hughes the previous autumn, Axel Wenner-Gren had further modified the yacht—giving it sophisticated radio and shortwave capabilities and super-long-range fuel tanks as well as arming it with heavy machine guns, a hundred and fifteen rifles, and antitank rockets—and then given it as a gift to Dr. Paul Fejos and the Viking Fund.

Fejos's name was not as familiar to me. Born in Hungary in 1896, Fejos had been a cavalry officer and pilot in the Great War, earned a medical degree, and then gone on to direct plays, operas, and motion pictures in his home country before becoming an American citizen in 1929. Unhappy with Hollywood's way of making films, Fejos had returned to Europe to make movies for MGM there. He had come back to the United States in 1940 and set up the Viking Fund in New York City in 1941. Chartered as a nonprofit organization to finance explorations with the goal of finding lost Inca cities in the Peruvian jungles—said explorations to be recorded on film by Paul Fejos and sold commercially despite the Viking Fund's nonprofit status—the FBI considered the organization a front for pro-German intelligence operations. The first contribution to the Viking Fund last winter had been Axel Wenner-Gren's gift of the modified 320-foot yacht the *Southern Cross*.

All this was of interest, but not nearly as interesting as the fact that Dr. Fejos's current wife was one Inga Arvad.

"Jesus Christ," I muttered a third and final time. These were just carbons and duplicates of Inga Arvad's file, but this excerpt must run to 150 single-spaced pages. I flipped through them, pausing at the photographs and photostats and transcripts of ELINT (electronic surveillance), TELSUR (telephone surveillance), and FISUR (physical surveillance). Inga Arvad had been and still was one heavily surveilled dame.

It was then that I recognized a phenomenon which I had witnessed scores of times in field work. Different agencies had followed different spoors to the same nexus, converging—as they were converging now on Arvad and the *Southern Cross*—without premeditation or plan. Donovan's COI soon-to-be OSS had become deeply interested in Axel Wenner-Gren, as had my own SIS. Fleming's and Stephenson's BSC were obviously interested in Wenner-Gren and the *Southern Cross*. U.S. Naval Intelligence was sure that the yacht had been modified as part of a scheme to refuel German submarines in the Caribbean or off the coast of South America or both. The FBI had become obsessed with Inga Arvad and followed her trail to the yacht, Wenner-Gren, and all the rest.

Inga Arvad's life—even the snippets of it I was skimming through in this abbreviated dossier—was the sort of true-life tale that Hemingway and his ilk could never get away with putting in their made-up stories. It bordered on the unbelievable—despite the fact that Inga Arvad was only twenty-eight years old and didn't seem old enough to have done all that was attributed to her here.

Inga Maria Arvad was born on October 6, 1913, in Copenhagen, Denmark. She had been a beautiful, precocious child, studying dance and piano under masters, and had been crowned Beauty Queen of Denmark at the ripe old age of sixteen. The same year, she competed in Paris for the title of Miss Europe, was offered a job in the Folies-Bergere, but chose instead to elope with an Egyptian diplomat when she was seventeen. She divorced him two years later.

There were numerous photographs of Arvad in the dossier. The first showed a very young and very beautiful blonde sitting next to Adolf Hitler in what looked to be a sports arena. The label on the back read "Inga Arvad and Adolf Hitler, Berlin Olympics, 1936". The accompanying report said that after Arvad had left the Egyptian diplomat, then starred in a Norwegian-based movie directed by Paul Fejos, and then begun an on-again, off-again affair with the director, she had suddenly gone off to Berlin as correspondent for the Copenhagen newspaper *Berlingske Tidene.* There had been no mention of any journalistic training before this, but it was becoming obvious that whatever young Miss Inga Arvad wished to do, she did.

Here there was an insert of an FBI interview with Arvad dated just a few months ago, December 12, 1941. In the transcript, Arvad stated that her assignments in Germany had been to interview prominent persons—including Adolf Hitler, Hermann Goering, Heinrich Himmler, and Joseph Goebbels—and that she "might have been present in Hitler's box on one occasion when the Führer was there." The FBI reports from that period suggested that the relationships had been a little more personal: that Arvad had been invited to Hermann Goering's private wedding ceremony, at which Adolf Hitler was the best man; that Hitler had described the young Arvad as "a perfect example of Nordic beauty" and had begged her "to visit me every time you return to Berlin."

It looked as if she had. Despite the fact that she had quit her job as "correspondent" before the Summer Olympics of 1936—after marrying Dr. Paul Fejos—she had been a guest of the Führer in his private box at the Olympic Games and had become good friends with Goering and even closer friends with Rudolf Hess. According to the FBI report, Arvad had made her last visit to Berlin in 1940, when she had been invited to work for the German Propaganda Ministry. In her December 12, 1941, interview with the FBI, Arvad said that she had turned down the offer, but a 1936 clipping from the International News Service stated that even then Hitler "had made her Chief of Nazi propaganda in Denmark." She had been twenty-two that year.

According to the dossier, Arvad had married Dr. Paul Fejos in 1936, but she had been the mistress of Axel Wenner-Gren before and after that wedding ceremony. When Fejos and Arvad had moved to the United States in 1940, it was her lover, Wenner-Gren, who had set up the Viking Fund, chartered in Delaware with its actual headquarters in New York City.

There followed several pages of Naval Intelligence threat estimates and photostats of the shipbuilder's designs of the

Southern Cross. I pulled out the design, folded it, and put it in my pocket.

"Hey!" shouted Delgado, straightening up from where he had been straddling the chair. "You can't take that."

"I need it," I said. "Shoot me." I checked my watch—five minutes left before I had to get back to the *finca*—and went on to the last section of the dossier.

The entire Arvad file was still active, but this last section was filled with recent surveillance reports, wiretap transcripts, bugging transcripts, and copies of letters photographed during FBI black bag jobs. All of it involved a romantic liaison between Inga Arvad and a young officer in U.S. Naval Intelligence, Ensign John F. Kennedy.

I realized from the notes that this was one of the sons of Joseph P. Kennedy, the millionaire and former U.S. ambassador to England. Everyone in the Bureau knew that Director Hoover was friends with Ambassador Kennedy—keeping the Irish patriarch up-to-date on classified information which might benefit him—but we also knew that Hoover distrusted Kennedy, considering him dangerously pro-German, and that there was a thick and constantly updated O/C file on the former ambassador. Surveillance on Arvad had reached a fever pitch since the previous December—shortly after Pearl Harbor—when Wenner-Gren's mistress and Hitler's favorite Nordic beauty had begun an extramarital affair with the twenty-four-year-old Ensign Kennedy. As an officer in the Foreign Intelligence Branch of the Division of Naval Intelligence, Ensign Kennedy was cleared for top-secret reports and was involved on a daily basis with rewriting decrypts from foreign stations for the ONI's various bulletins and in-house memos.

Since December, both ONI counterintelligence and the FBI had been monitoring the Kennedy-Arvad affair with the assumption that not only was there a security leak in progress but that Kennedy might be an active participant in a Nazi espionage operation. It was obvious that the FBI part of the surveillance included mail chamfering, black bag jobs, phone taps, physical surveillance, and interviews with everyone from one of the young Kennedy's sisters, who had introduced him to Arvad at the paper where they worked, to statements taken from janitors, mailmen, and bellboys at the hotels and apartments where the couple held their illicit meetings.

December 12, 1941—A memo to Director Hoover states that Frank Waldrop, editor at the *Washington Times Herald*, contacted a special agent in charge at the Washington field office to report that Miss P. Huidekoper, a reporter at that paper, had stated to Miss Kathleen Kennedy, another reporter at that paper, that their mutual acquaintance Inga Arvad, a columnist for the *Times Herald*, was almost certainly a spy for some foreign power. The memorandum sent to Hoover that day was headed "Mrs. Paul Fejos, alias Inga Arvad". Since Hoover had been keeping a confidential file on Arvad since the day she and her husband had arrived in America in November 1940, the revelation was small surprise to the director.

December 14, 1941—Full-scale surveillance is set up at Arvad's apartment at 1600 Sixteenth Street, #505. Dr. Fejos had left the country that day—bound again for Peru as part of his mysterious Viking Fund project—and Arvad's secret lover had appeared to spend successive nights in the married woman's bedroom. It seemed that Axel Wenner-Gren's mistress's lover was a U.S. naval ensign who wore "a gray overcoat with raglan sleeves and gray tweed trousers. He does not wear a hat and has blonde curly hair which is always tousled... he is known only as Jack."

Within twenty-four hours, the Office of Naval Intelligence has identified "Jack" as John F. Kennedy, son of Ambassador Kennedy, an ONI ensign assigned to Washington Naval Intelligence Headquarters. But the FBI is still in the dark. The file begins to fill up with intercepted communications between Kennedy and Arvad, Hitler's "perfect Nordic beauty."

January 1, 1942—Telegram from Kennedy, in New York, to Arvad:

> They are not keeping them flying so I won't be there until 11:30 by train. I would advise your going to bed, but if you come, buy a thermos and make me some soup. Who would take care of me if you didn't?
>
> Love, Jack.

On that same New Year's Day, FBI Special Agent Hardison acknowledges that all attempts to solve the identity of the assumed agent codenamed "Jack" have proved to be "entirely unproductive" but that the Bureau is still working on it.

Meanwhile, ONI—based on its memos included in the dossier—is becoming worried. An interdepartmental intelligence conference on December 31 includes notes on a conversation between Assistant Director Captain Klingman of the ONI to top FBI officials Tamm and Ladd "relative to Ambassador Kennedy's son, who is reported to be going to marry a woman who will divorce her present husband." The follow-up FBI memo by Ladd stated to the director: "Captain Klingman stated that they find this boy is 'right here in our midst,' and he wanted to know more of the circumstances..."

So while Special Agent Hardison and his men were puzzling over the identity of Arvad's New Year's Eve lover, Director Hoover was on the phone checking it out himself. A memo from the director reported: "Captain Klingman stated that he will handle the matter properly."

January 9, 1942—A copy of a request from the Chief of Naval Operations to the Bureau of Navigation requests that Ensign "Joseph F. Kennedy" be transferred immediately out of Washington, D.C. They meant "John F. Kennedy." The Bureau of Navigation, according to a separate ONI report, took no action. Surveillance on the suspected female Nazi spy and her intelligence service lover continued and intensified.

January 11, 1942—An intercepted letter from Dr. Paul Fejos, currently working for Axel Wenner-Gren's Viking Fund front organization, to his wife, Inga Arvad:

> You, dearest, can be more cryptic than the prophets of the Old Testament. You write that if you would be eighteen, you would probably marry Jack. I suppose it means Jack Kennedy. Then you follow up with, "But I would, might probably, choose you instead." Now, my inconsistent child, what is all this about? Has anything gone wrong with yours or Jack's love? Or is this again your sweet charity feeling toward me?

> Anything but that please. You see, Darling, you have made me some very difficult days with those charity attempts, and honestly it is far more human if you don't do them. Slowly I will get used to it, that I am without you, and that you cannot be reached, had—and things will heal (I hope) and there would not be any use to try to be charitable and therefore unwillingly, but in the final result: Cruel.
>
> There is, however, one thing I want to tell you in connection with your Jack. Before you let yourself go into this thing any deeper, lock stock and barrel, have you thought that maybe the boy's father or family will not like the idea?

I stopped reading and looked at my watch. Time was up. But there were just a few more pages of dossier to scan, a few more photographs. Hemingway could wait a few minutes.

What the hell kind of impotent asshole was this Dr. Fejos, writing his wife this sort of whining garbage? I looked back at the photographs of Inga Arvad. Short, curly blond hair. Pencilled eyebrows. Full lips. Perfect complexion. Beautiful, all right, but not worth this sort of demeaning behavior. But then, what woman would be?

I studied the photos another moment. Though they might be sisters, this was not the woman I had seen swimming naked early this morning. Inga Arvad looked like a natural blonde.

I flipped through the last twenty pages of the dossier.

January 12, 1942—While FBI counterintelligence experts are still working on the identity of the Arvad contact "code-named Jack," Walter Winchell's syndicated column announces: "One of ex-Ambassador Kennedy's eligible sons is the target of a Washington gal columnist's affections. So much so that she has consulted her barrister about divorcing her exploring groom. Pa Kennedy no like."

January 13, 1942—Ensign John F. Kennedy is transferred out of Washington to a navy base in Charleston, South Carolina.

January 19, 1942—Special Agent Hardison's surveillance report:

Ensign known only as Jack is confirmed to have definitely spent the nights of January 16, 17, and 18 with subject Arvad at Arvad's apartment. Bureau continues 24-hour surveillance. It is the opinion of Agent Hardison that this man lives someplace in the immediate neighborhood and after spending the night with the subject, goes to his own apartment, changes to his uniform and then returns to her apartment for breakfast.

January 19, 1942—ONI surveillance confirms that Ensign Jack Kennedy has flown from Washington to join his father in Florida before beginning his assignment in Charleston.

January 19, 1942—Intercepted letter from Inga Arvad to Jack Kennedy's new naval base postal box in Charleston:

> January 19, 1942—the first time I missed anybody and felt lonely and as though I was the only inhabitant of Washington.
>
> Loving—knowing it, being helpless about it, and yet not feeling anything but complete happiness. At last realizing what makes Inga tick.

January 24–25, 1942—Agent Hardison and his crack team "lose" Inga, report that her whereabouts are "unknown." The accompanying ONI report shows that Inga Arvad was waiting for Ensign Kennedy in Charleston when he reported for duty at his new assignment.

January 26, 1942—An intercepted letter from Arvad to Kennedy:

> The further the train pulled away, the less visible was the young handsome Boston Bean... I slept like a log. At midday we arrived to the Capital of the United States. To that same Union Station, where I went on January the First 1942 as happy as a bird, without a care, a fear or trouble in the world—just in love—remember?
>
> "Have you started making the baby yet," was a question asked me today. Guess by whom?

And so the love letters continue. And around the lovebirds, more agencies become involved in surveillance and countersurveillance. It becomes obvious in the reports that Director Hoover had used the Arvad affair to resume hostile surveillance of Colonel Donovan of the COI. Out of self-defense, Donovan's group begins a countersurveillance of Arvad and the host of FBI and ONI agents watching her.

On the same day that Arvad is writing her January 26 love letter to young Kennedy, Hoover is alerting the attorney general of the United States about his "current investigation of this woman as an espionage suspect," concluding that Arvad may well be "engaged in a most subtle type of espionage activities against the United States."

January 29, 1942—The special agent in charge of the investigation, taking over from the clueless Hardison, notes that the Arvad case has "got more possibilities than anything I have seen in a long time."

February 4, 1942—The director of the Alien Enemy Control Unit at the Department of Justice writes Hoover demanding a "report of all information you have in your files in respect of... Mrs. Inga Fejos, 1600-16th St., NW, Washington, D.C. which I desire in considering whether a Presidential Warrant of apprehension should be issued."

Hoover, of course, does not want Inga Arvad arrested. Her simultaneous affair with Wenner-Gren and the young Kennedy has given the director a carte blanche to open surveillance on half of the director's enemies in Washington.

The FBI telephone intercepts at the end of January and beginning of February run to many pages:

KENNEDY: I want to see you in Washington next week...if I can get away.

ARVAD: I'll fly to Charleston, darling. If that is more convenient for you.

KENNEDY: Will you? Of course it's better if you come here, but there is no sense in you doing all the traveling, so I'll come up there next time.

ARVAD: I will be happy to meet you halfway, Jack, darling. I will meet you anywhere you want, whenever you want. You can do anything you want, darling. If you want to go somewhere else, you're welcome.

KENNEDY: No, no, I'm coming to Washington. If I can get away at one o'clock, I can get that plane, otherwise, if I have to work I'll get away at six o'clock Saturday.

ARVAD: Good God. Do you have to work Saturday?

KENNEDY: Yes.

ARVAD: When are you sailing?

[A scrawled note on the transcript here: "Seeking classified information?"]

KENNEDY: I don't know.

ARVAD: Is that going to be soon?

KENNEDY: No.

ARVAD: I think it is.

KENNEDY: No.

ARVAD: Are you sure?

KENNEDY: I told you, I'll tell you.

And so on, for page after page. The special agent in charge searches these conversations for clues as to whether critical information has been exchanged between the Naval Intelligence officer and the German spy. He is especially interested in this cryptic exchange some days later:

KENNEDY: Did you say MacDonald was better dressed than I was? Did you say I should go to his tailor?

ARVAD: That's a lie! I don't care what you wear, darling. I love you as you are. Darling, you look best without anything.

Around the first of February, during a late-night phone call. Ensign Kennedy first teases Arvad about "a big orgy" he had heard she had held in New York, but ends up worrying about Dr. Fejos's opinion of him.

KENNEDY: What else did your husband say?

ARVAD: Why, he said I could do what I wanted. He said he was sad to see me doing things like this. I'll tell you about it and I swear that he is not bothering us and that you needn't be afraid of him. He's not going to sue you though he is aware what he could do by suing you.

KENNEDY: He would be a big guy if he doesn't sue me.

ARVAD: He's a gentleman. I don't care what happens, he wouldn't do things like that. He's perfectly alright.

KENNEDY: I didn't intend to make you mad.

ARVAD: I'm not mad. Do you want me to come this weekend very much?

KENNEDY: I would like for you to.

ARVAD: I'll think it over and let you know. So long, my love.

KENNEDY: So long.

Evidently Arvad did not think it over for long. From February 6 to February 9, she and Ensign Kennedy rarely left their room at the Fort Sumter Hotel in Charleston. An excerpt from the FBI Savannah field office report:

"5:45 P.M., Friday, Feb. 6, 1942—Subject Ensign Kennedy arrives Sumter Hotel in 1940 black Buick convertible coupe. 1941 Florida license 6D951. Kennedy goes to Subject Arvad's room and remains there, except for forty-one minute break for supper, until late Saturday morning."

Except for a few other brief breaks—one for mass on Sunday morning—Kennedy and Arvad remained in bed until Monday morning, February 9. Specially bugged rooms had been set aside for the couple at the Fort Sumter Hotel. Electronic surveillance reports refer to "sounds of strenuous sexual intercourse." In late February, the wily Inga tries to throw off Hoover's G-men by having Kennedy book a room for her at the Francis Marion Hotel, but the Savannah Branch FBI agents take an adjacent room while six agents of Naval Security listen against the wall of the opposite adjoining room.

"A great deal of the conversation which passed between the subject and Kennedy in the hotel room was obtained," reads the February 23 report from Special Agent Ruggles. "It was learned that the subject was quite worried about the possibilities of pregnancy as a result of her two previous trips to Charleston, and she spoke of the possibility of getting her marriage annulled. It was noted that Kennedy had very little comment to make on the subject."

It appeared that Ensign Kennedy was having second thoughts about marriage to this twenty-eight-year-old woman.

At this point, the record became as complicated as such things usually become. Inga was obviously aware of the dozens of FBI and ONI listening devices and was taking clever precautions to outwit them. In early March, Director Hoover made a personal call to Ambassador Kennedy, explained that the surveillance had now spread to the ambassador himself and that an arrest of his ensign son by Naval Security was a distinct possibility.

Joe Kennedy appears to have almost had an embolism. A phone intercept that same day between Joseph Kennedy's Hyannis Port home and Assistant Secretary of the Navy James Forrestal showed Kennedy beseeching his old Wall Street colleague to transfer his son's ass overseas.

"He's liable to get killed in the South Pacific, Joe," reads the Forrestal intercept.

"Better killed than remaining in that Arvad bitch's clutches," reads the Joseph Kennedy transcript.

Forrestal then called Director Hoover. The director recommended the transfer "for security reasons." Evidently Joe Kennedy's younger son was expendable in the ambassador's eyes. Word was that he was grooming his oldest son for the presidency someday.

JFK shipped out days later.

THE DOSSIER ENDED with the note from naval intelligence that Fejos's/Wenner-Gren's/the Viking Fund's ship the *Southern Cross* had sailed from New York Harbor on April 8, 1942. The navy had spotted it refueling in Bahama on April 17. Since then, the mystery yacht's whereabouts and mission had remained unknown.

I closed the dossier and handed it back to Delgado.

"Put the page back," he said.

"Fuck you," I said.

Delgado shrugged and curled his lips in that mocking smile. "It's your funeral, Lucas. I have to report that you took classified and confidential material without permission."

"You do that," I said, and headed for the door. I was twenty minutes behind schedule.

"Lucas?"

I stopped at the door.

"Did you hear about the murder last night?"

"What murder?"

"Some poor fuck named Kohler. A radio operator from the *Southern Cross*. The same boat you're so interested in. The same boat whose plans you just stole. Some coincidence, huh?"

I waited. Delgado sprawled in his chair and stared insolently at me. His cheeks and chest were damp with sweat.

"Who murdered him?" I said at last.

Delgado shrugged. "Word is that the Havana police are looking for a whore named Maria. They think she did it." He smiled again. "You wouldn't know where to find a whore named Maria, would you, Lucas?"

I stared at him. I had not openly lied to Delgado yet. After a second, I said, "Why should I know where she is?"

He shrugged again.

I turned to go and then looked back at him. "You said that a man from the Cuban National Police was following me the other day."

Delgado's strange lips curled up again. "And you didn't happen to notice. Even though he's a big fucker."

"What's his name?" I said.

Delgado rubbed his nose. It was very hot in the safe house. "Maldonado," he said. "The locals know him as Crazy Horse. And he is, too."

"Is what?"

"Crazy."

I nodded and went out, jogging the two blocks to where I had left Hemingway's Lincoln. There was a pack of bare-chested boys around the car, obviously considering what to steal in which order, but for the moment, it looked intact.

"Fuck off," I said.

The boys scattered and then regrouped to flash me two fingers in obscene salute. I wiped the sweat from my eyes, started the big car, and drove like hell for the Finca Vigía.

12

I STOOD ON THE FIREBOAT, which bobbed at anchor just inside the entrance to Havana Harbor. I was dressed in a fireman's heavy jacket and helmet, making small talk in Spanish with the eight other idiots there and waiting for the fireworks show to commence. Occasionally I would raise my binoculars and look out at the *Southern Cross* where it was anchored beneath the guns of the Battery of the Twelve Apostles. The yacht's superstructure glowed with lights. I could hear a piano playing across the expanse of dark water. A woman laughed. I could see that the lookouts were at their places on the bow, stern, and starboard side. The motorboat patrolled in circles, interdicting any small craft entering or emerging from the entrance to the Bahía de La Habana and staying between them and the anchored yacht until the boats had passed out of range. Then the motorboat would rush back to its patrol arc like an especially well-trained guard dog circling its master.

This was the dumbest goddamn mission I had ever volunteered for.

When I had returned to the *finca* guest house after my meeting with Delgado, no one had noticed that I was late. Hemingway and everyone else still there—Guest, Ibarlucia, Sinsky the Sailor, Roberto Herrera, Don Andres, several of the wharf rats—looked as if someone had died.

"What's the matter?" I said.

Hemingway rested his strong forearms on the long table for a minute. Then he lifted them to rub his eyes. "Plan's off, Lucas," he said.

"Can't get all the ingredients together?"

"We have all the goddamn ingredients," said the writer. "Except for the exact location of Kohler's berth. Norberto talked to one of the *Southern Cross* crew members about the dead man, and the sailor said that Kohler had bunked in the berth right next to his, the one just aft of the galley storage area."

"So? That seems specific enough."

Hemingway looked at me as if pitying my stupidity. "We haven't been able to find out where the galley storage area is. Norberto, Juan, and some of the other wharf boys were sure that they could get on the boat today to check the layout, but the yacht's not letting anyone aboard. Not even the police. The captain went downtown to discuss the murder with the Havana cops."

"That's good," I said. "It means Maldonado's people haven't grabbed the book ahead of us."

Hemingway shook his head. "You'd never have time to search the yacht in the few minutes this plan would give you. And without knowing exactly which berth was Kohler's, it's a waste of time. You said yourself that the book would most probably be in his berth rather than in the radio shack. And we don't even know for sure where the radio shack is."

I nodded, took the copy of the ship's plans from my coat, and laid it on the table. Hemingway stared at it, stared at me, and then stared at the plan some more. The other men gathered around. I thought that I noticed Winston Guest appraising me with a look of respect mixed with suspicion.

"Do I dare ask where the hell you got this?" said Hemingway.

"I stole it," I said truthfully.

"From where, *Señor* Lucas?" asked Roberto Herrera. "These are copies of the original shipbuilder's plans."

I shrugged. "It doesn't matter." My finger stabbed down on a small square marked on the lower deck. "Galley storage area. It's two ladders down from the radio shack but directly beneath it. Makes sense that Kohler would berth there. Probably has a cot in the shack as well. Did anyone find out if there was a second radio operator?"

"There was not," said Father Don Andrés Untzaín. "They are flying in a replacement tomorrow."

"Then I guess we have to do this tonight after all," I said.

Hemingway nodded, rubbing his palm across the ship plan as if trying to reassure himself that it was real. "One other thing, Lucas," he said. "The *Southern Cross* won't be going anywhere for a while. Both Norberto and Sinsky talked to members of the crew this afternoon. There's a bearing out on one of the two main shafts—it chewed up part of the shaft and gearing before they got into harbor. They're shipping parts from the States."

"Dry dock?" I said.

Hemingway shook his head. "Uh-uh. They're going to try do the repairs at the Casablanca shipyards."

I had to smile. The American ambassador had just made provisions for Hemingway to send the *Pilar* to the Casablanca shipyards to be fitted out as a Q-boat.

"Yeah," said the writer, and showed his teeth in a broad smile. "Maybe the two boats will be dockmates." He gestured Guest, Ibarlucia, and the others—including me—to move closer to the table. "Sinsky, you get the word to the boys that tonight's show is still on. Wolfie, you go get the ordnance we'll need. Patchi, you and Lucas and I had better go over the plans again."

MARIA WASN'T IN VIGÍA-GRADE A when I walked over to it. I had begun to think of the cottage as *la casa perdita*—"the little lost house."

Hemingway's people—the houseboy, René; the chauffeur, Juan; and possibly one of the maids—had done a good job cleaning up the shack. The floorboards were freshly swept, the fireplace was clean and workable, the broken windowpane had been covered over with cardboard, two cots were set out with blankets and pillows in the smaller room—as if the whore and I would be sleeping together in there—and a table and chairs had been set up near the fireplace.

"Maria?" I said softly. No answer. Perhaps she had run away after all. Perhaps she had gone home to her village to face the wrath of her father and lustful brother rather than be killed by Crazy Horse. I did not give much of a damn either way.

There was the sound of water running outside. I stepped out into the little courtyard between the house and the empty dairy barn and found Maria Marquez at a pump, filling galvanized basins with water. She jumped when my shadow fell over her.

"I called out," I said.

She shook her head so that her dark hair moved gracefully. "I did not hear you," she said in Spanish. "The pump made too much noise."

"There's a pump in the house," I said.

"It does not work, *Señor* Lucas. I wanted to wash the dishes they loaned me."

"I suspect that the dishes are clean," I said. "And you can still call me José."

She shrugged. *"Cómo le gusta mi cuarto, José Lucas?"*

"No está mal," I said. "It's cleaner than it was."

"Me gusta," said the girl. *"Me gusta mucho. Es como én casa."*

I looked at the little shack, the broken window, the outside pump, and the grassless courtyard. The air still smelled of manure. I imagined that it did seem like home to her. *"Bueno,"* I said.

Maria took a step closer and stared up at me. Her eyes were bright and sharp, her mouth tight. "You do not like me, José Lucas. *Por qué no?"*

I said nothing.

She took a half step back. *"Señor* Papa likes me. He gave me a book."

"Which book?" I said.

She carried her buckets of water into the shack, set them on the counter, and lifted a checkered dish towel. Under the towel were Hemingway's *For Whom the Bell Tolls*—the same title as the one he had signed for Ingrid Bergman—and the long-barreled .22 pistol which he had tried to give me that first night.

"He says that there is a character in this book with my name," said the young woman.

I picked up the pistol, opened it, saw that it was loaded,

shook the bullets out into my hand and set them in my pocket, and laid the empty pistol back on the counter. "And what did he say to do with this?"

The girl shrugged again. "He said that if *Caballo Loco* were to come here that I should run. If I could not run, I should use this to defend myself. Now I cannot do this because you have all the bullets." She looked as if she was going to cry.

"These bullets would only make *Caballo Loco* angry," I said. "You're more likely to hurt yourself or someone else than shoot Lieutenant Maldonado. I'll keep the bullets."

"*Señor* Papa will not be happy that you—"

"I'll talk to *Señor* Papa," I said. "You read your book and leave the pistol alone."

The whore pouted like a child. "I cannot read, *Señor* Lucas."

"Then use the pages for tinder when you start the fire tonight," I said. "*Tengo que ir. Tengo mucho que hacer.*" And I did. Much to do before the evening's fun in Havana Harbor.

THE FUN WAS SUPPOSED to start at fifteen minutes after midnight, but it was twelve-twenty-two before the five boats in Hemingway's flotilla came roaring and plowing out of the harbor entrance, firing off skyrockets as they came.

I counted two speedboats and three fast fishing boats—the *Pilar* was not among them, of course, since none of the craft were local boats. Through the binoculars I could see that the boats' names had been painted over or concealed by a seemingly carelessly flung roll of canvas and that all of the men aboard wore hats pulled low and were roaring drunk. *Seemed* to be roaring drunk. The men shouted and hooted across the water at each other as the careering small craft wove drunkenly out toward the lighted yacht.

I swung the glasses back on the *Southern Cross* and saw the lookouts pointing and shouting. An officer came out of the bridge and studied the flotilla. One of the lookouts pointed to the fifty-caliber mount, but the officer shook his head and went back onto the bridge. A moment later, the bald man we had seen with the swimming woman came on deck with the officer. The bald man was wearing a dinner jacket and was smoking another cigarette, this one in a long, black cigarette holder.

I looked back at the flotilla. The orbiting patrol boat was attempting to block their approach now, but the five boats had spread out and there was nothing the sentry boat could do but swing back and forth like someone trying to herd marbles uphill. I could see the two men in the cockpit of the sentry speedboat; they were holding Thompson submachine guns in plain sight and looking plaintively at the yacht for instructions. The first officer, standing next to the bald man on the *Southern Cross*, shook his head and waved his arms in a negative signal. The submachine guns disappeared. The patrol boat growled back to the immediate vicinity of the yacht.

I could make out Hemingway near the bow of the lead fishing boat. His face was only shadow beneath the low brim of the straw fishing hat, but I recognized the powerful upper body and the massive forearms. The men around him were laughing and tossing whiskey bottles into the rough water of the strait as their boats came out of Havana Harbor between the old fort on the hill and the old fort in the city. Someone fired another skyrocket into the air above the yacht. The officer on the *Southern Cross* shouted through a megaphone for the fishing boats to stand off, but the sound was lost in the explosions of firecrackers, cherry bombs, and popping skyrockets.

One of the flotilla's speedboats began circling the yacht at high speed, staying fifty yards out but drawing the attention of the lookouts and the sentry boat. That is when I saw Hemingway load the flare pistol and aim it at the yacht.

Two of the boats in the flotilla had men firing off rockets, seemingly at random, but most of the starbursts exploded above the *Southern Cross*. I could see through the binoculars that the men on the fishing boats were using those stupid bamboo stalks as bazookas. A fiery red blossom exploded just ten yards above the bow of the yacht, and the patrol boat roared out to shoo the careering fishing boat away.

Hemingway fired the first flare. Its parachute opened twenty feet short of the yacht and it drifted down into the water, sputtering and hissing.

"Hey! Goddammit!" shouted the bald man on the deck of the big boat. He dropped his cigarette holder in his agitation. "Stop that, you swine!" His voice was almost lost across the water.

Our fireboat had edged out away from the abandoned slips near the point on the city side, the engine gurgling at lowest throttle, and the eight men and I stood tensely. Our running lights were out.

Hemingway stood in the bow and fired again. The flare popped open above the stern of the *Southern Cross* and drifted over its port railing. The lookouts were shouting. The sentry boat roared away from the fishing boat it was herding and accelerated toward Hemingway's boat.

Someone fired a skyrocket directly at the bridge of the yacht. The first officer and the bald man ducked. The sound of the piano had stopped, and now men in tuxedos and women in evening dress were coming on deck. The first officer herded them back inside as two more white rockets exploded just above the bow of the ship.

One of the lookouts raised an automatic rifle and fired three warning shots in the air.

Ignoring the shots and the bedlam all around him, Hemingway stood on the bow of the advancing fishing boat, disdainful of the patrol boat rushing at them with searchlights flashing, and stood easily against the chop while lifting the heavy flare pistol a few degrees higher. For an instant all the other rocket and firecracker noise seemed to stop as Hemingway pointed, paused, and fired.

The flare arched in a flat, red streak, hit the mahogany deck of the yacht behind the bow, skittered across the deck—scattering lookouts and watchers—and disappeared under the canvas tarpaulin pulled tight over the crates just forward of the main superstructure. A skyrocket from another boat exploded just above the tarp five seconds later. Flames broke out beneath the canvas.

The guards on the patrol boat began firing across the bow of Hemingway's boat. The entire flotilla put hard over and accelerated in different directions, shouting insults in Spanish and continuing to fire rockets and lob cherry bombs at the fast boat. One of the flotilla speedboats lunged toward the yacht in a feint, drew the patrol boat back, and then took off to the west at high speed.

Our fireboat gained speed, throwing back a white wake at the same time that all of its running lights, searchlights, emergency lights, and sirens came on. It was a real fireboat, Hemingway had assured us, although it had only been used twice: once in 1932 when a freighter had caught fire in the middle of the harbor and burned to the waterline while the fireboat played its low-pressure hoses on the charred hulk, and a second time the previous year when a Cuban navy ammunition ship blew itself to bits eight miles off the coast and the fireboat had arrived in time to poke among the floating wreckage and retrieve bodies. The eight-man crew was made up of volunteers—all friends of the writer—who spent far more time drinking and fishing from the leaky tub of a fireboat than practicing rescue drills.

Now we leaped forward, the spray threatening to push the fireman's helmet off my head, the searchlight stabbing over my head and illuminating the yacht in a bobbing white circle. The patrol boat made to cut us off and then roared aside as the man at its wheel realized that our old boat was not turning or slowing. Shouts and curses followed us the final fifty yards to the starboard side of the yacht, where we were greeted by more shouts, curses, and warnings from the deck.

The five men around me ignored the noise and the deluge of water from our poorly aimed forward firehose nozzles as they rushed to our port side and made ready the fenders and boarding ladders.

"Stand off, stand off, stand off, goddammit!" shouted the first officer aboard the *Southern Cross.*

"No lo he entendido," shouted our helmsman, bringing us up alongside. *"Tenga la bondad de hablar en español!"*

Three of our "firemen" grabbed the railing with grappling hooks while two more tossed boarding ladders up the side. One of the ladders caught, and instantly two of the men were climbing, fire axes and hoses in hand.

"Get *off,* you slime!" screamed the bald man, rushing forward to stop the first of our volunteer firemen. Unfortunately for the bald man, the first of our men aboard was El Canguro, the Kangaroo, the powerful jai alai player. Suddenly the bald man was flying backward while the captain of our squad, an actual fireman, was shouting in broken English for the officers and lookouts and civilians to get out of his way, that the Havana Harbor Municipal Fireboat had authority during such emergencies, and would they please lend a hand in securing that fire hose that had been handed up?

The fire on the bow was almost out, but the smoke still billowed across the deck and obscured the superstructure. *Southern Cross* crewmen ran through the dark smoke, carrying fire extinguishers and axes, cutting away the smoldering tarp, hacking through tie-down lines, and pulling heavy crates out of the fire's way.

I was the fifth man up. I jogged forward, an ax in one hand, a flashlight in the other, paused at the hatch to the radio shack, waited for two shouting crewmen to run past me, and then stepped in.

Second door on the left was the radio room. Hatch was open. room dark. I found a fire Klaxon lever just where the wiring diagrams had shown it to be, and pulled it down. Suddenly the interior of the yacht began echoing with the shrill hooting.

I flashed the light around the radio room: shortwave, ship-to-shore, telegraph, voice transmitters, more electronic equipment than I had seen in a non-naval ship. Only a few books set in a recessed shelf. I stepped closer and ran the light across the books there. Standard radio room reference guides and troubleshooting manuals. A radio log that I flipped through quickly. Kohler would not have logged any covert transmissions or receptions.

Footsteps pounded in the corridor outside. I switched off the flashlight and waited while several officers and men ran past, undogged the outer hatch, and ran shouting onto the main deck.

Out the door, left, down the gang ladder. Left. Fans were sucking the smoke down into this corridor. The alarm bells were still echoing through the darkness. Down another short ladder.

The woman I had seen swimming naked stepped around a

bend in the corridor. Her eyes were shining. She wore a long, silk gown, scooped low in the front, that hugged her figure, and a simple string of pearls against her throat.

"What are you doing here?" she said. "What is going on?"

"Fire," I growled, lowering my head so that my helmet covered much of my face as I turned and pointed to the gangway up. "Get on deck. *Now!*"

The woman took a breath and rushed past, climbing the stairs with a scrape of her slippers.

I counted doors. Third hatch, galley. Fifth hatch, galley supply room. Sixth hatch, Kohler's room. I undogged the hatch and stepped in, ready to shout at anyone sleeping there.

The berth was small and empty. Three bunks, one table with an inset bookshelf above it, barely room to turn around. The fire Klaxon stopped blaring. I could feel bumps against the hull. The fire was probably out, the "firemen" chased off, the fireboat pushed away. Leaving the light off, I played the flashlight across the books there.

Only seven titles, four of them more radio reference books. The fifth was a novel, *Drei Kameraden* by Erich Maria Remarque, the sixth was a copy of Haushofer's *Geopolitík,* and the seventh was an anthology of German literature. I picked up the books to be sure that they were all in German, noted the publication dates, saw some pencil checks on different pages, and set them back carefully.

Then I was back in the corridor and heading up the fire ladder.

On the main level without meeting anyone, ready to turn right out the corridor I had come in through, then hearing voices and footsteps there. Shadows of men with guns.

I jogged down the corridor, took a left, heard shouts behind me, and stepped out through a hatch on the port side, away from where all the action had been. I dogged the hatch behind me and looked around.

The fireboat had already been pushed away. The smoke had let up. The lookouts would be back any second. I reached up and used the ax to smash the electric lamp above me. This section of deck dropped into darkness.

I walked to the railing, stepped over, balanced, dropped my ax, heavy coat, boots, flashlight, and metal helmet into the sea.

"Hey!" Someone coming around from the bow, shouting at the shadow he could just barely make out.

I dropped into the water, wearing nothing but the swimsuit I had worn beneath the fireman's coat.

I dived deep, came up fifteen yards out, dived again, came up farther out, my head low between the three-foot waves. The water was cold. There was noise and confusion on deck, but no shouts, no shots. I dived again, came up on the backside of another wave, and swam hard into the darkness.

13

HELGA SONNEMAN IS COMING to dinner tonight," said Ernest Hemingway. "You're invited if you buy a new shirt."

"Great," I said, not looking up from the codebook. "Is Teddy Shell coming as well?"

"Of course," said Hemingway. "You don't think Helga would go out for an evening engagement without Teddy, do you?"

I stopped working numbers and looked up at the writer. "You're serious? You can't be serious."

"Absolutely serious," said Hemingway. "Was introduced to Helga this morning when I was visiting the embassy. Liked her right away. Invited both of them."

"Mother of God," I said.

Helga Sonneman was the woman I had seen swimming naked and then almost run into in the smoky corridor of the *Southern Cross*. Teddy Shell was her playboy boyfriend. We knew a lot more about them now than we had a little more than a week earlier when we had pulled the fireboat trick.

"Eight P.M.," said Hemingway. "Drinks about six-thirty. Do you think we should invite Xenophobia?" Hemingway was amused by all this; I could tell from the firm set of his jaw. Teddy Shell, aka Abwehr Agent Theodor Schlegel, would most certainly like to meet Maria.

"Maybe you could dress her up and introduce her as an important guest from Spain," I said, joking. "Have her eat dinner next to the man who has his people out looking for her all over Cuba. The man who would probably shoot her the second he found her."

Hemingway grinned, and I realized that he was considering that idea, enjoying all of the ramifications. He shook his head. "Won't work. Upset the balance. Marty likes to have an equal number of males and females at the table whenever possible."

Teddy Shell, Hemingway, and I would make three males. Helga Sonneman and Martha Gellhorn... "Who's the third woman tonight?" I asked.

"The Kraut's coming this evening," said Hemingway.

"Which kraut?"

Hemingway shook his head again. "*The* Kraut, Lucas. With a capital *K. My* Kraut."

I asked nothing else. Hemingway did not explain. I would find out that evening.

It had been eight days since the midnight fireworks show in Havana Harbor. The Havana Police and Harbor Patrol had not been amused, but the fireboat's crew professed innocence of any intent except putting out the fire, the fishing boats and drunken fishermen had never been found or identified, and Mr. Teddy Shell of Rio de Janeiro, the civilian in charge of screaming "Swine" from the scientific ship the *Southern Cross*, had been such an arrogant swine himself when dealing with Cuban and U.S. authorities that no one wanted to help him too much.

Finding copies of the suspected code reference books had taken longer than we had thought. Remarque's *Drei Kameraden* was new enough and popular enough that we found a copy the next day in Havana's one bookstore that carried German titles, but Haushofer's *Geopolitík* and the 1929 anthology of German literature had taken a while. Finally, almost a week after our escapade, an airmail package had arrived from New York with copies of both books.

"I knew that Max wouldn't let me down," said Hemingway.

"And who is Max?"

"Maxwell Perkins," said Hemingway. "My editor at Scribners."

I had only the vaguest idea of what an editor did, but I was thankful that this one had combed used bookstores in New York until he had found the books that Hemingway had cabled him about.

"Goddammit, shit," said the writer. He was reading a note that had been in the package with the books.

"What?"

"Oh, that goddamned Garden City Publishing Company wants to reprint 'Macomber' and Max wants to give them permission."

"What's 'Macomber'?" I said. "One of your books?"

Hemingway looked at me without exasperation, accustomed to my ignorance by now. "'The Short Happy Life of Francis Macomber,'" he said. "It's a story of mine. Long short story. Took me as much work and blood to write as a novel would've. I used it to head up a collection of my short stuff in 'thirty-eight. That collection has never made money for Scribners or me, and now this Garden City outfit wants to reprint it in a cheap-shit sixty-nine-cent edition."

"Is that bad?"

"Es malo," said Hemingway. *"Es bastante malo.* It means that my work's competing with itself—not just with the original Scribners edition but with the Modern Library edition that's coming out as well. *Eso es pésimo. Es fucking tonto!"*

"Could I have them?" I said.

"What? Have what?"

"The two German books I need to decode the intercepts," I said.

"Oh," said Hemingway, and handed me the books. He crumpled up the letter from his editor and tossed it into the weeds, where one of the cats went after it.

IT HAD BEEN A BUSY WEEK for the Crook Factory. As the mean heat of early May settled into the stultifying heat of a Cuban summer, Hemingway's amateur operatives had begun keeping track of Lieutenant Maldonado, who was heading up an island-wide search for the whore named Maria, suspected of murdering the radio operator from the yacht the *Southern Cross.* I suggested to the writer that putting a tail on someone who was simultaneously a cold-blooded killer, a member of the National Police, and the chief investigator searching for the woman we were hiding near the *finca* was risky business, but Hemingway had just stared at me and said nothing. Meanwhile, some of his other operatives were merely lying low—a skill many of them had perfected in Spain and elsewhere—until the flap over the fireworks incident went away.

The wharf rats and longshoremen reported to Hemingway that the new radio operator for the yacht had arrived—flying in from Mexico City—but that the damage to the bearings and driveshaft was more extensive than first thought and that replacement parts would not arrive for another week at least. Even while the *Southern Cross* was stuck at anchor in Havana Harbor, Hemingway and his first mate, Fuentes, took the *Pilar* down to the Casablanca shipyard, where Fuentes stayed with the ship to oversee its refitting for intelligence operations while I drove the Lincoln down to pick up the writer. Over the next week, we received regular reports from Fuentes and Winston Guest, who drove daily to the shipyard to check on the work.

The *Pilar*'s dual engines were overhauled and improved for better speed. Additional auxiliary fuel tanks were squeezed in for longer-range patrolling. The Cuban navy had planned to install two removable .50-caliber machine gun mounts, but the U.S. Navy adviser overseeing the construction agreed with Fuentes that the mounts and guns would be too heavy for the 38-foot boat and the weapons were never actually mounted. Instead, carpenters built hidden closets, cupboards, and niches in which to hide Thompson submachine guns, three bazookas, two antitank guns, some small magnetic mines, a cache of dynamite charges, fuse cord, blasting caps, and several dozen hand grenades. Fancy "glass holders" were built to store the grenades out of sight.

When Guest returned with the news of these improvements, Hemingway grunted and said, "If the old girl catches fire at sea, then we'll all have the best Viking funeral the Caribbean's ever seen."

The U.S. Navy provided state-of-the art radio equipment, including direction-finding apparatus for triangulating on ship-to-ship, ship-to-shore, or submarine transmissions in cooperation with shore-based naval bases and Allied warcraft at sea. When Hemingway protested that he did not have time to learn how to use it or train his crew in its operation, Ambassador Braden and Colonel Thomason attached a U.S. Marine to Operation Friendless. The radio operator's name was Don Saxon; he was about my height, dirty blond, had boxed welterweight division in the Corps; and his résumé included the ability to field-strip a .50-caliber machine gun in the dark. Unfortunately, as Hemingway explained to the Marine over dinner at La Bodeguita del Medio, we had no .50-caliber machine guns, but Saxon would be in charge of all radio operations and our codebooks. We did not tell him about the German codebook we were trying to decipher in Hemingway's guest house.

The last touch in the *Pilar*'s conversion to Q-boat status was the installation of a quickly removable sign which read AMERICAN MUSEUM OF NATURAL HISTORY. "That ought to confuse the kraut skipper as he peers through his periscope at us," growled Hemingway on the day he went to the shipyard to bring the *Pilar* home. "Maybe he'll be so curious that he'll surface close by to send a boarding party over to see what the hell we're all about and we'll use the submachine guns on the boarders and the anti-tank guns and bazookas on the U-boat."

"Yeah," I said. "Or maybe all the German captain will be able to read is the word *American* and he'll stand off half a mile while sinking us with one shot from his hundred-and-five-millimeter cannon."

Hemingway folded his arms and glowered at me. "Seven-forty-class German boats don't have hundred-and-five-millimeter guns," he said disdainfully. "Just one eighty-eight-millimeter with some twenty-millimeter jobs for antiaircraft work."

"The new Class IX model has a hundred-and-five-millimeter cannon," I said. "And its fifty-caliber machine guns would cut the *Pilar* to pieces before you could ever get a bazooka or anti-tank gun on deck, much less loaded."

Hemingway gave me a long look and then grinned. "In that case, Lucas, my mysterious friend, we are—as I told the good colonel—well and truly fucked. But you'll be well and truly fucked along with us."

THE DAY AFTER THE FIREWORKS show, I knew that I was well and truly fucked. I'd put myself in a position where I could choose to report my evening's activities—breaking and entering a U.S.- registered yacht owned and operated by a legitimate U.S.-registered nonprofit organization, not to mention being an accomplice in setting fire to said yacht—and almost certainly lose my job, or choose *not* to report the unorthodox black bag job, have Delgado or someone else report my involvement when they discovered it, and certainly lose my job. Plus there was the problem of the missing codebook and the missing whore. I had put off reporting both of these minor facts, and the longer I waited, the more obvious my incompetence and/or disingenuousness would look when they did come to light. But if I *did* all this, it would seem that I had been failing in my role as a spy on Hemingway's operation while doing the writer's bidding at the expense of the Bureau.

I put it all in a report the day after the yacht business and stopped by the safe house to deliver it to Delgado while running around Havana on Crook Factory business.

Delgado arrived a few minutes after our arranged meeting time, wearing a clean *guayabera* and a straw hat pulled low. He tore open the seal of my report in his usual insolent manner, read it, and looked across the table at me.

"Lucas, Lucas, Lucas." He sounded amused and disgusted.

"Just send it on," I snapped. "And see if you can get the Bureau to identify the woman and bald guy on the yacht. I'll get photos of them and fingerprints if necessary, so we can send for their dossiers, if they have any."

Delgado tapped my report. "If I send this to Mr. Hoover, you won't be on this mission or in the SIS long enough to read those dossiers."

I stared at him. Not for the first or tenth time, I thought of how I would go at his gut and face with my fists if it came to a match. It would not be easy. Delgado would use his hands to try to kill me, I knew, not to box. "What do you mean?" I said. "It's not the first black bag job I've had to do."

"It's the first one you did without authorization," said Delgado with his infuriating curl of a smile. "Unless you count Hemingway's orders as authorization."

"I was told to obey his orders in order to earn his trust," I said. "I can't do my job if Hemingway doesn't trust me."

"What makes you think he trusts you?" said Delgado. "And do you really think the director wants one of his SIS boys hiding whores from the legally constituted Cuban police? A murder suspect, no less."

"She didn't kill Kohler," I said.

Delgado shrugged. "Don't be too sure, Lucas. Anything is possible in this business."

"Just send the report."

The lean man shook his head and tossed the manila envelope onto my side of the table. "No," he said.

I blinked.

"Rewrite the report so that it's vague about how you got the codebook and the names of Kohler's reference books," said Delgado. "Make it sound ambiguous—as if Hemingway's clowns are stumbling across this stuff. Leave the whore out of it altogether. That way you'll keep your job and we won't have to restart this mission from scratch."

I leaned back in my straight-backed chair and looked at the other agent. *Why the hell are you doing this, Delgado... whatever your real name is?*

As if reading my thoughts, Delgado curled his smile, took off his hat, and wiped the brim with a handkerchief from his trouser pocket. "What hidden motives can I have in ordering you to do this, Lucas?"

"You can't order me to do anything," I said flatly. "You're my liaison, not my controller in this. I was told to report through you directly to Mr. Hoover."

Delgado kept his smile, but his gaze was flat and cold. "And as your liaison to Mr. Hoover, I'm telling you to rewrite that fucking report, asshole. Keep the facts. Downplay your involvement. If the director thinks that you're jumping to Hemingway's tune, he'll pull you out of here so fucking fast that your beaner head will swim. And then what? Hemingway's not going to accept another 'liaison' person. I'll be doing ten times the amount of surveillance from outside the Crook Factory with those fuck-heads from the Havana branch of the Bureau breathing down my neck."

I looked at my typed report and said nothing. I wondered who had been more competently trained in lethal hand-to-hand combat—Delgado or me? It would be interesting to find out.

Delgado reached into his bag, pulled out two thin dossiers, and set them on the table. "I thought you might be wanting these." He stood and stretched. "I'm going to walk down the street to get a drink. Read 'em and leave them on the table. I'll pick them up when I get back."

I knew that he did not mean that I should leave classified material sitting in the empty safe house. He would be outside somewhere, waiting for me to leave.

I opened the thinner file first. This was not one of Hoover's O/C files—merely a basic Bureau dossier. I saw from the first-page synopsis that there would be no surveillance reports or transcripts, no chamfering photostats or agent analyses; this woman had an FBI file similar to the files of millions of other American citizens—a result of isolated contacts with other subjects or groups under Bureau surveillance, or because of anonymous tips, or simply because this person's name had come up somewhere, sometime, and a file had been begun.

Helga Sonneman had been born Helga Bischoff, in Düsseldorf, Germany, in August 1911. Her father had died serving the Kaiser in 1916, gassed during the Battle of the Somme. Helga's mother had remarried in 1921, this time to Karl Friedrich Sonneman. Herr Sonneman had two daughters and three sons by a previous marriage; one of those half sisters to young Helga was Emmy Sonneman, the future wife of Hermann Goering.

Helga had met Inga Arvad in 1936 through her half sister Emmy. Arvad was in Berlin as a correspondent and had contacted the future Mrs. Goering for an interview. The women had gotten along so famously that Emmy Sonneman invited Inga Arvad first to her country home—where she met the twenty-five-year-old Helga, who was visiting Germany to view the glories of the Third Reich—and then to the private wedding itself.

According to the brief report, Helga Sonneman had moved to the United States in 1929, shortly after the stock market crash, first as a student at Wellesley College—where she had majored in both anthropology and archaeology—then briefly as the wife of an American surgeon from Boston, then—through the second half of the 1930s—as a U.S. citizen in her own right, divorced from the surgeon, living in New York, once again under her own name. Helga Sonneman had made her living for the past decade as an independent authenticator of ancient artifacts—specifically, Mayan, Incan, and Aztec carvings and pottery. She had worked for several top American universities and was currently on retainer by the New York Museum of Natural History.

The report noted the connection to Goering and other top Nazi officials—the Sonnemans were especially friendly with Rudolf Hess, it seemed—but Helga's trips back to Germany during the '30s had been infrequent and apparently uneventful. It seemed that the attractive blonde had no interest in politics. Her travel over the past ten years had taken her to Europe occasionally, but much more frequently to Mexico, Brazil, Peru, and other parts of South and Central America.

References to Inga Arvad appeared in the dossier, of course. Besides knowing her from Germany and several trips to Denmark, Helga had been one of the people Inga had looked up after arriving in the United States in 1940. Indeed, Arvad had stayed at Sonneman's New York apartment for some weeks until Dr. Paul Fejos had arrived from Europe. Cross-reference notes in Helga Sonneman's file referred to comments in surveillance of Arvad at restaurants or parties with Axel Wenner-Gren, mentioning only "Miss Helga Sonneman, a friend of Mrs. Fejos, was also in attendance."

In the late autumn of 1941, shortly after Inga's lover, Wenner-Gren, had donated the *Southern Cross* to the Viking Fund, Dr. Fejos and the fund's board of directors had hired Helga Sonneman as the expedition archaeologist and curator of discovered antiquities. A hastily typed note mentioned that she had flown to the Bahamas on April 15 of the current year, presumably to join the Viking Fund ship, the *Southern Cross,* which had been observed refueling there on April 17, 1942. End of file. There was no mention of Teddy Shell.

Teddy Shell's dossier was much more substantial than Helga Sonneman's.

According to photographs and fingerprints sent to the Bureau this week from Special Agent in Charge R. G. Leddy (Havana Office), the bald businessman known on the *Southern Cross* as Mr. Teddy Shell was definitely one Theodor Schlegel, an Abwehr agent wanted by the Brazilian federal police, by DOPS (the Delegacia Especial de Ordem Politica e Social—the Brazilian political police, specializing in counterintelligence)—and the FBI (SIS), for espionage activities in Brazil.

Theodor Schlegel had been born in Berlin in 1892. A soldier in World War I, Schlegel had been discharged as a twenty-six-year-old lieutenant in 1918 and had begun a successful career in business, becoming an executive in a major German steel firm based in Krefeld. In 1936, the steel company had sent Schlegel to Rio de Janeiro to dissolve a money-losing branch firm there. He had quickly completed that assignment and then set up a new affiliate—Companhia de Acos Marathon—henceforth referred to in the dossier as "the Marathon Steel Company." During the years that the Third Reich lurched toward war and domination of Europe, Schlegel remained stationed in Brazil, running the Marathon Steel Company from its headquarters in Rio de Janeiro with frequent trips to its branch office in São Paulo. He also made frequent trips home to Germany, as well as trips to the United States to tour steel companies there. By 1941, Schlegel frequently visited New York under the passport name of Theodore Shell—a Dutch-German businessman and philanthropist. One of the U.S.-based nonprofit organizations to which Mr. Shell contributed, an IRS statement showed, was the Delaware-based Viking Fund. The social circles in New York knew the bald, bow-tied Mr. Shell as "Teddy." There was a photograph in the dossier of "Teddy Shell" posing, drinks in hand, with a grinning Nelson Rockefeller.

The report could not state exactly when Theodor Schlegel, aka Teddy Shell, had been recruited by the Abwehr, but best estimates suggested as late as his annual trip to Germany in 1939. By 1940, DOPS and its American FBI advisers suspected that Schlegel was the German agent known as "Salama," who reported on Allied shipping via a secret transmitter in or near Rio. At the same time, funds and coded messages were traveling to and from Salama by way of the German company Deutsch Edelstahlwerke, a firm which did business with steel executive Schlegel by day and transferred his bulkier messages to the Abwehr in Berlin by night.

Schlegel had come under initial suspicion because of reported contacts with a German engineer named Albrecht Gustav Engels, an Abwehr master spy and radio expert known to South and Central American counterespionage experts as code name "Alfredo."

I did not have to read the intelligence summaries on Schlegel's friend Engels. My work in Mexico, Colombia, and elsewhere had made me all too familiar with Alfredo.

Engels, theoretically Theodor Schlegel's radio contact in Brazil, had been so successful in setting up his Nazi intelligence operation that by 1941 his central transmitter in Rio de Janeiro—code-named "Bolivar" by the SIS—was the hub of Abwehr information being sent from New York, Baltimore, Los Angeles, Mexico City/Quito, Valparaiso, and Buenos Aires. More than that, Alfredo—Herr Albrecht Gustav Engels—controlled several hundred agents operating without hindrance in all of those cities and a dozen more.

I knew from my own experience that in October of the previous year, 1941, Dusko Popov—the same "Tricycle" whom Ian Fleming had enjoyed trailing through Portuguese casinos the previous August—had flown to Rio to confer with Engels about the possibility of setting up a major clandestine radio station in the United States. According to the notes in this dossier, Theodor Schlegel had been present at that meeting and had flown back to New York with Popov under his alias of Teddy Shell.

And it had been Engels who had passed along the queries from Berlin to Popov—queries from the Japanese about the defenses at Pearl Harbor, Hawaii.

I thumbed to the end of Schlegel's dossier.

In the spring of the current year, U.S. military authorities had been pushing the Brazilians to crack down on German espionage activities centered in their country. U.S. Chief of Staff George Marshall had sent a personal letter to General Goes Monteiro of the Brazilian army, begging and demanding that the Brazilian police and military take action. General Marshall had included excerpts of classified ONI and BSC—intercepted transmissions from Engels's "Bolivar" transmitter—broadcasts which had sent the position and sailing times for the *Queen Mary*, then traveling without escort and carrying nine thousand American troops to the Far East.

The FBI had intercepted and copied General Marshall's letter. One of the closing paragraphs read: "Had this boat been sunk with the inevitable loss of thousands of our soldiers, the incident would have imperiled the historic friendship between our countries had any suspicion of the manner of the betrayal of the vessel to its enemies reached the public...."

Translation: If the *Queen Mary* had been torpedoed due to the "Bolivar" transmissions and because of Brazilian inaction and incompetence, U.S. aid, military support, and goodwill would have been flushed down the crapper.

In response, the reports went on, DOPS and the Brazilian federal police—guided by ONI, BSC, SIS, FBI, and U.S. Army monitoring units and surveillance information—had lethargically begun making arrests in the Rio and São Paulo areas.

Theodor Schlegel had not been one of those picked up. The arrests had begun in mid-March and continued to the end of April. On April 4, according to the last report in the dossier, Theodor Schlegel—traveling as Teddy Shell and evidently ignorant of the roundup of his colleagues—had flown to the Bahamas and thence to New York. In Nassau, he had met with his friend Axel Wenner-Gren. In New York, he had met with Dr. Fejos and the board of directors of the Viking Fund, who had—in response to another philanthropical contribution from businessman Shell—appointed the bald, bow-tied German as director of the first expedition of the Viking Fund exploration vehicle, the *Southern Cross*.

"Jesus Christ," I muttered, wiping the sweat from my forehead. This stuff made the fabled Gideon knot look like a Boy Scout's simple sheepshank.

I left the dossiers on the table and went out into the heat and sunlight.

THE DEAD MAN'S CODEBOOK was driving me crazy with frustration.

I confess that cryptography had never been my strong suit,

either at Quantico or at Camp X. I had sounded smug enough explaining the Abwehr system to Hemingway earlier, but the truth was that although I had encountered German code often enough in Mexico and elsewhere, usually all I had to do with it was to send it along to the SIS experts in the field or back at the Bureau in Washington. Actually, the FBI was no great shakes at breaking code either, often farming out the job to ONI or Army G-2 or even State Department Intelligence, that nebulous branch of security for which Hemingway thought I was working.

My basic premises were correct, I was almost sure of that. The grids in Kohler's personal codebook were in the standard format. One thing about the Germans: once they found an elegant system they stuck with it even though that was idiocy in a world where even the best code could be beaten by opposition experts. Although I had never confirmed it in my spying at the BSC camp in Canada, rumors were rife that the British had already broken the most difficult German codes and that many of the Brits' cleverest commando raids and sea victories were based on that fact. On the other hand, German victories at sea and on the Continent continued to multiply, so if the British had actually shattered the German master codes and coding devices—especially for the Nazi submarine fleet—then the British high command was paying a huge price in lost ships and lives to keep that fact secret.

Meanwhile, all I had was the most basic Abwehr *Funker* (operator) code in front of me.

The basis for it was, I was certain, as simple as I had described to Hemingway. One or more of the books in Kohler's berth almost certainly held the key word or phrase that was the basis for each encrypted transmission. The grids were all preset for twenty-six squares across and five down, so it would be the first twenty-six letters on the appointed page of the appointed book. But frequently only parts of the twenty-six grid spaces across were used, the first word on the appointed page of the appointed book determining the number.

But which appointed page in which appointed book?

I knew that for the full twenty-six-letter encryption, the Germans had the habit of assigning one page of the book for each day of the year. That left Erich Maria Remarque's *Drei Kameraden* out—the little novel was only 106 pages long. I assumed that *Drei Kameraden* was the source for the "first word" that would decide how the grid was partitioned. But which page? That would have been sent in a coded signal prior to the actual translation. And did the encrypted transmission we had in the book relate to the twenty-six-letter code or the first-word code?

No matter, I thought. I had Kohler's jotted notes for the transmissions themselves: *h-r-l-s-l* / *r-i-a-l-u* / *i-v-g-a-m*... and so on. All I had to do was sort out which transmission went with which code based on which words or phrases from which books on which pages.

Ah, well. A hundred and six pages was finite enough...I would just substitute the first word on each of the 106 pages, block the grids accordingly, and see how the encrypted message played. First, though, I found myself sliding into the simple prose of Remarque—"*Meinen letzten Geburtstag hatte ich im Café International gefeiert...*"—and paying attention to the tale of automobiles, love, disease, friendship, and loss. I stopped myself sixty-one pages in—"*Und da kam sie, aus dem Gebrodel der Nacht, die ruhige Stimme Kosters...*" This was no time to read my first make-believe book.

Many of the first words could be discarded as too short—*Ich, Und, Die,* and so forth. Many of the rest—*uberflutete* (page 11), *mussen* (page 24), *Gottfried* (page 25), and so forth—started promisingly but led to nonsense when I tried to block the grid and transpose the transmission sequence.

By the afternoon of our dinner party with Helga Sonneman, Teddy Shell, and the mysterious "Kraut," I had gotten precisely nowhere. The Kraut was to stay in the guest house for a few days, so I helped Hemingway pack away our Crook Factory maps, files, dossiers, and typewriter—setting Kohler's codebook and the three German books in the safe in the main house—and then I packed up my own gear and carried it to Vigía–Grade A, *la casa perdita,* where Maria Marquez greeted my moving in with a raised eyebrow and a slight curve of those full lips. Xenophobia had been allowed to eat with the servants at the big house and to lounge by the pool in the afternoons when Hemingway was around to protect her, but today the *finca* was strictly off-limits and the girl was in a pouty mood.

I was supposed to run half a dozen errands in Havana before the Lincoln was due back at the farm. Whoever the Kraut was, Hemingway was going to the airport to pick him or her up at four-thirty that afternoon. I had two hours.

I stopped at the first pay phone. The voice on the other end of the line said, "Of course, Mr. Lucas. Come right up. We will be waiting for you."

The Nacional was the most expensive hotel in Havana. I had parked the car near the waterfront and walked several blocks, doubling back, darting in front of traffic, checking in shop windows, and generally using careful tradecraft to make sure that I was not being followed. There was no sign of Maldonado, Delgado, or any of the other parties who had been taking an interest in me recently. Still, I hesitated before going in the wide double doors of the hotel. Everything else I had done to this point might be explained to the Bureau. Omitting my primary role in the fireworks caper and holding off on reporting on the possession of the codebook until it was decrypted might be explained away if the rest of my mission was successful.

What I was about to do violated Bureau rules, SIS procedure, and interagency protocol.

Fuck it.

"Ah, come in, come in, Mr. Lucas," said Wallace Beta Phillips, at the door of Room 314.

There was another man in the room and it was not the driver from the other day, Mr. Cowley. This man was a professional, tall, slim, silent. He kept his jacket on in the dim heat. I guessed that it was a large-caliber revolver in his shoulder holster. Mr. Phillips did not introduce us. The hairless dwarf nodded and the other man went out onto the balcony of the suite, pulling the doors shut behind him.

"Scotch?" said the little man, pouring one for himself.

"Sure," I said. "A bit of ice."

Phillips sat on one of the gilded chairs and waved me to a place on the couch. The rumble of Havana traffic came through the tall windows and doors. I noticed that the hunchback's feet did not quite touch the floor as he sat. His shoes were brightly polished, his cream-colored suit as impeccably tailored and sharply pressed as the outfit he had worn in the car the last time I'd seen him.

"To what do we owe this pleasure, Mr. Lucas?" The ice clinked in his crystal Scotch glass as he drank. "Information to share, I hope?"

"A question to ask," I said.

The hairless man nodded and waited.

"Hypothetically speaking," I said, "would your interest in this Hemingway situation extend to offering some help in decrypting some radio intercepts?"

Wallace Beta Phillips showed no surprise. "Hypothetical radio intercepts, of course."

"Of course."

"Your Bureau has an extensive decryption department, Mr. Lucas. Failing that, they could always go through channels to Mr. Donovan or ONI, as they are wont to do."

I waited.

Phillips smiled slightly. "Or perhaps this hypothetical exercise involves less formal chains of command."

"Perhaps," I said.

"Pose the question, please," said the former Chief of Naval Intelligence for Latin America.

I sipped Scotch and set the glass down carefully. "Let's assume that someone found an Abwehr radio codebook," I said. "Standard grids per page. Several transmissions jotted outside the grids."

"One would need to know the books that operator had been using, of course," said Phillips, studying the amber fluid in his glass. The light danced on crystal and filtered through the whiskey.

"Yes," I said.

Phillips waited calmly. I noticed how dry and smooth his pink skin looked. His nails had been recently manicured.

What the hell, I thought. I was already in over my head. I gave him the three titles.

Phillips nodded again. "And the question, Mr. Lucas?"

"Any suggestions on how to find pages and key words?" I said. "The Abwehr changes the pattern frequently."

"Quite frequently," agreed the dwarf. He drank the last of his Scotch and set the glass down on the Louis XV end table. "May I ask how OSS or ONI cooperation at this point could benefit either or both of these agencies, Mr. Lucas?"

I made a gesture. "Hypothetically, Mr. Phillips, any decoded information that would pertain to COI... excuse me, OSS... or ONI operations could be passed along."

Phillips regarded me for a long moment. His eyes were very blue. "And who would determine whether such hypothetical information was relevant to OSS operations, Mr. Lucas? We or thee?"

"Me," I said.

Phillips exhaled and studied the pattern in the Persian carpet beneath his polished shoes for a moment. "Do you know the expression 'buying a pig in a poke,' Mr. Lucas?"

"Sure," I said.

"Well, I believe I am about to purchase a porcine in such a package." He crossed the floor, picked up my glass on his way to the bar, poured two more drinks for us, handed me mine, and walked to the tall window. "You know about the crackdown in Brazil?" he said.

"Yes."

"I believe the Abwehr does not know the full extent of the arrests or DOPS operations there," said Phillips. "Your FBI found it to their advantage to continue some clandestine radio traffic through the 'Bolivar' nexus, and Mr. Donovan's analysts concur that Admiral Canaris and his people have not yet discovered that Engels and some of his top people have been arrested."

I frowned. "I heard about the move against the Rio transmitter at the end of March," I said. "How could the Abwehr not know that their organization was compromised?"

Phillips turned around. His silhouette against the bright window reminded me of a diminutive J. Edgar Hoover. "Engels—code-named 'Alfredo,' you may remember—was among the first arrested in mid-March. But as I mentioned, his transmissions have continued."

I nodded. The FBI had pulled this trick before, continuing

sending classified information to the enemy in order to reap the benefits of the contact later. "It must be run straight out of the U.S. embassy in Brazil," I said. "None of the SIS traffic has carried this."

"It is," said Wallace Beta Phillips. "Do you know Special Agent Jack West?"

"No, but I've heard the name. Works under D. M. Ladd."

"Precisely. Agent West was dispatched to Brazil in March shortly after the *Queen Mary* incident on March 12..."

That "incident" had been when the Rio transmitter had broadcast the sailing dates for the British ship carrying nine thousand American troops.

"...and he personally oversaw the arrests with the Brazilian federal police in Rio and São Paulo," finished Phillips. "The Abwehr has received sporadic transmissions from 'Alfredo' since then, warning of increased police pressure, necessitating that the organization lie dormant for a while..."

"Not knowing that they're dormant in jail cells," I said. "But the Bureau can't continue that for long."

Phillips lifted a palm in a dismissive gesture. "Long enough."

I understood then. Long enough for Theodor Schlegel to leave on his Viking Fund mission without suspecting that Engels and his other comrades were either under arrest or being watched. Long enough for Admiral Canaris to be reassured...to what end? To continue whatever Abwehr project existed on or around Cuba.

For a second my blood literally ran cold. Both British and American intelligence services *had run the risk that German subs would torpedo the British* Queen Mary *with nine thousand U.S. troops on board rather than compromise this operation.* What the hell was going on?

I could simply ask Wallace Beta Phillips, but I knew that the little man would not tell me. Not now. Whatever my role in this labyrinthine game was meant to be, I would have to act it out myself before I found any answers. But Phillips *was* willing to buy his pig in a poke, risking more than I was. Obviously, ONI and Donovan's new OSS already *had* some or all of the German code if they were monitoring the FBI's 'Bolivar' and 'Alfredo' transmissions.

"What's the key?" I said. "Where in *Drei Kameraden*?"

Phillips smiled again. Unlike Delgado's leer, the hunchbacked dwarf's smile was quite pleasant, never taunting. "Since late April, the Abwehr and Schlegel have been using *Geopolitík* and the German literature anthology you mentioned, dear boy. I'm afraid that Remarque's book simply isn't in it."

"Then why did Kohler have it with him?" I said.

Phillips returned to his chair and hopped into it. "Perhaps he simply likes a good book."

"The page code?" I said.

"They are currently using April twentieth as 'day one/page one,'" said Phillips. "That was the day the key was changed, and I am aware of no further changes at this time."

"Books?" I said.

"My guess is that the word-based code is in *Geopolitík* and the alphabet-based key in the anthology," said Phillips.

I nodded, set my empty glass on the end table, and went to the door.

"Mr. Lucas?"

I held the door and waited.

"Do you happen to know the significance of April twenty?"

"It's Adolf Hitler's birthday," I said. "I didn't know that Admiral Canaris was so sentimental."

Phillips was still smiling. "Nor we, Mr. Lucas. We suspect that our friend in the harbor, Herr Schlegel, is the sentimental... if not to say simple-minded... one who suggested that date."

I turned to go.

"Mr. Lucas?"

The hallway outside was empty. I stood in the open door and looked at the tiny, hunchbacked figure, now standing in a trapezoid of rich light.

"You will be liberal in deciding what might be of interest to the OSS, yes?"

"I'll be in touch," I said, and went out the door.

I TOLD HEMINGWAY that I had to see the codebook and reference books again. The writer was bustling around, tying his tie and preparing for the trip to the airport, but he opened the safe for me.

"You can't work on that in the guest house," he said. "The Kraut's staying there tonight."

"I'll take them to Grade A," I said.

"Don't let Xenophobia see what you're doing."

I stared at him. Did Hemingway think that I was a fool?

"Oh...and Helga and Teddy Shell are coming earlier than six-thirty," he said, pulling on a linen jacket. Gellhorn brushed past us in the hallway, called for Juan the chauffeur to hurry up, and told Hemingway to hurry up in the same tone she had used for the chauffeur. The writer paused by a mirror to run his palms over his slicked-back hair. Whoever the Kraut was, Hemingway wanted to make an impression.

"We're going to have a little party by the pool before the cocktail hour," said Hemingway, "although there'll be cocktails enough by the pool as well. Bring swim trunks if you have them."

"Swim trunks?"

Hemingway showed all of his teeth in a wide grin. "I was talking to Helga on the phone this afternoon. She was delighted to learn that we have a pool. It seems that she just learned that there are sharks in the waters around Havana Bay...and she likes to swim."

"Ernest!" It was Gellhorn's shout from the car. "I swear to God, you won't let me get my makeup on and then you keep me waiting."

"Good luck with those," said Hemingway, handing me the four books as if in afterthought before he jogged out to the waiting Lincoln.

I walked up to *la casa perdita*, wondering where I was going to exile Xenophobia while I decrypted the Nazi radio transmissions.

14

THE THREE WOMEN in their swimsuits were not hard to look at. Martha Gellhorn wore a white, one-piece, elastic suit with piping around the bodice. Helga Sonneman had on a two-piece cotton swimsuit with stripes on both the halter top and the shortslike lower piece. Marlene Dietrich wore a trim suit of a navy blue so dark as to appear almost black. In body types, they ran from Sonneman's athletic but lush, almost luscious, Germanic fullness, through Gellhorn's American mixture of sharp lines and soft curves, to Dietrich's angular eroticism.

I had not been overly surprised when the "Kraut" turned out to be another movie star... this one in particular, actually. What little I had known about Hemingway a few weeks before included his friendship with this woman. I did not go to the movies that often, but when I did, I usually chose westerns or gangster pictures. I had seen Dietrich in that Jimmy Stewart movie—*Destry Rides Again*—just before Hitler had invaded Poland. I usually liked Jimmy Stewart, but I had not liked that movie very much; it seemed to be making fun of other westerns, and the Dietrich character, although speaking in her thick, German accent, was called "Frenchy." It seemed silly. Then I had seen her last summer in *Manpower*—a forgettable tough-guy movie starring two of my favorite tough guys, Edward G. Robinson and George Raft. Her character had seemed weak, almost superfluous, in that movie, and all I remembered of her were scenes where she showed her legs—still shapely even though she must have been forty years old by then—and a scene where she was cooking up a storm in a small kitchen. While sitting in the Mexico City theater, thinking of other things and ignoring the Spanish subtitles, I had realized—*She's really cooking that stew.*

Before I could go to the pool party, I'd needed to hide the codebook and reference books. Using Wallace's system, it had taken me less than fifteen minutes to find the reference words, block the grids accordingly, and work the codes. I was eager to show the result to Hemingway, but when I walked over to the *finca*, the writer was busy showing his home to his guests, and I thought that it was less than a good idea to bring the codebook to him in front of Teddy Shell, aka Theodor Schlegel, the man who had almost certainly hired Martin Kohler to send and receive those secret transmissions.

I couldn't leave the books in the dairy cottage. There had been no problem with Xenophobia when I arrived earlier; she was simply gone. The young whore was not supposed to wander off by herself, but she had been upset by being excluded from the *finca* all day, and I could only guess that she was wandering around the hillsides or even as far as San Francisco de Paula, down the hill. I hoped to hell that she had not gone into one of the bars or stores in that village, since both the National Police and Schlegel's people were reported to be looking for the girl, and the friendly villagers were almost certainly frightened enough of *Caballo Loco* to tell his people what they wanted to know. Not to mention that Schlegel's bribes would find eager tongues in that poor village.

I told myself that Maria Marquez was not my problem. My problem was finding a secure place for these books, especially the codebook, until this stupid party was over and I could talk to Hemingway. Picking up my books and notes, I changed into swimming trunks, wrapped the books in the checkered cloth from the counter, carried them in the back entrance to the *finca* while everyone was laughing and splashing out by the pool, opened Hemingway's safe—I had watched intently from across the room when he had opened the little safe that afternoon—

and locked the books away before going out to meet the Abwehr spy, the keeper of ancient artifacts, and the movie star.

IT WAS OBVIOUS that Dietrich had never been to the *finca* before. Earlier, I had caught the tail end of the twenty-five-cent tour of the house, with Helga Sonneman making polite comments but obviously put off by the animal trophies, Theodor Schlegel sipping his drink between polite grunts, but Marlene Dietrich exclaiming over everything—the hunting trophies, the books, the artwork, the long, cool rooms, Hemingway's writing place at the tall bookcase near his bed, everything. Her German accent was almost, not quite, as thick as I had heard it in the movies, but there was something much more relaxed and friendly about her tone than I had ever picked up sitting in a theater.

Now, as the women swam, the three of us men sat by the poolside, drinks in hand. Hemingway looked tan and comfortable in a much-washed yellow T-shirt and trunks so faded that I could not even guess at their original color, and Theodor Schlegel—I could not think of him as "Teddy Shell"—looked hot and uncomfortable in a high-collar, white dinner jacket, black bow tie, straight black dress trousers, and shiny black pumps. There is something proprietary in the act of three men watching three scantily clad women swim, and there was no question that Schlegel watched Helga Sonneman with a possessive eye. Hemingway was in good form, telling jokes, laughing at Schlegel's weak excuses for wit, calling to Gellhorn and Dietrich in a bantering way, and carrying drinks to poolside for Sonneman whenever the blonde surfaced. His possessiveness seemed to include both his wife and the actress, and possibly even Sonneman.

It was interesting to see Hemingway around women. It helped me to understand him a bit. On one hand, the writer was formal, almost shy, with females—even around the whore, Maria. He paid attention when they spoke, rarely interrupted—even when his wife was haranguing him on some point—and seemed truly interested in what they had to say. On the other hand, there was a slight aura of judgment hanging around Hemingway's dealings with the opposite sex—not the usual dismissive, locker room talk, in spite of occasional lapses such as the comment about "irrigating" his wife twice before breakfast—but in a sort of silent assessment, as if he were always in the act of deciding if this woman or that was worth his time and attention.

Obviously Dietrich was. Even after just half an hour of poolside banter, I could sense how ferociously intelligent the actress was, and how Hemingway enjoyed that. He seemed at his best around intelligent women—his wife, Ingrid Bergman, Leopoldina la Honesta, now Marlene Dietrich—and I had rarely seen that trait in active, charismatic men. Such men usually exhibited their strengths around other men and often seemed lost in the company of women—especially women not their wives. My uncle had been like that. I suspected that my father had. Not Hemingway. Whatever secret test he held for women to pass in terms of wit, appearance, conversation, and intelligence, it was obvious that Dietrich had long since passed it with flying colors.

Theodor Schlegel apparently had not passed whatever test Hemingway had concocted for men...or for secret agents, for that matter. Schlegel certainly did not look the part of the dashing German spy: a bland, round face under an almost bald scalp; a soft mouth; jowls; and basset hound eyes that looked like they might cry given only a small bit of provocation. His German accent was as pronounced as Dietrich's, but as sharp-edged and ugly as the actress's was soft and sensuous. I did admire the skill with which Schlegel had tied his neat bow tie. The agent's conversation with Hemingway had been as smooth and meaningless as that tie's knot—all silky surface.

Helga Sonneman spoke very little, but I was surprised to note that her voice held no hint whatsoever of a German accent. For someone who had been born in Germany and lived there until coming to the States for college, her lack of accent was remarkable. If anything, she held a very slight New England, upper-crust accent—not nearly as pronounced as Martha Gellhorn's Bryn Mawr drawl—modulated by New York City vowels.

I had been introduced as a guest and colleague of Hemingway's on his upcoming seagoing scientific venture, and that had seemed to satisfy everyone. I watched Sonneman's face very carefully as we were introduced—waiting for that telltale tightening of a muscle around the mouth or the inadvertent widening of her pupils at the shock of recognizing me as the fireman belowdecks—but there seemed to be no recognition there. If she was acting, she was a better actress than Dietrich. Of course, that was true of most real spies—we played our roles twenty-four hours a day, and often for years without interruption.

At about seven P.M., everyone except Schlegel went to their respective rooms to change for dinner. My last glimpse of the Abwehr agent before I jogged up to Grade A was of the bald man strolling through Hemingway's library, frowning at the titles as if they were somehow inappropriate and smoking cigarette after cigarette. I suspected that Teddy was nervous.

Somehow, Hemingway and Gellhorn had prevailed upon Ramón, the temperamental Chinese cook, to prepare traditional Cuban fare for dinner this night. Hemingway had told me that Ramón sneered at Cuban dishes, although the writer loved them. At any rate, the menu for this meal included *sofrito*—a paste of finely chopped onion, garlic, and green pepper sizzled in quality olive oil—for starters, then *ajiaco*, a country stew which included yuca, malanga, and boniato with *tostones*—refried wedges of green *plátano*, or plantain—and then more *plátano* on the side as *fufú*, a dish that Hemingway assured us had migrated from West Africa and which consisted of boiled plantain chunks sprinkled with olive oil and decorated with crunchy fried pork rinds.

The main course was roast pork—the bottom round *palomilla* steak which Havana gourmets loved best—with black beans, white rice, and more plantains. Spices I could detect included spearmint, cumin, oregano, parsley, sour oranges, and *ajo*—which was garlic in garlic with more garlic. I noticed that Schlegel's pale cheeks were growing more florid with each course, but Hemingway seemed to love the food and urged second and third helpings on everyone.

As always, the writer had chosen his favorite wine—Tavel, a French rosé—and poured for everyone, holding the bottle by the neck.

"Ernest," said Dietrich as he finished filling her glass again, "why do you hold the bottle such, my darling? It seems so clumsy for such a graceful man."

Hemingway only grinned. "The bottles by the neck," he said. "Women by the waist." And he refilled Sonneman's and Schlegel's glasses. Gellhorn and I signified that we were satisfied with what was left in our glasses.

We were at the dining room table, with Hemingway at one end, Gellhorn at the other, Dietrich at the writer's right-hand side, Schlegel across from the actress on Hemingway's left, Sonneman across from me at Gellhorn's right. As was always the case when I had been at the writer's table, conversation flowed even more freely than the wine, helped along but rarely dominated by either Hemingway or his wife. There was a good feeling at Ernest Hemingway's table, a flow of energy from the writer to all those around him, and this was true even when one of his guests was a pasty-faced spy and another a mystery woman with Nazi connections. Dietrich was obviously very fond of both Hemingway and Gellhorn—especially of Hemingway—and her energy matched that of the writer's without ever being overbearing.

All of the essentials of Schlegel's and Sonneman's reasons for being in Havana with their yacht had been discussed by the pool. All of the mandatory admirations of Dietrich's performances had been offered and brushed away by the actress. Sonneman and Gellhorn had engaged in some good-natured banter about their alma maters—evidently some rivalry existed between Bryn Mawr and Wellesley College. In the end, the two women agreed that for too many female students at each institution, the schools existed as a sort of breeding farm for future wives of Harvard, Princeton, and Yale men. Conversation had then turned to the food, the political situation, the strange energy of Cuba in general and Havana in particular, and the war.

"This dinner, Ernest and Martha," said Dietrich. "It is like a meeting of the Bund, yes?"

Schlegel blanched. Sonneman looked quizzical.

"All of us Germans," said the actress. "I would not be surprised if the FBI was peering in from the kitchen."

"That's only Ramón," said Hemingway with a chuckle. "He's checking to see if we actually eat this Cuban stuff."

"This Cuban stuff is delicious," said Sonneman with a smile

not unlike Ingrid Bergman's. "The best I've had since we arrived."

After the somewhat uncomfortable moment had passed, Hemingway began to question Helga Sonneman on the goals of the *Southern Cross*'s archaeological expedition to South America. She led him on a lively and exceedingly intelligent overview of the empire-building era of the pre-Colombian Incans. They would search for new ruins near the Peruvian coast.

My eyes had begun to glaze over with this lecture, but Hemingway seemed fascinated. "Didn't the Incas have a policy of resettling conquered people throughout their empire?" he said. "Moving ethnic groups around?"

Sonneman sipped her wine and smiled at the writer. "You *do* know your Incan history, Mr. Hemingway."

"Ernest," said the writer. "Or Ernesto. Or Papa."

Sonneman laughed softly. "Yes, Papa. You are right, Papa. From Viracocha's day to the Spanish conquest in 1532, the Incans resettled conquered people around their empire."

"And why did they do that?" asked Gellhorn.

"To provide stability," said Sonneman. "To make revolt that much more difficult by distributing ethnic groups."

"Perhaps that is what Hitler will do with conquered Europe," suggested Hemingway mildly. The war news this week had been bad.

"Yes," said Schlegel, enunciating carefully. "It is possible that the Germans will do just that when they subjugate the Slavic peoples and the Soviet empire."

Dietrich's lovely eyes flashed. "Oh, Herr Shell? Do you believe that the Russian people will be beaten so easily? That the Germans are invincible, perhaps?"

Schlegel reddened further and shrugged. "As I mentioned earlier, madam, I am Dutch by birth. My mother was German, yes, and we used that language much at home, but I hold no allegiance to either Germany or its myth of invincibility. But certainly the news from the eastern front has suggested that the Soviets do not have much time left."

"And last year," said Dietrich, "it seemed that was true of England, but the British flag still waves."

Hemingway refilled glasses. "But their convoys are taking a terrible beating, Marlene. No island can wage war if its sea-lanes are cut."

"Are the wolf packs taking such a toll in these southern waters?" asked Sonneman brightly. "We heard tales before sailing from Nassau, but..." She trailed off.

Hemingway shook his head. "No wolf packs this far south, Daughter. The U-boats hunt in packs in the North Atlantic, but down here it's the solitary submarine stalking the merchant ships. And yes, ships are going down at an alarming rate. About thirty-five per week, I'm told at the embassy. I'm surprised that your captain isn't more alarmed at the possibility of being sunk by a Nazi sub...or at least boarded."

Schlegel cleared his throat. "We are a peaceful scientific expedition ship composed of civilians," he said formally. "No submarine would bother us."

Hemingway chuckled. "Don't be too sure, Teddy. One look through a periscope at that destroyer-sized yacht of yours and your curious German sub commander just might come up for a look-see and sink you out of sheer pique." The writer looked at Sonneman again. "But of course I hope not," said Hemingway, "since your ship will be research headquarters and hotel while you hunt for those ruins."

"Precisely," said Sonneman. "And a very comfortable hotel it is." She drew one shapely finger down the tablecloth as if drawing a map. "The Incans left more than twenty-five hundred miles of road along the coast and an equal length of highway heading inland. Our hope is to find one of the lost cities in the southern reaches of that coastal highway." She smiled. "And even though the Viking Fund is a nonprofit organization, there is much money to be made if certain artifacts are discovered."

"Pottery?" said Gellhorn. "Artwork?"

"Some pottery," said Sonneman. "But the most exciting thing...May I tell them about the Toledo tapestry, Teddy?" she said with a glance at Schlegel.

It was obvious that Schlegel had no idea what she was talking about. After a judicious moment, he said, "Yes, I believe that would be permissible, Helga."

Sonneman leaned forward. "Viceroy Toledo wrote to Phillip the Second—the letter is still in the Archives of the Indies and I have a copy—saying that he was sending back to Spain four gigantic cloths, huge maps of his Andean realm, the beauty and richness of which exceeded all the tapestries and cloths hitherto seen in Peru or the Christian world. The letter arrived, but never the textiles."

"And you think it might be in the jungles of Peru?" said Dietrich with wonder in her voice. "Would not cloth rot in such a climate?"

"Not if packaged properly and buried deeply," said Sonneman, her voice almost vibrating with enthusiasm.

"Enough, please, Helga," said Schlegel. "We must not bore our hosts with our little interests."

Ramón and two of the serving girls came in with flaming desserts. After traditional Cuban fare, the Chinese cook had not been able to resist his instincts for elaborate dessert: in this case, Baked Alaska.

"SO WHY CUBA?" repeated Hemingway over dessert. "Why bring your exploration ship here?"

"The ship was fitted and modified on the Atlantic seaboard," said Schlegel stiffly. "The captain and crew are conducting sea trials while the scientists refine their equipment and search techniques. Currently we are repairing some damage... to the driveshaft, I believe. Within the month, we should sail for Peru."

"Via the Canal?" said Gellhorn.

"Naturally," said Schlegel.

Hemingway sipped his wine. "So how long did the Incan Empire last, Miss Sonneman?"

"Please call me Helga," said the blonde. "Or 'Daughter,' if that pleases you. Although you are only ten years or so my senior, I think, Ernest."

The writer showed his winning smile. "Helga it is."

"To answer your question, Ernest," said Sonneman, "one might say that the true Incan dynasty lasted only about two centuries—from perhaps the early fourteenth century, during the expansion of Capac Yupanqui, to 1532, when Pizarro returned with his small army to conquer their empire. The area then stayed under Spanish control for more than three hundred years."

Hemingway was nodding. "A few hundred Spanish in armor defeating... how many Incas, Helga?"

"At the time the Spanish arrived," said Sonneman, "it is estimated that the Incas controlled more than twelve million people."

"Good God," said Dietrich. "To think that so many could be overthrown by so few invaders."

Hemingway gestured with his dessert fork. "I still can't help but think of our friend Hitler. He plans a thousand-year Reich, but I wonder if this year might not be the high-water mark for his little empire. There's always some tougher son of a bitch coming along... like the Spaniards for the Incas."

Schlegel stared stonily. Sonneman smiled and said, "Yes, but we know that the Spanish arrived during another struggle for succession to the Incan throne... and during a time when disease was ravaging the empire. Even the amazing system of Incan highways... much more advanced than anything in Europe, I might add... helped the Spanish in their conquest."

"Like Hitler's autobahns?" said Hemingway with another grin. "My guess is that Patton will be driving Sherman tanks down those fancy German highways in two or three years."

Schlegel was obviously uncomfortable with this entire line of discussion. "I think that perhaps the Germans will be too busy fighting the Communist hordes to worry about expansion," he said softly. "I am not, of course, sympathetic with Nazi aims, but it must be admitted that in many ways Germany is fighting for Western civilization in its battle with the Slav descendents of Genghis Khan."

Marlene Dietrich hooted. "Mr. Shell," she said sharply, "Nazi Germany knows *nothing* about Western civilization. Trust me, I know this. The Russians you so despise... our allies... let me tell you, Mr. Shell, I have a mystical link with those Russians. There were many of them in Berlin when I was young. They had fled there after the revolution. I loved their enthusiasm, those brave Russians, their vigor, the way in which they could drink all day and all night without losing consciousness—"

"Here, here," said Hemingway.

"Toasts all day long!" said Dietrich, her voice rich with German accent and feeling. She raised her glass of wine. "Tragic children...that is what the Russian people are, Mr. Shell. Noel Coward said of me not long ago, 'She is a clown and a realist.' You have there a perfect definition of the Russian soul, Mr. Shell. In that sense, I am more Russian than German. And just as I would never surrender to Nazi beasts, neither shall the Russian people!"

She drank the last of her wine and Hemingway joined her in the silent toast. I wondered what J. Edgar Hoover would make of this conversation. Someday I should look at Dietrich's O/C file.

"Yes," said Schlegel, glancing around the table as if seeking support, "but surely you...certainly you must..."

"The Nazis know *nothing* of Western civilization," repeated Dietrich, her smile still pleasant but her voice sharp. "The Nazi hierarchy consists of degenerates...impotent perverts...vicious homosexuals...I am sorry, Martha. This is not dinner table talk."

Gellhorn smiled. "At *our* table, any abuse of Nazi Germany is acceptable and encouraged, Marlene. Pray continue."

Dietrich shook her head. Her blond coiffure fell forward around her sharp cheeks, then snapped back along her neck. "I am finished, except that I wish to know the Spanish word for such perverts, Ernest?"

Hemingway was looking at Schlegel as he answered. "Well, there's the standard word for 'queer,' of course—*maricón*—but Cubans use that to refer to homosexuals who are passive. The dominant homosexuals are called *bujarones,* meaning something like the word *butch* applied to lesbians."

"My," said Gellhorn, "the conversation *is* deteriorating isn't it?"

Hemingway gave her a flat look. "We're still talking about Nazis, my dear."

Dietrich's smile was as pleasant as before. "And which term, dear Ernest, would be the more insulting?"

"*Maricón,*" said the writer. "The local code of *machismo*

would have even more contempt for a passive, feminine homosexual. The word connotes weakness and cowardice."

"Then it is *maricón* that I shall reserve for the Nazis," said Dietrich with an air of finality.

"Well," said Martha Gellhorn, and paused.

Well, I thought. *Interesting.* Dinner with an Abwehr agent—most probably *two* agents—but most definitely with the half sister of Hermann Goering's wife... If all this talk of *maricónes* and perverts was upsetting Helga Sonneman, she certainly showed no sign of it. Her smile was as fresh and seemingly sincere as ever, as if she were being amused by a private joke—although whether the joke was all this crude talk about her Nazi acquaintances or "Teddy Shell's" growing unease, or both, it was difficult to tell.

Gellhorn had begun talking, discussing her own travel plans for the coming weeks.

"I'll be going to St. Louis next week to visit my family," Gellhorn was saying. "But later in the summer... probably in July... I've arranged an interesting project."

Hemingway's head snapped up. It was my guess that this was the first he had heard of this interesting project.

"*Colliers* is willing to pay me to go on a six-week fact-finding cruise around the Caribbean," said Gellhorn. "The islands in wartime and all that rot. There's a thirty-foot sloop they're willing to hire for the trip and even pay three Negro crewmen to travel with me."

"That's my wife!" boomed Hemingway in a strong voice that I heard as being a bit hollow. "Planning to spend our summer sailing around the islands with three Negroes. Thirty-five ships sunk a week and it's bound to get worse. Is *Colliers* paying for the insurance policy, Marty?"

"Of course not, darling," said Gellhorn with a return smile. "They know that the U-boats would never harm the wife of such a famous writer."

Dietrich leaned closer to Gellhorn. "Martha, darling, it sounds wonderful. Fascinating. But a thirty-foot boat... it is small for a six-week journey, yes?"

"Yes," answered Hemingway, rising to bring a bottle of

brandy back to the table. "Eight feet shorter than our own *Pilar.*" He stood holding the bottle by the neck and looked at Gellhorn as if he wished it were her neck in his hand. "Patrick and Gigi are coming in July, Marty."

Gellhorn looked up at him. Her gaze was not quite defiant but definitely unflinching. "I know that, Ernest. I'll be here for the beginning of their visit. And you've said for years that you wanted more time alone with them."

The writer nodded solemnly. "Especially with this goddamn war closing in." He seemed to shake himself from his low mood. "Enough of this dark talk. Shall we have our brandy out on the terrace? It's a clear night, and the breeze will keep the mosquitoes away."

GELLHORN AND DIETRICH HAD GONE BACK in the house to look at something. Schlegel was smoking a cigarette in moody silence, the long, black cigarette holder adding to his Prussian aristocrat image. Sonneman sat close to Hemingway in the comfortable wooden chairs. It had rained earlier, and the night smelled of wet grass, moist palm fronds, dripping mango trees, and the distant sea. The stars were bright, and we could see lights far below the hill. We could also see lights up the hill from us... and hear laughter and the sound of a piano.

"Damn that Steinhart," muttered Hemingway. "Another party. I *warned* him."

Oh, Christ, I thought.

But this time Hemingway did not call for the bamboo tubes and the fireworks. Instead, he suddenly said, "We'll be doing some scientific research this summer."

"Oh?" said Sonneman, her eyes sparkling even in the faint light of the candles in hurricane lamps set around the patio. "What kind of research, Ernest?"

"Oceanographic," said Hemingway. "The American Museum of Natural History has asked us to do some studies of currents, depths, migratory habits of marlin... that sort of thing."

"*Really?*" said Sonneman, glancing at Schlegel, who appeared drunk. She swirled the last of her brandy in the big glass and said, "I have several friends at the American Museum. Who is it that authorized this fascinating research, Ernest? Was it Dr. Herrington, or perhaps Professor Meyer?"

Hemingway smiled, and I realized that he was also quite drunk. The writer never showed the effect of the day's drinking in his speech or balance or general mannerisms, but I realized that enough alcohol made him mean and a bit reckless. It was a fact that I took note of. "Damned if I remember, Daughter," he said smoothly. "It was Joe here they sent down to work with me on it. Who authorized it, *Señor* Lucas?"

Sonneman turned the full radiance of her smile on me. "Was it Freddie Harrington, Mr. Lucas? It would seem to be his department."

I frowned slightly. Schlegel had roused himself sufficiently to glower at me in a sort of piggy insolence. I wondered if all the talk of *maricónes* and *bujarones* had hit a little too close to home for the soft, bald man. To Sonneman I said, "No, Harrington is in the ichthyology department, isn't he? Except for the marlin study, we're concentrating on oceanographic soundings, temperature readings, isobathic readings, chart updates...that sort of thing."

Sonneman leaned closer. "So it was Professor Meyer who found the money? He was always involved in their oceanographic program, as I remember."

I shook my head. "Dr. Cullins in cartography and oceanographic studies is the man who hired me."

The woman frowned slightly. "Peter Cullins? A short little man? Ancient as Methuselah? Tends to wear plaid vests that clash with his suits?"

"Dr. Howard Cullins," I said. "He's not much older than me. Thirty-two or thirty-three, I'd guess. He just took over the department from Sandsberry. I think Professor Meyer was in charge of diorama displays, wasn't he? He died last December, I believe."

"Oh, my, yes," said Sonneman, shaking her head at her own foolishness. "It must be the wine. I don't believe I've ever met Dr. Cullins, but I hear that he is famous for his cartographic knowledge."

"He published a book about two years ago," I said. "*The Unknown Seas*. A sort of history of seagoing scientific expeditions from the voyage of the *Beagle* to modern-day arctic explorers. It actually sold to the public."

"Cullins probably got my name from the ichthyologist Henry W. Fowler," said Hemingway. "I've been sending Henry information on marlin migration for more than ten years. In 1934, I took Charlie Cadwalader out on an oceanographic exploration from Key West. I've been dabbling in this stuff for years."

"Charles Cadwalader?" said Sonneman. "Director of the Museum of Natural Sciences Academy of Philadelphia?"

"The same," said Hemingway. "He loved drinking Tom Collinses while trying to land marlin."

"Well," said Sonneman, turning to squeeze Hemingway's hand, "good luck to all of you in your scientific mission. Good luck to all of us."

We drank the last of our brandy in toast.

JUAN DROVE SCHLEGEL and Sonneman back to the dock where a speedboat from the *Southern Cross* would be waiting. Helga had promised to come back for the *finca*'s Sunday soirée. There were hugs and handshakes. Theodor Schlegel roused himself from his sullen torpor long enough to thank his host and hostess for "a very illuminating evening."

I started to excuse myself, to leave the Hemingways alone with their actress friend, but Hemingway told me to stay. One more glass of brandy later, Dietrich announced that she was sleepy and was ready to turn in. Gellhorn led her down the path to the guest house, the two women still talking with animation.

When we were alone, the writer said, "Where the hell did you get all that stuff, Lucas? The American Museum stuff?"

"You'll find two very expensive long-distance calls to New York on your phone bill," I said.

"You're lucky," said Hemingway. "Usually it takes hours to get through to New York. If we can at all."

I looked him in the eye. "Why did you feel the need to play

that game? If one or both of them really works for the Abwehr, it was dangerous and stupid."

Hemingway looked down the path. "What do you think of her, Lucas?"

I was startled by the question, then realized that he had to be talking about Sonneman. "Helga?" I said. "She's very, very cool. If she's a German agent, she is twenty times the actor that Teddy Shell is."

Hemingway shook his head. "The Kraut," he said softly. "Marlene."

I had no idea why he was asking me for an appraisal of his friend. Then I remembered that the writer was very drunk. It was easy to forget with his measured diction and steady hands. "She's a lady," I said. "Very beautiful."

"Yes," said Hemingway. "She has that beautiful body... the timeless loveliness of her face. But you know something, Lucas?"

I waited.

"If Marlene had nothing but her voice... nothing but that... she could still break your heart."

I shifted uneasily. This sort of personal conversation was not part of our arrangement. "Do you want to..." I began.

Hemingway held up one finger. "You know," he said, still looking down the path where his wife and the actress had disappeared into the lighted cottage, "I'm never happier than when I've written something that I know is good and she reads it... and likes it."

I followed his gaze into the darkness. He could have been talking about Gellhorn, but I was sure that he was not, that he meant Dietrich.

"I value the Kraut's opinion more than the most famous critic's, Lucas. Do you know why?"

"No," I said. It was late. Dietrich was staying for the weekend, they had their damned parties ahead of them, and I wanted to show Hemingway the codebook and get some sleep.

"She knows about things," said Hemingway. "Knows about the things that I write about in my books. Do you know what I write about, Lucas?"

I shook my head. "Make-believe people and events?" I said at last.

"Fuck you," said the writer, but he said it in Spanish, softly, and with a smile. "No, Lucas. I write about real people, and the countryside, and life, and death, and matters of honor, and behavior. And I value the Kraut's opinion because she knows about those things... all those things. And she knows about love. She knows more about love than anybody you've ever met, Joe Lucas."

"All right," I said. I lifted my empty brandy glass from the wide arm of the wooden chair and ran my finger around the rim. "Do you want to see the codebook?"

Hemingway's eyes seemed to come into sharper focus. "You did it? You decoded it?"

"Yeah."

"Well, goddamn," said the writer. "What are we standing out here for? Marty will be down there gabbing with Marlene for at least half an hour. Let's go into the old kitchen and see what the Nazis were saying to each other out there in the sea and the dark."

We had retrieved the codebook and were almost to the old kitchen when there was a pounding on the front door. I slipped the book into my jacket pocket just as Hemingway opened the door.

Two policeman were standing there. They were keeping a tight grip on a squirming, struggling, protesting, weeping Maria Marquez.

15

HEMINGWAY ASSESSED the situation immediately.

In Spanish, he cried to Maria, "Where have you been? We've been looking for you!" Then he stepped forward and took the struggling girl from the surprised policeman.

These were not National Police, or even Havana cops. They wore the dirty uniforms of the provincial constabulary. One of the men had no cap, and his greasy hair hung down over his right eye. Both looked as if they had been struggling with a panther. The taller and older of the two straightened his rumpled uniform before addressing the writer in Spanish.

"*Señor* Hemingway, we regret to intrude upon your household at his time of night, but..."

"It is completely permissible," Hemingway said, still in Spanish. "We have been dining until only minutes ago. Come in. Please enter."

The two policemen stepped into the foyer. Both were glowering at the whore as if uncertain whether they should grab her again. But Hemingway had his right arm linked under Maria's left arm now, his big hand around her thin wrist, and he was holding her as if she were a skittish colt. The young woman's hair was wild and her face was lowered, but sobs still wracked her.

"*Señor* Hemingway," began the senior man again, "this woman...she says that her name is Celia. She was reported by people in San Francisco de Paula. It seems that she has been wandering there all evening...we found her sleeping in a barn belonging to *Señorita* Sanchez."

Hemingway was smiling at the policemen, but his voice was

hard when he said, "Is it against the law to sleep in someone's barn, Officer?"

The older policeman shook his head, realized that he was still wearing his cap, and took it off quickly, tucking it under his arm. Hemingway might have been a *yanqui*, but he was still an important man, a famous writer, a friend of many important people in Havana and in Cuba's government. "No, no, *Señor*... I mean, yes, it is technically a crime of trespass... but no, we are arresting this girl because the National Police have asked us to look for such a person. An Havana *jinetera* named Maria wanted for questioning in a murder..." The cop had used the polite word for "prostitute." He cleared his throat and began again. "This woman, she says that she works for you here in this house, *Señor* Hemingway..."

"Of course she does," boomed Hemingway, grinning at the policemen again. "She's worked here for months... although 'work' might be an exaggeration. Her mother said that she would be a good servant, but so far all the girl has done is mope from homesickness." He turned to the whore. "Celia, were you running away home again?"

Maria kept her face lowered, but she nodded and snuffled.

Hemingway patted her head affectionately. "Ah, well... a good staff is so hard to find these days, gentlemen. Thank you, Officers, for returning her. Would you care to stay for a nightcap?"

The two policemen looked at one another, obviously feeling control of the situation slipping out of their hands. "I think..." said the older one. "I mean, *Señor* Hemingway, we should probably bring this girl into Havana. I mean, the National Police warrant had said—"

"No need for that," said Hemingway, walking to the door. "If you drive her down there, someone will just have to drive her back here before morning. You've done your duty, Officers. Are you sure you don't want a small drink?"

"No, no, thank you, *Señor* Hemingway." The older man put his cap back on as the writer escorted them out the door onto the front terrace.

"Then you must stop by for one of our Sunday barbecues," Hemingway said expansively. "Mayor Menocal will be here this Sunday. Please honor us with your presences, Officers."

"Yes, yes, thank you," said both men, knuckling their foreheads as they backed down the path toward the gate.

Hemingway waved from the terrace, using his left hand to wave because his right hand was still locked around Maria's wrist. As soon as the officers' ancient car wheezed down the drive, he pulled Maria inside where I was waiting.

"You," he said softly to the whore, "please go in the new kitchen and sit there until we call for you."

Marquez nodded and went without a word.

"Maldonado will hear about this and come up here," I said. "To check it out."

The writer shrugged his large shoulders. "Then I will have to shoot Maldonado," he said. "It is overdue." He was still speaking in Spanish, even though I had spoken to him in English.

I OPENED THE CODEBOOK on the table in the old kitchen. No one else was in the house except for Maria, who could not hear through the walls and thick doors.

My notes were in the codebook, but I had not yet filled in any of Kohler's grids. I jotted the word *Brazilians* above the first grid and blocked out the appropriate spaces.

The grid looked like this:

B R A Z I L I A N S

"How did you get that key word?" he said. "And how did you know which spaces to block out?"

"It was the first word on page one hundred nineteen of *Geopolitík*," I said.

"How did you know which page to look at?"

"The preface to the transmission said that it was page nine and it was transmitted on April 29," I said. "They were using April 20 as their baseline."

"Why?"

"It doesn't matter," I said. "April 20 was zero. That's the one hundred and tenth day of the year. So 'page nine' is actually page one-nineteen. The first word on that page is *Brazilians*."

"All right," said Hemingway. "What about the blacked-out squares?"

"They assign numbers according to the key word—*Brazilians*," I said. "The first letter in the word is *B*—which is the second letter of the alphabet. So I blacked out the second space. In this case, they were using a simple alphabet substitution for numbers…*k* being zero and *x* being a dummy letter. The preface transmission was '*x-k-k-i-x*'…which translated as 'page zero-zero-nine,' which…starting from the April 20 zero point, was page one-nineteen."

Hemingway nodded.

"The second letter of *Brazilians*," I pointed out, "is *r*, which, not counting the letter *k* reserved for zero, is the seventeenth place. So I counted seventeen spaces from the first blocked-out square here in the second spot and blocked out another one. Then the letter *a* is the first letter, so—"

"I get it," Hemingway said impatiently. "Where's the code?"

I showed him Kohler's notes on the facing page. "Subtract the two opening groups of five," I said, "because they're dummies, then take away the page code '*x-k-k-i-x*', and the actual transmission for April 29 begins here." I pointed.

> *h-r-l-s-l / r-i-a-l-u / i-v-g-a-m / v-e-e-l-b / e-r-s-e-d / e-a-f-r-d / d-l-r-t-e / m-l-e-o-e / w-d-a-s-e / o-x-x-x-x*

"I still don't see…" began Hemingway, and then said, "Ahh…" as I began pencilling in the letters. "They go vertically," he said.

"Yeah," I said. "Columns of five."

I quickly filled in the rest of the grid.

"Let me see," said the writer.

B R A Z I L I A N S

H	■	U	M	B	E	R	T	O	A
R	R	I	V	E	D	D	E	■	■
L	I	V	E	R	E	D	M	E	S
S	A	G	E	S	A	L	L	W	E
L	L	A	L	■	F	R	E	D	O

He read the message aloud, but very softly. "Humberto arrived, delivered messages, all well, Alfredo." He looked up at me. "Who's Alfredo?"

"A radio operator's code name," I said. *Albrecht Gustav Engels,* I thought. *Formerly broadcasting from clandestine station 'Bolivar' in Rio, now residing in maximum security.*

"Kohler's, do you think?" said Hemingway in the voice of an excited boy.

"Possibly," I said. "But probably a land-based operator."

Hemingway nodded and looked back at the codebook, holding the book almost reverently, as if he were Tom Sawyer and this were a real treasure map. "And who's Humberto, do you think?"

I shrugged. Actually, the last dossier Delgado had brought me had covered that. "Humberto" was the Abwehr code name for one Herbert von Heyer, a forty-one-year-old Brazilian who had been born in Santos but who had gone to school in Germany and had been trained as Engels's assistant there. "Humberto" had been a go-between for Engels and our dinner guest that evening, Theodor Schlegel. They had arrested von Heyer two days after Schlegel had left on his Viking Fund mission.

"What else?" said Hemingway excitedly. "What's the rest of this code here?"

The facing page was covered with Kohler's tight script.

"All right," I said. "This next transmission referred to page seventy-eight."

"Of *Geopolitík*?"

"No, of that thick anthology of German literature," I said.

"This cipher prefix keyed on the first twenty-six letters on that page." I wrote the excerpt—"it took years for him to realize."

"Wait a minute," said Hemingway. "This is in English."

"Very perceptive," I said. "The original is *auf Deutsch.* Their last curve was to translate it before transcribing the code."

"Tricky bastards," muttered Hemingway.

I had to smile. This was the simplest code the Germans used—mostly for the convenience of their field operators in areas where they felt that monitoring would be very unlikely.

"Yes," I said. "Well, here they used a different cipher. I think it's because this *was* Kohler's transmission, sent on May seventh on the high seas. Those first twenty-six letters become the key group. Kohler assigned each of the letters a numerical value... one for the *a*'s, two for all the *e*'s, three for the letter *f*..."

"Wait a minute," said Hemingway. "What happened to the... oh, I see. There were no *b*'s, *c*'s, or *d*'s in the phrase 'it took years for him to realize.'"

"Precisely," I said. "So that phrase would be translated numerically as 5-12-12-9-9-6-13-2-1-10-11-3-9-10-4-5-8-12-9-10-2-1-7-5-14-2."

"Hmmm," said the writer.

"Now it does get a bit tricky," I said. "Kohler was transmitting letters in the same five-group clusters, but instead of starting with the first column down, the first transmission group would go under the first *a*. In this case, the *a* in *years*."

I circled the mass of Kohler's scrawl on the facing page holding the entire second transmission:

o-t-o-d-o / v-y-l-s-o / c-s-n-e-m / o-d-b-u-m / e-e-d-t-w /
o-y-r-t-d / e-s-i-a-a / b-l-r-e-r / n-i-f-t-i / s-s-t-b-r / s-d-o-i-a /
e-e-e-t-r / c-g-e-i-l / t-n-y-r-i / i-e-n-m-d / y-e-e-i-e / r-t-n-n-t /
n-r-f-e-r / t-r-c-n-t / g-e-a-m-o / v-o-f-s-e / r-s-d-t-i / i-o-a-e-n /
r-t-n-n-t / h-e-o-n-d / s-t-o-e-o

"I see," said Hemingway. He took the pencil and filled in the first five letters—*o-t-o-d-o*—under the first *a* in *years*. "Then this second cluster would go... under the next *a* in the message?"

"Yes," I said.

Hemingway jotted the *v-y-l-s-o* under the *a* in *realize.*

"And this third cluster," he said. "It should go under the first *e.* The next letter in the alphabet here."

"You've got it," I said. I watched as Hemingway quickly filled in the rest of the grid.

i	t	t	o	o	k	y	e	a	r	s	f	o	r	h	i	m	t	o	r	e	a	l	i	z	e
b	r	i	t	i	s	h	c	o	n	v	o	y	t	e	n	c	a	r	g	o	v	e	s	s	e
l	s	o	n	e	d	e	s	t	r	o	y	e	r	s	i	g	h	t	e	d	y	e	s	t	e
r	d	a	y	n	o	o	n	o	f	f	r	e	c	i	f	e	u	n	a	b	l	e	t	o	d
e	t	e	r	m	i	n	e	d	e	s	t	i	n	a	t	i	o	n	m	u	s	t	b	e	t
r	i	n	i	d	a	d	m	o	r	e	d	e	t	a	i	l	s	t	o	m	o	r	r	o	w

Hemingway read the message aloud, filling in the missing words as he went—"British convoy of ten cargo vessels and one destroyer sighted yesterday at noon off Recife. We were unable to determine its destination but it must be Trinidad. More details tomorrow."

He sat back in the chair and dropped the pencil on the table. "Jesus Christ, Lucas, this is for real. These fuckers are helping to sink ships."

I nodded. "We're only speculating that this was Kohler's transmission, though. Perhaps it's another broadcast from Brazil...or even from Cuba...that he intercepted. It could even have been broadcast from the sub we saw."

Hemingway was rubbing his cheek. "What about the rest of these code groups?"

I grinned. "Now it gets interesting. As far as I can tell, Kohler translated these either the day he was killed or the day before." I picked up the pencil, blocked the next grid, jotted down the key twenty-six letters, and filled in the columns at lightning speed: *"May 15—three agents landed, U-176, position: lat. 23 deg. 21 min N. long. 80 deg., 18 min W. All safe."*

"Me cago en Dios!" cried Hemingway. *"Estamos copados!"*

I had to blink at the vulgarity of the first part of that comment: "I shit on God! We're surrounded."

He ran into his office to get nautical charts. I walked the short distance to the new kitchen and peeked in on the whore. She was sitting meekly at the table, a glass of water in her hands. She looked up at me with red eyes. I nodded at her, shut the door, and walked back to the old kitchen, laying the codebook and notes out again.

Hemingway was spreading a map of Cuban waters. It was an old map with many notations in pencil and grease pen. "Here," he said, his blunt finger stabbing down. "That's about seven, eight miles southwest of the old lighthouse at Bahía de Cadiz Key. I know that fucking spot. It would be a perfect place to land enemy spies. The surf's not bad, and they could hike to the highway in twenty minutes. *God damn it!*" He pounded his fist down.

"There are two more transmissions," I said. I didn't even bother to block the grids, merely showing him my notes.

The first message read: "June 13, U-239, three agents"—and gave latitude and longitude. Then the cryptic: "Alum. Corp. Amer., Niag. Falls hydroelect., NY water supply."

"I think those are the targets for sabotage," I said softly. "The Aluminum Corporation of America. The big hydroelectric complex at Niagara Falls, New York. And New York City's water supply system."

"June thirteenth!" shouted Hemingway so loudly that I had to hush him so that the whore would not hear. "That hasn't happened yet. They must be trying to get to the States through Cuba. We can trap those bastards, sink the U-boat *and* the spies' raft! No, wait till they land and then grab them by the *cojones*."

He jumped to his feet again and pored over his charts. "Wait a minute," he said after only half a minute. "Those numbers are way off. This isn't in Cuban waters. Wait here."

He came back again with a large atlas. Opening it, he began flipping pages. "Here," he said at last. "Holy shit. Holy Mother of God. Christ on a stick."

I leaned over to see where he was pointing, even though I had looked up the coordinates in the same atlas before joining the pool party that afternoon. "Long Island," I said. "Interesting."

"Right near Amagansett," said Hemingway. He almost collapsed into the chair. "They can take a goddamn bus to Niagara

Falls and their other targets. Well, shit and damn. We can't intercept them ourselves, but..." He grabbed my wrist. "We have to get this to the embassy...to the FBI, to the navy, Lucas. They'll be able to grab that sub and those Nazi agents. Catch them in the fucking act."

"Yeah," I said. "There was one more message here. It just reads: 'June 19, four agents,'—and gives these coordinates. Those are southern waters, aren't they?"

"Not Cuban," said Hemingway, and began flipping pages again. He pointed. "Up here. The coast of Florida. Not far from Jacksonville." He ran his hand through his hair and slumped back again. His hair had been slicked down for the evening's party, and now dark strands stood up. "My God, Lucas. They're coming ashore like rats. We should take these to the ambassador now."

"In the morning should suffice," I said.

"Are there any more messages?" He looked at the codebook scribbles almost hungrily.

I shook my head. "But if Kohler's replacement doesn't change the code, we may intercept more at sea."

The writer nodded. "We'll have to put to sea immediately. Get Don Saxon on board to monitor the radios and direction-finding gear, and go trolling for subs."

"We'll have to figure out what to do with Maria," I said.

"What? Xenophobia? Why?" Hemingway brushed his hair back into place.

"I think you're right about Maldonado checking up on the provincial cops' report," I said. "*Caballo Loco* will be up here soon, sniffing around."

"We'll think of something in the morning," said the writer, still looking at the code grids. He suddenly grinned. "Hell, worse comes to worse, we can take her with us."

I thought that he was joking. "As a cook?" I said.

Hemingway looked completely serious as he shook his head. "Gregorio's our cook. The best any boat ever had. Xenophobia can mend socks and pass the ammunition when things get hot."

Christ, I thought.

Suddenly the writer stood and squeezed my shoulder very hard. "You did good, Lucas. Very good. I still don't know who or what you really are, but as long as you give the Crook Factory information like this, I'll be happy to keep you on." He took the codebook and notes. "I'm sleeping with these tonight. I'll drive down to see Spruille Braden in the morning."

I nodded.

"Good night, Lucas," said Hemingway, still grinning as he switched off the lights of the old kitchen. "Good job."

UP IN GRADE A WITH MARIA, we did not risk turning on lights. While she was in the smaller room undressing and getting ready for bed in the dark. I pulled the .38 pistol from its hiding place behind the loose bricks of the fireplace, checked to make sure that it was loaded except for the chamber under the hammer, and slid the pistol under my pillow. It was very dark out and starting to rain. I had dragged my cot into the outer room, but before I was under the covers, the whore was dragging her cot and blankets out next to mine. I frowned at her.

"Please, *señor*," she whispered. "Please. I will only lie here next to you. I will not touch you. I am so scared." She crept under the blankets. Her cot was less than a foot from mine.

"What the hell were you doing down there in the town?" I whispered harshly. "By all rights, *Caballo Loco* should be interrogating you now."

She began to shake. Her whisper was ragged. "I was so lonely. I was so unhappy. I went down there... I was not thinking. I could not go home. I had no money for a bus. I thought that I might find something... some way. I do not know, *Señor* José. I will not leave the grounds of the farm again, I swear on my mother's eyes."

I sighed and stared at the ceiling. After a moment, I heard a soft movement of her blankets and her small hand touched my bare shoulder. Her fingers were cold and still trembling. I did not reach up to squeeze that hand, but neither did I push it away.

Jesus, I thought as the rain pounded on the roof and the wind ruffled palm fronds outside. *And summer's just beginning.*

16

MAY PASSED AND TURNED INTO JUNE, and I became convinced that somewhere a noose was slowly but inexorably tightening. But which noose and around whose neck, I had little idea. The tropical heat grew from impressive to ridiculous, and when the trade winds did not blow, one's skull felt like it was being pounded by a hammer of sun glare against an anvil of blinding sea.

The was news from both theaters was mostly bad, with just enough reassuring facts to keep the fainthearted from despairing.

On the first day of June, Mexico declared war on the Axis.

"Well, that's it then," said Hemingway when we heard the news on the new shortwave radio on the *Pilar*. "Hitler and Tojo will probably throw in the towel when they hear this. All those divisions of crack Mexican troops should be invading Europe and the Home Islands before the month is over."

On June 4, the Japanese launched a huge attack at Midway Island. Everyone aboard the *Pilar* listened to the bare news reports of the fighting for four days; everyone except me had strong opinions about this new age of naval warfare. Hemingway insisted that the days of battleships and naval gunnery were gone, as extinct as crossbows, and that the type of fighting we were hearing about now—carriers launching aircraft to strike at enemy fleets from a distance of hundreds of miles—would decide the war. Evidently Admiral Ernest King, commander in chief of the U.S. fleet, agreed with Hemingway, because even while the outcome of the battle was in doubt, King admitted to reporters that the result of that battle would alter the course of the war. By June 7, the navy was claiming victory, but it would be months before we all realized how important and decisive that victory had been.

Also on June 4, word came from occupied Eastern Europe that a Czech patriot had assassinated SS Chief Reinhard Heydrich in that country. I knew from my black bag jobs at the BSC's Camp X in Canada that this "act of a Czech patriot" was actually a carefully planned British operation using Czech nationals. It had been William Stephenson's and Ian Fleming's idea to kill Heydrich. I was also not surprised when we heard on June 10 that the Nazis had destroyed the entire Czech town of Lidice and executed more than 1,300 of its civilian inhabitants in reprisal for Heydrich's assassination. The only reason given for the Nazis' choosing Lidice was that there had been a rumor that one of the assassins might have spent a night there.

And so the war progressed. By the middle of the month, Field Marshal Rommel was kicking British ass all the way across North Africa. The Japanese grabbed two islands in the Aleutian Islands and U.S. aircraft blasted six Jap ships along that Alaskan chain of islands. Despite Marlene Dietrich's inspiring words about how tough the Russians were, it was becoming obvious that the Germans were continuing to drive the Soviets back across the steppes and that Sevastopol, Russia's major Black Sea naval base, was on the verge of being captured.

On June 13, FDR authorized the creation of the Office of Strategic Services, consolidating and enlarging the authority of Wild Bill Donovan's former COI. I was tempted to send Mr. Wallace Beta Phillips a congratulatory card, but I had already sent Phillips the gift of the coded message regarding the British convoy—knowing that this was old material to Donovan's people, but fulfilling my part of the bargain—and when I had tried to call Phillips at the Nacional in late May, I was told that the little man had checked out and left London as his forwarding address.

IN NEWS MORE PERTINENT TO OUR EFFORTS, U.S. and Havana papers announced on June 29 that eight German saboteurs had been captured on Long Island by the FBI. This report turned out to be erroneous in almost every particular, but it was the first response we had heard from Hemingway's bold report more than a month earlier.

Hemingway had been disappointed about the lack of excitement surrounding his report. Ambassador Braden had been profuse in his praise, admiring Hemingway's covert operations and expressing certainty that the FBI and the navy would act immediately upon receiving and confirming the details. Colonel Thomason had sent Hemingway a coded note of congratulations through the embassy's diplomatic pouch. But there was an undercurrent of skepticism in both men's praise that infuriated Hemingway.

I handed my own report to Delgado and was not surprised when his only response after reading it was a slight rise in one eyebrow and a curl of his lip. It was a month later that I learned the details of the "saboteur arrest" through Delgado.

No German spies had been arrested on Long Island.

Despite Hemingway's report to the U.S. embassy and despite my report through Delgado directly to Director Hoover, the German spies had come ashore on June 13 without being interdicted or challenged by the FBI or the navy. Their landing would have gone unobserved except for their accidental encounter with a lone, young Coast Guardsman named John Cullen. This young man was patrolling an empty stretch of beach near Amagansett, Long Island, on the night of June 13 when he came across four men wrestling a large raft through heavy surf. Cullen waited for the men to come ashore. They assured him—with only slight German accents—that they were fishermen, that their boat had foundered, and that they were walking to town for help.

Cullen was not totally convinced. Besides the German accents and the fact that the four men were dressed like city civilians, there was the fact that one of the men apparently forgot himself and addressed the others in rapid-fire German. Also, the men were clearly armed with Lugers. Finally, there was the additional detail that in the predawn light the German submarine was plainly visible on the surface only some 150 feet from the beach, struggling to free itself from a sandbar.

The crack Abwehr agents did what any well-trained, cold-blooded spies would in such a circumstance—they offered John Cullen a bribe of $260, obviously all the folding money they had in their wet pockets at the time. With one eye on their weapons and another on the German U-boat, Cullen took the money and jogged back to his Coast Guard station, where his superiors promptly ignored his report for several hours. Had they believed him and acted before dawn, they would have found the four Nazi agents impatiently waiting for the 6:00 A.M. train at the Amagansett station of the Long Island Railroad and the U-boat still churning in a noisy attempt to free itself from the sandbar.

Eventually the Coast Guard did send Cullen and a patrol back to check on things. The agents were gone and the submarine had escaped, but they found signs of recent digging in the dunes and excavated a cache of high explosives, blasting caps, timers, fuses, and incendiary devices in the form of gift pen-and-pencil sets. There were also crates of German uniforms, brandy, and cigarettes. The Coast Guard officials responded to their years of training, put their heads together, and decided that these details were inconclusive. They would wait to report them.

Later that same day, the FBI learned of the landing from a Long Island police chief who had been watching the Coast Guard dig things up all morning. By mid-afternoon, the Bureau had sprung into action, sending half a dozen crack special agents to the beach to carry out a "discreet surveillance." Their discreet surveillance of the area was joined by that of approximately thirty civilians who had dragged beach chairs out to the excavation site to watch the Coast Guard finish its digging.

Meanwhile, the four German agents had taken the train to New York City and split into two pairs. They proceeded to get expensive hotel rooms and to eat expensive lunches. That same day, Director Hoover ordered a news blackout and put all of the FBI's field offices on full alert on what turned out to be the largest manhunt in the Bureau's history. But the Abwehr agents had disappeared without a trace.

"This," explained Delgado later, "is where it really gets good."

Two of the German agents—the leader, George John Dasch, and his partner, Ernst Peter Burger—had decided independently that they were not going through with their mission. Dasch had lived in the United States for almost twenty years before being enlisted by the Abwehr, and apparently his loyalty to Germany was not rock solid. Burger had just decided to take the $84,000 Admiral Canaris had provided for their mission and to make a run for it. Each had secretly decided to kill the other if he did not agree to the betrayal of the Fatherland.

The two men talked it over. Dasch took the money and went out to call the Bureau's New York field office to turn himself and his partner in. The special agent taking calls that day listened to Dasch's detailed report of their Long Island landing, of their mission of sabotage, and of the $84,000 they were willing to turn over to the FBI if someone would come and pick them up.

"Yeah," said the special agent, "and yesterday Napoleon called." And he hung up on Dasch.

Insulted but not discouraged, Abwehr agent George John Dasch packed the money in a suitcase and took a train to Washington so that he could meet personally with J. Edgar Hoover. After a long afternoon at the Justice Department of being sent from one office to another, Dasch finally was given five minutes with D. M. "Mickey" Ladd. Evidently, Ladd was as unimpressed as the New York field office agent had been and was in the process of leading Dasch to the door when the German agent dumped his suitcase of money all over Ladd's floor.

"Holy cow," J. Edgar Hoover's third-most-important assistant and the chief of the Domestic Intelligence Division is reported to have said. "Is this shit real?"

The Bureau interrogated Dasch for eight days. During that time, according to Delgado, the German agent spilled his guts about the Abwehr team's contacts, codes, targets of sabotage, and timetables. When the FBI's interest waned, Dasch went on to give extra information about Nazi war production, weapons' plans, and details of the submarine that had brought them to Long Island. He also told the Bureau about the Jacksonville, Florida, landing which Hemingway had predicted in his report.

On June 20, Burger and the other two agents in New York were arrested. They also sang like canaries.

Hoover waited for the Florida-dropped saboteurs to meet their assigned contacts in Chicago before he arrested all four of the German agents there on June 27. On the same day, he broke the story to the press, providing no details of how the FBI had broken the case. "That will have to wait," the FBI spokesman said officially and officiously, "until after the war." But, as Delgado explained, in a series of memos from Hoover to President Roosevelt and in a series of "off-the-record, background-only" briefings to reporters, Hoover gave the definite impression that a specially trained FBI agent (or agents) had not only infiltrated Abwehr command—and been trained at the same school of sabotage where the hapless German saboteurs had been taught—but had also infiltrated the Gestapo and quite possibly the German High Command. Hoover also let it be understood without ever having to say it aloud that he, personally, had been on-site on Long Island and in Florida to watch the doomed German agents land.

A month and a half after the landings, I asked Delgado what reward George John Dasch and Ernst Peter Burger were going to receive for turning themselves in, betraying their comrades, and providing all of this information to the Bureau.

"The secret trials have already been held," said Delgado. "All eight were sentenced to death. Six have already been electrocuted in the District of Columbia jail. For their service to the United States, Burger's sentence was commuted to confinement at hard labor for life, Dasch's to hard labor for thirty years."

"The director's getting sentimental in his old age," I said. Then I said, "What the hell happened to our reports? Hoover *could* have been on the beach, waiting for those idiots to come ashore."

Delgado shrugged, "I just pass on the shit you give me, Lucas. I can't make anyone read it."

EVEN THOUGH THE *SOUTHERN CROSS* would not be repaired and ready for sea until mid-June at the earliest, Hemingway began his patrols in the *Pilar* in May and began training his crew hard for longer patrols in June. Sometimes Hemingway would bring along his entire crew—his "executive officer," Winston Guest; first mate and cook Fuentes; Sinsky the Sailor, Juan Dunabeitia; Patchi Ibarlucia; the exiled (and, I thought, unreliable) ex-Barcelona waiter Fernando Mesa; Roberto Herrera; the U.S. Marine radio operator Don Saxon; and me.

I began learning the landmarks that all fishermen use to find their way. For us, an old house on the coastline near Cojímar was the sign that we were reaching the Hondón de Cojímar, an underwater abyss that provided excellent fishing. We called our landmark the Pink House or the House of the Priest. From there it was a little more than a nautical mile—what we called "Hemingway's Mile"—to the shooting range at La Cabaña, a fortress at the mouth of Havana Bay. Hemingway and Ibarlucia assured me that this area was thick with marlin when the current was strong, but we had no time for marlin on these "training cruises."

The Gulf Stream flows by Havana in an easterly direction, a great river within the sea some sixty miles wide and with a current that varies between 1.2 and 2.4 knots. It picks up speed as the sea deepens, and the water of the Gulf is a much more intense blue than the coastal waters around it. Onto that blue river cruised the garbage scows of Havana, heading to deeper water to dump their reeking heaps of refuse; around and behind those scows flitted hundreds of gulls and dozens of local fishing boats, all after the fish that fed on that garbage. Sometimes Hemingway would take the *Pilar* out at the end of that convoy—garbage scows, gulls, fishing boats, and us—the survey vessel from the American Museum of Natural History often towing its little auxiliary, the *Tin Kid*. "Look at it, Lucas," he called one hot, sunny morning. "The sea gives us everything—life, food, weather, the sound of the surf at night, hurricanes to keep things interesting—and this is how we repay her." He gestured at the tons of garbage being dumped overboard into the deep blue waters.

I shrugged. The ocean seemed big enough to take a little garbage.

Hemingway designated an area around Cayo Paraíso—Paradise Key—as our training base. We would haul stacks of fuel drums out for target practice. Instead of just dumping the things and practicing with the Thompson submachine guns and other weapons, the writer insisted that we paint faces on the drums—usually shocks of dark hair hanging over evil eyes and a Charlie Chaplin mustache. No wonder the crew began talking about taking out a cargo of "Hitlers" to practice on.

We often tied up near a buoy there and practiced with hand grenades. Patchi Ibarlucia and Roberto Herrera were the champions at this, throwing the heavy "pineapples" farther than I would have thought possible—and dropping them within a ten-foot circle more often than not.

"Right down the conning tower," Hemingway would call from the flying bridge, where he was watching the explosions through his field glasses.

There was a half-sunken freighter off the north point of the key, and here Hemingway would run boarding drills, closing quickly to grappling distance of the high side of the wreck, then throwing lines, and all of us boiling up from below decks, submachine guns and grenades in hand, going hand over hand up the ropes and dropping onto the tilted, rotting cabin of the freighter shouting "*Hande Hoche!*" and other pertinent German phrases until the invisible Nazi crew surrendered without a fight. Sometimes, though, Hemingway would indicate that the crew wanted to resist, so we would lob grenades and dynamite down hatches and then run and slide down the ropes like bloody hell.

On a much more realistic basis, we also conducted lifeboat drills—our lifeboat consisted of an inflatable raft given to us by the U.S. Navy. The raft was bright yellow and its oars were small, foldable, orange paddles. I don't believe I've felt or looked more foolish than during these lifeboat drills—eight or nine of us crowding into that idiotic little raft, paddling like fools against a current dedicated to taking us to Europe, each of us wearing our "scientific sombreros," wide-brimmed native hats that Hemingway had purchased for Operation Friendless, called "scientific" because *everything* aboard the *Pilar* those days was classified as "scientific" because of the stupid sign hanging from our bow.

"So this is where they take us prisoner and shoot us, right, Ernesto?" said Guest during one of these lifeboat drills.

Hemingway had only frowned, but once back aboard the *Pilar* and drinking cold beers, he showed us something. The document had been typed on thick, rich paper with an impressive letterhead:

OFFICE OF NAVAL ATTACHÉ AND ATTACHÉ FOR AIR
AMERICAN EMBASSY
HAVANA, CUBA

18 May, 1942

To Whom It May Concern:

While engaged in specimen fishing for the American Museum of Natural History, Sr. Ernest Hemingway, on his motor boat PILAR is making some experiments with radio apparatus which experiments are known to this Agregado Naval, and are known to be arreglado, and not subversive in any way.

[signed]
Hayne D. Boyden
Colonel, U.S. Marine Corps
Agregado Naval de los Estados Unidos, Embajada Americana

"This is our Letter of Marque," said Hemingway. "Just like in the old days, orders of marque give us a legal status... make us something other than spies and pirates... and will keep the Germans from shooting us if luck goes against us during our attack on their sub. The Germans are bastards, but they're finicky about legal niceties."

Hemingway had to explain at greater length what orders of marque were back in the days of sail and buccaneers, and all the while he was explaining, all I could do was stare at the writer and wonder if he actually thought that this piece of paper would save us from 9-millimeter slugs in the backs of our skulls if and when the German submarine crew captured us in the act of trying to sink their boat. Not for the first time, I realized that Sr. Ernest Hemingway not only constructed elaborate fictional worlds for his books but tended to live in them as well.

On some days, just Hemingway and I would take the *Pilar* out, and these days would be given over to exercises in navigation and radio operation. Hemingway was surprised when I told him that I could operate the coded shortwave radio and the direction-finding equipment. "Hell," he said, "we didn't need Don Saxon."

"You do on those days when you leave me behind to watch the Crook Factory," I said. Those days were frequent—about every other day—and I would spend them either traveling around to meet with the writer's "operatives" to receive their reports or sitting in the *finca* guest house receiving those reports from furtive visitors who arrived through the fields and hedges and departed the same way.

In the days just before the *Southern Cross* was due to sortie again, the *Pilar*'s log read like this:

June 12, 1942:	Patrolled to Puerta Purgatorio. . . . Return 5:30.
June 13:	Watch from 2 A.M. to 7. Out before daylight, patrolled 12 miles out until dark. In at 8 P.M. Win Guest went to Bahí Honda in auxiliary.
June 14:	Watch from 4 A.M. Out at daylight. 7:20. Patrolled until 1 P.M., then anchored inside at 4 P.M. with supplies.

That terse entry that said "Win Guest went to Bahía Honda in auxiliary" concealed some minor drama. Six of us had been aboard that day, searching for subs in an area where Cuban fishermen had reported sightings, when a coded radio message from the U.S. Navy had arrived ordering us to a point to pick up orders. The weather was bad that day—serious storm cells to the north and west of us, the seas rough with five-foot swells—

but Hemingway had dispatched Winston Guest and Gregorio Fuentes in the *Tin Kid* to make the crossing to Bahía Honda, where the secret orders were waiting.

"The weather's pretty shitty, Ernest," said Guest, bracing himself on the deck of the *Pilar* against the slapping waves.

Fuentes had said nothing, but his frown and squint toward the horizon conveyed the same message.

"I don't give a damn what the weather's like," snapped Hemingway. "These are *orders*, gentlemen. The first since we started this operation. Dead or alive, I want you back here before dawn with those orders."

The rich man and the leathery Cuban had nodded, packed some water and other provisions, and scrambled into the little boat. Later, they reported that the crossing had been as miserable as they expected and that they had not gotten into Bahía Honda until almost nine that evening, when they met with their American contact and received a sealed envelope in a waterproof pouch. Not opening the envelope—that would be Hemingway's prerogative—Guest and Fuentes had something cold to eat and slept a couple of hours before beginning the rough trip back to the *Pilar*.

At sunrise, Hemingway had taken the sealed orders and gone below. It was some time later that he came up and ordered Fuentes and Ibarlucia to weigh anchor.

"We're going back to Cojímar," he said, laying a chart across the control board on the main bridge of the *Pilar*. "Get some provisions. Lucas, you'll stay at the *finca* and run the Crook Factory. The rest of us have been ordered... here..." His finger stabbed down on the chart.

All of us craned to see. Hemingway was pointing to a series of keys north of Camagüey, an area off the northern coast of central Cuba where we had not yet patrolled.

"Lucas," he said during the choppy ride back to port, "besides minding the shop, you'll have to keep an eye on the *Southern Cross* and radio us as soon as she shows signs of heading out."

"Sure," I said. Whatever the details of his "secret orders" were, Hemingway was not telling me. That did not bother me, but I was sorry that I would be sitting ashore while the *Pilar* headed off on a real voyage. I liked the sea better than the farm, and as silly as some of our practice runs had been, any time at sea was more real than the Crook Factory business.

DURING THE DAYS the writer was gone, I ran the spy ring, watched over the whore, and thought about Ernest Hemingway. "Find out who he is" had been Director Hoover's order. I was not sure if I had even begun that process.

But as I waited on land, I thought of the Hemingway I had watched at sea.

There were, I thought, a few things that tested the true nature of a man. Being in a combat situation might be one, but I did not know, for I had never gone to war. My own battles had been private and hidden from sight, over in seconds or minutes, and survival had been the only award given. Dealing with a threat to one's family was another such test, I thought, but I had never had a family to protect...or to lose—since I'd grown to manhood, at least.

But the sea...this test I understood.

Hundreds of thousands of men go to sea, but to go out of sight of land in one's own boat as Hemingway did regularly, this was a more rare and challenging thing. One could see a man's mettle in whether he treated the sea with indifference or the respect it deserved, and whether his ego blinded him to the true power that surrounded a man or men alone on a wide ocean.

Hemingway treated the sea with an adult's respect. He'd stand on the flying bridge, his bare legs apart and braced without conscious thought against the pitch and roll of his boat, his bare chest brown with the sun, the dark hair there gleaming with sweat, his face stubbled with two days' beard, and his eyes hidden in the shadow of the long bill of his cap. *Hemingway paid attention to the sea.* There was none of his bully-boy bluster when it came to watching the weather, studying the currents and tides, heading in when even a hint of storm darkened the horizon or lowered the barometer, or facing that storm head-on when it was not possible to run for safe harbor. Hemingway never shirked in his boat... never failed to take the dog watch or the early watch, never begged off working in reeking bilge water or covering himself with grease at the engine or bailing shit out of the clogged head by hand if necessity demanded. He did what had to be done.

I had been six years old when my father died in Europe. He left home when I had just turned five. According to the two photographs we had of him, my father looked nothing like Hemingway. The writer was barrel-chested and bandy-legged, with a thick, bullish neck and a big head, while my father was thin and graceful, with long fingers, a narrow face, and skin that grew so dark in the summer that he was regularly called "nigger" by strangers in our Texas port.

But something about Hemingway at sea stirred up my few memories of my father and even more of my uncle. Perhaps the way he braced himself so gracefully or the way he carried on a conversation without ever relaxing his attention from the sea and weather around him. Hemingway was not a graceful man—already I had seen that he was prone to stupid accidents and that his eyesight was poor—but on the *Pilar* he moved with the grace given only to the true sailor.

I had begun to understand that Ernest Hemingway gave his full attention to the sea the same way that he focused his attention on what women—or at least women who interested him—were saying to him. And perhaps he did so for much the same reason: he thought that they had something to teach him.

And Hemingway learned quickly, that much I had already gleaned. In our conversation, it had become apparent that he'd had no contact with the real ocean as a boy and little as a man, except to cross and recross the Atlantic in large ships—first to go off to war as an ambulance driver, to return as a wounded veteran, to go back to Europe as a reporter, then to return as a married man planning to settle down in Canada with his wife, and so on. It was not until 1932 that Hemingway began going to sea regularly in a small boat, *Anita*, belonging to a friend of his named Joe Russell who lived in Key West. Russell had taught Hemingway the rudiments of navigation and boat handling—as well as running bootleg liquor, according to the writer—and then had introduced him to deep-sea fishing and the island of Cuba.

Recently, according to Ibarlucia and others, Russell had come to Cuba to visit his friend and had been treated like a beloved grandfather by Hemingway, who took the old bootlegger out on the *Pilar*, served him lemonade and kept asking, "Are you comfortable, Mr. Russell?" Hemingway had honored his old teacher, though the roles of teacher and pupil had long since traded places.

This, I realized, was another attribute of Hemingway's that tended to be overlooked and underestimated by those around him. The writer was one of those rare individuals who allowed others to introduce him to a passion of theirs—bullfighting, say, or trout fishing, or big game hunting, or deep-sea fishing, or appreciating fine wine or gourmet meals, or skiing, or reporting a civil war in Spain—and within years, sometimes months, it was *Hemingway* who had become the expert, who reported to others on the beauty and private aesthetics of whatever sport or activity had absorbed him and which he had absorbed in return. And then even his former teachers would bow to Hemingway's expertise, treating the obvious amateur as the expert he had become.

Hemingway was still a dilettante in espionage; so far he had been creating everything out of whole cloth. What would happen if I began tutoring him in the realities of the game? Would his playacting become deadly expertise in a matter of months? Would he begin to understand the intricacies of spying and counterspying the way he understood the deadly, indifferent vagaries of the ocean now?

Perhaps. But I had no reason to teach him. Not yet.

—

DELGADO WAS NOT SLOW to see the irony in my being in charge of the Crook Factory during the writer's first ten-day mission to the Camagüey archipelago. "You were sent down here to observe this idiocy," said Delgado. "Now you're running it."

I had no response to that. I was too busy to argue.

The *finca* was relatively quiet with Hemingway and his

friends gone. Pichilo, the gardener, puttered around in the flower beds and hedges, Pancho Castro, the carpenter, was hammering and sawing, building more bookcases and cupboards for the house, Ramón, the cook, could be heard shouting curses on occasion, and René Villarréal, Hemingway's chief servant, moved cat-quiet around the grounds, keeping the other servants on task and overseeing the compound in the absence of Roberto Herrera, the *finca*'s usual manager. Roberto was currently at sea with the boss.

All through May and early June, Hemingway and Gellhorn had continued their pattern of long Sunday parties at the *finca*. The gatherings were gay and crowded, with the usual people filling the grounds on Sundays—Ambassador Braden and his wife; a mob of Basques, including the usual core of jai alai players; contacts from the embassy such as Ellis Briggs, Bob Joyce, and their wives and children; some Spanish priests—often including Don Andrés Untzaín—as well as some millionaires, Winston Guest and Tom Shevlin were regulars, but also visiting yachtsmen. Helga Sonneman had attended two or three of the Sunday gatherings while the *Southern Cross* was being repaired, but Theodor Schlegel never returned to the *finca*. In addition, there would be colorful sorts who just happened to drop by and stay for dinner and evening drinks—Shipwreck Kelly, famous local fishermen like Carlos Gutierrez, and old friends who had crossed from Key West just to spend the day with the writer and his wife. Now the parties were in hiatus and Sunday afternoons were so quiet that I could hear the bees buzzing in the garden as I read reports in the guest house.

We had solved the problem of keeping Maria Marquez out of Lieutenant Maldonado's clutches by hiding the whore in plain sight. Xenophobia...I had begun to think of her by that nickname...still slept at Grade A, but during the day she worked at the *finca* as part of the domestic staff. Martha Gellhorn had insisted that the young prostitute never touch any of the food being prepared, but other than that restriction—and the fact that Gellhorn did not want to see the girl—Maria blended into the schedule and rhythm of work at the farm. When Gellhorn was absent—which she was much of the time in June, Juan

Pastor Lopez, the chauffeur, driving her off to Havana in the big Lincoln in the morning and not returning until late in the evening—Xenophobia was allowed to relax near the pool or wander the grounds between simple housekeeping duties.

Lieutenant Maldonado had not come hunting for the girl. I knew from the Crook Factory reports that the National Police were still looking for the missing Havana whore, as were some of Theodor Schlegel's Falangist contacts in Cuba, but I also knew from those reports that both Maldonado and the Abwehr agent were too busy to spend much time in personal pursuit of the murder suspect.

As I collated reports from Hemingway's operatives and began to take a more directive role in the operation, I began to appreciate the writer's spy network in a new light. There are two ways to create an effective espionage or counterespionage ring. The first and most common is to partition the field agents into "cells"—each cell autonomous and ignorant of the other cells, with those controlling the cells knowing names, contacts, codes, and mission objectives on a strict "need to know" basis. This was effective in the way that watertight compartments on a big ship could be effective: a breach in one or more of the cells could be contained and sealed off, allowing the ship to survive. The other way to create an effective group—especially for counterespionage—is to have everyone know one another. Such a cadre solves many security problems because it is almost impossible to infiltrate or subvert such a group and different agents can share information and objectives. Professional spy groups rarely use this form—the British Security Coordination group was an exception—because a breach of one of these watertight cells would sink the whole group.

But in the case of the Crook Factory, the motley arrangement was working astonishingly well.

It became apparent that neither Lieutenant Maldonado nor his boss, Juanito the Jehovah's Witness, was making much progress in finding Maria Marquez because they were too busy accepting bribes and running errands for both the FBI and German intelligence.

At first I was dubious of these conclusions, but as the Crook

Factory surveillance reports began to overlap and then re-overlap, a mosaic of *Caballo Loco*'s corruption became more visible. But none of it made sense.

It seemed from the reports that Hemingway's amateur operatives missed nothing in and around Havana. The bellman at the Hotel Plaza reported that Lieutenant Maldonado and Teddy Shell, aka Theodor Shlegel, had met six times in a suite Shell maintained at that hotel. Each time, the National Police lieutenant had left with a heavy briefcase. Twice, a girl who worked in the beauty parlor on the Prado had followed Maldonado to the Banco Financiero Internacional on Linea Street. Four other times, Maldonado was successfully followed from the Hotel Plaza to the bank by one of Hemingway's operatives known only as Agent 22. I did not know who Agent 22 was, but he was effective at surveillance, although his written reports were so poorly spelled and crudely done in pencil that it looked as if a ten-year-old was writing them. A former Spanish nobleman who now served on the board of directors for the Banco Financiero Internacional reported that Lieutenant Maldonado had no private account at that bank but that there was a special account set up under the name of Orishas Incorporated—literally, "Gods Incorporated"—and that Maldonado had deposited sixty thousand American dollars into that account, while his boss, Juanito the Jehovah's Witness, had deposited another thirty-five thousand.

Why was the Abwehr paying the Cuban National Police? Not protection money, I was sure. The Cuban police already looked the other way when it came to Nazi sympathizers and Falangist right-wingers and German agents in the country.

But then the FBI came into the picture. A Chinese waiter at the Pacific Chinese Restaurant twice had seen *Caballo Loco* meeting an American named Howard North in front of their establishment. The blind old man in the Parque Central knew the sound of Howard North's 1936 Chrysler and reported that it had headed northeast down the Prado toward the Malecón on both occasions. On that second occasion, our intrepid Agent 22 had somehow followed the Chrysler out Quinta Avenida to the port town of Mariel and then managed to get close enough to watch the National Police lieutenant and *Señor* Howard North walking alone on the empty docks there. North had given Lieutenant Maldonado a small, brown briefcase. That same afternoon, according to our contact at the bank, Maldonado had deposited fifteen thousand American dollars in the Orishas account. There had been an identical deposit on the date of the first meeting with Howard North.

Howard North was a special agent for the Havana field office of the Federal Bureau of Investigation.

I had not asked Delgado to confirm this fact. On Thursday of the week that Hemingway was in the Camagüey archipelago, I had brought the weekly report to Bob Joyce at the embassy and asked casually if there was a new FBI agent in town.

"How did you know about that?" said Joyce, looking at the sanitized report I had typed up for him. He looked up and grinned. "Raymond Leddy, the Bureau's top guy and our liaison here at the embassy, is quite upset about getting a new man. Special Agent North. Sent down from Washington ten days ago. I guess he wasn't asked for and really isn't needed…there are already sixteen agents here in Havana."

"Is Special Agent North here on some important business?" I asked. "I mean, don't tell me if it's classified, of course. I was just curious if it might relate to Hemingway's operation."

Bob Joyce chuckled. "I don't think that Special Agent North is going to be involved in any operation," he said. "He's some sort of accountant. That's why Leddy and the other guys at the Havana field office are ticked. They think that North was sent down here to go over their books…make sure all the pennies and pesos are accounted for."

"Somebody has to do it, I guess," I said.

Tens of thousands of dollars flowing from both Theodor Schlegel and the FBI to the Cuban National Police. What the hell was going on? One had to assume that the Abwehr's bribes related directly to the intelligence operation being run out of the *Southern Cross*, but what was an FBI accountant doing paying off *Caballo Loco* and his boss? And what made it more curious was that it seemed as if the local Bureau people did not know what was going on.

In the third week of June, just before Hemingway and his pals returned from their secret mission, I called in Agent 22.

It was Tuesday, June 23, and I happened to be at the *finca* sitting in the shade with Dr. Herrera Sotolongo and discussing the Crook Factory when Agent 22 finally reported.

The doctor knew about Hemingway's spy activities, of course, but he had refused to be enlisted in the campaign the way his brother had.

"Ernesto insisted," said the doctor, "but I refused. He had even chosen a code name for me—Malatobo—but I only laughed and refused again."

I laughed as well. A *malatobo* was a type of fighting cock.

"Ernesto and his code names," mused the doctor, sipping at his gin and tonic. "Did you know, *Señor* Lucas, that he calls himself Agent Zero-eight in this spy game he is playing?"

I continued smiling. I did know that Hemingway signed all of his reports "Agent 08."

"Why is it that you do not wish to participate in these activities, Doctor?" I asked. I knew that Herrera Sotolongo hated fascism more than most of the men who were out on the *Pilar* with Hemingway that day.

The quiet doctor set down his drink and surprised me by pounding his fist against the arm of the chair. "I won't be a policeman!" he said in adamant Spanish. "God damn it, I was a soldier and I would be a soldier again... Hippocratic Oath or no Hippocratic Oath... but not a policeman! I never liked police or spies!"

I had nothing to say to that. Then the doctor picked up his drink again and looked me straight in the eye. "And now Ernesto is surrounded by spies. Surrounded by people who are not what they say they are."

Returning the doctor's steady gaze with my own, I said softly, "What do you mean?"

Herrera Sotolongo swallowed the last of his gin and tonic. "This millionaire... this friend... Winston Guest."

I admit that I blinked. "Wolfer?"

The doctor snorted. "These nicknames that Ernesto awards us with. It is like a sickness. Did you know, *Señor* Lucas, that

Señor Guest has told Fuentes and the other less-educated members of Ernesto's crew that he, Guest, is Winston Churchill's nephew?"

"No," I said.

"It is true," said the doctor. "*Señor* Guest was a much-respected polo player in England. He was also a much better big-game hunter than Ernesto. You know that they met in Kenya in…I believe it was 1933?"

"*Señor* Hemingway mentioned that they met in Africa, yes."

"It is true," said Dr. Herrera Sotolongo, "that *Señor* Guest is *muy preparado*. You know this phrase?"

"*Sí*," I said. "Highly cultured. Well educated."

"More *preparado* than Ernesto knows," muttered the doctor. "*Señor* Guest is a spy."

"Wolfer?" I said again, just as stupidly as the first time. "For whom, Doctor?"

"For the British, of course. Everyone in Havana has seen him—"

That is precisely the moment when a ten-year-old street urchin in rags came up to us at the pool and touched his forehead in what I later realized was a salute.

"Yes, what is it, boy?" I said softly. I recognized the boy as the child who had run ahead of me to the Finca Vigia on my first visit there. If one of Hemingway's people was sending in a report via this child, I would have to call them in and give them a lecture on security and sanity.

"I am Santiago Lopez, *Señor* Lucas," said the boy. The child's shirt was open—it had no buttons—and his ribs were clearly visible. It looked as if he had not eaten for days. Whatever he wanted, I was going to send him in to the kitchen and tell Maria or one of the others there to make him a good meal before he went back to panhandling in the streets of Havana.

"Yes, yes?" I said, trying not to be cross with the child.

"You sent for Agent Twenty-two," continued the boy, his voice firm, although I could see his legs shaking slightly.

I looked at Dr. Herrera Sotolongo and rolled my eyes. Any hopes I had been harboring about the effectiveness of Hemingway's Crook Factory were evaporating with the fact of this child's being sent with a report.

"Could he or she not come in person?" I said.

"He or she did, *Señor* Lucas," said the child. "I mean, sir, I *did*. As soon as I received your order, sir."

I looked at the good doctor again, who returned my blank gaze with his wise but weary smile, and then I took Agent 22 into the shade of the ficus trees to question him further about the comings and goings of the murderer, Lieutenant Maldonado.

17

THE WEEKS THAT FOLLOWED were relatively uneventful ones for the Crook Factory, and rather seemed dominated by Hemingway's family matters. Later, however, I would look back on that June and July as a calm before a storm...and though I had no idea what—if any—storm was brewing, I remember every day as colored by the same kind of tension any sailor feels as he watches thunderheads massing on the horizon while racing for home.

Hemingway turned forty-three on July 21, 1942. I spent much of that night and the next talking with the writer in the cabin of the *Pilar*.

We had been out on antisubmarine patrol for six days. Hemingway's sons were aboard—Patrick and Gregory, or Mousie and Gigi, as he called them—but the only other crew consisted of Fuentes, Winston Guest, and me. For three days we had stalked the *Southern Cross* on its seemingly aimless and endless sea trials, monitoring the radios, occasionally hearing the static-lashed communications of sub captains talking to one another in German, us keeping in contact with the small base at Cayo Confites, and generally waiting for the Viking Fund yacht to make the first move. Then, on the fourth day, we lost the big ship in a serious storm. But following radio and direction-finder hints of a sub broadcasting from the vicinity of Key Romano, we turned in that direction on the evening of the fifth day.

Hemingway helped me with the tricky navigation as we approached Key Romano in the dusk. First we crossed the mouth of Punta Practicos until we raised the lighthouse at Maternillos on Key Sabinal. Then we cut the throttle far back as we crept through the treacherous Old Bahamas Channel. Fuentes stood on the bow then, keeping a sharp eye out for reefs and sandbars.

Once in the inner zone of keys, the way became a maze of shallow waterways—often drawing two feet of water or less—many of these channels turning into streams and shallow rivers that ran out from the key. In a small harbor there was the village of Versailles—half a dozen houses, most on stilts, and half of those abandoned. We anchored there at a point called the Punta de Mangle and spent three days exploring the inlets and channels in the *Tin Kid*, asking the few local fishermen if they had seen a huge yacht or motorboat in the main channels, and trying to triangulate on coded transmissions we were picking up.

Hemingway's birthday was as pleasant as we could make it while stuck on the *Pilar* on the ass end of nowhere amidst the mangrove roots and pepperbush forests. Patrick and Gregory had brought brightly wrapped presents for their Papa, Winston Guest presented Hemingway with two bottles of very fine champagne, Fuentes had carved a small wooden figure which amused the writer deeply, and we had a special dinner that evening. I had brought nothing for the man, of course, but I raised a glass of champagne in his honor that evening.

I remember the meal, which I'd watched the first mate cook. The appetizer was a spaghetti dish. Fuentes took an entire roll of spaghetti and broke it in half before dropping it into the boiling water. He had taken a chicken out of the icebox, and he cooked it in a special broth made with beef and pork bones. When the chicken was done, he strained the broth, took the crisp crumbs left in the strainer, and added the concoction to the chicken. Then he added salt and ground it up. Already the tiny galley was beginning to smell so good that I could have started eating right then.

Fuentes then took some Galician ham and chorizo—a type of Spanish sausage—and ground that as well. He mixed that with the ground chicken and simmering broth, added paprika, and cooked everything over the low flame on the tiny stove. Then he removed the spaghetti from the boiling water and served it with a few pinches of sugar. He poured the sauce into a separate dish, set all this on the table, and bellowed for everyone to drop what they were doing and get their asses into the galley to fill their plates.

While we were all eating this amazing spaghetti dish, Fuentes was finishing up the main course. We had caught a swordfish that morning, and earlier he had cut off six large slices and marinated them. Now, as we ate spaghetti and talked and drank good wine, Fuentes melted half a pound of butter and started frying those swordfish slices over a low flame. Still taking part in the conversation, he would squeeze lemon on the slices and turn them to keep them evenly browned. The aroma was amazing, better than steak cooking. Then he set each slice on a plate, added a pinch of salt, and served each plate with fresh salad and vegetables he had been simmering. For Hemingway, he had made a side dish of a special sauce made with peppers, parsley, black pepper, raisins, and capers, cooked next to the swordfish in a frying pan with very finely chopped asparagus.

"I am sorry, Ernesto," said the first mate and cook as we all dug into this delicious meal. "I had planned to make you fresh crabs with lemon and fricassee of octopus, but we have seen no crabs and have caught no octopus this week."

Hemingway clapped Fuentes on his back, poured him a tall glass of wine, and said, "This swordfish is the best I have eaten, *compadre*. It is a birthday gift worthy of a king."

"*Sí*," agreed Fuentes.

IT WAS THE NIGHT of the day after his birthday that Hemingway and I shared the dog watch and he talked more to me than ever before. At first it was a dialogue, discussing the chances against us finding the *Southern Cross* again and plans if we did find it, soft comments on the strange turns that the Crook Factory surveillance had taken in the past few weeks, then softly bitter comments about his missing wife—Gellhorn had taken off on her Caribbean cruise for *Colliers*—and finally a monologue there in the cockpit, dark except for the softly glowing binnacle lamp and the slowly wheeling stars that hung over us like a canopy and did not dim even where they dipped down and shone between the shrubs and mangrove trees that surrounded our little bay.

"So what do you think, Lucas? Will this splendid little war last a year... two years... three?"

I shrugged in the dark. We were drinking bottles of beer that were still cold from the *Pilar*'s ice chest. The night was quite warm and the bottles were beaded with cool sweat.

"I think it will last at least five years," said Hemingway, speaking softly, perhaps so as not to wake the boys and the two sleeping men, more probably because he was tired and a little drunk and essentially speaking to himself. "Maybe ten. Maybe always. It depends what we've promised as war aims. One thing's for sure... it will cost a goddamn fortune. This country can pay the bill... we haven't tapped our resources in the United States... but countries like England, they're fucked even if they aren't overrun by the Germans. This sort of war will bankrupt their empire even if they win, Lucas."

I sat in silence, looking at the writer in the dim light. Hemingway had given up shaving in the past two weeks—he said that the constant sun had irritated his skin too much to allow shaving—and his beard was growing in dark and piratical. I suspected that the piratical part was the true reason for the shrubbery.

"I'm doing my part to pay for the goddamn war that I never wanted," continued the writer, enunciating carefully in the slow way that told me that he had drunk far too much. "Had to borrow twelve thousand bucks just to pay my hundred-and-three-thousand-dollar income tax last year. Pardon me for mentioning money, Lucas. Never do. But... Jesus fucking Christ... a hundred and three thousand dollars in income tax. Can you believe that? He whom the gods will destroy, first they make successful at his trade. I mean, I have to pay that loan back and get enough ahead this summer, next winter, whenever, that I won't be completely wiped out and broke when I come back from the war. If I ever *go* to this goddamn war."

He drank his beer and leaned farther back against the cockpit cushions. Some night bird called from the mangrove thicket thirty yards astern of us.

"My second wife, Pauline, gets five hundred bucks a month from me every month, Lucas. Tax free. This year I haven't done much writing...shit, I haven't done hardly any...so that's a serious drain on capital. In ten years that would take...what? Sixty thousand dollars. I'd be wiped out in less than five years. So it's not all so simple, being a successful writer."

The *Pilar* creaked at her moorings, and Hemingway got ponderously to his feet, checked the stern anchor, and slouched back to his place in the cockpit next to me. The binnacle light illuminated his dark eyes and sunburned nose.

"Marty knows nothing about money," he said slowly, softly. "She saves terrifically on pennies and lets large sums go without a thought. She has a brave child's attitude toward it, but she doesn't know that when you get older you have to have a steady something to live on between books—books get further apart as you get older, Lucas. At least they do if you write only good books."

Several minutes passed in silence except for the lapping of waves against the hull and the soft creakings that were the sounds of any small ship.

"Hey," he said at last, "did you see the gold medal that the shooting club gave Gigi?"

"No," I said.

"Damned impressive," said Hemingway, his voice suddenly lighter. "It says, 'To Gigi as a token of admiration from his fellow shooters, Club de Cazadores del Cerro.' Christ, Lucas, you should have been there last week. At nine years old he beat twenty-four good men, all good shots, and many of them very fine shots, shooting live pigeons. He was using a four-ten against men using twelve-gauges. And live pigeon shooting isn't just trick shooting like skeet. Every bird is different. And you don't have to just hit them, you have to kill them dead inside a certain distance. And Patrick is even better as a wing shot. Right now Patrick is outshooting Gigi, but he does it so modestly and quietly, and with so little form or style, that nobody notices it except the old-timers and the bookmakers, while Gigi is known in the papers as *el joven fenómeno Americano*, and the day before we left on this patrol…I think it was the day before…an article in the paper called him *el popularísimo Gigi*."

Hemingway fell silent for a minute. Then he repeated, "*El popularísimo Gigi*," and his voice was thick. "So now I have to say, Go down to the post office and get the mail, *popularísimo*. Or, Time for bed, *popularísimo*. Or, Don't forget to brush your teeth, *popularísimo*."

A meteorite streaked from the zenith toward the horizon. We both sat silent for several minutes, heads back, watching the sky, waiting for another one. The sky did not disappoint us.

"I wish I could see some of the warmongers who brought on this war go fight in it before I have to, or before my boys have to," said Hemingway very softly. "Bumby…you know Bumby's my oldest…he'll be in it. He bought an old car. That's all we talked about when Bumby was here in the spring. His mother, Hadley, my first wife…"

Hemingway seemed to lose his train of thought and trailed off for a moment.

"His mother just wrote me that Bumby wants to drive the wreck across country, bring it all the way back east," he said finally. "But I'm going to write her and tell her that it doesn't make any sense. He'd use the tires up driving it back east, and gas rationing's so severe up there these days that a car really wouldn't be of much use once he got there. Besides, Bumby says that it doesn't even have a spare, so I doubt if it would survive a transcontinental trip. Better that he leaves it where it is and has it there when he goes back…or when he comes back from the war. *If* he comes back from the war."

The writer seemed to hear what he had just said, for he paused, shook his head, and swallowed the last of his beer.

"Wasn't that swordfish good, Lucas?"

"It was."

"Isn't fishing lovely, though? I would hate to die, Lucas, ever, because every year I have a better time fishing and shooting. I like them as much as when I was sixteen, and now I've written enough good books so that I don't have to worry about that, I would be happy to fish and shoot and let somebody else lug the ball for a while. My generation carried it plenty, and if you don't know how to enjoy life, if it should be only one life we have, you are a disgrace and don't deserve to have it."

Somewhere beyond the bow, a large fish jumped. Hemingway listened a while and then turned his face back toward me. His eyes were bright but vague in the yellow light from the binnacle lamp.

"Of course, it's just my luck, Lucas, that I happen to have worked hard all my life and made a fucking fortune at a time when whatever you make is confiscated by the government. That's bad luck. But the good luck is to have had all the wonderful things and good times I had...we had...especially Hadley and me. Especially when we were so poor that we literally didn't have a pot to piss in. Young and broke and writing well and living in Paris and drinking at the cafés with friends until the sky got light and the men or boys in white aprons began hosing down the sidewalks outside the bistros, and then staggering home to make love and then up early and black coffee... if we had any coffee... and then writing all day and writing well."

Hemingway leaned farther back against the cockpit cushions. He was looking at the sky as he talked. I do not think he remembered that I was there.

"Christ, I remember the races out at Enghien and the first time we went to Pamplona by ourselves, that wonderful boat... the *Leopoldina*...and Cortina D'Ampezzo and the Black Forest. I've been lying awake the last few nights...can't sleep...and I just keep remembering these things, all these things, and the songs.

A feather kitty's talent lies
In scratching out the other's eyes.
A feather kitty never dies
Oh, immortality.

Hemingway had a pleasant tenor singing voice.

"You notice my cats at the *finca*, Lucas?" He was looking at me again, aware that I was there and listening.

"Yes," I said. "They're hard to miss."

Hemingway nodded slowly. "You don't really notice them during the day... they're all over the damn place... but when it's feeding time, it's a goddamn migration, isn't it? When I can't sleep at night at the *finca*, I bring three cats into the room and tell them stories. The last night before the patrol, I invited in Tester—she's the smoke-gray Persian—and Dillinger, the black-and-white male whom we also call Boissy D'Anglas, and that half-Maltese kitten we call Willy. And I tell them stories about other cats that I've had... that we used to have. I tell them about F. Puss and about our greatest and largest and bravest cat, Mooky, whom we had out west, and who once fought a badger. And when I say 'The *badger*!' Tester has to get under the sheets, she's so frightened."

We sat there in rocking silence for a while. Clouds were slowly moving in to occlude the stars. The small breeze had died but the waves continued slow and regular. There were no mosquitoes.

"Are you still awake, Lucas?"

"Yeah."

"Sorry about all this nostalgia crap."

When I said nothing, Hemingway added, "It's a prerogative of living forty-three years. If you live that long, Lucas, you'll know what I mean."

I nodded very slightly and watched the tired man finish his beer.

"Well, another day of this screwing around out here chasing radio phantoms," he said, "and we'll head in. Gigi and I shoot in the Championship of Cuba on Sunday, and I want him to have a good night's sleep ashore before the competition." He grinned suddenly. "Did you see that the boys have armed themselves for when we find the sub, Lucas? Pat has his three-oh-three Lee Enfield, and Gigi's cleaned and oiled his mother's old Mannlicher Schoenauer. I remember when Pauline used that in Africa, hunting lions..."

"Why did you let them come along?" I said. "The boys."

Hemingway's grin faded. "Are you questioning my judgment, Lucas?"

"No," I said. "I'm just curious."

"When the patrols get serious," said the writer, "we'll leave the boys at the little Cuban naval base on Cayo Confites while we go out sub-hunting during the day. Until then, they might as well enjoy the adventure. God knows, life is serious enough without bleeding all the fun out of it."

I sipped the last of my beer. It was late. The stars were almost completely hidden by low clouds. It felt late. It smelled late.

"Christ," whispered Hemingway, "I wish Bumby was going to be here this weekend. He shoots pigeons beautifully. Almost as well as the little *popularísimo.* One of the Havana shooting critics wrote that there aren't four shots in Cuba who can beat the combination of Bumby, Papa, Gigi, and Mouse. I only wish Bumby could be here on Sunday, because he shoots as coolly as he is nervous playing tennis."

Hemingway got to his feet, and for the first time on the boat, I saw him struggle for a brief second to find his balance. "I'm going below, Lucas. Going to check on the boys and turn in. Wolfer will be up to relieve you in an hour or so. We're going to head out north of Cayo Romano a little after first light...see if we can pick up the *Southern Cross* just by luck and by God."

The writer moved forward, under the covering of the bridge, into the darkness, down the few steps to the forward compartments. I could hear him humming softly in the night and I could hear the words:

A feather kitty's talent lies
In scratching out the other's eyes.
A feather kitty never dies
Oh, immortality.

THE BOYS HAD SHOWN UP in the second week of July, shortly before Gellhorn had left. I knew nothing about children except that they usually fell into two categories—impossibly irritating and mildly irritating—but Hemingway's two boys seemed all right. Both were thin and freckled, with tousled hair and open smiles—although Gregory, the younger boy, was much quicker to show a smile or any other emotion than was his older brother.

Patrick was fourteen that summer of 1942—his birthday had been in late June—and he was just attaining that serious gawkiness of adolescence. Despite Hemingway's comments to me about his nine-year-old son's beating everyone at pigeon shooting, Gregory was ten that summer. The boy told me that his birthday was November 12 and that he had been born in 1931. I did not know if it was common for parents to lose track of their children's ages, but I could see how it could happen to Hemingway—especially if he saw them only once or twice a year.

The *Southern Cross* had taken forever to repair her driveshaft and was back in the Casablanca docks twice for further repairs, so it was July before she ventured out to sea, and for three weeks her captain put her through careful sea trials that rarely took her out of sight of land. Nonetheless, Hemingway was anxious and eager to tail the big yacht, so the boys were drafted onto the crew of the *Pilar* almost immediately.

I happened to be walking behind the *finca* on a warm night in mid-July, heading up to *la casa perdita* and dinner with Xenophobia there, when I heard Gellhorn and Hemingway discussing the fact that he would be taking the boys on patrol with him. Gellhorn's voice had reached that vicious, glass-shattering tone that women seem to find so useful in domestic arguments, and Hemingway's voice started out soft and contrite, building in volume only as the discussion continued. I did not pause to eavesdrop, but between the backyard and the road, I heard enough.

"Are you out of your mind, Ernest? What if your stupid sub-chasing game flushes a real submarine with the boys aboard?"

"Then they get to watch us sink it with grenades, I guess," came Hemingway's voice. "Their names will be in every paper in the States."

"Their names will be in a lot of papers if you make a sub angry at you and it pulls away to a thousand yards or so and blows the *Pilar* right out of the water with its six-inch deck gun."

"Everybody says that," grumbled Hemingway. "It's not going to happen that way."

"How do you know how it's going to happen, Ernest? What do you know about war? *Real* war?"

Hemingway's voice was agitated now. "Don't you think I know the realities of war? I had enough time to contemplate those realities while the doctors picked two hundred thirty-seven pieces of fucking shrapnel out of my leg in the hospital in Milan—"

"Don't you dare use that sort of language with me," snapped Gellhorn. "And the last time you told that story, it was two hundred and thirty-*eight* pieces of fucking shrapnel..."

"Whatever," growled Hemingway.

"Love," said Gellhorn flatly, "this time, if your silly little grenades miss that thirty-inch hatch you're so desperate to get close to, they won't find two hundred and thirty-eight pieces of *you*. Or of the boys."

"Don't talk that way," said Hemingway. "You know I wouldn't put Mouse and Gigi in harm's way. But the project's gone so far now that I can't stop it. All the equipment's tested and signed for. And the crew is terribly excited..."

"That crew would be excited if you promised to toss them a beef bone," said Gellhorn.

"Marty, they're all fine men—"

"Oh, yes, fine men," said Gellhorn, her voice dripping sarcasm. "And serious intellects, too. The other day I found Winston Guest reading *The Life of Christ.* I asked him why he was reading so quickly, and he said he couldn't wait to see how it ended."

"Ha, ha, ha," said Hemingway. "Wolfer's a good man, and loyal. Jesus, I've never known anyone more loyal. If I were to say 'Wolfie, jump out of this airplane; I know you have no parachute but one will be provided on the way down,' Wolfie would merely say, 'Yes, Papa,' and go diving out the door."

"As I said," came Gellhorn's voice. "An intellect to be reckoned with."

"...and Wolfer fits in perfectly," continued Hemingway in a rising voice. "He's got plenty of seagoing experience."

"Yes," said Gellhorn. "I think Guest's uncle went down on the *Titanic*."

I listened for Hemingway's response, but there was only angry silence.

"And your Marine radioman," continued Gellhorn. "My God, Ernest, all he does is sit around and read comic books. And have you noticed, dear? His feet smell something awful."

"I think Saxon's all right," grumbled Hemingway. "He's got combat experience. Maybe he's just had too much war...battle fatigue or something. And as for his feet...maybe it's jungle rot. You know, that fungus they get in the Pacific?"

"Whatever it is, Ernest, you had better have it taken care of before you cram all of your friends into the poor little *Pilar*. You smell bad enough at the end of these patrols as it is."

"What do you mean, we smell bad?"

"I mean, dearest, you stink when you come off that boat. All of you, but you the most, Ernest. You smell of fish and blood and beer and sweat, and you're covered with fish scales, and you're dirty, Ernest, *dirty*. Why don't you take a bath more often?"

I was just about out of earshot at this point, but I could hear Hemingway's voice. "Look, Marty, fish and blood and beer and sweat are what boats are all about. And we don't bathe on the boat because we have to conserve the fresh water. *You* know that—"

Gellhorn's voice was still quite sharp and audible. "I'm not talking just about on the boat, Ernest. Why don't you bathe *here* more often?"

"God damn it, Marty," shouted Hemingway, "I think you need a vacation. You've got battle fatigue worse than Saxon."

"I've got terminal claustrophobia worse than any of you," agreed Gellhorn.

"All right, Kitten. Cancel that stupid *Colliers* boat tour of yours. We could go down the coast to Guanabacoa instead, and you could do that other piece you wanted to write for *Colliers*..."

"What other piece?"

"You know, the one about how the Chinese down there water the human feces they sell to the truck farmers...the one you promised *Colliers* about how the buyers have to sample the stuff with a straw to decide whether it's thick enough. I'll give you a ride down on the *Pilar* and provide the straws so that you can..."

I heard no more voices as I turned up the road to the dairy.

The sound of breaking crockery was clearly audible all the way to Grade A.

FOR A WHILE toward the end of July, it seemed that Hemingway was more interested in entertaining his boys than in running either the Crook Factory or the antisub patrols. From the boys' point of view, it must have started as one hell of an enjoyable summer vacation. Besides introducing them to the excitement of the shooting competition at the Club de Cazadores del Cerro, the exclusive and expensive shooting club about five miles from the *finca*, Hemingway would knock off work in late morning—shortly after Patrick and Gregory began to stir—and play tennis with them, or take them fishing off the *Pilar*, or play baseball.

The baseball team started when Hemingway caught some of the local boys from the village of San Francisco de Paula throwing stones at his mango trees. It had become an obsession of Hemingway's that his beloved mango trees not be bruised by the boys' stones.

"Look," said Patchi Ibarlucia one day while we were typing reports at the guest house, "don't you want these kids to become good baseball players? Throwing rocks is good practice for them!"

Hemingway decided then and there that playing baseball would be better practice for them. He ordered baseball uniforms for them and bought bats, balls, and gloves. The players' ages ranged from seven years to sixteen. They named the team Las Estrellas de Gigi—"Gigi's Stars"—after Gregory, and they immediately began playing other pickup teams in the Havana area. Hemingway drove the team around in the repaired *finca* pickup truck and acted as their manager. Within two weeks, another fifteen boys had shown up to watch Gigi's team practice, and Hemingway decided that his backyard league needed another team. Once again he wrote a check, and now there were two uniformed teams playing every afternoon and evening in the empty field on the flat area between the *finca* and the village. Agent 22—aka little Santiago Lopez—was on this second team, and despite his prominent ribs and stick-thin arms and legs, Agent 22 was a solid place hitter and had a wicked arm when throwing in from left field.

In the evenings, after Gellhorn left on her *Collier's* cruise, Hemingway would take his two boys to dinner at the Floridita or to the rooftop Chinese restaurant called El Pacífico. I accompanied them on several of these trips, and I thought that just the elevator ride to the fifth-floor restaurant was an education for the boys. The elevator was ancient and open, with only a sliding iron grille for a door. It stopped at every floor. The second floor was a dance hall with a five-piece Chinese orchestra blaring away in a cacophony not unlike Hemingway's cats going at it in the moonlight. On the third floor was the whorehouse where Leopoldina la Honesta was working once again. The fourth floor housed a working opium den, and as the open elevator rose past the open doors, I saw the two boys get fast glimpses of the skeletal figures curled around their pipes in the smoky interior. By the time we arrived at the fifth-floor restaurant, one's sense of adventure was as stimulated as one's appetite. There was always a special table set aside under a flapping awning, with a fine view of Havana at night. The boys would order shark fin soup and listen to their Papa's story of how he had eaten monkey brains right out of the monkey's skull when he was in China with Marty the year before.

After dinner, Hemingway would often take the boys to the Frontón for the jai alai. Both Patrick and Gregory seemed to love the fast-paced game as the players—many of whom they knew well—leaped from the court floor to the walls, catching and firing the hard balls with the five-foot-long, curved wicker baskets—*cestas*—strapped to their wrists, the balls flying so fast as to be almost invisible and very dangerous. The boys obviously loved not only the game but the betting. The odds change with every play in jai alai, and the crowd wagers all through the thirty-point match. What Gregory and Patrick seemed to enjoy most was stuffing Hemingway's wager into the hollow tennis ball and throwing it down to the bookmaker, who always threw the receipt back and then waited for the ball to be returned at high speed. Between the leaping players, the high-speed jai alai balls ricocheting, the incessant shouting and bellowing of odds, and the dozens of wager-filled tennis balls in the air at any given second, it was a game to delight children's hearts and to make anyone a bit dizzy. Hemingway obviously loved it.

I knew nothing about parenting, but I began to think that Hemingway's affection for the boys sometimes crossed the line into serious indulgence. Both Patrick and Gigi were allowed to drink as much as they wanted on the *finca* grounds and at restaurants, and both boys showed a willingness to drink. One morning I was reading reports outside the guest house and saw Gregory drag himself out to the pool at around ten A.M.

Hemingway greeted him. The writer had finished writing for the morning and was sitting in the shade with a Scotch and soda in his hand. "What do you want to do today, Gig? Lunch at the Floridita? Gregorio says it's too rough for fishing today, but we could shoot a few practice pigeons in the afternoon."

The ten-year-old staggered to a chair and collapsed in it. His face was pale and his hands were shaking.

"Or maybe we should just take it easy today," said Hemingway, leaning closer to his son. "You don't look so good, pal."

"I feel like I'm coming up with something, Papa. It almost feels like I'm seasick."

"Ahh," said Hemingway, sounding relieved. "You've just got a hangover, Gig. I'll fix you a Bloody Mary."

Five minutes later, the writer was back with the drink, only to find Patrick draped across the chair next to Gregory.

"Guys?" said Hemingway, handing the drink to the younger boy and looking at the older one carefully. "You think maybe you should cut down on the drinking? If you don't" — he folded his arms across his chest in mock seriousness — "discipline will have to be enforced. We can't send you back to Mother at the end of the summer with the D.T.'s."

A POLIO EPIDEMIC WAS SHUTTING DOWN public gatherings in Havana that summer, and not long after Hemingway's birthday cruise, Gregory came down sick with suspicious symptoms. The boy was put to bed with a sore throat, fever, and aching legs. I was sent in the Lincoln to fetch Dr. Herrera Sotolongo, who called in two Havana specialists. For three days, the doctors came and went, tapped at Gregory's knees, tickled the soles of his feet, consulted in whispers, and then went and came again.

It was obvious that their diagnosis was not optimistic, but Hemingway ignored them and banished everyone from the boy's bedroom except himself. For almost a week he slept on a cot by Gregory's bed, fed him, and took his temperature every four hours. Day and night, we could hear the soft murmur of Hemingway's voice coming through the open windows and occasional laughter from the child.

Later, when Gregory had recovered from whatever the ailment had been, we were sitting on the hillside one afternoon when he suddenly began telling me about his quarantine.

"Papa would lie beside me on the cot every night and tell me stories, Lucas. Wonderful stories."

"What kind of stories?" I said.

"Oh, about his life up in Michigan as a boy. How he'd caught his first trout and how beautiful the forests were up there before the loggers came. And when I admitted that I was scared that I had polio, Papa would tell me about all the times he'd been scared as a boy, how he used to dream about a furry monster who grew taller and taller every night and then, just as the monster was about to eat him, it would jump over the fence. Papa said that fear was a perfectly natural thing and nothing to be ashamed of. He said that all I had to do was learn how to control my imagination, but that he knew how hard that was for a boy. And then Papa would tell me stories about the bear from the Bible."

"The bear from the Bible?" I said.

"Yes," said Gregory. "The bear he'd read about in the Bible when he was a little boy and wasn't very good at reading. You know, Gladly, the Cross-eyed Bear."

"Oh," I said.

"But mostly," said the boy, "Papa would just tell me stories about how he had fished and hunted in the Michigan north woods and about how he wished he could have stayed my age forever and lived there forever and never had to grow up. And then I would fall asleep."

A WEEK AFTER Gregory had fully recovered, we took the *Pilar* out to shadow the *Southern Cross*—just the boys, Hemingway, Fuentes, and me—and when the yacht turned back to Havana Harbor, the writer took the boat out to some coral reefs offshore so the boys could swim around a bit. This day, I was on the flying bridge, Hemingway was swimming near the deepwater reef with the boys, and Fuentes was out in the *Tin Kid*, taking fish off their three-pronged spears as they speared them. What we did not know at the time was that Gregory had tired of swimming back to the dinghy with his catches and had begun threading them through their gills onto his belt, leaving a trail of fish blood in the water around him.

Suddenly the youngest boy began screaming. "Sharks, sharks!"

"Where?" shouted Hemingway, who was treading water about forty yards from the boy. Fuentes and the *Tin Kid* were another thirty yards farther in, and Patrick was almost back to the *Pilar*, where it bobbed fifty yards from the dinghy and almost a hundred yards from Gregory. "Can you see them, Lucas?" shouted Hemingway.

I did not need binoculars. "Three of them!" I shouted back. "Just beyond the reef."

The sharks were huge, each longer than eighteen feet, and they were cutting toward Gregory in slow S-shaped curves, obviously following the scent of blood from the fish he had speared farther out. Their slick bodies were black against the deep blue of the Gulf Stream.

"Lucas!" shouted Hemingway, his voice tight but controlled. "Get a Thompson!"

I was already sliding down the ladder and running toward the closest weapons locker. When I emerged, it was not with one of the submachine guns—the range was much too great for those—but with one of the two heavy BARs aboard. The

Browning Automatic Rifles, massive, gas-powered automatic weapons had only recently been brought aboard to substitute for the missing .50-calibers.

Hemingway was swimming toward his son. And toward the sharks.

I raised the heavy BAR and propped it on the railing of the flying bridge. There was too much chop. Now both Hemingway and the boy were between me and the accelerating shark fins cutting through the waves breaking against the reef. I had no clear shot.

"Okay, pal," called Hemingway to the boy, "take it easy. Throw something at them to get their attention and swim to me."

Looking down the sights of the BAR, I saw Gregory's face-mask go below the waves as he fumbled with his belt. A second later he threw three or four small grunts in the direction of the oncoming sharks and began swimming away from the reef with the speed of Johnny Weissmuller.

Hemingway met the boy halfway and lifted him onto his shoulders, trying to get as much of the child's body out of the water as possible. Then the writer began swimming back toward the dinghy with strong strokes. Fuentes was pulling hard, but there was still forty or fifty yards of open water between them.

I clicked the safety off the BAR, made sure the short ammo clip was locked in, and sighted just over Gregory's head. The sharks had stopped just beyond the reef. Water roiled and their fins thrashed as they fought over the grunts. Hemingway kept swimming with his son on his shoulders, looking back occasionally and then glancing at me. When they reached the dinghy, Fuentes helped pull the sobbing, shaking boy into the boat and Hemingway made sure that his son was safely out of the water before he pulled himself up and out.

Later, on the *Pilar*, Hemingway said softly to me, "Why didn't you fire?"

"The boy was in the way and they weren't close enough. If they had come across the reef, I would have opened up on them."

"The BAR was just brought aboard," he said. "We never practiced with it."

"I know how to fire it," I said.

"Are you a good shot, Lucas?"

"Yes."

"Would you have killed those three fish?"

"I doubt it," I said. "Not all three. There's no better barrier to bullets than water, and all they would have had to do to get to you was dive six feet during their attack run."

Hemingway nodded and turned away.

A few minutes later, when Gregory admitted that he had been keeping the fish strung on his belt, Hemingway began the process of verbally ripping the boy a new asshole. The process continued all the way back to Cojímar.

18

THESE REPORTS AREN'T WORTH SHIT, Lucas," said Delgado, who was not oblivious to the fact that nothing much had been happening for weeks.

"Sorry," was all I said. I could not—or would not—allow my sense that something big was about to occur to be expressed in my reports.

"I'm serious. It's like reading about some goddamned Andy Hardy film. All that's missing is Judy Garland."

I shrugged. We were meeting at the end of the dead-end road just beyond San Francisco de Paula. Delgado had his motorcycle. I was on foot.

Delgado stuffed my two-page report into his leather satchel and straddled the motorcycle. "Where's the writer today?"

"He's out on the boat with his boys and a couple of friends," I said. "Following the *Southern Cross* again."

"And you haven't picked up anything from the boat's radio?" said Delgado.

"Nope. Nothing in the Abwehr code."

"So why are you here if Hemingway's at sea?"

I shrugged again. "He didn't invite me along."

Delgado sighed. "You're a sorry excuse for an intelligence agent, Lucas."

I said nothing. Delgado shook his head, fired up the motorcycle, and left me standing in a cloud of dust. I waited until he was out of sight and then I went into the thick bushes by the abandoned shed. Agent 22 was waiting there on a smaller motorbike... the one he frequently used to follow Lieutenant Maldonado.

"Move over, Santiago," I said. The boy jumped off, waited for me to straddle the seat, and then clambered on behind me.

The boy put his arms around my waist. I turned to look down at his dark hair and dark eyes. "Santiago," I said, "why are you doing this thing?"

"What thing, *Señor* Lucas?"

"Helping *Señor* Hemingway... risking injury... is this a game for you?"

"No game, *Señor*." The boy's voice was absolutely serious.

"Why then, Santiago?"

The boy looked away toward the shed, but I could see his dark eyes fill with tears that I knew he would never shed. "It is because of what they call *Señor* Hemingway... that is true for me. His is the name of that man I never had."

For a moment I did not understand. Then I said, "Papa?"

"Sí, Señor Lucas," said the boy and looked up at me, his thin arms tight around my waist. "When I do a good job for him, or when I play well with the baseball while he is watching, sometimes Papa looks at me and there is something in his eyes that is also there when he looks at his real sons. Sometimes then, I pretend—for just a moment—that I also may call him Papa and that it would be real and that he would hug me the way he hugs the boys who are truly his sons."

I could think of nothing to say.

"Please be careful driving this, *Señor* Lucas," said the ten-year-old. "I need it to follow *Caballo Loco* tonight and someday I must return it to the gentleman from whom I borrowed it."

"Don't worry," I said. "I haven't bent it yet, have I? Hang on, my friend." The small engine started with a racket and we accelerated down the road in the direction in which Delgado had disappeared.

WITH HEMINGWAY DEVOTING SO MUCH TIME and attention to his boys, I was free to run the Crook Factory and to sort out the confusing intelligence reports that were filtering back to me.

Very little had made sense since the beginning of this operation, and I was trying to rearrange the pieces on the board. Why had the director been so interested in Hemingway's penny-ante operation down here? Why the visits from the BSC's Ian Fleming and the OSS's Wallace Beta Phillips? Why assign someone as serious and deadly as Delgado as liaison? Why should the radio operator from the *Southern Cross* be murdered and who had murdered him? What was the real mission of the *Southern Cross* and why assign a weak sister Abwehr agent like Theodor Schlegel to head it up? Was Helga Sonneman in on this Abwehr mission and, if so, what was her role in it? Did she take orders from Schlegel or give orders to him? Was it pure, stupid luck that got Martin Kohler's radio codes to Hemingway, or was something more complicated going on? What the hell was the FBI doing funneling large sums of money to the Cuban National Police through a killer like Lieutenant Maldonado at the same time Schlegel and the Abwehr were paying the man?

I sent instructions out to the Crook Factory operatives over Hemingway's name and tried to make sense of the information coming back. After a few days of this, I began to wonder—not for the first time—just who I was working for. I had never trusted Delgado, and I no longer trusted J. Edgar Hoover's motivations. I had been cut loose from my usual SIS contacts, and I had no connections with the local branch of the FBI except for the occasional agent tailing me. Both the British secret service and Donovan's new OSS had made overtures to me, but I never flattered myself into thinking that they were interested in my well-being. Both agencies had a vested interest in this confused and confusing operation...I just did not know what those interests were. Meanwhile, I spent every day with Ernest Hemingway, spying for him, spying *on* him, telling him only a fraction of what I knew about the situation surrounding us, and wondering when I would be ordered to betray the man.

I decided that I would continue gathering information, get some sense of just what the hell was going on, and then decide who I was working for.

Which led to following Delgado. For the past four days, I had spent all of my free time doing just that. One thing the FBI is good at is surveillance; it is because they always have enough agents to assign to each job. One person covertly following one person is a near impossibility—especially when the person being followed has been trained in tradecraft. To do any surveillance correctly, you need several teams following on foot, one or two teams in vehicles, at least one team *ahead* of the surveillance target, and other teams ready to take over if and when the subject becomes suspicious.

I had Agent 22. But so far we had done all right.

WE FELL IN BEHIND DELGADO on the Havana Road just as he reached the heavy city traffic. We were about sixty yards back, and the highway was filled with honking cars, lumbering trucks, and flitting motorbikes just like ours. Nonetheless, I kept us tucked behind a truck carrying a tall stack of lumber and swerved out just to keep the other agent's motorcycle in sight. It looked as if he was heading downtown again. During the past few days, we had followed him to his room at the cheap Cuba Hotel, to various restaurants and bars, once to a whorehouse... not the one below the Chinese restaurant... twice to the FBI headquarters near the park, and once to the Malecón, where he had taken a long walk along the breakwater with Lieutenant Maldonado. Little Santiago wanted to run along the wall right next to them to hear what they were talking about, but I convinced the boy that the first job of a secret agent on a serious surveillance mission was to keep from being burned. We did not want Maldonado or Delgado to take notice of him. Santiago agreed reluctantly, and we watched the two men chatting from fifty yards away.

Now it was the afternoon of Monday, August 3, 1942. Before that day was finished, I would have a major new piece of the puzzle and very little would ever be the same again.

July had ended with Gregory's illness and recovery and Hemingway's continued irritation that the FBI and Naval Intelligence, much less his friends at the embassy, had not got back to him with congratulations for the Crook Factory's advance warning on the Amagansett spies' insertion into the United States. He had vowed not to feed them any more radio intercepts until we had checked them out ourselves. "Bring them the next bunch of Nazi agents tied up and gagged and see if they can ignore that," said the writer.

August began with more bad war news. The Germans had completed their capture of Sevastopol on the Black Sea and were continuing their advance, pushing the Soviets back in a drive that was obviously designed to end in the capture of Leningrad, Stalingrad, and Moscow. The Japanese had invaded East New Guinea at the end of July. U.S. Marines were said to be ready to invade Guadalcanal or some other island in the Solomons, but fighting in the South Pacific had gone from terrible to obscene in its ferocity. The Japanese were not giving up an inch of conquered territory without a bloody fight. Meanwhile, the French... the good old collaborationist French... were using their entire Parisian police force to round up foreign-born Jews—thirteen thousand of them, according to newspaper reports—and to lock them up in the Winter Velodrome before helping the Germans ship them out to God knows where.

"Hadley and I used to go to bicycle races in the Velodrome," Hemingway had said sadly when he read the report in late July. "I hope that there *is* a hell, just so that Pierre Laval can burn and rot there forever and ever."

The FBI was announcing more arrests of "Nazi agents" almost daily—158 back on July 10 alone—but these "agents" were, I suspected (and Delgado confirmed), just German aliens of dubious allegiance whose crimes tended to be on the level of belonging to the German-American Vocational League in New York.

On the local front, Martha Gellhorn was still absent—cruising the subinfested Caribbean with her three Negro retainers, our continued surveillance of Maldonado had not shown any more money drops, Theodor Schlegel was spending most of his time aboard the *Southern Cross* these days, and Helga Sonneman had twice gone out on the *Pilar* for fishing cruises with Hemingway and his buddies. I had suggested that this might not be a good idea, what with all of the weapons and sophisticated radio equipment hidden around the boat, especially if *Fraulein* Helga was the German agent we suspected her of being, but Hemingway had shrugged off my advice and taken the woman out for evening dinner and marlin-fishing cruises. He enjoyed her company.

Elsewhere on the local front, Hemingway's editor, Perkins, had written that Gary Cooper's movie *The Pride of the Yankees* had premiered in mid-July. Perkins had praised Cooper's acting in the film, but Hemingway had only laughed when reading that to me. "Coop throws like a girl," said the writer. "Gigi's arm is ten times stronger. Hell, our little left fielder…Santiago…could outrun, outthrow, and outbat Coop. Why they put Cooper in a movie about Lou Gehrig, I'll never know." That same week, a telegram arrived from Ingrid Bergman. Evidently, the director of *For Whom the Bell Tolls* had hated the daily rushes of the other actress, had fired her, and had then offered Ingrid the part of Maria. "I told her I'd fix it," said Hemingway smugly, folding the telegram away. Given the writer's schedule over the previous two months, I doubted that he had taken time to "fix" anything. Hemingway had a habit of taking credit for events in which he had taken no part.

On the very local front, things had become complicated between Maria Marquez and me.

I COULD SAY THAT I did not know how it happened, but that would be a lie. It happened because we were sleeping in the same room, because she was a woman lying there in nothing but a thin cotton nightdress, and because I was a fool.

She had brought the cot in and put her hand on my shoulder that first night when we thought that Maldonado was coming to kill her, and I did not make her remove her hand that night or the cot the next day. Sometimes Maria would be asleep in her cot by the fire when I got back to Grade A. Sometimes I would be gone for days with Hemingway in the *Pilar,* but when I came up the road from the *finca* in the rain, Maria would be there, sometimes sleeping but more often waiting for me, coffee boiling on the stove Juan and the boys had brought in, the fire in the fireplace cracking softly if the night was chilly. It was as close to a home as I had had in the last dozen years or so, and I grew lazy and complacent with the companionship and comfort.

One night in late July—it must have been the weekend of

the championship shooting competition at the Club de Cazadores del Cerro, because no one had been at the *finca* all evening—I had gone to sleep about midnight with Maria on the cot next to me. There was no fire that night. It had been hot and sultry all day and the windows were open to catch any breeze.

I awoke suddenly, feeling under the pillow for the S&W .38. Something had awakened me from a sound sleep. At first I thought it was the storm outside, lightning illuminating the dairy barns, thunder echoing down the hill, but then I realized that it was Maria's hand that had awakened me.

I admit that I had grown used to her sleeping close—used to her breathing and to the soft scent of her and to the childlike touch of her hand on my shoulder each night, as if she were afraid of the dark.

There was nothing childlike about her touch this night. Her hand had slid down my belly into my pajama bottoms and her fingers were clutching and stroking me.

If I had been awake, perhaps I would have pushed her away. But my dream had been hot and erotic—begun, no doubt, by her touch as I slept—and this warm, sweet friction seemed like nothing more than an extension of that dream. I did have time to think—*She's a whore, a* puta—but then all thought was lost as her hand tightened and moved more quickly. She shifted her weight from her cot to mine, and then my hands rose purposefully—not to push her away but to pull her loose shift over her head and off her body.

Maria's hair swung free from her nightgown as she rose above me. Her hands tugged down my pajamas. For a second the cool night air was a shock, but only for a second, and then the hot warmth of Maria's leg, belly, and groin replaced the warmth of her hand. We began moving smoothly and swiftly then, saying nothing, not kissing, Maria's back arching as she straddled me, her breasts beaded with sweat and glistening in the flashes of lightning. I no longer heard the thunder. Or, rather, the thunder was pounding in my ears now as my pulse raced and the world dimmed.

I had not been with a woman for more than a year. This encounter lasted only a minute. Maria seemed as rushed and starved for release as I had been, and she cried out and collapsed on me only a few seconds later.

And that should have been the end of it. But as we lay there on the single cot, sweating and panting, entwined not so much in an embrace as in a mere confusion of limbs and discarded garments, everything began again. This time, it lasted much more than a few minutes.

The next day, neither the young woman nor I said anything about what had happened in the night. There were no smirks, no tears from her, no knowing glances, only a silence that deepened and communicated more each time we were around each other. And that night, after I returned from a long planning session in the guest house with Hemingway, Ibarlucia, Guest, and others, Maria was awake and waiting for me. Five candles burned on the old mantel and on the floor near our cots. It was another hot night, but there were no storms brewing in the dark, at least not outside. But these inner storms continued to rage night after night when I was not out in the *Pilar* or—more recently—following Delgado late past midnight.

I cannot explain those weeks of intimacy. I cannot excuse them. Maria Marquez was Xenophobia—a young whore being chased by several killers—and I had no business being with her in any capacity except as an agent charged with her survival. But something about what was going on every day around me there at the *finca*—Hemingway's growing estrangement from his wife, the strange warmth of the boys' visit, the long summer days and evenings out at sea, and the general sense of vacation and timelessness surrounding the farm and all of us—conspired to make me relax, to look forward to the shared meals and shared evenings in the Grade A cottage, and to look forward even more to the nights of sweat and urgent, silent lovemaking.

On a night in the second week of this, Maria did weep. She lay against my chest in the night, and I felt her tears and the small, unbidden sobs that moved through her. I lifted her face then and kissed her tears away. Then I kissed her on the lips. It was the first time we had kissed. It was the beginning of countless more.

I thought of her now less as a whore than as a confused young woman from a small fishing village who had fled violent men there only to find more in Havana. She had chosen few things in her life—probably had not even chosen to become a whore when she had first accepted Leopoldina la Honesta's largesse, not understanding the consequences of that help—but now she had chosen me. And I had chosen a human side to life which I had never indulged in before: coming home to the same woman every evening that I was on the island, sharing meals with her in the cottage rather than alone or under the hostile gaze of the *finca*'s cook, and then going to bed—knowing what was going to happen each night, anticipating it—with the same woman. I began to learn her needs even as she worked to learn mine and anticipate them. This was also something new for me. Sex had never been more than a temporary liaison leading to a needed release of tension for me. This was... *different.*

One night, long after midnight, as we were lying together on my cot, Maria's leg looped over mine and the top of her head tucked into the hollow under my chin, she whispered, "You will tell no one of this, yes?"

"I will tell no one, yes," I whispered back. "It is between us and the sea."

"What?" said the girl. "I do not understand... the sea?"

I blinked at the ceiling in confusion, sure that this was a common Cuban saying. Certainly she would have heard this in her small village. Then again, her village was in the hills some miles inland. Perhaps the men there did not speak in the same idiom as the fishermen in the coastal villages.

"It is our secret," I said. Whom did she think I would tell? Was she worried that *Señor* Hemingway would no longer be courteous to her if he knew that she was "my woman"? What did Xenophobia fear now?

"Thank you, José," she whispered, setting her long fingers on my chest. "Thank you."

Only later did I realize that she was thanking me for more than agreeing to keep her secret.

THE OTHER TIMES Santiago and I had followed Delgado, even the time he met with Lieutenant Maldonado, the agent had not worked very hard to avoid being followed. This afternoon, August 3, Delgado was using every bit of his tradecraft to shake any possible tail. Still, I was certain that he had not spotted me or the boy.

Delgado drove his motorcycle through thick traffic to Old Havana, parked his machine in an alley off Progreso, went into the Plaza Hotel, came out through the kitchen exit, crossed Monserrate, and went into the elaborate Bacardi Building, with the statute of the giant bat atop its tower. I dropped Santiago off at the corner and circled the block in heavy traffic. When I came back onto Monserrate, the boy was waving wildly from the curb.

"He went out the back, *Señor* Lucas. He is on the Number Three bus going up O'Reilly." The boy leaped onto the back of the motorbike as I gunned it and swung up narrow O'Reilly Street.

Santiago had not let the bus out of his sight. Delgado was still aboard—and almost certainly checking out the rear window of the crowded bus to see if anyone was following him. I kept in thick traffic, passed the bus, and stayed several car lengths ahead of it while Santiago watched over his shoulder. Delgado leaped out at the Plaza de la Catedral, and Santiago slid off the back of the bike to follow as I stayed with traffic up San Ignacio past the Havana Cathedral.

Circling back, I followed the boy jogging down the sidewalk. For a minute after I picked him up, Santiago was too winded to talk, but he gestured at a taxi headed down Aguiar. I kept the taxi in sight as it circled back through La Habana Vieja, past the Floridita, until it returned to the Parque Central, only half a block from where Delgado had parked his motorcycle. We stayed hidden in traffic as Delgado crossed the street and walked into the Parque Central district.

I pulled the bike up onto the sidewalk near the old stone walls that had once circled Old Havana, and we put the machine up on its kickstand. "He's going to double back in the Parque Central to make sure that he's not being followed," I told the boy. "You cut across the corner of the park and keep him in sight. If he comes out the south or west side, go down to the corner by the Gran Teatro to watch. I'll head up to the Hotel Plaza and watch both intersections. Wave your bandanna waist-high to let me know that he's come out."

The Parque Central was not just a park, but the center of a

capital that the newly independent Cubans after the Spanish-American War had planned to be as grand as Paris or Vienna. All around and above the green palm fronds of the park rose the ornate, rococo, neo-baroque private and public structures that were Havana's pride. I watched Delgado disappear into the crowds around the white marble statue of José Martí at the center of the shady plaza and knew that anyone trying to follow him into the park would be spotted. He was very good. If I had guessed wrong about which way he would exit the park, we would lose him.

I stayed within the heavy sidewalk traffic at the north end of the Parque Central, walking back and forth between the Plaza Hotel on the north side and the elaborate Hotel Inglaterra on the west side, watching the crowds. Several minutes passed and I was almost certain that Delgado had doubled back again and crossed up by the Bacardi Building and lost us when I saw Santiago near the curb in front of the Gran Teatro. He was waving his red bandanna at belt level.

I jogged down the street. The boy pointed south toward a perfect copy of the Capitol Building in Washington, D.C. "He went into the Capitolio Nacional, *Señor* Lucas."

"Good job, Santiago," I said, patting the boy's thin shoulders. "You stay out here."

I went up into the capitol building, down its echoing halls, past the diamond in the floor of the lobby that was the declared center of Havana. The main corridor was empty, but the sound of a door closing echoed down a side hallway. I moved lightly on my boat shoes, trying not to let the soles squeak on the polished floor. Pausing at the frosted door, I opened it a crack and peeked through just in time to catch a glimpse of Delgado's panama suit twenty yards down the dimly lit corridor. I closed the door softly just as the other agent turned around.

I was sure that he would wait at the end of the corridor until he was sure that no one was behind him. But I had a hunch where he was going.

I moved quickly back to the main hallway, jogged up marble stairs to the mezzanine, moved quickly to the east wing of the building, tried several doors until I found one that was unlocked, and then went into the second-story level of the Museo

Nacional de Ciencias Naturales. It was a sad excuse for a natural history museum, its display cases mostly empty or filled with poorly preserved animals with dusty glass eyes, but it would be a perfect place for Delgado to watch reflections and stare back the way he had come. I circled the narrow mezzanine until I saw his white shoes on the south side of the central display area, and then I stepped back quickly, almost holding my breath. After an interminable ten minutes, Delgado turned on his heel and went out the locked south door of the museum.

I had to use my fist to rub grime off the upstairs window, but the dirt finally cleared in a large enough circle that I could make out Delgado crossing the wide boulevard south of the capitol building and going into the hulking mass of the Partagas Cigar Factory. I did not think that this was just another maneuver. This, I thought, was the agent's destination.

I went out the east door of the museum and crossed the boulevard at the corner. Delgado had gone in the main door of the cigar factory, but I went south half a block and then down the alley to the loading docks. Inside the huge warehouse section of the building, I knew how hard it would be to find Delgado. On the other hand, I knew that most cigar factories had small bars just off the main rolling and packaging areas. That would be a good place for a rendezvous, if that was Delgado's goal.

Walking confidently, as if I had business in the factory and knew my way around, I went through the warehouse doors into the main room. Here more than a hundred workers sat at their benches, their *galeras*; the hand-rollers using their rounded cutting knives to trim the leaves and then roll them. A "reader" was at his podium at the far end of the room, reading excerpts from some cheap romance novel. I knew that this practice of reading to the cigar workers dated back to the last century, when José Martí had made the rollers listen to pro-Nationalist propaganda while they worked. These days, it was newspapers in the morning and adventure or romance novels in the afternoon.

I walked through the *galeras*. Most of the hand-rollers were too busy to look up, but a few looked at me quizzically. I nodded to them as if approving their work and moved on. Some of the rollers were working on the *tripa*, the small leaf that gives the cigar its form. Others had finished with the *tripa*, and were rolling the *hoja de fortaleza*, the "leaf of strength" that gives the cigar its flavor, while others were already cutting and rolling the *hoja de combustión* that allowed the cigar to burn evenly. The final benches were applying a rice-based glue to the final large leaf, the *copa*, that gave the cigar its ultimate shape. Half of the workers here were men, and most of them—men and women alike—were smoking cigars as they did their work. It had taken me less than two minutes to cross the wide floor, and in that time, the old man near the exit door had cut and rolled all of the leaves of a cigar as I watched.

I went out through a side room where *depalillos* were removing the stems from the thin leaves and passing those leaves to the *rezgagados*, who sorted them according to grades. Beyond the sorting room, I caught a glimpse of the *revisadores* pulling cigars through holes in wooden boards to make sure that the size of each was perfect. Patchi Ibarlucia had once shared with me several ribald jokes about this quality control practice present in every Cuban cigar factory.

In the dark hallway just outside the *revisadores*' room, I saw the frosted glass and wooden doors of the little bar that sold cigars, rum, and coffee. There was a Closed sign on the door. I paused a second in the hallway and then opened the door a crack.

Delgado was in the third small booth, his back to the door. The man across from him looked up as the door opened, but I closed it before he could have seen me clearly. One glimpse was all that I needed.

I moved quickly down the hallway and ducked into the men's toilet just as the door to the bar opened and footsteps moved down the hall. There was a frosted window that opened onto the alley. I shoved up the window, went out, dangled six feet above the littered bricks of the alley, and let myself drop. Then I was up and running and around the bend in the alley before anyone appeared in the open window.

MARIA AND I made love all that next night, our passion ending only when there was a soft tapping on the door of Grade A just after dawn. The tapping was Santiago, whom I had told to report early, and the little boy tapped only once before going to wait in the courtyard of the dairy as instructed. I do not know why the young whore and I were so excited and persistent that long night. Perhaps she perceived what I had discovered—that the foundations of our little fantasy world there were crumbling and that reality was ready to blow in like a hurricane.

The previous evening, Hemingway had announced that we would be leaving early in the *Pilar.* Don Saxon's infected feet had finally reached the point where he could not serve as radioman on the boat for this trip and no one wanted him aboard until his feet were better. I was to come along and handle the communications gear. Naval Intelligence had sent the writer a coded communiqué ordering him to head down along the Cuban coast to a point where they suspected that German submarines were using certain caves as supply depots. Hemingway's crew was to consist of Fuentes, Guest, Ibarlucia, Sinsky, Roberto Herrera, me, and the boys—Gregory and Patrick. The writer guessed that we would be gone about a week—do some tracking of the *Southern Cross,* which was headed for the same waters—but my own guess was that he was not taking the mission very seriously if he was taking the boys along.

"I should stay here," I said. "Who's going to look after the Crook Factory?" After that afternoon's revelation in the cigar factory, I did not want to be out of touch and out at sea.

Hemingway had shown his teeth and waved away the objection. "The Crook Factory will take care of itself for a few days. You're going with us, Lucas. That's an order."

I came out of the Grade A cottage that morning to find Santiago waiting patiently, sitting on the low stone trough in the center of the courtyard. I walked with him down the road past the *finca.*

"Santiago, I'm going out on *Señor* Hemingway's boat for several days."

"Yes, *Señor* Lucas. I have heard."

I did not ask the child where he had heard the news. Agent 22 was fast becoming our most able operative. "Santiago," I said, "I do not want you following Lieutenant Maldonado while we are gone. Nor the man we followed yesterday. I do not want you following *anyone*."

The boy's face fell. "But, *Señor* Lucas, am I not doing an adequate job?"

"You're doing an excellent job," I said, touching the boy on the shoulder. "A man's job. But it will serve no purpose for you to follow *Caballo Loco* or the other man... or anyone we have been watching... while *Señor* Hemingway and I are at sea."

"You do not wish to know with whom the lieutenant is meeting?" the boy said quizzically. "I understood that it was important that we knew these things."

"It is important," I said. "But we know enough now that there is no reason to continue our surveillance until I return. Then I may have some very important jobs for you."

The boy's face brightened again. "And when you all return, we will play baseball again against Gigi's Stars? And this time you might play with our team the way *Señor* Hemingway sometimes plays on his sons' team?"

"Perhaps," I said. "Yes, I would like that. Truly." I was telling the truth. I loved baseball and had been frustrated watching the teams play while I sat idly on the grassy sidelines. One of the few things that I had carried everywhere in my duffel bag over the years had been the fielder's mitt my uncle had given me when I was eight. I had used that glove in college and at law school and at pickup games on the White House lawn when I was still regular FBI. I would not mind striking Hemingway out.

The boy was grinning and nodding. "Is there anything that I *should* do while you are away, *Señor* Lucas?"

I gave him three dollars. "Have some ice cream at one of Obispo's shops," I said. "Purchase some food for your family."

"I have no family, *Señor* Lucas," said the boy, still smiling but staring dubiously at the bills in his palm. He offered them back.

I folded his fingers around the bills. "Purchase almond cakes on the Calle Obispo," I said. "Have dinner at one of the *bodegas* where they know you. Agents must keep up their strength. There are difficult missions ahead."

The boy's grin lit up the morning. "*Sí, Señor* Lucas. I thank you for your generosity."

I shook my head. "It is your salary, Agent 22," I said. "Now run along. Return the unknown gentleman's motorbike if you please. We will find you another one... a *legal* one. I will see you in a week or less."

The boy had run down the dusty road past the *finca* in a cloud of dust.

THE *PILAR* PURRED OUT OF Cojímar's harbor on a cloudless day with the *brisa*—the locals' name for the trade winds out of the northeast—blowing just hard enough to cool us but not hard enough to churn the Gulf Stream into a heavy sea. Hemingway was in an expansive mood and kept pointing out landmarks to the boys: La Terreza, the big old house that was one of their favorite restaurants along the beach there, the big tree beyond La Terreza where the writer liked to sit and drink and chat with the local fishermen, and then he challenged the two boys to differentiate the fishermen from the *guajiros*, the countrymen, at this distance of three hundred yards and more.

"We cannot see their faces at this distance, Papa," Gregory said.

Hemingway laughed and put his arm around the younger boy. "You don't need to see their faces, Gigi. You see, the *guarijo* is nervous when he comes to town or the coast and he wears those formal shirts... the ones with the pleats... and the tight trousers, and the wide hats, and the riding boots."

"Yes, of course!" cried Patrick, who had gone to the flying bridge with the large binoculars. "You've pointed that out before, Papa. And they always carry their machetes. You can see them here without the glasses."

Gregory was nodding, happy in the circle of his father's arm. "Yes, I see now, Papa. It is like a costume that the *guarijos* wear. But what about the fishermen?"

Hemingway laughed and pointed at Gregorio Fuentes, standing comfortably on the narrow ledge on the port side of the cabin. "The fishermen are cheerful and self-confident, Gig. They wear whatever they damned well please. Bits and pieces and scraps of old clothes. And if you were looking through

Mouse's field glasses, you could tell them from the *guarijos* by how scarred and gnarled and brown their hands are."

"But the countrymen are brown as well, Papa," said the younger boy.

"Yes, Gigi, but the hair on their hands and arms is dark. Can you see, even from this distance, how bleached the hair on the arms of the fishermen is... worn white by the sun and the salt?"

"Yes, Papa," said the boy, although now we were far enough out toward the breakwater that the shapes of the fishermen on the shore were barely visible, much less their bare arms.

We headed southeast along the north coast of Cuba that day. The plan was to spend the night at the new little Cuban navy base on tiny Cayo Confites and search for the caves and the *Southern Cross* farther east along the coast the next day. The Gulf waters were blue and purple, the sky remained cloudless, the *brisa* continued blowing softly out of the northeast, and the sea was dotted with numerous fishing boats and pleasure craft, most using sails because of the wartime shortage of gasoline. It was a perfect day for cruising, but the perfection was shattered when it became apparent that the executive officer, Winston Guest, had forgotten to load the three cases of beer that Hemingway had pronounced the minimum amount necessary for a six- or seven-day mission. I was below, making notes and thinking about the ramifications of Delgado's rendezvous in the cigar factory, when the screaming and obscenities in Spanish and English and French began on deck. I rushed up, thinking that a German sub had surfaced—which, of course, they almost never did in daylight—and that we were on the verge of being boarded or sunk.

Everyone, even the boys, was cursing Guest soundly for forgetting the beer. The millionaire stayed steadfastly at the wheel, his ruddy cheeks growing redder and redder, but his eyes were lowered and his expression had become sheepish.

"It's all right, Wolfer," Hemingway said at last, cutting off the flow of invective. "They'll probably have laid in beer along with other provisions for us at Cayo Confites."

"If not," said Sinsky in an ominous murmur, "we shall have to mutiny and take this boat back to Havana."

"Or up to Miami," said Patchi Ibarlucia.

"Or just raid their base at Cayo Confites and seize the Cubans' homemade still," said Roberto Herrera.

"Or maybe there'll be beer in the secret German caves," said Patrick. "Ice-cold Bavarian beer hidden in the backs of the caves alongside the stacked jerricans of fuel."

"Bavarian beer and sauerkraut and sausage," cried Gregory. "Only we'll have to get past the sentries and those snarling German shepherds standing guard."

"I will create a diversion by setting fire to *Señor* Guest," said Sinsky.

"And we'll rush in while they're dousing Wolfer," said Patrick from the flying bridge. "Deprive the entire kraut sub fleet of their booze and vittles. Morale will plummet. The Nazis will abandon the Caribbean. The navy will give us a Silver Cross."

"A golden church key," said Ibarlucia.

Fuentes, who had been watching with squinted eyes and listening with a pained expression, said, "All this talk of cold beer is making me thirsty."

Hemingway pulled himself up the ladder to the flying bridge and took the wheel. Below, Winston Guest sighed and sat down on one of the cockpit cushions.

"Courage, lads!" called Hemingway from above. "With God's help, relief will come soon."

I shook my head and went below to puzzle out the current status of cross and double cross surrounding the Crook Factory.

19

MY HEADQUARTERS for thinking was the "radio shack"—actually, the *Pilar*'s former head, now crammed with $35,000 worth of government radio equipment. There was barely room to sit down on a tiny stool between the banks of shortwave receivers and navy transmitters. The two books I had taken off the *Southern Cross* were in a watertight bag stuffed beside the main radio, where the old toilet paper dispenser had been. When I took notes, I had to prop the notebook on my knee. It was very hot and stuffy down there with the door closed, but at least the door closed. With nine males aboard the *Pilar*, there was no private place to sleep and no private place to perform the duties for which the once and former head had been designed. The running joke—especially popular with the two boys—was that our first war casualty would be whoever fell overboard while trying to take a crap on rough seas.

With the radio earphones on, most of the horseplay and noise from above decks was silenced. Now I tried to empty my mind of the nonsense of this seagoing "mission" so as to concentrate on what was important.

I HAD GLIMPSED THE MAN sitting across from Delgado in the cigar factory for two seconds before I had pulled the door shut, but I had no trouble at all identifying him. I had seen his photograph in a dossier two years before in Mexico City and had read his name and code name recently in the Theodor Schlegel file that Delgado had shown me. It was the same man: the dark hair combed straight back in the South American style, the long hair on the sides touching the tops of his ears, the sad puppy dog eyes, his right eyebrow heavier than the left (but only the left one had been raised in surprise as the door had opened a crack), his full, sensuous lips, only partially tempered by the precise dark mustache. He had been expensively attired in a pale suit with a burgundy silk tie, impeccably knotted, the tie showing unobtrusive diamond patterns in gold thread.

This was Hauptsturmführer Johann Siegfried Becker of the SS...perhaps *Captain* Becker by now, if the April SIS intelligence estimates were correct. In April, it had been reported that Becker had been ordered to report back to Berlin from Rio in early May for reassignment and a possible promotion.

Becker was twenty-eight, close to my age. He had been born in Leipzig on October 21, 1912, and had joined the Nazi Party immediately after graduating from high school in Leipzig. He was admitted into the SS in 1931. It was highly unusual for a nineteen-year-old to be inducted into the dreaded, black-uniformed Schutz-Staffel, the Nazi "protection squadron"—Hitler's original private group of bodyguards from the 1920s, now grown into the most frightening of all frightening Nazi organizations, identified with the Gestapo and death camps and the SS's own intelligence service, the SD—but Johann Siegfried Becker was an unusual young man. Nazi Party documents attested to the fact that he was a superb organizer and an indefatigable worker. On April 20, 1937, Becker was promoted to an SS second lieutenant and was immediately shipped off to Buenos Aires, where he arrived on May 9 aboard the *Monte Pascoal.* There he worked undercover as a representative of the Berlin-based firm Centro de Exportacion del Comercio Aleman until the previous month, when he had been recalled to Berlin for another promotion and further orders.

The FBI and SIS in Central and South America knew Johann Becker as the finest Nazi agent in the Western Hemisphere. The Argentine police had almost closed the circle on Becker in 1940, but the SS man had moved to Brazil, where he had offered his services to the flailing Abwehr operation there run by Albrecht Gustav Engels—Theodor Schlegel's boss and the "Alfredo" of our decoded radio transmission. In a Berlin-bound communiqué intercepted by ONI in 1941, Engels himself had described Becker as the "only real professional agent" in both his network and South America and admitted that the SS man had "supplied the brains and energy" necessary to make the complicated Rio-based spy network viable. What made this so unusual that it had come to my attention in Colombia and Mexico was that Becker was SD—the intelligence arm of the SS—and Engels's network was an Abwehr operation.

The SD and the Abwehr hated and loathed one another almost as much as their respective chiefs—Reinhard Heydrich and Admiral William Canaris—hated and loathed each other. Each man wanted his own agency to be the one, true intelligence organization of the Third Reich. The competition was similar to the BSC's rivalry with MI5, or the FBI's unrelenting dislike for what was now the OSS, only in Germany such rivalry had been known to end up in machine gun massacres and literal backstabbings.

And now Johann Siegfried Becker—SS man, SD spy—had been newly promoted to captain by the Führer and presumably given much more responsibility. In fact, an unprecedented kind of responsibility that actually *united* Abwehr and SD espionage efforts in South America under the auspices of Becker's directorship. And now this man was meeting in a Havana cigar factory with my liaison and only lifeline to the Bureau, Special Agent Delgado.

I had to think about this.

Forty-five minutes of thinking later, I realized that there were still only four possibilities:

First, Delgado had turned double agent and was meeting with Becker to arrange some sort of betrayal of me, of Hemingway, of the Bureau, and of the United States.

Second, Delgado was working a much more important mission than overseeing my vacation with the Crook Factory—a more important mission that somehow included turning Hauptsturmführer Johann Siegfried Becker into a double agent working against the Reich.

Third, Delgado was working under cover himself, possibly

posing as an agent or paid informant working under Becker, or offering himself as a double agent in order to pass along misinformation to the German.

Fourth, some other scenario that I could not puzzle out.

Of these choices, the third was the most plausible—I had just stumbled on Delgado doing what we SIS agents do, what I had done many times myself when working under deep cover—but I was still uneasy.

Much of the uneasiness, I realized, came from the timing of things and this strange cooperation between the SD and the Abwehr. The timing was strange not only because of the almost absurd concentration of intelligence operatives in Cuba and around Hemingway's amateur operation but also because both Schlegel and Becker were carrying out their Cuba operation—whatever the hell it was—several months after almost being nabbed in the Brazilian/FBI crackdown on their networks there. It was possible that neither man knew about the arrests and phony transmissions now coming from Rio, but it seemed unlikely. On the other hand, Schlegel had left Brazil before the arrests had come too close to him, and SIS intercepts had reported that Becker was having trouble getting back to Berlin this spring because the Italian transatlantic airline had suspended flights after Pearl Harbor.

More troubling was this cooperation between the Sicherheitsdienst—the SD, Security Service—and Abwehr intelligence. Over the past six years, I had done more reading and investigation on this matter than most SIS field agents. Hell, I had probably studied it about as much as anyone in this hemisphere outside of Donovan's OSS specialists. If nothing else, it made use of my study of German in college and law school.

On the surface, the separation of missions and jurisdiction between the SD and the Abwehr seemed logical enough: Heydrich's SD had been in charge of all political espionage worldwide; Canaris's military Abwehr had exclusive responsibility for all military intelligence. This *modus vivendi* had been arrived at late in 1936, when the rivalry between Himmler's SS and the traditional Abwehr intelligence apparatus had reached such a frenzy that Hitler himself had been forced to demand a peace.

The "peace" was actually another huge step in the growing power of the SS and its intelligence wing, the SD.

Heinrich Himmler had originally consolidated the SS's power on the last day of June 1934, during the Night of the Long Knives, when—under Hitler's direct command—the SS had assassinated Ernst Rohm and hundreds of other leaders of the SA, the Sturmabteilung brownshirts who had been Hitler's shock troops all through his rise to power. On that one bloody night, Himmler had taken the SS from a minor power to the single, terrifying power of the Nazi Reich, assassinating not only the homosexual leaders of the brownshirts but destroying the power of the two-million-man street army. Less than three weeks after the massacre, Himmler had appointed young Reinhard Heydrich as the new leader of the party's intelligence branch, the Sicherheitsdienst.

Since 1934, Heydrich's chief enemy had not been foreign intelligence services but Canaris's venerable Abwehr. After the 1936 pact was signed, both groups had agreed to abide by the *Zehn Gebote*—the Ten Commandments of German Intelligence—separating the responsibility of the two agencies. In practice, Heydrich and his boss, Himmler, worked constantly to undermine and destroy Canaris's credibility with the Führer. Their ultimate goal was to dissolve the hundred-year-old Abwehr and bring *all* police, intelligence, and counterintelligence power under the Nazi Party security umbrella.

Heinrich Himmler ran the SS as well as the SD. Reinhard Heydrich had—until his assassination in June—headed up the Reichsicherheitshauptamt, the RSHA, the Reich Security Administration. Heydrich's RSHA consisted of several key departments:

RSHA I was personnel. RSHA II was administration. RSHA III was domestic intelligence. RSHA IV was the dreaded Gestapo. RSHA V consisted of detectives. RSHA AMT VI was foreign intelligence.

Since 1941, the director of AMT VI had been a handsome young SS brigadier named Walter Schellenberg. Only thirty-two years old, Schellenberg seemed much more urbane and sane than his recently murdered boss—Heydrich had been known as a whoremaster, a cold-blooded schemer with spidery hands, and had been called "the Butcher of Prague" during his brief reign as acting protector of Bohemia and Moravia—but reports suggested that Schellenberg was every bit as determined to dominate and destroy the Abwehr as Heydrich had been. In espionage circles, Schellenberg was famous for his daring kidnapping of two British agents in Holland in 1939. The Nazi had disguised himself as a "Major Schemmel," interested in joining a plot of German generals planning to overthrow Hitler and make peace with England. British Intelligence had bought the ruse and had sent two agents to meet with Schellenberg in the Dutch town of Venlo on the morning of November 9, 1939. Schellenberg had signaled his men, who had crashed through the frontier barricades in a rushing automobile, and then he had handcuffed the two surprised British agents and dragged them off to Germany for interrogation, after fending off pistol fire from other British operatives.

The incident had done little to hurt Schellenberg's standing with either Heydrich or Hitler.

In 1940, Schellenberg had almost pulled off another kidnapping—this one of the Duke of Windsor, the former King Edward VIII of England. Because of the duke's pro-Hitler statements, the Germans thought that the idiot would make a good mouthpiece for the Third Reich. Schellenberg planned an elaborate scheme to kidnap the duke and duchess in Spain while the former king and the woman he loved traveled to their post-in-exile in the Bahamas. Despite elaborate attempts only discovered later by BSC and the SIS, Schellenberg missed the duke when the royal changed his plans at the last moment and did not return to Spain.

This failure had not visibly slowed Schellenberg's rise to power, however, and Heydrich had made him his favorite, finally appointing him to command of RSHA AMT VI just a year before, in June 1941.

I had been curious about Schellenberg and AMT VI. While the Abwehr had blundered repeatedly in Mexico and South America, leading to the arrests of most of its agents, the SD operatives had been much more successful. Schellenberg evidently trusted no one and admired boldness. The Department VI headquarters was set apart from most of the other SD offices, quartered in the southwest-central section of Berlin at Berkaerstrasse 32, on the corner of the Hohenzollerndamm. Schellenberg's office there was—according to debriefings of British agents who had been there—equipped with two machine guns hidden in his desk, ready to murder anyone attempting to assassinate him.

This was the man who had called Johann Siegfried Becker back to Berlin in May to reassign him to some special operation in South America or the Caribbean. Presumably, that operation had been authorized—and perhaps designed—by Becker's chief, Heydrich, or the head of the SS himself, Heinrich Himmler.

Why are they cooperating with the Abwehr on this operation? What the hell does it have to do with the Southern Cross *and Hemingway's farce? Where does Delgado fit in?*

A noise cutting through static made my eyes snap open. I quickly tugged the earphones tighter and reached for my notebook and the watertight bag.

Somebody was transmitting on the frequency reserved for the *Southern Cross.* And it was in the same cipher used in the dead radio operator's codebook.

THERE WAS NO TIME to talk to Hemingway in private about the radio transmissions that afternoon or evening. And I had no intention of telling him with the others around.

We anchored off Cayo Confites just before nightfall. The spit of land was too small to be called an island, almost too small for the term "key." Young Gregory said that it looked like the skating rink at Rockefeller Center—only about a hundred yards in diameter and quite flat, featureless except for the shack in the center. The Cuban navy had built the shack as a communications post and resupply center for Hemingway's Operation Friendless and a few other naval projects, but the only signs that it was a military outpost were the tall radio antenna atop the shack and an oversized flagpole next to it. The Cuban flag was flapping as we raised the key, but just as we dropped anchor, three Cubans in naval uniforms marched out of the shack in tight formation. One stood at attention by the ropes as the officer stared at his watch, then signaled the third man, who blew a ragged cascade of notes on a rusty trumpet.

"Papa, look," said Gregory, "only the officer has an old ragged tunic on. Those other two are just wearing khaki shorts."

"Shhh, Gigi," said Hemingway. "They wear what they have. It doesn't matter what they wear."

The youngest boy looked crestfallen at his *faux pas*, but Patrick said in a stage whisper, "What is that rusty rope on the officer's shoulder, Papa?"

"I think it's supposed to be braid," said Hemingway.

The three Cubans had hauled down their flag. The awful trumpeting ended. One man carried the flag into the shack while the officer and the other enlisted man in shorts watched us drop anchor.

Ibarlucia, Herrera, and Guest had the *Tin Kid* free and were rowing for the beach before the *Pilar*'s anchor had kicked up silt. Ten minutes later they rowed back, and one glance at their faces showed that the base had not stocked any beer for us. A strange wailing was coming from the dinghy, but I could not believe that it was actually coming from the three men.

"Any beer?" called Hemingway from the stern.

"No!" The voices of the three men blended with the caterwauling. They seemed to be struggling with something.

"Any orders?" yelled the writer.

"No." It was Roberto Herrera in the bow of the dinghy. Guest and the jai-alai star were still wrestling with what sounded like a child being strangled, but Herrera's body blocked our view.

"Any sightings of the *Southern Cross*?" queried Hemingway.

"Uh-uh," called Herrera. They were within twenty feet now. The noise from the dinghy was incredible.

"Any provisions for us?" shouted Fuentes from the bow.

"Just beans," yelled Ibarlucia. "Twenty-three cans of beans. And this." He and Winston Guest held up a squealing pig.

Patrick and Gregory were laughing and slapping their bare legs. Their father looked disgusted. "Why are you bringing it aboard tonight? We don't want the goddamn pig sleeping with us."

Ibarlucia grinned up at us. His teeth were very white in the twilight. "If we leave our pig on the island tonight, Ernesto, the soldiers here will be having bacon for breakfast and ham sandwiches at noon. I do not think they will share with us."

Hemingway sighed. "Leave the damned thing in the dinghy. And *you*," he snapped, turning to the Basque named Sinsky, who was laughing and guffawing next to him. "*You* get to clean out the dinghy in the morning."

WITH A SQUEALING PIG in the dinghy and nine snoring, grumbling, farting men taking up every available horizontal surface on the *Pilar*, sleep was problematical that night. Around three A.M., I went up the ladder to the flying bridge, where Winston Guest was leaning against the railing, staying upright and alert for his watch. What we were watching for, I will never know. Perhaps Hemingway feared that a U-boat would come in close to the reef and attempt to sink the Cuban's shack.

"Nice night," whispered Guest as I leaned on the railing opposite him. It was a nice night: the sound of the waves breaking on the surf, the phosphorescent curl where they broke almost blending with the glow of the Milky Way spilling across the dome of black above us. There was not a cloud in the sky.

"Can't sleep?" whispered the millionaire. We were only six feet above the heads of the men sleeping on the cushions surrounding the cockpit, but because of the breeze, the waves lapping against the hull, and the surf breaking on the reef, no one could hear a whisper from the flying bridge.

I shook my head.

"Worried about the caves tomorrow?" he whispered. "That maybe the U-boat could still be there?"

"No," I said softly.

Guest nodded. Even with just the starlight for illumination, I could make out his sunburned cheeks and nose and his easy smile. "I guess I'm not either," he whispered. "I wish they would be there. I wish we could catch just one."

The way he said that made me think of a child wishing on a star. If Winston Guest *was* an agent, British or otherwise, he was one hell of a good actor. But then, as I had already noted, aren't we all who follow this trade?

"Did you see Ernest reading by flashlight when the others were sleeping?" whispered Guest.

I nodded.

"Do you know what he was reading?"

"No." I hoped that this would not be more melodramatic garbage about secret orders or somesuch.

"One of Martha's manuscripts," whispered Guest, his voice so low now that even I could barely make it out above the surf noise. "A book she's working on that she sent in from her goddamn cruise. *The Purple Orchid*, or some damn title. She wants Ernest to read it and tell her what he thinks, and he does... after fourteen hours at the wheel today."

I nodded and looked at the Cuban shack, glowing in the starlight. There had been lantern light for a while after dark, but the garrison of three had turned in early.

Guest said, "Yeah, those poor sons of bitches are stuck out here for the duration. Ernest said that the officer was probably assigned to this shithole of a key because he'd been screwing the commandant's wife and the other two were serving their sentences here for petty thievery."

I nodded. I had not come up to the flying bridge for conversation, but if Guest wanted to talk, I did not mind. I was still thinking about the two radio transmissions I had intercepted earlier.

"Speaking of wives," whispered Guest. "What do you think of her?"

"Who?" I said. I had no idea what he was talking about.

"Martha. Ernest's third."

I shrugged in the dark. "She has a lot of nerve," I said, "if she's still trolling around the Caribbean in that small boat."

Guest made a noise. "Balls, you mean," he whispered very softly. "Martha's always thought that she ought to wear the balls in the family."

I looked at the bulk of the sportsman, silhouetted against the glowing waves breaking across the reef. After a moment, Guest went on in a rapid whisper. "Ernest has shown me a few pages of this book she's writing... *Liana*, I think it's called. It's all about a man and his wife living in a place a lot like the *finca*.

And the man's always barefoot and in shorts and dirty and drinking too much and saying stupid things and this damn thing and the other. It makes me mad, Lucas. She's obviously writing about Ernest, painting this ugly picture of him. And here he is, dog tired, his belly hurting, his head aching from fourteen hours of sub patrol in the sun today, and he's making notes and treating her stuff like literature and she's just taking advantage of him, that's all."

I leaned on the railing. After a moment, Guest let out a long breath.

"I know I shouldn't be talking like this, but you live up there at the *finca*, Lucas. Well, not right at the *finca*, but close. You've seen them. You know what I mean."

I said nothing. Guest nodded as if I had agreed with him.

"A week or so before she left on her stupid *Collier's* cruise," whispered the other man, "Ernest asked me to go running with her... with Martha. It was when he was away with the boys during the first round of that pigeon shoot, and he didn't want her to get lonely. So I ran with her. She can't run worth shit. So I'd run half a mile ahead, then double back to her, then half a mile ahead, then back to make sure she was still moving... you know the drill."

A gull flew over in the starlight. We both watched it. It made no noise. Guest raised a make-believe rifle and sighted on the gull until it disappeared beyond the Cubans' shack.

"Anyway," he whispered, "all of a sudden... one of these times when we're running together for a few paces... she asks me what I thought of her choice of a husband. I said, 'What do you mean? Do you mean what do I think of Ernest?' And Gellhorn says, 'No... I mean what do you think of my choice?' And then she goes on—between panting like a dog ready to drop from exhaustion—she goes on to say that she'd picked Ernest mostly because he was a very good writer... 'Not a great writer,' she said, 'but a very good one'... and he could certainly help her grow as a writer and help her career. 'And,' she said, 'there's always the money from the books he's already written. That's nice.'

"Well, Jesus, Lucas, you could have knocked me over with a

feather. What a ball-breaker. What a tough, mercenary, self-serving bitch. To talk about Ernest like that in front of me. She didn't imply that she loved him at all, do you know what I mean? Just that he could help her career. What a bitch."

The millionaire's whisper was getting louder. I could hear the emotion in his voice. I nodded toward the sleeping men. Hemingway was sleeping belowdecks forward, with the boys, but someone might hear at least the tone of Guest's agitated whisper. I raised my eyebrow.

He nodded as if chastised and dropped his whisper to an almost inaudible level. "And besides, everyone in Havana and Cojímar... everyone except Ernest... knows that Martha's been having an affair an with José Regidor."

"*El Canguro?*" I whispered in surprise.

"Yeah," said Guest. "The Kangaroo. That handsome jai alai player. Just Marty's type. And Ernest's good friend. That bastard. Oh, that bitch."

I shook my head noncommittally, then whispered, "I'm going below. Unless you want me to relieve you now. It was a long day."

Guest shook his head. "Patchi will be up in half an hour to take the watch." He patted my shoulder clumsily. "Thanks, Lucas. Thanks for talking with me."

"Sure," I said, and slid noiselessly down the ladder.

THE NEXT MORNING we headed southeast, losing track of Cayo Confites and Cayo Verde astern, catching only a glimpse of the landmasses of Cayo Romano and then Cayo Sabinal to the south—both extensions of the mainland rather than true keys—and continuing along the edge of the Gulf beyond Punta Maternillos. The pig was driving us crazy. The animal was still in the *Tin Kid*, but squealing constantly now.

"Let me kill him and scald him and scrape him," said Fuentes. "That will quiet him and calm our nerves."

"I don't want the mess right now," said Hemingway, at the wheel in the cockpit. "And I don't want to lay up so that you can do it in the dinghy."

Fuentes shook his head. "I think that we will all be as crazy as that pig before we reach the caves."

Hemingway nodded. "I have an idea."

The *Pilar* swung north toward what appeared to be a white mirage floating in the blue sea. It was a small key—a fourth the size of Cayo Confites, its high point less than a foot above sea level. There was no reef and no real vegetation. No other land was in sight. I estimated that this key was about twenty-five miles from Confites and about twenty from the mainland.

"This is not on the charts," said Guest.

Hemingway nodded again. "I know, but I marked it the last time we patrolled this area. It looks perfect for our purpose."

"Our purpose?" said Guest.

Hemingway showed his teeth. "We need a pen for the pig." To Fuentes, he said, "Go on aft, Gregorio. Take the *Kid* and *el cerdo* on up through the shallows and show him his new home. We'll pick him up tonight or tomorrow morning on the way back."

The boys laughed to watch the pig run to one end of the island, dip its trotters into the lapping surf, squeal, and then run to the other end.

"He won't have anything to eat, Papa," said Gregory. "Or to drink."

"Watch," said Hemingway. "I told Gregorio to cut open that coconut with his machete and fill one half with water so the pig does not suffer until we return. Then we will eat it tomorrow."

"The coconut or the pig, Papa?"

"The pig," said Hemingway.

We reached the suspected submarine caves in mid-afternoon. U.S. Naval Intelligence had sent us on this mission, and as was usual with Naval Intelligence, the mission was more joke than job. Hemingway put in at a local village on the mainland to see if they knew of any large coastal caves, and the people there said of course they did, that they were a famous Cuban tourist attraction. They appointed a boy about Santiago's age to show us the way.

A mile down the coast, the boy showed us where to anchor, and with Fuentes staying aboard the *Pilar*, the rest of us took turns ferrying into a small cove. A weathered sign above the white spit of beach read in poorly spelled Spanish SEE THE SPECTACULAR CAVES—THE TENTH WONDERS OF THE NATURAL WORLD.

"La cuevas espectacular," Hemingway muttered darkly to himself. His face was redder above his new beard than sunburn alone would explain. He was in a vile mood.

"The boy says that no tourists have come here since the war started," said Guest. "The Germans could be using it."

"Yes, Papa!" cried Gregory. "The cave is probably filled with food and ammunition."

"I just hope there's some fucking beer," muttered Ibarlucia, whose mood was even darker than Hemingway's.

We followed the boy and the faint path up the beach, through a tumble of rocks, and into the largest of several cavities in the cliff. Hemingway was carrying his *.22* pistol in an old holster, Ibarlucia had one of the submachine guns from the boat, and Patrick carried his mother's old Mannlicher .256. Standing just inside the cave entrance, we could see only rough rock floor that stretched away into total darkness, but echoes suggested that the cave was very large. A cool, damp breeze breathed out of the depths at us and felt very good after the long day in the sun and the heat.

"I brought a lantern," said Roberto Herrera.

"We have flashlights!" cried Hemingway's boys.

"It is not necessary," said the little Cuban boy. "I will turn on the lights."

"Lights?" said Hemingway.

Hundreds of colored bulbs came on. They were strung around the huge cave like Christmas lights, hanging from and between stalactites, arching over dark apertures, one string rising to the high point in the cave almost a hundred feet above us.

"Wow!" said Gregory.

"Jesus fucking Christ," muttered Hemingway.

"Look, Papa," called Patrick, running ahead. "You can see where it narrows way over there. That has to be it! That's where the Germans have hidden their supplies. That probably leads to another giant tunnel. They wouldn't leave their things out here!"

The Cuban boy did not know where this tunnel led, only

that it was "much favored by lovers." There were no electric lights there, so we lit lanterns and turned on flashlights and followed Patrick and Gregory for several hundred yards down a narrow, winding corridor. While pausing at one juncture, Sinsky cut his hand on a sharp rock. Guest had a handkerchief but could not stop the bleeding, so he, Sinsky, Herrera, and the Cuban boy headed back. "You bring out the German sausage and beer and we'll picnic on the beach," called Guest as he disappeared back up the narrow passage.

Patrick, Gregory, Hemingway, and I pressed on. I watched the back of the writer's head as he ducked under rocks and stalactites, carrying the lantern, trying to keep up with his excited sons. At some places we had to crawl through the mud or over slick rock. At others we had to skirt pools that were either an inch deep or connected with the bottomless sea. And still the tunnel stretched on. We walked and crawled and squeezed through for what seemed like hours. Why was Hemingway doing this?

At that moment, I began to understand something about the man and the way he mixed reality and fantasy. Hemingway had seen war, and he knew what was coming. He knew that his oldest boy would certainly be in it—and quite possibly these younger ones as well if the conflict dragged on. The writer was giving his sons a taste of boyish adventure this last summer before the grim reality of war settled in on America. The Crook Factory, the sub patrols—it was all a way to restructure this terrible world war into something small and personal and romantic, with a dash of danger but very little of the mundane misery and terrible vulgarity and sickening tragedy of a real war.

Either that or he was nuts.

I felt a surge of anger then, but it was interrupted by Gregory. "Papa! Papa! It narrows here. It's not as large as the forward overhead hatch on the *Pilar*! I bet this is the entrance to their secret storehouse!"

We crouched at the tiny opening. It was actually a little below the floor of the cave, a ramp of slick rock going down into darkness beneath the sharp bottom of a boulder. The boys were right about one thing...the main tunnel ended there.

"Can you fit into that, Lucas?" asked Hemingway, lying on his belly and playing one of the flashlight beams into the darkness. The narrow passage turned to the left in an even smaller aperture.

"No," I said.

"I can, Papa!" cried Patrick.

"Me too!" said Gregory.

"All right, boys," said Hemingway, handing the flashlight back to his youngest son. "Gigi, you're the smallest, so you go first. Mouse, pull Gig out by the ankles if he gets stuck."

"Can I carry the pistol, Papa?" said Patrick. The fourteen-year-old sounded out of breath.

"You'll need your hands free to dig," said Hemingway. "And it may get hung up in your back pocket. I'll hand it down to you if you need it."

The older boy looked disappointed but nodded.

Hemingway patted both boys on the back. "Go on to the end, boys—if there *is* one. Good luck. I know you won't quit. You both know what it means if we find the depot."

They both nodded, eyes bright in the lantern light, and then Gregory squeezed into the opening and disappeared. Patrick followed a few seconds later. Both boys made it through the first two tight places. Hemingway continued calling to them after they were out of sight, but only Patrick's voice could be heard—faintly—echoing back up the narrow tunnel. Then there was silence.

The writer leaned back against the cave wall. I could see burst capillaries in his cheeks and nose—tiny hemorrhages that were not usually visible in the sunlight. He looked very happy.

"What if they get stuck?" I said softly.

He looked at me with a steady gaze. "Then I guess they've had it," he said. "But I'll put them in for a Navy Cross."

I shook my head. It was the first time we had been alone together since I had received the two radio transmissions, but this did not seem like the right time to mention them. Hemingway had no trouble mixing his fantasy and reality, but I still liked to keep the two separate.

Ten minutes later there was a muffled noise from the passage and the soles of Patrick's sneakers appeared. We helped pull the older boy back up the last bit of tunnel. A few seconds later, Gregory scuttled out backward. Both boys were covered with mud from head to foot. Gregory's shorts were torn in a score of places. He had removed his plaid shirt and wrapped it around something bulky. The bundle clinked. In some places, blood from small scrapes mixed with the mud on Gregory's chest and back, and both boys' hands were a mess. They were very excited.

"Right at the end, Papa!" said the younger boy, his voice so loud that it echoed in the dark tunnel. "It was right at the end, too narrow even for me to crawl forward, and I thought that we'd failed... but then I found *these*!"

"He did, Papa! I helped him wrap them. We thought it was empty, but we found these!" Patrick's voice was as excited as his younger brother's.

Hemingway held the lantern closer as Gregory unwrapped the bundle with shaking fingers. "Good work, lads. Good work!" Hemingway's voice was as excited as the boys' voices. Suddenly I felt like an intruder, an adult stumbling into a boys' universe.

"You did it, Gig! You did it!" Hemingway was saying, patting the boy on the back so fiercely that the ten-year-old could hardly untie his package. "Let's see what you got!" said Hemingway.

Gregory pulled out four bottles, their brown glass visible through the patina of mud.

"They're German beer bottles, Papa," said Patrick, trying to wipe the grime off one. "We looked at them in the flashlight beam down there. They're really German!"

Hemingway's face had fallen as he took one of the bottles in his hand and held the lantern above it.

"*They've* been here, Papa!" Gregory was saying. "The krauts. We thought that the tunnel just ended, but then we found these. I mean, their main depot must be at the end of one of those other little tunnels that led off the main passageway. We can't search them all today, but we can come back tomorrow morning! I'll go into the narrow ones. I wasn't afraid at all, Papa... not even when my shoulders got stuck and I had to wiggle but couldn't go forward or back until Patrick pushed me hard. Really I wasn't, Papa!"

Patrick was looking at his father's expression. "They *are* German bottles, aren't they, Papa? That one has a label still and the words are in German..."

Hemingway set the bottle down. "They're German beer bottles, all right," he said. "But made in the States by naturalized Germans. This one was brewed in Wisconsin. They were probably just tossed down there by picnickers. Tourists who came down this long tunnel for... something or the other."

There was a silence broken only by the hiss of the lantern flame. Suddenly Gregory turned his face to the cave wall and burst into tears. His shoulders moved up and down in silent sobs. I could see Patrick biting his lip; the older boy was also crying. Hemingway looked like he was ready to cry any minute as well. He put his big hand on Gregory's small shoulder. "You gave it your best shot, old man. I'm proud of you. In fact..."

Hemingway waited, but the boy kept his face turned away while he cried. Patrick looked up. "In fact, I'm recommending both of you for the Naval Cross for leading this expedition. And also..."

This time Gregory turned around. He was still crying softly, but he was listening.

"And also," said Hemingway with a chuckle, "an eventual transfer to Naval Intelligence."

THE CUBAN BOY TOOK HIS DOLLAR TIP—a fortune—and walked back to his village. We anchored in Spectacular Cave Cove that night. Hemingway authorized the opening of the Ethylic Department, and everyone was rationed three glasses of whiskey, even the boys. We built a large driftwood bonfire on the beach and made a serious dent in our provisions. We had not paused to catch any fish during our rush down the coast, so Fuentes laid out bread, canned beef, chilled chicken and sliced beef from the cooler, various vegetables, and freshly made potato salad. Hemingway ate several thick sandwiches of raw onion on dark rye bread, washed down by his ration of whiskey.

No one kept watch that night.

The next morning we detoured a few miles north to what the boys had named Cayo Cerdo to pick up our pig.

"Well, I'll be goddamned," said Hemingway.

"Our pig's gone," said Gregory.

"The bloody island is gone," said Winston Guest.

The island was there, actually, only it was about three feet underwater—a nasty little sandbar more than twenty miles from the nearest land.

Gregory was studying the horizon with binoculars. "I wonder if Cerdo swam for it," he said softly.

"Probably straight to the mainland," said Hemingway. "Unless he went north and east instead of south and west."

"I have seen this before," muttered Fuentes. "This reef is high enough to hold the sand between the tides. But when the high tide comes…*swisshh*. Gone."

"Poor Cerdo," said Gregory.

"We should have left him with the Cubans," said Sinsky.

"Fuck the Cubans," said Hemingway. "Let's skip Cayo Confites and make straight for home. We can't go after the *Southern Cross* or anything else without the provisions that were supposed to be waiting for us at Confites. We'll restock and head back out in a few days."

"It will be a very long day and night for you at the wheel, Ernest," said Guest.

Hemingway shrugged. Ibarlucia and the boys discussed what the here-now, gone-tomorrow island should be called on their revised chart. They settled on Cayo Cerdo Perdido—"Lost Pig Key."

LATE THAT NIGHT, during the last stages of the approach to Cojímar, I had some time alone with Hemingway on the flying bridge. I pulled out the codebook and showed him the first intercepted transmission.

"God damn," said the writer. "It's definitely from the *Southern Cross?*"

"Same Abwehr code as Kohler's," I said.

Hemingway tied the wheel off and held the flashlight closer to steady the grid.

[TWOAGENTSTOLAND 13/8 LT 21°25'—LG 76°48'30" 2300 HRS U516]

"God damn," he said again. "That thirteen/eight must be August thirteenth, less than a week from now. U-516 must be the number of the sub that's dropping the two spies off. I'll have to look at my charts, but I would think those coordinates would be near Bahía Manatí, Point Roma, or Point Jesus."

"They are," I said softly. "Point Roma. I checked the charts."

"Why in hell didn't you tell me this earlier?" snarled Hemingway.

"When?" I said. "We'd decided not to let the others in on this part of things."

"Yes," said Hemingway, glaring at me in the starlight, "but... goddammit, Lucas..." He unlashed the wheel and watched the ocean and approaching blackness of coast for a few minutes. "It doesn't matter. Point Roma would be a perfect place for two agents to infiltrate. There used to be a light there, but it's been out of order for five years. The bay is shallow, but it's deep water right up to the point. The Manatí Sugar Mill is abandoned, but they can see the old stack from deep water, and once they land, the infiltrators can follow the old railroad line all the way to the highway."

I waited for several minutes while Hemingway thought. Eventually, he said, "We're not reporting this, Lucas."

I was not surprised.

"Those bastards at the embassy and the FBI didn't give me any credit last time," continued the writer, his voice very soft but very firm. "This time, we'll drag in two prisoners and see what they have to say."

"What if the two prisoners don't feel like being dragged in?" I said.

Hemingway grinned at me in the dark. "They will, Lucas, trust me."

I looked toward land for a while. It was a following sea, rougher tonight, and we were charging down it like a runaway horse on a steep slope.

"What is it?" said Hemingway.

Without turning toward him, I said, "You think this is all a game."

I could only hear his voice, but I could *feel* him still grinning behind me. "Of course it's all a game. All of the good and hard and even bad things in life are just a game. What the hell's wrong with you, Lucas?"

I said nothing. Toward dawn, we raised the harbor at Cojímar.

IT WAS RAINING and gray in mid-morning when I went up to the *finca,* walked through the front door, and pounded on Hemingway's bedroom door. He opened it in his pajamas. His hair was tousled and his eyes were vague. A large black cat—the one named Boise, I think—glared at me from the rumpled bed.

"What the hell..." he began.

"Get dressed," I said. "I'll be out front in the car."

Hemingway was out two minutes later. He had a drink in a cork-lined thermos. I thought that it was tea until I smelled the whiskey.

"Now will you tell me just what the hell you think—" he began.

"A boy came," I said, driving the Lincoln very quickly down the muddy lane, through the gate I had already opened, down the hill, through the village, and out onto the Central Highway toward Havana.

"Which boy?" said Hemingway. "Santiago? One of the—"

"No," I said. "A black boy we don't know. Be quiet a minute."

Hemingway blinked, noticed how fast I was driving the Lincoln on the rain-swept roads, and stayed quiet.

Six miles toward Havana, just down the long hill where he

always told his chauffeur, Juan, to coast, I turned right down an unpaved road. Mud and water splashed by the side windows. The road ended in a tumble of abandoned shacks where a cane field had been left untended. The colored boy was waiting there on his motorbike. I slid the Lincoln to a stop and stepped out into the rain. Hemingway took a drink, left the flask on the front seat, and got out.

The other motorbike was just visible beyond the ditch. Someone had cut some branches in a sloppy effort to conceal it, but the rear wheel glistened wetly in the gray light. No one had made an effort to conceal the body.

Santiago was lying head down in the grassy ditch. His skinny legs looked very pale in the rain, there was some wet grass matted to his right knee, and he had lost his left sandal. The sole of his foot looked white and wrinkled, like fingers that have been in bathwater for too long. I resisted the insane urge to place the cheap sandal back on his foot.

Even though he was lying with his head down the slope and in a contorted position that looked terribly uncomfortable, Santiago's eyes were closed easily, his face was upturned, and he was smiling slightly as if he was enjoying the cool rain on his face. His hands were open and palms up and slightly curled as if he were trying to catch some of that rain. His throat had been cut from ear to ear.

Hemingway made a noise from deep in his throat and took a step back from the ditch.

I nodded at the black boy and he started his motorbike and headed back toward town, taking care not to slide on the rutted, muddy road.

"When?" said Hemingway.

"His friend found him during the night," I said. "About the time we saw the harbor lights."

Hemingway stepped into the ditch, ignoring the mud that squelched around his boots, and went to one knee next to the child. Hemingway's large, tanned hand touched the dead boy's small, white palm.

"Do you still think it's a fucking game?" I said.

Hemingway's head snapped around and he glared up at me

in pure hatred. I returned the stare. After a moment, the writer looked back at the boy's face.

"Do you know what comes next?" I said.

For a minute there was only the sound of the rain on the grass, on the puddles on the road, on our backs, and on the boy. Then he said, "Yes."

I waited.

"First we bury our dead," said the writer. "Then we find Lieutenant Maldonado. Then I kill him."

"No," I said. "That's not it at all."

20

CONFIDENTIAL MEMO
FROM FBI/SIS AGENT J. LUCAS
TO FBI DIRECTOR J. EDGAR HOOVER
AUGUST 9, 1942

Your charge to me upon accepting this assignment was to observe and report on the "true nature" of Mr. Ernest Miller Hemingway, an American citizen, age 43. This memorandum will attempt to summarize my observations on the subject to this point in time.

Ernest Hemingway is not, this observer is certain, an agent, willing or unwilling, of any foreign government, agency, power, or group. He *is*, however, a man living the life of a deep-cover agent—one of those dedicated, tormented, paranoid, and persistent moles of whom all counterespionage professionals live in fear. Why he has given up the flesh and bones of his identify to live in the shell of a self-made persona is difficult to understand.

Ernest Hemingway is a man addicted to words and thoughts. A man who reportedly glorifies action in his writing and life, Hemingway often confuses action with mere impulse, reality with self-inflicted melodrama. As a man among men, Hemingway makes friends easily and loses them even more easily. He assumes leadership in both senses of the word "assumes," and leads other men with the naturalness of nobility. As an acquaintance, he is loyal and treacherous. In daily life, he intersperses acts of great generosity with intervals of unremitting mean-spiritedness. In the course of a single day, he can exhibit great compassion and empathy followed by acts of a bone-deep selfishness. As a confidant, he is someone to be relied upon frequently but never fully trusted. As the captain of a small boat, he is skillful and instinctive. As a handler of weapons, he is careful but frequently immature. As a parent, he is deeply caring and frequently reckless. As a writer... but I have no idea what kind of writer Ernest Hemingway is.

I can say that Mr. Hemingway is the most bookish man with whom I have ever spent time. He reads newspapers in the morning, novels while on the toilet, magazines such as the *New Yorker* and *Harper's* while drinking by his swimming pool, books of history while eating lunch, more novels while sitting in the cockpit of his boat when others are at the wheel, foreign newspapers while drinking at the Floridita, letters between breaks in shooting competitions, collections of short stories while waiting for a fish to strike his line far out on the Gulf, and his wife's book manuscript by oil lamp while his boat is tied up behind a nameless key off the coast of Cuba during antisubmarine patrol. Hemingway is acutely sensitive to memory and nuance. He is also hypersensitive to praise and insult. Such tendencies would—one would think—lead the man to be a college professor or a prisoner of his own ivory tower. But instead we are confronted with the persona Hemingway has built for us—the hairy-chested brawler, the big-game hunter, the heavy-drinking adventurer, and the sexual braggart.

Hemingway is physically graceful and imposing, Mr. Director, while at the same time the man can be as clumsy as an ox in a phone booth. His vision is not good, yet somehow he manages to be an excellent wing shot. He hurts himself constantly. I have seen him run a fish hook through the ball of his thumb, split a gaff and ram splinters into his leg, slam a car door on his foot, and slam his head into a door frame. If he has a religion, it is exercise; he urges all those around him to immerse themselves in one violent form of exercise or another—even to the point of ordering his executive officer on the *Pilar*, a millionaire named Guest, to do road work and run several miles a day with the current

Mrs. Hemingway. Yet at the earliest sign of a sore throat or cold, Hemingway will take to his bed for hours or days on end. He is a habitual early riser, yet he often sleeps in until late morning.

I would assume that you are not a boxer, Mr. Director—and if you have ever sparred, it was with a fawning sparring partner from the Bureau, some suckling subordinate who would prefer to have his brains knocked out through his nose than to deliver a serious punch to your bulldog snout—but Ernest Hemingway has boxed. The other week, while Hemingway was drinking by the pool with a friend of his, a Dr. Herrera Sotolongo, I heard the writer spinning some elaborate boxing metaphor about his work: "I tried for Mr. Turgenev first and it wasn't too hard. Then I trained hard and I beat Mr. Maupassant, but it took four of my best stories to beat him. I've fought two draws with Mr. Stendhal, and I think I had an edge in the last one. But nobody's going to get me in the ring with Mr. Tolstoy unless I'm crazy or getting better. But I guess that's not true, because my ultimate goal is to knock Mr. Shakespeare on his ass. Very difficult."

I know nothing about writing, Mr. Director, but I know that this was—please excuse the term—bullshit.

There is another incident involving boxing that does, I think, describe Mr. Ernest Hemingway much better than his bragging.

Not long ago, when we were out on his boat one night, the writer told me about a time when he was sixteen or seventeen—still in high school in Oak Park, Illinois—and he found an advertisement in a Chicago paper for boxing lessons. Hemingway was eager to learn how to box, so he paid his money and signed up. It sounded, he said, like a good deal, because the instructors included several of the best boxers in the Midwest—Jack Blackburn, Harry Greb, Sammy Langford, and others. What Hemingway did not know was that this was an old con: the students would pay their tuition in advance and then be knocked out in the first lesson. Few ever showed up for the second.

Hemingway's first lesson went according to their script: he was knocked out by a local pro called Young A'Hearn. (I once sparred with Young A'Hearn, Mr. Director, but he was an old man of almost forty-five then, punchy, and going from gym to gym offering to spar in exchange for a few quarters or a drink.) At any rate, Hemingway surprised the con men by showing up the next Saturday for the next lesson. This time the fighter "teaching him"—someone named Morty Hellnick—ended the bout by punching Hemingway in the pit of his stomach after the bell had rung. Young Hemingway was puking for a week. In the next lesson, Hellnick deliberately hit the boy below the belt. "My left ball swelled up nearly as big as my fist," the writer told me. But he came back the following Saturday.

The point is, Mr. Director, that this kid finished his boxing course despite all of the punishment. He may have been the only "student" who ever completed the curriculum. He kept coming back for more.

I do not know exactly who or what Mr. Ernest Hemingway is, Mr. Director, or why you sent me here to spy on him and betray him—or possibly kill him—but I feel that I should warn you, the man does not quit or fold or go away easily. Whatever use you expected to put him to, be warned that this man is stubborn, and tough, and used to pain, and amazingly persistent.

That is the end of my observation and analysis to this point.

I SAT AT THE TYPING TABLE in the *finca*'s guest house and re-read my memo to Hoover. I had no intention of sending it anywhere, of course, and I would not have written it if I had not spent much of the night drinking whiskey and brooding, but it gave me some pleasure to read the words on the page in daylight—especially the part about the director's sparring only with fawning subordinates too afraid to deliver a punch to his bulldog snout. In the minute or so before I set fire to the sheet of paper and dropped it into the oversized ashtray, I wondered if this was the freedom that Hemingway felt while making up lies rather than sticking to facts when he wrote. Probably not—I had not made anything up in this report.

I put my actual two-page report in a manila envelope, slid the .38 into the back waistband of my trousers underneath a loose vest, and went up to the main house before driving into Havana to meet Delgado.

After the previous day's long, gray rain, it was a beautiful Sunday—cooler, blue sky, the trade winds blowing steadily from the northeast. The royal palms fluttered as I went by the pool to the house. From down the hill, I could hear the shouts of Gigi's Stars playing the other baseball team, known only as Los Muchachos. One of the *muchachos* was missing, but no one had asked about Santiago. One of the other boys had taken his place in the field and the game had gone on.

WE HAD BURIED THE BOY the day before, Saturday, the same day we found him, lowering his crude pine coffin into a grave in a remote part of the potters' field cemetery between the old viaduct and the smokestacks of the Havana Electric Company. Hemingway and I were the only ones there except for the grizzled old gravedigger whom we had bribed to bring a pine coffin out from the city morgue and to find us a grave plot. Not even Octavio, the Negro boy who had been Santiago's friend and who had found his body, had come to the hastily arranged graveside gathering.

After the gravedigger, Hemingway, and I lowered the small coffin into the muddy hole, there was an awkward pause. The old gravedigger stepped back and removed his hat. The rain ran down his bald scalp and scrawny neck. Hemingway had an old fishing hat on—he did not remove it—and rain dripped off the long bill. He looked at me. I had nothing to say.

The writer stepped to the edge of the grave. "This boy did not have to die," he said softly, his words barely audible over the patter of rain on the nearby foliage. "And he shouldn't have." Hemingway looked at me. "I let Santiago join our..." He glanced over his shoulder at the gravedigger, whose rheumy eyes were firmly fixed on the muddy ground. "I let Santiago join our team," continued Hemingway, "because every time I drove down to the Floridita before going to the embassy, a cloud of boys would surround the car, asking for money or begging me to let them shine my shoes or letting me know that they had a sister who was available. They were street boys, urchins, outcasts. Their parents had abandoned them or died of tuberculosis or drunk themselves to death. Little Santiago was one of these boys, but he never thrust his palm at me or asked to shine my shoes. He never spoke. He would hang back until the Lincoln started moving, and then—as the other boys fell away and went back to their begging posts on the corners—Santiago would jog alongside the car, never tiring, never asking for anything, never looking at me, but keeping up until I reached the embassy or we got out onto the main road."

Hemingway paused and looked up at the tall smokestacks of the Havana Electric Company. "I hate those fucking stacks," he said in the same tone he had been using for the eulogy, if eulogy it was. "They stink up the entire city when the wind blows in over the mountains." He looked back down into the grave.

"Rest well, young Santiago Lopez. We do not know where you came from nor where you have gone. But we know you've gone where all men go, and where we'll follow someday."

Hemingway looked at me again, as if suddenly self-conscious about what he was saying. But he continued, looking first at me and then at the narrow grave. "A few months ago, Santiago, another of my sons, John, my Bumby, asked me about dying. He was not afraid to go to war, he said, but he was afraid of being afraid of dying. I told Bumby about when I was wounded in 1918 and how afraid I was—I could not sleep without a night light, I was so afraid of dying suddenly—but I also told him about a very brave friend of mine named Chink Smith who quoted a bit of Shakespeare to me. I liked it so much that I had him write it out. It came from *The Second Part of Henry the Fourth*, and I've learned it and kept it with me since then, wearing it like an invisible Saint Christopher's medal.

"'By my troth, I care not; a man can die but once; we owe God a death... and let it go which way it will, he that dies this year is quit for the next.'

"You are quit for the next, Santiago Lopez. And you were a brave man, no matter what age you were when you paid God his debt."

Hemingway stepped back. The old gravedigger cleared his throat. "No, *señor*," he said in Spanish. "There must be words from the Bible before we put the earth over this child."

"Must there?" said Hemingway, his voice almost amused. "Will not *Señor* Shakespeare suffice?"

"No, *señor*," said the old man. "The Bible is necessary."

Hemingway shrugged. "If it is *necesario*," he said. He raised a clump of dirt... mud... and held it over the boy's grave.

"From Ecclesiastes, then—'One generation passeth away, and another generation cometh; but the earth abideth forever.... The sun also ariseth, and the sun goeth down, and hasteth to the place where he arose." He dropped the clod of mud onto the small coffin, stepped back, and looked at the old man leaning on his shovel. "It is proper now?"

"*Sí señor.*"

DRIVING BACK FROM THE FUNERAL in the rain and evening gloom, Hemingway said, "Tell me one reason I shouldn't hunt down Lieutenant Maldonado."

"Because he might not be the one who did it," I said.

Hemingway had glared at me. "Who else could it be? You told me last week that Agent Twenty-two was following *Caballo Loco*."

"Don't call him that," I said.

"*Caballo Loco*?"

"Agent Twenty-two."

"Who else could it be but Maldonado?" demanded the writer.

I had looked away from the rain-streaked windshield. "I told Santiago not to follow him... or anyone... while we were away. I don't think he would have done it after I ordered him not to."

"He must have been carrying out surveillance on *somebody*," said Hemingway.

I shook my head. "That road where Octavio found him goes to the shacks where he used to live when his mother was alive. The Negro said that Santiago used to go out there sometimes to sleep when things in the city got too crazy."

Hemingway drove for several minutes in silence. "Lucas," he said at last, "who else would have killed the boy?"

"I'll tell you later," I said.

"Tell me now or forget the fucking later," said the writer. "Tell me who you are and who you work for and who you think might have killed that boy, or get out of the fucking car now and don't come back to the *finca*."

I hesitated. If I told Hemingway any of what he'd asked for, I would no longer be working for the FBI or the SIS. The wipers slapped back and forth on the windshield. The heavy rain on the taut convertible top of the Lincoln sounded much as the rain had on the boy's coffin. I realized that I no longer worked for the FBI or SIS.

"I've been working for the FBI," I said. "J. Edgar Hoover sent me down here to spy on you and to report back to him through a liaison."

Hemingway pulled over to the side of the road. Trucks splashed past us. He turned sideways on the front seat and watched me as I spoke.

I told him about Delgado. I told him the background on Teddy Schlegel and Inga Arvad and Helga Sonneman and about Johann Siegfried Becker. I described the Abwehr and FBI money drops to Lieutenant Maldonado and his superior, Juanito the Jehovah's Witness. I told him about my contacts with the BSC's Commander Fleming on my way to Cuba and with the OSS's Wallace Beta Phillips once I arrived. I told him about the rifle shot during the fireworks attack on his neighbor Steinhart's party and about the second radio transmission I had intercepted during our trip to the tourist cave.

"What does the second one say?" demanded Hemingway, his voice flat.

"I don't know," I said. "It's in a numerical code I've never seen before. I don't think we were meant to decrypt it."

"Are you implying that we were *supposed* to intercept and decode the first transmission... the one about the two agents landing next Thursday?"

"I think so," I said.

"Why?"

"I don't know."

Hemingway looked out past the thrashing wipers. "They're

all circling around us—the FBI, maybe ONI, your British group...what's its alphabet soup?"

"BSC," I said. "I think so."

"OSS," continued Hemingway. "German intelligence..."

"Both branches, I think," I said. "Abwehr and RSHA AMT IV."

"I haven't a fucking clue about that," said the writer. "I didn't know that there *were* two branches of German intelligence."

"I know," I said. "You really don't know shit about any of this."

He glared at me. "But you do?"

"Yes," I said.

"Why are you telling me all this now?" demanded Hemingway. "And why the fuck should I believe *anything* you say, since everything you've told me until now has been a lie?"

I answered only his first question. "I'm telling you because they killed the boy," I said. "And because they're setting us up for something that I don't understand."

"*Who* killed the boy?"

"It could have been Maldonado," I said, "If Santiago was careless and the lieutenant knew he had been followed, *Caballo Loco* could have waited until we were gone, followed the boy out to those shacks, and cut his throat."

"Who else?" demanded the writer.

"Delgado could have done it."

"*An FBI man?*" Hemingway's voice was contemptuous. "I thought that you fucking draft dodgers only shot other draft dodgers."

"Delgado is...a special case," I said. "If he's who I think he is, he's killed other people. And I'm not sure who he's working for anymore."

"You think he's gone over to the krauts?"

"Possibly," I said. "The German intelligence networks in this hemisphere aren't worth shit, but they have lots of money. They could buy a mercenary like Delgado."

"Who else could it have been, Lucas? Who else could have done that to the boy?"

I shrugged. "Schlegel, although he doesn't seem the type. Schlegel could have paid one of the Germans or German sympathizers around Havana to do it. Helga Sonneman could have done it—"

"Helga?"

I went into more detail on the woman's dossier.

"Jesus fucking Christ," muttered Hemingway. "Does everyone know Hitler and his pals on a personal basis?"

"Even your guests," I said.

"My guests?"

"Ingrid Bergman's met him," I said. "Remember? And Dietrich was approached by German intelligence to work for them."

"And she told them to go fuck themselves."

"So she says."

Hemingway showed his teeth. "I don't like you, Lucas. I really don't like you."

I said nothing.

After a moment of silence—even the rain had stopped—he said, "Give me one good reason I shouldn't kick your lying ass out of the car now and shoot you if you ever come near the *finca* or my kids again."

"I'll give you one," I said. "Something complicated is unraveling here. Someone *wants* you to intercept those two agents being landed on the thirteenth."

"Why?"

"I don't know," I said. "But there's a complex game going on, and your pissant Crook Factory is being used as a pawn in it. I think you'll need my help."

"So that you can report everything to J. Edgar Hoover?"

"I'm finished with that," I said flatly. "I'll still be reporting, but nothing important is going to the Bureau until we get this worked out."

"And you think this is dangerous?"

"Yes."

"For Gigi and Mouse, or just to me and you?"

I hesitated. "I think that everyone around you right now is at risk."

Hemingway rubbed his chin. "The FBI would actually kill an American citizen and his family? His friends?"

"I don't know," I said. "Hoover prefers to destroy people through leaks, innuendo, blackmail, and the IRS. But we don't even know for sure that the danger is coming from the Bureau. The British are involved here somewhere, as are the OSS and both branches of German intelligence."

"*Estamos copados*," said Hemingway. "We're surrounded." He liked the sound of that phrase, I knew, but this time his voice was very serious.

"Yes," I said.

He got the Lincoln back on the Central Highway and drove us back to the Finca Vigía.

I WENT INTO THE MAIN HOUSE before driving to the rendezvous with Delgado. Hemingway was in the living room, in his flowered chair next to the tray-table full of bottles and glasses. There was a large black cat on his lap and eight or ten more lying on the carpet nearby. I saw that he had opened at least one can of salmon and two small tins of sardines. Hemingway was holding a glass of what looked to be straight gin on his knee. From his rock-steady gaze and molded expression, I knew that he was very drunk.

"Ah, *Señor* Lucas," he said. "Have I formally introduced you to my dearest friends, *los gatos*?"

"No," I said.

"This dark beauty is Boissy D'Anglas," said Hemingway, stroking the back of the purring cat's head. "And you know Friendless. And that smaller one is named Friendless's Brother, although he's a she. And that is Tester, and the skinny one is Tester's kitten, a wonder cat. And the chubby one at the edge of the carpet there is Wolfer, and next to him is Good Will, named after Nelson Rockefeller, our esteemed goodwill ambassador to this poor, ignored gaggle of insignificant countries south of the great and powerful Estados Unidos.

"Friendless has been drinking milk and whiskey along with me all morning, Lucas, but he has had enough and so will not perform for you now. Cats do not perform for anyone, Lucas. Did you know that? They just do what they damn well please, but will drink whiskey with milk for you if they love you and if they damn well please at that moment. And, oh, this is Dillinger, named after the dead gangster with the big cock, of course. I think the name gave him a superiority complex, but no longer... Marty had Dillinger and the other males neutered when we were out on our first sub patrol. Did you know that, *Señor* Lucas, *Señor* spy Lucas, *Señor* informer Lucas?"

I heard your brawl, I thought. *I heard you screaming at her and she at you.* I said nothing.

Hemingway grinned. "Bitch." He rubbed Boissy's neck. "Not you, baby. I sent her a cable today, Lucas. Marty. Didn't know where the fuck she is now, so I sent copies to Haiti, Puerto Rico, Saint Thomas, Saint Barts, Antigua, Bimini, and all the other stops on her fucking agenda. Want to know what the cable said?"

I waited.

"It said ARE YOU A WAR CORRESPONDENT OR WIFE IN MY BED?" Hemingway nodded as if satisfied, set the black cat delicately on the carpet, and stood carefully to pour three more fingers of gin. "Want a drink, Special Agent Joe Lucas?"

"No," I said.

"Conceited bitch," said the writer. "Calls Operation Friendless rot and rubbish. Says we're all jerking off. Says I haven't written a word worth reading since I finished *For Whom the Bell Tolls*. Bitch, I said. They'll be reading my stuff long after the worms have finished with you, I said." He sat down, took a drink, and squinted at me. "Did you want something, Lucas?"

"I'm going to town," I said. "Taking the car."

Hemingway shrugged. "Sure you don't want a drink?" he said.

I shook my head.

"If you don't want to drink good gin with me," he said pleasantly, "I could arrange to get you some cold tea. Or you could drain a bucket of snot and then suck the puss out of a dead nigger's ear." He smiled again and gestured toward the table covered with liquor bottles, ice buckets, and glasses.

"No thanks," I said, and went out of the living room, out the door, across the terrace, and down to the car parked in the drive.

ON THE WAY INTO TOWN, trying not to rehearse the imminent meeting and possible confrontation with Delgado for the thousandth time, I thought about Maria.

I had not told the whore about the boy's death, of course, but Maria seemed to sense that something was wrong all last evening and had been quiet and sensitive to my need to be alone. When I had tried to sleep, she had lain on the cot next to mine, her hand touching my cot but not me, her eyes watching me as I stared at the ceiling. When I rose to go up to the guest house and work on my idiot memo to J. Edgar Hoover, she had found my canvas sneakers and my denim shirt, bringing each without a word and looking at me with sad eyes. For an instant then, I had imagined what it would be like to be a normal human being, sharing one's sadness with another, talking about things that ate one to the marrow. I had shaken off that thought the night before with whiskey and my fantasy memo to the Director, and now I shook it off as the twin smokestacks of the Havana Electric Company came into sight down the Central Highway.

The .38 was on the seat next to me. It was uncomfortable driving with it against my back. I had loaded an extra cartridge in the chamber I usually left empty under the hammer and put half a dozen extra cartridges in the pocket of my vest. That last was almost certainly a silly gesture: if Delgado and I had things to settle today, they would be settled before I needed to reload. But then again, it was always better to carry extra ammunition and not need it than to... etc., etc.

I parked the car in Old Havana and started the six-block walk to the safe house. I should arrive right at the appointed time.

Wallace Beta Phillips had been accurate, of course, in his assessment of what had happened that night on Simón Bolívar Street in Veracruz, Mexico. The two Abwehr agents had arrived ninety minutes before the rendezvous time and positioned themselves in the front room to ambush me. By that time, I had been there, hidden in the closet just inside the hallway, for almost two hours. Phillips had mentioned that one of the neighbors had seen "a child throwing a rock" at the front door just before the shooting began. It had not been a child but a fifty-three-year-old barfly dwarf named El Gigante whom I had paid one hundred and fifty pesos to throw the rock and run like hell.

Today I would not be arriving early.

The .38 pressed into the small of my back, but the way I had it rigged, Delgado should not be able to know it was there unless he searched me. The vest was loose, and I had practiced reaching under it and drawing the weapon many times. It was still a clumsy place from which to draw and fire a pistol, but a shoulder or belt holster would be too obvious, as would my usual habit of tucking the weapon into my beltline just above the left front trouser pocket. I found myself wishing that I had brought the .357 instead of the .38, in case I had to fire through the old walls or doors of the safe house, but the larger gun was too difficult to conceal.

If I were Delgado and I wanted to eliminate any threat from Special Agent Joe Lucas, where would I be waiting? Possibly outside or in one of the ramshackle huts or rotting tenements along this narrow street. But there was always the chance that Special Agent Lucas might take the alley or another approach to the safe house. *Where in the house?* In the small, windowless room off the larger room. Perhaps lying on the floor, in the dark, the back door barricaded so that no one would come in that way, then wait for Lucas to silhouette himself in the front doorway. Perhaps wait another second or two for Lucas to come all the way into the main room with nothing but the small table to hide behind, the wall behind him stopping the slugs and muffling the sound of the shots. Then just walk away and leave the body for the rats.

The safe house door was open slightly. The windows were paneless and dark. I resisted the urge to check the .38 in my back belt and walked up to the rotting stoop, then in the door.

Delgado looked up from his usual place across the table. He was straddling the chair and resting his chin on the back of his right hand, on the back of the chair. I had noticed that he was left-handed. His left hand was out of sight at his side. Instead of the usual white panama suit, he was wearing a crisp, loose *guayabera* today. His skin looked more darkly tanned and his hair lighter than usual.

I set the manila envelope on the table and remained standing, watching the other man's cold, gray eyes as his left hand came up into the dim light.

As was his habit, Delgado tore open the sealed envelope and read the report. "You're kidding," he said at last.

I stood at ease, balanced with my legs apart, my left hand in my left pocket, my right arm hanging easily at my side.

"A fucking tourist cave?" he said. "Kids finding beer bottles? Pigs committing suicide on a disappearing sandbar? That's it?"

"It was ONI's call," I said. "They sent us."

Delgado snorted. "ONI." He tossed the two pages onto the table. His left hand went below the table's edge while his gaze stayed hard and level on me.

"You didn't see the *Southern Cross* during all of this dicking around?"

"No," I said. "But she's back in Havana Harbor. They have a berth over at Casablanca now."

"And you didn't pick up any ship-to-ship or ship-to-shore transmissions from her?" asked Delgado.

I shook my head, studying his reaction intently. Delgado was very quick when he wanted to be. If he began to move, I would have to go for a body shot...a head shot would be too risky. I did not know where his weapon might be—it could be rigged under the table and aimed at me now, in which case I was fucked—but other than that, it did not matter so much how quick each of us was but how steady we were once we began firing. I had loaded hollow points and had notched the noses of the slugs with my knife. If even one of those found flesh, there should not be any more argument. But, of course, Delgado would have done the same.

His left hand came up quickly. I did not start and my right hand did not move.

He tossed the black and white photograph onto the table. "Do you know this man, Lucas?"

"Yeah," I said, my voice staying disinterested. "I've seen his file. Johann Siegfried Becker. SD. What about him?"

"He's not in Brazil anymore," said Delgado, watching me.

"I know," I said. "May's SIS threat estimate said that he was in Berlin."

Delgado shook his head slowly. "He's in Havana." After a minute, he said, "Aren't you going to ask why?"

"Does it relate to my job here?" I said.

"Not one fucking bit," said Delgado. "Which is to say, you're not really *doing* any job here, are you?"

Two boys ran across the lawn outside. I watched them without turning my face away from Delgado. I had stepped to my left upon entering so that my back was not to the open door. I had no idea how many people were working for and with Delgado. One might be waiting across the street in the abandoned tenement, waiting for me to leave, the scope of his rifle all sighted in on a spot I would have to pass on my way back up the street. Well, there was nothing I could do about that except concentrate on keeping the small hairs on the back of my neck from writhing.

"Becker is here because his network is being rounded up in Brazil," said Delgado. "The Hauptsturmführer isn't sure about heading back into that shit storm. He's opened negotiations with some...ah...local representatives about either turning state's evidence or working both sides of the street."

"Why are you telling me?" I said.

Delgado rubbed his lower lip. Sweat ran down his cheeks and dripped from his chin. It was very hot in the little room. "I'm telling you, Lucas, because we don't want you bumping into Herr Becker in some *bodega* and blowing his head off or turning him over to the local constabulary until we complete our negotiations."

"We?" I said.

"Me," said Delgado.

"All right," I said. "Anything else?"

"Not from me."

I went to the door, never quite turning my back on him.

"Lucas?" His left hand had gone beneath the table edge again. Standing half in the sunlight as I was, I had trouble seeing him well in the dim interior. "Sorry about the kid," he said.

I put my hand behind me as if to scratch an itch. "Do you know who did it?" I said.

"Of course not," said Delgado. "I just heard about the burial and put two and two together. You should tell your writer pal not to use kids in his spy games."

"You don't have any idea who killed Santiago?" I said, watching his eyes.

Delgado's lips curled in his simulacrum of a smile. "Was his name Santiago?"

THE *FINCA* GROUNDS SEEMED EMPTY when I got back. Then I remembered that the servants were off that evening and that Winston Guest and Patchi Ibarlucia had planned to take the boys to El Pacífico for dinner.

I knocked, received no answer, and walked into the main house.

Hemingway was sitting where I had left him, in his ugly floral chair in the center of the room with the drinks tray to his left, but now all of the cats were gone. Instead of Boissy D'Anglas on his lap, he had the Mannlicher .256 from the boat between his legs and the muzzle just under his chin. The butt of the rifle rested on the rough weave of the carpet. His feet were bare and his big toe was inside the trigger guard, just resting on the trigger.

"You're just in time, Joe," said Hemingway. "I've been waiting for you. I want to show you something important."

21

I STOOD FIFTEEN FEET from Hemingway and watched him prop the muzzle of the Mannlicher under his chin. I did not know if the weapon was loaded. I did not like it that the writer had called me "Joe." In private, he never called me by my first name.

"*Estamos copados,*" said Hemingway. "And this is what we do when we're surrounded, Joe." He put both hands on the barrel and leaned it forward, his bare toe moving tighter on the curve of the trigger. Hemingway was wearing only a stained blue shirt and dirty khaki shorts.

I said nothing.

"In the mouth, Joe," he said. "The palate is the softest part of the head." He moved the muzzle to within inches of his open mouth and pressed the trigger down with his big toe. The hammer dry-clicked. Hemingway raised his head and smiled. I recognized it as some sort of a challenge.

"That's fucking stupid," I said.

Hemingway moved very carefully as he propped the rifle against the arm of his chair and got to his feet. He might have been very drunk, but he was balancing easily on the balls of his feet as he flexed his fingers. "What did you say, Joe?"

"That was fucking stupid," I said. "And even if it wasn't, putting the barrel of a firearm in your mouth is something only a *maricón* would do."

"Would you like to repeat that, Joe?" said Hemingway, enunciating carefully.

"You heard me," I said.

Hemingway nodded, walked to the back door, and beckoned me outside. I followed.

Standing by the pool, he took off his dirty shirt and folded it carefully on the back of a metal chair. "You will want to remove your shirt," Hemingway said in Spanish. "I plan to spill very much of your blood on it."

I shook my head. "I don't want to do this," I said.

"Fuck what you want," said Hemingway. "And fuck you." In Spanish, with a thick Cuban accent, he added, "I shit on your whoring mother."

"I don't want to do this," I said again.

Hemingway shook his head as if clearing it, stepped forward quickly, and launched a left jab at my face. I ducked it, raised my fists, and began circling to my right, working from the assumption that vision in his left eye was worse than in his right. Hemingway jabbed again. I deflected it.

His opening jabs were—much like the Cuban insult—mere provocations. I realized at once that, like me, he was a counterpuncher. The beginning of a bout between counterpunchers can be deadly dull.

I smiled at him. "*Piropos, señor?*" I said mincingly. Then, flatly, "*Pendejo. Puta. Maricón. Bujarón.*"

Hemingway came at me then. In the two seconds before the real fight began, I realized that I could kill him easily but had no idea if I could beat him in a fistfight.

He aimed a solid left jab at my mouth. I blocked it and he swung a hard right hook around to my belly. I danced back, but his huge fist still caught me solidly in the ribs, knocking much of the wind out of me. Hemingway followed with another left and a right hook over my guard that should have broken my cheekbone but careened off the top of my skull instead.

Hemingway had a very heavy punch. That's an advantage, of course, but one that can work against amateur fighters who get too used to depending on a knockout or knockdown in the first minute of a fight. They forget that they sometimes have to go the distance.

Hemingway moved in close, grabbed my shirt with his left hand, and chopped a right hook down at me again. I took the blow on my shoulder, crouched low, and hooked him three times in the belly.

The air went out of him with a soft *whoof* and he closed on me, pulling me tight, using me to prop himself up while he caught his breath, but trying to do damage at the same time. His belly had been soft, but he had been ready for the blows and was not about to go down. He grabbed at my hair, but it was too short to give him much grip. He drove me back toward the wall of the *finca*, using his bulk and greater weight to move us across the patio. I buried my chin in his shoulder and pressed hard against him, not giving him a shot at anything except my back. His kidney punches still hurt like hell. Backpedaling, realizing that once he got me against that rough wall he could use his weight to do real damage, I butted him in the chin and pushed him away when his head snapped back.

Hemingway shook sweat out of his eyes and spat blood. I slapped him hard across the face with a fast backhand, heard him growl, and caught him with a good right hook as he charged in.

He did not go down. I was out of fighting shape, but not *that* out of shape. That hook—even though it had caught him on the side of the head instead of the jaw—had taken care of bigger men in the past. Hitting Hemingway's skull had been like punching an anvil.

He moved in again and grabbed my arms, his thumbs moving fast and tight, squeezing hard on the insides of my elbows between the upper muscles and my forearms, trying to damage the tendons at the bases of my biceps. I raised my knee, but he swiveled fast enough to take the blow on his hip instead of his testicles. I kicked again, he released my arms, and I caught him twice on the right ear with my left as he moved back. His ear began swelling immediately, but I realized that his thumbs had done some damage—my left arm was almost numb and my right forearm tingled as if it had fallen asleep. This son of a bitch had learned his tricks well as a kid in Chicago.

Hemingway was panting heavily now as we circled again, moving toward the pool. He backed into a metal chair and kicked it out of his way. As he was doing that, I moved in with a combination, but he blocked both blows and caught me above the left eye as I backed out. I shook the blood out of my eye. The brow was swelling quickly, but not low enough to blind me before the bout was over.

Hemingway came in again, breathing hard. I could smell the gin on his breath and in his sweat.

His right fist came in low and hard and would have smashed my balls into pulp if I had not levitated back and up. I took the blow on my inner thigh and felt my right leg go numb even as Hemingway's left fist clubbed down against my right temple hard enough to send me spinning.

For several seconds I could not see anything except red spots or hear anything except the roar and rush of the blood waterfall in my skull. But I stayed on my feet, completed my spin, and unleashed a right uppercut to where I expected the bigger man to be moving in.

I was off by inches, but my fist still went through his guard and caught him square on his bare chest. Through the waterfall noise, the blow sounded like a sledgehammer in a slaughterhouse.

I backpedaled and covered up, waiting for his continued attack, kicking the overturned patio chair away again, shaking my head to clear my vision, and hoping that I was not going to back into the swimming pool. No attack came for several seconds, and I had time to shake away the worst of the roaring and get some of my vision back.

Hemingway was leaning forward, vomiting onto the patio stones. His right ear was obscenely swollen—looking like a bunch of red grapes—there was blood and vomit in his beard, and his left eye was almost closed from a blow I did not remember landing. I dropped my guard halfway and staggered a few steps closer, opening my mouth to say something about a truce.

Still retching, Hemingway threw a roundhouse right that would have taken my head off if I hadn't ducked under it. I stayed down, duck-stepped closer, and hit him twice in the belly.

The writer staggered closer, grabbed my shirt as if for support, pulled me upright, came up quickly, and butted me in the chin.

I felt a side tooth splinter as my head snapped back. I tried to backpedal, but Hemingway was hanging on again with his left hand, punching me hard in the ribs with his right. His big teeth were snapping as he tried to bite my ear, my throat. I heard my battered shirt rip down the front as I pulled away and caught him on the cheekbone with two short, hard, straight lefts. His guard went down, and I came around with a perfect hook to his solar plexus, remembering at the last instant to hold back just enough so as not to kill him.

He doubled over and reeled away, but still did not go down. A second later, gasping and staggering backward, he tripped over the metal chair and fell heavily onto the paving stones.

I stepped forward, wiped more blood out of my left eye, and waited.

Hemingway got slowly to his knees, then to one knee, and then to his feet. His right ear was swollen and bleeding. The flesh around his right cheekbone was purple. His left eye was closed now from swelling, his mouth and short beard were covered with blood, and his chest hair was matted with blood and vomit. Hemingway grinned at me with bloody teeth and staggered forward, his arms rising again, his swollen fists closing.

I grabbed his arms, pulled him into a clinch, and buried my chin in his shoulder again so he could not butt me or push me away. "Tie," I gasped.

"Fuck... that," gasped the writer, and dug a weak left into my ribs.

I pushed him away, swung a hard right at his bloody chin, missed, and went to one knee.

Hemingway brought his fist down against the side of my head hard enough to make sparks leap in my vision, and then he sat down on the patio stone next to me.

"You... take... back that... *maricón*?" gasped Hemingway.

"No," I said. I felt around between my swollen lip and gums until I found the splinter of broken tooth. I snapped it free and spit it out. "Fuck you," I said. "And the *maricón* horse you rode in on."

Hemingway laughed, stopped laughing, held his ribs, spat blood, and chuckled more carefully. "*Muy buena pelea,*" he said.

I started to shake my head but stopped quickly when the patio began to tilt and spin. "No... such thing... as a good fight,"

I said between gasps for air. "Fucking waste of... time... energy." I rubbed my mouth again. "Teeth."

I looked at my hands. The knuckles were swollen and scraped. It felt as if someone had run over them with a small car.

Hemingway rolled to his knees and moved toward me. I got to my knees to meet him, my arms coming up so slowly it felt as if there were lead weights on my wrists. *This son of a bitch is forty-three fucking years old,* I thought. *What did he fight like when he was my age?*

Hemingway's arms came around me clumsily. I waited for the blows and butts, then realized that he was patting my back with his swollen hands. He was saying something, but I had trouble hearing him through the renewed waterfall in my skull.

"... inside, Joe. Marty had a steak in the freezer," he said. "Good bottle of Tavel on ice."

"You're hungry?" I said as we helped each other to our feet, each leaning against the other for support. There were drops of blood spattered over most of the stones by the pool, and the evening wind was blowing long, blue streamers of what I realized had been my shirt.

"Yeah, I'm hungry," said Hemingway, steering me toward the door. "Why not? My stomach's empty."

THAT NIGHT, Maria was even more solicitous than she had been the night before. "Poor, poor, José," she murmured, putting cool, wet towels on my face, hands, and ribs to slow the swelling. "I have seen this before with my brothers. Did the other man suffer?"

"Terribly," I said, wincing slightly as the cool towel touched my battered ribs. I was lying on my back and wearing nothing but my undershorts. Maria wore only her thin cotton shift. The lantern was turned low.

"Is there any part of you that does not hurt, my José?" she whispered.

"Just one part," I said.

"Show me," whispered Maria.

I showed her without pointing.

"Are you sure it does not hurt?" she whispered. "It looks all red and inflamed."

"Shut up," I said, and drew her down onto me. Gently.

"We will not kiss on the lips in honor of your poor mouth," she whispered. "But I can kiss elsewhere, yes?"

"Yes," I said.

"We must make the swelling go away, no?"

"Shut up," I said.

Toward morning, we slept.

THE BOYS WERE gone the next day, out on the *Pilar* fishing with Guest, Ibarlucia, and Sinsky. Hemingway and I shuffled around the *finca* like two eighty-year-olds who had been in a train wreck. We decided that we needed nourishment, and agreed that the nourishment had to be liquid in nature.

After he opened the second gin bottle, we locked the doors and got down to business. The dining room table was soon covered with nautical charts. Chart Number 2682 was the one we wanted. According to a legend on the chart, these coastal waters had been charted in 1930 and 1931 by the U.S.S. *Nokomis.*

"Longitude seventy-six degrees, forty-eight minutes, thirty seconds," he said, checking the decoded transmission and looking back at the chart. "Latitude twenty-one degrees twenty-five minutes." He stabbed a swollen finger down on the chart. "It's Punta Roma," confirming what we'd first seen on the *Pilar*'s chart.

I studied the charts again. Point Roma was far down the north coast of Cuba, not too distant from where we had explored the tourist caves. It was beyond the scattering of large keys—Sabinal, Guajaba, Romano—where the *Southern Cross* had been carrying out its sea trials and where the *Pilar* had spent so many fruitless days, and southeast of the large Bahía de Nuevitas.

"It's a good place for a landing," said Hemingway. "This is mostly empty coast along here. There's not much of anything between Nuevitas and Puerto Padre. Manatí Bay has a tricky channel that runs five and six fathoms, but much of it has silted up since the Manatí Sugar Mill closed on the southwest part of the bay, and there are only a few shacks in that entire area. Nothing on the coast here." He ran his finger in a circle at the entrance to Bahía Manatí. "You see why a sub would like this approach, Lucas."

I checked the fathom markings. The area just off the beach ran six to eight fathoms, but fifty yards out, the shelf dropped off to a hundred and ninety-five, then two hundred and twenty-five fathoms. A U-boat could easily pull within two hundred yards of Point Roma and Point Jesus at the narrow entrance to the bay without fear of finding a sandbar or reef.

"They can see the old Manatí stack from the entrance to the bay," said Hemingway. "They can use that as a reference point through the periscope by daylight, then launch small boats toward those coordinates after dark."

I nodded and touched a Y of rail lines halfway along the bay line between the sugar mill and the entrance to the bay. "These go to the cane fields?"

"They did," said Hemingway. "The short line hauled the cane into the pressing sheds and the old docks there. All abandoned now."

"And *Doce Apostoles*?" I said, pointing to a cluster of dots across the inlet from the abandoned rail lines.

"The Twelve Apostles are large rock formations," said Hemingway. "There used to be workers' shacks at the base of them, but they're overgrown as well." He ran his hand northwest up the coast a short distance. "You see here, right behind Point Roma and the abandoned lighthouse there, Enseñada Herradura."

I nodded. The inlet was broad and shallow, three-quarters of a fathom, according to the chart. "You don't think they'll come in there, do you?" I said.

"No," said Hemingway. "No need. I think they'll come ashore by raft right at the old light on Point Roma. No rocks or cliffs there, and it's free of mangroves and other crap. But we could take a small boat into Enseñada Herradura and hide it there in the mangroves."

"Small boat," I said. "The *Tin Kid*?"

Hemingway shook his head. "I want to keep the dinghy with *Pilar*. We don't want to bring the *Pilar* into water that shallow, especially if the wind is from the east, and I don't think we could conceal her anyway. We'll have to get something else."

"A turtle boat?" I said. "Borrow a skiff?"

The writer scratched his chin stubble and then winced. "I can get something faster that can get us in and out of a rain puddle. Tom Shevlin's rich and has a beautiful, old twenty-two-foot speedboat tied up at Cojímar. He owes me a favor and gave me permission to use the boat if I wanted. I think he named it *Lorraine*, after his wife. Shevlin can't use it because of the gas shortage."

"Fast?" I said.

"Sure," said Hemingway. "A hundred and twenty-five horsepower engine—almost twice as powerful as the *Pilar*'s, with less than half the weight to push. Shallow draft. Extra-long-range fuel tanks."

"Sounds like it ran booze north during Prohibition," I said.

"Exactly," said Hemingway. He pointed to the map again. "Look at how nice this will be for them. This coming Thursday, the sub checks out the area in the daylight, then comes right up to the entrance to Bahía Manatí after dark. What time did the transmission say?"

"Eleven P.M.," I said.

The writer nodded. "There's a crescent moon, but it rises after midnight on the thirteenth. They come ashore at Point Roma and follow the old cane roads and railways to the abandoned sugar mill on the southwest bend of the bay. From there, they just walk out the old spur line that ran from the mill to the town of Manatí, twelve miles farther inland. Someone picks them up in Manatí and from there it's a simple drive down the highway through Rincón and Sao Guásima to the Central Highway, then turn right to Havana and the U.S. air base at Camagüey, or left to Guantánamo." He looked at me. "Twenty-three-hundred hours on Thursday the thirteenth if we're going to greet them. When do you think we should get there, Lucas? Before sunset on the thirteenth?"

I thought of Simón Bolívar Street in Veracruz. Someone had been waiting there. I knew that someone would be waiting for us here.

"Way before sunset on the thirteenth," I said. "Before noon."

"You have to be fucking kidding."

"I have to be fucking serious," I said.

Hemingway sighed and rubbed his short beard. He winced again and looked at his swollen fingers. "All right. Leave on the day after tomorrow. How do we do this? Should the kids and the *Pilar* stay here?"

"I don't think so," I said. "Let's all make a show of leaving early Wednesday morning. The kids, your usual crew, me, everybody. Drop me somewhere along the coast and I'll head back to Cojímar to get Shevlin's speedboat and I'll meet you at the base on Cayo Confites Wednesday night. We'll go ahead to Bahía Manatí the same night."

"Gregorio, Patchi, Wolfer, and the others won't like being left behind," said Hemingway.

I looked at him.

"Yeah," he said. "That's just too bad." He ran his hand through his hair. "There's a lot to do between now and then. We'll have to bring the *sombreros científicos* and a couple of the *niños* from *Pilar* when we go in."

I knew that he was not talking about his children. Hemingway had ordered Fuentes to make special leather cases with oil-soaked, sheepswool linings for the Thompson submachine guns. When the crew of the *Pilar* was at action stations, the cases hung by straps from the railing around the flying bridge and elsewhere. Ibarlucia had commented that the swinging gun cases looked like rocking cradles, thus the automatic weapons were nicknamed "little children." It was at times like this when Hemingway was at his cutest that I had the urge to hit him again.

I looked at my swollen hands and shelved that idea.

The writer rolled up the chart. "So you and I are there hiding in the weeds or the mangrove roots or the rocks or whatever, the German agents show up at twenty-three hundred hours on the thirteenth...and then what?"

"That's what we're going to see at twenty-three hundred hours on the thirteenth," I said.

Hemingway gave me a disgusted look. I took it as my cue to

leave, and went back to the guest house to do some Crook Factory business.

MY MAJOR CONCERN WAS the second coded transmission that I had intercepted. I had told Hemingway the truth when I said that it was in a different code that I could not decipher, but I had not explained the details.

The transmission had been in groups of five letters, exactly like the book code—*q-f-i-e-n* / *w-w-w-s-y* / *d-y-r-q-q* / *t-e-o-i-o* / *w-q-e-w-x* and so forth. The problem was that it was *not* the book code. There was no page number given. There were no key words or first sentences.

Since I had encountered both Abwehr and SD AMT VI transmissions before, my guess was that this was the latter. The Nazi intelligence agency—as opposed to the German army intelligence—liked number-based ciphers for fast and secure transmissions. Such a code would be based upon a string of numbers, perhaps six or seven digits long, chosen at random by the agent transmitting. He would give that string to the person or persons receiving his transmission. The numbers would tell the receiving station how many letters up or down in the alphabet to count to find the actual letters.

For instance, if the randomly chosen number had been 632914, the first letter in the transmission—*q*—would actually be six letters up or back in the alphabet—*w* or *k*. The second letter transmitted—*f*—would be three letters up or down—*i* or *c*—and so forth.

A decent cryptology department could break such a code, given enough time and computers. "Computers" were people—usually women—who worked in the number-crunching department of decrypt groups, plugging in various possible numbers, studying the thousands or tens of thousands or millions of combinations, looking for repetitions, letter frequency probabilities, and so forth. But with dummy inserts, false transmission groups, and other simple transmission devices, decrypting even such a simple code was a months-long, infinitely laborious task. And I had never been good at arithmetic.

What bothered me about this code was that I had become almost certain that we were *meant* to decipher the previous book code transmission. The whole operation had been too easy—discovering Kohler's codebook, finding the two reference books on the *Southern Cross*, the later transmissions being in the same code. Someone wanted us to know about the rendezvous at Point Roma. But that same someone did *not* want us to read the ancillary transmission.

This bothered me. I did not believe in intuition or any paranormal powers—not even the "sixth sense" that intelligence agents were supposed to develop with time—but all of my training and experience was warning me on a subconscious basis that this number-encrypted code was bad news.

Given my suspicions about Delgado, I could not give the intercept to him and ask him to send it to SIS/FBI labs for decryption. It did not seem feasible that I could saunter into the FBI's Havana field office, explain my mission to Special Agent in Charge Leddy, and expect any help without bringing down J. Edgar Hoover's wrath for going out of channels and blowing my cover. Besides, it could literally take months to break even a simple numerical code, and we did not have that kind of time.

I had been considering a crude but effective shortcut to the decryption problem when Agents 03 and 11 arrived at the guest house.

Agent 11 was the aged bellman at the Ambos Mundos Hotel. Agent 03 was "Black Priest," Hemingway's friend Father Don Andrés. I was used to seeing the priest at Hemingway's Sunday-afternoon parties, where Don Andrés usually wore a bright red sport shirt. But today he was in his black outfit with a Roman collar. He looked older this way and much more solemn.

"We have come to tell Don Ernesto that the rich man from the boat, *Señor* Shell, is leaving in one hour," said Father Don Andrés. The bellman nodded vigorously.

"You are sure of this?" I said in Spanish, looking at both men for confirmation.

The bellman said, "Yes, *Señor* Lucas. *Señor* Alvarez at the desk confirmed *Señor* Shell's airplane reservations for three o'clock. *Señor* Shell has asked for a car to be brought around at one-thirty for a ride to the airport."

I nodded. Teddy Shell—Theodor Shlegel—had been staying ashore for most of the time the past month, moving from hotel to hotel. He had not met with Lieutenant Maldonado for more than two weeks, and he stayed aboard the *Southern Cross* only during the yacht's occasional forays down the coast.

"What is his destination?" I asked.

"Rio de Janeiro," said the Black Priest. Hemingway had explained this nickname recently. It had not been one of the writer's creations but had come about after the Church had assigned Father Don Andrés to a parish in the worst and poorest section of Havana as a punishment for his previous behavior, including his years as a machine gunner in the Spanish Civil War. Most of Father Don Andrés's parishioners were from the lowest levels of Cuban society—Negroes, in other words—and so the nickname Black Priest.

"You're sure of this?" I said. I knew that the only three P.M. flight out of José Martí Airport was to Rio.

The bellman looked offended. "Yes, *Señor* Lucas. I saw the ticket myself."

"Round-trip or one way?" I asked.

"One way, *señor*," said the bellman.

"We think he's flying the coop," said Father Don Andrés. "Don Ernesto should know."

"I agree," I said. "I will tell him. Thank you for your diligence, gentlemen."

"It is important?" said the bellman, grinning through missing teeth.

"It may be important, yes," I said.

The priest looked uneasy. "Should we not report to Ernesto in person?"

"I will tell him, Father," I said. "I promise you this. Right now, the writer is resting. He has a bad headache this morning."

The priest and the bellman exchanged knowing glances. "Should we follow *Señor* Teddy Shell to the airport?" asked Father Don Andrés.

I shook my head. "This will be taken care of. Thank you again for your professionalism."

When they were gone, I walked past the swimming pool, around the dilapidated tennis court, to the small garage. Juan, the chauffeur, was washing the Lincoln in front of the garage and looked at me suspiciously as I approached. Juan frequently acted as if he was constipated and out of sorts, and I do not believe he liked me much.

"May I help you, *Señor* Lucas?" The words were correct, but his tone was slightly insolent and challenging. The staff at the *finca* was never quite sure how to treat me; I was something slightly higher than hired help but definitely lower than an honored guest. Also, it had been decided that I was the one responsible for bringing a whore into the *finca* household family. The servants seemed to like Maria, but I suspected that they held it against me that I had lowered the tone of the place.

"Just looking for something," I said, walking into the dimness of the little shed. The garage had the reassuring smell of garages everywhere.

Juan put down his sponge and stood at the open door. "*Señor* Hemingway does not wish for anyone but him and myself to touch his tools, *Señor* Lucas."

"Yes," I said, opening the metal toolbox and rooting through the contents.

"*Señor* Hemingway is very strict about this provision, *Señor* Lucas."

"Of course," I said. I chose a roll of gray duct tape and a large, flat-headed screwdriver about eight inches long. I closed the toolbox and looked around the wooden countertop. There were cans of paint, dusty two-by-fours, coffee cans of nails... ah, yes. I lifted the small can of axle grease and checked under the lid. About a third of the can left. That would do. I picked up a ten-inch length of lead pipe and put that in my back pocket.

"*Señor* Hemingway is *extremely* strict about no one except myself and himself being allowed to touch..." the chauffeur was going on, forgetting his syntax in his growing agitation.

"Juan," I said sharply.

The little man blinked. "Yes, *señor*?"

"Do you have a uniform coat and cap to wear when you drive *Señor* Hemingway or his guests for formal occasions?"

Juan squinted at me again. "Yes, *señor*... but he rarely asks me to..."

"Go get them," I said, just sharply enough to brook no argument but not so sternly as to offend the man.

Juan blinked and looked at the wet Lincoln. It was washed but not yet toweled off. "But, *Señor* Lucas, I must—"

"Get the uniform and cap," I said with finality. "Now, please."

Juan nodded and jogged away. His home was down the hill in the tin-roofed cluster of shacks that was the village of San Francisco de Paula.

A few minutes later he was back with both articles. The cap and jacket smelled of mothballs. As I had expected, the jacket was too small for me, but the cap fit. I took the cap and said, "Have the car dried and waxed and ready in twenty minutes."

"Yes, *Señor* Lucas."

I walked up to Grade A. The cottage was empty. Maria was helping clean at the *finca*. I took the .357 Magnum out of its hiding place, checked the chambers, and slid the large handgun into my belt. Then I went to the clothesline where my dark jacket was hung—it had been freshly ironed by Maria—and pulled it on. The dark pants, jacket, and cap looked more or less like a uniform.

The car was gleaming when I returned to it with the keys. I had picked up a bottle of whiskey in the house and was carrying it in a brown paper bag along with the screwdriver, pipe, roll of tape, and can of grease. Juan stood next to the vehicle and looked wistfully at his cap.

"*Señor* Hemingway is sleeping," I said. "Do not wake him, but when he wakes, tell him that I borrowed the automobile for a short time."

"Yes, *Señor* Lucas. But..."

I drove down the driveway and out the gate.

I DID NOT LOOK MUCH like a chauffeur: my face and hands were swollen and bruised, and although my complexion had darkened even further from months of exposure to the sun, I did not look especially Cuban. Still, I trusted Schlegel not to pay attention to a mere driver or remember me from our dinner together at the *finca*. Schlegel was the type who never looked closely at the hired help.

I drove through the squalor of San Francisco de Paula, under the gigantic Spanish laurel that arched over the entire roadway, and down the hill on the stone of the old Central Highway. I drove past the café called El Brillante, with its crude wall painting of a huge, sparkling diamond, and then down the long grade toward the outskirts of Havana.

Memories of the previous day's fight with the writer bothered me more than my aching knuckles or swollen lip. A fistfight was life's best example of pure, unadulterated idiocy. I had provoked Hemingway into fighting because I had recognized the look on his face when I walked into the living room to find him staring into the muzzle of the Mannlicher. I had seen the same look on the face of ex-NKVD chief Walter Krivitsky a year and a half earlier in a room in the Bellevue Hotel in Washington, D.C.

"*Estamos copados*," Hemingway liked to say. "We're surrounded." I think he liked the sound of it in Spanish. That had been my message to Walter Krivitsky on the evening of February 9, 1941, as I sat with him in his room in the Bellevue Hotel. The little man was tough and clever, and had been on the run for four years, escaping or outwitting his own Russian intelligence service, GPU assassins, both European and American Abwehr networks, Office of Naval Intelligence agents, and FBI interrogators. But toughness and cleverness can carry one only so far when your enemies are relentless.

Krivitsky's eyes had shown weariness, and Hemingway's eyes had reflected that same sense of siege. *Estamos copados.*

At the end, Krivitsky had turned to me for help. "I'm not here to help you," I said. "I'm here to make sure that the Germans don't get you and interrogate you before they kill you."

"But surely the FBI will—"

"You've told the FBI everything you know," I said to the former Russian agent. "Everything you know about the Soviets *and* the Germans. The FBI doesn't need you. No one needs you."

Krivitsky had looked at the stained wall of his hotel room and laughed softly. "I borrowed a gun, you know. In Virginia. But I threw it out the window of the train."

I had taken the .38 from my shoulder holster and handed it to the shaggy-browed little man.

Krivitsky had checked to make sure it was loaded and then held the pistol loosely in his right hand, the muzzle pointed in my general direction. "I could kill you, Special Agent Lucas."

"Sure," I said. "But Hans Wesemann and the others will still be out there. They'll be waiting when you try to leave in the morning."

Krivitsky had nodded and taken a long drink from the vodka bottle on the nightstand. Hans Wesemann was part of a Todt Team—a death team whose only mission was the assassination of one man, Walter Krivitsky. Krivitsky knew that once a Todt Team was assigned to a target, that target rarely survived.

We continued to talk into the night. The subject was hopelessness. *Estamos copados.*

In the end, Krivitsky had used the .38 on himself, of course, holding it to his right temple rather than putting it in his mouth. Hemingway was right about the palate being softer and a more certain spot to place the slug—more than a few would-be suicides had ended up drooling vegetables after bullets bounced off their skulls and removed only part of their brains, not all of them. But the .38 bullet had been very successful in ending Walter Krivitsky's paranoia.

That morning, before we had consulted the nautical charts, Hemingway had shown me a manuscript he had just finished. I glanced at it. It was the introduction to the *Men at War* anthology. The piece ran to more than ten thousand words, almost fifty typewritten pages. I was surprised at how bad Hemingway's spelling was—he rarely dropped the *e* before adding the *ing*, for instance, and made other simple mistakes that would have gotten me fired if I had submitted an FBI field report like that—and I was surprised to see all of the handwritten insertions, substitutions, and corrections.

"Read it," Hemingway had ordered.

I read the piece, in which Hemingway argued that the

anthology could render a patriotic service by acquainting American youth with the true nature of war throughout human history. He talked about how he reread the same piece—Frederick Manning's *The Middle Part of Fortune; or, Her Privates We*—every July on the anniversary of his wounding at Fossalta di Piave. It's "the finest and noblest book of men of war," he wrote, and his purpose for reading it was always the same—to remind himself of how things had really been so that he would never lie to himself. That was the purpose of this anthology, he wrote, to show what war was really like rather than how it was supposed to be.

But the look in Hemingway's eyes the previous morning had told me that he still dreamed of how war should be—Quixotic contests on the high seas between the *Pilar* and a German submarine—rather than how it was, with a child dead in a ditch with his throat cut.

Krivitsky had understood the reality of things. *Estamos copados.* He had been perched on the brink of the abyss for years, much as I sensed Hemingway had been. All Walter Krivitsky had needed was some vodka, some late-night conversation, and the loan of a .38.

Is this why you sent me down here, Hoover? I thought as I drove up to the Ambos Mundos Hotel. *Is that the way this is supposed to play out with Hemingway? Is that my role in all this—to drink and talk with Hemingway until it's time to hand him the gun?*

THEODOR SCHLEGEL DID NOT recognize me. For a second I thought he recognized the black Lincoln, but taxis and hired cars in Cuba ran the gamut of makes and models, so after a cursory glance he settled into the back seat while the porters scrambled to put his two bags in the trunk. He did not tip them, merely saying "*Aeroporto*" and nodding at me to drive off. All that illicit Abwehr money, and he couldn't even tip his hotel porters a few cents.

Schlegel read a newspaper as I drove out of town. He did not lower the paper as I turned onto the dead-end road just on the outskirts of town. He did not look up until I stopped.

"Why are you—" he began in bad Spanish, and then stopped when he saw the muzzle of the .357 pointed at his face.

"Get out of the car," I said.

Schlegel's eyes were wide as he stood by the side of the Lincoln. He raised his hands.

"Put your hands down," I said as I unlocked the trunk and removed his bags, tossing them onto the side of the road with one hand as I held the pistol in the other.

Schlegel looked at his bags and then blinked at his surroundings. I had stopped only ten yards from where we had found Santiago's body. There was growing alarm in the chubby Abwehr agent's eyes, but no shock of recognition at the place. This answered one of my questions.

"I know you," Schlegel suddenly said with something like relief in his shaky voice. "You were at the—"

"Shut up," I said. "Turn around." I patted him down. He had no weapon on him. "Pick up your bags and walk straight ahead to that shack."

"What do you—"

"Shut up!" I said in Portuguese, and slammed the barrel of the .357 against the back of his neck just hard enough to draw a red welt and a few drops of blood. "*Spazieren Sie,*" I snapped. "*Schnell!*"

We walked to the first shack, Schlegel panting slightly as he carried his heavy bags up the muddy hill. No one was around. Insects made noise in the thick underbrush beyond the shacks. The building had been burned out some years before, leaving only the charred walls with no roof.

"*Zurücklegen,*" I said when we were inside the shell of the building. Schlegel dropped the bags. I noticed that he was stepping carefully, trying not to get soot or carbon black on his white suit. It was very hot out of the breeze.

"Look here," Schlegel said in English. "I remember that you were a decent sort. There's absolutely no reason for you to aim that pistol at me. If it's money you want, I am willing to—"

His voice was sounding more confident, although it was still shaking slightly. He had started to turn when I tapped him on the side of his head with the lead pipe I had wrapped with duct tape.

IT TOOK SCHLEGEL almost ten minutes to regain consciousness, and I had begun worrying that I had hit him too hard when he started moaning and stirring. I had used the time to go through his bags: clothes, underwear, shaving kit, eight bow ties, a business appointment book with no immediately obvious codes or cipher, and a folder filled with papers relating to his job with the Companhia de Acos Marathon in Rio. There was also a 9-millimeter Luger and $26,000 in crisp, one-hundred-dollar bills in the bottom of his larger suitcase.

Schlegel moaned again and tried to move. I stood behind him and to one side and watched. He stirred again. I saw his eyes flicker open and then grow wide as he remembered what had happened and realized where he was and what was happening to him.

That last fact might have been the hardest for him to piece together. In front of him and in his field of view were the open suitcases—the Luger and the money atop his scattered clothes in one suitcase—and his white suit coat, trousers, blue shirt, white shoes, and red bow tie folded and stacked neatly atop the other pile of clothes. I watched as Schlegel tried to look down at himself, realized that his hands were taped behind his back and that he was wearing only his undershirt, boxer shorts, and black socks. Then he moaned as he realized that he was draped over an oil drum. The moan was muffled by the duct tape I had placed across his mouth.

I stepped closer and set my foot on the backs of his legs, pushing slightly so that he rocked forward on the rusted barrel. His face grew red as gravity forced the blood forward and down. I took the double-wide strip of tape in my hand and pressed it over the German's eyes before he could twist his head away. The man moaned through the tape over his mouth, and then I rocked him back so that his toes could touch the ground and he could breathe more easily.

"Schlegel, listen to me," I said in rapid German. "What you say in the next few minutes will determine whether you live or die. Be very careful. Tell me only the truth. Hold nothing back. Do you understand me?"

Schlegel tried to speak and then nodded.

"*Sehr gut,*" I said, and ripped the tape from his mouth. Schlegel cried out and then fell silent as I held the blade of my knife against the side of his neck.

"Your name," I snapped. I had long since decided that German was by far the best language in the world for interrogation purposes.

"Theodore Shell," said Schlegel in English. "I am technical adviser to the Marathon Steel Company, headquartered in Rio de Janeiro, Brazil, with a subsidiary in São... Ach! Stop! Do not do that! Cease!"

I used the knife to finish cutting the length of his undershirt, then slipped the razor-sharp blade under the elastic of his shorts and cut them away. The process had drawn blood here and there.

"Your name," I said again.

Schlegel was panting in fear now. He wiggled on the oil drum, his black socks trying to find purchase in the loose soil, his face redder than ever. "Theodore Schlegel," he whispered.

"What is your code name?"

Schlegel licked his lips. "What do you mean? I have no—"

I drew the point of the blade across the cheeks of his buttocks. Schlegel screamed.

"You can scream all you want," I said. "There is no one to hear you. But every time you scream, you will be punished."

The bellowing stopped.

"Your code name?"

"Salama."

"Do you work for Abwehr or AMT VI?"

The overweight man hesitated. I slipped the knife into my left hand, lifted the screwdriver in my right, and dipped the metal end of the screwdriver in the open can of grease.

"Who are you?" whispered Schlegel. "What do you want? Is

it the writer who is paying you? I can pay you more. You've seen the money…Ahh! Jesus! Stop! Jesus Christ! Acchh! Oh, my Jesus."

"Shut up," I said. When he was silent except for the gasping, I said, "Abwehr or AMT VI?"

"Abwehr," said Schlegel. "Please do not do that again with the knife. I will pay you any amount—"

"*Silence!*" I took a breath. In his shock, Schlegel had urinated against the oil drum and his legs. "Tell me about Alfredo," I said.

"Alfredo?" said Schlegel. "No, wait! Wait! Stop! Yes…I forgot the code name. Alfredo is Albrecht Engels. In Brazil."

"His transmitter?"

"We call it 'Bolívar.'"

"Do you use it?"

"*Nein…nein!* It is true. Last year I paid twenty contos…a thousand dollars…of my own money to build our transmitter in Gávea."

"Operator's name?" I snapped.

"George Knapper was the first. He was sent to the United States a year ago. Rolf Trautmann is my current operator."

Was, I thought. Trautmann had been rounded up in the FBI/Brazilian police operation almost four months ago while Schlegel was traveling on the *Southern Cross*.

"How does Hauptsturmführer Becker figure into your present operation?" I said.

I felt Schlegel's body stiffen. As terrified as he was, he seemed more terrified of Becker. "Who?" he began. Then he screamed, "No…*you cannot do that!* Mother of…stop! Just stop! I will tell you! No! Christ, just stop!"

I pulled the head of the screwdriver away and wiped it on the grass. "Becker," I said.

"He has worked with us in Brazil," panted the German. His legs were quivering. Tears flowed from beneath the duct tape and trembled on his cheeks and jowls.

"Is he Abwehr or SD?" I said. So far, I had asked no questions for which I had not known the answers.

"SD," gasped Schlegel. "AMT VI."

"Is he your superior in this operation?" I asked, laying the knife against Schlegel's spine.

"Yes, yes, yes."

"Describe this operation," I said flatly. "Goals. Purpose. Timeline. Agents involved. Status report."

"I don't... Yes, no! Stop! Please!"

I waited while the man stopped sobbing.

"Operation Raven," he gasped. "Joint Abwehr/SD mission. Authorized by Admiral Canaris and Major Schellenberg."

"Goals?"

"Infiltration of the Viking Fund. Use of—"

"Infiltration?" I said. "The Viking Fund doesn't know about your objectives?"

"No, they... Oh, stop! Christ! No! It is true! The boat was purchased for them. We have... I have... contributed money to the fund. But they think, they do not know... Jesus, I tell the truth!"

"Continue."

"We use the radio equipment on the *Southern Cross* to communicate with U-boats and Hamburg," gasped Schlegel.

"Objectives," I said again.

Schlegel shook his head. "I do not know them. Becker has not... Ahhh!"

This time the scream went on for a long minute. I looked over my shoulder at the open door. There was no guarantee that no one was within hearing distance, but I trusted the Cubans' well-honed sense of survival to insure that we would not be disturbed.

"Truth!" said Schlegel, weeping openly. "Hauptsturmführer Becker has not told me. We have paid much money to the Cuban National Police, but I do not know what the money is for."

"Who receives it for the Cuban National Police?" I said.

"Lieutenant Maldonado," said Schlegel, his body quivering on the oil drum. "He conveys it to his superior officer, the one known as Juanito the Jehovah's Witness. He, in turn, pays General Valdes."

"What is the money for?"

"I do not know." Schlegel's body flinched in anticipation, but I made no move.

"How can you not know, my friend?"

"I swear to you! I swear on my mother's soul! Hauptsturmführer Becker has not confided in me."

"Name all of the other agents," I said, touching the blade of the knife to his back for a second before transferring the knife to my left hand and picking up the screwdriver again.

Schlegel was shaking his head. "I know only Becker, the current radio operator on the boat... Schmidt... who is an SS sergeant, very stupid... and no one else... Wait! No! Please, no! Stop!"

I did not stop for some seconds. By this time, Schlegel was certain that a knife had been tearing his vitals apart, but no real damage had been done to anything but his pride. The screwdriver was cold steel but well lubricated. I thought of Hemingway's introduction to *Men at War.* The writer boasted of knowing "what war is really like rather than what it is supposed to be." He had no idea.

"Who else?" I said. I wanted this over with. "You used agents to hunt for the missing whore. Who?"

Schlegel was shaking his head so violently that sweat and tears struck me three feet behind him. "Truly, I tell you truly. I know of no one else. We used Falangists... sympathizers... to look for the girl. We did not find her. We used no real agents. But there will be landings... one is scheduled for the thirteenth... No! Stop!"

"Tell me the purpose of the landings," I said.

"I do not know. I swear. They are Abwehr men. Two. To be landed by submarine at some location on the Cuban coast. I do not know where."

"Why?" I did not expect an answer to this question.

"To meet with the FBI," gasped Schlegel.

I almost dropped the knife and screwdriver. "Continue," I managed to say after a second.

Schlegel was still shaking his head. "I discovered this by accident. I swear. Hauptsturmführer Becker did not tell me. I know this from the Cuban... Lieutenant Maldonado... who said that Herr Becker was to meet with the FBI and that there will be further contacts after a submarine insertion of agents."

"Who from the FBI?" I said.

"I do not know. I swear to you. I do not know. Please let me go. I beseech you, as a man. As a Christian."

"What is the purpose of this rendezvous with the FBI?" I said.

"Please. I beg of you. I have a wife. I am a good man. You must not... Stop! Oh, Jesus fuck! *Fuck!* Shit! Stop!"

"The purpose?"

"I am not supposed to know... but I am aware... these things were rumored in Rio... Becker has made mention, indirectly..." Schlegel was gasping and babbling, a phrase in German, a fragment of a sentence in Portuguese, words in English. I waited patiently.

"There is some contact between the Abwehr and the FBI," he panted. "It has been rumored for at least a year."

"And the landing has to do with that contact?" I said.

"I think so... I do not know... perhaps... I think so. Becker said that this is a very important operation. That the future of the Reich depends upon it. Oh, please let me go."

"Who killed the boy?" I said.

"Boy? What boy?" said Schlegel, and his terror was in not knowing how to answer the question. "Please, what boy?" He clearly knew nothing of Santiago's death.

"Name the operatives other than the radioman and Becker," I said.

Schlegel started to shake his head. "Wait... wait! No, wait! Wait! Stop! There are two others in Cuba."

"Who?" I said. I was trying not to vomit in the heat and stink of the burned-out shack. "Where?"

"I do not know. They are a Todt Team. That is a team trained to—"

"Names," I said.

"I know no names. Honestly."

"Is Helga Sonneman an agent?"

"I do not know—"

Schlegel screamed and screamed again. When he got his breath, he said, "I swear by all that is holy and by my faith in the Führer, I do not know their names. I do not know if Sonneman is an agent or simply a rich, foolish bitch. I know that one of the Todt Team members is close to Hemingway's group. Becker receives constant information from that agent about what the writer's amateur organization is doing."

"What is that agent's code name?"

"Panama."

"And the other's code name?"

"Columbia."

"The Todt Team," I said. "Are you sure that there are only two?"

"Two. I am certain. Two. Becker receives transmissions from two."

"Male or female?"

"I do not know. I swear to you, I do not know."

"Who are they going to kill?" I said softly.

Schlegel shook his head so fiercely that sweat pattered in the ashes and struck the burned-out beams. The gray tape over his eyes wrinkled as he furrowed his brow. "I do not know. I do not think the transmission has been sent yet with authorization for them to... to complete their mission."

Here we were. This was the reason for all this. I said, "Give me the cipher base for the numerical-based transmissions."

"I do not... Christ! Stop! Please! No!"

"The cipher base," I said.

"You must believe me. It is Becker's code. He had me deliver it to the radioman aboard the *Southern Cross*, but I have no memory for numbers and do not remember... No!"

The screaming stopped eventually. I said, "If you have a bad memory, you wrote it down somewhere. If you want to live, Herr Schlegel, find it for me within the next ten seconds."

"No, I cannot... Wait! Stop! Yes! In my appointment book! On the third to last page. There is a column of phone numbers."

I retrieved the book and checked the page. Beside a list of Rio-based businessmen's names, there were phone numbers. Brazil used a seven-digit system.

"The fifth number down," gasped Schlegel. "I had to write it down to remember it."

"Two-nine-five," I said. "One-four-one-three?" Something in Schlegel's tensed muscles told me that this was not all.

"I will discover if this is not correct," I said softly. "You will not leave here until I know. And if it is not..."

Schlegel's body collapsed then, that is the only way to describe it. It was as if all the air went out of the man and he simply deflated and became a vaguely human-shaped jellyfish draped over the oil drum. I am ashamed to admit that I had seen this before.

"It is the number," he said, sobbing loudly. "It is reversed."

I dropped the screwdriver into the ashes, stepped closer, raised the knife blade, and cut through the tape that bound his wrists. I ripped the tape away from his red and swollen eyes.

I picked up the Luger and dropped it into my jacket pocket. Walking to the door and looking out at the ditch where little Santiago had been murdered, I said, "Clean yourself. Get dressed. Repack your suitcases."

Ten minutes later, I followed him back to the car. Schlegel walked like an old man, and his body continued to shake. I had planned to use the lead pipe a final time, spill whiskey over him, deliver him to the airport, and pay some boy a few dollars to help my "inebriated friend" meet his flight to Rio. But I had been clever enough for one day. Too clever. And fat little Teddy Schlegel had been through enough. I knew that he would kill me in a second if he got the chance, but not this day. Nor soon.

I drove him to the airport. He rode all the way with his shoulders sagging and his head down. Once there, I took his bags from the trunk and set them on the curb. I had not touched the $26,000.

Schlegel stood shaking on the sidewalk, his eyes still lowered.

"Of course, there will be others watching you until you board your plane," I said softly. "If you call anyone from here or talk to anyone, these others will gather you and return you to me. Do you understand?"

Schlegel nodded, his face still lowered and his legs now also visibly shaking.

"Board your aircraft," I said. "Go to Rio. *Never* return to Cuba. If you mention this to no one, I will mention it to no one. No one need know that you spoke with us."

Schlegel nodded. His fingers were trembling. Why some people are chosen for intelligence work, I will never understand. Why any of us continue to do it, I also will never understand.

"Go home," I said, and got in the car and drove away.

On the Central Highway back to San Francisco de Paula, I opened the bottle of whiskey I had brought along to splash over Schlegel's clothes as part of the cover story. Instead, I drank most of it before I drove through the gates of the *finca*.

"*Estamos copados,*" I said. Unlike Hemingway, I did not like the sound of the words at all.

22

WE HAD FOUND SANTIAGO'S BODY on Saturday, August 8. Hemingway and I had held our idiot fight on Sunday, August 9. I had driven Schlegel to the airport on Monday, August 10. Lieutenant Maldonado came to the *finca* on Tuesday, August 11, the day before we were scheduled to depart in the *Pilar* to meet the August 13 landings.

Hemingway had spent much of the morning provisioning his boat. He had decided that along with Gregory and Patrick, the crew would consist only of Winston Guest, Patchi Ibarlucia, the recovering Don Saxon to man the radio, and his indispensible mate, Gregorio Fuentes. The *Southern Cross* had left the Casablanca shipyards for what was supposed to be a short trip up to the area around Key Paraíso and back by sunset, and Hemingway had finished the preparations on the *Pilar* and sent her out to shadow the yacht. He had appointed Wolfer as the acting captain in his absence. Don Saxon, the Marine, was along for the afternoon to man the radio. Hemingway stayed behind to clean and oil the *niños* and to study the charts of the approach to Bahía Manatí. He had cabled Tom Shevlin, received additional permission to take the millionaire sportsman's speedboat on a trip, and we were planning to drive back to Cojímar in the evening to meet the returning *Pilar* and prepare the *Lorraine* for its adventure.

"Tom says that there are two long, hidden compartments aft of the engine housing," said Hemingway. "Left over from the rum-running days. We can stow the *niños*, the grenades, and one of the BARs there."

"You're bringing a BAR?" I said. "Why?"

"In case we have to engage the submarine," said the writer.

"If we have to engage the submarine," I said, "we're fucked."

USING SCHLEGEL'S KEY, it had taken me only a few minutes on Monday afternoon to decode the numeral-based transmission I had intercepted during our last outing. First I copied the transmission as I had received it:

q-f-i-e-n / w-u-w-s-y / d-y-r-q-q / t-e-o-i-o / w-q-e-w-x / d-t-u-w-p / c-m-b-x-x

Then I wrote the repeating cipher base above the transmission:

3 1 4 1 5 9 2 3 1 4 1 5 9 2 3 1 4 1 5 9 2 3 1 4 1 5 9 2 3 1 4 1
q f i e n w u w s y d y r q q t e o i o w q e w x d t u w p c m b

I had neglected to ask Schlegel which direction the cipher went in the alphabet—up or down—but there were only two choices, and in a minute I realized that during encryption for transmission, the cipher moved the letters *up* the number of spaces indicated by the digit above it, which meant that during decryption I would count *down* that same number of letters. Thus, three spaces back from *q* gave me *n*, one space back from *f* gave me an *e*, four spaces back from *i* gave me another *e*, and so forth. I tossed out the last two *x*'s as filler.

The message now read:

NEEDINSTRUCTIONSANDFUNDSCOLUMBIA

So, for *that*, Schlegel had endured what he endured and I had further eliminated any sense of honor in my life.

But it did tell me something. First, if Schlegel was to be believed—and I believed that he had told me everything he knew—then this transmission was being relayed to Hamburg via the radio operator on the *Southern Cross*. Furthermore, the captain and crew of the yacht probably did not know that these transmissions were being sent via their shortwave. Also, this confirmed Schlegel's statement that there were two members of the SD assassination team in Cuba—this Columbia and the one code-named Panama. It was Panama whom Schlegel had said was close to Hemingway's operation. It was Panama's partner, Columbia, who was asking for instructions and money.

Who could Panama be? Who was close enough to the Crook Factory to relay reliable information about it? Delgado, of course, because I had been passing him information. Winston Guest? Dr. Herrera Sotolongo had said that he believed the sportsman to be a British agent. If a British agent, why not a double agent for the Germans? But I found it hard to believe that the impulsive, likable Wolfer was a trained SD assassin. Dr. Herrera Sotolongo himself refused to join Hemingway's band but knew enough about the operation of the Crook Factory to be the source. Who else? One of the Basques? Sinsky or Patchi or Roberto Herrera? The Black Priest? One of Hemingway's servants who was inserted long ago and had been living under deep cover all that time? I had seen stranger things.

Of course, it did not have to be someone that close to Hemingway. He had more than twenty operatives in his Crook Factory, and there was no security within the group. Any one of the bellmen or waiters or wharf rats or drinking cronies of Hemingway's whom he had enlisted for this farcical operation could be the assassin.

It was feasible that Panama was Lieutenant Maldonado, receiving money from the Germans and possibly using it to bribe one of Hemingway's amateurs. That way, Panama could be reporting updated information to Becker without being too close to the day-to-day operation of the Crook Factory. And we knew that Maldonado was a killer. He could easily have sold his services to the Germans and been trained in their Todt Team tactics.

But Maldonado was not Aryan. And the SD was particular about whom it chose as its cold-blooded assassins.

Columbia could be Hauptsturmführer Becker himself. But

Schlegel had said that Becker had been receiving messages *from* both members of the Todt Team. If the chubby Abwehr man had been correct, then it made more sense that our friend Johann Siegfried Becker was the agent in charge of Operation Raven in Cuba and that Columbia was someone else, quite possibly someone I had not seen and had never heard of before.

Two RSHA SD AMT VI assassins, awaiting instructions, waiting to be unleashed, awaiting word from Hamburg or Berlin to kill their target or targets.

Who was their target?

So far we had two dead people: Kohler, the first radio operator from the *Southern Cross*, and poor Santiago. Both had their throats cut. It seemed probable that Maldonado had killed Kohler, and the boy had been following the lieutenant just days before the murder. Perhaps the SD had loosened its preference for Aryan killers in this instance.

Finally, there was one other factor that would—I hoped—make Schlegel's ordeal worthwhile. If the Abwehr man did not cable Becker upon his return to Rio—and there were several good reasons that Schlegel might not be eager to share the details of his interrogation or the fact that he had ratted out an SD assassin team—then Becker and his Todt Team would think that their numeral-based code was secure. For a few days at least, we might be able to intercept more of their secret transmissions.

And a few days, I thought, *should be all that we need.*

And that is when Maria burst into the guest house. Her eyes were wide with terror and her voice was shaking so badly that I could hardly understand her.

"José, José, he is here. He has come for me. He is here to kill me!"

"Calm down," I said, holding her shoulders and shaking her to stop her from rolling her eyes and panting like a spooked horse. "Who's here?"

"Lieutenant Maldonado," gasped the girl. "*Caballo Loco.* He is in the main house. He has come to take me away!"

I had taken to keeping the .38 in my belt. I wanted to give Maria a weapon while I went up to the main house, but I did not want to face Maldonado unarmed. I went into the guest room and took Schlegel's Luger from the nightstand.

Pulling Maria into the guest room bathroom, I held out the pistol, slapped in the clip of 9-millimeter slugs, chambered a round, and clicked off the safety. "Stay right here," I said. "Lock this door. If Maldonado or anyone else unfriendly tries to come in, just aim and squeeze the trigger. But make sure it's not me or Hemingway before you shoot."

Maria was weeping softly now. "José, I do not know how to operate such a—"

"Just aim and squeeze the trigger when you know it's a bad guy," I said. "But be damned sure it's a bad guy."

I stepped out and waited until she locked the door. Then I went up to the main house.

I HAD NEVER SEEN Hemingway so angry, not even the day of our fight. As he stood blocking the front doorway, stopping Maldonado and three other Cuban uniformed goons from entering, the writer's face was pale, his lips were white, and his hands were clenched so tightly that I winced to see those bruised knuckles turning purple and white.

"*Señor* Hemingway," the lieutenant was saying, glancing once at me as I walked up behind the writer and then paying me no further attention, "we regret the necessity of this intrusion—"

"There's not going to be any intrusion," snapped Hemingway. "You're not entering this house."

"Regrettably, we must, Don Ernesto," said Maldonado. "It is a matter of police priority. A young woman who is a primary suspect in a recent murder has been reported in this area, and we are searching all homes where she might—"

"You are not searching this home," said Hemingway.

The confrontation bordered on farce. The lieutenant was speaking in English, which his three goons probably did not understand. Hemingway was speaking in formal Spanish. Every time he said no to *Caballo Loco*, the eyebrows of the three underling cops went a bit higher in shock and surprise.

I had forgotten how tall Maldonado was. The Cuban looked to be six feet four inches tall, with one of those physiques that seems to be all long bone and gristle. His facial features were exaggerated in size—long chin, heavy brows, cheekbones that threw shadows onto his lower cheeks—and even his mustache seemed more pronounced than a normal man's. Maldonado often dressed in plainclothes, but this afternoon he was in full uniform, and he rested his knobby thumbs on his black gun belt as he spoke. The lieutenant seemed very relaxed, almost amused by the confrontation, and this seemed to make Hemingway all the more apoplectic.

The writer was wearing the same soiled shirt and shorts he had on the evening of our fight, only now that long-barreled .22 target pistol was tucked into his wide belt. Maldonado did not seem to notice the weapon, but his three goons could not keep their eyes off it. I was afraid that the lieutenant's insolent manner and perfect English were going to so enrage Hemingway that the writer would pull the .22 and there would be a gunfight right there in the front hallway of the *finca*. I decided that if this happened, I would have to take out Maldonado with the .38 before drawing down on his underlings. Somehow, I did not believe that Hemingway's .22 would stop the tall Cuban before he drew the Colt .44 from its holster and blew the writer all the way back into the dining room.

This is nuts, I thought. And one hell of a way for a trained agent of the SIS to die—a gunfight with the Cuban National Police.

"*Señor* Hemingway," Maldonado was saying, "we will make the search as quick and unobtrusive as possible—"

"No, you won't," said Hemingway in Spanish, "because there's not going to be any search. This house and grounds are American property... U.S. soil."

Maldonado blinked at this. "Surely you jest, *señor*."

"I am totally serious, Lieutenant." One look at Hemingway's face would have convinced anyone of this statement.

"But I am sure that under international law, only the United States Embassy and certain military bases such as Guantánamo and Camagüey would be considered U.S. soil on the island of Cuba, *señor*," said the lieutenant in calm tones.

"Bullshit," said Hemingway in English, and then switched back to Spanish. "I am a citizen of the United States of America. This is my home and property. It is protected by the laws of the United States of America."

"But surely, *señor*, Cuban sovereignty in this matter is—"

"Fuck Cuban sovereignty," said Hemingway. He was watching Maldonado's eyes very carefully, as if he believed in that old gunfighter's maxim that the eyes showed you when your opponent was going to draw his weapon.

The three goons were angered by the last statement. Their hands moved to the pistols on their own belts. I wondered if Hemingway was going to watch all of their eyes. I kept my own gaze locked on Maldonado's right hand where it rested on his belt in front of his holster.

The lieutenant smiled. He had large, perfect teeth. "I understand that you are agitated, *Señor* Hemingway. We mean no offense, but our duty requires—"

"I take offense, Lieutenant. This is American property, and any unauthorized entry would constitute an invasion of U.S. soil at a time when my country is at war."

Maldonado's right hand came up, and he rubbed his long chin as if seeking a way to be reasonable with this *gringo*. "But if all foreign residents in Cuba claimed that their homes were the property of their respective nations, *señor*, then..."

"I make no claims for anyone else," snapped Hemingway. "But I am a U.S. citizen, working on war-related scientific projects under the direct authorization of Ambassador Spruille Braden of the United States embassy, Colonel Hayne D. Boyden of the United States Marine Corps, and Colonel John W. Thomason Jr., Chief of U.S. Naval Intelligence for South America. Any unauthorized entry of this home will be considered an act of war."

Lieutenant Maldonado seemed to be at a loss as to how to deal with this glorious illogic. His three goons kept their hands on their pistols and looked to their tall leader for a sign.

"I understand that these are sensitive times, *Señor* Hemingway, and even though our duty to search for this alleged murderess is clear and indisputable," said Maldonado, "we do not wish to disturb your harmony or offend the sensibilities of so preeminent a resident and friend of the Republic of Cuba. Therefore, we will honor your request not to disturb your home if you give us your word that the woman we seek is not here, and we shall then restrict our search to the adjoining grounds and outbuildings."

The goons goggled at this endless flow of English from their superior.

"I give you my word on nothing but the certainty that your men will be shot as trespassers if they set another foot on these grounds," said Hemingway, looking up at Maldonado.

Neither man blinked for a long, silent moment. The air smelled of sweat.

Maldonado bowed slightly. "Very well, *señor*. We understand your feelings and respect your need for privacy in these troubled times. If you see or hear of a young woman such as the one we seek, please contact me at—"

"Good afternoon, gentlemen," said Hemingway, speaking in English for the first time and stepping forward to close the door in their faces.

Maldonado smiled, stepped back, and nodded for his goons to follow him as he walked back to the green Chevrolet parked in the driveway.

Hemingway closed the door and went to the window to watch them drive away. I started to say something light to break the tension, but then I noticed his pallor and clenched fists and decided against it. I had no doubt that the writer would have pulled the little .22 and begun blazing away if Maldonado had put his huge foot across that threshold.

"That cocksucker's the one," whispered Hemingway. "I'm sure that he killed Santiago."

I said nothing.

"I sent Xenophobia down to the guest house," he said, looking at me for the first time. "Thanks for coming up."

I shrugged.

"Is that a pistol in your belt," said Hemingway, "or are you just happy to see me?"

I pulled my jacket back far enough to show him the .38.

"Stranger and stranger, Special Agent Lucas," said Hemingway. He went over to his drink table by the floral chair and made himself a Tom Collins. "Drink, Special Agent Lucas?"

"No thanks," I said. "I'll go tell Maria they're gone."

Hemingway sipped his drink and looked at the painting on the nearest wall. "I guess I'll have to quit calling her that."

"What's that?" I said.

"Xenophobia," said Hemingway. "The girl has real enemies. They really want to kill her."

I nodded and went back out past the pool to the guest house.

In the bedroom, I called Maria's name once, started to knock, paused, stepped to one side of the door, and then knocked.

The 9-millimeter parabellum slug came through the door head high, went through the wall just above the bed, and probably tore through one of the royal palms outside before passing over the main house.

"Goddammit, Maria!" I yelled.

"Oh, José, José," cried the whore, throwing open the door and rushing out to throw herself into my arms.

I pulled the Luger out of her hand and clicked on the safety before allowing her to collapse against my chest. I had the urge to knock her across the room. It was one thing to die an absurd death in a gunfight with Cuban National Police goons, quite another to be mistakenly shot to death by a Cuban whore. I was not sure which would have amused my old friends in the Bureau more.

I told her what Hemingway had said to them, and that *Caballo Loco* and his little *locos* were gone for the day and probably for good. She remained hysterical.

"No, José, no, no!" she cried, wadding my shirtfront into a wet mass. "They will be back. They will return. They will come for me. Tomorrow you and *Señor* Hemingway and the little ones and the smelly sailors and all the rest will go away on *Señor*

Hemingway's boat and then no one will be left here to watch over me except Ramón the cook, who is crazy, and Juan the chauffeur, who wants to take me to bed but does not like me otherwise, and then *Caballo Loco* will return and they will rape me and then kill me for something that I did not do, that *Caballo Loco* himself did, and you will return but I will not be waiting in the cottage for you as I have done each night and you will wonder, Where is Maria? But Maria will be dead and cold and—"

"Maria," I said softly, squeezing her arms. "Maria, darling. Shut the fuck up."

She looked at me in shock.

"I'll talk to *Señor* Hemingway," I said softly. "He will take you with us on the boat."

"Ah, José!" cried the whore, hugging me so tightly that my bruised ribs almost gave way.

THE REST OF THE AFTERNOON was busy and instructive. Hemingway invited Maria to the main house for lunch, and blushing wildly, the young whore accepted the invitation and rushed up to Grade A to get into her finest dress. She was flustered when I told her that I wasn't going to join them for lunch—Hemingway had not invited me—but pleased when I said that I would pack her things in the same travel duffel that I was carrying. Before going across the hill to lunch, Maria set out her few borrowed pieces of clothing, her hairbrush and modest makeup kit, and her extra pair of sandals. After she left, I packed it all away carefully and then looked through the small box where she kept her things. There was nothing of importance left.

Then I spent the better part of an hour wandering the grounds—checking the "corpse well" up the hill, the old outbuildings beyond the overgrown tennis court, the shed where the swimming pool supplies were stored, the garage and storage lean-to behind the garage, and then back to Grade A, where I wandered through the dairy barns and clambered into the lofts. Lieutenant Maldonado and his boys were nowhere in sight. But under moldering hay in the back corner of the loft, I found a long package wrapped in canvas. I brought it with me when I went into Cojímar to check out the *Lorraine* and to load it with supplies. We had planned to do this later in the evening, when the *Pilar* returned, but Hemingway had decided that it would be a better idea for me to take the speedboat out while it was still light and leave it at a private dock in the old seaside town of Guanabo, about ten miles up the coast.

Juan drove me to Cojímar since he then had to drive up to Guanabo and pick me up. The driver was sullen and silent, which suited me fine since I had my own reasons for silence. It was a thoughtful drive. When we arrived at Shevlin's private dock, I told Juan to relax in the shade of the car while I emptied the stuff from the back seat and the trunk and loaded the boat.

The *Lorraine* was a beautiful boat, a 22-foot runabout handcrafted of mahogany and chrome, fitted with leather cockpit seats and other expensive materials, built in the States by the Dodge Boat Works during the late '20s when craftsmanship in small boats was at its height. Luckily, Shevlin had replaced almost all of the mechanicals with updated equipment: the Lycoming V-8 engine was only two years old and as clean as an engine could get, the steering mechanism had been modernized, the hull had been cleaned of barnacles recently, there was a brand-new magnetic compass on the dash, and a powerful searchlight had been mounted next to the windshield. Shevlin had modified the boat for the comfort of his passengers by moving the engine compartment farther aft and combining the two cockpits into one spacious, leather-lined space.

No one but Juan watched me unload the car. In addition to the canvas package, I was lifting out heavy boxes of food, six five-gallon containers of potable water, three large boxes of hand grenades—what Hemingway insisted on calling "frags"—and two Thompson submachine guns in their sheepswool-and-leather cradles. Hemingway had insisted on bringing a dozen extra clips for the *niños*, and I dutifully carried them aboard and set them in place. I locked all of these things away in the starboard aft compartment that Shevlin had told us about. If one did not know the long panel behind the cockpit cushions was there, it would never be found.

In the portside compartment, I loaded two of the *sombreros científicos* from the *Pilar*, a couple of green tarps, a tan tarp, a hundred feet of clothesline, several nautical charts rolled into cardboard tubes, canvas jackets, extra boat shoes, and some other clothing. I also packed away a military first aid kit, a separate bundle of sealed surgical dressings, my .357 Magnum and sixty rounds of ammunition locked away in a waterproof pouch, a box of Hershey bars, two bottles of insect repellent, two sets of binoculars from the *finca*, two powerful flashlights, a small Leica camera, two hunting knives, a couple of canvas bags with carrying straps, and a pump gun filled with Flit.

I went up to the dock and rigged two wide boards as a ramp down to the *Lorraine*, and then called Juan to help me roll the two fifty-gallon drums of gasoline down into the cockpit. The chauffeur grumbled, but he helped me get the drums in place against the sternboards without scratching the mahogany or staining the leather cushions. Juan went back to the car to smoke a cigarette while I used some of the rope to lash the drums into place, making sure that they were secured well enough to stay in place come hell or high water. The heavy gasoline drums ruined the perfect trim of the little craft, making her ride too low at the stern, but there was nothing for it.

When I was sure that everything was loaded and secured, I waved to Juan, took Shevlin's silver key out of my pocket, and started the speedboat with a satisfying roar of its 125-horsepower Lycoming engine. Letting it idle, I cast off the bow and stern lines myself, settled into the luxurious leather seat, swung the beautiful wooden showroom stock Duesenberg auto steering wheel hard aport, and grumbled out through evening traffic of returning fishermen who looked at the speedboat with a mixture of disdain and envy.

Once beyond the rocks of the breakwater, I opened her up to within a tick of a red line on the tachometer. She immediately jumped up on plane and sliced through the rows of easy swells like a bullet through soft cotton. There was the sound of the hull pounding, but no bad vibration at all. I throttled back a bit, but let her continue to fly with her bow free. The rush of air was exhilarating after the hot, sultry days ashore with almost no breeze. If I had an unlimited amount of fuel, I realized, I could hold her at thirty-five knots all day on a sea like this. I throttled back until her lovely bow came down and set my course east along the coast.

The hills and fields near Hemingway's Finca Vigía were arid, dusty, and mostly treeless where orchards had not been planted, but this section of coastline east of Cojímar looked like a tropical paradise from half a mile out to sea: a long stretch of white beaches, the crests of sand dunes catching the setting sun and throwing shadows on the sea grapes and other shrubs, fluttering lines of coconut palms glowing gold and green in the sunset. There was no real harbor at Guanabo, but a lovely curve of bay with the old town huddled under palm trees at the apex of the curve and lines of white bungalows in the trees near the points. The cottages had been built in the 1920s and 1930s to handle the growing number of *Norteamericano* tourists, but now their paint was peeling and most sat empty and boarded up, waiting for the end of the war.

I tied up at a private dock on the eastern end of the bay. The *Lorraine* had a canvas tarp that covered the cockpit, and it took a few minutes for me to figure out how to rig it properly with its myriad of chrome snaps and elastic loops. Hemingway knew the old man who owned the pier and the fishing gear shack on it, and the old fellow assured me that the beautiful speedboat would be there when we wanted it the next day. I paid him *Señor* Hemingway's compliments and a dollar bill. Juan and the Lincoln arrived eventually, and we rode back to the *finca* in silence broken only by the rumble from approaching thunderclouds in the twilight.

Maria was excited to see me, excited about the next day's adventure, and mostly excited about her long lunch and conversation with *Señor* Hemingway. The writer had just left to meet his boys and buddies at Cojímar, so Maria and I had a light meal at the Grade A cottage and watched the heat lightning flash to the west. Despite her excitement, she admitted that she was still terrified that Maldonado might return, and she jumped every time thunder rumbled. After the dinner dishes were washed and the lanterns were lit, she went to the door.

"Where are you going, Maria?"

"Just for my evening walk, José."

"Aren't you afraid of *Caballo Loco*?"

She smiled at me but glanced nervously out at the darkened courtyard.

"Besides," I said, "don't we have better things to do than a walk? We might not be alone again for several days."

Maria's eyes widened at this. Bedtime initiatives had almost invariably been hers. "José," she whispered.

I walked to her, closed the door, and carried her back to our shoved-together cots.

23

THE TRIP BEGAN MERRILY, like a family outing on a sunny day. Before it was over, one of our party would be dead on the ocean and I would be busy digging bullets out of a dead man's spine.

Hemingway got the *Pilar* under way shortly after sunrise on Wednesday morning. All of his crew except me were in high spirits—with Maria and Hemingway's two boys aboard, the trip had the feel of a weekend jaunt. That impression was augmented by the pack of fishermen and buddies who showed up at the dock to wave the *Pilar* off. The group included Roberto Herrera; his brother, Dr. Herrera Sotolongo; Sinsky the Sailor; Fernando Mesa; and the other former crewmen left behind, as well as the Black Priest, Don Andrés; and a cluster of Cojímar regulars who were having Bloody Marys for breakfast at La Terreza.

Maria loved the boat but was terrified of the sea. She confided in "Papa" that she could not swim, that her youngest brother had drowned while working out of the Port of Santiago on a fishing boat, and that she was happiest sitting in the precise middle of the *Pilar* and would be saying many prayers to the Virgin Mary for good weather during our trip.

"Yes, Daughter," said Hemingway, "you say the prayers and I shall consult the barometer. We want good weather for our voyage."

Once out to sea, Patrick and Gregory took charge of the young whore—I do not think they had any idea where Maria was from or what her background was, only that she was "another pretty friend of Papa's"—and they competed in showing off the boat's capabilities, the outriggers, the fishing tackle on board, and their own spearfishing gear. Their Spanish was rough in spots, but the occasional lapse in grammar or syntax was compensated for by their obvious enthusiasm.

"Once we get to Cayo Confites," I overheard Patrick telling her, "I will take you spearfishing."

"But I cannot swim," said Maria.

Patrick laughed, and I realized that the boy—just like his younger brother—was probably smitten. "Nonsense," he said, "the water is so salty there and the waves so small inside the reef that you couldn't sink. All you have to do is take this mask and put your face in the water."

"You could wear a life jacket, if you wish," said Gregory, joining the conversation despite his brother's scowls and obvious signals to piss off. "Although it's harder to swim around that way," continued the younger boy, also obviously enjoying Maria's company.

"Are there not sharks?" said the young woman.

"Oh, yes, scores of them in the area," said Gregory brightly, "but they rarely come across the reef around Cayo Confites, and then only at night. And I'll be there to protect you."

"With grunts strung on the belt of his swimming trunks," said Patrick, "to attract the sharks."

Gregory glared at his older brother, but Maria only smiled and said, "And aren't there barracuda?"

"Barracuda never bother us," said Patrick, regaining control of the conversation. "They'd only hit you if the water was very muddy or too roily. Or if they just got a glimpse of you and struck by mistake. We don't go spearfishing when the waters are that roiled up."

"Barracuda are really curious," added Gregory, "and they swim around us all the time, but they always go away. They never attack us."

"Unless you were swimming with fish on a stringer," said Patrick, still needling his younger brother. "Or on your belt. But who would be stupid enough to string bleeding fish on his belt?"

Gregory ignored him. "But you can swim between Mouse and me, Maria. Nothing will bother you that way."

The young whore laughed and shook her dark hair. "Thank you, thank you both. But I do not swim and will stay on the island and watch you catch fish and cook them for you when you bring them in."

"It isn't an island," said Patrick, obviously still miffed at his brother and angry that the woman was not planning to swim with him. "It's a little pissant of a key." He had said "pissant" in English.

Maria nodded and smiled.

THE *PILAR* PAUSED just beyond the bay at Guanabo while Hemingway took me in to the dock in the *Tin Kid.* The little outboard sputtered and popped but kept running as the dinghy cut through the lines of small waves and then seemed to float across the transparent waters of the bay.

"You forgot to load this yesterday," said the writer, patting a long object wrapped in two rain slickers.

I pulled away one end of the closest slicker. One of the two BARs. Hemingway kicked an ammo can of ammunition with his foot. I nodded, resigned to carrying the heavy weapon with us.

"You'll get to Confites before us unless there's shitty weather," said Hemingway. "Just be sure that you don't go scouting Point Roma by yourself."

"No," I said.

Hemingway squinted back at the *Pilar*, its green paint gleaming as the larger boat bobbed beyond the point. The boys were showing Maria how to fish from the stern chair. "I'd feel better if you were bringing Xenophobia down in the *Lorraine*."

"I offered," I said. "She's too afraid of the water to come in the small boat. And I thought you weren't going to call her Xenophobia any longer."

Hemingway shrugged. He brought us up to the dock, and the old-timer there chatted amiably with Hemingway while I got the cover off the speedboat, secured the BAR, still wrapped in its rain slickers, set the can of ammo away, double-checked the hoses and pump for the auxiliary gasoline drums, and cast off the stern line.

Hemingway lifted the loop off the bow line and stood looking down at me. He was wearing an old African safari shirt, rolled up and buttoned at the sleeves, open most of the way down the front. Sweat glimmered on his forearms and chest hair. He was very brown.

"What did you tell the girl about this trip?" he said.

"Nothing. Just that she could come with us."

The writer nodded. "I've got two of the big canvas tents in the *Pilar*. Gregorio will pitch them when we get into Confites and she and the boys will stay there while Wolfer and the others do... scientific business."

I nodded and looked back at the *Pilar* again. The canvas that rose to the waist height around the flying bridge had been laced on, and the two long boards were hanging on either side amidships, proclaiming MUSEUM OF NATURAL HISTORY in twelve-inch-high letters.

"Keep Saxon awake," I said. The Marine had the habit of dozing off in the heat of the radio room, and I didn't want him missing possible transmissions.

"Yeah." Hemingway squinted to the east. It was still a beautiful morning. "We'll get them going early tomorrow—Wolfer and the others—out on sub patrol to the northwest of Confites. We don't want them intercepting the real sub."

I smiled at that thought.

Hemingway tossed the coiled bow line to me. "Don't break Tommy's boat, Lucas," he said, and walked back to the *Tin Kid*.

I brought the *Lorraine* out of the bay at a conservative speed and swung the bow east just beyond the point. Hemingway was halfway back to the *Pilar*. Patrick, Gregory, and Maria waved at me from the stern of the bigger boat as I opened the throttle a bit and brought the *Lorraine* up on plane. They looked like three happy, sunburned children out on a boat ride.

THE CUBAN LIEUTENANT and his men were happy to have company that evening and shocked that a woman was visiting their key. All of the men disappeared into their shack while Fuentes and the rest of us set up the old safari tents, and when the soldiers returned, they were still in rags but now in their best and cleanest rags. Maria was gracious and chatted with them in rapid-fire Cuban Spanish while we carried in boxes of food and cooking materials.

The lieutenant had seen no enemy activity during the previous week and only a few turtle boats. A broadcast had come from Guantánamo that a PBY out of Camagüey had engaged an enemy submarine off the west coast of Bimini three days earlier, and the lieutenant had put his men on alert and Cayo Confites on defensive status, but there had been no sightings. Hemingway thanked the lieutenant and his men for their diligence and invited them to our evening cookout.

After the sun set and a wind had come up to blow the worst of the mosquito clouds toward the southwest, Fuentes built a large driftwood fire and began grilling large steaks. There were baked potatoes and fresh salad enough for everyone, and this time Wolfer had not forgotten the beer. The mate had baked a Key Lime pie for dessert, and after that whiskey bottles were handed around to everyone, including the boys and Maria. The Cubans turned in around midnight, but the rest of us sat and lay against driftwood logs for another hour or more, watching the sparks rising from the campfire go drifting among the constellations and talking about submarines and the war. When we spoke in English, Maria showed little understanding, but she never ceased smiling and seemed to be enjoying herself very much.

"In the morning," said Hemingway, talking to Wolfer and Patchi, "I want you to take the *Pilar* up toward Megano de Casigua. Keep your eyes peeled for sub activity and keep Saxon's ears plastered to the 'phones for some sound of the U-boats communicating with the mainland or the *Southern Cross*. All he heard today were some squirts in German from the wolf packs way up north."

"I thought that we might see the yacht on our trip down here," said Winston Guest. "She was last sighted heading in this direction."

"You may see her tomorrow," said Hemingway. "If you do, feel free to shadow her."

"And if *Señorita* Helga is aboard?" said Ibarlucia, raising the whiskey bottle in toast.

"Feel free to fuck her for me," said Hemingway. Then he started like a guilty boy and glanced at Maria, but evidently her English did not include this most basic terminology of her profession.

"Anyway," continued the writer, "Lucas and I are going to take Shevlin's little darling in past Puerto de Nuevitas beyond Cayo Sabinal and investigate some of those rivers and inlets there, charting the area and checking for possible refueling bases."

Fuentes rubbed his chin. "I am surprised *Señor* Shevlin loaned his beautiful craft for this business."

"Tom's in the Hooligan Navy," said Hemingway. "He wants to do his bit. And for *Lorraine* to do hers." He looked at Winston Guest across the dying campfire. "Wolfer, make sure that the boys and Maria have everything they need for some spearfishing and putting around tomorrow."

Guest nodded. "I'm leaving the *Tin Kid* for their fishing," he said. "The lieutenant's promised to watch over the boys until we get back tomorrow night."

"Lucas and I will bivouac somewhere around Puerto Tarafa," lied the writer. "And we'll see you on Friday morning. Don't leave on patrol until we get back."

If we get back, I thought.

WE LEFT BEFORE SUNRISE. Hemingway looked in on his boys, sleeping in the tent, and then we rowed the *Tin Kid* out to where the *Pilar* and the *Lorraine* bobbed at anchor. The morning was windy and cooler than most had been that summer. Fuentes had fussed about the *Pilar* the previous evening, rigging one bow anchor and two stern anchors before being assured that she would ride out any morning squall properly, but the *Lorraine* lunged and dipped at her single anchor line like a dog eager to be off the leash.

Hemingway slid behind the wheel and took us out. He was wearing the same safari shirt as the day before and had a long-billed cap pulled low. He kept the rpm down, not wanting to wake the boys. As we passed the *Pilar*, Fuentes stepped out on deck and gave his boss a two-fingered salute. Hemingway saluted back, and then we were out beyond the reef, the engine growling at a higher note as we crashed through the chop.

The writer checked the compass, set our course at 100 degrees, and rested his wrist on the Duesenberg steering wheel. "Do we have everything?" he said.

"Yeah." I had been out on the *Lorraine* the night before while the others were finishing their meal. The checklist was complete.

"No, we don't," said Hemingway.

"We don't?"

He looked stern, reached into his safari jacket, took out two short, broad corks, and tossed me one. I looked at it and raised an eyebrow.

"Asshole corks," he said, and swiveled back to watch the sun rise just to the north of our projected course.

WE HEADED EAST OF THE Archipelago de Camagüey, staying on the edge of the Gulf Stream just in sight of land. The wind and wave action stayed moderately high, but the sun broke through scattered clouds and the heat of the day returned with a vengeance. Just before we turned southeast toward Bahía Manatí and Point Roma, I took the glasses out of the waterproof case and began studying the northern horizon.

"What are you looking for, Lucas?"

"Cayo Cerdo Perdido."

Hemingway chuckled. "Your bearings are right, but your timing's off. It's just about high tide. Lost Pig Key should be under water by now. That's a nasty little reef."

"Yes," I said. "That's what I was confirming."

Hemingway swung the bow to heading 160, and the following sea pounded against our port and stern sides. With less power, the speedboat would have wallowed sickeningly, but the writer applied just the proper amount of throttle to keep us cutting through the waves without wasting too much fuel.

As we came in off the blue of the Gulf, I looked back to the north. Somewhere out there, below periscope depth, scores of men huddled in a long, clammy, dripping tank smelling of sweat and diesel oil and cabbage and dirty socks. They were down there in the darkness and had been for weeks, their bones and skulls throbbing to the constant beat of the engines and pistons that drove their boat, their skin itchy with too many days without bathing or shaving, their ears attuned to the moan and creak of the steel hull under pressure. They spent their days in the cold dark of the depths and rose only at night to recharge their batteries and suck in some fresh air. Only the captain and perhaps his first officer were privileged to look through the periscope as they took their bearings against landmarks on the mainland or closed on their prey; the rest of the men listened and waited in silence for orders—to man battle stations, to fire torpedoes—and then waited some more for the unmistakable sounds of explosions and the hull of a merchant ship breaking up under pressure as it sank. And then waited again for the explosion of the depth charge that might sink them.

One hell of a life.

If the intercepted transmission had been real, two of those men sitting out there in the depths right now were preparing to come ashore. Were they nervous on their last day aboard the U-boat—checking their maps and code words and equipment one last time as they got into civilian clothes and oiled and re-oiled their pistols? Of course they were. They were men. But they were probably also eager to get out of the dark stink of the boat and get on with what they were trained for.

What were they trained for? Teddy Schlegel hadn't seemed to know their mission. Meeting with the FBI? That was almost beyond belief.

"There's the point," said Hemingway. "Get the *niños* out."

We had agreed that we would reconnoiter the entire area before settling on a vantage point and hiding place. That meant that we were going into Manatí Bay as well as checking out the points and seacoast. If this was a trap, it probably was designed to snap shut on us in the daytime when we arrived. I went back to the hidden storage compartments and brought out two Thompson submachine guns and a canvas bag of extra clips. The metal of the weapons was oily to the touch.

"Some frags, too," said Hemingway from the wheel.

I opened a box of hand grenades. They were gray, heavy, and cool to the touch as I lifted out four and set them in the bag with the extra clips.

"Keep the *niños* out of the salt spray," said Hemingway. He was bringing the *Lorraine* in quickly from the northeast.

I laid the submachine guns between the seats, out of the spray under the teak and mahogany and chrome dash, and studied the coastline with the twelve-power glasses. When one has studied charts long enough, it seems as if one has already visited a place when one arrives. But I had never seen these points or this bay before. On our previous trips along the coast here, we had been too far out to sea to make out details. Now reality came into focus. It was much as the charts had suggested.

The entrance to Bahía Manatí was wider than I had thought—about forty yards from point to point. Point Jesus, on the east, projected farther out to sea than Point Roma, on the west side of the inlet, but I could see why Point Roma had been chosen for the beacon light: the cliffs on the Point Roma side were higher, rising about thirty feet above sea level, as opposed to the ten- or twelve-foot cliffs on the Point Jesus side. I could see the gradual bight of Enseñada Herradura, to the west of Point Roma, a long, gradual curve of inlet disappearing into mangroves and swamps. The rest of the coastline here was sharp, with rocks and reefs along Point Jesus and more shoals and boulders to the west of Enseñada Herradura. There was little real beach as such, but a nice sandy spit became visible beneath the beacon light on Point Roma.

I studied the light through the binoculars. The metal was rusted and corroded through here and there, obviously not maintained, but the real problem was that someone had stolen the lenses and the light assembly. It looked as if the beacon had been out of commission for some time. Looking beyond the broken beacon light, I could see untended cane fields on the bluffs above the sea as far as I could pan to the west and the east. This was not real jungle here; I could see a few scrubs and palm trees above the mangrove thickets, but most of the land had been given over to raising cane before it had been allowed to return to a wild state. Besides the broken beacon light, the only sign of civilization visible from the sea was the Manatí smokestack rising above the cane on the west side of the bay.

"I'll take us in for a look around the bay," Hemingway said softly. "Be ready to get out on the bow with a pole if the channels are't marked. And keep your *niño* with you."

I nodded, lifted the weapon, and let the binoculars hang around my neck. The submachine gun on my lap felt a trifle silly; I had been trained in the weapons, of course, both at Quantico and at Camp X, but I had never really liked the so-called tommy guns. They had little range and less accuracy. Essentially they were just pistols with an amazing rate of fire, useful for hosing things down at very close range. Good for blazing away in the movies, but not as useful as a good rifle for long work or a trusted pistol for close-in business.

Surf broke on the rocks to the east and on the reef to the west as we slowed and grumbled our way into the center channel. Beyond the entrance, various stakes—some just dead branches wedged in the mud of the banks—marked the narrow channel. Some of the stakes were obviously missing and others were tilted so their tops were just under the surface.

Hemingway slowed *Lorraine* to just above idle and kept to the center of the channel as I watched the points and cliffs and cane fields on either side for any sign of movement or a glint of sunlight on metal or glass. Nothing is as impenetrable to the eye as a cane field.

We curved slightly to the left as the inlet wound east a bit before turning south again. We had planned this—to arrive just after high tide, much as it would be at eleven that night—but even so, we could see where the channel had silted up after years of neglect. The way was relatively clear ahead of us so that I did not yet have to crawl out on the bow with a lead rope or pole, but behind us, our passage had roiled the water to a muddy concoction the color of coffee with too much cream.

"Is she throwing any mud?" said Hemingway, his voice terse.

"Just from this starboard bank. You might want to hold her hard against that port bank through here."

Hemingway tapped the chart laid out on the dash. "This says eight fathoms, six through here, five around the bend of the cut. I bet there aren't two fathoms through here. And that's only ten feet wide. It's all mud bank beyond that."

"Yeah." *Doce Apostles* became visible on a point to our left. The coastal cliffs were behind us here in Manatí Bay, and the cane fields and mangroves now came right down to the water, but a small hill ran back from the bay where the twelve boulders were visible through the greenery, and below the rocks half a dozen tumbledown shacks were being reclaimed by vines and weeds. A maze of old paths ran along the bank and down to a dock, but the paths showed no recent use and the dock had collapsed into the bay.

I watched the black windows of the shacks and clicked the safety off on the Thompson.

"There are the tracks and the stack," said Hemingway softly.

The bay was opening up. I could see that the end of it was about a mile to the southwest, with a deep inlet running out of sight southeast of the *Doce Apostoles*. In the center of the bay, dead ahead, there was a single, tree-covered island. To starboard, where Hemingway was looking, the green tangle of the overgrown cane fields was broken by two openings where rusted tracks ran back into the fields. By the southernmost track, the brick smoke stack rose thirty or forty feet. There were several brick buildings here at what had been Puerto Manatí, and two piers running out into the bay where the track ended, but the glass panes on the buildings had been broken, one of the docks had collapsed and the other ended in water that was now less than a foot deep, and the dirt roads along the bank were overgrown.

"Shit," said Hemingway. "Chart says that there should be five fathoms here. We're drawing less than one. Get out there with the pole."

I slung the Thompson over my shoulder and clambered out onto the bow with the long staff. "That was a silt bank," I said. "It's almost a full fathom ahead."

The engine rumbled and we moved ahead, churning up

mud behind us. The little island marked "Cayo Largo" on our chart loomed ahead. Another hill rose above the cane on the shoreline to the right, this one about twice as tall as the Twelve Apostles. Beyond it, more ruins were visible at the southeast edge of the bay.

"That's the main Manatí mill," Hemingway said softly as we moved slowly around the small island. There were a few shacks on the island, but these had been almost completely overgrown by trees and vines. My head was swiveling like a fighter pilot's as I tried to watch the brick buildings on shore, the area around the stack, the old mill, and the island houses for any sign of movement. Suddenly there was an explosion of sound and color as twenty or thirty flamingoes took flight from a sandbar along an inlet. I admit that I swung the Thompson up in that direction before lowering it sheepishly. The birds flapped noisily along the southwest curve of the bay and landed along another spit of sand in an area marked "Estero San Joaquin" on the chart.

"*Cocos,*" said Hemingway, killing the engine and letting us float with the mild current.

I looked toward the hill where he was pointing. A dozen or so of the wood ibis he was talking about fluttered in the lagoon between the abandoned piers near the stack and the hilly point. Closer in, a pair of roseate spoonbills waded delicately across one of the few mud banks still above the waterline at high tide.

The largest part of the bay lay ahead of us, but most of it was visibly too silted up even for the shallow draft *Lorraine.* "I bet there's not ten inches of water in most of that," said Hemingway, swinging his bruised fingers in an arc that took in the wide expanse of bay.

"No," I agreed. "But a rubber raft could make it."

"Yeah. And they could come in here tonight and go straight to the pier or to the old road over there, but I still don't think they will."

"Why not? It's more secluded here."

"Yeah," said Hemingway, "and I think that's one of the reasons they won't come all the way into the bay. I think they'll want to be in sight of the sub—communicate to them by flashlight or somesuch that they've landed successfully."

I nodded. Hemingway was speaking from intuition, but my experience suggested that he was right.

"Besides," continued Hemingway, "they're scheduled to come in an hour before moonrise, and it would be a pain in the ass to navigate the first part of that channel in the dark, even if their raft draws only six or eight inches."

I sat back on the burning hot wood of the bow, cradling the long pole and the submachine gun on my knees. "I agree," I said. "Point Roma seems to be the spot. Shall we head out and find a place to park *Lorraine*?" Even though it was just midday and there was a mild breeze, clouds of mosquitoes and sand flies were drifting out toward us.

"Yeah," said Hemingway. "Let's get the hell out of here."

IT TOOK US A LITTLE MORE than an hour to find a place to conceal the *Lorraine* in the swampy inner curve of the Ensenada Herradura, reconnoiter the area above the Point Roma light, and then haul our gear there. The best hiding place for the boat was in the mangrove lagoon directly west of the point, and naturally that was a mass of mud and swarming mosquitoes. It would have been wiser to drop our gear at the sandy point and then hide the boat, but we were both eager to conceal the *Lorraine* and get on with things, so we ended up making two trips up and down the hill through thickets, bugs, and mud.

Deciding where to conceal ourselves was serious work. We wanted to see the point, of course, but also get a clear view of the inlet in case the German agents defied our expectations and rafted straight into Bahía Manatí. We also wanted a clear view out to sea and needed to be able to retreat easily in case we had to reposition ourselves or just make a run for the speedboat. Finally, we needed concealment.

This was a test of Hemingway's military prowess, and I was impressed by his decision. There was a perfect place near the crest of the hill—just out of the encroaching cane field, sheltered under a low tree, and offering a 270-degree panorama of the beacon light, the inlet, the northern part of Manatí Bay, and even of the enseñada, behind us. There was even an old trail to this high point, running down to the spit to the north and south toward the old mill road, all of which would make it easy to haul our gear up. Hemingway pointed it out immediately and said, "Too obvious. We'll look lower on the hill."

He was right. Part of this deadly game which we could not afford to forget was that it was probable that we were *expected* to be here. It was hard to understand why either of the German intelligence agencies would want to ambush us, but if it was to be an ambush, there was no reason for us to make it easy for them.

Hemingway chose a site about a third of the way down the slope to the west of the point. There were no real dunes along this stretch of coast, but erosion had carved innumerable gullies along the face of the low cliffs, and Hemingway chose one of those fissures on the ridge of the slope that ran between the point and the inlet where we had hidden the boat. The gap was narrow and steep on the northern—ocean—side, but wider and filled with trees and then thick undergrowth on the southwestern approach along the edge of the cane field. From the high point in this gully, we could see the beacon light, the trail that ran along the high point of the ridge, the sandy point at the inlet, and a wide stretch of open sea. From the gully we could move under cover to the top of the ridge to check the bay and the old mill road, and if there was movement on the old road or along the old rail tracks behind us, we could beat a retreat either down our gully or into the cane field and from there back down to the speedboat.

It was hot. We hauled up two tarps and strung them across the narrow trench, tying them off to roots and rocks, staking them down so they would not flap even in a high wind, letting them sag so as to look like part of the gully, then dumping more soil and branches on top of them as camouflage. From thirty feet away it made our perch damned near invisible in the daylight. At night it should conceal us from anyone coming along the path on the ridgeline.

The sand flies were vicious—their bites raised instant welts—but Hemingway sprayed the area around our covered foxhole with Flit and handed me the bottle of repellent. The writer had not insisted on dragging the BAR up the hill with us—it was too clumsy to carry easily if we had to abandon our position in the night and run for the boat—but he had insisted that we get the long gun out of its wrappings and thread an ammo belt before leaving the *Lorraine.* I think he was preparing for us to shoot our way free of a trap if we had to.

Along with the tarps, the Thompson submachine guns, a bag of grenades, a bag of extra clips, the binoculars, the Flit gun, knives and personal gear, the sombreros, the first aid kit, pistols in holsters for each of us, and binoculars, we had also hauled a small cooler of beer and sandwiches up the sandy slope to our hideout. In early afternoon we paused to eat—corned beef sandwiches for me, thick fried egg and raw onion sandwiches for Hemingway, washing it all down with cold bottles of beer. I had to smile when I thought of how Director Hoover would react if he learned that one of his special agents was drinking beer in the middle of a stakeout. Then the smile faded when I realized that I almost certainly no longer had a job with Mr. Hoover's Bureau.

All through that long afternoon and early evening we lay in our gully, taking turns watching the ocean through the glasses and trying not to scream from the sand fly and mosquito bites. Occasionally one of us would scuttle to the top of the ridge and over, checking the bay, the *Doce Apostoles*, the old road, and the abandoned mill for movement. But most of the time we just lay there.

At first we whispered when we wanted to communicate, but soon we realized that between the surf breaking beyond Point Jesus, the waves hitting against the low cliffs east of Point Roma, and the wind in the cane fields behind us, we could talk in normal tones and not be heard ten feet away.

By late evening, after the sun had set behind the cane fields and the rocky Point Brava far to the west, and with the ocean sounding louder in the gloom, I felt as if we had been hiding there for a week or more. We had taken turns napping so we would be sharp through the night, but I don't think Hemingway slept ten minutes. The writer was in good spirits, showing no signs of nerves. His voice was easy, his manner relaxed, and his humor evident.

"I heard from Marty before we left," he said. "She sent a cable from Basseterre on Saint Kitts. Her three Negroes finally got tired of adventure and marooned her on that island. The cable was censored, of course, but I got the impression that she's been sailing from island to island hunting for German subs and adventure."

"Did she find anything?"

"Marty always finds adventure," said Hemingway with a grin. "She's thinking of heading for Paramaribo next."

"Paramaribo?" I said.

"It's in Dutch Guiana," said Hemingway, rubbing the sweat out of his eyes. I noticed how swollen his ear was and I felt bad about it.

"Yes, I know where Paramaribo is. Why is she going there?"

"*Quién sabe?*" said Hemingway. "Martha's idea of adventure is just going somewhere very far away and very uncomfortable and letting things happen to her while she bitches and moans about it. Then she'll write a brilliant essay that will have everyone laughing. If she survives."

"Are you worried about her?" I said. I tried to imagine how I would feel if I were responsible for a mate and she was rattling around through jungle and sub-infested waters where I could do nothing to help her if something went wrong. I tried to imagine being responsible for a woman at all.

Hemingway shrugged. "Marty can take care of herself. Do you want another beer?" He used the handle of his knife to pop the cap on another bottle.

"No. I think I should be at least partially sober when the German U-boat arrives."

"Why?" said Hemingway. After a while, when the shadows were merging into true darkness, he said, "Wolfer may have said a few things to you about Marty. Unkind things."

I raised the binoculars to look at the dimly lit horizon and said nothing.

"Wolfer's jealous," said the writer.

I thought that this was a strange thing to say. I lowered the glasses and listened to the night wind stir the cane.

"Don't believe anything too outrageous that Winston might have said," continued Hemingway. "Marty's a very talented writer. That's the problem."

"What is?" I said.

Hemingway belched softly and shifted the submachine gun in front of him. "She's talented," he said flatly. "At writing, at least, I'm more than talented. There's no worse hell on earth than constantly being confronted with genius that you can't quite attain yourself. I know that. I've felt it myself."

He was quiet for several minutes. He had made the statement so softly, so matter-of-factly, that I realized first that he was not bragging and second that it was almost certainly true.

"What are you going to write next?" I asked, amazed that I was asking that question. But I was curious.

Hemingway also seemed surprised. "You're interested? *You?* The once and future fiction illiterate?"

I looked through the binoculars again. The horizon was a dim line. The surf seemed very loud in the gloom. I checked my watch. It was 9:28.

"Sorry," said Hemingway. It was the only time he ever apologized to me. "I don't know what I'll write next, Lucas. Maybe, someday, after the war, I'll write about this confused shit." I saw him look at me in the gloom. "I'll put you in it. Only I'll combine the worst parts of you with the worst parts of Saxon. You'll have the fungal foot rot as well as your shitty disposition. Everyone will hate you."

"Why do you do it?" I said softly. The breeze blew a few mosquitoes away from my face. The line of surf was glowing in the late twilight.

"Do what?"

"Write fiction rather than write about true things."

Hemingway shook his head. "It's hard to be a great writer, Lucas, if you love the world and living in it and you love special people. It's even harder when you love so many places. You can't just transcribe things from the outside in, that's photography. You have to do it the way Cézanne did, from inside yourself.

That's art. You have to do it from inside yourself. Do you understand?"

"No," I said.

Hemingway sighed softly and nodded. "It's like listening to people, Lucas. If their experiences are vivid, they become a part of you, whether or not their stories are bullshit or not. It doesn't matter. After a while, their experiences get to be more vivid than your own. Then you mix it all together. You invent from your own life stories and from all of theirs, and after a while it doesn't matter anymore which is which... what's yours and what's theirs, what was true and what was bullshit. It's all true then. It's the country you know, and the weather. Everyone you know. Only you have to avoid showing off... parading all the things you know like marching captured soldiers through the capitol... that's what Joyce and so many did, and why they failed." He gave me a sharp look. "Joyce is a man, not a woman."

"I know," I said. "I remember the book on your shelf."

"You have a good memory, Joe."

"Yes."

"You'd make a good writer."

I laughed. "I could never lie like that," I said, realizing what I had said as I said it.

Hemingway also laughed. "You're the biggest liar I've ever known, Lucas. You tell lies the way a baby sucks his mother's tit. It's instinct with you. I know. I've had experience at that tit."

I said nothing.

"The trick in fiction is like the trick in packing a boat just so without losing the trim," he said. "There are a thousand intangibles that have to be crammed into every sentence. Most of it should not be visible, just suggested. Have you sever seen a Zen watercolor, Lucas?"

"No."

"Then you wouldn't understand if I said that a Zen artist paints a hawk just by putting a dab of blue for the sky without a hawk."

"No," I agreed, although part of me did understand.

Hemingway pointed toward the ocean. "It's like that goddamn submarine that's out there right now. If we see the periscope, we know that all the rest of it is down there... the conning tower, the torpedoes, the engine room with all its dials and pipes, the dutiful Germans huddled over their sauerkraut... but we don't have to *see* all that to know it's there, we just have to see the fucking periscope. A good sentence or paragraph is like that. Do you get it now?"

"No," I said.

The writer sighed. "Last year when I was in Chungking with Marty, I ran into a young navy lieutenant named Bill Lederer. There was almost nothing to drink in that godforsaken hellhole of a country except rice wine with dead snakes and birds in it, but word got out that Lederer had bought two cases of whiskey at a Chinese auction. The dumb shit hadn't even opened any of it yet... he was about to be transferred and he was saving it all for one big blowout. I told him that not drinking his whiskey was like not fucking a pretty girl when he had the chance, but he was adamant about saving it for a special day. Following me so far in this, Joe?"

"Yeah." I kept watching the surf.

"I wanted the whiskey," said Hemingway. "I was thirsty. I offered him real money... dollars... lots of them, but Lederer wouldn't sell. Finally, in desperation, I said, 'I'll give you anything you want for half a dozen bottles.' Lederer scratches his head and says, 'Okay, I'll swap you six bottles for six lessons on how to become a writer.' All right. So after each lesson, Lederer gives me a bottle. At the last lesson, I said, 'Bill, before you can write about people, you must be a civilized man.' 'What's a civilized man?' says Lederer. 'To be civilized,' I told him, 'you have to have two things—compassion and the ability to roll with the punches. Never laugh at a guy who has had bad luck. And if you have bad luck yourself, don't fight it. Roll with it—and bounce back.' The way I rolled with your punches, Lucas. Do you see where I'm headed here?"

"No idea," I said.

"It doesn't matter," said Hemingway. "But the truth is, I've given you more tips to good writing than I gave Lieutenant Lederer. And my last advice to him was my most important."

"What was that?"

"I told him to go home and sample his whiskey," said the writer, grinning so that I could see his teeth glowing in the starlight. "The chinks had sold him two cases of lukewarm tea."

We were silent for several minutes. When the wind came up, the tarp above us barely stirred, but the dry cane stalks rattled like fingerbones in a tin cup.

"Anyway, the fucking trick is to write truer than true," said Hemingway at last. "And that's why I write fiction rather than fact." He lifted his binoculars and peered out at the dark ocean.

I knew that the conversation was closed, but I persisted. "The books live longer than you, don't they?" I said. "Longer than the writer, I mean."

Hemingway lowered the glasses and looked at me. "Yes, Joe. Perhaps you see the hawk and the submarine after all. The books last longer. If they're any good. And a writer spends a lifetime alone, facing eternity or the lack of it every goddamn day. Maybe you do understand." He raised the binoculars again. "Tell me everything again. Everything about this cross and double cross. Tell me everything you can tell me that you haven't told me."

I told him everything except the details with Schlegel and about the package in the dairy barn.

"So you think that first transmission was to get us here?" he said.

"Yeah."

"But not just the two of us. They probably assumed that we'd bring the *Pilar* and the others."

"Probably," I said. "But I don't think that's the important part."

"What is the important part, Joe?"

"That you and I are here."

"Why?"

I shook my head. "I can't quite figure that out. Schlegel said that the operation involved the FBI, but he must mean just Delgado. I can't believe that Hoover's involved with the Germans. It doesn't make sense."

"Why not?" said Hemingway. "What does Hoover most fear? Nazis?"

"No," I said.

"Communists?"

"No. He's most afraid of losing his power... of losing control of the Bureau or of the Bureau's losing clout. A Communist overthrow of the United States would be a distant second on Mr. Hoover's fear list."

"So how would this confused mess in Cuba fit into your Mr. Hoover's fear?" said Hemingway. "People are motivated more by fear than any other emotion. Or at least that's been my observation."

I thought about this for a while.

THE RAFT CAME IN through the surf precisely at twenty-three hundred hours—eleven o'clock on the nose. Then we saw two dark figures dragging the raft through the shimmering lines of surf onto the narrow sand spit glowing in the starlight, and then the two figures opened a box or chest, removed a shielded lantern, and flashed signals toward the darkness of the ocean.

Ten seconds later, there was the tiniest flash of light from a conning tower or periscope several hundred yards out—two dots, two dashes, one dot. Then there was only darkness again and the sound of surf.

Hemingway and I watched while the two agents collapsed their raft, dragged it up into the closest gully—three fissures east of our own—and buried it with much noise from their shovels and soft cursing in German. Then the agents moved up the hill toward the tree on the ridgeline which had seemed a perfect place for us to hide.

The writer and I crawled backward out of our blind and knelt in the brush to watch the two Germans climb the hill not seventy feet from us. The surf and wind drowned most of their conversation, but because the wind was behind them, we could hear a few words in German. Only their heads and shoulders were visible in starlight above the brush and then those disappeared as they moved into the darkness under the big tree.

Hemingway set his lips next to my left ear. "We'll have to follow them."

I nodded.

Suddenly their signal lantern blinked twice again. Thirty yards to our right and on the ridgeline, almost concealed by cane breaks and shrubs, a different light—a smaller one—blinked once.

"Fuck me," whispered Hemingway.

We began crawling up the hill on our bellies, the Thompsons' slings around our forearms but the weapons aimed muzzle-first ahead of us.

Then, without warning, the shooting began.

24

THE FIRING WAS NOT COMING FROM where we had seen the second lantern flash, but from near where we had last seen the two German infiltrators. I dug my face in the sandy slope, assuming that the two agents had seen or heard us and were firing on us. Evidently, Hemingway made the same assumption, for after ducking while the first four shots cracked out, he raised his Thompson, obviously preparing to return fire. I slapped his submachine gun down.

"No!" I whispered. "I don't think they're shooting at us."

The firing had stopped. There was a single, loud, terrible moan from the darkness under the tree on the ridgetop, and then silence again. The surf rolled in, mingling with the pounding of my pulse in my ears. The crescent moon was not yet up, and I found myself trying to do as I had been trained for night fighting in very dim light—attempting to sense movement out of the corners of my eyes, using peripheral vision rather than straight-on viewing to get a sense of where my opponents were. Nothing.

Hemingway was tense and ready next to me, but he did not seem rattled by the gunfire. He leaned closer and whispered, "Why don't you think they were shooting at us?"

"No sound of bullets overhead," I whispered back. "No hits on the shrubs above us."

"People fire high in the dark," whispered the writer, still hugging the slope and moving his head rapidly from left to right.

"Yeah."

"You make the weapon that was fired?" whispered Hemingway.

"Pistol or machine pistol on single shot," I whispered. "Luger. Schmeisser maybe. Sounded like a nine millimeter."

Hemingway nodded in the dark. "They could be flanking us to the right. Through the cane field."

"We'd hear them," I whispered. "We're okay here." We were all right for the time being. Even though whoever was shooting now held the high ground, no one could approach us from our left without making too much noise on the fifteen-foot sea cliff or from the right without crashing around in the cane field. The hillside between us and the ridgeline was overgrown with pepper bushes and low scrub oak; both Hemingway and I had found ways to crawl up in the daylight, but at night it would be impossible to come charging down at us without noise.

Unless whoever was up there had carefully reconnoitered the hillside and knew just where to crawl in the dark.

Or unless there were others coming up the hillside behind us from the swampy cove even as we lay there with our attention focused on the ridgeline.

"I'm going up," I whispered.

Hemingway gripped my upper arm, hard. "I'm going too."

I leaned closer so that my whisper was almost inaudible. "One of us should head to the right where the answering lantern flash was. The other should try to approach the tree... see if the two men are still there." I knew that splitting our force of two in the darkness was dangerous—if nothing else, we might end up firing at each other—but the thought of someone still out there on the right made my neck hairs crawl.

"I'll head for the tree," whispered the writer. "Take your flashlight. We don't want to open up on each other."

We had taken thick squares of red flannel cloth and wrapped them over the ends of our flashlights so that only the dimmest of red glows filtered through. It was supposed to be our recognition signal.

"Meet back here as soon as we check the areas," whispered Hemingway. "Good luck." He began squirming his way up under the low oak branches and roots.

I crawled out to the right, up and over the rim of our gully, all the way to the cane field before beginning to climb the slope toward the ridgeline. There was no sound now except for the wind in the cane, the surf, and my own muffled panting as I squirmed forward on my knees and elbows, remembering to keep my ass down. The moon would be up any minute now.

I knew when I had reached the top of the ridge only when I crawled out of the thick tangle of pepper bush and felt the grassy but hard-packed trail under me. To my left, the trail wound along the ridge to the tall tree. To my right, it curved left around the wall of cane and stayed on the east-facing slope as it dropped down to the bayside road that ran back to the railroad tracks and the abandoned mill. I scurried across the path and crouched behind a low oak, raising my head slowly and carefully.

No movement in either direction. I could not hear Hemingway fifty feet away as he approached the tree. I glanced down at the bay. Dark water and the rustle of royal palms from the opposite shore under the *Doce Apostoles.* I must have been almost exactly where the second lantern had been flashed, but I could see no track or sign in the darkness. My guess was that whoever had been here had gone back south on the trail toward the bay, the tracks, and the mill.

Or perhaps they were waiting just behind those low scrub oaks around the bend in the trail.

I slung the Thompson over my head, barrel down under my left arm, and pulled the .357 Magnum from my holster, sliding off the safety and setting my thumb on the hammer. Moving in a crouch and only for quick bursts, I started south down the trail, dodging from side to side, squatting behind cover and pausing to pant and listen. No sounds but the rattling cane and the increasingly distant surf.

There was a bare patch of trail on the hillside and I crossed it in a crouch sprint, weaving all the way, my stomach muscles tensed and waiting for the shot. It did not come. At the bottom I waited twenty seconds for my breathing to calm before stepping out on the old roadway that ran along the shoreline here. If Hemingway got in trouble now, it would take me a couple of minutes to run up the slope and down the ridgeline to get to him. And quite possibly run into another ambush.

This isn't smart, Joe, I thought. Then I began moving south down the old road. When the mill had been working, this road probably had been smooth gravel, but now grass and vines grew waist high in the center and only two faint ruts showed. I ran while crouching, trying to keep my shoulders at about the height of the grass, the pistol raised and ready. My instincts told me that in this high grass and darkness, knife work might be called for.

Someone moved about a hundred yards ahead of me, right where the wall of cane was broken by the old railroad lines. I dropped prone and aimed the pistol with both hands, knowing the figure was out of range but waiting for another movement. Nothing. I counted to sixty and then got up and began sprinting in that direction, jumping from rut to rut at random intervals, feeling the tall grass whip at my legs and elbows.

There was no one on the road at the terminus of the first abandoned railroad line. The rusted rails running into the cane field curved out of sight about fifty yards in. The cane was so high and dark in there that it looked like a railroad tunnel. Far ahead and to the left, I could see the two abandoned docks running out into the bay. Both were empty.

The goddamned crescent moon was rising. Because my eyes had adapted to the dimness of the starlight, it seemed like someone was suddenly shining a searchlight on the bay and hillside. I stayed to the left, in the shadow of the high grass there, and loped to where I could see the smokestack and the docks.

There were two abandoned brick buildings about a hundred and twenty yards ahead, where the processed cane had once been loaded onto flat-bottomed barges. The broken windows and rooftops were perfect sniper roosts now. I lay on my belly in the grass of the road and considered my options. The road curved around the hillside here toward the buildings, the hill beyond, and the actual sugar mill, a quarter of a mile beyond the docks. Unless I tried to cut through the jungle and cane field behind these first buildings, I would have to pass them along the road with the moon behind me. Even crawling, I would be a target for anyone on the second floor or roof of the old buildings. I had the Thompson and the Magnum... neither of which would be worth shit to me for another seventy or eighty yards. Someone with a rifle and scope near the stack could take me out as soon as I came around this curve of the hill.

If it had not been the two infiltrators firing, then there had to be at least two other people out here tonight—the one with the lantern and the one who had done the shooting. It had sounded like a Luger or Schmeisser firing, but God alone knew what other weapons they were carrying. Or how many other men were out there.

It was time to be a coward.

I turned and crawled on my belly until I was around the bend and out of sight of the buildings and the docks. Then I ran in a loping crouch back the way I had come.

The ridgeline was still silent. I could crawl straight ahead and see if Hemingway had checked out the area from where the shooting had come, but I decided to head back to our duck blind first. I crawled along the edge of the cane field until I reached the gnarled oak that had been my landmark, and then started down the hill toward our gully. Ten yards out, I rose just enough to hold up the flannel-covered flashlight and flash it once, very quickly. Then I dropped back into the shrubbery and waited, pistol aimed. An interminable fifteen seconds later, a dim red circle flashed once in the gully. I holstered the Magnum and crawled ahead.

"THEY'RE BOTH DEAD," whispered Hemingway. He was sipping from a silver whiskey flask. "The Germans who came ashore," he said. "Both dead under the tree. Shot in the back, I think."

"Anyone else around?"

He shook his head. "I checked the east slope all the way down to the bay road. Crawled through the brush on either side of the ridgeline. Then I covered everything on this side of the hill back to the *Lorraine*. No one's here." He took another sip. He did not offer me a drink.

I told him about the glimpse of the figure by the railroad tracks and my decision to turn back.

Hemingway just nodded. "We can check it in the daylight."

"Be even better for snipers then," I said.

"No," said Hemingway. "They'll be long gone. They did what they came to do."

"Kill the two men who landed," I said.

"Yeah."

"But why?" I said, knowing that I was just musing around. "Why would the Todt Team... if that was who it was... kill their own agents?"

"You're the professional," said Hemingway, setting the flask back in the pocket of his safari jacket. "You tell me."

We were silent for a while. I said, "What can you tell me about the bodies?"

Hemingway shrugged. "I didn't crawl down to them. Good chance they're booby-trapped. Two dead. Men. Both in German army uniforms. Moonlight was on one of them. Young. A boy. Some gear and crap littered around them... the lantern they used to signal, a courier pouch, some other stuff."

"Uniforms?" I said, surprised. Secret agents arriving by raft in enemy territory did not make a habit of arriving in uniform.

"Yeah. Basic Wehrmacht infantry, I think. I didn't see any insignia or division patches or anything... probably removed... but both are definitely in uniform. One of them is lying face up... the one in the moonlight... and I could clearly make out that goddamned *Gott Mitt Uns* belt buckle they like to wear. The other one, face down, was wearing one of those soft, wool German infantry caps."

"You're sure they're both dead?" I said.

Hemingway gave me a look. "The crabs are already busy at them, Lucas."

"Okay, we'll take a look at first light."

"Five fucking hours from now," said Hemingway.

I said nothing. Suddenly I was very tired.

"We'll have to secure the area," said Hemingway. "Keep watch up there to make sure that no one comes back to loot the bodies."

"Two-hour watches?" I said. "I'll take the first one." I grabbed a canteen and a spoon from the mess kit and started crawling out of the gully. Hemingway grabbed me by the leg to stop me.

"Lucas? I've seen lots of dead men. The first war. Reporting in Turkey and Greece and Spain. Lots of corpses. And I've seen men die... in the bullring, on the battlefield."

"Yeah?" It seemed an odd time to brag about that.

Hemingway's tone shifted, became the voice I had used as a boy in the confessional. "But I've never killed a man, Lucas. Not personally. Not face-to-face. Not at all, that I know of."

Good, I thought. *I hope to hell that doesn't change tonight or tomorrow.* I said, "All right," and climbed up the slope.

IT WAS LIGHT ENOUGH by five A.M. to inspect the corpses.

Hemingway had been right about most of the particulars. Two very young men—one blond, one with wavy, brown hair—both in uniform, both shot twice in the back, both quite dead. The land crabs had come up from the beach and were busy when we arrived in the first light. A few scuttled away, but half a dozen were too busy around the boys' faces and showed no sign of leaving. Hemingway had removed his pistol and aimed it at one of the bigger crabs that was standing its ground, claws raised, but I touched the writer's wrist, tapped my ear to signify noise, and used a stick to bat the crab halfway back to the sea.

We crouched by the bodies, Hemingway on one knee and watching the weeds and the ridgeline while I studied the corpses. There were no grenades rigged—no booby traps.

Boys. He had been right about that. Neither man had been older than twenty. The blond one on his back looked to be about Patrick's age. The crabs had taken both his eyes and been busy with his pug nose and girlish lips. The smell was very strong and rigor mortis had long since set in.

Both men had been shot in the back, evidently by someone concealed on the east slope. It must have been fairly short range—probably no more than twenty feet away.

"We have to hunt for the brass," I said.

Hemingway nodded and moved down the east slope, keeping his eyes peeled down the ridgeline but also checking the ground. A few minutes later he was back. "The sand's scuffed in several places. Boot marks, but indistinct. No hulls."

"Our killer is tidy," I said softly. I had rolled the brown-haired boy onto his back and was checking his tunic pockets. Nothing. Hemingway had been right about the uniforms: basic Wehrmacht issue, but without insignia or unit designation. Very strange.

Each man had been shot twice, once in the lower spine, once in the upper body. The lung shot on the blond man had exited high in his chest, creating quite a mess and an opening for the crabs, but both of the bullets were still in the other man. I rolled him back onto his face and checked his trouser pockets. Nothing. The same with the blond boy. The trousers were thick wool. These men would be sweltering today if they were alive and had not yet changed clothes.

"Do you think they planned to change clothes once they made contact here?" said Hemingway, seeming to read my thoughts.

"Probably." Each man had been carrying a Luger. The blond-haired boy's was still holstered; the boy with curly hair had drawn his before being gunned down and it now lay in the weeds a foot beyond his splayed fingers. I checked the weapons. Neither had been fired.

Most of the gear they had dropped was not worth investigating closely: the broken lantern; a folding entrenching tool; an ammo box filled with compasses, cooking gear, and flare pistol; a rucksack stuffed with ponchos and two pairs of black, civilian street shoes; two Wehrmacht-issued bayonets still in their scabbards; some rolled charts of the area with only Point Roma and this area circled in grease pencil. But one canvas ditty bag was heavy and pliant. I let Hemingway open the brass fastener and root through the bag. He pulled document after document out of smaller waterproof pouches in the bag.

"Good Christ Almighty," whispered the writer. He showed me a page. It was a photostat of a nautical chart of Frenchman Bay, Maine, showing the proposed route for submarine U-1230 through the bay, complete with morning and afternoon stops clearly marked, culminating in scribbles showing the nighttime disembarkation of two Abwehr agents at a place called Peck's Point on Crab Tree Neck, north of Mount Desert Island.

"Save that a minute," I said. "I want to make absolutely sure there are no shell casings around here."

It was a relief to move upwind from the bodies while we crawled on our knees to check the sand under and around the shrubs in widening circles with the bodies as the locus. We went all the way down to the spit of sand below the cliffs to the north, the bay to the east, and our own gully to the west. Hemingway had been right. There were scuffs in the sand about eighteen feet away on the east slope, in a concealed area just off the ridgeline, where the ambusher had done the deed. One person. Boot marks but nothing distinct. No brass.

"All right," I said as we moved back into the shade and the stench under the tree. "We'll check the rest of that bag in a minute. I think that's what this landing was all about. But I need to see something." I rolled the dead blond-haired boy onto his face. His arms were so stiff that it was like turning over a department store mannequin. The entrance wounds through the shirt and just below the high belt of his wool trousers were much less dramatic than the exit wound on his chest. I pulled up the young man's gray wool blouse and dingy undershirt, reached around to undo his belt, pulled it off, handed it to Hemingway, and tugged down his trousers so that the upper parts of his buttocks were exposed. The boy was very pale except where the blood had settled along his back and buttocks during the night. There the flesh was so livid as to be almost black.

I removed my own shirt.

"What in hell are you doing, Lucas?" hissed Hemingway.

"Just a minute," I said. I clicked open my pocketknife, took out the spoon I had brought from our picnic mess kit, and began cutting into the boy's back. Gasses had swollen the corpse considerably already, even before the heat of the sun had struck him, and the flesh there was pulled as tight as a drumskin. I knew that the bullet had traveled upward from the entrance wound just above the coccyx, but there was still a lot of digging involved before I found the slug embedded in the third sacral vertebra.

Then the digging and prying began in earnest—dulling the scalpel-sharp point of my knife and almost snapping the bowl of the spoon off at one point—before I managed to leverage out the flattened slug.

I wiped my knife and hands on the grass, tossed away the bent spoon, wiped the bullet with my handkerchief, and held it up in the light. The head of the slug had been flattened by bone, but the black nose was still visible, as was the short twist of rifling at the base. I was glad. I did not want to dig around in the other boy's upper thoracic cavity until I found another slug.

I showed it to Hemingway. His gaze was fixed on me. "Who *are* you, Lucas?"

I ignored that. "Nine millimeter," I said as I pulled on my shirt.

"Luger?" said the writer.

I shook my head. "Black heads. From a Schmeisser machine pistol."

Hemingway blinked and looked at the slug. "But the killer wasn't firing on full automatic."

"No. Single shots. Very careful. One each in the lower spine. One each in the upper back. He took his time."

"It's a nasty place to shoot a man," Hemingway said softly, as if speaking to himself. "Why not in the head?"

"It was night." I put the bullet in my handkerchief and the handkerchief back in my trouser pocket. "Let's have a look at those documents."

"All right," said Hemingway. "But let's move upwind first."

THE SUN ROSE as we studied the documents. The first one was the photostat of U-1230's course in Frenchman's Bay.

"This can't be real, can it?" said Hemingway.

"Why not?"

"It must be...what do you call it in espionage? Disinformation. There's no reason for two German agents to be carrying this during an infiltration, is there?"

"None," I agreed. "Unless their mission was to deliver this stuff to someone. Notice that there's no date set on this sheet for

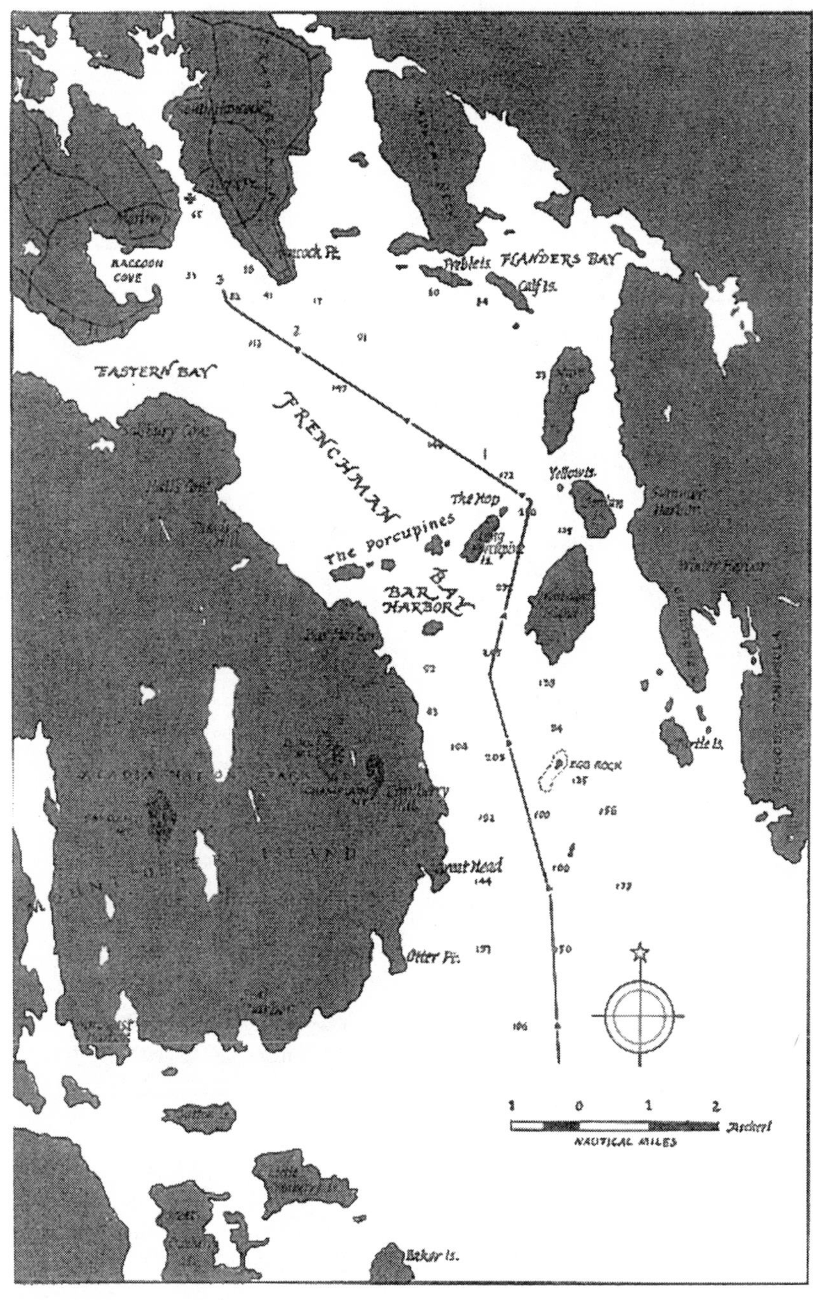
RACCOON COVE
Preblels
FLANDERS BAY
Calf Is.
EASTERN BAY
FRENCHMAN BAY
Yellow Is.
The Hop
The Porcupines
BAR HARBOR
EGG ROCK
Turtle Is.
Otter Pt.
Baker Is.
NAUTICAL MILES
1 0 1 2

the landing. If it hasn't happened yet, it's possible that the photostat is just a tease...that they're negotiating some price for the date and time."

The next photostat was more cryptic:

		3	6	2	9
8			К	Ф	
5		А	Л	Х	
1		Б	М	Ц	
4		В	Н	Ч	
0		Г	О	Ш	
2		Д	П	Щ	
9		Е	Р	Э	Ы
7		Ж	С	Ю	Й
3		З	Т	Я	Ь
6		И	У		
		I	II	III	IV

"Code?" said Hemingway.

"It looks like a German attempt to decode a Russian cipher," I said. "The date down in the corner says 5 March, 1942. It's recent enough. This one is from German Army Group North and seems to be an intercept of a communication from the Soviet 122nd Armored Brigade."

"Is it important?" said Hemingway.

"How the hell should I know?"

The next document was also from the Eastern Front.

"Translation?" said Hemingway. "I mean, I can read some German...'Leningrad Front—Top Command Net'? But what are the numbers? Kilohertz means radio frequencies, right?"

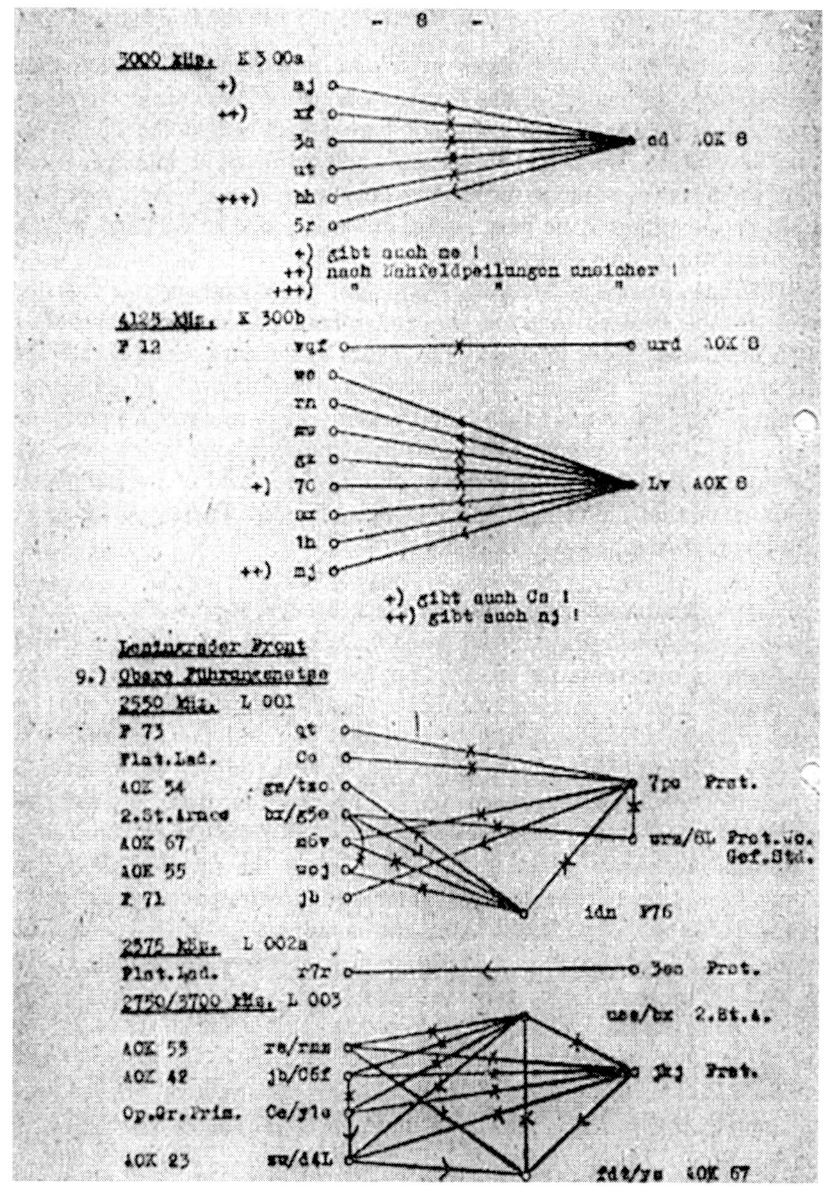

"Right," I said. "It looks like recent German radio reconnaissance of Soviet communications nets. This is a network marked K300a broadcasting on 3,000 kilohertz. The Germans are mapping a station with the call letters *ed* that seems to belong to the Russian Eighth Army. This other network designated L001 broadcasts at 2,550 kilohertz. The diagram shows who communicated with whom between the rear stations, front staff, and advanced front staff battle post. I think the battle post is this nexus marked '8L'. The notes down here at the right seem to suggest stations belonging to both the Soviet Fifty-fifth Army and what they call '2.St.A', which I think stands for what the Soviets call their Second Shock Army."

"Who's this going to?" asked Hemingway.

"I have no idea."

"Would U.S. intelligence want to know this stuff about the Soviets? They're our allies, after all."

"I don't know if American military intelligence would want this," I said truthfully. "Probably. Intelligence gathering becomes a goal of its own after a while. It matters less who we spy on than the fact that we *can* spy."

Hemingway scratched sand out of his short beard. "You're cynical for an agent, Lucas."

"That's redundant," I said. "Look, this photostat looks like it's from the Crimea."

"Reconnoitered Enemy Batteries," read Hemingway.

"Last November," I said. "That's probably during the fighting south of Sevastopol."

"This is German intelligence of Soviet positions from that battle?"

"Uh-huh," I said. "I think this is what's called a sound-and-light-ranging battery map. They've numbered all of the Russian gun and battery positions including this one here, noted by a cartoon of a ship. It looks like they're counterbombarding this one position."

"Except for the Frenchman Bay U-boat chart, this is all information about the Soviets," said Hemingway.

I lifted another document out of its watertight pouch and showed it to the writer.

"This isn't a photostat," I said. "It's a page ripped out of someone's notebook."

"So?"

"So this is raw Abwehr intelligence data."

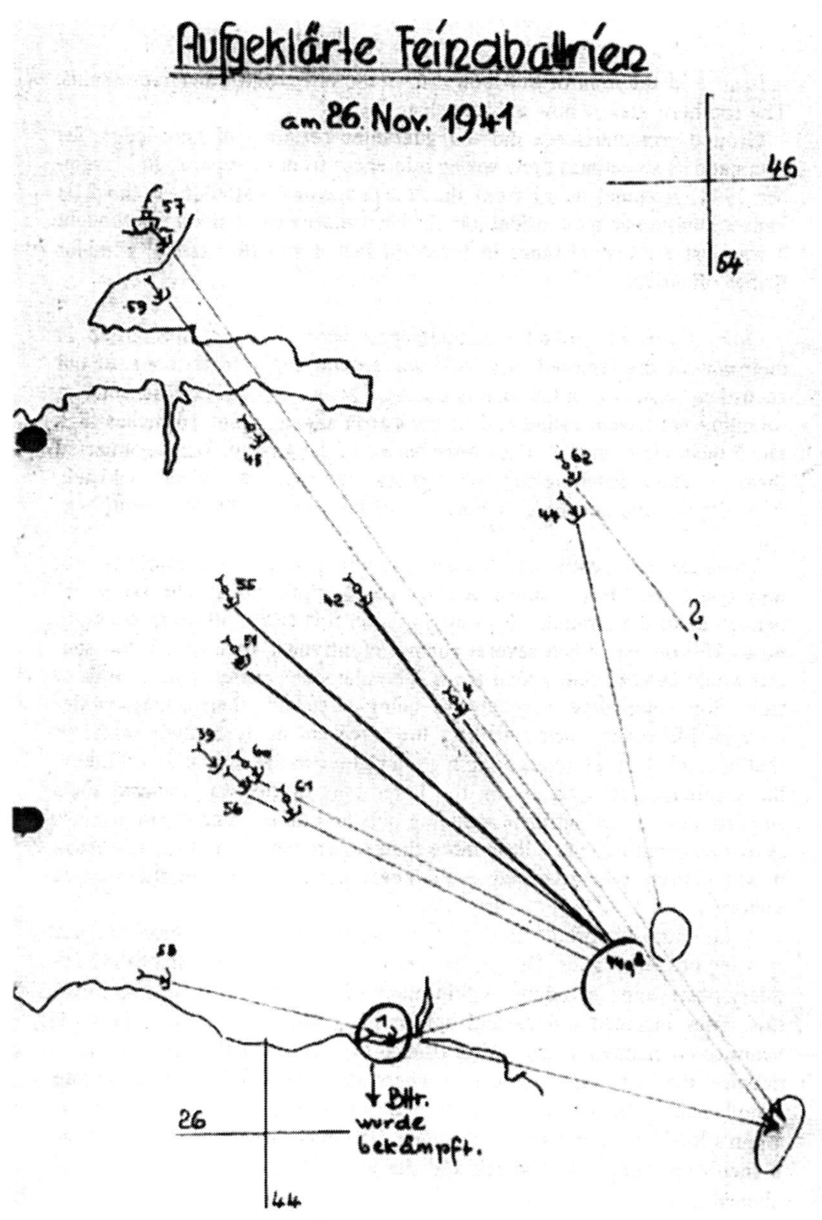
Aufgeklärte Feindbatterien
am 26. Nov. 1941
46
64
57
59
48
62
44
?
55
42
51
4
39
40
56
41
58
1
Bttr.
wurde
bekämpft.
26
44

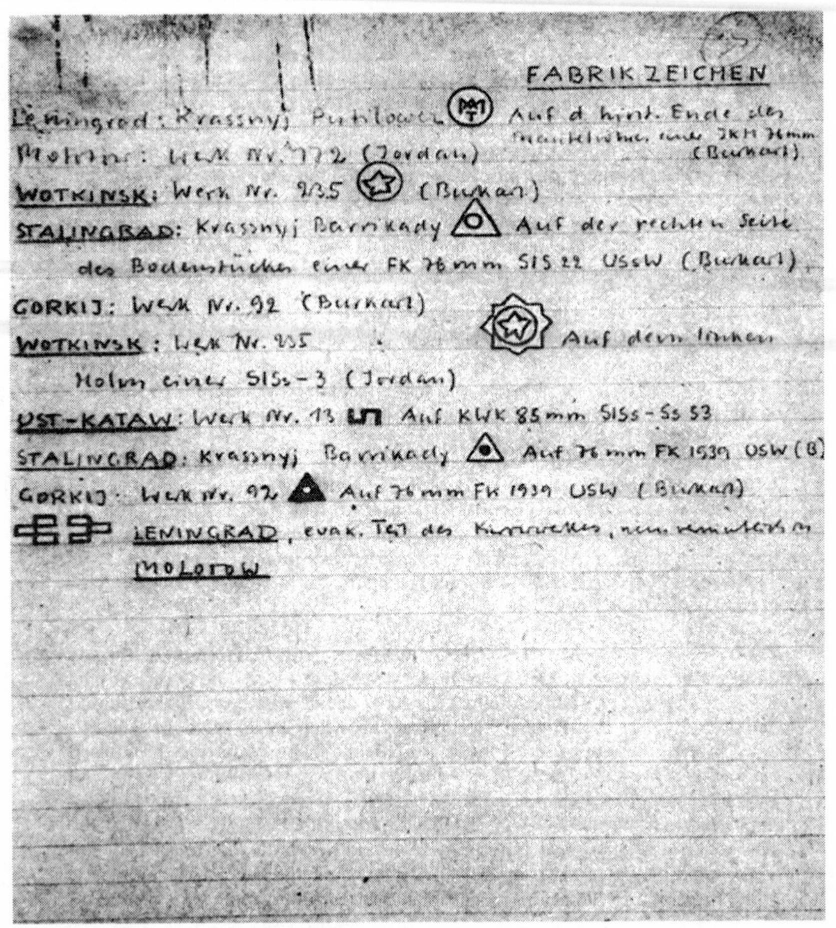

FABRIK ZEICHEN

Leningrad: Krassnyj Putilowez Auf d. hint. Ende des [illegible] (Burkart)
Molotow: Werk Nr. 172 (Jordan)
WOTKINSK: Werk Nr. 235 (Burkart)
STALINGRAD: Krassnyj Barrikady Auf der rechten Seite des Bodenstücken einer FK 76mm SIS 22 USSW (Burkart),
GORKIJ: Werk Nr. 92 (Burkart)
WOTKINSK: Werk Nr. 235 Auf dem linken Holm einer SISs-3 (Jordan)
UST-KATAW: Werk Nr. 13 Auf KWK 85mm SISs-Ss 53
STALINGRAD: Krassnyj Barrikady Auf 76mm FK 1939 USW (B)
GORKIJ: Werk Nr. 92 Auf 76mm FK 1939 USW (Burkart)
LENINGRAD, evak. Teil des [illegible], [illegible] MOLOTOW

"What does it mean?"

I looked at the script for a moment. "I think it's just a list of marks put on tanks by different Soviet factories. It's probably a way the Abwehr is estimating Russian tank production."

"Is that significant?"

"I don't know if the data is," I said, "but how it's presented is."

"What do you mean, Lucas?" Suddenly the writer looked over his shoulder at the ridgeline under the tree. There had been a sound. "The land crabs are back in force," he said, settling back

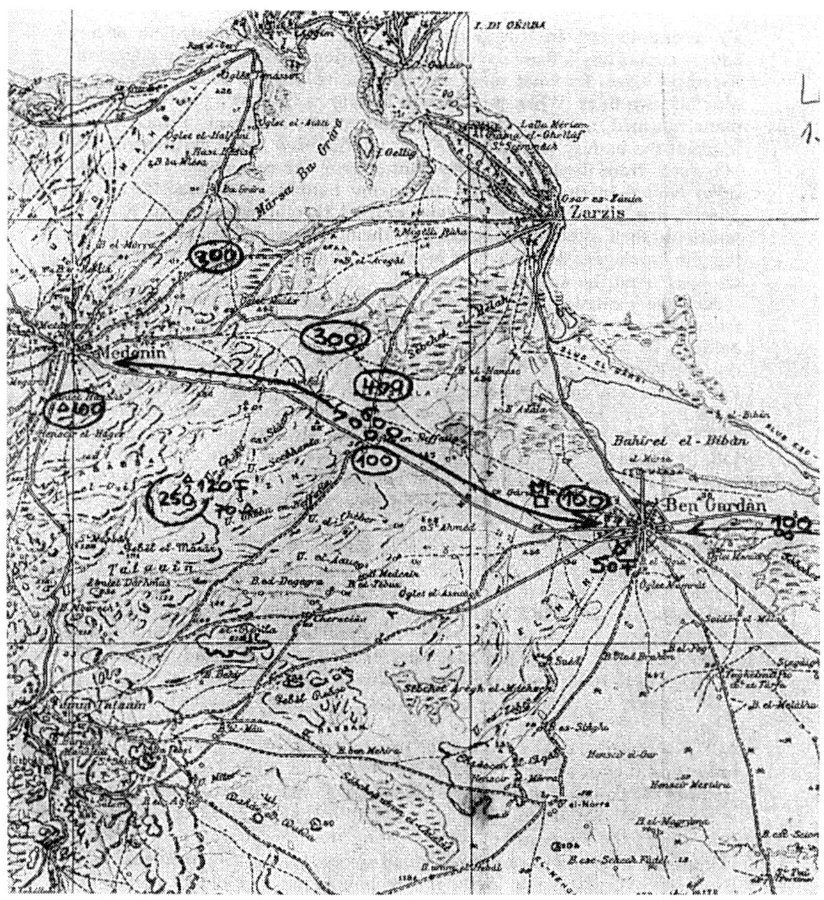

onto the sandy slope. "What do you mean the way it's presented is important?"

"It's raw, original Abwehr intelligence," I said. "This would tell U.S. or British intelligence more about how the German military intelligence goes about its job than about the Russian tanks."

Hemingway nodded. "So it's not just someone peddling information on the Russians. German sources are being betrayed."

"Yes," I said. "And if you think that it's only intelligence from the Eastern Front, look at this."

The next document showed notes from a German aerial

SECONDARY MONITORING UNIT SA-2
NORTH CHARLESTON, S. C.

UNIT CASE # SA-2-7-111446 WASHINGTON CASE # 56
N. CHARLESTON, S. C.
DATE : APRIL 5, 1942
OBSERVER : F. STEWART JONES

CALL : STATION CALLING "AOR" AND STATION ANSWERING TO "AOR".
FREQUENCY : 14,550 & 14,560 KCS. AND 14,385 KCS., (MEASURED)
EMISSION : A-1
BEARING : NONE
RECORDING : NONE (PAGE5)

GMT
1713 (14,385 KC.) VVV OK OM GA GA K VVY VVY VVY RR OK OK GA GA
K VVV VVV VVV VVV VVV - RRR QTC OK GA GA K

1714 (14,560 KC.) VVV VVVV - QSAG PSE QSV K K

1715 (14,385 KC.)VVV VVV VVV VVV VVV VVV VVV VVV VVY VVV VVV
VVV VVV VVV VVV OK OK OK VVV VVV VVV

1716 (14,550 KC.) RPT RPT RPT

1716 (14,385 KC.) OK QTC OK GA K VVV GA GA OK OK QTC OK

1718 (14,560 KC.) - - SRI RPT ALL KA - YENOV (GROUP MISSING)
ERILJ EOBRI PHEBR ENELE TIUNO ITACQ GYOFB EEEE GYGFB
XNMAY QTXNE INUDR TISHI MYYSN TXLXO FSL NQRIX NUS

1722 LRXFX YOEYE QAUNE CERXA SEION AR CODE OF 3 OK? QSV K

1722 (14,385 KC.) VVV VVY VVY VVV VVY VVV VVY VVV VVY VVV VVY
OK OK GA GA K

1722 (14,560 KC.) R GLAD GLAD NW KA KA DYRE DYRE ILIC ILIC
SUA SUA ILL ILL - - GLDTG GLDTG TTELR TTKSR XTSRI XTSRI
IPKIN IPEBB TXAEX TXAEX GRLUD GRLWB EGZNG EGZNG ORAWW
ORABW FTNLH FTNLN SRREI SNREI FSIKE FSIKE SOIEU SOIEU
SOELP BOELP SHERS SHERS LAHNB LAHNB NAXSA NAXSA GHISB
GHIBB ZARVG ZARVG BUERB BUERB NRAIA NRAIA PTFXM PTFXM
AWERU AWERU SLNGB SLNBZ NEONE NEONE ZRWEG ZRWEG EEMEN

reconnaissance mission over North Africa. The battle in the desert east of Ben Gardan had been in the news less than six weeks before.

The sun was fierce now. The smell of death was almost overpowering. It reminded me of what these scrawls on a map had led to—British and German corpses rotting in the desert sun.

"I can read this," said Hemingway. "Fifty tanks south of Ben Gardan.

A hundred vehicles parked on the west side of town. A hundred Allied vehicles traveling in both directions on the road east of the city and six hundred moving on the road west of it. But what use is a two-month-old situation map?"

"No idea," I said.

"Then what about this one?" Hemingway handed me a carbon copy of a typewritten page.

"Shit," I said. I did understand the significance of this form. "This is an FBI or U.S. Army or Navy Intelligence intercept of a German spy station radioing Hamburg," I said. "April five. It's a basic Abwehr book code, being transmitted on 14,560 kilocycles. The Abwehr listening station is responding at 14,385 kilocycles. See where the agent transmitting made a mistake about halfway down and keyed a series of dots...*E*'s here...to indicate his error? Then he transmitted the correct group following it."

"Can you read it?"

"No."

"Why did you say 'Shit'?" Hemingway was frowning at me in the strong morning light.

"The only reason this would be in the packet is to show... whoever they were delivering this to...that the Abwehr has a source inside the FBI or inside U.S. military intelligence," I said. "This carbon was stolen or purchased directly from an American source."

"Shit," said Hemingway.

Precisely, I thought. *April five of this year was during the time that Inga Arvad was having her fling with young Naval Intelligence Ensign Jack Kennedy in Charleston and just before the* Southern Cross *had sailed. The son of Ambassador Joseph P. Kennedy.* "Shit indeed," I said, wiping sweat and sand out of my eyes. "What is it?" I said.

Hemingway was chuckling as he looked at a thick sheaf of typed papers. I could see the German Fraktur on the letterhead and even make out the double-lightningbolt keystroke that Third Reich typewriters used for the SS.

"Oh, nothing," said Hemingway, still chuckling. "Just a carefully typed, absolutely complete list of the postings and personnel distribution of every branch of the Hamburg Abwehr post, dated 1 April, 1942. Want to know how many counterintelligence case officers they have there? Twenty-six. Four enlisted men. Fifteen civilian employees. One radio maintenance man hired on a contract basis. Twenty radiomen. Seventy-two radio clerks. One photographer. One noncommissioned officer for transportation... I presume that's a chauffeur. Two bicyclists... Jesus Christ, Lucas."

I nodded. "Stuff it all back in. We'll take it with us."

"You're goddamned right we'll take it with us. We're going to get this back to Ambassador Braden and the others as soon as possible... tonight, if we can."

"No," I said firmly. "We won't."

Hemingway looked at me.

"We'll get the camera," I said. "We have to photograph the two dead men, the junk around them, and the bullet. Then we have to dig up their raft and photograph it. Then we have to bury it again. And then we have to bury them."

"We have to bring back the Naval Intelligence people," said Hemingway.

"No," I said again. "We won't."

Hemingway did not argue. He waited. For a second the wind died and the stench from the hilltop was almost overwhelming.

"I'll tell you when we get the *Lorraine* out to sea," I said.

Hemingway just bobbed his head once and went off to get the camera and the other entrenching tool.

25

THE *PILAR* WAS SAFELY at anchor and most of the crew and the kids were finishing a late breakfast around a campfire when Hemingway and I put into Cayo Confites.

We had almost broken the back of the beautiful *Lorraine* during our wave-pounding return trip to the key. Staying up on plane the entire way, spray flying, kicking up a rooster tail, it seemed that we were trying to outrun Satan. Tom Shevlin's beautiful speedboat drank all of its own fuel and was deep into the gasoline drum reserves before we raised the island. When I pointed out the fuel consumption to Hemingway, he said only, "Fuck it... the Cubans have more for us at Confites."

The writer let me take the wheel during the return trip. As we slowly left *Enseñada Herradura*, passed through a gap in the reef with great care, and watched Point Roma recede as we brought the little craft up to speed, Hemingway sat on the leather rear bench and held the loaded BAR across his knees and our bag of fragmentation grenades next to him. I did not ask him, but I suspected that he was hoping the previous night's submarine might appear out of the Gulf blue like a sea monster rising from the cold depths. That image was the crux of my view of Hemingway that summer—the tired and bearded knight hoping for his dragon to appear.

We sighted no submarine during our breakneck return trip.

The boys and the men greeted us around the morning campfire.

"How was your trip, Papa?" asked Patrick.

"Did you find a refueling base?" said Gregory.

"Did you see any submarines?" asked Guest.

"We saw some flying fish but no Germans," said Gregory.

"Did you and Lucas find anything important?" said Ibarlucia.

"We're glad you're back, Papa," said Gregory.

Hemingway sat on a log, took a metal cup of steaming coffee from Guest, and said, "Nothing interesting, boys. Lucas and I poked around in the channel behind Cayo Sabinal and explored a few dead-end creeks. Slept on a beach last night. A lot of bugs."

"Where's Maria?" I said.

Ibarlucia pointed to the *Pilar* where it was anchored sixty feet from the beach. "Don Saxon got really sick last night. Vomiting, diarrhea, the whole enchilada. He wanted to stay by the radio, but finally Gregorio tucked him in the big bunk in the forward compartment and Maria stayed with him last night." The jai alai player shot me a glance. "I mean, taking care of him. He was really sick."

"How is he this morning?" I asked.

"Sleeping," said Winston Guest. "Gregorio and Maria brought the *Tin Kid* in a couple of hours ago to have breakfast with us. She went back out by herself to check on Saxon." The sportsman shook his head in appreciation. "That little girl is terrified of the water, but she handled that little boat like a trooper. If I get sick, I want her as my nurse."

"I think I'll go say good morning to her," I said.

"She should be bringing the dinghy in pretty soon," said Patrick. "We were going to show her the reef where we were spearfishing yesterday."

I nodded, walked to the beach, shed my gritty shirt, trousers, and sneakers, and waded in wearing only my undershorts. The lagoon water was already warm, but it felt good after the heat, blood, sand, and sweat of the long night and morning. I swam out to the *Pilar*.

Maria was surprised to see me standing there almost naked and dripping water. "José!" She set down her cup of coffee, jumped up the last step from the galley, and threw her arms around me. Then she blushed, stepped back, cast one shy glance down at my clinging underpants, looked over her shoulder toward the forward compartment, and said, "*Señor* Saxon is sleeping, José, and the little boat is tied up here, if you—"

I patted her hair. "I came out to invite you on a picnic, Maria."

Her eyes grew as wide and excited as a young girl's. "A picnic, José? But we just finished breakfast and..."

I smiled. "That's okay. It'll take a while to get to the place I want to show you. We'll have an early lunch there. Get some things together in the galley and I'll find my duffel and get dressed." She smiled and hugged me again, and I patted her on the rump as she scrambled back to the galley.

In the small compartment where we stored our bags, I pulled on clean shorts, a threadbare denim shirt, and my one extra pair of canvas boat shoes. Then I went into the big forward compartment and shook the snoring Marine awake. "Feel any better?" I said.

"I...feel...terrible," said Saxon, squinting at me and smacking his dry lips. "Hung over. Headache."

"Maria took care of you last night?"

"Yeah, she—" The big radioman stopped and squinted up at me. "Don't get the wrong idea, Lucas. I was puking my guts out. Hardly knew where I was. All she did was—"

"Yeah," I said. "Did you pick up any coded transmissions during the patrol yesterday?"

"Uh-uh," said the Marine, holding his head in his two huge hands. "But one came in after we put in last night. Late. Must have been almost midnight."

"And you managed to catch it even though you were so sick?"

"Yeah. I was on the floor in the head with a bucket between my knees and the earphones on. Hemingway kept repeating how important it was that I keep monitoring last night."

"Did you write it down?"

Saxon squinted at me. "Sure I did. It's the only entry on page twenty-six of the radio log. Couldn't understand it, of course. That fucking new code."

I patted him on the shoulder and went into the tiny radio shack. The "radio log"—a grubby spiral notebook—ended with notes on an exchange between a British destroyer east of Bimini and a Panamanian cargo ship. Page twenty-six was missing. I went back in and shook Saxon awake again.

"Are you sure you wrote it down? Page twenty-six isn't there."

"Yeah. I'm sure. I mean, I think I did... I remember getting some stuff on the notebook when I was sick, but I didn't tear out *that* page. I don't think. Damn."

"Don't worry about it," I said. "You don't remember any of the groups, do you?"

Saxon slowly shook his head. His scalp was badly sunburned beneath his tight crewcut. "Just that it was in five-letter groups. Twelve or thirteen groups, I think. Not much repetition."

"Okay. By the way, there's no carrier tone on the receiver."

"Damn and hell," said Saxon. "The motherfucking, ass-licking, cocksucking turd of a piece of cornholing pisswad nigger junk was going out the entire pigfucking day on me yesterday. Piece of goddamn cockpuss farthole Navy surplus bubbleshit junk."

"All right," I said, and thought, *Never try to talk to a Marine with a hangover.*

Maria was still packing a picnic basket when I took the *Tin Kid* in to the beach and had Fuentes ferry me out to the *Lorraine*. The Cubans helped us refuel the auxiliary drums, and Maria was waiting when I rumbled back to the *Pilar*.

"*Señor* Saxon is sleeping," she said as she carefully stepped over the gunwales of the speedboat and carried the picnic basket to the center of the rear couch. She was wearing a clean, blue-checked dress.

"Good," I said, pushing off from Hemingway's bigger boat and steering toward the break in the reef. Patrick and Gregory were shouting from the beach, obviously upset to see Maria leaving, but I just waved at the boys.

"Can we really do this, José?" said the young woman. "Just leave everyone on such a day?"

I held out my hand and she came up to the passenger seat to hold it. "Yep," I said, "we can. I told *Señor* Hemingway that I was taking the day off. I've earned it. Besides, the *Pilar*'s not leaving until much later today. We'll be back in plenty of time." She continued to hold my hand as I brought the *Lorraine* out into open sea and opened the throttles to within two grand of the red line on the tach.

Maria still acted nervous in the small boat, but she seemed to relax after half an hour or so. Even with a bright red scarf tied over her head, her dark hair whipped back in the strong breeze of our passage and droplets of spray caught in the fine hairs on her right arm where it rested on the gunwale. It was a beautiful day as the sun climbed toward mid-morning and we continued to pound our way east through the slight chop.

"Are we going so far, then, for our picnic?" said Maria, peering toward the southern horizon, where the mainland was little more than a suggestion of low haze.

"Not so far," I said, throttling back. This was a place of dangerous reefs even though we were only an hour or so away from high tide. "There," I said, pointing to the northeast.

The little island was only about twenty feet across and ten inches or so out of the water, with waves from the Gulf rolling up on the gravel.

Maria looked at me as if I was going to announce the joke as I brought the speedboat in carefully, tossing the bow anchor out just twenty feet or so from the beach. "José, it is so low and rough... so many rocks in the sand."

"It's just the top of a reef that gets exposed at low tide," I said. "It'll be gone in..." I checked my watch. "About an hour. We'd better get our picnic stuff over there and eat fast."

Maria pouted, obviously disappointed. "I would rather eat in the boat, José, if you do not mind. The water there makes me very nervous. I do not swim well, you know."

I shrugged. "Whatever you want, kid."

She brought out thick roast beef sandwiches with plenty of horseradish—one of my favorites—and cold potato salad, along with several bottles of beer. The beer was wrapped in wet towels to keep it cool. She had even packed tall glasses and poured our beer with some ceremony.

I lifted the glass in salute to her, set it carefully on the tablecloth she had spread on the engine compartment behind us—I did not want to leave a ring on Shevlin's mahogany—and said softly in German, "What did you give Saxon last night to make him sick?"

Maria looked at me uncomprehendingly. In Spanish, she

said, "What did you say, José? I understood *Señor* Saxon's name but... why did you speak to me like that? Is that German?"

"It doesn't matter," I said, still *auf Deutsch.* "I don't suppose you kept the page of the radio log?"

She stared at me, obviously concerned but seemingly only that I was prattling at her in a language she did not understand. Then she suddenly smiled broadly. "You tease me, José," she said in soft Spanish. "Are you saying sweet things?"

I smiled and switched to English. "I'm saying that I will probably have to kill you if you don't start talking to me, bitch. I may kill you anyway for what you did to little Santiago, but your only chance is if you drop the shit and talk. Did you transmit a message this morning before you disabled the radio?"

Maria continued to stare at me, smiling tremulously but apparently not afraid, only confused.

"All right," I said in German. "Come aft. I have some nice gifts to show you."

She did not seem to understand the invitation until I hoisted myself over the seat and moved to the rear of the cockpit. Still smiling, she accepted my hand, stepped between the console and the seat, and walked carefully to the back couch.

I opened one of the concealed compartments and took out the curved knife that I had taken from one of the dead German boys. "Do you recognize this, Maria?" I said in Spanish.

She smiled immediately, obviously relieved that I was speaking in a way she could understand. *"Sí,"* she said, "that is a cane-cutting knife. It is used by the men in the cane fields."

"Very good," I said in Spanish. "You know that... but you didn't know the expression 'Between me and the sea.' You should have known that, Maria. I should have figured everything out then. Any little girl growing up near the coast in Cuba would have heard adults using that expression. Are you Spanish or German with Spanish parentage? The dialect, by the way, is excellent."

Maria stared at me wide-eyed. "What are you saying, José? I—"

"If you call me José again," I said, "I may have to shoot you sooner rather than later." I took the .357 Magnum from its place in the compartment and held it casually with the muzzle toward her.

"Sprechen Sie!" I snapped.

Maria's head pulled back as if I had slapped her.

Tired of the playacting—hers and mine—I did slap her. Once. Fairly hard. She sprawled backward onto the cushions and then slid to the deck. She raised her fingers to her cheek and stared at me, her head against the gunwale. The wickedly curved cane knife was where I had set it, in the center of the rear bench, slightly closer to me than to her. I still held the .357.

"All right," I said in English. "Let's go over it, and then you can correct the mistakes. You're half of Becker's Todt Team. Panama. You always have been. You were inserted into Cuba months ago. If I go to visit your village—what was it? Palmarito, near La Prueba, near Santiago de Cuba?—odds are that no one there has ever heard of the Marquez family...certainly not a Marquez family with a daughter who ran off after her brother raped her. Or was there a Maria Marquez whom you murdered?"

Maria continued to hold her palm against her reddening cheek and stare at me as if I had turned into a venomous snake.

"Very good," I said, sliding into German. "Martin Kohler, the poor, stupid, Abwehr radioman from the *Southern Cross*, comes to the rendezvous with you at the whorehouse as planned. Or perhaps he was there to meet Lieutenant Maldonado? It doesn't matter. You waited until the Cuban policeman was gone and then cut Kohler's throat...locked yourself in the bathroom and started screaming. Very neat, Maria. Hemingway and I get the codebook we're supposed to get and you get inserted into life at the *finca*. God in heaven, I was such an obliging shithead."

Maria blinked once but did not smile at my use of *Scheissköpf.*

"You'd already been to the *finca*, of course," I said. "The first night I was there when you took a shot at us when we were playing cowboys and Indians on Frank Steinhart's property. But who were you shooting at, Maria? Hemingway? That doesn't make any sense. Me? That doesn't make any sense either, since you people wanted me there to guide the amateur Hemingway through all of this nonsense. *Somebody* had to decode the radio transmissions for him and keep him alive during all of this. *Somebody* had to help him get to the right place at the right time so we could be your courier in delivering this..."

I took out the German courier packet and tossed it onto the long leather cushion next to the cane knife. Maria looked at it the way a lost soul in the desert would look at a cold cup of water.

"Maria, you'd better tuck in your dress," I said in casual German. "The way you're sitting with your knees up, I can see your underpants and pubic hair."

The woman reddened further and began pulling her dress tight. Then she stopped and glared at me, showing hatred in her eyes for the first time.

"It's all right," I said in Spanish. "You're very good. It's just been a bad day."

She got up and sat in the rear corner of the bench, studiously ignoring the knife and the courier packet between us. "*Señor* Lucas," she said slowly in her Cuban Spanish, "you have the wrong idea about me, I swear to you on my mother's soul. I *do* know just a little German and English... I learned it in the madam's house where I—"

"Shut up," I said evenly. "Who *were* you shooting at that night at the *finca*? Was it just part of the script, to keep me interested in the play? Or was there someone in the party you wanted to warn... or even kill? Another agent? British, perhaps? Winston Guest?"

Her eyes gave me nothing.

I shrugged. "So you stayed close, picking up information any way you could and giving it to Haupsturmführer Becker... it was Becker controlling you, wasn't it?"

She said nothing. Her face might have been carved out of ivory. Not a muscle twitched.

"All right," I said. "Then you killed little Santiago. Probably used the same knife you'd used on Kohler in the whorehouse. You're good with knives, kid."

She did not look down at the cane knife, nor at the .357 I held loosely in my lap.

"It was a bit too tidy when Lieutenant Maldonado showed up hunting for you after all those weeks," I said softly in English. "Too clever by half, as the Brits like to say. But it worked... you got invited along on this jaunt. But now what, kid? You were close to your target... if Hemingway's your target." I watched the muscles around her eyes, but they still gave me nothing. "Of course he is," I said. "And probably me as well. But when? And why? After we deliver this stuff..." I patted the canvas courier bag. "Are we an embarrassment after we play our part in the delivery? And why did Columbia...your Todt Team partner...kill those poor German boys last night? Couldn't it just have been arranged for them to drop these documents somewhere we'd find them?"

Maria put her hand over her eyes as if she were ready to weep.

"No, I guess not," I said. "Those boys were taking orders from Admiral Canaris and the military. The Abwehr doesn't have a clue, does it, Maria? It thinks it's running one operation in Cuba while you and Becker and Himmler and the late Heydrich and your Todt partner are running another one. One that betrays the Abwehr. But betrays them to whom...and for what, Maria?"

She sobbed softly. "José...*Señor* Lucas...please believe me. I do not understand most of what you are saying. I do not know what you—"

"Shut the fuck up," I said. I reached deep into the compartment and pulled out the long, canvas-wrapped bundle I had dug from the straw of the dairy barn the night before we all left. I unwrapped the Remington .30-06 and dropped it heavily onto the deck. The six-power scope took a nick out of the polished mahogany. "It was stupid to keep it so close, Maria," I said in rough German, using a Bavarian dialect. "But, then, you might need it soon, mightn't you? Are those your specialties, knife and long gun? I know you're a *Vertravensmann* and a *Todtägenten*, but are you one of those superagents...one of those *Groassägenten* that we Bureau boys used to be so afraid of?"

"José..." began the woman.

I slapped her very hard, backhanded. Her head snapped back but she did not tumble off the cushions this time. Nor did she raise her fingers to touch her red cheek or to wipe the blood from her mouth.

"I told you that I would kill you if you called me José again," I said very softly in Spanish. "I mean it this time."

She nodded slowly.

"Tell me who the other Todt Team member is," I snapped. "Delgado? Who?"

The woman I had called Maria for months smiled slightly. She said nothing.

"Do you know how I got Teddy Schlegel to talk?" I said in German. I took a long screwdriver out of the toolbox in the aft compartment and dropped it on the cushion next to the cane knife. "There are more options with a woman," I said, and showed her my teeth in a grin.

If the force of hatred in a gaze could kill, I would have died then.

"You'll tell me," I said in English. "And you'll tell me the details of the operation. Take off that dress."

Her eyes snapped. "What?" she said in Spanish.

I grabbed both of her wrists and pulled her to her feet. Setting the .357 in my belt, I continued holding her wrists in my left hand while I used my right hand to grab the front of her dress and rip it all the way down, white buttons flying and rolling on the deck next to the empty .30-06 Remington. Releasing one of her wrists, I tore the dress to rags as I ripped it off her. I threw the rags overboard.

Maria used her free hand to claw at my eyes. I slapped her back onto the cushions at the far corner of the stern bench. I had always noticed how white and chaste her brassieres and underpants were—for a theoretical whore—and today was no exception. The white cotton gleamed in the heavy morning sunlight. Her breasts looked heavy, white, and vulnerable above the brassiere as she half lay back against the gunwale, and the insides of her thighs were pale.

"All right," I said, turning to reach deep into the side compartment again. "One more thing to show you and then—"

She was very fast—faster even than I had expected. I barely had time to whirl and catch her right wrist as the cane knife came around in an arc that would have cut my kidneys out if it had continued. If it had been a pointed, stabbing knife rather than a form of scythe that had to be swung laterally, she would have had me.

She was also stronger than I expected. All those nights rolling on the cots and the floor of the cottage—feeling the power in her thighs and upper arms as she hugged me tighter and deeper—should have warned me. She almost managed to pull her knife hand free from my grip while her left hand scrambled at my belt, tugging at the .357 Magnum tucked there.

I used both hands to shake the knife out of her grip. It clattered across the already cluttered deck, but Maria managed to pull the pistol free. She jumped back to the corner of the cockpit and raised it at my face before I could grab the weapon back. She held the pistol straight-armed with both hands, and her finger was on the trigger. There was no way I could cover that distance before she squeezed that trigger.

"Maria," I said, my voice shaky. "Whatever your name is... we can do a deal here. No one knows about this but me and I won't—"

"*Schwachsinniger!*" she snarled, and pulled the trigger. The hammer fell on an empty chamber. I had a second to react before she pulled the trigger again, but I did not move. The hammer came down again and dry-clicked again. A third time.

"I was sure," I said in English. "But I had to know without a doubt." I stepped forward and took the empty pistol away from her.

She elbowed me in the stomach and lunged for the cane knife, on the deck.

Gasping for air, I grabbed her around the middle and pulled her back. We both fell on the cushioned bench and the speedboat bobbed ever so slightly. Maria clawed backward for my eyes, but I had buried my face between her shoulder blades so that her nails only raised blood on the back of my neck. I flung her into the rear corner again and got to my feet.

Maria bounced up, quick as a proverbial panther, and went into a professional's fighting stance. Her right arm was cocked and rigid, the fingers straight as a wedge and reinforced with a folded thumb. She took a half step and jabbed for my belly in the kind of blow designed to come in up and under the ribs and pulp the heart.

I parried the blow with my left forearm and slugged her on the chin. She flew backward onto the deck like a heavy bag of laundry, her head banging the chrome gunwale hard enough to make a noise like a gunshot. She sprawled there, legs apart, sweat between her breasts and in the crotch of her chaste white underpants, eyes fluttering. Pinning her wrists, I slapped her gently on both cheeks to bring her around. I had not hit her hard enough to kill her or keep her out long, but the bump on the head had been nasty. There was blood on the gunwale.

Her eyes fluttered open.

"I don't suppose you kept the page from the radio log," I said. "You're too smart for that. But we might as well check." I lifted her with one arm and tore the brassiere and underpants off her. No folded page. I had not thought there would be. Part of my mind was watching like a disinterested referee, critically trying to decide if I was enjoying any of this. I do not think I was. I felt like I might be sick over the side any minute.

"Okay," I said. "Time for our picnic." I lifted her off the deck and threw her far over the side.

The water brought her to full consciousness, and she flailed her arms to get back to the boat. I lifted the fishing gaff and held her off. She turned around and dog-paddled the thirty feet to the dwindling key, pulling herself up on the rocky bit of exposed reef and sand. Her hair dripped saltwater onto her breasts and knees as she turned to glare at me.

I stowed the gaff, the .30-06, the cane knife, the canvas pouch, and the .357, pulled up the anchor, and tossed the remains of our picnic overboard. I threw her a full canteen. She caught it by its strap with one hand.

I started the engine and swung the bow west. "I'm going back to Confites," I called. "Get some iodine on these scratches on my back. It should be high tide in about thirty-five minutes. The reef top will be underwater by then and the riptides will be fierce, but maybe if you sink your feet in the sand and find a niche in the coral, you can hang on by your toes."

"José!" cried the woman on the spit of sand. "I truly cannot swim."

"It doesn't matter too much," I said. "It's twenty-five miles or so to Cayo Confites." I pointed to the south. "About twenty to the mainland or the Camagüey archipelago. The tide would be with you, but the sharks are plentiful. And, of course, there are only a few places where the reef wouldn't tear you to ribbons going in."

"Lucas!" screamed the woman.

"Think about it," I said. "Think about my questions. Maybe I'll check back while you're treading water. Your ticket for a ride is just a few answers. Do you want to chat now?"

She turned her back on me and watched the waves eat away a bit more of her key. Whoever she was, enemy agent and vicious killer, she had a beautiful back and backside.

I pushed the throttle far forward and the *Lorraine* leaped ahead west. I did not look back with the binoculars until I was two miles out. Cayo Cerdo Perdido was already invisible, but it must have still been above water because I could see the pale sheen of Maria's flesh silhouetted against the blue of the sky and the deeper blue of the Gulf. I think she was looking in my direction.

The *Pilar* was just over the horizon, waiting at precisely the empty point on the chart where we had arranged to rendezvous. Only Hemingway was aboard. He slid down from the flying bridge and dropped a fender between us as the speedboat bobbed next to his green-and-black boat.

"Did she tell you anything?" he said, hooking the *Lorraine* tight around a stanchion with his gaffe and holding her in place.

"She called me a *Schwachsinniger*," I said.

Hemingway was not amused and I guess I wasn't either.

"Everyone thinks we're nuts today," he said, looking back toward Cayo Confites.

I nodded and scratched my cheek. Without planning it, I was growing my own little beard on this trip. I looked at my watch. My stomach hurt where she had elbowed me hard. Or perhaps it just hurt of its own accord.

"What's next?" said Hemingway.

"I'm not going to beat her up any more or torture her," I said, my voice sounding dead even to my own ears. "I'll head back when the water's lapping around her ankles, but if she doesn't talk then, we'll just have to bring her back to Havana with us."

"And do what with her? Turn her over to Maldonado and the National Police? To your friend Delgado?"

"I'll just have to turn her into the Havana field office of the Bureau," I said. "Leddy and the others there won't like it, and we'll probably never figure out just what this Operation Raven was all about, but they'll arrest her and Becker. Maybe Becker will tell them who else is involved and what the plans were."

"Or maybe he won't," said the writer, frowning at me as we bobbed up and down on the rising blue sea. "Or maybe your buddies at the Bureau already know very well what it's all about. And maybe Xenophobia will tell them about the dead agents last night and about the documents, and maybe we'll have to turn over the photostats and pages to the FBI or be shot as traitors ourselves, and maybe it'll all go the way they planned after all."

I checked my watch again. "Maybe," I said. "But one thing's for certain...if I don't get back to Cayo Cerdo Perdido in the next few minutes, all this will be academic. We won't have any prisoner to hand over."

I started the engine again as Hemingway shoved us apart and pulled in the kapok fender. "Hey!" I called over the rising gulf to him. "The name...Xenophobia...it was an in-joke for you, wasn't it? You never trusted her or believed her, did you? Not from the start."

"Of course not," said Hemingway, and went back to his flying bridge.

TWENTY MINUTES LATER I caught up to the *Pilar*. Cayo confites was still over the horizon to the west. He throttled back and glared down at me as I cut my own engine, but he did not come down the ladder from his high bridge.

"Where the hell is she, Lucas? What'd you do with her?" He was scanning the open cockpit of the speedboat as if I had hidden her under the cushions.

"I didn't do anything with her," I said. "She was gone when I got back there."

"Gone?" he said stupidly, looking back to the east and shielding his eyes as if he might see her swimming out there.

"Gone," I said. "There was still a few square feet of dry key left. But she was gone."

"Holy fuck," said the writer, taking his sombrero off and rubbing his mouth with his forearm.

"I made several swings to the south, between the key and the mainland, but didn't find anything," I said, my voice sounding strange to me again. "She must have started swimming."

"I thought she couldn't swim," he called from his high perch.

I glared up at him and said nothing.

"Maybe a shark snatched her right off the reef top," he suggested.

I drank some water from the canteen I had found bobbing half a mile south of the key. I wished I had some whiskey aboard.

"Do you think last night's U-boat might have picked her up?" asked Hemingway.

I thought about that. It had its humorous dimensions. The U-boat captain would not have known that she was a German agent, of course, as he peered through his periscope at this naked woman apparently standing on water twenty miles from land. If she had been picked up by a submarine whose crew had been away from land for several months, whatever was happening to her now would be far beyond anything I might have planned to make her talk. Of course, she could have explained her situation and identity in rapid-fire German, but I did not think that would have changed the outcome.

"Not a chance in hell," I said. "She either swam for it or was knocked off the key by a wave and drowned."

Hemingway looked to the east and nodded. "Before I left, Saxon said that he'd checked the radio."

"And?"

"She broke one of the tubes. He doesn't have a replacement, so we can't send or receive until we get back and order another fucking vacuum tube."

I said nothing. The chop and the sight of the *Pilar* bobbing up and down were making me sick to my stomach. But then, I had felt sick to my stomach before that.

"All right," I called up to him, "we get the kids and your pals and head home."

"What do we say happened to Miss Maria?"

"We tell them that she got homesick and I took her to the mainland so she could go home to her village," I said. I looked back to the southeast. Palmarito, near La Prueba, was in that general direction.

"We won't have another chance to talk in private," said Hemingway. He had put the battered sombrero back on, and tiny trapezoids of sunlight illuminated his face. "What happens when we get back but don't deliver the courier packet as planned?"

I sipped from the canteen again and then capped it and strung it over the back of the driver's seat. I wiped my mouth. Sunlight dancing on the wavetops and chrome was making me dizzy. "When we don't do our part, they'll either call off their operation and go away or..."

"Or?" called Hemingway.

"Or send the other member of their assassination team after us."

"After *me*, you mean," said Hemingway.

I shrugged.

"Can't we do anything to preempt them?" he said. "Go after this fucking Hauptsturmführer Becker, maybe?"

"We can try," I said. "But my guess is that Becker's dived deep. He'll get word to his agents to do what they have to do and he'll be on the next boat to Brazil or back to Germany. He may already be gone."

"You think he was the one with the lantern last night? I think that our dead German boys saw the man before the one in hiding killed them. They thought they were home safe. Do you think it was Becker acting as a Judas goat?"

"Yeah. Maybe. How the fuck should I know?"

"Don't get testy, Lucas." He looked back to the east. "This is inconvenient."

"What is?"

The big man stood easily, legs apart to balance himself against the rocking of the *Pilar*, and grinned down at me. "Now we have to rename that disappearing little key for our charts. How does Cayo Puta Perdida sound?"

I shook my head, thumbed the engine to life, and pointed the bow west by northwest.

26

I HAD NEVER BEEN QUITE sure why they called them safe houses. Some very unsafe things took place in safe houses.

I arrived on time and walked in without caution or preamble. Delgado was in his usual chair opposite the door, straddling it in his usual manner, with his usual contemptuous half-smile hovering around his mouth. He looked tanned and bored. His white snap-brim fedora was on the table next to a bottle of Mexican beer. From time to time he took a sip of beer. He did not offer me any. I sat and placed both my hands on the tabletop.

"So? Did you all enjoy your cruise?" His voice was as self-amused and sarcastic as ever.

"Sure."

"You're bringing the women and children along these days," said Delgado, his pale eyes looking through me. "Has Hemingway given up any semblance of using our taxpayers' gasoline for government service?"

I shrugged.

Delgado sighed and set the bottle back on the table. "All right, where's the report?"

I held out my empty hands. "Nothing to report," I said. "Nothing sighted. Nothing found. Even the radio got broken, so nothing heard."

Delgado smiled and stared. "How did it get broken, Lucas?"

"Clumsy Marine," I said. "Then people got tired and sunburned and sick, so we came home."

"With no report?"

"With no report."

Delgado shook his head slowly. "Lucas, Lucas, Lucas."

I waited.

Delgado drank the last of his beer. It looked warm. He belched. "Well," he said softly, "I don't have to tell you what a disappointment this operation…and you…have been to Mr. Ladd and Director Hoover and the others."

I said nothing.

Delgado gestured with his thumb. "You carrying that .357 in your belt for a reason?"

"Havana's a dangerous city," I said.

Delgado nodded. "Are you blowing your cover with Hemingway, or don't you give a shit anymore?"

"It's Hemingway who doesn't give a shit anymore," I said. "He doesn't care who I am or who the opposition is. He's getting bored with his Crook Factory game and of chasing phantom submarines."

"So are we," said Delgado, his gaze flat and cold.

"Who is we?" I said, returning that gaze.

"The Bureau," said Delgado. "Your employers. The people who pay your salary."

"The taxpayers are getting bored with the Crook Factory?" I said.

Delgado did not smile. Or, rather, his curled half-smile did not change. "You realize, don't you, Lucas, that it's just a matter of days before you get pulled off this assignment and dragged back to Washington to be held accountable?"

I shrugged. "Fine with me."

"It won't be fine with you when it's over," said Delgado, his voice finally carrying a message other than sarcasm. Threat. He sighed again and stood up. I noticed for the fiftieth time that he sometimes carried his weapon in a shoulder holster under his left arm and at other times wore it in a holster on his belt, on the left side, just as I preferred. I wondered how he decided which way he would dress when he got up in the morning.

"Okay," he said, smiling broadly now. "I think that does it with us down here, Lucas. This was bullshit from the start, and you turned it into even deeper bullshit. A total waste of my time as well as the Bureau's. I'll fly back today or tomorrow to report in person. I'm sure you'll be hearing from Mr. Ladd or the Director through regular channels."

I nodded and watched his hands. He held one out.

"No hard feelings, Lucas? Whatever happens."

I shook the hand.

Delgado left his empty beer bottle on the table and walked to the door, squinting out at the brilliant sunlight. "I hope my next assignment is in someplace cool."

"Yes," I said.

He started to go and then paused, leaning back in with his hand on the door frame. "Hey, how is your little whore doing? I didn't see her when you guys docked last night."

I smiled politely. "She's doing fine. She was below deck, sleeping."

"Sound sleeper if she can snooze through all that banging around and shouting."

"Yes," I said.

Delgado put on his white hat, snapped down the brim, and tapped a one-finger salute against it. "Good luck with whatever they send you next, Lucas." Then he was gone.

"Yeah," I said to the empty safe house.

ON SUNDAY, August 16, knowing that he might very well be the target of a ruthless Sicherheitsdienst assassin, Hemingway had one of his weekend pool parties. Most of the usual suspects were there—Ambassador Braden and his lovely wife and their two daughters; Bob Joyce and his wife, Jane; Mr. and Mrs. Ellis Briggs and their two kids; Winston Guest, wearing an expensive blue blazer and looking completely different with his hair combed and slicked back; Patchi; Sinsky; the Kangaroo; the Black Priest; a bunch of the writer's other Basque and athlete friends; the Herrera brothers; some of his Club de Cazadores Cuban shooting pals such as Rodrigo Diáz, Mungo Peréz, and Cucu Kohly; Patrick and Gregory and half a dozen of their baseball-playing buddies—and even Helga Sonneman showed up, announcing that the *Southern Cross* had finished its work in these waters and was ready to head for Peru.

I did not have time for the party, which is just as well since I was not invited. The previous evening, I had tailed Delgado to his hotel, waited across the street through the night, and followed him to the airport in the morning. He left on the eleven A.M. flight to Miami. The woman at the ticket counter said that he had purchased a connecting flight to Washington, D.C.

This meant nothing, of course. If he was the other Todt assassin, his departure could have been for my benefit. Or he might be a double agent but was leaving the country much as Schlegel had. Or he might be the loyal FBI agent he appeared to be, returning to the Justice Building to report on his success in whatever operation he had been running to turn Becker at the same time he was reporting on my failure.

It worried me, being away from Hemingway, but I had set Delgado at the top of my threat assessment checklist. The writer was so busy preparing for his Sunday soirée that he did not notice that I had the Crook Factory agents—at least those not drinking his whiskey at the party—coming and going through his hedges and flower gardens like gophers.

Lieutenant Maldonado was my second most serious worry, but he had been seen in Havana during the previous few days, and I had some of the waiters and wharf rats downtown keeping a watch on the policeman. I posted boys in San Francisco de Paula to cut across country to the *finca* with a warning if they saw Maldonado's car coming down the Central Highway. I had all of the Crook Factory's remaining operatives keep a watch for Haupsturmführer Johann Siegfried Becker in Old Havana, Cojímar, the dock areas, the coastal areas, and wherever German sympathizers lived or hung out. I paid two of the best young operatives twenty-five dollars each—a fortune—to stay at the airport and keep watch for Delgado's return. They were warned repeatedly not to let him spot them, but to telephone the *finca* or rush there on their motorbikes if they saw him.

Finally, I ordered Don Saxon to alternate shifts in the *Pilar*'s radio room with me, around the clock. He was sullen to the point of rebellion about this, and it was incredibly inconvenient for me, since it took almost as long to drive to Cojímar from the *finca* as it did to drive to Havana, but I had little choice. The only sophisticated radio available to us on this part of the Cuban coast was in Hemingway's boat.

Odds were that we would not catch a transmission in Cojímar anyway, but the *Southern Cross* was in Havana Harbor just down the coast, there had been reports of submarine sightings as close as Key Paraíso, and I had a hunch that messages would come to Columbia via local broadcasts. Also, I had no other choice.

All that day, Monday, August 17, there was an excess of normalcy. Lieutenant Maldonado went about his police business; Hauptsturmführer Becker continued to be absent or invisible; there was no sight of or word from Delgado; no one tried to kill Hemingway or his boys at the end-of-the-summer shooting competition at the Club de Cazadores; the radio hissed and popped through the afternoon or carried coded naval chatter that meant nothing to us or occasionally snarled in static-lashed German from the real U-boat war many hundreds and hundreds of miles to the north.

Then a little after one A.M. on the morning of Tuesday, August 18, I snapped awake as the familiar keying of shortwave beeped in my earphones. I was taking notes before I was awake. A minute later, using just the flashlight to read my notes and trying to drown out Saxon's snores from the forward compartment, I realized that this was a book code—based on *Geopolitík*, page 198. The signal had been strong, probably coming from less than twenty miles away. It was my hunch that it was being broadcast from a powerful transmitter from land near Havana, or from a boat nearby.

It took me only a few minutes to block the grid and translate.

OPERATION RAVEN SHUT DOWN REPEAT SHUTDOWN

But this was in the compromised book code. We were *meant* to know what was transmitted via this code. Twenty minutes later, another strong signal came through, apparently from the same local transmitter. But this time, it was in the numerical code I had bullied from Schlegel. It took longer to record and decrypt this and then translate it from the German:

COLUMBIATO U296ANDADLHAMBURG
AUGUST29BRITSC122DEPARTSNYHARBOR
SEPT3BRITHX229DEPARTSNY
SC122[51VESSELS13COLUMNS]
HX229[38VESSELS11COLUMNS]
POINTALPHASC122STEER67DTHEN49DNORTH40DEAST
POINTALPHAHX229STEER58DTHEN41DNORTH28DEAST

This was hard intelligence being transmitted from Cuba to a submarine in the Caribbean and to Hamburg. On August 29, a British convoy—SC122—with fifty-one vessels sailing in thirteen columns was to depart New York Harbor. Equivalent information was given for British Convoy HX229, departing September 3 with thirty-eight vessels. The data in the last two lines were specific sailing instructions for the convoy at "Point Alpha"—a predetermined point in the North Atlantic obviously known by the German U-boat wolf packs.

Agent Columbia was still in Cuba and was now transmitting hard information to the waiting subs.

A little after three A.M., an even longer message from Columbia came through, encrypted in the "secure" numerical code and directed to the RSHA control in Hamburg and Berlin:

PRIORITY. HAVE AUTHENTICATED PREVIOUS REPORTS OF FORTHCOMING ALLIED LANDING IN FRANCE. NATURE OF OPERATION: LIMITED TO ONE DIVISION STRENGTH. NOT REPEAT NOT FULL SCALE INVASION. TARGET: DIEPPE AND WEHRMACHT FIELD HQ AT QUIBERVILLE. TROOPS 2ND CANADIAN DIVISION. COMMANDER GENERAL CRERAR. CODE NAME: OPERATION RUTTER. DATE OF OPERATION: WAS SET FOR MIDSUMMERS DAY. DELAYED BECAUSE OF WEATHER. NOW SET FOR PERIOD AUGUST 19–AUGUST 21. CHECK WITH AFUS IN GB RE RADIO TRAFFIC. UPON CONFIRMATION ALERT WEHRMACHT. FOR YOUR INFORMATION PANAMA DISAPPEARED. DO NOT REPEAT DO NOT INFORM ABWEHR. COLUMBIA.

I could only stare at the notepad and wipe the cold sweat from my forehead. The "Check with AFUS in GB re radio traffic" must refer to having other *Agentenfunkgerät*, or agents with secret radio transmitters in Great Britain, check British military radio traffic. Which meant that the Germans had broken at least some of the British army or naval code.

A little after four A.M., Saxon came in to relieve me. I told him to go back to sleep. At 4:52 A.M., this message came in weak but clear from German shortwave relayed from a U-boat somewhere in the Caribbean:

CONTROL TO COLUMBIA. OKM SAY RN SIGNALS HAVE BEEN MENTIONING OPERATION JUBILEE SINCE MAY. WHAT DO YOU KNOW ABOUT JUBILEE?

This confirmed my suspicions. "OKM" stood for *Oberkommando der Marine*, the German navy. "RN" had to be the Royal Navy. The Nazis had definitely broken the Royal Navy's code. At 5:22 A.M. this arrived strong and clear, obviously from a transmitter not many miles away from the *Pilar*:

JUBILEE DEFINITELY SECURITY COVER NAME FOR OPERATION RUTTER. ORDER OF BATTLE INCLUDED IN NEXT TRANSMISSION. AWAITING ORDERS. COLUMBIA.

Twenty minutes later, another, shorter, message came through in SD numerical code:

COLUMBIA GOOD WORK. CONTINUE TRANSMISSIONS AS INFORMATION ARRIVES. PART ONE OF OPERATION RAVEN COMPLETED. YOU ARE AUTHORIZED TO KILL GOETHE. GOOD LUCK AND HEIL HITLER.

"TELL ME AGAIN," said Hemingway later that same Tuesday morning. "Why do you think it's me they want to kill?"

"'Goethe,'" I said. "It's a lazy man's code for 'writer'...and you're the only writer I can think of in all this mess."

"Marty's a writer," said Hemingway. "And her former last name begins with *g*."

"And she's safely... where?" I said. "Dutch Guiana?"

"Why would they use such an obvious code?" grumbled Hemingway.

I shook my head. "You're forgetting... this was in their one-time SD AMT VI numerical code. Schlegel hasn't yet admitted that he spilled the beans. In fact, Schlegel was probably arrested as soon as he returned to Brazil. He might have had a fair trial and been executed by now."

Hemingway looked skeptical.

"Besides," I said, "we'll know in a few days if this information on the upcoming British-Canadian Dieppe raid is accurate."

"If it is," said Hemingway, touching his swollen ear, "it will be one hell of a slaughter."

"Yeah," I said. "But more importantly, it will tell us that they're not aware that this code has been compromised. They'd never risk our turning this over to the FBI or OSS or ONI if it's real."

"*Are* we going to turn it over to the FBI, OSS, or ONI?" said Hemingway.

I shook my head again. "I don't think it would help if we did. If these possible invasion dates are accurate, we'd only have three days at the most to try to stop the raid. Something that big doesn't grind to a halt that quickly."

"But if those Canadians go ashore with the Wehrmacht knowing they're coming and waiting for them..." said Hemingway, and stopped, his eyes focused on something not in the *finca*'s living room.

I nodded. "That's a constant problem with this sort of thing. Right now, it's a certainty that both British and American military planners are allowing ships to be sunk and even battles to be lost rather than reveal that they've broken German or Japanese codes. I'd bet anything on it. In the long run, it pays off."

"Not to the poor Canadian fucks who are going to be ground up like hamburger on the Dieppe beaches," snarled Hemingway.

"No," I said softly.

Hemingway shook his head almost violently. "Your profession stinks, Lucas. It stinks of death and rot and old men's lies."

"Yes," I said.

He sighed and sat in his flowered chair. The big black cat named Boissy jumped onto his lap and squinted at me suspiciously. Hemingway had been drinking a Tom Collins when I came in, but now the ice was melted. He sipped the drink anyway while he rubbed the big cat's neck. "So what do we do, Lucas? How do we make sure that this doesn't pose a threat to Gigi and Mouse?"

"Whoever the second Todt agent is," I said, "he's a professional. I don't think the boys are in danger."

"That's reassuring," the writer said sarcastically. "He's a professional so I'm the only one who ends up dead. Unless whoever it is decides to blow up the entire *finca* with a bomb while the boys are sleeping here."

"No," I said. "I think it will have to look like an accident. Just you. An accident."

"*Why?*" demanded Hemingway, his voice rough.

"I'm not sure," I said. "It's part of their Operation Raven... I just don't understand it all yet. But the message says that part one of the operation is completed. Evidently you're not needed for part two."

"Great," said Hemingway. "Look, I was planning to leave later this week to take the *Pilar* down the Camagüey archipelago to shadow the *Southern Cross* when it departs. Helga tells me that the captain has decided to take the yacht around the tip of South America rather than through the canal and that they're going to make a stop in Kingston. Wolfer and I have some theories on where these U-boats are refueling. We'd make sure that the yacht actually left Cuban waters and then we'd snoop around the east end of the island before swinging down to Haiti, putting in at Kingston, and coming back up and around the west end of Cuba. We'd be gone for a week or two. Should I cancel it?"

I thought a minute. "No, it might be the best thing."

"We're pretty visible with our Museum of Natural History

signs," mused Hemingway. "A Nazi sub could sight us and sink us. I could be making it easier for the SD to get me."

"I don't think so," I said. "These communications are between Columbia and Hamburg and Columbia and some SD intelligence man aboard one German boat. I doubt if any German sub skipper has any idea who you are or what Operation Raven is. You'd be as safe as any small boat in these waters."

Hemingway looked grim. "I was talking to Bob Joyce and a couple of the Navy Intelligence boys on Sunday. It's all classified, but they're projecting more than fifteen hundred Allied merchant ships to be sunk this year. At the rate the Germans are going, they'll sink between seventy and eighty ships in the Caribbean just this month and next... between two and three hundred in the Caribbean before the year is over. And to think that Marty was out sailing around in that carnage." He looked at me again. "Do you think I should take the boys?"

"What was the plan if you don't?"

"They were going to stay there at the *finca*. The staff would be here, and Jane Joyce was going to look in on them every once in a while."

I rubbed my cheek. I had slept an hour or two before driving over here from Cojímar, but I was very tired. The last few days and nights tended to blur together. *Could there be a potential hostage situation in all of this?* I could not categorically say no. "It might be best if you took them with you," I said.

"All right," said Hemingway. He grabbed my wrist. "What do these people *want*, Lucas? Other than me dead, I mean."

I waited until he released me. "They want us to send along the documents we got from the dead Germans," I said. "I feel certain of that."

"And as long as we don't, I'm in no danger?"

"I'm not sure," I said. "My guess is that they plan to kill you one way or the other."

"*Why?*" demanded the writer. His voice held no hint of a whine, only curiosity.

I shook my head again.

Hemingway set the black cat down carefully and got up to pad off to the bathroom in his sandals. Before leaving the room, he looked at me over his shoulder. "For an intelligence agent, Lucas, you don't know very much."

I nodded.

I NEEDED EITHER another radioman or another me. Crook Factory reports kept coming in all that long, hot Tuesday—Lieutenant Maldonado's movements in Havana, continued negative surveillance for Becker, still no sign of Delgado at the airport or hotels—and I tried to catch a few more winks of sleep before heading back to the *Pilar* for my graveyard shift on the radio. I did not want to leave Hemingway alone. The writer started carrying that little .22 target pistol in his belt as he wandered around the grounds of the *finca*, but other than that, he showed no outward concern about the death threat. That evening, he put on a clean shirt and long pants and went in to the Floridita with friends to drink.

They'll make it look like an accident, I kept telling myself. And for that they will probably want privacy. But then I thought of the Havana traffic and how easy it would be for a car to accelerate out of an alley or down a side street and finish Columbia's assignment.

They'll want the documents first, I also kept telling myself. We had not trusted any hiding place at the *finca*, so I had been carrying the German courier pouch around in a duffel bag slung over my shoulder. It lay at my feet in the *Pilar*'s radio shack during the night. Not subtle, but I reassured myself that anyone wanting them would have to come straight at me before dealing with Hemingway.

Which wouldn't be much of a problem for them given your current state. I was exhausted. I brought along pills that I had carried in my gear for years and popped them when I became too sleepy to concentrate on the earphones.

The only radio intercept achieved on August 18 happened while Don Saxon was on duty in the early afternoon. He sent Fuentes to the *finca* with the transcript of the transmission. It was in the SD numerical code. I went down to the guest house and decrypted it. Fourteen lines giving the specifics of the order of battle of the Canadian troops headed for Dieppe. The message began by saying that the small fleet had already disembarked and that the invasion was imminent.

On Wednesday the nineteenth, Havana radio broadcast the news that a British attack on the coastal city of Dieppe had begun. Six beaches were said to be occupied by gallant Allied forces. The announcer was very exited—perhaps this was the opening of the long-awaited Second Front! Details were sketchy, but the invasion was said to be serious—transport ships and landing craft had brought thousands of Canadians supported by tanks on the ground and swarms of RAF fighter planes overhead.

By the next day, August 20, 1942, even the censored news reports could not hide the fact that the experimental invasion had been a disaster. Most of the troops had been killed or taken prisoner. The transport ships had been blown up or beached or had fled. The RAF fighters had been beaten off by Luftwaffe aircraft that had been moved to nearby airfields before the raid. The six beaches were still covered by Canadian corpses. The Nazis were bragging that *Festung Europa* was invincible and were openly inviting the British or Americans to try it again.

"I guess that's what you call a confirmation," said Hemingway that afternoon. We were in the guest house. Patrick and Gregory were splashing and shouting in the pool outside. "Your Columbia must have gained some status with SD AMT VI with his Monday-night transmission." Hemingway looked me in the eye. "But where's he getting all this, Joe? Where is a German agent in Cuba picking up all this high-level intelligence on the Brits?"

"Good question," I said.

That night, sometime after one A.M., I startled awake on the *Pilar* to the sound of code beeping in my earphones. I had been so sound asleep that I had missed the first five code groups, but the sender obligingly rebroadcast his transmission three times at thirty-minute intervals.

It was the old book code, based on the anthology of German folk tales. There was no additional transmission in secure SD numerical code. After the third transmission, I clicked on the twenty-watt bulb over the table and stared again at the grubby little radio log notebook.

COLUMBIA RENDEZVOUS WITH PANAMA 0240 HOURS 22 AUGUST WHERE PALE DEATH ENTERS BOTH HOVELS AND THE PALACES OF KINGS UNDER THE SHADOW OF JUSTICE.

It was hot and humid in the tiny radio shack—the air moving sluggishly through the tiny porthole stank of spilled diesel fuel, dead fish, and sewage heated by the hot summer day and night—but my skin felt cold as I read and reread the message.

I did not believe for a moment that Panama—Maria—was to meet with Columbia at 2:40 A.M. the next morning, but certainly the rendezvous site would be appropriate for that. Columbia had obviously decided that Hemingway and I had killed Maria. Perhaps he now suspected that we had also compromised the SD number code. At any rate, I was now supposed to carry this message to the writer as dutifully as I had the previous ones, and just as we had been present for the fatal landing of the two German agents, so would we be present for this fateful "rendezvous." Only this time, no Germans were scheduled to die.

On that Friday morning, I argued with Hemingway. I had not told him about the radio intercept. We were at the Floridita, having a breakfast of hard-boiled eggs and daiquiris. The only other customer was an old man sleeping on his stool at the opposite end of the bar.

"Look," said the writer, "the *Southern Cross* is sailing on Sunday at the earliest. Why should we take the *Pilar* out tonight?"

"I have a hunch," I said very quietly. "I think it would be best if you got the kids away from here for the weekend."

Hemingway salted his egg and frowned deeply. His beard had grown in full and symmetrical over the summer, but where the beard ended, his skin carried a rash from the sun. His swollen ear looked better. "Lucas, if you're planning some grandstand play..."

"Uh-uh," I said. "I just want a few days to run the Crook Factory without worrying about your and my security. It'll be easier keeping a low profile with you and the boys and your pals out of the way."

The writer looked unconvinced.

"You can go up to Key Paraíso or down to Confites and wait for the yacht to sail," I said. "Sonneman told you that it was sailing around the east side of the island…"

"She might not be the best informant," growled Hemingway.

"So? You could still catch it before it reached Kingston even if it sailed west. I'll keep your operatives watching and we'll radio you on the regular marine band channels or call Guantánamo and have Lieutenant Commander Boyle reach you with their big transmitter."

"So you just stay behind for a week or two?" said Hemingway.

I rubbed my eyes. "I need the vacation."

Hemingway laughed. "You do at that, Lucas. You look like shit."

"*Gracias.*"

"*No hay de qué!*" He ate the last of his hard-boiled egg and reached for another. "What do you do if you need help back here?"

"Same thing," I said. "I'll give you a call using the Cojímar radio or have Bob Joyce authorize the Guantánamo call."

"In code?" Hemingway seemed fascinated with the code games.

I shook my head. "Saxon's no good with real code. We'll just make it a personal code you could understand."

"Such as?"

"Oh," I said, "if I need help here, I'll say that the cats are lonely and need feeding. If we need to rendezvous somewhere else, I'll radio that, say, we need to meet where the Cubans raise their flags."

"Cayo Confites."

"Yeah," I said. "But you'll have a lot to do if you're sailing tonight. You'll need to get busy."

"Why tonight?" said Hemingway. "Why sail after dark?"

I drank the last of my daiquiri. "I don't want anyone to know you're gone until tomorrow at least," I said. "I have things to do tonight."

"Things you don't want to tell me about?"

"Things I want to tell you about later," I said.

Hemingway ordered two more tall drinks and another basket of hard-boiled eggs. "Okay," he said. "I'll get Wolfer and the others together today and arrange to cast off after dark. We'll wait for the *Southern Cross* at Confites. Most of the gear and provisions are aboard, so it won't be a problem leaving tonight. But I don't like it."

"You're just leaving a day early," I said.

The writer shook his head. "I just don't like the whole thing," he said. "Something stinks somewhere. I have a feeling that we're not going to see each other again, Lucas... that one or both of us is going to be dead soon."

I paused with the new daiquiri poised in midair. "That's a hell of a thing to say," I said softly.

Suddenly Hemingway grinned. He tapped my glass with his. "*Estamos copados, amigo*," he said. "Fuck 'em. Fuck 'em all."

I touched glasses and drank.

27

THE CEMENTERIO DE CRISTÓBAL COLÓN IS one of the largest necropolises in the world. Columbus's Cemetery takes up the equivalent of dozens of city blocks some distance southwest of the hotel district and separates the areas of Vedado and Nuevo Vedado. I reached it that night by driving around the harbor, staying south of Old Havana and cutting over west past the Castillo del Príncipe.

The cemetery had been created in the 1860s when Havana had run out of regular church catacombs. Hemingway had told me that there had been a competition for the design of the necropolis, won by a young Spaniard named Calixto de Loira y Cardosa. The designer had planned the huge cemetery on a medieval grid pattern in which interlocking crosses of narrow lanes were to separate the dead according to status and social class. Set west of Old Havana, whose own streets and alleys were no wider than oxcarts, the huge cemetery seemed an extension of the city of the living into the city of the dead. Hemingway had told me that upon completing the design and original construction on the necropolis, Calixto de Loira y Cardosa had dropped dead at the age of thirty-two and become one of its first residents. The story had seemed to amuse the writer.

At the main entrance to the Cementerio de Colón, the Latin motto inscribed in stone reads PALE DEATH ENTERS BOTH HOVELS AND THE PALACES OF KINGS.

The rendezvous was supposedly set for 2:40 A.M. I parked Hemingway's Lincoln on a side street and approached an east entrance just after one in the morning. The gates of the cemetery were all closed and locked, but I found a place where a tree grew close to the tall iron fence and clambered over, dropping heavily to the grass within. I was wearing a dark suit coat and trousers and a dark fedora pulled low. I carried the .357 in a quick-release holster on my hip, my gravity knife in my trousers pocket, and one of the powerful flashlights from the *Pilar* in my jacket pocket. Over my left shoulder was looped thirty feet of coiled line, also from the *Pilar*. I was not sure yet why I needed the rope—to tie up a captive, to set some sort of trap, to climb some fence—but it had seemed like a good idea to bring it.

Months earlier, Hemingway had told me about how bizarre the necropolis was—how important Havana families had vied with one another for almost eighty years to build ever more elaborate tombs and monuments there—but I was not prepared for the block after block of morbid architecture. I stayed off the empty, silent streets that crisscrossed the cemetery and moved quietly down the narrow walkways and lanes between the tombs. The place was a stone forest in the moonlight—crucified Christs staring down at me in agony, elaborate Grecian temples with frescoes and pillars gleaming, angels and seraphim and cherubim hovering above graves like so many circling vultures, Madonnas looming out of the dark like women in shrouds, their upraised fingers looking like pointed revolvers in the dark, Gothic mausoleums with iron gates throwing ink-black shadows across my path, urns everywhere, hundreds of Doric columns throwing shadows to conceal waiting assassins, and everywhere in the cooling night the stench of decomposing flowers.

That afternoon, I had gone to a local tourist bureau and bought a cheap map of the cemetery. I checked it now by moonlight, not wanting to switch on my flashlight for even a second. This was precisely the kind of situation SIS agents were trained never to find themselves in: arriving at a rendezvous which was almost certainly an ambush, on the enemy's territory, not knowing how many of the opposition there would be, leaving all the initiative to the other side.

Fuck it, I thought, and refolded the map and moved on. I found a life-sized sarcophagus of a man lying supine with a life-sized statue of a dog at his feet. Beyond that, a four-foot-high chess knight stood guard over a stone slab under which lay the remains of one of Cuba's greatest chess players. All right, that was on the map...just another few hundred yards to the Monument to the Medical Students. I passed a dark monolith and realized that it was a tombstone in the shape of a domino with two threes on it. The legend on the map had explained that the woman buried there had been a fanatical domino player who had died of a stroke when she failed to draw a double three during an important tournament. I turned left. A short distance beyond the domino lady was a low tomb literally buried in flowers. This had to be the grave of Amelia Goyre de la Hoz. Hemingway had enjoyed telling me her tale. She was buried in 1901, her child in a separate grave at her feet; they had exhumed her for some reason years later only to find the skeleton of the infant in her arms. Cubans loved that sort of story. So did Hemingway. Women from throughout the island made pilgrimages to this grave—thus the giant mound of flowers. It smelled like all the funeral parlors I had ever been in.

The Monument to the Medical Students was in the oldest section of the cemetery. Several lanes converged there. In 1871, eight young Cuban men were executed for desecrating the tomb of a Spanish journalist who had criticized the burgeoning independence movement. There was a tall icon of Justice over the tomb, but the statue wore no blindfold of impartiality and the scales she raised in one hand were definitely tipped to one side. "Where Pale Death enters both hovels and the palaces of kings under the shadow of justice" had read the radio transmission.

It was 1:40 A.M. It had taken me bloody damn forever to find this tomb and now it took me longer to find a hiding spot.

Just down the pedestrian lane from the Monument to the Medical Students was a mausoleum that looked like a miniature of the Taj Mahal and must have been thirty-five or forty feet tall. The thing had carved niches, angels and gargoyles carved along each face with more standing guard on the two set-back roofs, and another robed angel perched atop the mosquelike dome. If I could clamber up that corner and get onto the first roof, I could conceal myself behind that tesselated parapet and look down on the Monument to the Medical Students, watch the empty streets and the broad intersection, and peer down into the many narrow paths and walkways on the approach to the monument. Of course, when the assassin or assassins did make their move, I would be stuck twenty-five feet in the air, able to shoot at them but not able to give chase... but, then, that was where the rope could come in handy. I could loop it around one of those corner statues and slide down in ten seconds. I congratulated myself on my prescience, moved to the shadowed side of the monstrous mausoleum, and began climbing.

It took ten minutes and a rip through the knee of my trousers, but eventually I pulled myself up and over the marble parapet. There was a ten-foot setback and then another wall rising to the dome, glowing in the moonlight. More angels or saints were above me, arms raised. The parapet was not fortress-wall high—it was only three feet from the top of the marble railing to the more prosaic asphalt and gravel of the roof—but I could crouch down and peer out through the ornamental cracks. If I had to, I could duck-walk my way around the roof and see in all directions.

I made my loop around a six-foot-tall statue on the southeast corner and coiled the rope out of sight by the wall. Then I knelt by the south rampart and watched the open areas around the Monument to the Medical Students. The hundreds of marble and granite statues seemed to be peering up at me like a pale army of the dead. A storm was coming in from the north. The moon was still bright, but lightning flashed occasionally and thunder rumbled over Havana. It was 2:00 A.M.

It was just as I was glancing at my watch at 2:32 A.M. that I heard a soft sound behind me. I started to turn, but at that second something cold and round touched the back of my neck.

"Do not move an inch, *Señor* Lucas," said Lieutenant Maldonado.

GOOD WORK, Joe, I thought. It should have been the last thought that went through my brain just before the .44-caliber slug from Maldonado's ivory-handled pistol followed it. I had managed to climb up to the Cuban National Policeman's sniper's perch, not check the back side of the roof, and then miss the sound of his footsteps on the roof because of the now almost constant rumble of thunder. *What a fuck-up.* Still no bullet. What was he waiting for?

"Do not move," Maldonado whispered again. I could hear the click of the Colt's hammer being cocked and smell the garlic on the man's breath. He pressed the muzzle of the handgun deeper into the soft groove on the back of my neck as he patted me down with his left hand, removed my flashlight and the .357, and tossed both away across the rooftop. Evidently he thought the knife too small to worry about. I took every second that he did not shoot as a reprieve of my terminal stupidity.

Maldonado stepped back. I could no longer feel the muzzle against my neck but I could feel the aim of the .44 still centered on the back of my head. "Turn around very slowly and sit on your hands, *Señor* Special Agent Lucas."

I did as he said, keeping my hands palms down on the rough rooftop. Maldonado was not in uniform; he was wearing the same sort of dark suit and hat as I had chosen, but he wore a tie with his dark blue shirt. Cubans are never very comfortable with informal dress, I had noticed. Hemingway was always shocking them with his shorts and grubby clothes.

Think, Joe, think! I forced my sluggish brain to concentrate on something other than giddy relief that the tall policeman had not yet executed me. I noticed that he was in his sock feet. He must have left his shoes on the other side of the dome so as to creep up on me even more quietly. He needn't have bothered—thunder boomed so loudly that it seemed like the Battery of the Twelve Apostles cannon from El Morro Castle across the bay had begun a barrage of the city. The moon still cast some light, but the clouds were quickly covering it.

Maldonado had crouched down and gone to one knee, perhaps so that he could see over the parapet behind me without being visible from the ground. Perhaps it was just more comfortable for him to shoot me from a kneeling rather than a standing position.

Concentrate. He has some reason for keeping you alive. He's not wearing shoes—a possible help if you close on him.

Another part of my mind was thinking, *You're sitting on your hands while he holds that large-bore Colt steady on your face. You'll never close with him for hand-to-hand combat.*

Shut up! I forced myself to think even while my body reacted as it always did to having a firearm aimed at it: my scrotum contracted, my skin prickled, and I had the overpowering urge to hide behind something—anything. I mentally shook away this reaction. There was no time for it.

"Are you alone, *Señor* Special Agent Lucas?" hissed the policeman. Only his long jaw and white teeth were visible in the shadow under his dark fedora. "Did you come all alone?"

"No," I said. "Hemingway and the others are down there now."

The teeth caught more of the fading moonlight as Maldonado grinned. "You lie, *señor*. I was told that you would come alone and you have."

He was expecting just me. I had just got my heart rate under control, and now it accelerated again. "You're not Columbia," I said.

"Who?" said Maldonado without real interest.

I smiled. "Of course you're not Columbia," I said. "You're just a stupid greaser spik taking orders and bribes. That's what you *pendejos* do."

The grin wavered and then widened. "You try to anger me, Special Agent Lucas. Why? Do you wish to die more quickly? Do not worry... it will be soon."

I shrugged... or tried to. It was not easy when one was sitting on one's hands. "At least tell me who ordered you to do this," I said, allowing my voice to quaver slightly. It was not difficult to do that. "Was it Delgado? Becker?"

"I will tell you nothing, you pig-fucking North American," said the lieutenant, but even in the fading moonlight I had seen the slight quiver of muscles around his mouth at the mention of Becker's name. *Becker, then.*

"Pig-fucking?" I said, and after a moment of silence, added, "What are we waiting for, Crazy Horse?"

"Do not call me that," the lieutenant said. "Or this will be more painful for you than it must." Thunder rumbled. I could see the lightning playing amidst the low buildings of Old Havana now, less than a mile to the northeast.

Advantages? I thought, forcing myself into a cold, dispassionate analysis. *Not many. A slug from that .44 will almost certainly end the argument at this distance, and he can easily pull the trigger twice before I can close the five feet that separate us. Still, he's too close. And he's on one knee—which will be awkward for him if things change quickly. And he's used to bullying and killing drunks, teenagers, cowards, and amateurs.*

Which of those categories do you fall into? asked another part of my mind. I was disappointed in myself. Not for the first time in my life and career, I wondered how many millions and millions of men had died with their last thought being a disgusted *Oh, shit!* at their own stupidity. I suspected that it went back to the caveman days.

I watched the storm approach. It was behind Maldonado. He could hear the thunder but could not see how close the lightning strikes and rain squalls were getting. I looked up at the darkening dome above him. No lightning rod that I could see. Perhaps he would be struck by lightning before he shot me.

That's about what your odds add up to, Joe. I felt loose gravel digging into my palms. I curled my fingers of both hands around the gravel. It hurt to sit on my curled fingers like that and in a couple of minutes it would put my hands to sleep, but I did not have to worry about things so far away as a couple of minutes.

Without taking his eyes off me for more than a split second, Maldonado raised his left wrist and glanced at his watch. *That's what we're waiting for. The 2:40 rendezvous time.*

Certainly we had passed that. Perhaps Maldonado had been instructed to wait a few extra minutes to make sure that no one else was with me before killing me. I realized then that he probably had a rifle propped somewhere on the other side of the wall surrounding the dome. He had been waiting up there with the long gun, had watched me arrive and seek out just this roost, and had retreated to the far side of the roof while I grunted and sweated my way up the side of the mausoleum. It must have amused the Cuban no end.

"What kind of rifle did you bring?" I asked in easy, conversational Spanish.

The question seemed to surprise him. He frowned a second, apparently analyzing whether answering it would give me any sort of advantage. He must have decided in the negative. "A Remington thirty-aught-six with a six-power scope," he said. "It would have been just right in the moonlight."

"Jesus," I said, forcing a chuckle. "Does AMT VI hand those out like union cards? It's just like the one I took away from Panama before I killed her."

There was no reaction. Either Maldonado was a consummate actor or he did not know her code name. I did not think he was acting. "Maria, I mean," I said. "I found her rifle before I drowned her."

This time he did react. His lips tightened and I could see his finger on the trigger also tighten. "You killed Maria?" The storm almost drowned his words. Perhaps that was what he was waiting for—no shot would be heard when the storm was directly overhead.

"Of course I killed her." I laughed. "Why would I keep the lying bitch alive?"

I had been hoping to enrage him into some action short of shooting me, but his only reaction was to smile again. "Indeed, why?" said Lieutenant Maldonado. "She was a murderous little cunt. I always told *Señor* Becker that someone should douse that woman with gasoline and light a match." He glanced at his watch again and smiled more broadly. "I place you under arrest, *Señor* Special Agent Joseph Lucas." His thumb moved away from the Colt's hammer.

"For what?" I said quickly, preferring conversation to a .44 slug in the forehead. I could see the wall of rain drawing across the rooftops of Old Havana like a black curtain. The moonlight was gone, replaced by the flash and blast of lightning just beyond the cemetery's northern and eastern boundaries. There was enough noise now for Maldonado to kill me with a cannon without being overheard on the streets outside.

"For the murder of *Señor* Ernest Hemingway," said the lieutenant with a grin. It was a final death sentence.

"Don't you want the documents?" I said quickly, my heart hammering at my ribs. "Didn't Becker tell you to get the German documents?"

Maldonado paused. I realized that his finger had already applied most of the necessary pressure on the Colt's trigger. "Hemingway has the documents," he said, the last word drowned out by a clap of thunder from a lightning strike only a hundred yards distant.

I shook my head and prepared to shout over the coming rain. He couldn't know that. We had decided that Hemingway should keep the courier pouch only as he was ready to leave on the *Pilar* that evening. It had seemed safer than my hauling them around town for a week. "No!" I said. "They're in my car. Becker will pay you extra for them!"

I could see his eyes now as his head tilted back a bit. Lieutenant Maldonado was mean and crafty but not all that intelligent. It took him four or five seconds to work out that he could indeed extort more money from the Hauptsturmfuhrer if he found the documents but that he did not need me alive to find them if they were actually in my car. He would simply shoot me, find the car, and take the documents.

Maldonado smiled and aimed the pistol more carefully—lower, at my heart.

The lightning did not strike the dome. It must have hit the statue of Justice above the Monument to the Medical Students. That was better—the flash was behind me, blinding Maldonado for a second or two while the clap of thunder sounded like an explosion in the mausoleum beneath us.

I threw myself to the left, hit hard on my shoulder, and rolled toward Maldonado. He fired, but the slug ripped over my right shoulder and took off a chunk of the marble parapet behind me. He fired again, but I was already leaping to my feet, and the bullet passed an inch under my crotch, burning the inside of my thigh. Maldonado was uncoiling to his full height as I tossed the two handfuls of gravel into his face. The third slug sliced a groove through my earlobe.

I got both hands on his right wrist and forced the pistol down and around even as I kicked the man's long legs out from under him. We both went down heavily, but I made sure that I went down on top of the policeman. The air whoofed out of him like a garlic-scented bellows.

Maldonado snarled and clawed at my face with his left hand. I ignored that and broke his right wrist, flinging the gun across the rooftop. My .357 was now closer than his Colt.

The Cuban screamed and threw himself sideways, flinging me against the marble wall around the base of the dome. He screamed again, cursing in Spanish, and struggled to his feet, clutching his broken wrist. I took two steps forward, perfectly visualized following through for a forty-yard field goal kick, and kicked the tall man in the balls so hard that he literally levitated. Two lightning bolts struck around the dome—one behind us and the other on a tall cross held high by a marble saint below. The double explosion of thunder almost but not quite drowned out Maldonado's bellow and grunt as he folded up like a six-foot-four accordion. His hat rolled across the rooftop.

Panting, I picked up the .357 Magnum and set it back in my holster, keeping both eyes on Maldonado as I did so. He might have a boot gun or switchblade in his cuff. It would have to be his left cuff to do him any good, I realized. His right hand was bent backward at an impossible angle on his wrist, and even as he rolled on the rooftop in silent agony after the scrotum punt, he tried to cradle the broken wrist.

I flicked open my gravity blade and stepped closer, putting one knee on the policeman's prominent Adam's apple as I pinned him to the roof with my weight. The rain began hammering down on us as I leaned over and set the blade just below his right eye. The razor-sharp point of the blade cut through flesh just beneath the curve of his eyeball.

"Talk," I said. "Who went to kill Hemingway?"

Maldonado's mouth opened, but he was obviously too terrified of losing his eye if he tried to move his jaw to speak. I released a bit of pressure on the knife and lifted my knee, ready to cut his throat in an instant if he began to struggle.

He did not struggle. He gasped and moaned.

"Shut up," I said, slicing away a flap of skin between his ear and the corner of his mouth. "Who went to kill Hemingway?"

Maldonado screamed. The worst of the lightning had moved beyond the cemetery now, but thunder still echoed across the necropolis. He shook his head wildly.

"Who's the other Todt Team member? How many are there?"

Maldonado moaned.

"Tell me," I said, raising the blade toward his right eye.

"I do not know, *señor*. I swear. I swear to you. I do not know. I swear. I was to wait for you... Becker said that you would come alone tonight... I was to wait ten minutes more to be sure and then to kill you.... If anyone discovered us, I was to say that you were shot while resisting arrest. If no one heard us, I was to bring the body to a place on the coast tomorrow afternoon..."

"What place?"

"Just a place far to the east. Nuevitas."

Nuevitas was below the *Archipiélago de Camagüey*, where Hemingway was waiting at Cayo Confites.

"Who ordered this?"

"Becker."

"In person?"

"No, no... Please, not so hard... the blade is cutting the corner of my eye..."

"In person?"

"No!" said Maldonado. "A phone call. Long distance. Very long distance."

"From inside Cuba?"

"I do not know, *señor*. I swear to you."

"Is Delgado part of this?"

"Who is... Delgado?" panted Maldonado, obviously looking for some opening just as I had been a minute before. His hands were still at his side. I knelt more heavily on his throat and laid the blade on the inside of his eye hard enough to draw more blood.

"If you move a finger," I said, "I'll pop this eye out like a grape on the end of my knife."

Maldonado nodded ever so slightly and pressed his hands hard against the rooftop.

I described Delgado in one sentence.

Maldonado nodded again. "I met with the man. It was to arrange payments of money."

"To you?"

"Yes... and to the Cuban National Police."

"Why?"

The lieutenant shook his head gingerly. "We are providing... liaison. Security."

"For whom? For what reason?"

"For the *gringos* and the Germans to meet secretly."

"What *gringos*? Which Germans? Becker?"

"And others. I do not know who or why. I swear to God... No, no, *señor*!"

I realized that this was going nowhere. "When is Hemingway supposed to be killed?" I said. The rain dripped from my nose and chin onto Maldonado's upturned face.

"I do not know—" began the lieutenant, and then he screamed as I knelt with all of my weight on his chest. "Today!" he screamed, his hands coming up to claw at me. "Sometime today... Saturday!"

I got off the man and walked over to pick up his Colt and my flashlight, allowing my back to be turned toward him for two seconds while I watched for movement out of the corner of my eye.

He moved all right, but not for a boot gun or switchblade. Maldonado leaped to his feet, jumped to the corner of the roof, and grabbed my rope to swing himself over the wall even as I dropped to one knee and aimed the .357.

He had forgotten about his broken wrist. He screamed once as he lost his grip and again the instant before he hit something solid down below. I walked to the parapet and looked down. Maldonado had fallen only about twenty-five feet, but his upper body had landed on a raised marble slab while his legs had struck a large urn. At least one leg was twisted at a terrible angle.

I walked around to the back of the dome, found Maldonado's .30-06 right next to an open door in the wall there, and took it with me as I went down a narrow staircase into the dark interior of the mausoleum. I used the flashlight to find the door on the south side. The metal gate screeched loudly as I stepped outside. The moonlight had partially returned even though it was still raining. Maldonado was gone.

I found him crawling down the narrow pedestrian walkway

around the north side of the mausoleum. He was using his elbows and left knee to leverage himself along. His right hand was useless, and it looked as if his right leg had suffered a compound fracture. *Something* sharp and white had punctured the dark fabric of his trousers and was protruding above the knee. When he heard me coming up behind him, he rolled onto his back with a groan and fumbled in his belt, coming out with a small pistol that gleamed in the rain. A .25-caliber Berretta.

I took the little gun away from him and snapped the .357 out of its holster, standing four feet away from him as I aimed it at his skull. I raised my left hand to protect my face from skull fragments and splatter. Maldonado did not raise his hand or flinch or curl away, but I could see all of his teeth as he clenched his jaws waiting for the bullet.

"Shit," I said softly. I stepped forward and swung the barrel in a vicious arc that knocked the policeman's head around on the cold stone. I checked his pulse. Soft and rapid, but there. Then I grabbed him by the collar and dragged him back into the mausoleum, laying him on the floor between two raised sarcophagi. There was a large brass key in his jacket pocket. Both the door and the iron gate of the tomb locked from the outside, of course, and I locked them both and tossed the key far out into the statuary before leaving the cemetery at a painful jog.

I checked my watch when I got back to Hemingway's Lincoln: 3:28 A.M. Christ, time sure crawled when you were having fun.

I BROKE EVERY CITY and national speed limit in my wild ride to Cojímar. It was still raining—the moon had disappeared again—and the roads were slick and dangerous. At least the traffic was nonexistent. I imagined my dialogue with a Cuban policeman if I was stopped for speeding with my .357 on my belt, a Cuban National Policeman's Colt .44 and Remington rifle in my back seat, and blood on my jacket, coat and ear. *Hell,* I finally decided, *I'll pass him ten dollars American and drive on. This is Cuba, after all.*

The departure at Cojímar seven hours earlier, just after sunset, had been the exact opposite of our tumultuous farewell a week earlier. No one was around except for a few disinterested fisherman. Hemingway had chosen Wolfer, Don Saxon, Fuentes, Sinsky, Roberto Herrera, and the boys to go with him. Patchi Ibarlucia had wanted to go, but he was playing in a jai alai tournament. Everyone—even the boys—seemed subdued and serious about this evening departure.

"What do you do if you need me and can't radio me?" said Hemingway as I handed him the stern line. "Or if I radio Cojímar or Guantánamo that I've found something and need you to get there?"

I pointed across the harbor to where Shevlin's speedboat was tied up. "I'll take the *Lorraine* if we're still allowed to use it."

"You shouldn't be after taking that huge gouge out of the deck," said Hemingway, but tossed the keys.

I had to think a minute before remembering the tiny nick in the mahogany when I had dropped Maria's rifle.

"It's still topped off," said the writer, "and we've put two new auxiliary drums on her. If you need to use her, be careful. Tom's a millionaire, but he can be cheap at times. I doubt if he has insurance."

I nodded. Then we decided that Hemingway should keep the courier pouch. I handed it over as Fuentes pushed the bow away from the dock.

"Good luck, Joe," said the writer, leaning across the gap to shake my hand.

I PULLED INTO THE COJÍMAR DOCKS a little before 4:00 A.M. There were lights on a few of the boats as fishermen prepared to get under way. The *Lorraine* was not at her berth.

I leaned over the steering wheel and rubbed my aching forehead. *What did you expect, Joe? Columbia's been a step ahead of you through all of this. He probably stole the boat while you were heading to the cemetery for your rendezvous.*

Which means that he doesn't have that much of a head start.

I looked around the harbor. There were no other speedboats there in Cojímar, only slow fishing boats, dinghies, skiffs, a couple of leaky turtle boats, a few rowboats, two dugout canoes, and one forty-six-foot yacht that had limped into port from Bimini a week earlier with engine problems and a petulant owner from California.

The Lorraine*'s fast. It'll beat the* Pilar *to wherever Columbia wants to lay in wait. I'll need a fast boat just to get down there by noon.*

Down where? Nuevitas? I decided to answer that question after I found a fast boat.

I drove back into the city as fast as I had raced through it half an hour before. There were a few good boats tied up at the city piers, and I might be able to hotwire some of them, but the owners of nice boats usually foresaw that eventuality and precluded it by keeping one or more vital engine parts with them when they left the dock area—the equivalent of lifting one's own distributor cap when parking in a rough neighborhood.

But there was one beautiful boat not tied up at the docks. The *Southern Cross* was anchored far out in the harbor, all set except for final provisions for its long trip through the canal and down the west coast of South America. It was scheduled to leave on Monday morning, according to the Crook Factory's most recent reports on Friday afternoon. They had been delayed one day because their new radioman had gone missing and could not be found in the usual bars and whorehouses. They were interviewing Cubans and Americans this time, according to our reports. The yacht obviously had a problem keeping its radio personnel. Hemingway and I had discussed it and decided that the only German agent aboard had probably left the country, much as Schlegel and Becker had before him.

I parked at the city pier, clambered over the chain-link fence, found a rowboat to my liking, tossed my various bundles in it, and began rowing across the harbor toward the huge yacht. Even at night it was white and beautiful, with spotlights fore and aft illuminating its sleek sides and approaches. I noticed that the rowboat was leaking, so I set my duffel and the Remington up on the thwarts and tossed the plaid blanket from the Lincoln across them. I sang loudly in Spanish as I rowed.

Hijacking the *Southern Cross* might not be completely practical, given its crew of almost a hundred and sixteen able-bodied seamen and officers, its passenger list of more than thirty scientists, and its reported possession of heavy machine guns and many rifles. But hijacking the *Southern Cross* was not exactly what I had in mind.

I had to sing especially loudly to wake the dozing guards in the Chris-Craft speedboat floating at anchor between the yacht and the shore. The two men in the guard boat were stretched out—one across the bench in the forward cockpit, one across the bench in the stern cockpit—and both were snoring loudly enough for me to hear them over my own drunken singing. I was within thirty feet of them before the one in the front cockpit snapped awake and turned a searchlight on me.

"Hey, *amigos*, do not do that!" I called in slurred Cuban Spanish. "It hurts my eyes." I continued rowing sloppily.

"Turn around," said the first guard, in front, using terrible Spanish in a *Norteamericano* accent. "This is a restricted area." He sounded sleepy. His partner was awake now, knuckling his eyes and squinting at me. They both saw a lone man in a rowboat. The man was stubble-cheeked under a hat pulled low, and his suit was wrinkled and stained. He had a bloody ear. He was obviously drunk. His boat was leaking.

"Restricted area?" I called in amazement. "This is Havana Harbor... the harbor of the capital of my nation and my people. How can it be restricted? I must get to my cousin's fishing boat before he leaves without me." I kept flailing at the oars, moving closer to the speedboat but in a crablike fashion.

The guard shook his head. "Stand off," he called. "Stay at least two hundred yards from the big white boat. Your cousin's fishing boat is not out here..."

I nodded, still shielding my eyes from their spotlight. The few stars that had peeked out between storm clouds were gone and the sky was paling despite the continued drizzle. "Where did you say my cousin's boat was?" I called, slipping against the oarlocks and almost falling onto the forward thwart. Both guards had Thompson submachine guns slung around their necks, but neither had shifted his weapon into a position where he could get to it quickly.

"Goddamn it!" called the man in the stern, reaching for a gaff to hold me off as the rowboat bobbed toward their beautiful twenty-two-foot speedboat.

"Do not move," I said in English, swinging the Magnum up and aiming it carefully. "Turn that fucking light off."

The guard in front switched off the light. In the sudden dimness I could see both of them readying themselves for some action.

"You'll both be dead before you can cock the bolt," I said, clicking back the hammer on the .357 and swinging the muzzle easily from one target to the next. The rowboat bumped against their speedboat. "You, in front, lean on the windshield. Both hands. That's right. You... lean over the stern. A little farther over. All right."

I tossed my gear over and then jumped into the small aft cockpit. The man in the stern made a foolish move and I clubbed him down as he turned. The guard leaning against the windshield looked over his shoulder. "I won't use just the barrel if you move," I said softly.

He shook his head.

I took their submachine guns and set them on the stern cushions and then held the Magnum steady as the conscious guard followed my orders and dragged his buddy over the gunwale and into the rowboat. The other man moaned.

I pushed them off with the gaff and pulled up the small anchor with my left hand, holding the pistol on the more conscious of the two as I did so.

The man was wearing a tight sweater that showed a bodybuilder's physique. He was obviously trying to save face, ransacking his memory for some line from the movies that would serve to show that he was unafraid. "You'll never get away with this," he said.

I laughed, started the engine, checked the fuel gauge—three-quarters full—and said, "I already have." Then I fired twice into the little rowboat.

Both men flinched away. The hollow-nosed .357 slugs tore impressive holes in the rotten wood of the rowboat's hull.

This speedboat was beautiful and expensive—a twin-engine, twenty-two-foot, barrel-topped Chris-Craft with its forward cockpit partitioned only by the mahogany trim behind the forward bench. The small aft cockpit was set behind six feet of mahogany-topped, chrome-railed engine compartment. I had checked on the boat the first time Hemingway and I had seen it on patrol. It was newly built—1938 or 1939—and sported twin six-cylinder 131-horsepower Chris-Craft Hercules engines, one a standard KBL and the other a KBO—the O for "opposite rotation." The props turned to the outside, the port to the left and the starboard to the right, providing high speed and negating each other's rotational torque. It made the boat amazingly maneuverable at speed, able to turn around in its own length.

"You can swim if you want to," I called over the rumble of the twin engines, "but you probably know that sharks like to come into the harbor before dawn to feed on the fish around the city sewage outlets. And the yacht might not get a ladder down in time. If I were you, I'd row hard for the docks."

I opened the throttle and headed for the harbor entrance. I only glanced back once before reaching the breakwater. It was raining hard again, but I could see lights coming on amidships on the *Southern Cross*. The rowboat was heading toward the pier with the bodybuilder guard rowing like hell while the other man bailed with his bare hands.

28

BETWEEN THE WORSENING STORM and the dropping fuel gauge needle, I was not sure that I would reach even Cayo Confites. I kept the rpm as high as I could without risking running out of fuel halfway there or tearing the hull out on the high waves that were pounding the speedboat. A second storm front had come in from the northeast, and I was soaked to the skin twenty minutes out from Havana Harbor. For most of the ride, I had to stand behind the wheel, bracing myself with one hand gripping the windshield while I peered ahead through the spray and rain, leaving my own tail of precipitation whipping off me as I roared south and east.

By that time the entire Cuban Coast Guard must have been alerted about the daring bandit who had made off with the friendly scientific Americans' Chris-Craft in the middle of Havana Harbor. The Cuban Coast Guard was known for machine-gunning unarmed European Jewish refugees trying to sneak ashore at night; they would dearly love to turn their huge .50-caliber weapons on a certified bandit.

About ten A.M. I spotted two Coast Guard boats—each gray and white and about thirty feet long—heading west to cut me off. I turned north and lost them in a heavy squall that almost capsized the speedboat. More fuel and time lost. As soon as I could, I turned southeast again and opened the throttles. The heavy pounding made all of my many bruises ache worse and gave me the grandmother of all headaches.

I raised Cayo Confites about 1:45 P.M. The fuel gauge had

been on empty for the last ten nautical miles and there was no reserve tank. I swung around to approach the little harbor and was elated for a minute when there was no sign of the *Pilar.* Then I saw the tents and the soggy campfire ring and the men milling around near the guard shack and my heart sank.

The engines sputtered and died as I came through the opening in the reef. The Cuban army lieutenant and his men had turned out with bolt-action rifles left over from the Spanish-American War, and Guest, Herrera, and Fuentes had come down to the beach with their *niños* before someone used their binoculars.

"It's Lucas," yelled Winston Guest, waving for the Cubans to lower their rifles. As I dug out an oar and laboriously paddled in through the lagoon—only the heavy storm surf allowed me to keep the heavy boat moving—Sinsky, Saxon, and the two boys came out of the tents and ran down to join the others.

"Where's Papa?" yelled Patrick.

"What happened to the *Lorraine*?" shouted Guest as he waded out to grab the bow of the Chris-Craft and help me pull it up on the gravel shingle of the key. "Where's Ernest?"

I jumped out and waded ashore as they made the speedboat secure. It was still drizzling, and I was soaked with seawater and shaking with cold. After the hours of pounding, my legs did not want to hold me upright. When I tried to talk, all I got out was the chatter of my teeth.

Sinsky brought a blanket from the tent and Fuentes brought a steaming cup of coffee. The Cuban soldiers and *Pilar* crew gathered around.

"What happened, Lucas?" said little Gregory. "Where's Papa?"

"What do you mean?" I managed to say. "Why should I know?"

There was a babble of noise. Saxon went up to the tent and came back with a crumpled sheet of paper. I recognized a page from the radio log.

"This came in clear in Morse on the marine band about ten-thirty this morning," said the Marine.

HEMINGWAY—NECESSARY THAT WE MEET IN THE BAY NEAR WHERE WE BURIED THE EUROPEAN ARTIFACTS. I HAVE FIGURED THINGS OUT. BRING THE DOCUMENTS. EVERYTHING WILL BE OK. BOYS SAFE NOW. COME ALONE. I WILL BE IN LORRAINE—LUCAS

"You didn't send it," said Guest. It was not a question.

I shook my head and sat on a camp stool. *Columbia is always one step ahead.* Now he would get both Hemingway *and* the courier documents. "When did he leave?" I said.

"About fifteen minutes after the message arrived," said Sinsky.

I looked at them. I said nothing, but my gaze said *And you let him go alone?* and they must have heard it. Herrera said, "He said that you two had arranged a meeting and that he had to go alone."

Winston Guest said, "Shit, oh shit, shit, oh shit." He sat on the sand. I thought that the big man was going to cry.

"Where's Papa?" said Gregory. No one answered.

I stood up and dropped the blanket. "Gregorio," I said, "would you please get me a thermos of coffee and some sandwiches? And the best binoculars you have, please. Wolfer, Sinsky, Roberto, I'll need your help refueling the speedboat. Lieutenant, do I have your permission to fill the tanks and take at least one of the extra drums?"

"Certainly."

"Patrick," I said. "Gregory. Would you run up to the tents and get any extra clips of ammo for the *niños* that your Papa left behind? And two of the grenades in that green ammo box? Be careful carrying them down...the pins should stay on. Thank you."

"We're going with you," said Winston Guest in a tone that would brook no argument.

"No," I said in an answering tone that ended the discussion. "You're not."

IT WAS STILL raining when I came in sight of the broken light at Point Roma. I had taken time to field-strip and oil the Remington while the others were fueling the speedboat. Sinsky had taken the two salt-soaked Thompsons out of the boat and handed me his—freshly oiled with a full clip. The boys had brought down a waterproof bag with six extra clips and two grenades; Fuentes brought down the food, coffee, and binoculars in another waterproof rubber duffel.

As we lashed the extra fuel drum in place in the aft cockpit, the Cuban lieutenant approached. "*Señor* Lucas," he said, his voice apologetic, "we have just received notice on the radio that a boat matching this description has been stolen at gunpoint. We are ordered to arrest or shoot the bandit if we sight him."

I nodded and looked the short lieutenant in the eye. "Have you sighted him, Lieutenant?"

The Cuban sighed and opened his hands. "Unfortunately, no, *Señor* Lucas. But I will have my men keep a close watch through the rest of the day and night."

"That is wise, Lieutenant. I thank you."

"For the gasoline, *señor*? It was brought here for *Señor* Hemingway's use."

"I thank you for everything," I said, and held out my hand. The lieutenant shook it firmly.

"Go with God, *Señor* Lucas."

I THOUGHT ABOUT MY DECISION to leave the other men behind as I headed south toward the mainland. Perhaps I was grandstanding... Saxon, Fuentes, and Sinsky certainly knew how to fight, while Herrera and Guest would give their lives in an instant for "Ernesto." Six armed men had to be better than one when going into harm's way.

Only I knew that this was not true. Six of us in the speedboat would get in one another's way, and the thought of six of us firing submachine guns at once made me wince. It would be chaos. No one on the *Pilar*'s crew except Saxon had the discipline and experience of having been under fire to be reliable in an emergency, and not even Saxon was ready to take orders from me. So they had grumbled and glowered, but they had let me go on alone when I insisted that Papa's life would be in greater danger if we all went barreling after him. I suggested that he would probably show up while I was out hunting for him, so it would be better if they remained on the key where he had told them to stay.

"Please tell Papa to come back, Lucas," said Patrick, looking me dead in the eye with a man's earnestness and intent.

I nodded and touched the boy's shoulder with no condescension, as one man would touch another's at a serious moment.

There was no sign of the *Pilar* in the Ensenada Herradura or north or south along the coast. Hemingway's boat was too large to conceal in the mangrove swamp as we had hidden the *Lorraine*, but I laid off the reef and put the glasses on every possible hiding place anyway. No boat.

The rain had slacked off as I raised the mainland, but the surf was crashing across the reef north to Point Brava and all along the rocks below Point Jesus and east. It was a miserable day. The high waves had obliterated the sandy spit and were chewing at the low cliff by the beacon where the German boys were buried. As I came in through the heavy surf and fought the wheel to make the inlet opening, the sudden stench of decay washed across me despite the trailing wind and the rain-sweetened air. The crabs or something larger had done their digging.

Then I was through the stench and the inlet and swinging hard to starboard to stay within the narrow channel. The railroad tracks and abandoned shack and sagging piers became visible to my right. The *Doce Apostoles* came into sight on my left. I throttled back, kicking up mud, and loosened the Thompson on its strap, my hand on the clip and trigger guard. At Castle Morro above Havana Harbor, the Twelve Apostles were cannon; here they were just big rocks and some abandoned shacks. But I felt like the boulders and black windows were gunsights zeroing in on me as I rumbled past.

There was the *Pilar*—anchored just west of the little bay island called Cayo Largo on the Nokomis charts—about sixty yards out from the western shoreline, just opposite the rocky hill that separated the abandoned rail line buildings and stack from the southeastern bend in the bay where the old mill sat amidst vines and cane fields.

I let the engines idle while I studied Hemingway's boat through the binoculars. Nothing moved. My skin crawled as it waited for the impact of a rifle bullet from the shore, but nothing came. The *Pilar* was held in place only by a bow anchor, and as the green-and-black boat moved slightly with the wind and current, I saw that the *Lorraine* was tied up behind it. Shevlin's speedboat also appeared to be empty.

I unhinged the windshield and dropped it flat onto the bow of the *Southern Cross* speedboat. Then I dropped to one knee on the front bench, lifted the Remington out of the waterproof gun case Guest had given me, actioned a round into the chamber, strung the sling around my left arm, and set the six-power scope on both boats. The magnification was not as good as the binoculars, but I could still see that there was no movement.

Strange. If Columbia was aboard the Lorraine *when Hemingway arrived, the agent either swam ashore, had another boat pick him up, or is still aboard the* Pilar.

Besides canvas curtains on the port side of the cockpit beneath the flying bridge and smaller glass windows next to that canvas, *Pilar* had a glass windshield that propped open at the front of the cockpit, three wooden rectangular porthole covers on the side of the raised forward compartment—all three of which were closed—a hatch opening halfway forward atop the main compartment, and a sliding hatch at the forward end of the compartment just where the last eight feet or so of bow began. I scoped all of that as the *Pilar* moved slowly at anchor. The gunwales were low toward the stern, but still too high for me to see if anyone was lying on the deck. As both boats pivoted toward me, the *Pilar* rotating to the current around its bow anchor and the *Lorraine* tied to a cleat on the starboard side of Hemingway's boat, near the stern—I could see that no one was in the cockpit behind the wheel of the *Pilar* and that all of the seats of Shevlin's speedboat were empty.

Minutes passed. Mosquitoes buzzed around my head, landed on my face and neck, and began to drink. I held the rifleman's pose, the scope bobbing slightly with the boat but steady enough to squeeze off a shot if and when I had to. I was wearing the street shoes, torn trousers, and blue shirt I had put on the night before. The jacket was on the rear bench of the forward cockpit. The .357 was in the quick-release holster on my belt and the Thompson was slung around my back. More minutes passed. I turned my head only to check the shoreline to the left and right, and occasionally to glance quickly behind me. No movement. No other boats.

I began to feel certain that Hemingway was wounded, lying on the floor of his boat and bleeding to death while I knelt there and watched through my scope, letting vital moments pass, allowing him to die. *Do something!* my imagination demanded. *Anything.*

I shut off my imagination and held my firing stance, remembering to blink and breathe normally, moving only when I had to restart circulation in my legs and arms. I could see my watch turned backward on my wrist above the taut rifle sling. Ten minutes passed. Eighteen. Twenty-three. It began to rain again. Some of the mosquitoes left. Others arrived.

Suddenly a figure bolted from the cockpit of the *Pilar* and leaped into the *Lorraine.* As he untied the speedboat, I confirmed that it was not Hemingway—too thin, too short, clean shaven. He was hatless, wearing tan slacks and a gray shirt and was carrying the German courier pouch slung over his shoulder. He had a Schmeisser machine pistol in his right hand. I fired just as he started the *Lorraine*'s engine. His left arm jerked and the windshield in front of him exploded, but I could not tell if it had been a clean hit because of the movement of all three boats and the sudden downpour.

The *Lorraine* roared ahead and disappeared behind Cayo Largo. I stood in my speedboat, bracing myself against the hinge of the flattened windshield, watching the *Pilar* for any further movement, and waiting for the *Lorraine* to come around the east side of the little island. Columbia—if that is who it was—had nowhere to go on that side of the bay: the water was less than a foot deep for most of that wide, muddy expanse of shallows.

Ten seconds later the *Lorraine* came roaring around the island, cutting back toward the deep channel behind it as it sliced through silty banks and sludge. The man was standing at the wheel, steering with the left arm I thought I had hit, and firing the machine pistol at me with his right hand. I saw the puffs of smoke and felt the *Southern Cross* speedboat vibrate softly to several impacts, but I had no time to pay attention to that as I tried to stand firmly on the bobbing boat and fire. I levered in another round, fired again, actioned in another round, fired again.

My first shot blew apart the spotlight next to the man's arm. The second shot missed. The third shot knocked the man off his feet onto the deck behind the seat.

The *Lorraine* roared by, throttle still wide open. I slammed the Chris-Craft's throttles forward and swung her in a tight arc, still watching the *Pilar* for movement. It would be a perfect ambush for a rifleman there to take me out now. Nothing.

I could see the man in the gray shirt flopping around on the deck like some great, gray fish as the *Lorraine* continued to roar straight down the channel between the semisubmerged marker sticks. He was wounded but trying to get to his feet, trying to get to the wheel. I pushed both throttles full forward and fishtailed from side to side, trying to see over the raised bow of my own boat and taking some evasive action as he found his machine pistol and began firing again. A bullet smashed the right windshield. Another tore leather and stuffing out of the seat cushion next to me. Two or three more thunked into the fifty-gallon gasoline drum behind me, and I immediately smelled the stink of gasoline as it poured into the rear cockpit. Nothing exploded or ignited.

The *Lorraine* seemed to know her own way out of the harbor and was making straight for the inlet at thirty-five knots. But I was gaining on her, sluicing mud as I cut it too close with the banks to my right—if I struck a real sandbar there at this speed I would go flying out over the windshield—and I dropped the Remington, raised the Thompson, and emptied the entire clip into the *Lorraine*'s cockpit as I came up on her starboard quarter.

The man twitched and danced like a poorly handled marionette and jacknifed backward against the port gunwale. I pulled out the empty clip, slammed in another, and began firing again, but stopped when I saw the left shoreline rushing at both boats.

I threw the starboard prop into reverse and cut hard to

starboard, throwing a curtain of water all the way to the narrow beach as I just missed the mud banks and shoreline. The *Lorraine* roared ahead as if determined to cut across the spit of rocky land below the ridge in its quest for open sea.

My own boat slammed across two mud banks and almost threw me out before I jammed both throttles forward again and regained the narrow channel, my stern toward the inlet. I killed the throttles and looked back just in time to watch the *Lorraine* tear herself apart on the rocks and mud banks.

The top of Shevlin's beautiful boat came apart and flew through the air in a shower of glass, chrome, mahogany, and wire as the hull—splintered and shattered but still driven ahead by the screaming engine—roared on through shallows, rocks, vines, and beach before tearing itself into ten thousand pieces on the hillside where we had buried the Germans. Flames erupted here and there, but there was no central explosion. The air smelled of gasoline.

The man's body had been thrown sixty feet and had landed face down in the water near the center channel. He floated with his arms and legs spread-eagled, blood from his wounds mingling with the billows of mud.

I turned the Chris-Craft around and advanced very slowly, the submachine gun raised and ready. Three minutes and he did not move except to bob up and down on the *Lorraine*'s dying wake. The courier pouch had been thrown free, and I could see documents in the treetops, the shallows, and sinking in the main channel. *Good riddance.* When my boat floated close enough, I could see the white of the man's spine peeking through the shreds of shirt and torn flesh.

I laid the submachine gun on the seat, got the gaff, and struggled to hook him to turn him over.

There were no serious wounds on the face, only an open-jawed expression of absolute surprise. So must it be for most of us. I reached down, grabbed him by the hair and shirt, and dragged him aboard. Water and blood ran across the polished deck of the speedboat and gurgled in the scuppers.

I did not know this man. He had a thin, pale face; some stubble; short, wiry hair; and bright blue eyes that were already clouding over. The bullets from the Thompson had caught him across the chest and groin. The inside of his left arm showed the grazing path of the first Remington slug and a larger entrance wound in his side showed where the second had knocked him down. Some impact in the crash had almost torn off his right arm.

I fished in his pockets. Amazingly, a billfold had stayed in his jacket pocket. A small, sodden card with no photograph identified him as SS Major Kurt Friedrich Daufeldt, officer of the Reich Security Administration, Sicherheitsdienst, AMT VI. A separate, typed note under the twin SS lightning strokes said simply that SS Major Daufeldt was carrying out sensitive and important work for the Third Reich and should be offered every possible courtesy and cooperation by any member of the armed forces or security apparatus or intelligence wing of the Third Reich. Heil Hitler! The note was signed by Reichsführer Heinrich Himmler, SS Lieutenant General and Chief der Sicherheitspolizei Reinhard Heydrich, and SS Major Walter Schellenberg, chief of RSHA VI.

Well, that's it, then. I put the ID and soggy letter in my pocket and looked at the stranger's dead face. "Hello, Columbia," I said. I doubted if there would be too many agents in Cuba with this rank and such a letter from the three highest men in the SD. One was now dead in Czechoslovakia, but the letter was still almost unique in the power it conferred on this corpse. Whatever Operation Raven had been, it had been important and approved at the highest possible levels in the Nazi hierarchy. I doubted if he had carried this card and letter around with him during his undercover work here, but perhaps he had been planning to leave this evening after dealing with Hemingway and wanted his bona fides with him. "Good-bye, Columbia," I said. "Herr Major Daufeldt. *Auf wiedersehn.*"

The corpse said nothing. The rain had let up, but a light drizzle continued to moisten the upturned face.

I shut off the engine and checked the damage to the Chris-Craft. There were three holes in the fifty-gallon drum, and gasoline had spilled everywhere. This was not good. It had been pure luck that the pooled fuel and fumes had not ignited—either by the bullets' impact or the hot engine just forward of the aft cockpit. The speedboat had one small console and I rummaged in it, coming up with some rags, a small bucket, and a roll of duct tape. I used the tape to seal the holes as best I could, rolling the drum around until the perforations were pointed skyward and then re-securing the heavy thing, and then mopping up the gas with the rags and throwing them overboard. I stripped the shirt off the corpse and used it as best I could to get the rest of the spilled fuel swabbed up, and dipped the bucket into the sea to wash down the cushions and deck until the reek of gasoline lessened. I checked the bilge, decided that not much of the gas had gotten in there and that the fumes were neglible, and then started up the small bilge pump to empty it. The speedboat did not explode.

Hurry! my subconscious kept shouting. *Hemingway may be hurt or dying.* Well, it would not help him if I blew up the boat only a few hundred yards away.

When the bilge was empty and all gasoline fumes vented, I crawled forward and dragged Major Daufeldt's corpse across the engine compartment and wedged him onto the deck of the aft cockpit beneath the gas drum. Then I finished mopping up the blood still soaking the deck of the forward cockpit.

Once under way again, I studied the *Pilar* through the twelve-power binoculars. Still no movement. But there had been none before Major Daufeldt had made his break for it.

I swung around to the west, coming up slowly on the stern of Hemingway's boat, the .357 in my hand now as I carefully avoided mud banks and sandbars. I could see into the cockpit and into the dark entrance to the forward compartments from this angle. Nothing. When I was twenty feet away, by standing upright, I could see the deck of the compartment almost to the stern bench.

A body lay face down there. I saw the shorts, the sprawled legs, the massive upper body under a sweatshirt with the sleeves cut off, the bull neck, the short hair, the beard. It was Hemingway. The back and side of his head were bloody, and the thick fluid stirred sluggishly as the *Pilar* yawed back and forth with the waves. He did not appear to be breathing.

"Aw, goddamn it," I whispered to no one as the Chris-Craft

crept up to the *Pilar*'s starboard quarter and bumped against the bigger boat. No movement or noise from the forward compartment. The side canvas was rigged and the windshield was lowered on the left side above the wheel. Hemingway might have been under way when the shot came, but *someone* had dropped the bow anchor.

Columbia... Daufeldt... shot the writer from the shore, near the pier, then took the *Lorraine* out here and dropped the *Pilar*'s anchor.

Maybe. I tied on to the aft starboard cleat, just where the *Lorraine* had been tied up, waited for the waves to match, and hopped aboard, the Magnum in my right hand and a grenade in my left, watching the stairs to the forward compartment and the hatch visible along the upper superstructure beyond the dropped windshield. Nothing. Only the sound of the waves.

I risked a glance at Hemingway. There was a lot of blood and at least one section of scalp lifted away from the bone above and behind his ear. Because of the motion of the boat, I could not tell if he was breathing. The swollen ear I had given him was covered with blood from the head wound. I felt another pang of regret for that fight.

I turned back toward the cockpit and that dark entrance just as a pistol came up and out of the forward hatch. I raised the .357, but too late. There were three short, sharp slaps and I felt two solid impacts on my upper right chest, then—as I was spinning, still trying to bring the .357 to bear—another cracking sound and a more terrible blow exploding in my left side.

I dropped the pistol and grenade and fell into the stern cushions, then over the stern board that Hemingway had modified lower than usual to facilitate landing big fish. I heard a distant splash as I hit the water. I do not know if the darkness that swallowed me was unconsciousness or just the black water as I sank toward the muddy bottom.

29

DAMN YOU, Lucas, don't die on me. Don't die on me yet."

Someone was slapping my face. Hard. The pain of the slaps was nothing compared to the hot pokers searing my chest and right arm and totally insignificant compared to the blowtorch burning away my left rib cage, but it kept me from sliding back into the comfortable darkness of drowning and death. I forced myself the rest of the way back and opened my eyes.

Delgado smiled and sat back. "Good," he said. "You can die in a minute. I have a couple of questions I want answered first." He was sitting on a backless canvas camp chair he had set up in the center of the *Pilar*'s cockpit. Hemingway's body still lay on the deck to our left, his face in the pool of blood. The pool was broader now. Delgado was wearing dirty white trousers, deck shoes, and his undershirt. His arms and shoulders were tanned and heavily muscled. He was holding Hemingway's .22 target pistol and tapping the long barrel against his knee as he watched me raise my head and bring my eyes into focus.

I lurched toward him, ready to grab him before he could bring the pistol up. My head jerked and my vision dimmed as the pain overwhelmed me. My arms were pinned behind me, and I could feel metal cutting at my wrists. Although my thoughts came slowly, as if moving through a thick sludge, I realized I was sitting on the bench along the starboard side of the cockpit and that Delgado had handcuffed me to the short length of ornamental brass rail below the gunwale there. Water poured from my clothes and squished from my shoes. I watched the water running off me with only a dulled interest, not leavened when I realized that much of the water was red. I was bleeding very heavily. Delgado must have fished me out and slapped me awake almost immediately after shooting me.

He slapped me again now, using the barrel of the .22 against my temples. I tried to focus my eyes and to pay attention to what he was saying.

"...are the documents, Lucas? The Abwehr documents? Tell me where they are and I'll let you go back to sleep. I promise."

I tried to speak. I must have hit my face going overboard, because my lips were cut and swollen. Or perhaps Delgado had been slapping me for longer than I thought. I tried again.

"...in...the...bay," I said. "Daufeldt...had them."

Delgado chuckled and pulled the SS major's soggy ID and Himmler's letter out of his trouser pocket. "No, he didn't, Lucas. And I'm Daufeldt. And one reason I pulled you out is that I needed these tonight. Now I need the Abwehr documents. Where did Hemingway hide them?"

I shook my head. That made the pain rise in my right arm and left side and brought the dancing black spots back. "In the... bay and...on the...beach. When...*Lorraine*...hit."

Delgado slapped me with his hand. "*Concentrate*, Lucas. Hemingway had the courier pouch or I never would have killed him. But the papers were from some bullshit manuscript, not the Abwehr documents. Kruger didn't have the real documents when he made a run for it. Where are they?"

I used all of my energy to raise my head and look at Delgado. "Who...is Kruger?"

Delgado's lips curled. "Sergeant Kruger. My dear, loyal SS radioman from the *Southern Cross*. You just fished him out of the bay, Lucas. Now, where did Hemingway hide the fucking documents?"

I shook my head and then let it drop. "Major...Daufeldt. Papers."

Delgado grabbed me by the hair and pulled my face up as he leaned closer. "Listen, Lucas. *I* am Major Daufeldt. We needed a diversion when you arrived. I convinced poor, cowardly Sergeant Kruger to take the Schmeisser and make a run for it in the *Lorraine*. I assumed you would kill him. The papers are *mine*. But where are the documents?"

"Is Hemingway... alive?" I managed.

Delgado glanced casually over his shoulder. There were flies circling around Hemingway's bloody head and the pool of blood that now reached to his shoulders. "I don't know," said Delgado. "I don't care. If he is, he won't be much longer." He looked back at me and smiled. "He had a boating accident. Hit his head when he drove the *Pilar* onto a sandbar. I used the gaff, but it could have been any sharp corner on the boat. I'll wipe the blood and hair off the gaff after I drop him overboard. Then I'll drive this boat onto a sandbar. After his body spends a few hours in the water, they won't be able to tell much about his wound."

I sat up as straight as I could and tried to move my hands in the cuffs. Delgado had clicked the handcuffs so tight that they had shut off all circulation. I could not feel or move my fingers. Or perhaps it was just the bleeding that had done that... shutting off feeling to my hands. The blood had soaked my shirt, trousers, shoes, and the leather bench. I tried to concentrate—not just on Delgado but on my own body. I remembered three impacts: one on my arm, one on my upper right chest or shoulder, the third—and the worst—in my left side. I looked down. Torn, wet shirt, much blood. It told me little. He had used the .22. That gave me hope. But the pain and bleeding and growing weakness were bad signs. One or more of the little slugs might have hit something important.

"Are you listening to me, Lucas?"

I focused my eyes again. "How?" I said.

"What?"

"How did you get Hemingway?"

Delgado sighed. "Is this supposed to be the point in the movie where I tell you everything before you die? Or, better yet, before you escape?"

I felt the cuffs tearing at my wrists and knew that there would be no escape. If I did get my hands free, I was too hurt and weak to do anything with my hands even if the feeling came back. I considered using my legs to grapple with Delgado, but after moving them just inches, I realized that they had almost no strength. I might be able to get them around his middle and squeeze for a few seconds, but I could not keep him in a scissors grip, and all he had to do was take the .22 and shoot me. I decided that I would conserve what little strength I had and wait for an opportunity. *An opportunity to do what, Joe?* The voice in my mind sounded weary and cynical. I looked at Delgado and worked to stay conscious.

"All right," he said. "How about I tell you how I got Hemingway and then you tell me where he might have put the Abwehr documents."

Though he must know that he held all the cards and didn't need to tell me anything, I nodded. Into my hazy consciousness came the idea that Delgado's cockiness might be my only hope. Though he'd made the sarcastic observation about this being the part in the movie where he told me everything, I could tell that, true to most of those movie characters, he was longing to do just that. Perhaps Hemingway's observation that fiction—even movie fiction—was truer than life would hold.

"We let the *Lorraine* drift here near the island," said Delgado, that infuriating half-smile still curling his lips. "Sergeant Kruger was aboard, face down in the cockpit, apparently hurt and unconscious. He was wearing your green shirt then, Lucas."

I must have shown some expression, because Delgado chuckled. "Elsa got it for us."

"Elsa?"

Delgado shook his head in the manner of an adult dealing with a very dull child. "Maria. Never mind. Perhaps later you can tell me how you killed her, but that's not important now. Do you want to hear the rest of your bedtime story?"

I waited.

"So while your writer was calling your name and tying up to the *Lorraine*," said Delgado, "I swam out from the island and came up behind him with the Schmeisser and had him hand over the .22 and that was that." He shook his head again. "But the stupid shit put up a fight. Tried to grab the Schmeisser. I could have shot him or killed him barehanded, of course—that was plan one, having it look like you had killed him—but until Lieutenant Maldonado delivered your body to Nuevitas, we had to make it look like it *could* have been an accident. So while the sergeant grabbed Hemingway, I took the back of the writer's head off with the gaff. You understand, we thought that he had the Abwehr documents in the cockpit with him, because we saw the courier pouch. But it was just some idiot manuscript about two people fucking in France. So I had Kruger watch your pal lie there and bleed while I searched through the boat. And then you arrived, Lucas, charging to the rescue. And I thought it was quite heroic of me to send poor Sergeant Kruger out with my Schmeisser while I waited here for you with nothing but Hemingway's little toy gun. I intended to put three slugs into you just to bring you down so I could get my papers back and find out about the documents, but that last one is probably fatal because you twisted when you were falling. Sorry. End of story. Where are the documents?"

I shook my head. I thought that the wind had come up and was rustling the palms on the nearby island, but I realized that the noise was just a rushing in my ears. "Tell me... more," I said, my voice sounding hollow. "I don't... understand. The documents. Becker. The dead German soldiers. Operation Raven. Why? What's it all about? I don't understand."

Delgado nodded affably. "I'm sure you don't understand, Lucas. It's one of the reasons you were picked. Smart... but not *too* smart. But I'm afraid that we don't have any more time for chatting, and if we did, I still wouldn't tell you shit." He raised the .22 and aimed it at a point between my eyes. "Where are the Abwehr documents?"

"Fuck you," I said. And waited.

Delgado's lips curled up a notch. "Tough guy," he said, and shrugged. "I hate to break it to you, Joey, but I don't really need the Abwehr papers now. There are more where those came from. The other side has already come through with its initial delivery, and now that the pipeline is open, I'll shovel more Abwehr information into it later. They trust us now, after Point Roma. We'll keep them happy."

"Keep who happy?" I said stupidly, thinking, *Just enough strength left in my legs to use them once... now would be a good time, Joe.* But Delgado had slid his canvas chair back a couple of feet and was out of reach.

He shook his head. "Sorry, Lucas. Out of time. So long, kid."

The black circle of the .22 muzzle had claimed almost all of my attention, but I saw the movement out of the corner of my eye as Hemingway got to his knees and then moaned and struggled to get to his feet.

Delgado lowered the .22 and half turned in his chair. "Oh, shit," he said tiredly. He stood then and watched patiently as Hemingway got to his feet and swayed there drunkenly on the bloody deck of his beloved *Pilar*. The writer's face was as white as the solitary cloud that floated in the sky behind him. As Delgado stood watching him rise, I hoped—for the second time—that the man's cockiness would override his immediate instinct to kill.

"Congratulations," said Delgado, taking a step back from the pale apparition. "You're one tough son of a bitch. That blow would have killed most men."

Hemingway staggered and flexed his hands, obviously trying to bring the little tableau of Delgado and me into focus.

He's too far from Delgado, I thought, my heart pounding hard enough now that I was afraid that I would bleed to death that much quicker. My left side felt like it was hemorrhaging much too freely. *He's too far away. And it doesn't matter because Delgado could kill him with his bare hands on Hemingway's best day.*

Delgado sighed. "I guess it's back to plan one. Writer found dead next to the body of the double agent who shot him." He raised the .22 and aimed it at Hemingway's broad chest.

I jacknifed my body back on the cushions, ignoring the raging wave of pain that cut through me, and kicked out as hard as I could, catching Delgado just above the base of his spine. The agent staggered forward and then caught himself from falling, but not before Hemingway grunted and swept his arms around him in a huge bear hug.

"Fuck that." Delgado laughed and freed himself by knocking aside Hemingway's left arm with a flat-handed judo chop to the inside of the bigger man's bicep. Delgado swept the target pistol up under Hemingway's jaw.

The writer grunted again and grabbed Delgado's right arm with both hands, forcing the muzzle of the pistol out and away. Delgado could have used his free left hand to kidney punch or judo chop Hemingway to his knees, but he instantly realized that the writer was forcing the barrel of the pistol his way, so he chose instead to grab his own right wrist with his free hand, adding leverage to keep the muzzle away. The target pistol stayed upright between them, the barrel pointing skyward in the few inches of free space between the men's sweating faces.

I coiled again, fighting away the dizziness, ready to kick out at Delgado if they came closer, but though the two men lurched around the wide cockpit in a terrible and clumsy dance, they did not come close enough.

Delgado obviously had the much greater skill in hand-to-hand combat, but his hands were occupied, he needed both legs to keep his balance, and Hemingway was using all of his great upper-body mass to keep the agent off balance. Hemingway was fighting for his life. Delgado was simply waiting for his chance to fire. The decisive factor was that Delgado had his finger on the trigger while both of Hemingway's hands were wrapped around Delgado's wrist. Wherever the muzzle was pointed, only Delgado would decide when to pull that trigger.

The two big men staggered in circles, bouncing off the canvas-covered side of the bridge, crashing into the wheel, careening into the port gunwale, then lurching into the center of the cockpit again. Hemingway forced the muzzle toward Delgado's face but it made no difference; the agent's finger stayed inside the trigger guard. They lurched again, and now the barrel moved toward Hemingway's face.

Before Delgado could fire, Hemingway tucked his head low on his right shoulder, out of the line of fire, grunted, and charged forward again. The barrel pointed straight up. Both men crashed into the ladder leading to the flying bridge. Delgado moved with lightning speed to change his grip, grabbing the pistol with his left hand to gain greater leverage, forcing the muzzle down toward Hemingway's face again.

The writer butted Delgado in the face and moved his own hands, risking a bullet in the face for the split second it took to change his grip. Now they were lurching together again, shoes squeaking and sliding on the bloody deck, but Hemingway's right hand was clasped over the cylinder of the target pistol now, his forefinger awkwardly jammed under the curve of the trigger guard above Delgado's trigger finger.

Delgado kneed Hemingway in the balls. The writer grunted but hung on, still straining, even while Delgado used the second to move his left hand higher on the barrel, forcing it down until the muzzle was directly under Hemingway's chin. The writer's eyes strained to look down. He could not move the barrel away. Gasping, the half-smile curling higher, Delgado jammed the muzzle into the soft flesh under Hemingway's jaw, thumbed the hammer back, and pulled the trigger.

Hemingway was already sliding his hand the endless two inches along the top of the pistol even before Delgado squeezed the trigger. Now the hammer fell, mashing the last joint of Hemingway's little finger as the writer kept his flesh and fingernail between the hammer and the firing pin.

Delgado ripped flesh off Hemingway's finger as the agent tugged the pistol back and away, freeing it, the two of them spinning and almost toppling together, then righting themselves and crashing into the ladder again. They were six feet away. I could not reach them with another kick. I felt my strength flowing out of me with the blood that soaked the cushions and then my legs went limp.

Delgado had freed the hammer for another shot, but he had inadvertently pulled the barrel toward himself while doing so. Now Hemingway's left hand flew to that barrel, leveraging it over. Dalgado freed his own hand, sitting it higher on the barrel, but the writer's fingers were already locked around it, giving no room. I was reminded of boys choosing up sides for a baseball game by moving their clenched fists higher and higher on the bat until there was no more space for fingers.

I could no longer see the barrel of the .22, only Delgado's straining hand locked over Hemingway's, their right hands lower, Delgado with his finger on the trigger and Hemingway with his finger jammed in over Delgado's.

Hemingway showed all of his teeth. Cords stood out on his bloodied neck. The muzzle moved in under Delgado's chin and was jammed mercilessly upward into the soft flesh there.

Delgado arched his head back faster than I would have

thought possible, but the wooden rung of the ladder to the flying bridge caught him on the back of the skull and kept him from moving it farther. Hemingway forced the muzzle up again, deep into the flesh under Delgado's jaw.

Delgado screamed then—silently—not in fear, but like a paratrooper readying himself to leap out of the door of a transport plane into wind and darkness. Both men continued to strain full force.

Hemingway squeezed Delgado's finger down on the trigger.

Black dots had been dancing in my vision for some time, and now they merged and closed around me for a minute. When I could see again, Hemingway had dropped the pistol and was the only one standing, swaying over Delgado's body where it was slumped against the ladder. With the nasty cut on Hemingway's scalp, it looked as if it was the writer who had been shot in the head, not Delgado. There was no exit wound on the top of Delgado's skull. Judging from the copious bleeding from Delgado's eyes, ears, and nose, as well as the mess under his jaw, it looked as if the *.22* slug had gone up and in through the soft palate and ricocheted around in the confines of the skull.

Hemingway was looking down at the body and then looked at me with an expression I shall never forget. It was not triumph, nor regret, nor shock alone, nor bloodlust—I could only describe that look as the disinterested gaze of a terribly intelligent observer. Hemingway was *recording* this: not only what he saw but the smells, the soft lurchings of the *Pilar*, the gentle afternoon breeze, the sudden cry of gulls from the direction of the inlet, and even his own pain and reactions. Especially his own reactions.

Then Hemingway's gaze focused on me and he stepped closer. The dancing black specks merged again, and I felt myself sliding, as if my bloody wrists had slipped out of the handcuffs and I was free... free to slide down into that painless darkness, free to float away from all this, free to rest at long last.

I came back because of the sharp slaps—again—and the demanding voice, Hemingway's clear tenor this time, saying, "Damn you, Lucas, don't die on me. Don't die on me, son."

I did my best to obey.

30

IN THE END, it was the Herrera brothers who probably saved my life. Roberto Herrera did not have his older brother's medical skills, but he knew enough to keep me alive until we got back to Cojímar, where Dr. José Luis Herrera Sotolongo was waiting with a surgeon friend. And it was also Ernest Hemingway who kept me alive.

I remember fragments of the events after Delgado's death. Hemingway reminded me later that his first instinct was to take the Chris-Craft—it would get us back to Cayo Confites and Cojímar much faster than the *Pilar* could. But after he had dug out the first aid kit and put sulfa and compression bandages on my wounds, I fainted for a few minutes and came to only when he was lifting me to set me into the speedboat.

"No, no," I mumbled, grabbing his arm. "The boat's... stolen."

"I know that," snapped Hemingway. "It's from the *Southern Cross*. That doesn't matter."

"It does," I said. "The Cuban Coast Guard is looking for it. They may shoot first and ask questions later."

Hemingway paused. He knew how trigger-happy the Cuban Coast Guard was. "You're a federal agent," he said at last. "FBI and whatchamacallit, your SIS. You commandeered the boat for police business."

I shook my head. "Not...anymore. Not an agent. Go to jail." I told him about my middle-of-the-night meeting with Lieutenant Maldonado.

Hemingway had laid me back on the cushions and sat down.

He touched his head. He had wrapped long bandages around his head wound, but the white gauze was already soaked with blood. It must have hurt like hell. "Yeah," he said. "That could be a problem if we bring you back to the hospital using the stolen Chris-Craft. The *Southern Cross* people could press charges, and even if Maldonado's dead, his boss—Juanito the Jehovah's Witness—probably knew that he was sent out to kill you."

I shook my head again, bringing on a blizzard of dancing black spots. "No hospital."

Hemingway nodded. "If we take the *Pilar*, we can radio ahead and have Dr. Herrera Sotolongo waiting for us. Or even put in at Nuevitas or one of the other ports and have a doctor ready."

"Didn't Delgado destroy the radio?" I said. I was content to lie absolutely still on the cushions of the starboard bench and watch the clearing sky. All of the clouds had gone now. The storm was past.

"No," said the writer. "I just checked. He must have tried it and found that it wasn't working."

"Broken?" I managed, my thoughts sliding away again. I suddenly remembered that Hemingway had injected me with an army morphine ampule from the medical kit. No wonder I was feeling hazy and lazy.

He started to shake his head, moaned softly, and said, "No. I took out some tubes and hid them. I needed the space."

I squinted at him. Either the wave action here in the bay had grown much stronger or I was getting dizzier. "Space?"

Hemingway held up a sheaf of papers in a manila folder. "The Abwehr documents. Thought I might tuck them away somewhere before coming into Manatí Bay to meet you. Glad I did." He gingerly touched the soaked bandage on his head and looked around. "All right," he said. "We'll take the *Pilar*."

"Photographs," I said. "Pictures. And we have to get rid of the bodies."

"This place is turning into a fucking Nazi cemetery," growled Hemingway.

I dimly remember the writer carrying out the grim task of laying the two bodies out, photographing them from all angles with the Leica, photographing the Chris-Craft, and then setting each of the corpses in a separate cockpit of the speedboat, casting off the speedboat, backing the *Pilar* away, and firing four shots into the gas drum with my .357. The stench of the gasoline brought me closer to consciousness as the rear cockpit of the beautiful speedboat filled with fuel again, and then Hemingway brought the *Pilar* closer, used a match to light a gas-soaked rag that I dimly recognized as my old green shirt, and tossed the burning brand onto the boat.

The stern of the Chris-Craft mushroomed into a blossom of flame that scorched some of the paint on the *Pilar*'s starboard side. Hemingway was up on the flying bridge and now he shielded his face from the heat and pushed both throttles open, getting the *Pilar* up to speed while taking care to stay in the narrow channel leading away from Cayo Largo. I sat up long enough to look back once. That was enough. The entire speedboat was engulfed in flames, as were the seated bodies of Delgado—*Major Daufeldt*, I corrected myself—in the forward cockpit, and Sergeant Kruger in the rear cockpit. We were about two hundred feet away when the main gas tank and the rest of the reserve drum exploded, throwing fragments and burning chunks of mahogany and scorched chrome across the bay. Some of the royal palms on the island caught fire, but they were so damp from the recent rain that the flames soon went out, leaving only blackened fronds to rustle in the wind of the bonfire. A few hot shards landed on the deck of the *Pilar*, but I was too weak to get up to throw them overboard, and Hemingway was too busy piloting from the flying bridge. They continued to smolder until we were through the inlet—which still smelled of German corpses in the sand at the point—and out through the gap in the reefs, cruising west-northwest toward the deep waters of the Gulf.

Hemingway came down the bloody ladder, used the bloody gaff to hook and toss overboard the burning bits on the deck, put out a small fire on the smoldering side canvas with an extinguisher he kept in the galley, and then came back to check on me. The sea was still rough after the storm and I could feel the waves of pain the pounding was causing, but I felt them only distantly because of the miracle of the morphine. I dimly noticed how pale and shaky Hemingway still was, and realized that the scalp wound must be hurting him enough that he could have used some morphine as well. But he couldn't use it—he had to drive us home.

"Lucas," he was saying, touching my good shoulder, "I've radioed Confites that we've had an accident and that they should have the big medical kit ready. Roberto's good at that stuff. He'll know what to do."

I closed my eyes and nodded.

"...these fucking documents," Hemingway was saying. I realized that he must be holding the Abwehr papers. "Do you know what Delgado wanted us to do with them? What was it all about?"

"Dunno," I mumbled. "But... have a theory."

I felt Hemingway waiting there beyond my closed eyelids as the *Pilar* pounded her way west.

"Tell you," I said. "Tell you... if I live."

"Then live," said the writer. "I want to know."

THE SURGERY WAS DONE QUIETLY at Dr. Herrera Sotolongo's home on a hill not too many miles from the *finca*. Delgado's first shot from the .22 target pistol had cut a clean little hole through the flesh of my right arm and had exited without creating a fuss or severing any major muscles or arteries. The second shot had caught me in the upper right shoulder, nicked the collarbone, and had ended up as a bump just under the skin above my right shoulder blade. Dr. Herrera Sotolongo and his surgeon friend, Dr. Alvarez, said that they almost could have extracted that slug with their fingers. There had been more internal bleeding associated with the path of this bullet, but nothing life-threatening.

The third bullet had done the mischief. Entering on my left side and headed directly for my heart, the slug had nicked a rib, been deflected just enough to cut a corner of my lung instead of the heart, and had ended up a millimeter from my spine. "Quite impressive for a twenty-two-caliber bullet," Dr. Herrera Sotolongo had said later. "If the gentleman had used the Schmeisser you described... well..."

"He liked to load the Schmeisser with hollow points with notched ends," I said.

Dr. Herrera Sotolongo had rubbed his chin. "Then we definitely would not be having this conversation, *Señor* Lucas. Now lie back and sleep some more."

I slept a lot. Three days after the surgery, I was moved from the good doctor's home to the guest house at the *finca*. There I took more pills, received more shots, and continued to sleep a lot. Both the surgeon and the doctor came frequently to approve of their work and to shake their heads at how minimal the actual damage had been considering all of that alien metal in my body.

Hemingway had also been on bed rest for a couple of days after his friend sewed up his lacerated scalp. The doctor echoed Delgado's sentiments. "You are one tough son of a bitch, Ernesto. And I say that with all respect and love."

"Yeah," agreed Hemingway as he sat on the edge of my bed in his bathrobe. The three of us—the writer, the doctor, and the ex-spy—were having a "medicinal libation" of straight gin. "I keep getting concussions. Have since I was a young man. A goddamn skylight fell on me in Paris when Bumby was a baby. Saw double for a week. A lot of bumps since, usually on my head. But the worst accident I've had was back in 'thirty when I was driving to Billings and rolled our car into a ditch. Your right arm looks like nothing compared to mine after that, Lucas. The inside of my arm looked like the part of an elk you have to throw away as unfit for human consumption when you butcher it out. Sort of like your left rib cage when I poured the sulfa on it in the *Pilar*."

"Great," I said. "Can we change the subject? How is Mrs. Hemingway doing?"

Hemingway shrugged. "There was a brief note waiting for me. She's seen Paramaribo in Surinam. Nothing there but sand chiggers, heat stroke, and bored GI's, she says. She's seen the sights of Dutch Guiana and the penal colony that's French Guiana and was thinking of heading home, but then she bought a map of the region and that changed her mind."

"What was on the map, Ernesto?" said Dr. Herrera Sotolongo.

"Nothing," said Hemingway. "She says that the map is almost empty except for the capital, a few settlements on the coast, and several rivers. The big river—the Saramcoca—weaves its way up from Paramaribo through green and white space. The green is jungle, she says. The white unknown. The river's a blue line that winds up through the green and white to a small cross that Marty figures is where the farthest traveler lay down to die. Beyond that cross, she says, even the river is unexplored... it's just a line of blue dots where they guess the damn thing goes. She's hired a local Negro named Harold to take her upriver to where the blue dots wind through white space."

Dr. Herrera Sotolongo sighed. "So many diseases there, I'm afraid. Everyone has malaria and indigenous dysentery, but it is also a very bad place for dengue—also known as break-bone fever. Very, very painful. Like malaria, it recurs for many years."

Hemingway nodded tiredly. "Marty'll catch it. She catches everything, sooner or later. She ignores mosquito nets, drinks the local water, enjoys the local produce, and then wonders why the hell she gets sick. I don't catch anything, I'm afraid." He gingerly touched his professionally wrapped head. "Except concussions," he added.

Dr. Herrera Sotolongo held up his glass of gin. "To *Señora* Gellhorn, Mrs. Hemingway," he said in toast.

We all lifted our glasses.

"To *Señora* Gellhorn, Mrs. Hemingway," said Hemingway, and tossed back the gin in one gulp.

EVERYONE WANTED TO KNOW what had happened, of course. Only Gregorio Fuentes never asked a question about our wounds, the disappearing Chris-Craft, the destruction of the *Lorraine*, and the mysterious radio message setting up our rendezvous. Evidently the tough little Cuban had decided that if his boss wanted him to know any of this, the writer would tell him. The others on the crew and back at the *finca* pestered us with questions. "It's classified," Hemingway had growled that first day, and that is the answer we stuck with. The others—including the two boys—were sworn to secrecy about everything, especially the Chris-Craft, and they grumbled but complied.

"What the hell am I going to tell Tom Shevlin when he gets back?" said Hemingway that last week in August. "If he makes me pay for that speedboat, I'm fucked. I wish we could send the bill to the navy or the FBI."

We had discussed reporting everything to Braden or Colonel Thomason, and then decided to say nothing to anyone. The puzzle of Operation Raven and the Abwehr documents still bothered us. "Swear Shevlin to secrecy and tell him everything," I suggested. "Maybe he'll be proud to have served his country."

"You think he'll regret that he had but one modified twenty-two-foot speedboat to give for his country?"

"Maybe," I said doubtfully.

Hemingway held his head. "Fuck, that was a beautiful boat. You remember how her bow light was integrated into the bow cleat? And the little sculpted mermaid bow ornament? And the instruments, all crafted by the same designer who did those beautiful 'twenties Gar Wood boats? And the Deusenburg steering wheel and the—"

"Enough," I said. "I'm getting a little queasy."

Hemingway nodded, still holding his head. "Well, Tom's a generous man and a patriot. And if we can't convince him to forgive us on those grounds, we'll just have to shoot him."

ON MONDAY, August 31, I was sitting up in the guest house bed eating some cold soup when Hemingway came in and said, "You've got two visitors."

I must have looked blank.

"A fancy Brit and a dwarf in a two-hundred-dollar suit," said the writer. "I told them that they could talk to you, but only on the condition that I be allowed to sit in on the conversation."

"Fine with me," I said, setting the tray on the bedside table.

Introductions were made, extra chairs were fetched, and Hemingway sent one of the houseboys for whiskeys all around. We made small talk until the drinks arrived and the boy was gone. I saw Hemingway taking stock of the fancy Brit and the dwarf in the two-hundred-dollar suit, and I watched Commander Ian Fleming and Wallace Beta Phillips doing the same with the writer. The Brit and the dwarf seemed satisfied with what they saw and heard; Hemingway appeared to remain dubious.

"So glad you survived everything, dear boy," said Fleming for the third time. The topic of my wounds was getting old.

"So can we talk about why these wounds and everything else happened?" I said.

Fleming and Phillips glanced at Hemingway.

"It's all right," said Hemingway in a stern tone. "I'm family. Besides, I came away with a few bruises of my own." He touched his still-bandaged head. "I'd like to know why."

The visitors looked at each other and nodded. It was a hot day, I was sweating in my pajamas. Hemingway was wearing a loose guayabera, shorts, and sandals, but he was sweating freely. Ian Fleming was sweating politely in a tropical wool blazer that looked to be more wool than tropical. Only Wallace Beta Phillips seemed cool. The little bald man looked so trim and contained in his perfectly tailored suit that it could have been a dry seventy degrees in the room, rather than a humid ninety.

I decided to do a second round of introductions so Hemingway would better understand the ground rules. "Ian works with the British MI6 boys," I said. "He's done some work with William Stephenson's BSC in this hemisphere."

The long-faced Brit nodded politely in Hemingway's direction and lighted a cigarette. I saw Hemingway frown at the affectation of the long cigarette holder.

"Mr. Phillips used to work with the Office of Naval Intelligence in this hemisphere," I said, "but now he's with Bill Donovan's COI."

"OSS now, Joseph," Phillips said softly.

"Yeah. I stand corrected. But I thought you'd gone on to a posting in London, Mr. Phillips."

"I have, actually," said the small man. I found his smile had just the opposite effect on me that Delgado's had—it relaxed me and made me want to like Phillips. Delgado's smile had made me want to kill the man.

Hemingway took care of that for you. I shook my head—the painkillers made me a little fuzzy about this time of day.

"I came back to chat with you," continued Phillips. He nodded in Hemingway's direction. "With both of you."

"So tell us about it all," said Hemingway. "Or do you need to know what happened last week?"

Ian Fleming removed the long cigarette holder from his

mouth and tapped ashes into the guest ashtray next to my dinner tray. "We have a pretty clear idea of that, but we would be delighted to hear the details of Major Daufeldt's demise."

Hemingway glanced at me. I nodded. He told them briefly and succinctly.

"And Lieutenant Maldonado?" said Wallace Beta Phillips.

I described the meeting in the Cementerio de Colón.

"But the lieutenant survived?" said Fleming.

I nodded. The Crook Factory had been busy bringing us information on this detail. "Some women bringing flowers to Amelia Goyre de la Hoz's grave heard him shouting in the mausoleum late the next day. They rushed Maldonado to Havana Hospital, managed to save his leg, and put him under twenty-four-hour guard."

"Why?" asked Mr. Phillips.

"To hear him tell the story," said Hemingway, "the lieutenant surprised ten Falangist criminals who were intent upon defacing the Monument to the Medical Students. He fought them off, but the Cuban National Police fears reprisals. Maldonado's quite the hero in Havana this week...at least to anyone who doesn't know him."

"Do you think he will seek revenge, old boy?" said Fleming, looking at me.

"I don't think so," I said. "Maldonado was an errand boy in all this, not a major player. He's got his money from both the FBI and the SD. He just failed in one of his errands. There's no reason he should pursue it further. Besides, the word is that he'll be on crutches for some months to come."

"All right," said Hemingway. "Let's hear some explanation of all this. Lucas has been saying he understands most of it, but he refuses to talk."

I adjusted the pillow behind me. "I thought we might have this conference," I said. "It would be easier if someone else could fill in the blanks."

Ian Fleming looked surprised. "You expected us?"

"Mr. Phillips at least," I said. "Although I thought someone from your group might be here, Ian. After all, it was your secrets that were being traded."

"Which secrets?" said Hemingway. "You mean the British convoys and Dieppe?"

Mr. Phillips steepled his fingers and smiled again. "Why don't you go ahead with your hypotheses, Joseph? We shall add what we know when it is appropriate."

"All right," I said. I took a drink of water from the glass on the tray. Outside, the palms rustled in the warm trade wind. I could smell the hydrangeas in Gellhorn's garden. "All right, I think it went something like this.

"The SD obviously made some deal with American counterintelligence... almost certainly with the FBI, probably with Mr. Hoover personally. On the surface, there was this joint SD-Abwehr intelligence operation going on in Brazil, Mexico, and Cuba. Teddy Schlegel and the other Abwehr operatives, including the poor soldiers they killed on the beach, didn't have any idea what was really going on."

"Which was?" prompted Fleming, posing with the cigarette holder and smiling slightly.

"Which was the SD—Becker, Maria, Delgado, Kruger, and their masters—selling out the entire Abwehr network in this hemisphere, and possibly in Europe as well."

Hemingway touched his bandage. His beard was longer now. "One Nazi spy agency selling out another?" he said. "That doesn't make any sense. They're fighting *us*."

"Mr. Phillips," I said, "you could probably explain this better than I can."

The bald man tapped his steepled fingers and nodded. "Actually, Mr. Hemingway, the SD almost certainly puts the United States and all of its various intelligence and counterintelligence apparati far down on its list of enemies."

"You mean Britain and the Soviet Union come first?" said Hemingway.

"They have greater priority in the international scheme of things, yes," agreed Phillips, "but the Sicherheitsdienst's greatest enemy is... the Abwehr." He paused to take a sip of his whiskey. "As I am sure Joseph has explained to you, Mr. Hemingway, the SD AMT VI intelligence group is a subset of the Nazi RSHA, the same agency which contains the Gestapo and the SS and which is, even now, creating and administering concentration camps and death camps throughout occupied Europe."

"Himmler," said Hemingway.

Mr. Phillips nodded again. "Reichsführer Heinrich Himmler. Perhaps the single most evil man alive on the face of the earth today."

Hemingway's dark eyebrows rose slightly under his crown of bandages. "More evil than Adolf Hitler?"

Ian Fleming tapped ashes and leaned forward. "Adolf Hitler dreams nightmares, Mr. Hemingway. Reichsführer Himmler turns these nightmares into realities for the Führer."

"We have reliable information," said Mr. Phillips, "that even now, Jews are being fed into death camps... not concentration camps, mind you, but huge institutions administered by the SS for no other purpose than the destruction of the Jewish race... in numbers that the civilized world will not believe."

Hemingway looked interested and sick. "But what does that have to do with Delgado and Maria and the Crook Factory and me?"

"On the surface," said Mr. Phillips, "Admiral Canaris of the army intelligence Abwehr and Reichsführer Himmler of the Nazi RSHA and the late Lieutenant General Rienhard Heydrich of the SD all got along marvelously and cooperated in the name of the future of the Thousand-Year Reich. In private, of course, Canaris loathed these particular Nazis, and Himmler and Heydrich had been planning for some time to destroy Canaris's agency and reputation."

"By transmitting all this Abwehr information to the FBI," I said. "Before that, the local SD strongman—Becker—destroyed the Brazilian and South American Abwehr networks. Then he and Delgado arranged to ship all of the classified Abwehr documents through us to the FBI. Or at least through us to Delgado and then to Hoover."

Hemingway shook his head. "That doesn't make any sense. If Delgado already had a pipeline to Hoover... worked for him, for Chrissakes... then he didn't need the Crook Factory or us as a way station for those documents."

"Ah, but he did, old chap," said Fleming, chuckling to

himself. "The fellow you know as Delgado had already made arrangements to move this information through the Cuban National Police, and when your Crook Factory exploit came along this past spring, everyone—Delgado; J. Edgar Hoover; Heydrich; Colonel Walter Schellenberg, in charge of Department VI; Himmler himself—they all saw how perfect it was. An amateur espionage ring in touch with all of the major U.S. counterintelligence agencies, authorized by the U.S. ambassador himself…and only ninety miles from the mainland. A perfect cut-out."

"Cut-out," mused Hemingway. "Meaning that we—the Crook Factory, Lucas, me—would be the fall guys if anything went wrong."

"Precisely," said Mr. Phillips. "As far as we can tell, J. Edgar Hoover was terrified about his slip-up in the Popov affair last winter. The FBI had documented evidence of the intentions of the Japanese to bomb Pearl Harbor many *weeks* before the actual attack, but Hoover and his men had dropped the ball. William Donovan has confirmed this. Hoover was frightened that President Roosevelt would learn about this and diminish the role of the FBI in intelligence affairs, or, in Hoover's most nightmarish scenario, remove him as Director of the FBI."

"Mr. Hoover would rather be dead," I said softly.

"Exactly," said Mr. Phillips. "And that's why he decided to go ahead with the plan that Major Daufeldt…your Delgado…had placed before him. The SD plan. The Himmler plan."

I raised one hand like a schoolchild. "But who exactly is…was…Delgado? I mean, I know he was Kurt Friedrich Daufeldt, SS major, but who *was* he?"

Ian Fleming tapped out his cigarette and removed it from the long, black holder. His expression and tone were more serious than usual. "As far as we can tell, dear boy, Daufeldt was the single most able intelligence agent in the entire German war effort." He smiled wanly at the writer next to him. "Which is not saying much, Mr. Hemingway. The Nazis have been extraordinarily incompetent in the field of gathering and analyzing field intelligence."

"Which is another reason Himmler and the other SD leaders had no qualms about surrendering Abwehr operations," said Mr. Phillips. "Most of those operations were and are disasters. They're a bit more competent in the Eastern Theater of Operations, but they were confident that Director Hoover would never share the Abwehr intelligence about the Soviets *with* the Russians."

"Then why did he want it?" said Hemingway. He smiled at his own question. "He's getting a head start against the Communists, isn't he?"

"Precisely," said Mr. Phillips.

"I think Mr. Hoover is much more afraid of the Communists than he is of the Japs or the Nazis," I said.

"This war is a bit of an inconvenience for our friend Edgar," said Fleming. "He really wants to get it out of the way so he can get on with the *real* war."

"Against the Soviets," said Hemingway.

Ian Fleming showed his crooked, stained teeth in a large smile. "Against the entire International Communist Conspiracy."

I raised my hand again. "Excuse me, but no one's answered my question. Who *was* Delgado?"

"Yes," said Mr. Phillips. "Who indeed? You remember, Joseph, that I suggested to you some weeks ago that your Mr. Delgado was the mythical Special Agent D? The gentleman theoretically responsible for the actual shooting of John Dillinger, Baby Face Nelson, and some of our other national embarrassments? Sort of a *special* special agent for Director Hoover?"

"Was he?" I said.

"We believe so," said the hairless man. "Actually, we have no idea what his real name was. When he came to Director Hoover's attention in 1933, Delgado was known as Jerry "Dutch" Fredericks, a hoodlum and FBI informant from Philadelphia. But we think now that he was not truly from Philadelphia at all but had been inserted in the United States by Himmler even then."

"He would have been young," I said.

"Twenty-six when Director Hoover enlisted him for... ah... his special operations. Your Special Agent D spoke English, German, and Spanish and was quite at home in all three cultures, as well as comfortable with the culture of the so-called Mob and the American criminal underground. In 1937, because of the attention within the Bureau after the Dillinger and other shootings, Mr. Fredericks went to Spain, where he worked for the Fascists and used the name Delgado for the first time. We have evidence that he was in Berlin in 1939 and was known as Major Kurt Fredrich Daufeldt. As I said, whether that was his true name or not is problematical."

"Busy guy," said Hemingway.

"Quite," agreed Mr. Phillips. "We were naturally concerned when Delgado/Fredricks/Daufeldt showed up in Cuba this spring. Or I should say, Mr. Stephenson, Commander Fleming, MI6, and the BSC were concerned. They tipped us to our friend Delgado's presence and activities." He nodded in Ian Fleming's direction.

The British agent smiled. "We weren't actually sure what Daufeldt and Becker were up to, you understand, but we did not anticipate that it would be overly beneficial to our side."

"Which it wasn't," I said. "It was classified information about *British* convoys and troop movements that Director Hoover had sold them."

Hemingway looked at me, then at the two other men, and then at me again. "The FBI was trading *British* secrets for the Abwehr documents?"

"Of course, old boy," said Fleming with a phlegmy laugh. "You don't think the director of the Federal Bureau of Investigation would pay off his German informants by revealing *American* secrets, do you? Good God, man, the fellow's a bloody *patriot*."

Hemingway folded his arms and scowled. "It's hard to believe. And why would Hoover want to *kill* me?"

"Delgado wanted to kill both of us," I said, feeling the pain medicine begin to wear off. What I gained in mental clarity tended to be canceled out by the distraction of the agony in my side and back. "But I don't think Hoover had decided that we had to die."

"Not his style, actually," murmured Ian Fleming. "You chaps served as a cut-out...a collective fall guy, as it were, should the intelligence transfer be discovered...but I suspect that

Edgar rather balked at killing one or both of you. Rather more his style to haul you up in front of a Senate committee investigating Communist infiltration and discredit you or send you to jail."

"There's no such thing as a witch-hunt committee like that," said Hemingway.

"There shall be, dear chap. There shall be."

"It was the SD that decided that we had to die," I said. "Himmler and Hoover could trust each other, because both their positions and power depended on maintaining secrecy about the arrangement. But we knew too much. Once we had received the Abwehr documents and passed them on to Hoover via Delgado, our role as patsies was completed."

"But we *didn't* pass them on," said Hemingway, his arms still folded. He was scowling.

"No, we didn't. But that didn't matter all that much. We had been in the right place at the right time. Delgado could duplicate most of the Abwehr information if he had to. And the Cuban National Police would continue to act as the pipeline after we were gone. We just had to *look* guilty if there was ever an investigation.

Mr. Phillips set down his empty glass. "And you certainly *would* have looked guilty, both being found dead, apparently at each other's hands, with the dead German lads buried nearby. Especially after Joseph's brutal attack on a hapless Cuban police lieutenant."

Ian Fleming lighted another cigarette. "What we hadn't actually anticipated was that Delgado would murder two of his own chaps."

"So it was definitely Delgado who shot the German boys on the beach?" said Hemingway.

"Oh, almost without a doubt." Fleming smiled. "Some of our chaps followed Mssrs. Delgado and Becker from Havana to the town of Manatí that evening, but then lost them on what we now know is the abandoned rail line to Manatí Bay. I rather suspect that the young German soldiers had been told to expect Hauptsturmführer Becker, and it sounds as if the gentleman illuminated himself by lantern light to allay their anxiety a scant few seconds before Delgado gunned them down with his busy little

Schmeisser. Best way to make sure the documents fell into your eager hands, don't you know?"

I shifted to make myself more comfortable. It did not help. "As long as we're tying up loose ends," I said. "What about Maria? Who was she?"

"An SD agent, dear boy," said Ian Fleming between puffs on his cigarette. "Half of the so-called Todt Team dedicated to eradicating you and Mr. Hemingway when your part of the scenario had been completed."

"Goddammit, I *know* that, Ian," I said, feeling the pain get my nerves on edge. "I mean, who *was* she?"

Mr. Phillips crossed his legs, running his fingers down the perfect crease in his trousers. "That's perhaps the most puzzling part of this, Joseph. We simply don't know who she was. A German national perhaps, raised in Spain. Or a very fine linguist. Very successful, deep cover. She is every counterintelligence director's nightmare."

"Was," I said. "Unless you know something that I don't about her getting off Cayo Puta Perdida alive."

"Cayo *what*?" said Ian Fleming, looking shocked.

Mr. Phillips shook his head. "Sorry. No intelligence to that effect. Of course, our few OSS operatives on this island are too few and too overworked. We shall certainly keep a sharp watch, should the lady ever reappear."

"Delgado called her 'Elsa'," I said.

"Ahh," said Mr. Phillips, and took a small leather-bound notebook from his jacket pocket. He opened a silver fountain pen and made a notation.

"And what about the Abwehr documents?" I said.

Mr. Phillips smiled. "Mr. Donovan and the OSS would be most pleased to take those off your hands, Joseph. Obviously we would never share them with Mr. Hoover or the FBI... unless, of course, we were forced to, in private, should the director ever again attempt to destroy our agency as he has worked so hard to do in recent months. And we would love to have copies of the photographs you took of the dead German couriers, of Delgado's and Kruger's bodies, and... if it would not be too inconvenient...

notarized, dated, and sealed affadavits from both of you describing the events you have suffered and witnessed."

I looked at Hemingway. The writer nodded. "All right," I said. I had to smile, despite the pain in my arm, shoulder, back, and side. "You're putting the director in a small box, aren't you?"

Wallace Beta Phillips returned my smile. "Yes, but with the security and interests of the United States of America our foremost priority," he said. "It might be best in the future if the OSS handled all foreign intelligence gathering. And it might also be best if the director of so powerful an organization as the FBI had some...ah...*discreet* checks and balances put on his power."

I thought about this for a moment. I could not disagree.

"Well, well, well," said Fleming, stubbing out his second cigarette, downing the last of his whiskey, and generally looking as if he was ready to leave. "We seem to have everything tied up in the appropriate knots, as it were. All conundrums and solutions present and accounted for."

"Except for one," said Hemingway.

Both visitors waited attentively.

"What the fuck do Lucas and I do now?" said the writer, glowering from beneath his bandages. "Joe doesn't have a job. Christ, he doesn't even have a country to go home to. I can't imagine that Hoover wouldn't find some way to make Joe's life a living hell if he tried to stay in his job or return to the States. Imagine the problems with the IRS."

Ian Fleming frowned. "Well, yes, there is that...."

"And what about *me*?" continued Hemingway. "The Infernal Revenue Service is already eating me alive. And if what you say is true about Hoover's favorite method of infighting, he'll be accusing me of being a Communist as soon as the war is over and the Russians aren't our allies any longer. Hell, maybe he's already started gathering information."

My gaze met that of Phillips and Fleming. We had all seen Hemingway's file. The earliest documents there were ten years old.

"Excellent points to consider, Mr. Hemingway," said Mr. Phillips, "but I can assure you that Mr. Donovan and a few others of us in...ah...influential positions within the OSS will not allow Director Hoover to vent his spleen on you. Another reason to prepare those affidavits for us."

"And you are an internationally respected writer, after all," chimed in Ian Fleming. "Hoover craves celebrity in himself but he fears the power of it in others."

"And your primary residence is in Cuba," I said to Hemingway. "That should give him pause if he ever sees an opening."

"Not to worry," said Mr. Phillips. "As Joseph so cleverly put it some minutes ago, Director Hoover is back 'in his box.' And our agency will do everything in its power to keep him there. In fact, Mr. Hemingway, should you ever require a favor..."

Hemingway only looked at the little man. After a minute, the writer said, "Yes, well, it all sounds good. But as soon as my wife is finished finding out what's beyond the little cross on the empty map, I'm going to see if she'll fly up to Washington to have dinner with her buddy Eleanor and chat with the old lady in the wheelchair about putting a leash on this particular dog."

"Cross on the empty map?" said Fleming, looking from Hemingway to me as if we had suddenly begun transmitting in cipher. "Old lady? Wheelchair? Which particular dog?"

"Never mind, Ian." Mr. Phillips chuckled. "I shall explain it to you on our drive back to the airport."

Everyone except me stood to go. I looked up at them and wished that it was time for my pain medication.

"Joseph?" said Mr. Phillips. "May I tell you my true reason for coming today?"

"Sure," I said. I was thinking about the truth of what Hemingway had just said about my never being able to live in the States again or hold down a job in counterintelligence. It was not a new thought—I had known it since the day I decided to tell Hemingway everything and work for him rather than for my true masters—but it made me sad beneath the morphine hangover and the waves of pain rolling across me.

"Mr. Donovan is very impressed with your...ah...ingenuity in this whole thing, Joseph. He would love to meet you and discuss future employment possibilities."

"For out of the country somewhere," I said dully.

"Well, yes," said Mr. Phillips, smiling. "But that is where

our agency does its work, isn't it? Do you think it would be possible for you to fly to Bermuda in a couple of weeks? Only if your recovery allows it, of course."

"Sure," I said again. "Why Bermuda?" That was British territory.

"Actually, dear boy," said Fleming, "it was arranged that Mr. Donovan would come to Bermuda to speak with you because Mr. Stephenson would also like the opportunity to chat with you before you make up your mind about any OSS offer. It was a bit more convenient for William...our William...to stay on British territory until Director Hoover gets over his inevitable petulance, if you get my drift."

"Mr. Stephenson?" I said stupidly. "He wants to talk to me?"

"The possibilities are quite exciting, old chap," said Fleming. "And after the war, after Adolf and Tojo and Benito and all these other aberrations are...as we keep saying today...put back in their boxes, there will be other challenges. And Britain might be a most pleasant place to live for a young American chap on a good salary."

"Work for MI6?" I said, sounding stunned and stupid even to myself.

Mr. Phillips smiled and tugged at Fleming's arm. "Nothing to decide today, Joseph. Come see us in Bermuda in a couple of weeks...or as soon as you are fit to travel. Mr. Donovan looks forward to meeting you."

Hemingway walked them out to the driveway. I sat there in bed, itchy beneath the surgical dressings, half sick with pain, and shook my head at all this. *Work for fucking MI6?* A few minutes later, Hemingway came back with my pain pills.

"You shouldn't take these with alcohol, you know," he said.

"I know," I said.

He handed me my two pills and a fresh glass of whiskey. He had brought a glass for himself. After I had swallowed the pills, he raised his glass. "*Estamos copados*," he said in toast. "But in the meantime—Confusion to our enemies!"

"Confusion to our enemies," I said. And drank.

31

ON MY LAST DAY at sea with Hemingway, we finally flushed a submarine out of hiding.

It is hard now, so many years later, to remember just how young and tough and resilient one was in one's youth. But I *was* young and tough. I healed quickly, even accounting for minor setbacks during the heat of that unusually warm Cuban August and early September of 1942. Every morning, Hemingway would bring several newspapers down to the guest house with him and we would have coffee together and read—Hemingway in the comfortable guest chair, me in the bed most of the time, although by the first of September I was sitting up in a chair for an hour or two a day.

The war news continued to be dismal. Field Marshal Rommel opened the month with a new attack on British forces in Egypt. Hemingway's old enemy in Spain, General Franco, ousted cabinet members and assumed full, dictatorial, Fascist control of that country, thus making Europe all but complete in the fall into its long night of tyranny. The Germans opened their attack on Stalingrad—waves of Stuka dive-bombers, thousands of tanks, and hundreds of thousands of troops attacking on the ground—and the Russian lines immediately buckled and were pierced. It seemed only a matter of time before Stalingrad and all of the Soviet Union collapsed. In the United States, the Baruch Commission was warning of "a full military and civilian collapse" due to the rubber shortages caused by the Japanese seizure of all sources of rubber in the South Pacific and Asia. As to the war at sea, it was now being revealed that the Germans had already sunk more than five million tons of Allied shipping, that their subs were sinking one of our ships every four hours on average, and that they were building subs faster than Allied navies and air forces could sink them. There would be more than four hundred German submarines in service in the Atlantic before the end of the year.

Patrick had to leave the second week in September to fly to New Milford, Connecticut, where he was entering a Catholic boy's school called Canterbury. Between the war news, the anticlimax after the summer's events, Hemingway's continuing headaches, and this sense of imminent dissolution of his temporary family, the writer was obviously feeling blue. The boys and the men hanging around the *finca* picked up on Hemingway's mood, and by the first week in September, it was a gloomy place to be recovering from gunshot wounds. As always, it was Hemingway himself who tried to pick up everyone's spirits—first by arranging elaborate baseball games at the Club de Cazadores in which Hemingway insisted on pitching several innings, and then by setting up the Operation Friendless Farewell Cruise, in which he would take everyone down the coast in the *Pilar* for four days, stop by Cayo Confites so the boys could say good-bye to the Cubans there, and fish their way back along the coast.

Dr. Herrera Sotolongo did not think it was advisable that I go along on this trip—the wave action alone could tear my stitches open, he insisted—but I pointed out that I was also leaving the next week and that nothing in the world could keep me behind at the *finca* during this final voyage.

We left Cojímar early on the morning of Sunday, September 6. I insisted on walking up the gangplank under my own power, but I admit that I was so exhausted when I got on the boat that I was glad to sit down. Hemingway not only insisted that I take the big bunk in the forward compartment during the trip, he had also brought along one of the overstuffed upholstered easy chairs from the living room of the *finca*, and he and the boys rigged this in the cockpit with lines cleverly tied to the same brass rail to which I had been handcuffed two weeks earlier, so that I could sit back with my feet up on the side bench without fear of sliding across the deck. It was embarrassing to be pampered like that, but I suffered it.

The weather was beautiful all four days. In addition to the boys and me, Hemingway had invited along Wolfer, Sinsky, Patchi, Roberto Herrera, his indispensable mate Gregorio Fuentes, and Roberto's brother, Dr. Herrera Sotolongo, to make sure that I did not die and ruin the trip for everyone. Still making amends for his error earlier in the summer, Guest loaded so many cases of beer aboard that even the hidden compartments were crammed full of cans and bottles. To add to the sense of holiday, Hemingway, Fuentes, and Ibarlucia had worked all week on building a sub-killing explosive device known only as the Bomb. Using a core of gunpowder triggered by several grenades, all encased in a metal shell with small handles that made the thing look like a diminutive garbage can, the Bomb could and would—according to Hemingway—blow the conning tower off any submarine that came within range. Of course, "range" was a relative term. After several practice throws with rocks and sand simulating the grenades and gunpowder, even athletes like Guest and Ibarlucia proved that they could lob the Bomb only about forty feet on a good day with the wind behind them.

"Fine, no problem," Hemingway growled. "We'll close on the sub, get too close for it to use its torpedoes or deck gun, and that range will be perfect." But in the days before we raised anchor for the farewell cruise, Hemingway and his two boys were seen in the field below the *finca* working on different variations of a giant slingshot made from large branches and old inner tubes, trying to improve the range for the Bomb.

On the first day out, Fuentes interrupted our lunch by shouting "Feesh, Papa! Feesh on the starboard side!" Hemingway had been munching a sandwich while he steered on the flying bridge, but he tossed the sandwich overboard and was sliding down the ladder even as the huge fish used its bill to knock the bait out of the outrigger. The writer immediately let the drag off the reel, the line humming a high note as it ran out into the blue Gulf waters, Hemingway chanting as it ran, "One chimpanzee, two chimpanzee, three chimpanzee..." until he hooked the monster hard on the count of "fifteen chimpanzee."

He fought the fish for only eighteen minutes, but it was an exciting eighteen minutes. All of us were cheering, and Dr. Herrera Sotolongo had to remind me to sit back and calm down before all of my wounds and incisions opened again. The marlin weighed six hundred pounds, and I watched as Fuentes carved a few fillets out of that great mass of fish and then tossed the rest overboard for bait. Twelve minutes later, Fuentes was shouting "Feesh! Feesh!" again. Hemingway was the first one to the rod, and this time he only counted to "five chimpanzee" before driving the hook home.

This battle lasted much longer, and the marlin broke the surface a hundred times in amazing leaps that had us all gasping at the beauty and the power of the great fish and at its will to survive. When Hemingway finally reeled the huge marlin in, he ordered Fuentes to release the hook.

Gregory, Patrick, Guest, Ibarlucia, and Dr. Herrera Sotolongo started shouting protests, but the writer insisted. As Fuentes worked to release the hook, the boys argued that the marlin be pulled aboard at least long enough for a photograph to be taken. "I'm leaving in three days, Papa," said Patrick, his voice not exactly rising to a whine but coming close. "I want something to remember him by."

Hemingway put his huge hand on his son's shoulder. "You'll remember it, Mouse. All of us will. We'll always remember those jumps. Beauty like that can't be captured in a photograph. I'd rather release him and give him his life back and have him enjoy it, than to 'immortalize him' in a grainy photograph. None of the best things in life can be captured. The only way we can immortalize anything is by appreciating it when it happens."

Patrick had nodded agreement, but he sulked for hours after the great fish swam away. "The photograph would have looked great on the wall of my dorm room," he muttered at our dinner of marlin steaks that night. Hemingway ignored the comment and passed him the potato salad.

On the second day, the *Pilar* pulled up alongside a sixty-foot whale shark that seemed to be lazing on the surface, its huge eye rotating to watch the *Pilar* approach but showing no sense of anxiety or eagerness to move on, even when Fuentes poked it in the side with an oar.

"Christ," said the first mate, "that thing, she is enormous."

"Yeah," said Hemingway. "It's almost a third the size of the sub we're going to find on this trip."

We anchored off Cayo Confites that night. Hemingway and his boys slept in sleeping bags on the deck above my forward compartment, and I could hear them through the open hatch cover, talking about the stars and constellations for a long time before I fell asleep. The writer had bought Patrick an expensive telescope the previous winter, and now the older boy was pointing out the North Star, Orion's Belt, and a score of other constellations.

The next morning started off badly, with Hemingway driving the *Pilar* aground somewhere west of Cayo Confites. He backed off immediately, but the sound was terrible, and everyone was in a foul mood as they rushed around the thirty-eight-foot boat, opening hatches and pulling up floorboard coverings to see if the impact had caused the hull to spring a leak. Everything was dry. I watched Hemingway's face during all of this and saw the sickness there. As little Gregory had said earlier that summer, "I think that Papa loves the *Pilar* most of anything in the world, after us, of course, and then his cats, and then Martha."

Things looked up after that when Hemingway called everyone up from breakfast with a shout of, "On deck, *amigos!* Looks like a schooner on a reef!"

The schooner was not actually in trouble on the reef, but anchored just inside it. It was the *Margarita* out of Havana and Hemingway was good friends with the captain's brother. They were seining the reef. The writer immediately brought the boys aboard, introduced them to the skipper, and arranged for Patrick and Gregory to help the crew all day as they encircled the entire reef with a long net dragged by three dories. The rest of us fished from the *Pilar* and watched the commotion as the men and boys struggled through the afternoon to bring up the endless net, the boys frequently diving to free it from snags on the coral. When the seine was finally lifted out, the water around the reef was suddenly filled with fleeing turtles and sharks, while captured pompano, snappers, jacks, barracuda, and baby sailfish flopped and squirmed in the cooling evening air.

The captain of the *Margarita* invited the crew of the *Pilar* aboard for dinner that night, and everyone went except Dr. Herrera Sotolongo and me. The doctor had the habit of turning in early—unusual for anyone in Cuba—and I was worn out from just watching the day's activities. Falling asleep that night, I listened to the laughter coming from the schooner and many long, formal toasts being offered in Hemingway's correct but stilted Spanish.

The next morning we were heading home when Winston Guest called from the flying bridge, "Submarine! Submarine!"

Hemingway and his sons were up on the flying bridge in five seconds, and everyone else was on deck and craning to see.

"Where?" said the writer. He was wearing a tattered T-shirt, shorts, and his long-billed cap. He no longer had to wear a bandage on his head, but looking up at him from the rear deck, I could see the patch of missing hair where the doctor had sewn his scalp back on.

"Ten points off the starboard bow and closing," Guest said, his voice trying to sound cool and military but quavering a bit with excitement. "Approximate range, one thousand yards. She just surfaced."

Hemingway raised the binoculars for a few seconds, lowered them, and said "Battle stations" in a clam voice. "No rushing," he added. "Normal movements. Patrick, keep fishing. Reel in whatever you've hooked there. Don't look at the sub."

"It's a barracuda on the line, Papa, but—"

"Stay with the fish, Mouse," said Hemingway. "Gigi will go forward and get your three-oh-three Lee-Enfield. Gregorio, why don't you break out the *niños* and then check the oil on the smaller engine? Patchi, Roberto, go below and bring up the bag of grenades and the Bomb, would you please?"

Everyone tried to act casual, but as soon as Gregory was out of sight, we could hear him running and crashing around, grabbing his mother's old Mannlicher and his brother's Lee-Enfield, spilling cartridges on the deck down there in his hurry to load the weapons.

"I will go down and get my medical bag," said Dr. Herrera Sotolongo.

"Jesus Christ!" said Winston Guest, his mouth dropping open as he raised his binoculars. "She's as big as a battleship. A fucking aircraft carrier."

I had struggled out of my lashed-down easy chair and was leaning over the starboard gunwale, ostensibly to watch Patrick bring in the barracuda, but also squinting across the diamonds of morning light on the low waves to catch a glimpse of the sub. It *did* look huge. Water poured from its honeycombed superstructure and dripped from its conning tower in a white spray. Even without binoculars, I could easily see the cover lashed over the single, huge deck gun.

"Lucas," Hemingway called softly, "why don't you sit down again? The Germans will *have* to turn about and board us if they see a skinny guy in a flowered armchair on the stern deck. Even Nazis would be curious about that. Everyone try to make your faces seem calm. We don't know how powerful their binoculars are."

Hemingway pressed the throttles forward and let Wolfer take the wheel while he slid down the ladder to help Roberto and Patchi manhandle the Bomb through the cockpit and up onto the flying bridge. Fuentes brought up the submachine guns and hung them on the railing of the flying bridge from the straps on their sheepskin-lined cradles. The bow was turned in the general direction of the submarine now, canvas was laced around the upper bridge, and the Bomb would not be visible to an observer on the U-boat no matter how powerful his binoculars were. The writer and Fuentes fiddled with the explosive device, setting fuses, pulling pins, or somesuch. I had the sudden image of the Bomb's blowing the *Pilar* and all of us to kingdom come by mistake.

"My God," said Guest, studying the sub through the twelve-power binoculars again. "She *is* big."

"But she's not getting any bigger," said Hemingway, taking

the glasses and holding them on the sub for a long minute. "Wolfer," he said, giving Guest the binoculars, "we're not *closing.* It's heading *away* from us." Hemingway's tone was under control, but I could hear the fury under the surface. "It's not only *heading* away, it's *pulling* away." He leaned over the back of the flying bridge and called down to Fuentes, who had opened the hatch cover and was fiddling in the engine compartment. "Goddammit, Gregorio, can't we get any more speed out of her?"

The little mate held up his hands. "She is doing twelve knots, Ernesto. That is all she can do with so many people and so much gasoline aboard her."

"Then maybe we need to throw some of the people overboard," snarled Hemingway. He took back the glasses again. There was no pretense of normalcy aboard now. Patrick and Gregory were near the bow: Patrick on the starboard side with his ancient Lee-Enfield; his younger brother on the port walkway with the Mannlicher Schoenaauer. Both boys were wet from spray and grinning like wolves.

"Goddammit," Hemingway said softly. "She's headed directly away from us. Range must be about fifteen hundred yards." Suddenly the writer laughed and turned to Ibarlucia. "Patchi, can you throw the Bomb fifteen hundred yards?"

The jai alai player showed his perfect teeth in a huge grin. "You give the word, Papa, and I'll try."

Hemingway clasped his friend's shoulder. Everyone began to relax. The submarine continued drawing away from us, its course north-northwest, its white wake the only disturbance on the morning's smooth sea.

As if on cue, everyone on the boat—including me—began cursing in a blue cloud of Spanish and English epithets. Ibarlucia had jumped down to the bow and was standing there, legs apart, fist raised, shouting, "Come back and fight, you yellow sons of whores!"

In five minutes, the sub was a small dot on the northwestern horizon. In eight minutes, it was gone.

"Lucas," said Hemingway, sliding down from the flying bridge, "if you feel like it, come on down with me. We'll radio in the sighting and give its last position, course, and speed. Maybe there's a U.S. destroyer in nearby waters or they can send a plane out from Camagüey."

I went below with him to send the message. After we had transmitted and repeated the same message for ten minutes or so, Hemingway said softly, "I didn't want to close with it anyway. Not with Gigi and Mouse on board."

I looked at him. Both of us were dripping sweat in the hot confines of the little room. We could hear the engine note drop as Guest throttled far back and put us on our original course.

"I bet a lot of the U-boat crew are just kids, too," Hemingway said. "Shit, it's trite to talk about war. Sherman said it all. War is necessary...sometimes. Maybe. I wonder, though, Lucas. I wonder."

Suddenly the two boys exploded down the stairway, wondering if the sub might return, hoping that it would, asking if they should act differently next time.

Hemingway put his arms around the boys' shoulders in the galley. "You both acted fine," he said. "Very fine." His voice suddenly rose, imitating an orator or a radio announcer or FDR. "As for me, my lads, someone else will fight for me on the beaches and in the hills and in the whorehouses. December seven, a day that will live in infamy, will be avenged by younger men. Hell, fix me a gin and tonic, will you, Gig? We're heading home."

32

PATRICK LEFT FOR SCHOOL ON FRIDAY, September 11. Gregory was ready to leave to visit his mother and go from there to school on Monday, September 14. I flew from Havana to Bermuda on Saturday, September 12.

"All my boys are leaving," Hemingway said gruffly that Thursday evening we put back into Cojímar and tied up the *Pilar* for the last time.

I could only look at the writer.

Dr. Herrera Sotolongo and the surgeon, Dr. Alvarez, both came by on Friday evening to check me over. They both recommended another two weeks' rest before going anywhere. I said that I was going the next day. Both doctors wished me luck and told me that my death would not be on their consciences.

Hemingway offered to drive me to the airport on Saturday morning. "Juan doesn't coast on the hills," he explained. "He's wasting my gasoline."

The drive to José Martí Airport was not a long one, but Hemingway talked most of the time.

"Tom Shevlin's back in town," he said.

"Uh-oh."

"No, it's all right. It turns out he *did* have insurance on the *Lorraine*. He wasn't too upset. He says that he's probably getting a divorce and he would have just had to rename the boat anyway."

"That's good," I said. "I guess."

We drove in silence for a few minutes.

"I've decided to give up running the Crook Factory," he said suddenly.

"You're shutting down the operation?" It seemed sensible to me. The amateur espionage operation had served its purpose as a lightning rod.

Hemingway scowled at me from his place behind the wheel of the Lincoln. "Hell no, I'm not shutting it down. I never even considered that. I just want to spend more of my time on Operation Friendless."

"Chasing subs," I said.

"*Catching* subs," said the writer. "*Sinking* subs."

"So who's going to run the Crook Factory?" I had a surge of hope and nausea at the idea that he was going to ask me to stay and run things. God, I was popular—weren't Bill Donovan and William Stephenson coming all the way to Bermuda to meet with me? Now this. Screwing everything up and getting shot three times, I realized, had been a great career move.

"I've decided to ask my friend Gustavo Durán to come down and run it," said Hemingway. "I've told you about Gustavo. I told Bob Joyce at the embassy that I needed a real pro to run the operation."

Hemingway *had* told me about Durán. The former Lieutenant Colonel Gustavo Durán had known the writer in Paris long ago when Durán had been a music student, art critic, and composer. When Hemingway had gone to Spain in the spring of 1937, Durán had been commanding the 69th Division at Torréjon de Ardoz and Loeches, east of Madrid. The two had renewed their friendship and Hemingway's admiration of the artist-turned-soldier almost seemed to reach the point of hero worship. Hemingway had told me that he had depicted a thinly disguised Gustavo Durán as one of the heroes of his last book, *For Whom the Bell Tolls*. After Ingrid Bergman's visit in May, Hemingway had described how he had worked hard to get a Hollywood job for Durán as a technical consultant on the movie version of his book, but the director—Sam Wood—was "scared shitless of the Red Menace" and had refused to hire the Spaniard, even though Durán had never belonged to the Communist Party. Hemingway had sent Durán—who was going through hard times—a

$1,000 check instead. The writer had described to me how the check had been promptly returned.

I felt a stab of discomfort from the wound in my side. Only later did I realize that it had not been the wound at all.

"Gustavo will be perfect," Hemingway was going on. "I've already cleared it with Ellis Briggs and Ambassador Braden at the embassy, and Bob Joyce has written a secret letter to the State Department. I kept it secret because we certainly didn't want J. Edgar Adolf Hoover hearing about it."

"No," I said.

"Gustavo's in New Hampshire right now, in the process of becoming an American citizen. Joyce's letter and some other things I set in motion should expedite matters. I cabled him just the other day, but I'm pretty sure that he'll accept the offer. He did a wonderful job with intelligence in Spain. He should be down here by early November, and his wife could join him later. I'll give him the guest house. He can continue to run things out of there and they'll both live there."

"Great idea," I said.

"Yeah," said Hemingway. We did not speak any more until we were at the airport.

Hemingway insisted on carrying my single duffel and seeing me through all the formalities of departure. We walked out on the tarmac where the silver DC-4 was waiting, its few passengers lined up at the ramp.

"Well, shit, Lucas," he said, and held out his hand.

I shook it and took my duffel from him.

I was walking toward the plane and it had started its port engine when Hemingway shouted something at me.

"What?" I said.

"I said you have to come back to Cuba someday, Lucas."

"Why?"

"Rematch!" he called over the engine noise.

I paused and cupped my hand like a megaphone. "Why? You want to try to get your title back?"

"Fuck that," called the writer, grinning through his beard. "I never lost it."

I nodded and walked to the ramp. There was a moment of

giving the stewardess my ticket and setting the strap of my duffel over my shoulder, and then I looked back to wave good-bye. Hemingway had gone back into the terminal and I could not see him through the crowds of Cubans and military personnel. I never saw him again.

33

I HAVE RECORDED THE FEW CONVERSATIONS that I had with Ernest Hemingway about writing. The one on the cliff above Point Roma on the night when we were waiting for the German infiltrators is the one I remember best, although the conversation aboard the *Pilar* the night of his forty-third birthday comes back to me occasionally. One other conversation about writing occurs to me now, however. He was not speaking to me at the time, but was sitting by the pool at the *finca* with Dr. Herrera Sotolongo. I just happened to be sitting close enough to eavesdrop.

The doctor had asked Hemingway how a writer knew when to end a book.

"As much as you want to finish the damned thing," Hemingway said, "another part of you never wants to end it. You don't want to say goodbye to the characters. You don't want the voice inside your head to stop whispering in the particular language and dialect of that book. It's like having a friend die."

"I think I understand," the doctor said dubiously.

"You remember two summers ago when I refused to get a haircut until I'd finished *For Whom the Bell Tolls*."

"Yes," said the doctor. "You looked very terrible with such long hair."

"Well, I finished the damned book about July thirteenth, but I didn't quit writing when the book was finished. I kept working through my birthday, writing a couple of chapters as a sort of epilogue, describing Karkov meeting with General Golz after the screwed-up Segovia offensive, the two of them driving back to Madrid together, then a whole chapter telling about

Andres visiting Pilar and Pablo's abandoned camp, Andres looking down at the wrecked bridge in the gorge... that sort of crap."

"Why is it crap, Ernesto?" said Dr. Herrera Sotolongo. "It was not interesting?"

"It was not necessary," said the writer, sipping his Tom Collins. "But I carried the manuscript up to New York in the middle of the hottest summer since the Creation and worked on it at the Hotel Barclay, feeling like a blind sardine in a processing factory, sending two hundred pages a day over to Scribners via a kid I hired as a runner. Gustavo Durán was visiting me with his new bride, Bonte, and I had him read the galleys to make sure that the accents were in the right place in the Spanish words and that my grammar was all right."

"And was it?" asked the doctor, sounding amused.

"Most of it," growled Hemingway. "But my point was that my editor, Max, just loved it all, including the epilogue chapters that I should have never put in. In Perkins's usual way, he just said that he loved it all and saved his criticisms for after I had cooled off from the writing. By late August, Scribners was asking me to take out a scene where Robert Jordan jerks off—"

"Jerks off?" said Dr. Herrera Sotolongo.

"Masturbates." Hemingway grinned. "Performs an act of onanism. But anyway, Max never said a word about the useless epilogue. Finally, when everything else was settled, I realized that Perkins was sending me his usual subliminal messages. 'I love the final chapters because, naturally, I'm so curious about what happens next, Ernest,' Max was saying, 'but in a real way, the book ends with Jordan lying on the pine needles waiting for death to arrive, just as you had him lie there sixty-eight hours earlier in the opening sequence of the first chapter. It is a wonderful symmetry, Ernest. A beautiful circle.'

"'All right, Max,' I'd said. 'Drop the last two chapters.'"

"Are epilogues not good, then?" asked the doctor.

Hemingway had scratched his beard, watching the boys splash in the pool. "They're like life, José Luis," he said then. "Life just keeps going on until you die... one damned thing after another. Novels have structure. They have a balance and design that real life lacks. Novels know when to stop."

I had watched the doctor nod in agreement, but I do not think he understood.

When I decided to write this narrative, I knew that Hemingway had been correct that night at Point Roma when he said that a good story had to be like the glimpse of a submarine's periscope. In later years, Hemingway was quoted as saying that a novel was like an iceberg—seven-eighths of it should be invisible. I *knew* that this was the best way to write our little tale, but I also knew that I would never be good enough as a writer to tell the story that way. I would never be a Zen artist, putting a brush stroke of blue on the canvas to portray the hawk. The only way I knew to tell any story was the way Hemingway had criticized that night at Point Roma—marshaling all of the facts and details and marching them all through the book like prisoners of war through the capital, letting the reader sort out the important details from the dross.

Thus this clumsy epilogue.

TRUE TO HEMINGWAY'S PREDICTION, Martha Gellhorn did catch dengue in her trip up the blue-dot river beyond Surinam. The break-bone fever was so terrible and painful that on her last day in Paramaribo, Gellhorn tried to lift herself from a chair because her legs would not work, slipped, and fractured her wrist. She hardly noticed, wrapping some adhesive tape around the broken wrist before flying away from that jungle hell.

Nonetheless, after receiving a cable from her husband, she flew straight to Washington, D.C., and had dinner at the White House. The fact that Gellhorn's meeting with the president and his wife did help to shield Hemingway from the wrath of J. Edgar Hoover was attested to by these memos, which I did not see at the time and only recently acquired—some fifty-five years later—through the Freedom of Information Act.

CONFIDENTIAL MEMO
FROM FBI DIRECTOR J. EDGAR HOOVER
TO FBI AGENT LEDDY
DECEMBER 17, 1942

Any information which you may have relating to the unreliability of Ernest Hemingway as an informant may be discreetly brought to the attention of Ambassador Braden. In this respect it will be recalled that recently Hemingway gave information concerning the refueling of submarines in Caribbean waters which proved unreliable. I desire that you furnish me at an early date results of your conversation with Ambassador Braden concerning Ernest Hemingway and his aides and activities.

CONFIDENTIAL MEMO
FROM FBI AGENT D. M. LADD
TO FBI DIRECTOR J. EDGAR HOOVER
DECEMBER 17, 1942

Hemingway has been accused of being of communist sympathy, although we are advised that he has denied and does vigorously deny any communist affiliation or sympathy. Hemingway is reported to be personally friendly with Ambassador Braden, and he is reported to enjoy the ambassador's complete confidence.

Ambassador Braden, as you will recall, is a very impulsive individual and he apparently has had a "bee in his bonnet" for some time concerning alleged graft and corruption on the part of certain Cuban officials.

Agent Leddy (Havana Field Office) has advised that Hemingway's activities have branched out and that he and his informants are now engaged in reporting to the Embassy various types of information concerning subversive activities generally. Mr. Leddy stated that he has become quite concerned with respect to Hemingway's activities and that they are undoubtedly going to be very embarrassing unless something is done to stop them.

Mr. Leddy has advised that Hemingway is apparently undertaking a rather involved investigation with regard to Cuban officials prominently connected with the Cuban Government, including General Manuel Benitez Valdes, head of the Cuban National Police; that he, Agent Leddy, 'is sure that the Cubans are eventually going to find out about this if Hemingway continues operating, and that serious trouble may result.'

Mr. Leddy stated that he can point out to the ambassador that he, Leddy, has not checked any reports from Hemingway concerning corruption in the Cuban Government; that he does not feel that Bureau agents should become involved in any such investigations, it being entirely without our jurisdiction and a matter in which the Cubans themselves alone are concerned and something that, if we get involved in it, is going to mean that all of us will be thrown out of Cuba "bag and baggage."

Agent Leddy stated he can point out to the ambassador the extreme danger of having some informant like Hemingway given free reign to stir up trouble such as that which will undoubtedly ensue if this situation continues. Mr. Leddy stated that despite the fact the ambassador likes Hemingway and apparently has confidence in him, he is of the opinion that he, Leddy, can handle this situation with the ambassador so that Hemingway's services as an informant will be completely discontinued.

Mr. Leddy stated that he can point out to the ambassador that Hemingway is going further than just an informant; that he is actually branching out into an investigative organization of his own which is not subject to any control whatsoever.

CONFIDENTIAL MEMO
FROM FBI DIRECTOR J. EDGAR HOOVER
TO AGENTS TAMM AND LADD
DECEMBER 19, 1942

Concerning the use of Ernest Hemingway by the United States ambassador to Cuba: I of course realize the complete undesirability of this sort of a connection or relationship. Certainly Hemingway is the last man, in my estimation, to be used in any such capacity. His judgement is not of the best, and if his sobriety is the same as it was some years ago, that is certainly questionable. However, I do not think there is anything we should do in this matter, nor do I think our representative at Havana should do anything about it with the ambassador. The ambassador is somewhat hot-headed and I haven't the slightest doubt that he would immediately tell Hemingway of the objections being raised by the FBI. Hemingway has no particular love for the FBI and would no doubt embark upon a campaign of vilification. You will recall that in my conference recently with the president, he indicated that some message had been sent to him, the president, by Hemingway through a mutual friend [Martha Gellhorn], and Hemingway was insisting that one-half million dollars be granted to the Cuban authorities so that they could take care of internees.

I do not see that it is a matter that directly affects our relationship as long as Hemingway does not report directly to us or we deal directly with him. Anything which he gives to the ambassador which the ambassador in turn forwards to us, we can accept without any impropriety.

CONFIDENTIAL MEMO
FROM FBI AGENT LEDDY [HAVANA FIELD OFFICE]
TO FBI DIRECTOR J. EDGAR HOOVER
APRIL 21, 1943

The writer has been advised in confidence by an Embassy official that Hemingway's organization was disbanded and its work terminated as of April 1, 1943. This action was taken by the American ambassador without any consultation or notice to representatives of the Federal Bureau of Investigation. A complete report on the activities of Mr. Hemingway and the organization which he operated is now being prepared, and will be forwarded to the Bureau in the immediate future.

CONFIDENTIAL MEMO
FROM FBI AGENT D. M. LADD
TO FBI DIRECTOR J. EDGAR HOOVER
APRIL 27, 1943

Mr. Hemingway has been connected with various so-called Communist front organizations and was active in aiding the Loyalist cause in Spain. Despite Hemingway's activities, no information has been received which would definitely tie him with the Communist Party or which would indicate that he is or has been a Party member. His actions, however, have indicated that his

> views are "liberal" and that he may be inclined favorably to communist political philosophies. At the present time he is alleged to be performing a highly secret naval operation for the Navy Department. In this connection, the Navy Department is said to be paying the expenses for the operation of Hemingway's boat, furnishing him with arms and charting courses in the Cuban area. The Bureau has conducted no investigation of Hemingway, but his name has been mentioned in connection with other Bureau investigations and various data concerning him have been submitted voluntarily by a number of sources.

Gellhorn finally asked Hemingway for a divorce in late 1944. She had stayed with him at the *finca* on and off during his long year of absences while on sub-chasing patrols in the *Pilar* through all of 1943 and into the spring of 1944. Writing to her while she was in London, Hemingway complained that the empty *finca* was lonelier than limbo. When she returned, their fights reportedly grew more and more wicked, their reconciliations less convincing. For two years, Gellhorn had been challenging Hemingway to quit "playacting war" and to go out and report it, but her husband had stubbornly stayed in Cuba with his boat, his friends, his cats, and his *finca*. Finally, in March 1944, when he took her up on her taunts, he did it in a way she would not soon forget or forgive. Any magazine in America would have paid Ernest Hemingway to be its correspondent. He volunteered to write for *Collier's*, Gellhorn's magazine. Since they had payroll and transit vouchers for only *one* correspondent at the time, Hemingway was sent to Europe first. When Gellhorn said that she would travel as a freelance writer with him, Hemingway lied and said that they did not allow women on the military flight. Gellhorn later learned that the actress Gertrude Lawrence sat next to Hemingway during the entire flight.

Hemingway flew to London on May 17, 1944, joking with Miss Lawrence about the fresh eggs she was carrying for her British friends and planning a pancake breakfast for everyone once they got to England. He told everyone that he was still angry at his wife for not saying good-bye to her special cat when she had left the *finca*. Martha Gellhorn had shipped out on May

13, the only passenger aboard a ship carrying a cargo of dynamite. The convoy suffered heavy losses during the hazardous twelve-day crossing.

Friends were not totally surprised when word eventually came of their separation and divorce.

INGRID BERGMAN AND Gary Cooper starred in the movie version of *For Whom the Bell Tolls*, and the film premiered on July 10, 1943. The film was beautiful to look at—as was Bergman with her short hair—but reviewers and audiences criticized it for being too slow and too long. In truth, there was no real chemistry between Cooper and Bergman. Years later, the film that people would remember was the hastily written, plot-confused, low budget movie she did while waiting anxiously for word of whether she would get into *For Whom the Bell Tolls*. The movie was called *Casablanca*.

GUSTAVO DURÁN DID COME TO CUBA and was in charge of the Crook Factory until it was shut down by mutual consent in April 1943, but he and his wife had several fallings out with Hemingway and Gellhorn, and the Duráns soon moved out of the guest house and took up residence in the Ambos Mundos Hotel. By mid-1943, Gustavo Durán was working as an intelligence officer for Ambassador Braden and the Duráns were the hit of Havana society.

After the war, both Durán and Ambassador Braden were accused of being Communists and were dragged before the Un-American Activities Committee. “The real leftist is Hemingway,” Gustavo Durán declared before the Senate. “And I met Braden in Hemingway’s house.”

Spruille Braden, devastated at being charged with disloyalty after so many years of government service, also testified that Ernest Hemingway was the American Communist in Cuba. Braden then flew straight to Havana and asked for Hemingway’s forgiveness. “He said he was sorry—that he had to lie to keep his job—and expressed all kinds of apologies and seemed to be sincere," Hemingway later told Dr. Herrera Sotolongo. "So I forgave him."

Bob Joyce, Hemingway's liaison with the embassy, quit to join the OSS about eight months after I did. I saw Joyce once in Europe a year later, but we were in the back of a darkened Dakota aircraft, waiting to jump into the night over Eastern Europe, our faces were blackened with burned cork, and I do not think that he recognized me.

I NEVER SAW Gregory or Patrick Hemingway again. Gigi became a well-respected physician, like his grandfather. Patrick became a big-game hunter in Africa, but returned to the States and became known as an environmentalist.

Oddly enough, it was the oldest son, John—the "Bumby" whom I'd never met while in Cuba—that I ran into in Hammelburg, Germany, in January 1945.

John H. Hemingway had joined the OSS in July 1944. Three months later, Bumby parachuted into France at Le Bosquét d'Orb, fifty kilometers north of Montpelier. His mission was to train local partisans on the art of infiltrating enemy positions. In late October, he was on a daylight reconnaissance along the Rhone Valley with a U.S. Army captain and a French partisan when they were attacked by an Alpenjäger unit. The Frenchman was shot in the belly and killed; Bumby and Captain Justin Green were wounded. During their interrogation by the Austrian officer in charge of the alpine unit, the officer realized that he had known Ernest, Hadley, and two-year-old Bumby in Schrüns in 1925. The officer canceled the interrogation and shipped the wounded, bleeding twenty-one-year-old Hemingway to a hospital in Alsace before he bled to death.

My team was sent into the POW camp near Hammelburg to help the prisoners escape. Young John Hemingway did get away that night, but he was recaptured four days later and taken to Stalag Luft III in Nuremberg, Germany. His father had to suffer the report that Bumby was Missing in Action until the young man was liberated in the spring of 1945, by which time he had survived more than six months in a succession of prisoner of war camps, each one with less food than the last. He flew to Cuba in June 1945 to be reunited with his father, his brothers, and his father's new bride, Mary Welsh.

LIEUTENANT MALDONADO RETURNED to his post with the Cuban National Police, although he walked with a limp for the rest of his life. A few years before Hemingway left Cuba forever, Maldonado was on patrol near the *finca* and was reported to have killed Black Dog, Hemingway's favorite pet at the time, bashing the canine to death with the butt of his rifle.

In the last days of Batista, Maldonado became famous for his power and brutality, driving through the provinces in a Willys jeep and shooting people almost at random. But he had chosen the wrong dictator with which to throw in his lot. *Caballo Loco* was arrested by the revolutionary government in 1959, the last of Batista's local officers to stand trial. Everyone was sure that the tall killer would be hanged, and during the public trial Maldonado wept constantly, until his sallow, pockmarked aide and co-defendant finally stood up in the courtroom and said, "Hey, pal, stop crying like a damn whore. You did the killing and so did I."

The aide was hanged. Inexplicably, Maldonado was sentenced to thirty years in prison. There were literal riots with the local Cubans demanding that the revolutionary government hold a new trial and condemn Maldonado to death. But that was the week that Fidel Castro ordered the halt to all executions of Batista's officers guilty of murder.

Hemingway was still in Cuba then, and he told a friend that week, "He's going to die of old age, damn it. That's what is going to happen. For the good of the town and the country, the best thing would be to see him dead and buried." It is reported that Hemingway volunteered to pull the trigger.

MARLENE DIETRICH, perhaps because she was born in Germany, became one of the most aggressive Hollywood celebrities in the race to serve and entertain the American GI's during the war. In

1943 she opened a USO Canteen in Hollywood for troops being shipped overseas. It was the only place where GI's could see famous movie stars brewing coffee, baking doughnuts, and washing pots and pans. Dietrich always insisted on washing the pots and pans.

In 1944 and 1945 she went overseas with the traveling USO shows, and there were few entertainers the troops enjoyed more. Mostly, I think, it was her legs. And her voice. And the sexuality which hung around the woman like a cloud of incense. Even from fifty yards away on a foggy night, a GI watching Dietrich sing and dance had no illusions that he was seeing the girl next door.

I saw her perform once in France, but I am sure that she did not notice or recognize me. Besides there being several hundred soldiers and local citizens there, I was dressed in French peasant garb and had a thick beard.

Dietrich celebrated the liberation of Paris with Hemingway by going with him to "liberate" the Ritz and to drink the best champagne from that hotel's cellars. She always professed her love and loyalty to the writer, and was devastated when he killed himself in 1961.

WINSTON GUEST LARGELY DROPPED OUT of sight in later years. In 1961, the year Hemingway died, Guest was the owner of Guest Aerovias de Mexico, S.A., the smallest of the three Mexican international airlines. We used that airline extensively for covert CIA operations during that decade.

After the Cuban revolution, Sinsky—Juan Dunabeitia—refused to follow the Ward Line merchant marine company he worked for to the United States. He returned to Spain, where he opened a maritime supplies store and eventually died.

Gregorio Fuentes celebrated his one hundredth birthday in Cuba in July 1997.

IN THE 1960S, while I was stationed in Berlin, I heard rumors of a female Soviet agent in her late thirties who had been recruited from Reinhard Gehlen's old Nazi intelligence network. Gehlen had run the most efficient and competent German operation of the war.

What made rumors of this female interesting to me was the fact that her name was Elsa Halder, that she was a distant cousin of the late Erwin Rommel, that she looked anything but Aryan—dark hair, dark eyes, dark complexion—that she had grown up in a German diplomat's family posted in Spain during most of the 1930s, and—of greatest interest to me—she had won a bronze medal swimming for Germany in the 1936 Olympics. Her specialty had been long-distance events.

I never looked deeper into her identity or whereabouts and never ran across her in my arena of operations.

NOR DID REICHSFÜHRER Heinrich Himmler give up his quest for total power within the Nazi intelligence community and within the Third Reich. In the OSS, we were certain that Himmler wished not only to be deputy Führer but to replace Hitler when the time came. That thought gave us chills and kept us diligent at our work.

All through 1943, Himmler and his RSHA SD AMT VI colleagues looked for ways to discredit Admiral Canaris and his Abwehr. In January 1943, Himmler appointed Ernst Kaltenbrunner head of the RSHA, and Kaltenbrunner's first act was to elevate Colonel Walter Schellenberg—Himmler's and Heydrich's co-author in Operation Raven in Cuba—as chief of Department VI. Kaltenbrunner's and Schellenberg's first priority was to destroy the Abwehr.

They got their chance in January 1944. After complicated machinations by the SD, a member of the Abwehr in Istanbul, a Dr. Erich Vermehren, defected to the British. On February 10, the British—guided by the hands of William Stephenson and Ian Fleming in MI6—confirmed Vermehren's defection.

Hitler exploded. Two days later, the Führer signed a decree that abolished the Abwehr as an independent organization, subordinating it to the RSHA and giving Heinrich Himmler complete control over all foreign intelligence. Canaris was immediately removed from the post in which he had served for nine years.

Later in 1944, after the failed plot to assassinate Hitler, Schellenberg himself arrested Admiral Canaris, whose only crime might have been knowing about the plot and not warning Hitler. The former intelligence chief was taken to a meat-packing plant and repeatedly hanged from a meat hook, his arms tied behind him with wire. The execution of all the conspirators was filmed, and Adolf Hitler spent his evenings watching these films over and over.

THEODOR SCHLEGEL HAD BEEN ARRESTED immediately upon his return to Brazil in the summer of 1942. Delgado and Becker had arranged for the rounding up of all the Abwehr agents and networks in South America, soon to be replaced by SD networks. Schlegel and six of his associates were brought before the Brazilian Tribunal de Seguranca Nacional in October of that year. Schlegel was sentenced to fourteen years in prison.

Hauptsturmführer Johann Siegfried Becker had fled to Brazil the day after Delgado murdered the two Germans at Point Roma, but Becker avoided arrest for two and a half more years, setting up SD networks to replace the betrayed Abwehr operations, generally creating mischief without many real results, until his arrest in April 1945, only a few weeks before the collapse of the Third Reich and the suicide of his Führer.

J. EDGAR HOOVER DIED ON TUESDAY, May 2, 1972, a national icon if not exactly a national hero anymore.

I was sixty years old that year, serving as a CIA station chief in Calcutta. Just another aging civil servant dreaming of retirement. I had not been in the United States for thirty years.

When news of Hoover's death reached me in the middle of the night over the secure line, I picked up another phone and called an old friend of mine in Langley, Virginia. My friend called a mole we had long since placed within the Bureau, who, in turn, soon set in motion the delivery of a letter to the new acting director of the FBI, L. Patrick Gray. This letter was sent via the attorney general's office to avoid interception by certain of

Hoover's old cronies. The letter was marked "PERSONAL—DELIVER TO ADDRESSEE ONLY." L. Patrick Gray read the letter on May 4, 1972.

The letter began: "Immediately after discovering Hoover's death, Clyde Tolson made a call from Hoover's residence to FBI Headquarters, presumably to J. P. Mohr. Tolson directed that all the confidential files kept in Hoover's office be moved out. By 11 A.M. they were all taken to Tolson's residence. It is unknown whether these files are still there. The point is—J. P. Mohr lied to you when he told you that such files do not exist—They do. And things are being systematically hidden from you."

Acting Director L. Patrick Gray immediately sent the letter to the FBI laboratory for examination. The lab reported only that different typewriters had been used: a Smith Corona, elite type, for the envelope; an IBM, pica type, for the letter; that neither the envelope nor the letter bore watermarks, and that the letter itself was a reproduction, a product of direct electrostatic process rather than the indirect, such as a Xerox.

Gray demanded an explanation from Assistant Director Mohr, who once again insisted that there had been no secret and confidential files. Gray wrote a personal note to Mohr—"I believe you!"

Miss Gandy, Hoover's private secretary for the past fifty-four years, had moved 164 private files to cardboard storage boxes which were taken first to Clyde Tolson's home and eventually to the basement of J. Edgar Hoover's home at Thirtieth Place NW. From there they disappeared.

My friend from Langley reached me again in Calcutta on June 21, 1972. You would recognize my friend's name. He was famous for ferreting out moles within the CIA. He hated Soviet moles, but he despised FBI moles just as much. Some called him paranoid. He had been a friend of Bill Donovan's during the old OSS days and had worked with me for years on the Special Desk dealing with the British and the Israelis. We had both dined with Kim Philby before that double agent fled to Moscow. We had both vowed never to repeat that oversight.

"I have them," said my friend that night on the secure line.

"All of them?" I said.

"All of them," said my friend. "They're stored in the place we agreed."

I said nothing for a moment. After all those years, I could now go home if I wished.

"They make for interesting reading," said my friend that night. "If we published them, nothing would ever be the same in Washington again."

"Nothing would be the same anywhere," I said.

"Talk to you soon," said my friend.

"Yes."

And I set down the telephone very gently.

34

I DID NOT COME HOME to the United States in 1972, nor when I retired from the Agency late in 1977.

I came home four days ago; almost fifty-six years to the day after I left the country, flying from Miami down to Havana to meet a man named Ernest Hemingway.

No one plans to be an old man, to watch most of one's friends fall by the wayside, but that has been my fate. Almost eighty-six years old. As a younger man, I had been shot four times, survived two serious automobile accidents and one dramatic aircraft wreck, was lost at sea in the Bay of Bengal for four days and nights, and once spent a week wandering through the Himalayas in the middle of winter. I survived it all. Pure luck. Most things are pure luck.

And my luck was good until ten months ago. I had my driver take me into Madrid for one of my regular, biannual physicals; my doctor, who seems old at the age of sixty-two, always chides me for coming to him. "How long has it been since even Spanish doctors made house calls?" I always joke.

But this day last August there was no joking. He explained to me the technical terms and the simple truth of it all. "If you were younger," he said, his eyes truly sad, "we would try surgery. But at age eighty-five..."

I had patted my doctor on the shoulder. "Could it be a year?" I asked. Hemingway had once told me that it took him about a year to write a book.

"Not a year, I am afraid, my dear friend," said my doctor.

"Nine months, then?" I said. My book would not be an act

of genius as Hemingway's books had been, so certainly I could write it in nine months. Nine months sounded like such a fertile period of time.

"Perhaps nine months," said my doctor.

On the way out into the hills to my home that evening, I had my driver stop by a stationery store so I could buy more paper for my laser printer.

IN 1961, the week I heard of Hemingway's death, I resolved to write about those few months with him in the summer of 1942. Last week, almost thirty-seven years after making that promise, I finished the first draft of this book. I know that there should be many more rewrites, much polishing, but I am afraid that is not possible. In a way, I feel like I am cheating discipline, and it pleases me.

I really did not begin reading fiction until after World War II. I began with Homer and spent a decade just working my way to Charles Dickens and Dostoyevsky. I did not read a Hemingway book until 1974. I started *The Sun Also Rises* the week that Nixon resigned from office.

I see the weaknesses in Hemingway's self-conscious prose and in his even more self-conscious philosophical stances. At times, especially in the later books such as *Across the River and Into the Trees*, the critics are right: Hemingway's style becomes a parody of Hemingway's style.

But ahh... when he was good. There indeed was the genius he mentioned that night on the sandy hillside above the beacon at Point Roma.

It is in the short stories that I best hear the voice of Ernest Hemingway. It is there in his short stories that I began to see the hawk in the dab of blue for a sky. It is there that I could catch a glimpse... not even of a periscope... but of the slightest hint of the wake of a periscope in the blue of the Gulf, and immediately see and hear and smell the workings of that submarine, the sweat of its crew, and the terror of the two boys waiting to go ashore and die.

One of my few regrets the past nine months is that it is

difficult to read when one is writing ten to twelve hours a day. I wonder how real writers deal with that. I remember Hemingway reading at all times of the day and night—by the pool, over meals, aboard the *Pilar*. Perhaps his deadline was less demanding.

THE UNITED STATES OF AMERICA IS TOTALLY CHANGED. Nothing remains as I remember it.

It is all familiar, of course, because of magazines, newspapers, television, CNN, a thousand movies on videotape and laser disk, and—more recently—the Internet. But it is totally changed.

I called one of my few friends still at the Agency—a young man I helped to train in my last years on the job, now one of the senior members of the firm—and asked for one final favor. He hesitated, but in the end I received the packet via Federal Express: the passport, well-used and frequently stamped, my photograph under someone else's name; the credit cards, including a gold American Express card; the driver's license, Social Security card, and other wallet detritus, including a fishing license. My friend had a sense of humor. But then, he knew something about me and could be certain that I would not be up to much mischief during my brief stay. The fishing license was scheduled to expire about the same time I was.

I came into the country through Toronto and perversely chose to drive to Idaho. Driving myself was a nice change—although I personally do not believe that unwell eighty-five-year-olds with one working eye should be allowed to drive at all—but driving on an American interstate highway is truly a new experience. So much more open and empty than an autobahn.

I bought a firearm in Spearfish, South Dakota. There was a mandatory waiting period while they checked to make sure that I was not a felon, but I did not mind waiting. The trip had tired me out, and the medicine I was taking tired me more. It also allowed me to take the trip. The medicine was very powerful, not legalized by the FDA or any other regulatory agency in any nation, but it works quite well. It would kill me if I were to take it for more than a month, but that will not be a problem.

The man at the gun shop called me at the motel a few days

later and told me that I could pick up the gun any time. The name under my passport photograph belongs to a solid, upstanding citizen with no felony priors or recorded incidents of violent mental illnesses.

I chose a Sig Sauer .38 because I had never owned one before or used one in the line of duty. It looks small and square and compact compared to the long-barreled weapons of my youth. It has been two decades since I last carried a handgun.

Yesterday I arrived in Ketchum. The town must have grown much since Hemingway bought a home there in the winter of 1959, but it still has the feel of a mining town. I found the site of the Christiana Restaurant, where Hemingway had insisted that FBI men were following him and demanded that his party leave before finishing their meals. Near there, I found a room at a motel and then went to a liquor store. I bought a presentation gift box of Chivas Regal, complete with two Scotch glasses with the Chivas emblem embossed on them.

The house he and his wife had bought in 1959 is still there. It is quite unpreposessing—a two-story chalet with steeply pitched roofs and sides of rough, poured concrete. The gravel road has been paved since Hemingway's day, and other homes have moved up the hill that must have been covered with nothing but sagebrush when the writer lived there, but the view is the same—rows of high peaks to the north and south, the double bend of the Big Wood River to the east.

Yesterday evening, driving around town before returning to my hotel, I found an empty lane, little more than two ruts through the sagebrush, that seems to cross the high plains forever before disappearing into the haze at the base of the mountains. That is where I will drive this afternoon, after this visit to the cemetery. I have my Toshiba laptop in the rented Taurus and will remember to save this last page or two to floppy disk before turning off the computer and taking a walk into the sagebrush.

Hemingway's grave is set between two fine pines facing the Sawtooth Mountains. The view is—especially on a warming spring day like this, with the snow still capping the high peaks—truly breathtaking. There were three other people at his gravesite and I had to wait in the Taurus almost half an hour before they left. I never considered the fact that Hemingway's grave must be a local tourist attraction.

Finally they are gone and I carry the gift box of Chivas over to the grave. I've forgotten my glasses and can't make out most of the writing on the tombstone, but I can see his name and the dates of his birth and death.

Despite the warm sun, my hands are chilled, and I have trouble tearing the plastic from the gift box. The cap on the bottle also gives me trouble. It's a pain in the ass being old and sick.

A few minutes ago, I set the two glasses of amber liquid on a level spot next to the headstone. The sun made the whiskey look like liquid gold.

I have always hated scenes in the movie where some asshole character gives a long soliloquy at a grave. It does not ring true. It is cheap. I would not even have come to Ketchum if I could have gone to Cuba... perhaps up to the *finca*, which is now a museum with the *Pilar* rotting away in the backyard. But I was certainly not up to that trip. One of the things that most pisses me off about dying now is that Castro will outlive me. I hope it is not by many months or years.

I lifted the first glass. "Confusion to our enemies," I said softly, and drank the golden whiskey in one gulp.

I lifted the second glass. "*Estamos copados*," I said. "*Estamos copados, Papa*."

ILLUSTRATIONS

ABOUT THE AUTHOR

Dan Simmons is the award-winning author of several novels, including the *New York Times* bestsellers *Olympos, The Terror,* and *Drood.* He lives in Colorado. For more information about Dan Simmons, visit DanSimmons.com.

Reading Group Guide

THE CROOK FACTORY

A novel by

DAN SIMMONS

A note from Dan Simmons on *The Crook Factory*

The incredible story of Ernest Hemingway's Cuban spy-catching, submarine-chasing, World War II adventures in my new novel, *The Crook Factory*, is—I think—all the more incredible for being 95 percent true.

Some years ago I decided to write a fictional version of Hemingway's Cuban spy adventures when I noticed just how cursorily that year, from May 1942 to April 1943, was covered by his many biographers. Usually the explanation went something like this—"In the first year of America's involvement in the war, Hemingway stayed home in Cuba even while his wife and friends went off to fight or cover the fighting. During that time, Hemingway set up a counterespionage group which he called the Crook Factory and which was composed of old friends from the Spanish Civil War, bartenders, prostitutes, rumrunners, fishermen, priests, and other cronies. He also convinced the U.S. ambassador to arm his boat, the *Pilar*, in an attempt to lure a German submarine to the surface and sink it with grenades and small arms. He did not succeed in sinking a German submarine, and his spy organization was terminated in April 1943."

What the biographies did NOT say was that Hemingway's adventures are still classified in the voluminous dossier which the FBI has kept on him since the 1930s. What we DO know about those months during which the writer ran the Crook Factory and his seaborne Operation Friendless is that the FBI was very upset about what Hemingway was discovering about espionage activity in and around Cuba, and, more precisely, what secrets his agents had discovered about corruption in the Cuban government and national police. What all but the most recent biographies also do NOT explain about this period is that it appears to be the basis for the raging paranoia in the last years of Hemingway's life—a period when the writer was certain that he was being followed by the FBI. The truth is that Hemingway *was* being followed by the FBI.

In *The Crook Factory* there is a fictional extension into the dark core of what we do not know about those months, but what we do know is amazing enough. Here are a few of the details in *The Crook Factory* that are based on confirmed fact:

J. Edgar Hoover and the FBI had warning of the Japanese attack on Pearl Harbor but failed to follow up on it because of infighting with rival intelligence agencies.

Hemingway's Crook Factory uncovered a nest of intrigue and corruption in Cuba.

Young Ian Fleming, later the creator of James Bond, was actively involved in espionage in the United States and Canada at that time.

Hemingway's lifelong friendships with the likes of Gary Cooper, Marlene Dietrich, and Ingrid Bergman all stemmed from this period.

Almost all of the spies and intelligence operations detailed in *The Crook Factory* were real people and real operations—as melodramatic and absurd as some appear.

All of the FBI memos in *The Crook Factory* are factual and reprinted verbatim.

The FBI surveillance of the sexual encounters between young naval lieutenant John F. Kennedy and a presumed German spy, Inga Arvad, was as depicted.

The secret transcripts of electronic and telephone surveillance on Kennedy and Arvad are reprinted exactly as the FBI recorded them.

The FBI's illegal surveillance of the vice president of the United States and the first lady, Eleanor Roosevelt, were exactly as depicted.

The New York–based Viking Fund—a philanthropic organization investigating Incan ruins—was real, and the FBI investigation into its Nazi connections is true.

The 300-foot yacht, the *Southern Cross*, outfitted by a German spy and given to the Viking Fund, was real, and it was suspected by the FBI of serving German subs.

The vicious infighting between J. Edgar Hoover and rival organizations such as the OSS and the British BSC—often at the expense of the war effort—was real, including one incident where Hoover arrested OSS agents breaking into the Spanish Embassy in New York.

The plots by Himmler and Heydrich of the Nazi SS intelligence organizations to trap and discredit Admiral Canaris and his Abwehr spy group were real and resulted in Hilter disbanding the respected Abwehr. Canaris was eventually tortured and executed.

The BSC's plot to kill Heydrich of the SS was real and planned in Canada's Camp X.

Camp X was real.

The details of Hemingway's Operation Friendless attempt to catch and sink a German submarine by posing as a Museum of Natural History research ship are real.

The South American German spies in *The Crook Factory* were actual agents, and their fates were as depicted.

The Marx brothers absurdity of the landing of Nazi agents on Long Island and the FBI's refusal to believe them even when they were trying to turn themselves in was real and as insane as depicted in *The Crook Factory*.

Hemingway's logs from the *Pilar*'s antisub patrols are given verbatim.

The vast majority of dialogue between Hemingway and other historical characters is based on real descriptions, and *all* of his comments to the fictional Joe Lucas about writing, the war, fiction versus fact, and so forth are based closely in Ernest Hemingway's comments and writings.

Hemingway's chase of the German submarine occurred exactly as depicted in the novel.

The depiction of Hemingway's Crook Factory spy operation is accurate.

Hemingway's real fear of the FBI in his last years and the details of his suicide are factual—as is the largely undisclosed actual interest the FBI still had in the aging writer. These newly revealed facts are confirmed through later interviews, new biographical information, and newly declassified FBI documents released through the Freedom of Information Act.

While the thrust of *The Crook Factory* is fictional, the vast majority of details, characters, incidents, dialogues, and wartime events are true. It was fun melding these almost fictional-sounding facts with the "truer than true" soul of fiction to create this book, and I hope it will be enjoyable for the reader to experience it.

—Dan Simmons

Questions and topics for discussion

1. How would you characterize Simmons's portrayal of 1940s Cuba—both the expat community there in which Hemingway played a central role, and the local population? How does his portrayal align or differ from what you know or pictured about the region during World War II?

2. When we meet Lucas, the news of Hemingway's suicide rocks him to his core. But when Lucas first meets Hemingway he knows nothing about him and isn't quite sure what to make of the author's larger-than-life persona. How would you characterize Lucas's relationship with Hemingway as he first gets to know him?

3. Lucas's at times fractious relationship with Hemingway changes over the course of the events depicted in *The Crook Factory*. What causes his feelings to evolve? Did your assessment of Hemingway, as depicted by Simmons, align with Lucas's assessment of the novelist, or were there moments when your opinion of Hemingway differed from Lucas's?

4. Were you surprised by Simmons's portrayal of Hemingway? How did the Hemingway in *The Crook Factory* differ from your image of Hemingway?

5. Hemingway, both as a writer and a person, is frequently linked with depictions of masculinity in American

society. How does machismo play a part in the story of *The Crook Factory*—not only in regards to Hemingway, but war and espionage as well?

6. How would you describe Hemingway's relationship with his two sons in *The Crook Factory*—and what might the novel be said to say about the father-and-son relationship through the prism of their interactions? Do you see a similar dynamic in effect anywhere else in the novel?

7. Marriage and romance play key roles in *The Crook Factory*—not only in the number of attractive women that cross Lucas's path, but in Hemingway's relationship with his wife, and with the other women who frequent his estate. What do you think Dan Simmons says about love and intimacy in *The Crook Factory*?

8. Lucas is frequently caught off guard by the number of high-profile guests that visit Hemingway socially at the *finca*, and historical figures like J. Edgar Hoover and Ian Fleming make guest appearances in Simmons's narrative outside of Hemingway's immediate purview. Which famous person's visit did you most enjoy reading about? Were they portrayed as you might have expected from reading about them, or your experience with their work?

9. In the report Lucas composes but does not send, Lucas writes: "A man who reportedly glorifies action in his writing in life, Hemingway often confuses action with mere impulse, reality with self-inflicted melodrama." Do you agree with Lucas's assessment of Hemingway's writing? Where do you see this characterization reflected in the events of *The Crook Factory*—or do you consider Lucas's description unjust?

MULHOLLAND BOOKS

You won't be able to put down these Mulholland books.

BREED *by Chase Novak*

SAY YOU'RE SORRY *by Michael Robotham*

BLEED FOR ME *by Michael Robotham*

THE HOUSE OF SILK *by Anthony Horowitz*

THE REVISIONISTS *by Thomas Mullen*

THE RIGHT HAND *by Derek Haas*

SEAL TEAM SIX: HUNT THE SCORPION *by Don Mann*

GUN MACHINE *by Warren Ellis*

THE WHISPERER *by Donato Carrisi*

HIT ME *by Lawrence Block*

EDGE OF DARK WATER *by Joe R. Lansdale*

YOU *by Austin Grossman*

THE CROOK FACTORY *by Dan Simmons*

BEAUTY *by Brian D'Amato*

Visit mulhollandbooks.com for your daily suspense fiction fix.

Download the FREE Mulholland app.

CPSIA information can be obtained
at www.ICGtesting.com
Printed in the USA
LVOW12s1936090118
562393LV00005B/917/P